I0760850

BONES OF THE PAST

Villains' Code: Book 2

DREW HAYES

Bones of the Past
Villains' Code: Book #2

Edited by Erin Cooley (cooley.edit@gmail.com) and Kisa Whipkey (http://kisawhipkey.com)
Cover by A.M. Ruggs

Acknowledgments

This novel is dedicated to my Star Puncher

Special thanks to my incredible beta readers for their irreplaceable help, especially on a book as long as this one. Shout-out to Bill Hammond, TheSFReader, E Ramos E, Amanda, and Priscilla Yuen.

Prologue

"Would you hurry up already? I'm not missing this because you couldn't be bothered to leave the lab. Chloe and I *will* go up to the roof without you."

Tori let out a long, exasperated breath and cursed her past self's naiveté. When she'd been setting up her new lab, tucked away in what was supposed to be three underground personal parking garages (which had undergone serious reconstruction and retrofitting) beneath her apartment building, the idea of an intercom had seemed like a stroke of brilliance. This way, Chloe and Beverly could easily reach her if something important came up without having to run down and potentially alert Tori's security system. Only after everything was put in place did it occur to her that perhaps she should have put in a function to mute them when the need arose.

Dropping her tools onto her workbench, Tori walked over to the intercom and held down the formerly white button, stained now with grease and oil from the weeks she'd spent toiling away down in her lair. "I'm almost done. Chill the hell out. It's not even supposed to start until nine."

"That's an estimate, and you know it. Nobody can be sure exactly when they'll arrive."

Personally, Tori had her doubts about such a statement. While it was true that the local news had been reporting on the impending phenomenon for the last two weeks—ever since someone at the Alliance of Heroic Champions first noticed the anomaly—many people had actually known about it several days prior to the announcement. Doctor Mechaniacal had sent out an email to all the scattered guild members, which self-deleted immediately after being read, cautioning them to the impending threat. Well, perhaps less cautioning, and more telling them to make sure to stay out of whatever it was that went down. There were more than a few Guild of Villainous Reformation members who couldn't resist a good slugfest, and this sure as hell had the potential to be one. Still, no one—at least no one still with the guild after Balaam's uprising—was going to disobey a direct order from Doctor Mechaniacal. He'd given the alert, and the arrival time, well before the capes had even admitted to knowing anything was going on. If he said they'd get here at nine, Tori was inclined to believe him.

"Give me five more minutes. I'm working on something special." Tori released the button and turned her attention back to her current project. For once, it wasn't the pieces of a red and black meta-suit splayed out on the giant workstation she'd set up in her first few days here. That was an ongoing project, one that would never truly be completed, though she had managed to finish an overhaul and upgrade along with all the repairs it had needed after the city-wide brawl. No, for now, her attention was on three sets of what had once been welder's goggles, though they were barely recognizable as such under all the gadgetry and tech Tori had added to them.

Much as Beverly might complain, she'd see it was a worthwhile use of time when Tori brought the ocular bad boys back to the apartment. These sorts of shows didn't come along very often, and she wanted to see every last detail. Besides, this project had made for a nice diversion, something to take her mind off what was coming.

Exciting as the night's festivities would be, they had nothing on what was coming over the weekend. Now *that* was something to be on time for.

Much as Ivan would have preferred to be with his children, Janet and her husband Juan had taken them out of the city, a decision that Ivan wholeheartedly endorsed. He had ample confidence in the AHC, especially now that Lodestar was once more at her post, but that didn't mean things still couldn't go sideways without warning. Better his children be far from the danger, somewhere away from all the chaos and madness of things to come. It had been hard enough to accept his youngest, Beth, acquiring meta-human abilities; the last thing he needed was her brother Rick ending up in the same boat.

Instead of watching the show at his townhouse—a poor replacement for the suburban home that was still being rebuilt—Ivan had taken advantage of his decades-old friendship with a billionaire and decided to watch from Wade Wyatt's downtown penthouse. This was partially because Wade always kept high-end food a mere phone call away, but also due to a lingering sense of worry. If something bad did happen, he'd prefer to have his old friend, Doctor Mechaniacal, at his side. Between the two of them, they could easily make the difference in a fight, should the need arise. While it was hardly an ideal situation, especially for a pair of semi-retired supervillains, the fact remained that they lived on this planet just as much as everyone else. A threat to Earth was a threat to their home, and they were not men who took such dangers kindly.

"Ivan, please calm down. I can see you gripping the armrest of that chair. Any moment now you'll snap it clean off, and it was made custom for this apartment." Wade dropped down next to Ivan, staring out one of the floor-to-ceiling windows that wrapped around his entire penthouse. They, like Wade himself, were deceptive in appearance. Each was fitted with a wide array of technological marvels, allowing them to zoom like a lens, go dark, serve as television screens, withstand a rocket launcher, and probably do all manner of other tricks Ivan had yet to witness.

As for Wade, he seemed as unworried as usual, relaxing in khakis and a polo, his thinning copper hair unstyled. The gentle smile Wade wore almost hid the brilliance of the mind behind it, that of the genius inventor who had won infamy as Doctor Mechaniacal, the man in the meta-suit that was powerful enough to challenge all but the strongest of capes. That was a long time ago, however. Nowadays, he was merely a billionaire tech mogul who led a secret guild of villains who worked smarter than the common criminal.

Perhaps things hadn't changed as much as Ivan thought.

"Sorry." Ivan released his grip on the armrest; there were finger indents still visible in the leather. "The timing just has me worried. We've kept our heads down for months, and now, suddenly, days before we're about to put things back in order, this happens. The timing just seems... suspicious."

"Come on, Ivan. You've been around long enough to know how these things go," Wade replied. "Where meta-humans are concerned, events and forces tend to pile together. Confluences are the best example, but they're far from the only one. Hell, it happens to regular people, too. Where do you think the saying 'when it rains, it pours' comes from?"

"I still don't like it." Ivan reached over to the table and helped himself to a handful of grilled shrimp. Wade had called up quite a spread for just the two of them. Then again, given how much Ivan had stress-eaten already, he might have gotten the exact right amount of food. That was Wade—brilliant and calculating, down to the last detail. Oddly, that thought made Ivan feel better. If the smartest person he knew wasn't worried about tonight, then maybe it was okay to relax.

"What you don't like is being on the sidelines," Wade told him. "Tori pulled you back in, and now you're hankering to throw some punches and make your strength known. Even if you know you aren't needed, you'd still prefer to be active than to watch from a luxury suite."

Much as Ivan wanted to deny that possibility, he couldn't. Wade was right. He'd gone back into battle, had remembered what it was like to be his full self for the first time in years, and now he was having to shake the craving all over again, like a relapsing addict.

"There's nothing to worry about. The AHC is doing a full-court press, a real show of force. After Apollo's attempted revolt and the ensuing fight with us, they're all over this sort of PR opportunity." Wade reached out and helped himself to a crab cake from the pile on a nearby table. "And even if that weren't true, Lodestar is going to be there. Do I really need to remind *you* that she's more than enough to handle nearly any threat? Add in Professor Quantum being back and Quorum getting off the sidelines, and the fight almost seems unfair."

Those three, the Champions' Congress, overseers of the AHC, were indeed a team that was not to be tested. Ivan knew it well; he'd experienced it firsthand. All the same, he'd feel much better when this evening was said and done.

Until then, he tried to force himself to relax and focus on the food.

"—and that about *wraps* things up!"

Though he groaned inwardly, Cyber Geek merely smiled for the cameras as Hat Trick posed next to the would-be muggers, bound now in the multicolored scarves she'd summoned from her sleeves. Hat Trick—Lucy, when she was out of costume—was kind, dedicated, brave, and trustworthy. Cyber Geek—Donald, when he didn't have to dress up like the superhero he still sometimes felt he wasn't—valued her as a teammate and liked her as a friend. However, she was an adamant fan of putting puns in her banter, and no amount of gentle coaching or careful suggestion would deter her from making those quips.

At least there weren't many reporters out tonight. They, like most of Ridge City, were busy covering the much-bigger news: eyes to the sky, waiting with bated breath to see how things played out. For his part, Donald would have loved to be watching things unfold with the rest of the citizens. But he wasn't a citizen. He was Cyber Geek, superhero of the Alliance of Heroic Champions, and that meant there was work to be done.

With all the big names and powerful capes occupied by the impending event, it had fallen to the newer recruits to make sure the streets stayed safe tonight. More than a few crooks had gotten the idea to take advantage of the distraction and pull off some capers. Already Cyber Geek and Hat Trick had foiled three muggings, two robberies, and a drunken man trying to make love to a post box. Medley and Cold Shoulder, the other two members of their team also known as Ren and Irene when out of costume, were a few blocks over, busting up a bar brawl. That wouldn't take long; one look at Medley and everyone sober enough to process fear would stop short. A living chimera composed of over a half dozen animals, including a tiger-like head, scales, fur, claws, and a sharp tail, Medley was a walking reminder that natural human defenses weren't at the top of the food chain. Cold Shoulder, with her ice powers, was equally dangerous, though she didn't look it. Cyber Geek pitied the poor bastard who tried to take a swing at her; Cold Shoulder was a big fan of shock and awe.

Originally, they'd planned to work the night as a team, but the need for capes had forced them to split off and spread themselves thin. Cyber Geek was shocked at how much crime there was; he'd lived in Ridge City all his life and had thought of it as one of the safest towns in existence. Maybe it was the excitement—or the fear—about what was coming. Maybe the whispers he'd heard in the AHC halls were true, and that guild they'd fought had kept the low-level crooks too scared to cause much trouble. Whatever the reason, it didn't matter; not tonight. What counted was keeping people safe, just like the stronger capes would be doing in the sky.

Still, it was a pity. If he'd been given the choice, been allowed to exist as Donald rather than Cyber Geek for the evening, he might have tried to watch things unfold with Tori. They hadn't gotten to talk much over the last few weeks, with Donald getting more responsibility from the AHC and Tori being promoted out of her intern-level work. Keeping connections with normal people was more difficult than he'd expected, but he wanted to keep trying all the same. Important as Cyber Geek was, he couldn't let Donald fade away completely.

Static buzzed in his ear communicators as new orders came in. Someone was trying to break into an antiques store ten blocks away. Hat Trick nodded —she'd heard the same thing he had—and, with a quick throw of her arm, sent another multicolored scarf shooting out from her sleeve. The fabric wrapped itself around a nearby building's ledge and just like that, she was off, swinging through the air. There were plenty of people who'd have thought finding an enchanted starter magician's kit made for a lame power, but Hat Trick had managed to prove she could be just as useful as someone like Medley, even if she lacked the brute force.

For his travel, Cyber Geek reached into the digital display he now always had with him and pulled out a gigantic blue boot large enough for a human to stand inside. It was an item from *Jump Jump Jones*, a video game from childhood that offered some strange, but useful, travel options. Getting inside the boot, Cyber Geek launched up from the ground, easily clearing twenty feet in the first bound, before landing unharmed on the street below.

There were more efficient ways to travel, when the need was dire, but he'd discovered that few things made the same impression on criminals as a massive shoe dropping down from the sky. After all, Cold Shoulder didn't have a patent on shock and awe.

Chloe and Beverly were already on the roof by the time Tori sprinted through the door, three sets of goggles hanging on her arm. From the top of their apartment building, they could see the other nearby roofs crowded with dozens of watchers using telescopes and cameras. Luckily, most of the people who lived in their building were the type to prefer viewing live news footage rather than standing in the slightly chilly late-Summer air. That left the trio alone, which was how they preferred it, anyway.

"About time! You know it's five minutes to nine," Beverly chastised. She was tall, with piercing green eyes that shifted color when Beverly turned into one of her several dragon forms. Of course, when that was the case, she went by Bahamut, as no villain worth their salt used their own name in a caper.

"Yeah, I cut it close, but at least I brought party favors." Tori held up the goggles, handing a pair each to Beverly and Chloe, keeping a set for herself.

"I'll be the one to ask: what the heck are these?" Chloe turned them over in her pale hands before slipping the goggles past her short, bleached-white hair and onto her face. She looked a tad like an owl who'd gotten really into steampunk as she twisted and turned, staring up at the night sky.

Tori walked over and gently lifted Chloe's hand up to the side of the goggles, where a dial could be felt. "Specialized watching devices. I figured we'd want to get a great view of the show. If you tweak this part here, you should be able to adjust the scope and focus of your lenses. Don't worry about glares from the ships or powers: I added enough neutralizing light filters that you could chart the stars at noon. Actually, daytime sky-gazing might be a fun use for these." Moving Chloe's finger across the dial, Tori heard her roommate gasp in surprise as the stars above them came into sharp focus.

"Holy shit. Now I feel bad about yelling at you to hurry." Beverly had donned her own pair after watching the demonstration and was currently looking up into the night. "These are awesome."

"Apology accepted, because hell yes, they are." Tori slipped on her own goggles, but didn't zoom in just yet. Despite her faith in Doctor Mechaniacal's calculations, the location of arrival could shift slightly in response to the AHC's presence, so she wanted to keep a wide view until then. "We'll be able to see the purple in Lodestar's eyes with these."

Before anyone could question the truth of that statement, it happened.

The ship burst into view above Ridge City, clearly alien from the first glance. It was oddly shaped in such a way that looking at it too long made Tori's head start to hurt, but it wasn't as large as she'd been expecting. Maybe that was why it had managed to get this close before being noticed.

All around them, in the streets and on the rooftops, people yelped in excitement and pointed to the sky. Even in Ridge City, visitors from outer space were not a common occurrence. It had been over a decade since the attempted Cernovian invasion, and at least five years since the cape known as Cresscriss arrived, fleeing his doomed planet. In the time since, they had yet to encounter any more alien presences—until this ship had been seen barreling toward Earth.

Tori was about to adjust her dial, but paused just long enough to check her watch first. Nine on the dot. Doctor Mechaniacal had been right yet again, not that she was surprised. Her respect for the legendary tech-based villain was second only to that for Ivan, the man who had once been feared across the world as the monstrous Fornax. That respect came not from admiration at what he'd built, though, but rather from the mentor he'd been to her when she first joined the guild. Ivan had done his best to shape her education and keep her alive. Without him, she might never have become the meta-suit-wearing villain known as Hephaestus.

And now, she was getting the chance to watch someone Ivan respected—and feared—in action. Twisting her dial, Tori searched the skies for the signature glow of the world's most powerful cape.

The Grzzniltan ship broke easily through the atmosphere, and the city below came into view. From behind the seat, the pilot could hear its navigator listing off information about the elements in the air. They'd have to do some extensive testing first, but remote scouts had indicated that this place might be perfect for terraforming. True, it would wipe out the native inhabitants; however, that was of little concern. These strange creatures with their vulnerable skin and primitive minds—they couldn't even travel between the stars. Cleansing them would be a kindness, really, saving them from their own ignorance.

It happened suddenly and with almost no warning, save for the streak of light that shot up from the ground below. The entire ship halted in midair, sending the pilot flailing. It grabbed onto the console with its tentacles in an effort to stay balanced. If they hadn't slowed in preparation for landing, such a violent stop would have turned it and the crew into pulp on the nearest wall.

The others were already scrambling, trying to understand what could have stopped them so instantly. It should have been impossible, but perhaps the native creatures had better defenses than they'd expected.

The large screen at the front of the room lit up with a new image, one much smaller than the picture of the ground below. Floating in the sky, glowing like the heart of a star, was a female creature similar to the native animals the Grzzniltan probes had reported in early scouting endeavors. Except that species didn't fly, or glow, or stop entire spaceships with a single one of their five-digited tentacles. Hands, these creatures called them. But of course, that was impossible. Even the mighty Wrexwren warriors, renowned for their raw power, couldn't halt an entire ship in midair. It was some sort of technology; that was the only explanation.

"Hi there!" She spoke in odd noises, yet moments later, the proper grunts and gloomfs reached the pilot's ears. "My name is Lodestar. I hope this translator is working right. Cresscriss said your ship was Grzzniltan and tried to whip something up so we could talk."

Cresscriss? A Paldomian name, yet there were no more Paldomians in the universe. They'd been wiped out, a necessary stepping stone on the road to others' progress. Was this creature lying, or had some truly escaped?

"Anyway, I wanted to let you know that this is Earth, and if you've come here seeking safety, peace, trade, or any sort of diplomatic relations, we welcome you with open arms. Should that be the case, we'd be happy to escort you to a safe landing site and open discussions."

As the Earth native spoke, more of her kind came into view. One wore glass in front of his eyes and a long white coat, his whole body sparking with blue energy as he floated in midair. Another had simple clothes, save for a silver belt around his waist that seemed to be keeping him aloft. Looking at that one, he seemed wrong, like too many creatures piled into a single section of space and time. Others rose from the ground, wearing all manner of shapes and colorful garb.

The pilot's navigator was shouting, trying to get the pilot's attention. It couldn't imagine what was so important; they clearly needed to wipe away these pests first.

Still, listening was an integral part of being in command, so the pilot oozed over to the navigator and looked at the screen. What it saw made two of his nine fluid sacks skip pulsations. The navigator had pulled up a program designed to sweep for any dangerous or profitable energy sources, and what stood before their ship was unfathomable. That much power, condensed into such minute forms… it boggled all sense of logical. Many of these creatures were dangerous, but the three at the forefront were a class of their own. As for the one who had seemingly stopped their vessel... the readings from her went beyond such primitive concepts as danger.

"We like to think of ourselves as a friendly planet," the human woman continued, unfazed by the effort of holding an entire spaceship suspended. "We've got some extraterrestrial folks who can vouch for that. But you should also know, we're not a species who likes to be stepped on or subjugated. If there were any Cernovians still around, I'd tell you to ask them. So, if you're here for peace, let me reiterate that we welcome you."

The creature—Lodestar she had called herself—paused long enough to move her arm. As she did, the entire ship shifted, dispelling any doubt about what had halted them mid-flight. It was a short display, but a potent one all the same. Once she'd finished, Lodestar resumed her speech.

"But if you've come here to cause trouble, then you should know that we are plenty capable of making that ourselves. And we would be *more* than happy to share."

Cheers burst from around them as the ship rose back into the sky, quickly fading from view for all those without telescopes or goggles whipped together by a tech-genius. Tori, Beverly, and Chloe all sat on the roof for some while, watching it vanish back into the space between the stars from whence it came.

Interesting as it would have been to access a new species of alien thoughts, culture, and technology, Cresscriss had already made the public aware that Grzzniltans tended to be opportunists and cowards, so they'd most likely flee when faced with a species capable of fighting back.

"I like to think I've seen my fair share of shit, but that was still pretty damn cool." Beverly yanked her goggles off and tried to hand them to Tori, who shook her head.

"Keep them. Maybe we'll come up here and do some stargazing. Or you can be a perv and watch that all-dude running club that goes by here every afternoon."

"Runners? No thanks. I like my men with more muscle than that. Stargazing sounds fun, though." Beverly carefully tucked the goggles into one of her pockets and let out a sigh. "You know, there was a time in my life where watching capes send a spaceship packing would have been the most amazing part of my year. But now, all I can think about is this weekend."

"You and me both," Tori agreed.

"Personally, I can't wait for this weekend," Chloe said. "With you two out of the house, I'm going to do a terrible movie marathon and try out some new casserole recipes. I'll save the best one for when you get home."

There wasn't much that could top a preemptively-foiled alien invasion; however, for them, one such event loomed bright on the horizon. In a few days' time, the thing they'd been anticipating for months would finally arrive.

This Saturday, the guild's new headquarters would officially open, and with that, they would begin their work as true members.

Chapter 1

When everything was said and done, the central blame for the day's events—and all that came about as a result of them—could be placed squarely on the aliens who were stopped before they ever touched down. True, they fled the moment they were met by much of the AHC (particularly Lodestar, Professor Quantum, and Quorum), but they also provided a huge shot of excitement on a Tuesday evening. Even after their departure, Tori had stayed up with Beverly and Chloe for several hours, talking about the stars and the potential mysteries beyond them. While they, like the rest of the world, were aware that extraterrestrials existed, not much more was known than that. The few refugees who'd found a place on Earth had either known little outside their own worlds or had been unwilling to part with such information. In a way, that was a blessing, for the uncertainty of what lay beyond the dark skies was as important as the twinkling stars themselves.

Of course, a night up late talking with her friends meant that Tori was sleep-deprived and grouchy, even by her standards. It didn't help that she'd been pulling all-nighters for the week before, working overtime to make certain her meta-suit was fully operational before the guild meeting. Neither she nor Beverly were entirely sure what to expect, but if Tori had learned one thing during her apprenticeship, it was to always be prepared to meet any challenge.

"You look rough." Ivan had barely glanced up as she set the stack of files on his desk, yet he wasn't too absorbed to snap off the quick remark.

"Fuck you, too." Tori glanced around quickly to make sure no one had overheard. Though she was supposed to be Ivan's niece—a necessary bit of subterfuge left over from when she'd lived over his garage—there was a limit to how glib she was allowed be in the office. Thankfully, no one was walking by Ivan's door right then, so the remark remained their secret.

"Cute. But I'm serious. You need to pull yourself together. We've got a big meeting this afternoon, and you're going to be around the upper management. This will be their first time seeing you as an executive coordinator instead of an intern; I want you to make a good impression." He was still looking at his desk, filling out forms without so much as a moment of hesitation between his pen strokes. Fornax was a powerful beast, Tori had seen that firsthand, but Ivan Gerhardt's capacity for multitasking was a feat she still found rather astounding.

Unfortunately, he was also right. While the title of Executive Coordinator really meant that she just did the same work she had as Ivan's assistant for several other managers, it had come with a bump in pay and put her on a solid career track. According to the development plan Vendallia Industries had made her fill out, within two years she'd be on track for an HR job, and after that, she could move into management herself. Granted, Tori didn't know how long she'd actually need to keep this cover job going, but until she had enough capital from respectable sources to start her own tech firm, she needed to appear normal. And there was nothing more normal than working a shitty corporate gig to slowly climb the career ladder.

Letting out a long groan, Tori smoothed her suit on reflex and dropped into one of the two chairs in front of Ivan's desk. With a quick motion, she pulled out her phone to go over the day's schedule. "Okay, it looks like I've got a small gap between your post-lunch presentation review and the meeting's actual start. Maybe I'll swing by Ridge City Grinders and grab some espresso. It won't turn me into rainbows and sunshine, but I should be able to smile my way through most of the afternoon."

"You're thinking too small," Ivan told her. Finally glancing up from his desk, he reached into a nearby drawer and pulled out his company credit card. "Call Chloe and have her set up an order for the group ahead of time. That way, you can walk in with a nice treat to get everyone over the post-lunch slump. Remember: taking the initiative earns you big points with the higher-ups."

Reaching slightly, Tori accepted the card and tucked it away in her pocket. "I already took bullets for the company. Now they want me to take initiative, too?"

"That was last quarter. You're only as good as your most recent accomplishments."

Ivan turned back to the task at hand, and Tori didn't object. She was one of the few people who knew how much work he needed to get done before their meeting kicked off. Instead, she headed out to drop off more documents with one of the other managers.

It was a little galling at times, when she really thought about the fact that Vendallia was a subsidiary of Indigo Technologies, the company that Wade Wyatt owned. They were trying to impress people who were supposedly higher on the food chain than them, when, in reality, she and Ivan had both shared beers with the man sitting at the tiptop of the ladder. If anything, other people should be kissing up to them. But that was the trouble with secret identities: you couldn't use the relationships your costumed self might have without raising questions. Tori Rivas was a low-level, white-collar worker, only recently promoted from intern.

If she wanted to climb higher, she'd have to do it with solid work and afternoon coffee.

"—and it looks like public perception of the AHC has gone up measurably after last night's spectacle. We'll have to wait to see if this is a temporary bump or a long-term gain; however, overall we do seem to be regaining people's trust after the Apollo incident."

Quorum set the report down and looked at the other two people in the room. Professor Quantum seemed bored, which was neither a surprise nor a slight. He always appeared to be some level of disinterested—when there were no cameras around, at least. For a man with his intellect, meetings like this probably felt like time-wasting torture, and yet he still came. They'd all seen what happened when the Champions' Congress drifted apart, and it was a mess they were working daily to clean up.

Lodestar, on the other hand, appeared engaged. While she was in costume, her power wasn't currently activated, meaning she had chestnut-colored hair and lacked the signature glow that often surrounded her. It made her less distracting, which Quorum appreciated during these private meetings. She was flipping through the handouts Quorum had made, looking over the figures their PR department had brought around to them this morning.

"We're still a long way from where we were in the public's eye," Lodestar noted.

"One of the AHC's leaders was put on public trial for colluding with a villain, planting evidence, and partially causing a city-wide brawl. Add in that it came to light we've been secretly letting criminals out of jail and I'm amazed we've made such strides of recovery at all."

Lodestar didn't bother to correct Professor Quantum about the fact that, legally, that part wasn't on the AHC. Mostly because it didn't matter. Technically, the government had created the Orion protocol, a caveat in the law that allowed convicted villains their freedom if they assisted in stopping potentially world-ending threats, but the government wasn't the face of keeping meta-human peace. That honor and burden had been thrust upon the Alliance of Heroic Champions, and they were the ones at the center of the scandal when the truth came out.

"On that note, I have an order of business to raise." Professor Quantum stood as he spoke, a habit from the older days when there had been more spectacle and protocol to these meetings. Despite being the oldest meta-human in the room (in fact, Professor Quantum was the first known meta-human at all, as *his* experiment had allowed new elements into the world, altering the laws of science as they'd then been understood), he never looked older than a man in his early forties. Twin streaks of gray ran along the otherwise dark hair at his temples, and his glowing blue eyes were hidden behind a pair of spectacles that did far more than correct poor vision, which he didn't have. As always, he wore the same outfit: a dark, tailored suit under a crisp white lab coat that floated out behind him.

"As you both know, earlier this week, my latest experiments arrived in Ridge City. Since we had the impending spaceship to deal with, I tabled the issue; however, now that the threat has passed, I'd like to discuss how we are going to manage their debut."

"We're not." Lodestar's reply was brisk and automatic. She set her shoulders, ready for Professor Quantum to fight her on the issue and unwilling to give ground. "We've already talked about this. No more debuts. No more managing every angle of a superhero's career and cherry-picking the ones who get media attention. Everyone does the best job they can because it's the right way to use our gifts. The people will love who they choose to love, and the rest will go to bed every night with the consolation prize of knowing they made the world a safer place."

"That's all well and good for some two-bit street urchin who gains the ability to chat with frogs or what have you, but you must realize we're talking about the continuation of a legacy. I have spent years developing this team to be the perfect combination of assets, appeal, and abilities. You want me to just turn them loose in the streets without so much as even a press conference?" Professor Quantum was staring right back at her, which was no small feat. Lodestar might be the public face of the AHC, and doubtlessly one of the strongest meta-humans on Earth, but Professor Quantum wasn't far behind her. He'd kept the peace and run his own superhero organization for decades before she came onto the scene.

"We didn't have any sort of media push when we started, and all of us managed fine. If your next generation can't do the same, are they really an improvement?" Lodestar was going after his pride, a tactic Quorum had seen her use many times in the past. It didn't always work, but Professor Quantum's ego was too large a target to miss completely.

"The world lacked constant media saturation when I began my work, and things were different even when you started. The internet was barely blooming, people weren't under a constant barrage of information coming out of their handheld devices, televisions, and screens at every..." Professor Quantum trailed off, realizing he'd slipped off into a tangent. "Very well, Lodestar. Perhaps you're right. Showing them special treatment could have a negative effect, make them seem pampered rather than deserving of their accolades. Does the Champions' Congress have any objection to me turning them loose as soon as possible? If they are to be judged by their deeds, then I would like to permit them to begin work. Today. Within the hour, if possible."

Lodestar threw a brief glance at Quorum, then nodded. "I don't see any issue with that. Granted, they haven't been formally vetted yet, but I've seen the footage from your island and shaken their hands. All four seem competent."

It was an olive branch, a compromise. Rather than making them jump through hoops or formality like any other new cape would, Lodestar was permitting the team to head out into the field. So far as Quorum could tell, it seemed a fair halfway point, so he nodded his head as well.

But it didn't escape his notice that Professor Quantum looked a bit smug as he retook his seat seconds later. While Quorum couldn't be entirely sure, he was almost certain this was the outcome Professor Quantum had been aiming for all along.

Tori was five steps out of Ridge City Grinders, her arms weighed down by the enormous plastic bag full of carefully packed to-go cups, as well as her own entire eight-ounce cup of espresso, when the explosion rocked the street. It was only thanks to her training that she stayed physical, resisting the reflexive urge to turn into living fire. While all her clothing was made out of a special material that would shift with her, that wouldn't do much to protect the coffee, and it certainly wouldn't save her secret from the dozens of panicking witnesses yelling and running through the street. Officially speaking, Tori Rivas was a perfectly mundane and normal human being. Hephaestus was the only one with powers, and not even the capes knew what lurked beneath the suit's metallic exterior.

As she backpedaled toward the sidewalk, her eyes scanned about, rapidly assessing the situation. Smoke was pouring out from a wall in one of the nearby buildings. If memory served, that place was a jewelry store. What kind of damn idiots were robbing a jewelry store in broad daylight in the same section of town where the Alliance of Heroic fucking Champions had their national headquarters? Tori shook her head, thankful yet again for the guild that had taken her in and shown her the proper way villains were meant to conduct themselves. This was the sort of thing that would get someone expelled from their organization in a very permanent fashion. Breaking the guild's code was a zero-tolerance sin, one that came with punishment carried out by people on the same level as Ivan.

From the smoke, Tori saw five figures emerge, each clad in all black, wearing ski masks and carting large duffel bags. One person, much taller than the other four, was strapped down with at least a dozen bags: meta-human with augmented strength, obviously. Already Tori could hear the sirens of the police making their approach, but with a brute in the mix, these crooks would be more than the brass could handle.

While Tori had admittedly not always been the most dutiful or attentive apprentice, some of Ivan's teachings had sunk in better than others. One of the most important lessons seemed quite relevant at the moment: if there were going to be capes in your vicinity, be somewhere else.

Lugging her bag of coffee—she would be *damned* if she was going to fill out the forms needed to use a company credit card and then lose the goods—Tori tried to head further up the sidewalk, back toward the office. It was tough at first, since she had to fight a terrified crowd, but they thinned out quickly. Most were hurrying inside nearby buildings, failing to realize that the structures they were trusting to keep them safe could easily be brought down on their heads by the wrong sort of meta. At least out in the open Tori had space to move.

She'd only gotten twenty feet away before the first cop car arrived; poor bastards must have been on patrol nearby. From the other end of the street came what looked like a retrofitted minibus, armored and strapped down with guns. As the crooks began loading their wares into the bus, the big guy dashed over to the police car. Tori's breath caught in her throat. Escape was one thing; doing nothing while innocent people got killed was a whole other issue. Where the hell were the capes, anyway? This was their town, and they could sure as shit use the publicity.

Thankfully, the police were clearly veterans of living in Ridge City. As the hulking criminal wrapped his hands around the top of their patrol car and lifted it overhead, both officers popped the doors and leapt out, rolling to safety and coming up with their weapons drawn. One squeezed off a shot that hit their attacker in the left leg, tearing a hole in his pants but otherwise doing no damage.

What it did manage to do, however, was draw the brute's attention. Even through the ski mask and at her distance, Tori could see the disdain in the meta-human's eyes as he glared at the cop who'd shot him. Without so much as a glance over his shoulder, the muscular beast of a man tossed the police car behind him like an unrepentant litterbug throwing away a burger wrapper.

Though the shot might have been unaimed, it still had plenty of power. The car soared through the air, away from the bus with the other criminals, clearing the small crowd of civilians and tumbling down on a direct course for the ground.

Unfortunately, the spot of street it was hurtling toward was exactly where Tori was currently standing.

Chapter 2

The blast of wind was her only warning before Tori found herself suddenly hurtling through the air, cradled in a pair of lean, strong arms. A horrific cacophony of smashing metal and shattering concrete barely reached her ears over the sound of the wind, the car crumpling down in the spot where Tori had been standing. It was so close, she could still see her bag of coffees only a few feet away; apparently, it had slipped from her hand in the rescue.

While the impact wouldn't have killed her—her fire form had an abundance of uses, and this occasion fit well within her wheelhouse—her savior had no way of knowing that. And, in truth, this did save her the complication of publicly using her powers. Just as Tori tried to twist and get a better look at her rescuer, the wind came to a sudden, unexpected halt.

The result of this unfortunate timing was that Tori found herself gazing upward at her helper right as they came to a stop in front of a small crowd of onlookers, most of whom had produced camera phones. To anyone viewing this from the outside, it no doubt appeared as though she was enraptured by this man, rather than trying to figure out what sort of facial features rested below the bright blue mask covering everything except his nostrils, eyes, and mouth. The mask clung so tight, it could almost have been mistaken for paint; there was no gap between the face and the covering.

"Sorry for the abrupt pickup, but I thought you'd prefer it to a total crash-and-burn."

Not the smoothest line she'd ever heard, but for a cape new on the scene, it was decent. Actually, now that she was really looking, Tori realized that this fellow appeared *much* too put together for a cape she'd never seen before.

He was of average height, lean and muscular—no surprise, given that he'd just shown off super-speed. Brown hair and eyes were the only features the mask gave away, and the rest of his costume was strikingly similar to the facial accessory: blue material, thicker in some places than in others, along with a telltale notch or switch that betrayed functionality. There was also a thick bracer on one wrist—most likely control terminals for whatever hidden systems were at work. This cape wasn't just rocking a costume: he had an outfit, something made specifically to help him fight crime. A stylized "T" was on his left pectoral, and Tori couldn't help but feel like she'd seen all of this before. Not quite the same, but unmistakably similar.

"Oh no!" In front of Tori, a man's eyes went wide as he looked back at the scene of the crime. She whipped her head around, jaw nearly dropping in surprise. One of the goons had lifted an automatic weapon and was starting to angle it toward the onlookers.

Holy *shit*. Were these people insane? Spraying down citizens might cause enough panic to cloak an escape, but the AHC would never stand for that kind of display of violence. And that was assuming they ever got the chance to lay a finger on these idiots. If anyone from the guild learned about this, they'd soak the earth in these idiots' blood, then give them transfusions to make it last longer. This was Ridge City; even villains had friends and family here.

Thankfully, as visions of the worst flickered through Tori's mind, the gun vanished from its owner's hands. Seconds later, the weapon crashed heavily to the ground, shattering on impact.

"Ma'am, I need to set you down now. There's still work to do."

Well, *that* was embarrassing. True to form, Tori had gotten so lost in her curiosity that she'd forgotten her surroundings, including the fact that she was still hanging on to the super-speed guy who'd helped her out. In the rush of speed, clinging to him had seemed natural, though now she realized it likely appeared quite different to the onlookers.

With as much dignity as she could muster, Tori freed herself from the blue-clad mystery cape, who vanished in a blur. He reappeared over by the criminals, where Tori could now see three figures wearing what seemed to be matching outfits standing just outside of proper view. Either this was the fashion-coincidence of a lifetime, or they had an entire team of capes here to help out. Despite their technically being on opposite sides, Tori was happy to see them. This was the sort of chaotic mess that neither organization approved of.

"Hey there, folks. Have no fear about the voice coming out of your phones and nearby speakers. Just one of my many tricks, and the reason they call me Presto. No, not the fast one who just saved that lady. His name is Tachyonic, master of speed and time. Watch him go—isn't he something?"

True to the voice's promise, Tachyonic zipped around one of the would-be robbers, easily knocking him over. With that kind of speed, everyone except the strong-meta should be already captured. This wasn't just about foiling a crime, then. Someone was throwing themselves a debut.

From the decked-out minibus, the sound of machinery engaging could be heard. Evidently, these robbers had come expecting resistance. It was significantly *less* likely they had been prepared for the beam of energy that carved neatly through the entire bus, cutting the section with the engine off from the rest of the vehicle entirely. Out of this divide stepped a woman whose costume matched Tachyonic's, though Tori noted that this one had a noticeably more revealing cut, emphasized all the more by the woman's figure.

"That bombshell is Plasmodia. Keep your distance, fellas. Anything that hot is bound to burn, and if her looks don't do it, then her power to conjure, shape, and direct raw plasma energy absolutely will."

The voice was starting to wear on her nerves. If escape had been at all possible, Tori would have been running for it. Unfortunately, between the fight to her fore and the giant crowd to her rear, there was no easily slipping away. Especially after being saved by Tachyonic. She could *feel* the stares and whispers, which only made it worse. Moving would trigger their attention. Her best shot was to wait until the capes won, then make a break for it in the ensuing celebration.

Big-meta wasn't too keen on seeing the bus get destroyed, it turned out. He slammed a mighty boot into the street and blasted forward, plainly intending to lay out Plasmodia. Rookie mistake, at a glance. After she'd sliced through reinforced metal with ease, this idiot should assume she could cut him, too. He'd know that, if he'd gotten proper guild training, just like he'd know to never make a big move in a situation like this.

The whole thing was a play. These capes were *way* too strong for this level of incident; they had the entire thing in total control. Which meant the only reason no one had touched the big, obviously-criminal meta was that they were leaving it for some remaining unnamed member of the team.

Sure enough, as the lumbering crook drew close, another person in a blue costume struck. This one was blond, taller and more muscular than Tachyonic by a wide margin, though not quite so huge that he gave himself away as a meta. From a size perspective, the criminal meta had the advantage. That was one more important lesson taught by the guild, however: size meant little in the world of super-human abilities.

With unexpected grace, the new cape caught his opponent mid-charge, executed a perfect flip, driving him into the ground, and then punched. Once. That was all it took to make the hulking crook go limp. Not a small feat, given the strength that robber had demonstrated. Whoever the new guy was, he definitely had power to spare.

"And that, my wonderful audience, is our leader. The inheritor to history's greatest superhero, the man who will usher in a new age of peace and justice. I give you, the one, the only... Agent Quantum!"

For the most part, the crowd had rolled with this incident pretty well. Outside of the moments when they'd felt directly threatened, the scene was more interesting than scary once the capes arrived. To many Ridge City citizens, this was old hat; it happened every time a new bunch of metas popped up. At that announcement, however, the entire crowd went silent in shock. Just in time, as it turned out, because the voice on their speakers was rising.

"That is right, folks. You are the fortunate few who can look back upon your life and say that you—yes, you—were there the day the New Science Sentries appeared to save the world. All right, team, time for the Big Finish!"

A final form clad in blue appeared, as if from nowhere. This one was covered head-to-toe in the material, not so much as an eyehole breaking the surface. Presto had appeared at last, and with a wave of his hands, the blue form made two of the criminals vanish. They reappeared fifty feet up, screaming as they dropped before disappearing five feet from the ground, only to once more pop out fifty feet up. Tachyonic zipped around, tying up all the remaining bodies, while Plasmodia yanked out the minibus driver and tossed him over for Tachyonic to wrap up. Once Agent Quantum was sure the big meta was down and bound, he leapt up, snaring both crooks falling from the sky in a single arm before settling them carefully down as they begged to be cuffed. If neither man started the day with a fear of heights, they would certainly have one now.

"Thank you, citizens of Ridge City!" Presto's voice echoed from the speakers, nearly beaten out by people's cheering. As they yelled, Tori felt the crowd loosen. She quietly moved toward the sidewalk, putting as much distance as possible between herself and the onlookers. She wasn't quite quick enough to escape the rest of Presto's spiel, though.

"We are the New Science Sentries, Ridge City's freshest, greatest team of superheroes. Be sure to tag us when you post pics and video of this!"

Thanks to years of learning to pass unnoticed, and perhaps a little guild training here and there, Tori managed to duck through several boutiques and small businesses, eventually making her way back to the Vendallia Industries offices. She was late, for sure, but had one hell of an excuse if Ivan tried to give her crap. At least she'd been smart about it. No revealing of powers. No getting involved with crooks or capes. Except for the getting saved part, she'd been a model bystander. While that bit was not-so-great, she couldn't think of a better move to have made. The pictures would be a short-lived embarrassment until another cape did some remarkable feat—probably Lodestar knocking out a kraken, or the like.

Tori was so absorbed in the fallout from her encounter that she didn't realize it hadn't ended quite yet. As she passed an alley, a form leapt out. Thanks to the flash of blue, she caught on in time and didn't roast him, but it was closer than it should have been.

"Miss, I think you dropped this." Tachyonic had appeared, holding her sack of what had to be spilled coffee. Of course he had. This was what capes did, especially when they were coordinating a debut.

"Thanks." Tori looked in the bag, noting that for the most part, the contents had held together just fine. God bless Chloe and her love for extra-durable packing. As she rifled through the bag, however, Tori realized there was indeed one thing missing. In the chaos of escape, she hadn't yet thought to miss it, but now, there was nothing she wanted more. "Wait, where's the receipt?"

That earned her a look of surprise. That's how she interpreted the widening eyes, anyway. "Do you think I shortchanged you on the contents?"

"I don't know, was that part of the show?" It wasn't fair, not really—she could tell the team hadn't caused the incident, they'd just made use of it—but that didn't lessen the tightening in her stomach as she hunted for the receipt.

"What... do you mean?" The unshakeable surety of Tachyonic was starting to slip, a keen awareness slipping into his eyes.

Setting down the bag, Tori kneeled on the sidewalk and dug in earnest, delving into the section of the bag where spills had occurred. "Come on. You had a team member hack the nearby speakers to emcee the whole thing. Do you seriously not realize we can tell you were toying with those goons? They had backing and muscle and equally no idea what to do with it. The whole fight should have been over in seconds, but that doesn't make for as viral of a spectacle, right? I don't know how Donald puts up with you image-obsessed assholes."

Her tirade had taken Tachyonic back a few mental steps. As it wound down, he appeared to find himself and dig in, going so far as to actually cross his arms. "Most people would be thankful to have gotten saved."

"Yeah? Welcome to Ridge City, where we hold our capes to higher standards. They save people first, show off second. If you can't live up to that, then this city isn't for you. Take your ass to Tampa. I hear they've got a solid rookie program." With great effort, Tori pulled herself up from the ground. The receipt wasn't in there. It was gone. "Maybe out there, they can teach you that if you save someone in the public eye, especially during your debut, it's not a great idea to leave behind the documentation that gives away my first name and employer."

She was a little surprised, but he seemed to get the implication at once. Part of her had been preparing to walk him through the issue.

"Ah. Someone out there has a picture of me saving you, along with at least your first name and who you work for. Pair that with my team making our debut today, while taking on the legacy of the greatest superhero team in history, and it makes for an easy human-interest angle. I don't suppose there was any chance you're one of those people who is secretly hoping for a lot of fame and attention from strangers?"

"Basically the exact opposite," Tori replied.

"I'll... see what I can do." Tachyonic vanished without another word—a wise decision in Tori's estimation. His empty promise was just that: empty. There was no power in existence that could tamp down on humanity's love of gossip or interest in capes.

Whether she liked or not—and she very much did *not*—Tori Rivas was about to get her fifteen minutes of fame.

Chapter 3

Working in downtown Ridge City meant that occasionally, an emergency broadcast went off, letting everyone know that there was some sort of meta-event happening and they should all stay indoors. Ivan felt minimal concern when one activated shortly after Tori left. The odds of it being near her were slim, and she was a villain of the guild. She could handle being around some action.

Still, his worry did arise when a call on his cell phone lit up. It was rare for people to reach out directly like this. Superiors preferred email, the guild had its own channels, and Wade managed to keep all guild members off telemarketing and robocall lists—though that was more for the marketers' safety than anything else. As his eyes fell upon the name, Ivan's worry was dispelled, replaced by the constant rock of terror he carried with him at all times. Janet was calling, which meant something was going on with their kids. It was the only topic they actively communicated over.

Snatching it up, Ivan immediately accepted the call. "Janet, always a pleasure. Is everything okay?"

"Rick hasn't suddenly developed powers, too, if that's what you mean." Ivan winced at that. Technically, they didn't know how Beth had been turned into a meta-human, though they shared the same suspicion that it was connected to Ivan's past in some way. "But we do have a problem. Beth's Starscout cluster is due to start having meetings again soon, and they keep kicking back her registration. There's a new cluster leader taking over for Dr.

Randall. I'm not sure if the replacement is trying to lower his headcount by shuffling Beth out, or if he's just terrible at paperwork. Either way, we need to handle it. I've got to do a guest lecture tonight, and Juan is taking Rick to his mathematics club. Can you go straighten this out?"

On the surface, it was a perfectly normal request for a wife to make of her ex-husband. The issue here was that Janet rarely reached out, and it was even less common for her to ask for a favor. While she'd accepted his presence in their children's lives, it didn't mean she went out of her way to make it easier. Some might have mistaken her attitude for spite, but Ivan knew better. Janet's focus was entirely on the safety of their kids. Having a famous villain as a father would make things endlessly more complicated for them, so she tried to put distance between that legacy and the innocent offspring who had nothing to do with Fornax.

All of which meant that if Janet was asking him to step in, there was a reason. "Any suspicion of what the issue might be? If I know the problem, it'll make finding a solution easier."

"I have a hunch. I think you should draw your own conclusions, though. Just make sure you take care of it. Beth's been in the same cluster since she started as a Sparkscout, with the same friends. Between her school falling down and turning into a meta-human, she needs some stability. Please don't let her down."

The please was unnecessary, as was anything beyond the request itself. Ivan knew quite well how much turmoil his daughter had seen. She would *not* lose this, too.

"I'll handle it after work. My evening is quite free."

No sooner had the words left his mouth than Tori burst into his office, looking quite a bit rougher than she had upon leaving and without any coffee in hand.

"Janet, I need to let you go. Looks like another situation has just come up."

Donald stood in the gym next to Ren, watching the silent, wall-mounted television along with the myriad of other sweating forms. When he'd become a superhero and joined the Alliance of Heroic Champions, part of him had thought moments like this were long past—seeing some new cape swing into action on a screen, being caught completely unaware by the sudden emergence of an incredible new force for good. Amazingly, though he'd racked up a few fights of his own now, he still felt that same sense of wonder he'd had while watching capes as a kid. If Donald was the only one feeling that way at first, he damn sure wasn't once *that* name was flashed across the screen.

"*What!?*"

It was impossible to say which of the many screeching voices owned that particular verbal expulsion, nor did it matter. The words easily summarized the general feeling in the AHC's gym.

The Science Sentries were the original, as in *original*-original, superhero team. Formed a few years after Professor Quantum's experiment tweaked the laws of physics, introducing entire new meta-elements and strange magical forces, the Science Sentries were in many ways a precursor to the League of Metas, which organized capes before the Alliance of Heroic Champions was formed. But they'd been disbanded since the mid-seventies, as everyone save Professor Quantum had either died or grown too old to keep doing the work. And now, decades later, he was just handing over the title to some new team?

No... that wasn't right. Donald kept watching the screen as the shaky cell-phone-camera footage jumped around. The news report was doing a hack job editing it all together; they'd jumped right in during the middle of the fray. Nevertheless, this team, whoever they were, had visible skill to burn. They were nothing like he and Ren had been in their first battle, even if that had admittedly been against an inter-dimensional monster. These four were coordinated, practiced, calm. If this really was their first official outing, then they must have trained for years prior to do it like this. That would make a lot more sense; Professor Quantum was a man who took care of his legacy. Handing over the name "Science Sentries" wasn't something he'd do easily.

"The competition just got tougher." Ren kept watching the screen—which usually showed exercise forms or cooking-contest shows, depending on who got to the remote first—but his arms picked up a pair of extremely heavy weights as he began to do curls. Seconds later, his tail snaked around a third weight and began to lift as well, though this one was notably lighter.

"They're our allies, not our competition," Donald pointed out.

Ren made an inhuman noise in his throat, the intended implication entirely lost on Donald. Being friends with someone who was mostly animal took practice, especially in the realm of non-verbal communication, but they'd made steady progress since first teaming up. "Do you see any inherent issue with trying to be the best superhero you can possibly be?"

"Of course not."

"Then you should accept that as much as these people are our friends and allies, they're also our competition. We all want to be the best. Me, you, Bloopston over there by the water fountain, Big Swing on the deadlift—even the established capes like Battle Cry and Dapper Doll are looking higher up the mountain to the Champions' Congress." Ren kept on lifting as he spoke, and Donald noticed his words seemed to be inspiring several of the others as well. Even he felt his fingers itch for a controller; playing games was the way Donald improved his digital inventory.

Had the screen not changed, Donald might have been tempted to point out the flaw in Ren's philosophy: none of them would ever be the best. As a team, that title could be claimed. However, on an individual front, the battle was lost before it started. There was only one person who was the strongest, the toughest, the surest. When everything and everyone else failed, Lodestar came through.

Donald had witnessed her in person only twice. Once in childhood, and once when they were breaking into the AHC headquarters to free Quorum. Both times were seared into his memory. Lodestar was the kind of person who left an impression.

However, before any of that could escape his lips, a new clip of footage popped up on the screen. This time, rather than focus on the fight, it was a clip of the one called Tachyonic saving a civilian from certain death. Donald almost couldn't believe his eyes as the scene played out, showing Tachyonic stop after a sudden surge of movement, carefully holding a very recognizable woman in his arms.

It was a painfully familiar image to Donald—one from his most private fantasies, where he held Tachyonic's position, finally showing his crush the kind of capable superhero he'd become. Seeing that she'd been in danger was bad enough; watching that unexpectedly soft gaze upon Tachyonic's face... Donald found himself markedly less excited about this new team than he had been seconds ago.

Setting down a weight, Ren pointed a claw up toward the screen. "Hey, isn't that Tori?"

"I'm not sure. The picture from the camera is a little blurry. Could be somebody else." Donald wasn't even sure why he bothered with the lie, other than to have a few extra moments to process the sudden surprise.

Ren called across the gym to a scaly woman with visible gills and webbed fingers. "Hey, Bloopston, give us sound!"

Bloopston picked up a nearby remote from the water cooler and cranked the volume as requested.

"—reports are coming in from the Alliance of Heroic Champions that these are indeed inheritors to the Science Sentries mantle, not pretenders with a false claim as we've seen before. Additionally, they would request that the civilians and police involved in the incident be left unbothered. While the woman in this video's name has been leaked online thanks to some active sleuths on the scene, we will of course not be repeating it here, and would like to encourage our viewers to please respect the AHC's plea for discretion."

As the anchor spoke, the runner on the bottom of the screen showing the broadcast's social media feed began to light up with posts, people spamming Tori's name over and over, proving once more that humanity was definitely not prepared for the level of technology it had access to. The reporter continued, oblivious to the fact he was being undermined as he launched into a history lesson on the original Science Sentries.

Donald paused only long enough to give Ren a quick glance before darting out on a direct course for his phone. This time, there was no issue in the communication, as Ren got immediately out of the way. When it mattered, they understood each other just fine, and this *definitely* mattered.

One day. One damn day, and Vernon's new team was already causing her trouble.

Helen sat at home, Penelope at her summer day camp, watching the video on replay. She'd already done a few soundbites for the media and made a quick call to Quorum, but that was all just to handle this new team's arrival on the scene. The bigger problem was that Tachyonic had gone and kicked a hornet's nest. Except hornets would be infinitely better than what lurked inside Tori's hive.

Her core dilemma was one of morality and information. A key aspect of the AHC was that it did *not* exist entirely outside the law; that was a League of Metas philosophy that was stomped out when the organization died. Yes, capes were empowered to take extraordinary actions, especially in dire circumstances, but they were not judges and juries themselves. Criminals, meta or human, went through the legal system; at least, the ones who let themselves be taken in. Technically speaking, there was no warrant out for Tori Rivas. She was an innocent civilian, so far as the law was concerned.

Hephaestus, on the other hand, was wanted in connection to a museum heist. The metal-suited crook was on the scene and had dealt with members of the AHC in the escape. The conundrum was that there was no evidence in Helen's possession that linked these two identities together. Quorum would put it together, and Vernon might, if he cared enough to realize she was Ivan's "niece" in documentation. As for the new team, there was essentially zero chance they'd realized they'd just put a potential supervillain on national television and framed her as a helpless damsel in distress.

After a few decades of this job, it was hard not to see the patterns. Peaks and valleys, the changing of the ages. Some parts held constant, though. Bank robbers always threw the gun when the bullets ran out, incompetent crooks had a strange knack for getting their hands on dynamite, and the media loved an image that told an instant story. A freezeframe of a new superhero holding what appeared to be an adoring woman he'd just saved fit the mold perfectly. That photo of Tori and Tachyonic was going to play. Given that her name was already out there, that meant attention.

First things first: she needed to get a protective detail around Tori. With the guild no longer capable of patrolling the underworld, things were changing. The old rules were starting to be ignored as up-and-comers decided to test their limits. So far, the AHC had been holding strong, but crime was increasing all over the globe. Helen couldn't assume that no one would try to take a run at Tori, just for the sin of being vaguely connected to a cape. People had tried more over less.

It wasn't that she was worried for Tori—that guild didn't admit members who couldn't handle themselves. No, Helen's worry was for what Tori or—gods forbid—Ivan would do to anyone that tried to move against her. While they might no longer be ruling over crime thanks to Apollo shoving them into the light, the guild did have an extremely clear process on what happened to those who attacked their members directly. Worse, they knew how to do it without leaving evidence behind.

As she picked up the phone, Helen decided her next call was going to be to Vernon, or rather, Professor Quantum, since this would be an official communication. They needed to have a talk about that team of his. Letting them skip ahead to fieldwork hadn't been entirely off base, not with the power they were displaying, but if these four were going to be in the AHC, then they needed to learn to do the job properly.

Chapter 4

There weren't many excuses one could offer up for missing a meeting with management, but being drawn into an attempted robbery's chaos was a hard one to argue with. Especially when there was documentation of the incident all over the news. Tori was formally excused from work for the remainder of the day; they even released Ivan, as well, since he was ostensibly her only local family. How much of that was management being kind and how much was Ivan using his unknown connections, Tori genuinely had no idea.

Rather than go to her own apartment, they instead headed straight to Ivan's townhouse. "By now, reporters have your address," Ivan explained as Tori tried to settle on the couch. This new place was slick, with high-end appliances and fancy furniture, but it lacked the authentic comfort of Ivan's real house. Sadly, that had played host to a meta-human brawl between Hephaestus and a traitor of the guild, which had left it in an... uninhabitable state. Until the repairs were completed, Ivan was stuck in this swanky place, not that he seemed to care. The only requests Tori saw him make when these arrangements were being set up were for a modern kitchen and rooms for both of his kids. Ivan had his priorities.

"Couldn't I turn the hose on them or something? It can't be legal to hang out in front of my building, hoping to harass me." Tori had been looking forward to a quiet evening of refining her meta-suit for the guild's reopening that weekend. Now she was wondering if she'd have to build some sort of hidden tunnel system just to attend. Actually, now that she considered it, some secret entrances and escape hatches were a good idea in general.

"The countless thespians, models, and other famous folk in your shoes have tried such methods, few of which were successful. While our media cycle has kicked up several notches, you're not the first person to get a shot of fame for being saved by a cape. Some try to turn it into careers of their own. Most fade away after a new story pops up. My advice is to lay low and wait it out. After a day or two, you can probably go home safely. Until then, feel free to use Beth's room."

Despite how unfunny the situation was, Tori still let out a short chuckle. "So, this was all just an elaborate plan to get me to be your housemate again. I respect the effort, but if you're lonely, maybe move in with Wade? He's one of the few people you like."

Ivan shuddered, albeit slightly, at the suggestion. "Impossible. We've already lived together, and the man is an abhorrent slob when at home—and do keep in mind that critique is coming from someone who's raising a teenager. The original reason he invented robots that do tasks like cleaning or driving was to appease me after a particularly strong argument over when a trash can needs to be emptied."

For a moment, Tori tried to picture it. Two of the world's most powerful villains, in their primes, having a heated discussion about who was dragging ass on their chores. Hard as she worked, the image of Fornax and Doctor Mechaniacal bickering about trash refused to form. Ivan and Wade, however, she conjured with minimal effort.

"Besides, how could I be lonely? Between you lot at the office, keeping an eye on the guild, and my actual children, it often feels like I go entire weeks without spare moments to rub together." Ivan's eyes darted to the watch on his wrist. "On that note, I'm afraid I have an errand to run. My sincere apologies, but I made the commitment before I was aware of your situation. Please get comfortable. I can grab us some fast food on the way back."

The room grew unexpectedly heavy as Tori narrowed her eyes. "Uh oh. What's going on?"

"As I said, an errand I need to run. No need to pull out the suspicious stare."

"Except you *never* do takeout when you can help it, and that goes double for fast food. You always stick to real meals, even when we get in late and doing something quick and greasy would be way easier. Sorry, Ivan, but you taught me that paying attention to details and listening to our gut helps us stay alive. If I'm not high enough in the guild to know or whatever, fine, but say that. I don't need to be lied to."

Ivan both cursed and complimented his past self; the education provided to Tori had clearly been a comprehensive one. "The lie was for me, not you. Janet called and asked me to help with Beth's Starscout cluster. There's been an issue with her registration."

"I didn't know Beth was a Starscout," Tori said. "Hope they've improved the uniforms. Those old collars used to itch like all hell."

It was one of the few times she'd seen Ivan actually reel in surprise. "*You* were a Starscout?"

Her laughing smile faded, and Tori looked away. "Mom thought I needed socializing, said I was too preoccupied with research and experimentation. Started me as a Sparkscout, then graduated into Starscouts when I was old enough. I never liked any of the camping or outdoorsy stuff one bit, but I got to do it all with my mom, so now I can't help loving the memories."

"It's a good organization. Everything the founder hoped for." Ivan pressed on, hurrying past his slip-up before Tori could ask how he would possibly know a thing like that. "My fear is the fact that Janet felt the need to get me involved at all. She is not a woman to be taken lightly, especially where our children are concerned. If she wants me to deal with this, then the most likely reasons are because the situation requires a dangerously firm hand, or she somehow thinks the problem is my fault and expects me to solve it. I'm worried what that means for Beth and her group."

After a brief moment of consideration, Tori hopped up from the couch. She'd never gotten settled on it, anyway. "I'll come, too. Sitting around a strange place with nothing to work on is just going to make me stir-crazy, especially after today. Plus, I can be your Starscout expert, in case anyone tries to trick you with fake rules or policies."

It was a stretch, and they were both keenly aware of that. Ivan didn't blame Tori. Her entire world had gotten shaken up on a coffee-run mere hours ago; she needed time to process. And company, apparently. There was a small amount of merit in her proposal, though. Ivan had more than enough magic to tell when a human lied to him, but having her there to call out any bullshit was a more mundane option that demanded less explanation. For people in their position, appearing normal was among the highest of priorities.

"Just so we're clear, Tori, this is a matter I take seriously."

"I know how you feel about your kids, and Beth probably saved my life when her school collapsed. I'm not going to fuck around with something that girl cares about," she replied.

"Good answer." Ivan walked over to the table and grabbed his keys. "But keep your head down as we drive. Remember, for the moment, you're a celebrity."

Tori let out a groan that sounded like it had crawled all the way up from her toes. "I don't suppose there's any way I could convince you to let me ride in my Hephaestus helmet, is there?"

In the early days, though not quite as far back as her post-event, pre-Lodestar days, Helen had trouble controlling her power. It came bursting forth at the slightest desire, suffusing her body and lighting up everything in a three-block radius with her glow. Over time, and with significant practice, she'd learned to master her abilities, drawing only as much power as she wanted. It was that level of self-control that permitted Helen to last seven years without using the burning power that dwelled within her.

That same control was how she managed to illuminate only her hair and eyes at that moment, shifting into the appearance of Lodestar without calling up so much strength that she risked ripping a door from its hinges. Even in her most mundane form, Helen's body was at peak human capacity for strength, agility, endurance, flexibility, and every other physical factor one could measure, so it wasn't as if she felt defenseless. Besides, they were in the heart of the AHC, and she was about to walk into a room with four other superheroes.

Already waiting for her in the lounge were the New Science Sentries and a thin man with a receding hairline who was running around checking their vitals. One of Vernon's—no, Professor Quantum's—men. It was important to keep those lines in place when she was wearing her costume. Even if the world already knew who he was, it didn't matter. Lodestar set the standard. If she got sloppy with official names, then others would think that was permissible—and it was *not*, even if she was annoyed with Professor Quantum for bringing a small staff along with his new team.

No matter how many times she had these sorts of meetings, she always took a deep breath for courage. Before grabbing the door handle, Helen drew in a single long gulp of air. Lodestar blew it out as she strolled into the room, smiling at the waiting team.

At the sight of her, Professor Quantum's lackey headed out the door as the rest of the room broke into a brief flurry of action.

The scramble wasn't new; she'd been famous for much too long. The team before her turned into a fray of limbs and movement as each and every one hopped to their feet. Only the shorter member, Presto, took his time rising. None were in masks, so she could see the excitement and terror shining out from each of their faces. It was hard to meet one's heroes; all the more so when they were *actual* superheroes. She'd stood where they were once and knew that feeling all too well, even so many years later.

"The New Science Sentries," Lodestar opened. "Those were some exceptional skills you showed off; I can see why Professor Quantum handed down the team name. But I'm getting ahead of myself. Let's start with introductions. I met you all briefly at the welcoming party, when you shook hands down the line, but I think we can do better than that. Agent Quantum, as leader, why don't you tell me about yourself and your team?"

Of them all, Presto looked the least nervous. That was, however, merely because he was a better actor than the others. Reading their body language, Agent Quantum appeared to be the one who actually *was* the least nervous, although it wasn't by a huge lead. He still stepped forward without fail, meeting her eyes as he spoke. Without the mask, it was clear he had the classic handsomeness so many capes prized: square jaw, bright eyes, and a smile that was commanding and friendly at the same time.

"Yes, ma'am. I'm Agent Quantum, but you can call me by my civilian name: Austin. Tachyonic and I were part of a prenatal setlium experiment prior to our births, which is where we both gained our abilities. Plasmodia and Presto were created through alternate means, and joined us on the island in late childhood. Our respective power sets are as follows: Tachyonic distorts the chronoflow around him to—"

"I'm up to speed on all your powers," Lodestar politely interrupted. "I was hoping to learn a little more about you as people. Let's start with an easy one, especially for recruits who have had their powers this long: what made you want to become superheroes?"

She considered this more of an icebreaker than a question. The answers people gave were usually off the cuff, either a quick pleasantry that had been practiced to death or the sort of sincere blathering that betrayed a lack of introspective thinking. The real reason was something one found out over time. Still, this was at least a conversational jump-off point that everyone who wanted to be a cape would be able to join in on.

"The chance to do great things." Tachyonic was the one who spoke up, and he was lying, badly. So badly, in fact, that Lodestar suspected he didn't expect or want this answer taken seriously. Interesting. She hadn't known what to expect from that one, and so far still didn't.

"I mean, let's be honest here. I'm short, not much of a looker, and most people tend to find me... I think 'abrasive' is the word they use when they're being nice. Guys like me have only one shot if we want to be rich, famous, and desired by lovely women all over the globe: superhero." Presto vanished, reappearing on a nearby chair so he could look Lodestar more easily in the eyes. "Please feel free to call me Ike, by the way."

Another liar, except this one *did* want to be believed. She shook his hand, absorbing the bluster to think over when she had more time.

As Lodestar turned away, she nearly bumped into Plasmodia, who had edged closer.

"I realize this sounds like I'm kissing up, but... the Day of Two Stars was what inspired me. I saw it from the ground, and even though I was a kid, I never forgot the way the sky lit up. I didn't use my powers before then; I thought they were too dangerous. Watching you was when I realized that sometimes the world needs dangerous powers."

"I haven't heard anyone use that term in a while." Lodestar noticed the flash of panic that ran through the young woman's eyes and quickly spoke to reassure her. "I like it, mind you, it's just one that fell out of fashion. Orion was a dangerous foe, and I wouldn't face another like him if I had the choice. But knowing it helped show younger capes what we can do makes the fight worthwhile."

Plasmodia nodded enthusiastically, a too-bright smile of capped teeth beaming on her face. "Oh! And I'm Eleanor, but everyone calls me Ellie! Sorry, should have opened with that."

"It's okay. There's no set order to introductions." Lodestar gave Plasmodia a quick wink before turning back to Agent Quantum. "And you, leader of the team? What got you into this field?"

"I was born for it. This is all I've ever known." The reply was quick and crisp; he'd been ready for this. "With respect, that's all I'd like to say for now, if that's acceptable, ma'am. The rest is a personal matter."

Lodestar closed her eyes for an extra-long blink. She didn't just understand Austin's reasoning; she'd expected it from at least one of them. Powers almost always came from chaos. It was the rare meta-human who gained their abilities in a peaceful, expected manner. And in that chaos, others often weren't so lucky. It was a sad constant that so many meta-human powers were forged in tragedy, yet it was one she had to be aware of all the same.

"Perfectly fine. You certainly have the right to your own privacy," Lodestar told him. "I'm not here today to pry as you get acclimated. I'm here to discuss your team, your performance today, and your future in the Alliance of Heroic Champions. My understanding is that Professor Quantum has been training all of you for years, both as individuals and as a team. Is that correct?"

All eyes darted to Austin a split second before he spoke. They were definitely cohesive as a unit, that much was clear. "Yes, ma'am. Our team composition wasn't officially set until roughly two years ago, so we've only had that long to work together. Prior to that, we all received at least five years of personal development education."

Once, before the AHC, before Lodestar, before the burning night that changed her life, Helen had been a young woman with dreams of acting. She'd even gotten in some training during her brief stint at college. That interest and talent had served her well many times through the years, and this was no exception. She successfully managed to keep the twist of incredulity from her expression. Two years of team training? Most were lucky to get two weeks before they were needed somewhere in the world. Professor Quantum had been polishing these four long past the point where it was worthwhile, just to make sure they'd do his legacy proud. Never mind that they'd have been better served doing the work and growing from experience: the image came first.

However, none of that was the team's fault, which was why Lodestar denied the frustrated expression any time on her face. "That's clear to see from watching the tapes. You're all very gifted, and you work together extremely well."

The foursome basked in the compliment like she'd breathed literal light into them. Even Presto's smile was glowing. It made the next line all the harder to speak, but she did so, anyway. Taking the tougher path was what being a cape was all about.

"Unfortunately, I think some of Professor Quantum's older, less-refined tactics might have slipped into your education. Today, for example. You all did an excellent job stopping the robbers, but it took at least four times as long as it should have with your skill levels. Any of them could have fired into the gathered civilians while you were taking turns putting on a show. Additionally, none of you were actually working crowd control. You are *extremely* lucky that your first job was in Ridge City, where the population knows what to do in a meta-fight. Another town, another country, people will try to get close for pictures and souvenirs. If things hadn't broken your way several times, the news would be reporting on the showboating new team who got civilians killed."

To an outside observer, it would appear like Lodestar had just slapped the

New Science Sentries without so much as a twitch of her hand. Eyes wide, mouths agape, they definitely hadn't been prepared to get dressed down, and damn sure not by Lodestar herself. Years of practice giving these speeches had taught her not to pause here. It was best to power through while they were stunned into silence.

"That's the bad news. The good news is this: teaching you to be better superheroes is why the Alliance of Heroic Champions exists in the first place. We'll get you up to date on optimal meta-response strategies, run some drills for you to practice, and in no time, I have faith you'll be a team as useful and beloved as the original Science Sentries."

They didn't exactly look great, but at least most of their mouths had managed to close. Since they were taking it well, Lodestar opted to push ahead and knock out the last major item. Professor Quantum had kicked up a fuss at first, until she once again reminded him that they'd both started under similar conditions.

"One thing you need to learn about the AHC, though: we own our mistakes. Tachyonic, you brought a civilian in front of a crowd of cameras, posed with her, then let her name get leaked to the public. You put that woman in a position she didn't ask for, one that comes with actual danger. That means you're the one who is going to make it right."

As the New Science Sentries leaned in, Lodestar explained what their next few days would entail.

Chapter 5

The laboratory was elegant: impeccably designed for both function and aesthetics, the work of someone who had spent untold years inside such research facilities. On a large screen, videos of the day's robbery played on a loop, cycling in new footage as soon as varying angles became available. Some were selected from public broadcasts; other bits were harvested from phones with poorly secured encryptions.

In the center of the lab, a gaunt man stood, watching the television. Average height, bland looks, and a slight stoop in his shoulders. The only parts of him that stood out were his perfectly bald head, unnervingly thin silhouette, and the shining intelligence in his eyes. Well, those features, and the small leak of dark smoke coming from his left wrist—but that could wait for the moment. His attention was rapt on the screen, and every time an anchor said the name of the new team, the man twitched as though it were a physical blow.

"About time you let them out. I was wondering how much more bait it would take. Those poor souls of yours have no idea who they're following. Someone should remedy that." He glanced down, noticing the steady stream of smoke, and frowned. "I'll have to make myself presentable first, get a handle on my excitement. Can't give away the turn too soon."

That bland face split into a wide-mouthed cackle, the man cracking up at his own pseudo-joke as he moved toward a massive machine taking up a full quarter of the laboratory. As the laughter rolled off him, so too did flecks of his skin, loosing more dark smoke into the air. With a single wave of his hand, the machine's door opened, and he vanished inside.

"Nice office." Tori took note of the faux columns on the exterior: not especially good-looking, but visibly expensive. In a way, the columns were a snapshot of the entire office: designed by someone who wanted to exude the appearance of wealth, yet lacked any actual sense of taste or refinement. Granted, she wasn't an especially swanky woman herself; Tori only developed a skill at gauging such factors because it mattered during her thief days. Knowing what a place was worth at a glance was part of using one's time efficiently.

"Real estate developers are evidently doing well in the wake of Ridge City's recent disaster." Ivan somehow managed to keep the words neutral, despite the fact that the "disaster" he was referring to had kicked off when Ivan let himself slip back into Fornax and had chased Apollo around the city. While it was true that the incident, like the rest of the fiasco, was mostly Balaam's fault, it didn't mean the public at large had forgotten Fornax. Especially since he was supposed to have been dead.

The office was mostly empty, not surprising since the workday had ended. They heard conversation coming from a break area and saw a few bodies shuffling through the halls, so at least they weren't meeting the guy in an empty building. That would have set off Tori's trap instincts, though that might have been pretty entertaining in and of itself, she quickly realized. Anyone trying to jump Ivan from a dark alley was in for the surprise of their soon-to-be-ended lives.

Winding their way back through the carpeted halls, Ivan led her to a door labeled "Haywood Gibson" that had been left cracked open. They paused before Ivan touched the knob and gave Tori a pointed look, which she answered with a simple nod. From here on, it was Ivan's show. She might not be his apprentice anymore, but she damn sure took a passenger position when it came to watching after Ivan's children. Whatever happened would be up to him and no one else.

One quick knock was all Ivan gave before he shoved the door open to reveal a handsome man in a gray suit, working at his desk. The moment his eyes fell on Ivan, a rapid flash of emotions ran through him. Much as he tried to hide his real feelings under professional friendliness, there had been something dark for a split second. Anger, maybe, or perhaps fear? Whatever it was, Tori knew Haywood wasn't happy to see them, regardless of the lies he was about to spit out.

"Mr. Gerhardt, glad you could make it, and right on time, at that." Haywood was up, extending a strong hand which Ivan shook. His frame and size betrayed the muscular definition beneath the suit, but if he was trying to intimidate Ivan with a squeeze, she doubted that Ivan would even notice. "Unfortunately, I'm afraid I don't have any better news to share. As I told your ex-wife, when Dr. Randall left Ridge City following that unpleasantness some weeks ago, the Starscouts had to be reorganized as personnel shifted to cover the gap. While I'm happy to be taking over for him as cluster leader, I don't have the power to change the fundamental makeup of the groups."

It was a fine story. Put the blame on bureaucracy, which was virtually impossible to disprove, and paint himself as a sympathetic ally. The trouble was... it was bullshit. Tori was able tell that much, so Ivan definitely could. Still, just in case, she should do what she was ostensibly here for.

"Weird. Because my cluster leader left when I was five, and no one had to break up my group or transfer anyone out."

"I also find it fascinating that this 'reorganization' appears to have affected only one single child: my daughter." Ivan stared hard at Haywood for a long second, then did the last thing Tori was prepared for. He smiled. "But we're in luck. I happen to know some higher-ups in the Starscouts. If the issue is one of simple red tape, that should be an easy matter to cut through, with their cluster leader's permission."

Was he lying? It seemed possible, especially given who was at the *top* of the Starscouts, but Tori made it a policy not to rule out anything. She had friends on the cape-side; maybe there were some hidden strings Ivan could pull. Besides, what mattered wasn't whether it was true or not, only if Haywood believed them.

On that account, there was no need to worry. Whether it was Ivan's magic or years of experience speaking with authority as a manager, Haywood's blanched expression made it clear he'd bought the story. "I'd be happy to help in any way I can, but since meetings are due to start next week, I'm afraid there's probably not enough time to get it resolved. If she would like to transfer back in over Winter Break, I'm sure we can manage something."

"Don't worry about that, Mr. Gibson. My contacts work fast. Beth will be back in her cluster before tomorrow evening. Unless there's some other issue I haven't been made aware of." Ivan was still smiling, still polite, and Tori could feel her stomach tying itself in knots.

She'd seen Ivan on a murderous rampage as Fornax. She'd seen him be an efficient killer of the guild as Pseudonym. And she'd seen him manhandle Balaam as a vengeful father. She'd seen her teacher's ire enough times that she'd begun to smell violence on the wind whenever someone near him walked a dangerous line. Tori took a few steps back, trying not to draw attention—not that she needed to worry. Both men's eyes were locked on one another.

Haywood broke the stare, affecting an "aw-shucks" air as he switched tactics. "Okay, you got me. I didn't want to bring this up, in light of you all knowing one another, but there's been some concern from the other parents. Beth's... condition makes her dangerous. She can produce sharp metal from her body on a whim, and that makes some parents nervous."

"Then you tell them to eat shit, because the founding principle of Starscouts is that it's for *everyone*. Any gender, any race, any species—meta, human, or in-between. Every child is welcome." Tori was surprised at the ferocity in her voice. She wasn't sure if the anger came from memories tied to her mother or the fact that of all the dumb stuff in the Starscouts, that part had always stuck with her.

"It's fine, Tori. The problem isn't with the parents. I know, because they are the parents of Beth's friends. After her change, we reached out to each one—even sat down with a few—to make sure they understood what had happened. Not everyone was in love with it, but none of them would try to kick her out of her cluster. That would be Mr. Gibson's decision." Ivan never so much as glanced at Tori, his attention fully on the now slightly sweating real estate developer who was glaring right back.

In what had to be one of the all-time greatest pointless gestures, Haywood puffed his chest a bit, emphasizing the size difference between him and Ivan. She wished with all her heart that this idiot would swing, but that was likely hoping for too much.

"Fine, Mr. Gerhardt, you've worn me down. Yes, I am the one who transferred Beth out, and I'm not going to apologize for it. The rest of the kids in that cluster are nice, normal humans, and you want me to let some girl with a power she can barely control be in there with them? Forget it. I'm putting my foot down as their leader. The safety of the cluster comes first."

For the first time, Ivan broke eye contact with Haywood, looking to Tori. "Is that excuse number three or four? I'm starting to lose count."

"One was a half-step between lies, so let's call it three, to be safe," Tori replied.

"I suspect this will be the last. False concern for others is often the bigot's final refuge, at least when patriotism is off the table." He turned back to

Haywood, no longer smiling. "Now then, Mr. Gibson, your worry for the safety of children is admirable, which is why Beth has received constant training to control her powers, a task at which she has excelled. Tell me, what hollow reason would you like to offer up next?"

It had taken some time and cracking through a few false fronts, but before their eyes, the real Haywood Gibson finally appeared. His pleasant face warped into an expression of tight, pinched anger, and he straightened to his full height, which was admittedly taller than either Tori or Ivan. That probably made him feel safe, a reminder that he still had the physical advantage—a delusion that would last only until it was tested, however.

"I'm supposed to just take your word for it, let her in the door because you say it's okay?" The tone was more belligerent now. He was done with diplomacy.

"I would recommend you take the word of the Alliance of Heroic Champions, who has been providing her and others in similar positions with the training," Ivan shot back. "They can produce reports, and did, which I know because we submitted them along with Beth's registration information. But you never read those, did you? You saw the word 'meta' and knew in that moment she wasn't going to be in *your* cluster."

Haywood wisely stayed silent. Implication was one thing; admitting to what he'd done with a witness in the room was another. Ivan just shook his head. "It doesn't matter. I was serious about knowing higher-ups in the organization. Congratulations on your brief tenure as a cluster leader, Mr. Gibson. By tomorrow, the position will be revoked, and I expect you'll be barred from the organization for violating one of its most fundamental tenets. Tori, we can leave now. Our business is concluded."

Not quite looking away yet, Ivan motioned for her to head to the door. Haywood, on the other hand, apparently didn't enjoy being talked down to. He'd gotten redder and redder as Ivan spoke, and Tori could see a vein bulging along his forehead. After a moment or two to absorb the chewing out, Haywood leaned forward, towering over Ivan.

"Listen here, asshole. I don't know who you think you are fucking with, but you've got no idea the connections I have in this town. Call all the people you want—call Lodestar herself—I'm telling you right now, there is no way I'm going to open my home to your little *abomination* for—"

Tori didn't see the punch. She could make out the spray of blood that splashed across the desk, and the half-shattered teeth clattering against a wall, she just wasn't able to track Ivan's fist as it obliterated Haywood's jaw. Her whole body went cold, unsure of what the hell was going on. There was no warning, no lead-up, just a savage blow and a now rasping man on the ground, trying to make noise through a mouth no longer shaped for it. With no small measure of fear, Tori looked to Ivan, unsure if it would be him or Fornax who awaited her.

As it turned out, it was Ivan. Purely Ivan. His eyes hadn't even turned inky and rune-filled, meaning he wasn't substantially using his powers whatsoever.

That didn't set her as much at ease as she'd have expected, though. The darkness on Ivan's face was something Fornax could never match; he didn't love anything enough to fuel that much hate.

"Since she was a child, Beth has always tried to help those in need. She made a habit of bringing home injured animals, from crushed snails to wounded birds. No matter how many times we told her it was pointless, she kept trying. And when she of course failed, we had to hold a funeral ceremony for each one of those lost souls. Every house I've lived in has become a makeshift graveyard, because that girl refuses to walk past when she sees a living being in pain. It's the same with other children, and people as a whole. That is who my daughter has always been at her core: someone who reaches out to help those in need, no matter how helpless their situation might be. She is so kind, so gentle; every day I am filled with gratitude and pride that she turned out *nothing* like her cruel, petty father."

With a casual ease, Ivan pressed a foot into Haywood's ribs, cracking several. "And now, because of something she had no choice in or control over, Beth is going to spend the rest of her life dealing with pieces of shit like you, people who try to take that goodness away from her. Tearing her down for the sin of existing. Telling her she's different, lesser, that the world doesn't have a place for her."

Reaching down, Ivan grabbed Haywood by the neck and lifted him into the air. Whatever illusions the developer had possessed about being stronger than his visitor were long since dispelled. He was visibly cowering now, broken mouth rasping out attempts at screams. As Ivan stared into Haywood's eyes, his own began to change. The irises expanded, swallowing up each eye into a pit of endless darkness. Then, from within the void, red runes began to glow.

If Haywood had been scared before, he was terrified now. His attempts to struggle doubled, and Tori thought she caught the scent of liquid fear emanating from his slacks.

For Ivan, the shifts were irrelevant. He reached up and broke Haywood's left arm in two places.

"Such a shame about the car accident. Crumpled in, really tore up your whole left side. Don't worry, we'll make sure people remember seeing you leave and drive off unharmed. We are exceptionally good at this kind of thing. Because you forgot, Mr. Gibson, that not all metas are capes. We don't all suffer silently and take the higher road. You won't remember this meeting, not truly, but you'll see me in your nightmares. Take this lesson to heart, and carry it with you always."

Ivan pulled Haywood in close until he was mere inches from those deadly glowing eyes. "Some of us fight back. Don't you ever dare forget that, because the next meta might not have my exceptional self-restraint. One last thing: if you ever go near the Starscouts again, in any capacity, I'll rip your fucking limbs off. Filth like you doesn't belong around anything that decent."

Part of Tori wanted to chuckle, but there was nothing funny about the look on Ivan's face. For her part, she took out a cell phone and punched in a familiar number. It was a line all official guild members had to know by heart, and one of the few services that had remained functional during their downtime.

"Yeah, it's me. I think we're going to need a cleanup team. What happened? Ivan got mad. No, not *that* mad. We don't need power washers."

From his position in Ivan's grip, Haywood let out a small squeak of terror before the pain and shock finally sent him into unconsciousness. When he awoke, his memory of acquiring the injuries would be quite different. The eyes would stay with him, though, in his darkest of nightmares. No amount of drugs or drink could drive them away.

Injuries might mend over time, but some wounds burned too deep to heal. Just as Ivan intended.

Chapter 6

Were he forced to explain as simply as possible, Ivan might say the difference between common criminals and villains of the guild was the concept of consequence. Criminals tried to live without them; villains accepted they were inevitable. Leave too much evidence, go to jail. Piss off the capes, end up hunted. Fight Lodestar, lose. Simple, inevitable equations that were easy to ignore in the short-term if one didn't mind losing in the long run.

Villains accepted these facts and were therefore able to work around them. They learned to obliterate their trails, to use the law as a shield, and to avoid getting mixed up with capes. Most of that last one came from just plain avoiding them, making it a point to be where the superheroes weren't. Sometimes, unfortunately, it wasn't that simple. Sometimes, accepting the consequences meant not getting away clean.

Ivan knew what he had to do, just as much as he knew he couldn't let Tori be a part of it.

After a largely silent car ride home, he pulled up in front of the townhouse. "There are several places nearby that deliver. My apologies that we didn't have time to pick something up."

"I... my appetite did well with recovery time, anyway." It was the gentlest way she could broach what had just happened. In the moment, all Ivan had seen was Haywood, but once they turned things over to the cleanup team, he'd realized the experience might have been hard on Tori. She'd witnessed him in the throes of madness, seen him act as a guild enforcer, yet she'd never watched him be so casually violent before.

"What you saw in there… I won't say I regret it, but I could have sent you from the room first. For that, I'm sorry."

Tori whipped her head back in surprise. "Whoa now, I think there's a misunderstanding. Yes, I'm still new enough for bloodshed to make me queasy, but I am on-fucking-board with what just went down. I'm replaying it in my head, subbing in some choice teachers I had who had interesting ideas about what 'kinds' of people should go into the sciences. You don't need to apologize to me for shit. I didn't call the cops, Ivan. I called a team to wipe up your mess. Let's not forget, I'm in this guild too."

She made a good point. In truth, Ivan should be taking her along; she would do well to see this next part. However, that wasn't his choice to make. The next errand revolved around someone else's secret. At the very least, he'd try to get the message across. Even if she was no longer his apprentice, Ivan had plenty of experience to share.

"Then you need to remember what comes after an indulgence like that: owning the fallout. Our team will handle the cleanup, but I just hospitalized a Starscout cluster leader a week before they were set to resume meetings. It is on me to go tell my Starscout contacts about the situation and help them make it right. That might mean paying for training the replacement out of pocket, or pitching in with some sort of manual labor at their next event. I could choose not to do that, but it would risk losing those contacts. A villain owns their actions and the consequences that follow."

After briefly considering the words, Tori popped her door open. "I get it, and I get that these contacts are probably not the kind you bring a new person around. One question, though: how do you know they won't make you take Haywood's place?"

"Because they know my *full* history, and I can't imagine anyone wants Fornax watching over a herd of children."

"Too bad. If we got a picture of you in the cluster leader uniform, I bet I could make a mint selling those around the guild."

"It's the digital age. The Bytes would just scan one and put it on a shared server," Ivan pointed out.

Tori climbed out of the car before poking her head back in. "Spoilsport. Good luck with your contacts. You know if you need me..."

"I know. Thank you." With that, Ivan drove off into the night.

Part of Tori was sorely tempted to follow him and see about these mysterious contacts, except she'd just received a very good reminder that Ivan was not to be tested on some matters. His kids were one of them; the code was another. Besides, after the drive home, she was feeling peckish, and by the time food arrived, Tori would be ravenous.

Whatever he was up to, Ivan could handle himself. Hell, so far as Tori knew, there was only one person in the world who could beat Ivan in a real fight, and what were the odds he'd run into her?

"Yeah, I got the call. Checking on it now." Dapper Doll clomped along through the rain, cursing her bad fortune to get patrols in a city under a storm cloud. She was ready to get out of Norwalk and back to the comforts of Ridge City—specifically, her dry room and clothes at the AHC. It wasn't that she minded getting wet for the job—had there been a civilian in need, Dapper Doll would have been racing to their aid. For a simple reconnaissance job involving someone spotting suspicious activity, however, the gusto was harder to conjure.

Stepping down a side street, toward what should have been a building's rear, filled with dumpsters and perhaps a few people sneaking smokes, Dapper Doll caught sight of movement. Music pulled at her ears, high-pitched and cloying. She slipped closer, thoughts of dryness abandoned. Clangs rose as she moved beneath a section of roof, blocking her momentarily from the rain.

Turning a corner, Dapper Doll couldn't believe what she saw. Burgers, pizza, fried chicken, hot dogs, cake—an entire smorgasbord of food presented on an immaculately decorated table. Only the food wasn't lying there, waiting to be eaten. Instead, it was moving around, singing, dancing, and generally partying like there was no tomorrow. Now that she was near, Dapper Doll could see the others watching, entranced: nearly a dozen civilians who must have stumbled upon the show. For a moment, she feared a trap, before noticing the giant banner that hung in the middle of the scene. Emblazoned upon it were three simple words:

"Expect the Unexpected."

Swallowing hard, Dapper Doll tapped her communicator to radio the office. The higher-ups were definitely going to want to know that Captain Bullshit was active again.

Beverly paused outside the apartment to wipe off her shoes, even though it hadn't rained all day. There had been a massive, stinky puddle to walk through in front of the building, along with a gaggle of smelly, soaked photographers who glared daggers at everyone who strolled inside. They were looking for someone, and having casually glanced at a TV in the last ten hours meant that Beverly knew exactly who. The assholes could wait all night; she'd already gotten a text from Tori that she was crashing at Ivan's place.

Were anyone else she knew staying at the house of an older gentleman they worked for, it would have thrown up a plethora of red flags. Tori and Ivan, thankfully, were a rare exception to the rule. They liked and respected one another, but even ten minutes around the pair made it clear how deeply platonic their relationship was. Beverly was glad for that, especially when Tori needed a place to crash while the guild was down. After this weekend, they'd both have a spot to lay low when the occasion demanded.

Walking into the apartment, Beverly found Chloe standing by the brick wall at the living room's far end, looking out on to the street and the photographers below. "Am I off base in guessing you're the reason all those paparazzi are wet and grumpy?"

"Debatable," Chloe replied. "I just happened to forcefully mention that 'Karma is a bitch' near them. I would argue that after that, anything negative that happened afterward is a consequence of their own choices… including a truck hauling used septic water springing a sudden and brief leak just as it drove past. I also think four of them have stubbed their toes. Guess Karma and I have the same opinion of their profession."

Being part of a guild filled with famous villains, Beverly often marveled at the raw power of her colleagues. Yet Chloe, of all people, worried her even more at times. That ability of hers was easy to underestimate and could have ridiculously potent effects. If it had to end up in anyone's hands, maybe it was best it had gone to neither a cape nor a villain, but to someone who only used the gift casually. And on deserving victims, in this case.

"Isn't septic water...?"

"Yeah, the front stoop needs a serious washing, and you might want to give a scrubbing to any shoes you walked through it with," Chloe confirmed.

"Glad I wiped my feet." Beverly hunkered down and popped her shoes off, wrapping them in a paper towel to be dealt with once she'd had a moment to relax. "You got Tori's message, I assume?"

Chloe walked over from the window, turning on the oven and yanking a container from the fridge. "Caught up in a new team's debut, became a media curiosity, laying low until it blows over. Means there's one less for dinner."

"That lucky bum is probably getting home cooking. According to Thu… someone I know, the person she's staying with is pretty good in a kitchen."

The statement earned Beverly a look of worried surprise. When they'd moved in with Chloe, she and Tori had been honest about their affiliation to the Guild of Villainous Reformation. It only seemed right, given that living with them exposed her to certain risks, plus Beverly had spilled most of the beans during the "Ridge City Riots" (as most media outlets had dubbed Balaam's attempted uprising.) Outside of that detail, though, Chloe knew very little of their world. She didn't ask, they didn't offer, and the balance had been holding well, so far.

"Sorry, there's no reason I should find that weird. Everyone eats, so some criminals probably cook well. Just not what I picture when I imagine famous villains, you know? Except for Doctor Mechaniacal, maybe. He always did remind me of a kitchen gadget gone awry."

Beverly laughed, but said nothing. Neither she nor Tori had told Chloe who'd been their mentors when joining the guild. It wasn't necessarily a secret, just a topic both took care not to broach accidentally. If Chloe asked, Beverly would answer, for what little that was worth. Her mentor, a surprisingly cultured giant called Thuggernaut, was mostly known as an enforcer who'd gotten on the law's wrong side—nothing overly shocking. When Chloe found out she was living with Fornax's apprentice, on the other hand, it might require a longer talk.

That was Tori's battle, and it could wait for another night. Beverly had her own shit to deal with. But she could also use some rest and entertainment after a long day's work. "Hey, Chloe, doesn't the cycling club usually come up the road not too long from now?"

"That they do," Chloe confirmed.

"I wonder if any of them will accidentally end up on the sidewalk, running over the paparazzi's feet?" Pouring herself a tall glass of wine, Beverly walked over to the window and took a spot opposite from where Chloe had been standing, gazing out on the street below.

As it turned out, no cyclists rode on the sidewalk, but one kicked up a spray of stray gravel that got into the eyes of three photographers and broke two cameras. It wasn't until they'd been rubbing their faces for several minutes that someone appeared to remember they were covered in septic water, which led to a mass panic as the three began running around in a tizzy about the impending pink eye.

No doubt about it, Chloe's power was scary as hell.

Things were getting interesting again. The lulls were unavoidable—without a valley, was there such a thing as a peak? Thankfully, just as inevitable was the eventual beginning of something new. So many times he had watched stories like this one, yet they were not quite the same. A shift in details, a difference of characters, all while the bones persisted: new team arrives in town, kicks up a fuss, encounters a stranger that is more than she appears to be.

It wasn't always Tori and Tachyonic. They weren't even always called the New Science Sentries. Sometimes, the debut went bad. Gunfire, people getting hurt, blood everywhere… a lack of real-world experience showing itself in the worst possible way. Those universes were rare, though. Professor Quantum had raised a powerful team, if nothing else. That part almost never changed.

To Nexus, the only things even close to being as interesting as the Singulars—beings who existed in only a single iteration of the multiverse—were those he considered to be Constants. These were fascinating in how little they varied across the infinite sea of possibilities. Lodestar was often a different person—such was the nature of that gift—yet whoever wore the power unfailingly upheld the same standard. That had confused Nexus for a time, until he unraveled the secret of her abilities.

Far more interesting were ones like Professor Quantum. He virtually never changed. In any universe where he existed, he was almost always the same: brilliant, prophetic, and dangerous. Even better, by this point there was usually a dash of desperation mixed in. Alone, that would have made Professor Quantum a boring target to watch, each iteration being nearly identical. However, although every Professor Quantum was often the same, the worlds they lived in varied tremendously, and that was what made him interesting.

The new team's composition this time was a surprise—Presto often didn't make the cut. This one was either talented or determined. Nexus could hardly wait to see which it would be as he sat on the roof-deck of Tori's building, enjoying the late-summer evening heat. Already, the gears were turning, old grudges rising. It was shaping up to be one hell of a show this time around. And it would be, no matter what.

Things were going to be interesting soon, even if Nexus had to *make* them interesting.

Chapter 7

"To be clear, your story is that you came by my home to tell me one of the Starscout cluster leaders was keeping a meta-human child, your daughter, out of her established group, and that said leader was also involved in a terrible car accident that will remove him from the role. The two things are, I'm supposed to believe, an unrelated coincidence. Good god, Ivan, you couldn't have brought this in when I was putting Penelope to bed? She loves a good piece of fiction."

The kitchen table was tense as Helen and Ivan both nursed their cups of coffee. As far as these sorts of talks went, it hadn't been a terrible one. She'd heard him out and hadn't interrupted, even during the section they both knew to be utter falsehood. Once the story was over, though, Helen had gotten a serious look in her eyes. She'd left the room briefly, made a few calls, and returned with a sense of purpose. Ivan had no idea what to expect when she put on that expression, only that she'd be the one to decide the next step.

"I'll ask out of obligation, is there any chance that I could find evidence to prove this wasn't just a car accident?"

"I can't imagine why you would. Ask the man himself. He'll tell you he got distracted on the road and spun out, eventually slamming into a tree. Not only is there a lack of evidence, there is, technically speaking, no crime to investigate."

Wordlessly, Helen finished her coffee, walked to the counter, poured a fresh cup, and then proceeded to dump in more fake sugars than Ivan could fathom before returning to her seat. Her holographic-generating glasses were perched on the side of the table, meaning that she looked her physical age at the moment. Somehow, watching what should be a nineteen year old with such a world-weary gaze always unnerved him slightly.

Ivan sat patiently as she worked, wondering what would come next. This was new ground for them. Part of her had to know these things happened, yet normally, Ivan kept it miles from her radar. Tonight was different; he'd messed with something of *hers*.

"Ivan, do you know the origins of the Starscouts?" Helen spoke after three test sips from her new cup of coffee.

"I recall the general shape of the tale," Ivan replied. "A pair of siblings accidentally kicked up a fuss when one wanted to join the Junior League of Heroes, Professor Quantum's old child-meta indoctrination ring, and the other was barred entry for being human. When they switched over, both attempting to join the Kid Adventurers, they found out that that organization didn't allow metas. In the media firestorm that followed, a new company wanted to start something to capitalize on the opportunity, but they were competing with established institutions, so they needed a big draw. The sort of face no one could ignore. They found her, but she demanded more than just certain humans and metas be allowed in. Lodestar watches over everyone, so every child was welcome in her organization. That was the deal if they wanted to use her as a spokeswoman."

Another sip from the cup. "This jerk isn't the first to try to break my promise. There are systems in place for that sort of thing. Whatever insult he hurled to get under your skin, you would have won out in the end. But from what I'm hearing, he got the absolute hell beaten out of him. These aren't the old days, Ivan. You can't go around punching everyone who annoys or—"

"He called my daughter an abomination. You want to throw me back into Rookstone, go right ahead. We both know you can do it. But the Earth will rot and the sun will die before I ever apologize for what I did tonight."

The serious veneer slipped slightly, revealing a shocked expression on Helen's face. "I wasn't expecting that."

"Thought better of me?" Ivan asked.

"Worse. I assumed if he'd crossed a line like that, you'd have killed him outright." Helen leaned back in her chair, hands absentmindedly drumming on the cup. "For goodness' sake, Ivan, you always keep things moving, I'll give you that. What am I supposed to do with this? We both know you broke the law, but I've got no provable victim, not even a crime to report. Capes aren't judge or jury outside of dire emergencies, and without proof, I'd just be wasting time and resources trying to pin you for this."

He didn't have an easy answer to give. This was the trouble with having friends on the other side. Sooner or later, it made things complicated. Although in the case of he and Helen, it had definitely been sooner. "It is a dilemma. If I can offer something to help make it right, I will."

Helen hopped off her chair again, this time going to a different section of the kitchen and returning with a bottle of dark rum. She poured a shot into her remaining coffee, then offered it to Ivan, who also accepted. Neither of them could get drunk off such a paltry offering; it was the act of drinking together that held significance.

"Here's the situation as I see it. You hurt a civilian tonight. Maybe one who had it coming, but still, you hurt a mundane. It's one thing when criminals fight one another—not even Lodestar can protect people from their own choices. Civilians are different; you of all people know that. You can't skate on this, Ivan. That said, you handled it the best way I could have hoped for, coming right over and reading me in on the situation, even being honest when pushed. It's possible, if I spent a *tremendous* amount of resources that would be better used elsewhere, that I *might* be able to get the courts to prosecute you for assault. Not a great option. So instead, we'll do this one off the books. No cops, no jail. You're serving *my* sentence. Can you handle that?"

Some might have jumped at the opportunity. Not Ivan. He stared into his coffee-cocktail, pondering the offer for a full minute before finally offering a reply. "I won't betray anyone who has put their trust in me. If the penance requires me to turn on the guild or other allies, then I'm afraid I must decline."

It was Helen's turn to think, though she didn't need as long. "I'm almost completely certain my idea won't cause you do that; however, if it comes up, we can agree to deal with it on a case-by-case basis."

With resigned determination, Ivan nodded. "Then I will abide by the punishment you decide."

"Good." Helen pulled out her phone and began to text. "I'm sending over some details. You'll need to go pick up a uniform before next week, plus review the information and resource packet long before the meeting. I don't care how dorky the uniform looks; you're wearing it."

The whiplash was so severe that not even Ivan's augmented body could bear it. His head swam as talk shifted from punishment to doing some sort of errand. It was only when Ivan looked at the text Helen sent that the pieces fell into place.

"You can't be serious. The other parents would throw a fit if they knew."

"They *will* know. They'll know that Ivan Gerhardt stepped in to take over as cluster leader after a supposedly unrelated car accident sidelined the current one. And since they all think of Ivan as a pillar of the community and a loving parent—a view I share—they'll have no objections to you filling the role." Helen was grinning a little now, making a half-effort to hide the smile behind her coffee cup. "Besides, you don't have to do it alone. Every Starscout cluster has a male and female leader, so you'll get someone at your side to help."

Ivan took a heftier drink, wishing he'd put more rum in the coffee. "I can only imagine what poor soul will be trapped with me as a partner."

"Seeing as Haywood's helper was going to be a secretary from his office, she's pulled out along with him," Helen said. "Don't worry. I already know a perfect sub. Great woman, won't take any of your shit, and has one hell of a hand at a crafting table."

"*You*? You're going to be a Starscout cluster leader? Isn't that a tad... self-indulgent?"

"Solid point. I'll let some other gal unknowingly pair up with a legendary supervillain to take care of a bunch of children." The smile faded slightly, her eyes growing firm once more. "Look, making you clean up after yourself is the best idea I have that doesn't involve a wild goose chase of investigation, but I also owe a responsibility to those kids. While you've got your talents, I think they'll do better with someone a little more personable, as well. So I'm going to help, because although you are a criminal and fast with the punches, you're also my friend."

It was a touching moment, cut short as she quickly added, "Oh, and Tori is going to be joining us as well."

The cup nearly shattered in Ivan's hand, his tension in the moment the only thing that left him aware enough to stop the reaction of surprise. "Why would we do that? On top of putting your identity at needless risk, Tori and I have roughly the same level of personal skills. Even Wade said as much when he paired us together, calling us both pains in the ass. I don't imagine that improves around children."

"She's not coming because we need the help. She's coming to get the lesson. Tori was with you during all of this, so she needs to see that even Fornax has to face the consequences of his actions."

Although he'd marshalled himself as she spoke, Ivan was still feeling unnerved. "How did you know about... never mind, I suppose it doesn't matter. Tori had no hand in the night's events. She was there only because she couldn't go home, thanks to an AHC cape putting her in the spotlight."

"Tachyonic and the others are already working on making right their mistakes. We're talking about you." There was a sternness to Helen's tone that made it clear she wasn't negotiating; however, it had softened slightly by the time she spoke again. "I assumed Tori was a bystander already, which is why I'm giving her the same role. She's going to be our assistant—or accomplice, as some might call it—just like she was tonight. Besides, I think it's time to meet your apprentice, especially now that she's tied to the New Science Sentries."

"What am I supposed to tell her about why, exactly, she suddenly has to start joining us for Starscout meetings?"

"I'd go with the truth," Helen suggested. "You're making amends and need her help. If she really pushes, you could tell her that the orders came from Lodestar herself."

Ivan's eyes widened in terror as he imagined taking that route. "I'll think of something else. That sort of statement raises more questions than it answers, and Tori's curiosity is already a dangerous thing. I'd hate to see it piqued in your direction." He glanced over, expecting professional interest and instead finding a sly smirk of excitement.

"I like her already. Now, let's dig into the Starscout meeting structure. You might want to grab a pen."

A secret, high-tech, guild-funded base this was not. The building had been a manufacturing plant for cheap plastic novelties that went belly-up a few decades back, then got further developed by a tech startup to use as a hip new office. Sadly, they also went bankrupt—in this case, before the renovation was even complete. The result of this was a strange, cavernous building with an unusual number of empty rooms, giant production machines covered in grime and dust, as well as the rare and wonderful luxury of working toilets.

The crew gathered around Deacon, whose eyes were shining brightly. Nobody was sure if Deacon was really a meta, like he claimed, or if he was just a smart guy with ambition and guts. His thin frame might have made him an easy target in a different organization, but a benefit of being the mastermind was that no one expected physical intimidation to be in his repertoire. Besides, that was why Darius stood on the opposite side of Emory, both of them flanking Deacon, sending the clear message that he wasn't alone.

While Deacon might not really be a meta-genius like he claimed, he was certainly smart enough to keep his bodyguards well compensated.

Darius was a standard bruiser, the sort of strong, tough meta one could find without much effort. He was a little older than some, which presented vulnerabilities, but also experience. Thus far, he'd been a useful asset to Deacon. Hell, a good chunk of this gang had been found through Darius's contacts. Emory himself was less bulky, yet substantially more unnerving. Scales on his gray-green skin gave away his condition before one could notice the sharp claws on his hand or the fangs in his mouth. Good as Darius was at handling the straightforward threats, some challenges called for a more flexible solution.

After a couple of weeks working for Deacon, Emory had begun to get a sense of the man. The talk had been going for five minutes already, and as he watched Deacon's posture straighten, Emory realized they were finally getting to the meat of the matter.

"—and so, you see, fate has offered us a rare chance. Thanks to today's events, we have an opportunity to do something few would ever dream. We can gain the advantage over a group of *superheroes*. Imagine it: grabbing a woman they've only just publicly saved and holding her hostage. For the life of a civilian, the superheroes will bend over backward."

From the back, a hand went up, followed quickly by the man shouting his question. "Won't one of the big capes just come save her?"

There was a murmur of agreement among the masses. No one had forgotten seeing the capes kick ass across Ridge City not so long ago, a solid reminder of what made them dangerous.

"A fair point, and one I considered myself. Worry not, I have a lead on some components that will render us impossible to find for even the most gifted of metas," Deacon assured him. "As for dealing with our targets, do not fret. We will conduct this operation in such a way that the New Science Sentries' own shame will keep them from seeking outside help, keeping our opponents' numbers manageable. They will try to deal with us themselves, and in the process, become even more vulnerable."

Another voice rang from the back. "How does this get us paid?"

The murmurs were much louder this time. Good plans or not, Deacon wasn't winning over this crowd without a dollar sign.

Apparently, he'd been ready for this, continuing without so much as a second of hesitation.

"A smart question to ask before any job. The answer is simple: we get paid for the act of committing the crime. Our talents have been recognized, and the employer is extremely interested in the New Science Sentries. We are not to kill any of them, but injuries will be highly rewarded, as will unmasking any members."

One of the less-public aspects of Emory's power was the gift of smelling emotions. Not every twinge in sentiment flung scents into the air, but the major ones usually came coupled with detectable pheromones. That was why Emory noticed the sting of fear across his nostrils at those words. Wordlessly, three of the criminals turned and walked out of the building without so much as a second thought.

"Don't worry about them," Darius assured Deacon softly. "Plenty in this line of work have a no-AHC policy. They won't run their mouth, but they aren't touching this sort of job regardless of pay."

In different circumstances, Deacon might have ordered them killed. The problem was that all three were connections of Darius, who would most likely get the execution order. If he said no, or stopped Emory from doing the job, Deacon's entire power structure would collapse—that much he was certainly smart enough to see.

"Very well. A greater split of the pay for us."

Deacon went back into his spiel, but Emory kept an eye on Darius. It wasn't him coaching a peaceful solution that was strange; Darius usually erred on the side of diplomacy. No, what bothered Emory was the continuing scent of fear.

The strongest source hadn't left with the others. In fact, it was standing opposite him, guarding the other side of Deacon. Why was Darius so afraid of this plan? What did he and those three seem to know that the rest of them didn't?

Most important of all: why weren't they sharing this concern with anyone else?

Chapter 8

An unexpected silver lining to Tori's sudden minor celebrity status was Vendallia making the call to let her work remotely for the rest of the week. That, or Wade put word through his channels and made it happen. One could never be sure how much influence that man exerted in his company, which, to Ivan's thinking, was exactly the way he liked it.

Pulling up to the Vendallia building, Ivan noted a person hanging out near the entrance. A frown tugged at his neutral expression, trying and failing to coax emotion onto his face. Security was supposed to keep the paparazzi away from the building, since this was privately owned property. This one must have been especially dedicated and foolhardy. Ivan would ensure the mistake wasn't repeated, not at *his* place of work.

Halfway across the parking lot, a familiar flash of copper hair triggered Ivan's memory. It couldn't be... could it? Given that he'd been living at the AHC all this time, the level of change was certainly possible. This man stood straighter and had noticeably more mass, but there was no mistaking Donald Moss. Technically speaking, he was still on the Vendallia payroll, though his deliverables had shrunk to a token level. It had been quite a few weeks since Ivan last laid eyes on his former programmer.

"Mr. Moss, to what do we owe this unexpected honor?" Ivan didn't bother to scan him into the building—not because he felt a need to keep Donald out, but because he suspected the man's reason for visiting wasn't here. "If you've come to check on Tori, I'm afraid she won't be present today. In light of the traumatic events, Vendallia is permitting her to work from home and stay out of the public view."

Even though Donald flushed at the assumption, Ivan knew he'd saved them both five minutes of Donald beating around the bush. This was still a workday, presumably for both of them. Cyber Geek patrolled a lot of local beats with his team; the AHC was helping them lay a good foundation of experience in a place where they still had veteran capes watching. It was hard to miss his antics, and Ivan was glad to see the young man finding his place.

"I wanted to make sure she was okay. And to apologize. Tachyonic isn't on my team, but he's part of the AHC, so it seemed like one of us should say we're sorry about all this."

As a villain, even a barely-involved one, Ivan was grateful Donald hadn't ended up with a more... potent ability. When people with these kinds of noble instincts got serious power, they made being a villain all the harder. To his thinking, there were enough capes like that already, and one *real* superhero spurring them on to greater heights.

"Very responsible of you, Donald. I'll pass the message along—unless you intend to reach out to her today?"

"I might send over a text. Thought it would be better to apologize in person, but I guess digital beats nothing." Donald paused, all pretense of their meeting exhausted. Not wanting to seem like he'd only come for Tori, Donald groped about for small talk. "How have you been, Mr. Gerhardt?"

"Healthy and busy. On that regard, if you'd like to visit socially, I'm happy to make time. However, I'm afraid the day's tasks are currently calling." It was best to put this conversation out of its misery. They both had better uses for their day.

Donald appeared to agree, hurrying away from the door to clear Ivan's way. "Of course! Sorry to bother you, Mr. Gerhardt."

Before he turned away fully, Ivan spoke up once more. "You're never a bother, Donald. I daresay many in the office miss your presence, myself included. They're all very proud of you. If you were to go up and look through the breakroom, I think you'd be surprised just how many of the mugs are emblazoned with Cyber Geek's branding."

The look between them stretched on for several seconds before Donald gave a slow nod. "Thanks, Mr. Gerhardt. You know, you're one of the only people who didn't look at me differently after everyone found out what I could do."

"I have always known the kind of man you are. Gaining powers merely offered you a new way to show that to the world. So long as you remember why you took this path, you never need to feel ashamed about who you are."

Another long look, this one ending with an unexpected smile before Donald finally walked away. Any other day, Ivan would have left out that last part, but the memory of Haywood's words from the prior night still rang in his ears. He could offer a little extra comfort to a fellow meta-human, even if Donald would likely never know it was a bond they shared.

Didn't it fucking figure? The morning prior, Tori would have said she'd trade anything to have the rest of the week off to tweak her suit. Now, she had the time, and one of the only places she couldn't spend it was at her apartment building where the suit was waiting. Plus, in the process of getting her free week, Tori had lost one of her most valuable assets as a villain: anonymity. In her civilian form, she was supposed to be no one of significance—the sort of person eyes would skim right past without another thought.

As she helped herself to Ivan's fridge, noting that he'd stocked some of her favorite beer, Tori mulled over the idea that while anonymity was her teacher's tactic, it wasn't the only one. Wade Wyatt himself proved that point perfectly. Unbeknownst to the rest of the world, famed billionaire investor and entrepreneur Wade Wyatt was really the famous supervillain known as Doctor Mechaniacal. True, everyone did still think of him as a criminal, but only in the ways that capitalism forgave by necessity. Even his most vicious of critics couldn't fathom who they were really talking about.

The more she dwelled on the notion, idly sorting through emails on her laptop in case someone decided to make sure she was putting in the hours, the more Tori began to consider that this might have been inevitable. If she wanted to follow Wade's path, found her own company to sell her tech, then Tori would be a public figure eventually.

Perhaps this could be more than ill-fortune. Notoriety had rewards along with risks. Opening a new browser, Tori brought up old articles on Wade Wyatt's rise to prominence. With an example to pull from and an opportunity to use, she might be able to turn this development to her advantage. Unfortunately, anything she tried would require charisma to pull off, which posed a challenge. When it came to technology and data, Tori spoke the language fluently. Interacting with people had never come as easily. Her best friendships had come from either trying to pretend to be something she wasn't (a normal office drone) or had been forged in the heat of battles with life-or-death stakes.

A problem to tackle down the line, she supposed. Right now, she needed to flesh out this half-formed idea while she still had the shape of it. If nothing else, it was something to fill up her day. She'd stretch her legs for lunch, but until then, Tori waded deep into the waters of the last few decades of meta-human history.

The scrawny boy appeared to be no more than eleven years old, which made the half-drunk glass of warm beer in front of him rather worrying. Stranger still was the way everyone inside the fetid building gave him a wide berth, save only for the waitstaff, who would occasionally venture near to refresh his beverage. Only two other patrons lingered—a pair of men in fatigues with prominently displayed weapons, both nursing a liquor that was bitter and potent.

A new shadow appeared in the door, the person who stepped through causing audible gasps from staff who happened to look over. She was unnaturally tall and thin, like her skin wasn't holding in quite as many organs and muscles as a normal human's might. Skin tinged the color of an old lime, hairless, she moved with dangerous grace, like a cougar roaming the brush. Despite the heat, most of her body, save for her arms, legs, and head, were concealed under a large purple coat with an absurd amount of buttons.

From his spot at the bar, the lone child briefly glanced over, then motioned to a waitress, tapping the empty space at his side. Within moments, another beer was waiting, appearing seconds before the strange woman took her seat.

"You shouldn't be here. We talked about this when we ran. At least, those of us who were sane enough to string words together. Scatter to the winds and lay low for as long as we can. Too many of us gather, the wrong people take notice, and next thing you know, *she'll* be kicking down that door and dragging us back."

His voice was appropriate to his appearance, plainly that of a child. Yet there was a worn quality to it as well, the tone of one who had seen a lifetime of sunsets and still had untold more to go. He appraised his unexpected guest as her unnaturally long fingers plucked the glass from the table and she slurped some of the contents.

"I have never understood your taste for squalor, Grantham." Her voice, like the rest of her, was a little off. Too high in places, too low in others, like someone doing an impression of human speech. "You are correct. Initially, our plan was to spread ourselves thin and stay hidden. Some have been making bolder moves since then. Blade God cut through an entire underground weapons dealer's warehouse hunting for a clue on his swords. Suh-Rak is gathering components for another summoning, some of Cobblord's labyrinths are showing up for sale again, and of course, no one knows what to expect next from Captain Bullshit. Not to mention there were rumors of some mythically powerful frost Viking killing a warlord's army and placing the entire encampment under his control."

At her words, a new tension filled the room. Every person there stopped, waiting to see what the child's reaction would be. It turned out to be finishing his beer and motioning for another. Grantham faced his guest fully as he waited for the refill.

"Come to scold me, Lozora? I didn't kill off some benevolent village leader or anything like that. I tore a criminal's head off, froze it, and put it on display as a warning to whoever tried next. That's how it works, right? We get to do what we want so long as we hurt other criminals? That's how they justified letting fucking Fornax out into the world, isn't it?"

Grantham slammed a fist on the word "Fornax," striking the bar and causing a thin sheet of ice to form along its top. He took a moment to compose himself, then allowed the bartender to set down his next beer. "If the AHC knew about this place, they would have come already."

"Not even superheroes can keep control over the entire world, but I suspect the AHC will make time for us, should they learn of our positions. You remember Captain Bullshit's warning: he has made us nigh impossible to find, but that protection fades once we reveal ourselves publicly, intentionally or otherwise."

Despite the snort that escaped his lips, Grantham had no doubt the protection was real. It was the only explanation for how, in this new, digital age, not a single escaped criminal from Rookstone had been caught yet. Besides that, Captain Bullshit's power was held in high regard. Were it in the hands of someone a little more focused, they might very well be the greatest meta in existence.

"That's why you came all the way out here? To remind me that I need to be careful?"

"No. I came because there might be another way. Someone is making covert hires at the moment. They are funding everything from street-level enterprises to recruiting specialists of our level. I can't say more at this juncture, but trust me when I say it is someone with experience."

Sipping off the top of his drink, Grantham smacked his lips. He had to go into the damn tropics to manage it, but here the natural aura of cold put off by his body was dulled enough to allow for warm drinks to touch his lips. It didn't seem like much, until the ten thousandth time a hot meal turned lukewarm the moment it hit his tongue.

"I'm not bending a knee to that guild. Call themselves villains all they like, but once you've got rules on you, you're a cog in the machine, same as everyone else. Been a cog once. Not going back to that."

Lozora shook her unnatural head. "Not the guild. Not anyone who's been inside Rookstone, actually."

Now *that* got Grantham's attention. "I thought she'd rounded up all the major players."

"There was a long time before her, before the AHC. Some enemies are older, smarter, and more patient. The largest, most fearsome alligators are the ones cunning enough to avoid hunters year after year. One of them is hiring, if that interests you."

For a few minutes, there was no sound save for the occasional slurps of warm beer. At last, Grantham set his glass down, slowly shaking his head.

"Nah. I'm gonna pass. I know where this ends for me: in battle. Always in battle. I've only been out for a little while; I'd like to enjoy myself some more. Give the mystery employer my best, and let them know if something really interesting pops up, I won't automatically kill an envoy—even if they aren't as fearsome as you."

"As expected. I cautioned them as much, but it was essential to try. Having the legendary Jokull on staff is the sort of opportunity that cannot be passed over."

Grantham's face tightened briefly, causing all the nearby staff to scamper back, but it relaxed seconds later. "No Jokull these days unless he's necessary. Luckily, he hasn't been needed since the last attempted insurrection. I think word has finally spread that shooting me while I'm like this only brings him forth."

The pair of armed men on the other side of the hut exchanged sudden, fearful looks, then walked out as casually as they were able. Given the clanks of weaponry as they moved, it was not a particularly successful endeavor.

With a weary sigh, Grantham moved to rise from his seat, until Lozora's hand fell on his shoulder. "Allow me. I'm heading out, anyway. A token of thanks, for your hospitality."

Her long legs unfurled as she stood, making it out of the bar in a smattering of steps. Seconds later, Grantham heard the telltale thud of weighted bodies dropping into the dirt. That was Lozora—when she decided it was time to strike, most never even had a chance to scream.

Part of Grantham was curious to see where her endeavor would lead, but he'd been at this too long to jump at the first offer. Best to wait and let the real schemers get their plans in order. That was what would lead to a fight worth having.

That was when Jokull would return.

Chapter 9

Thursday evening was an unexpectedly busy one in Ivan's townhome. Between having a cluster of Starscouts to prepare for next week and a clandestine organization of criminals reopening that weekend, Ivan was swamped. Some of the work had spilled over onto Tori, who was finding herself dealing with uncomfortable levels of nostalgia as she worked through the old Starscout materials.

Just as the sun was going down, Ivan got a call that had him leave the room. That in itself was par for the course; when they'd been living together, Tori had seen Ivan seek solitude for calls from Vendallia, the guild, and his kids. The man enjoyed his privacy. This time, however, he came back with an expression that was hard to read. Ivan always looked a little too serious for any given situation, yet this was different. Worry, she'd seen enough of on his visage to catch, but unless she was mistaken, there was a small twinkle of amusement in his eyes. It was the sort of potentially dangerous tell she'd learned to watch for years ago.

"I am pleased to announce that you are officially cleared to return to your apartment. The paparazzi gave up faster than we expected. Seems the ones who camped out always had an especially bad time, and the countermeasures to ensure your safety have been put into place. You're free to head over as soon as you like."

"Uh huh. And are we just going to skim past the word 'countermeasures' like that's not some shit I should be read in on?" Tori paused her current work-in-progress—cutting out a few dozen cardboard circles that would be part of a crafting project for the Starscouts. "You've got a look about you. Is this something I should be concerned with?"

While it might have been Tori's imagination, Ivan seemed to smile slightly, just for a sliver of a second. "Yes, it is, but if I were to forewarn you, it might complicate things further. The wheels are in motion. It's not in our power to stop without experiencing serious repercussions. But the countermeasures were put in place by someone I trust, so in the end, I have faith that they'll prove useful."

If it was someone Ivan trusted, then that narrowed down the pool substantially. Outside of his kids, the only people Ivan seemed to trust were some of his fellow guild council members. The most likely candidate was Doctor Mechaniacal, except anything he added to the building, they all knew Tori would find and take apart. Maybe someone with magic, the polar opposite of her specialty. Arcanicus was on the council now and had stayed loyal to the guild during that nasty Balaam business. That made the most sense, and magic was weird, so it could account for why her knowing in advance would matter.

"Doesn't seem like I have much choice in the matter."

"You could move," Ivan suggested. "Get a more secure place, and we'll have our people protect the records so the new home wouldn't slip out. Not pleasant, but sometimes, that is the best solution."

It was true. She had no real attachment to the apartment; they'd only been there a few months. Except... this was the first home she'd *chosen* in a long time. Not a base, or a hideout, or a shelter: a home. Ivan's garage apartment had been a nice stepping stone, but this was different. No one was driving her out until Tori was ready to go.

Besides, it would take too long to get a new lab up and running.

Tori brushed the shards of cardboard from her hands as she stood. "Fuck that. I'm not going anywhere. In fact, if you don't mind, I'd like to head over. I've got some last-minute suit work I can pack in before things kick off this weekend."

"I understand the sentiment to stay planted a little too well," Ivan replied. "By all means. I appreciate the help you've already given. Go home, get *some* rest if you can manage it, and I'll see you after work tomorrow."

Tomorrow. The guild reopened tomorrow. It wasn't like Tori had some grand scheme to rob a stock exchange cooking in the back of her mind, yet she'd been surprised to find that once the Guild of Villainous Reformation had vanished from her life, she suddenly missed it. That was especially strange, given how she'd found her way into it, but she couldn't deny the flutter of excitement in her chest at the thought of tomorrow. Some of the world's most powerful, deadly people would be gathered together, making small talk, and Tori would be right there with them.

No, actually, that wasn't quite right. Hephaestus would be the one in attendance, which was all the more reason Tori needed to get to work. She couldn't very well show up to an event like that in unkempt attire. Beverly would have her head on a platter.

"I'll be there with bells on. Well, with *some* kind of metal covering on."

Ivan groaned, but Tori was almost positive she caught of a hint of chuckle in there as well.

The people walking past the newspaper box paid it no mind. These metal contraptions lingered despite their less frequent use, gravestones for print media even as it desperately grasped at the last vestiges of life. It was old, faded green, and had a dent on one side from an enthusiastic teen with a steel-toed boot. There was nothing of note about it, until there was.

No one could say where the package came from. A box, white as a page, bound with a ribbon the shade of purple that reminded those who saw the hue why purple was the color of royalty. The ribbon ended in a crisp bow with a single end poking out. One tug is all it would take to undo the immaculate ribbon, and upon seeing it, every possessor of hands in the vicinity wanted to be the one to make that tug.

It was a child who was there first, her line of sight and position allowing her to reach the prize before anyone else. For curiosity's sake, that was ideal. An adult would have had considerations, hesitations, thoughts and fears that would have stayed their hands. Children had no such hurdles to clear. When it came to presents, there was an immediate and optimal strategy: open it.

The ribbon gave with a single pull, fluttering lightly to the ground. Fast she could, the girl slipped a thumb under that pristine lid and yanked it up. For an instant, the box seemed empty. Not as if there was nothing inside, but rather as if it contained a vast and endless void, a chasm in existence through which one could slip and be lost forever. Then, from within that void came a voice that burst forth, thundering throughout the entire street.

"Expect the unexpected!"

A squeal broke from the girl's lips as birds burst out of the box, which she quickly dropped and ran away from. They were all species and colors, an avian enthusiast's dearest dream made manifest. So many, too many; the rainbow of wings began to blot out the sky, the roar of their flaps drowning out all other sounds. Within seconds, it was too loud to talk, the world growing dim as more and more birds sealed it off from the sun. Only when the sky was fully blanketed did the flapping stop.

No warning. One minute, all of the street in downtown Dash City was under birds. The next, they suddenly halted their wings. Rather than fall, every bird began to expand, growing, inflating, and finally bursting entirely. Rather than the expected rain of blood and viscera, each bird produced only a small puff of something in their demise.

Like the birds themselves, the strange puffy materials ranged the color spectrum, drifting down to cover everything below. It was once more a child who discovered this material's true nature, knowing it on sight and popping it into their mouth before a very worried parent could stop them.

Cotton candy. The birds were exploding into cotton candy, which was now coating the street like a sugary snowstorm. It was bizarre, nonsensical, and disturbing on multiple levels. Only the younger people in attendance actually needed that signature line at the beginning. The rest had been around long enough to know a Captain Bullshit production when they saw one.

The car, piloted by one of Wade's robotic drivers, dropped Tori off at the curb before her building. While there were no cameras or reporters there as Tori yanked her bag of clothes and sundries from the trunk, she did have to deal with a large moving van blocking off most of the front entrance. It was thanks to that van that she didn't notice Beverly and Chloe coming up from the other side of the street, nearly colliding with the pair.

"Oh hey, Tori's back just in time." Chloe held up a large bag filled with to-go containers from a nearby noodle shop. "Beverly said you'd be here. This is pretty quick, though."

"I got a text you were on your way just when we were ordering." Beverly's stare was harder than necessary, most likely because Tori hadn't been the one to send any sort of message. It had no doubt come from Ivan, possibly relayed through another guild member like Thuggernaut.

Tori ignored the stare, reaching over instead to take one of Chloe's plastic bags. "Must have caught the good traffic. You two got dumplings, right?" Her eyes were scanning the bag, hunting for any container that might have the proper dimensions.

"Somehow, we remembered your favorite dish from the place we eat at weekly." Beverly threw an arm around Tori as they headed into the building, squeezing her tight. "I'm glad to see you're okay. Curious about why they let you come back so soon, but that's probably a discussion for closed doors."

All three climbed the stairs, reaching their floor—the third—in short order. Here, however, they encountered a dilemma. Stretching out from the door two apartments down from their own was a giant couch. It was caught at an awkward angle, slightly too long to make the door's corner as it came in from the hallway. Since it wasn't able to go in, that left a hunk of furniture jutting out into the hall, blocking anyone from getting past. Even more odd was that this sizable couch was being held up by one man. Since his back was to them, they could only make out his substantial frame and golden hair.

"Austin, would you try pushing now? *Gently*!"

There was something familiar about that voice, something in the cadence. Tori couldn't place it, though, and in seconds, she had something new to occupy her interest. In front of them, the big man shifted his weight, moving the couch slightly forward.

Snap.

"What was that?" The man holding the couch was the one yelling this time. There was a casual ease to his voice, an exact opposite of the tightly wound tone they'd heard coming from the apartment. It was strangely soothing and oddly calm, given the situation.

"One more thing to fix, apparently. Hang on. Ike's going to grab a screwdriver, then Ellie and I will take the door off its hinges. Just... give me a minute."

Since everyone involved in the move seemed content to wait, Tori loudly cleared her throat. Unloading a cumbersome couch was hardly a sin, but she wanted to get to dinner while it was hot. After so many days away from home, hitting a snag mere steps from the door was especially infuriating.

At the sound of her voice, the man holding the couch—presumably Austin—turned to face them. He was handsome, a classic chin paired with shaggy hair and eyes that were a tad too blue. Those eyes took in the scene, then stopped, suddenly.

Without warning, the couch went slamming to the ground with a worryingly loud thud. Tori braced for a charge, expecting some enemy that had slipped in and was about to ambush them. The attack never came. Instead, she realized that Austin had begun to blush and was hurriedly trying to pick the couch back up over the cries of protest from inside the apartment. Had he been holding that thing up on his own, and from the back end?

"My apologies, ladies—I mean, ma'ams, er... my apologies. We got caught up in the task at hand and I didn't notice your arrival. Give me a moment, and I'll make some space."

While Austin was fumbling with the couch, acting strangely weak given what they'd all seen him do, new faces poked out from the doorway. The first was lean, with brown hair and serious eyes. Next was another blonde, this one female, and made up like she had somewhere fancy to be. Lastly was the lowest in the doorframe, a shorter fellow with a mischievous grin already in place.

"Oh! It's you." The woman, Ellie by process of elimination, stared right at Tori for a full three seconds before the dark-haired man next to her gave a quick elbow. "I mean, it's you, our down-the-hall neighbors."

"Either that, or you picked the worst time to come tour one of the available units." When he spoke, the lean one confirmed himself to be the owner of the tightly wound voice. Most of that vanished as he stepped forward, however, adopting a far more relaxed demeanor. "Sorry about the bad first impression. I'm Kyle, the lunk handling most of the couch is Austin, the guy next to me is Ike, and that just leaves Ellie."

Beverly took charge of their end, sparing Tori and Chloe the trouble. "I'm Beverly. This is Tori and Chloe. You all seem nice, but we've got hot food we'd like to eat soon, so if it's not too much trouble, could you make a gap that we can squeeze past?"

At Beverly's words, Austin had stopped working entirely, but the moment her request was verbalized, he sprang into action. Another loud *snap* echoed from within the apartment as Austin hurriedly jammed the couch into a new angle, this one offering enough clearance for a person to fit through. Although Tori saw Kyle wince at the noise, he said nothing.

"Thanks... Austin, wasn't it?" Beverly paused as she walked past. "When we're not in such a hurry, I'll bring these two over and we'll do proper introductions."

"That sounds lovely." Despite the fact that she and Chloe were right on Beverly's heels, Austin's attention hovered on them cursorily, only flickering their way long enough to ensure they made it through the gap safely. The rest of the time, his eyes seemed to be at war with themselves, trying to look at Beverly, then stopping and jerking away.

Without any further delays, Tori and the others made their way into the apartment. While Chloe went about unpacking the bags, Tori and Beverly took a short detour into Tori's bedroom. Not every part of the apartment could be adequately isolated on a budget, but Tori had spent the extra cash to equip her room with dampening tech. It wouldn't stop Professor Quantum from listening in; however, any bug off the street would get nothing but static.

Walking briskly into her room, Tori shut the door, and then flicked some hidden switches on her nightstand. Spinning around, she motioned to Beverly that it was okay to talk. A good thing, because the words came bursting from Beverly's mouth the moment they were permitted.

"It's not just me, right? That has to be them... except, how? How did they end up here, in our building, on our floor? And seriously, do they really think they're hiding it?"

All prudent questions, but Tori decided to tackle the confirmation that Beverly was, in fact, correct in her suspicion.

"It's not just you. That was definitely the New Science Sentries. For some reason, we're now living down the hall from the AHC's newest team of capes."

Perhaps she should have given more thought to moving after all.

Chapter 10

"Is there any chance we're wrong about this?" Beverly had a hopeful expression, and with good reason. While Tori had already been a thief when she was recruited by the guild, Beverly was merely someone who had unexpectedly found herself with a power she couldn't control. Initially, working with the guild had been about getting a grip on her abilities—her only option, given that Beverly *hated* anything to do with Professor Quantum. Not without reason, either. However, such was not their concern tonight. The issue was that four capes might have just moved in down the hall from a pair of guild-member villains. That didn't bode well, especially if Beverly was hoping to transition back into a normal life.

Tori turned the fact around in her head, but there wasn't much wiggle room. "The sizes and general looks all match up. Austin was showing off some clearly enhanced strength, which corresponds with what we've seen from Agent Quantum. Plus, I recognize Kyle's voice. Not from when he was in front of the crowd, but from when he talked to me after. Must have let his guard down and slipped into more natural tones. Wow, they are *bad* at this."

At her own words, understanding suddenly clicked into place for Tori. A cape moving in down the hall from someone they'd saved in the same week was essentially an impossible coincidence. But the AHC forcing a cape who'd inadvertently put a civilian into harm's way to watch over that civilian... shit, Ivan had even said they were going to make amends.

This was what he'd meant? How in the hells had Ivan signed off on the idea? Tori didn't have to wonder this time; she already knew the answer. He'd said yes because that was the answer a normal person would give. People loved the capes, especially in Ridge City, so rebuking their offer would definitely stick out in people's heads. Of course, there was also the possibility that Ivan hadn't gotten any say in the matter. They had, at best, a lightly diplomatic relationship with the Alliance of Heroic Champions. That didn't mean the guild had veto rights on whatever plans the AHC put into motion.

Much as Tori might have liked to offer false hope, this was not a situation where it was smart to keep her ally in the dark. Methodically, Tori broke down her suspicions for Beverly, who, by the end, actually *was* sporting a cheerier face.

"Okay. That's not so bad. Yeah, it sucks that they're around, but it's not because they know who we are. And I'm relieved to hear that you're their main focus. After Austin kept looking at me in the hall, I thought he was trying to figure out which masked criminal I am." As Beverly grinned, the green of her eyes brightened momentarily. No one would know her mask, largely because she only ever wore her costume around the guild. In the field, she was always transformed, and it would be quite the detective who realized Bahamut the terrifying dragon-shifter was in fact this capable young woman.

"No, I'm pretty sure that look had nothing to do with Bahamut and everything to do with Beverly." To her surprise, given their predicament, Tori felt a chuckle try to bubble up. "I mean, the guy saw you and literally dropped a couch. Doesn't get a lot more overt than that."

"Or he was trying to cover up for using his strength in public," Beverly countered.

Tori let it go, for the moment. They had bigger issues to tackle. "Assuming the guild knows about this and we're stuck with the situation, what are we going to do? If that team really is here to keep an eye on me, they'll probably try getting closer to us."

"Is telling them to 'fuck off' not an option? It tends to be your go-to move when strangers try interacting with you."

"That's for randos on the street," Tori replied. "This is trickier. If we let them into our lives a little, then that's the method they'll use for surveillance. If we tell them to eat shit, they'd still have to do their job, which would mean watching us covertly."

It was easy to see Beverly's symmetrical features and mistakenly believe beauty to be her greatest feature, but those who knew her well were keenly aware there was a sharp, dangerous mind behind those mesmerizing green eyes. "I get it. We either let them in on our own terms, or we deal with being spied on for the foreseeable future."

"Or both," Tori added. "They could just as easily do both, assuming we're even right about it all." She paused, giving her next words proper consideration. "Look, this might be about me, but I think you should get to make the call. To me, the Science Sentries are just one more team from the past, a reboot to something I never cared much about. To you, it's personal. I'm not going to ask you to grit your teeth and smile at those capes. Not in our home."

Beverly's usual confidence flickered for a moment, surprise and old pain both rising to the surface. After nearly half a minute of silence, she finally met Tori's eyes. "I might not have set out to join a guild of villains, but I still did it. I made that choice. Part of that means, for better or worse, I'm always going to be a little bit tied to the capes. My grudges can't be more important than my current life, or the relationships in it. Sooner or later, I have to learn to at least minimally deal with capes, unless I want to draw suspicion toward myself and my friends. If I can cope with Professor Quantum's new team, I'll be able to handle anyone. I won't promise it will always go well, but I'll stay as civil as possible."

A loud banging on the door reminded them that this was not a two-person apartment, no matter how deeply they got lost in discussion. "Come on, you two. Dinner is getting cold. Hold your clandestine meetings after we eat."

Both women laughed as the somber mood that had descended was quickly dispelled. Beverly rose first, a smirk lingering on her lips. "Chloe's right, let's not try to bite this off all at once. We know they're here, and we suspect why. The next move is theirs. Although, if you wanted to talk to Wade about any tech upgrades..."

"If we use a piece of Doctor Mechaniacal tech and they find out, we then have to explain how we got it," Tori interrupted.

"Right. That stuff isn't exactly commercially available. Guess we'll come up something, and by that, I mean my genius inventor roommate who brought the capes here with her will find a solution."

"But no pressure, right?" Tori asked.

"Well, a little pressure." Beverly gave her friend a pointed look. "Or have you forgotten that we definitely need to slip away unnoticed tomorrow?"

Shit. Tori actually *had* forgotten, in all the excitement of their new neighbors. Tomorrow night, the Guild of Villainous Reformation opened the doors of its new headquarters. Not the sort of event one wanted to miss, especially when the guests were famed criminals of incredible power.

While it wouldn't be much help in the moment, this was one more reminder that she *really* had to install some secret tunnels into this building already.

Cyber Geek was nearly to his destination when a voice from one of the AHC's many coordinators crackled in his ear.

"Cyber Geek, your team is to halt approach immediately. We just detected a tremendous amount of energy spiking in that area. They've either got some sort of dangerous item or a meta who was shielding their true potential. This situation has escalated beyond your capabilities."

The words stung, even as he turned to halt the others. Medley looked especially ferocious tonight, claws extended and fangs on full display. Cold Shoulder was already inside a moving ice-construct, putting her on equal intimidation grounds with Medley. Even Hat Trick had put on a serious face. They didn't know much about the job, only that someone had broken into a residential building to supposedly rob a hidden vault. While there were civilians in the building, none were near the scene of the crime, so they weren't considered to be in immediate danger. Having a meta with lots of power changed that; it put the civilians in play, so deep down, Cyber Geek knew this was the right move. The job called for someone more experienced.

Still, seeing the flickering lights coming from the ground floor, Cyber Geek's stomach turned. In his non-masked form as Donald Moss, he'd been forced onto the sidelines for most of his life. Never brave or strong enough to make a difference. Doing it now, though, was different. It was almost more than he could bear, knowing that people were in danger.

"How long until our reinforcements arrive? The lights are getting brighter, seems to be building to something." Cyber Geek didn't intend to break orders, but he also wouldn't cool his heels if civilians were in danger. That wasn't the kind of superhero he was training to be.

"I wouldn't exactly call her 'reinforcements'. Count your lucky stars, rookies. Most people go years before they happen to catch her in the field." There was a smugness to the voice that Donald didn't have to wonder about.

From the east—states away if she was coming from Ridge City—a golden bolt tore out of the night sky. It zipped into the building and out the other side. With the golden bolt vanishing, so too did the pulsing glow. Squinting, Cyber Geek noticed a bright red flash high up in the sky, perhaps past the limits of their very atmosphere.

The crooks came running out the front of the building, slipping and falling atop one another in a desperate race for a van parked not far from the entrance. They were halfway there when the golden light returned, landing directly between the four would-be masterminds and their escape vehicle.

Around him, Cyber Geek could hear lungs go still as they unintentionally all held their breath. While they'd met her briefly during the Ridge City Riots, this was most of the team's first time to see her on the job in person. Only a young Donald, many years before his Cyber Geek days, had caught the show once prior. It was an experience that had been locked into his mind.

One could forget many things, but a front row seat to watch Lodestar save the day was a memory that endured.

"You're all probably panicking right now, and with good reason. Yes, your scheme is undone and you've been caught, so you'll be going to jail. That said, you've still got a trial ahead of you, so don't ruin your own cases by doing something stupid like—"

In that moment, Cyber Geek wondered if the criminal had shot at that precise moment on purpose, or if Lodestar had known exactly how long it would take and had timed her speech appropriately. The first was more likely, but there was something about the way Lodestar controlled the situation that left Cyber Geek slightly unsure.

The bullet, as countless had before it, struck Lodestar and bounced harmlessly to the ground. She let out a tired sigh, looking from it to the shooter. "As I was saying, don't be stupid and try to shoot me, since—"

At that moment, all four men opened fire. Looking more disappointed than mad, Lodestar stopped each one by standing still and letting the bullets hit. When the final casing was spent, one crook, the original shooter, reared back and hurled his weapon at Lodestar's head. This one, she caught, crumpling the firearm effortlessly in her fingers.

"I guess it's nice to know some things never change. Seriously, did you expect that to work after all the bullets did nothing?"

The now-gunless gunman didn't respond. He'd turned around and began to flee, sprinting away at top speed. Whatever bravery he'd held had broken; he was now in a mad dash for freedom. The effort was understandable, but pointless. He was a hunk of driftwood trying to float away from a tidal wave.

In a literal flash, Lodestar was there. Moving almost too fast to see, she knocked her target carefully to the ground, then zip-tied his arms and legs. The others attempted to scatter as well, but in less than thirty seconds, she'd gathered them all into a neat pile.

"Situation resolved. They had some kind of hyper-advanced bomb to blow the safe. Based on how big it was, even at the edge of space, that thing would've taken out this whole building and a fair chunk of the block. Let the police know that, if at all possible, we want to know where they got it. This is the third crew with gear above their station just this week, and each one has been in a different part of the country. We need a handle on this, and soon."

Lodestar glanced over to where Cyber Geek and the others were waiting. To their surprise, she greeted the team with a warm smile and waved them over. Tentatively, all keenly aware they were approaching a living legend, they made the trek over.

"Hey there, nice to see you all again. Sorry to horn in on your scene, especially when we finally let you out of Ridge City, but this job keeps us all on our toes no matter how long we do it. Have to roll with the surprises, especially the potentially devastating ones."

Lodestar paused, taking the time to look each of them in the eyes. "You did the right thing. I know it's not easy to wait when people need you. I really do. But the powers in this world run a wide gamut, and getting killed easily by someone out of your league doesn't help anyone. Not you, not your fellow superheroes, and certainly not any civilian who might have needed you in the future. I want you to know that even if it wasn't easy, you did well tonight. That's what makes a superhero, more than the fighting or the powers: doing the right thing, especially when it's hard."

None of them had been sure what to expect when Lodestar waved them over. Even the most optimistic hadn't imagined they'd be getting a speech praising them for following orders. The more cynical part of Cyber Geek wanted to believe her speech was formulated to condition newer recruits to do as they were told. But the truth was, he understood what she was getting at. Cyber Geek had seen Fornax return, had watched him slap around a cape as strong as Apollo. Some threats were too big for them, and no matter how their pride might buck at the idea, there would be times they had to put their trust in the stronger superheroes.

"How will we know when we're ready for more?" Medley was the one to ask it, because that was who Ren was at his core: always competitive, always striving to be better. In his human days, that tendency might have been more subdued, but since his transformation, being a superhero was his only major positive outlet. More and more of who he was had been poured into that identity, and the work that went with it. "I know we have to start small, but I also like to test myself and measure my growth. It's hard to do that when we're always working the lowest-risk jobs."

She looked at Medley, truly took him in, and nodded. "I can understand

and respect that. However, I hope you can in turn see why the time to take the inherent risks of such tests should never be done in the field, when civilian lives are in play. Yes, the job will push you to and past your limits, but we do not seek those situations. That's called courting death. It is a fair request, though, so I'll think on setting something up for you. Back in the day, we used to... well, I'll talk to the Champions' Congress first."

Lodestar stepped forward, clapping them each on the shoulder in turn. "Until then, I need you four to do me a favor. Stand guard over these crooks until the police arrive. There's word of some giant meta-beast rampaging in Uruguay, so I need to get moving. Stay alert, and watch one another's backs. You're not home safe until you're home, safe."

With that, she leapt into the sky, a golden light that tore quickly out of sight.

From behind Cyber Geek, Hat Trick started to gasp for air and fell onto Medley's shoulder.

"By Houdini's handcuffs, I was so nervous I forgot to breathe."

Although his lungs had kept working, Cyber Geek understood the sentiment. Even after months at the AHC and growing accustomed to thinking of himself as a real cape, the older heroes still intimidated him. And those were just the normal ones. Being around Lodestar drove home to them all just how large the divide between some meta powers was. Merely standing in the same space as her was daunting. Perhaps that was why she was so warm, to try to undercut some of the legacy that lived on her heels.

Whatever the case, Cyber Geek was just thankful Lodestar was on their side. It was scary to admit, but if Lodestar turned evil, he wasn't entirely sure there *was* another meta who could stop her.

Chapter 11

The car came precisely at six in the evening, whispering up to the curb with the sort of undeniable perfection Tori had begun to associate with Doctor Mechaniacal's mechanical drivers. Both women had just stepped out of the building, holding bags. For Beverly, a simple gym duffel was enough to contain the secret attire she was carting around, but Tori required something more substantial.

To even a well-trained eye, Tori merely appeared to be dragging a sizable rolling suitcase, the kind too large for even the most foolishly optimistic of travelers to attempt stowing in the overhead compartment on a plane. It was, in fact, exactly that; however, it was also a tad more. Though Tori had yet to perfectly reproduce the miniature gravitational anomaly generator that Ivan had gifted her—even the base component costs for that model were out of her reach—she *had* successfully managed to create weaker versions of it. None that would get a heavy meta-suit airborne on their own, but two built into a custom suitcase were potent enough to make it transportable.

No sooner had they exited their building than the car was there, human-appearing helper bots coming to cart away their luggage. If Wade wanted, he could have upended the entire travel industry overnight with these helpers, to say nothing of slotting them into manual labor jobs. Tori hadn't seen everything behind the curtain, but she had a hunch these inventions were what kept a massive structure like the guild functioning. She'd certainly never seen

Thuggernaut or Xelas scrubbing toilets. The latter would probably blow one up if she tried.

It was one more pointless, nervous thought atop an array of them. Despite her soft spot for the guild, going back would always be a slightly scary prospect. The people she'd aligned herself with were not to be trifled with. Even trying to live under the radar, there was an inherent danger to all of them. Ivan, easily the most domesticated villain of any she'd met, had proven that point earlier this week. These people lived by their laws, not society's, but breaking them still carried consequences.

"Where do you think we're going?" Beverly was looking out the window as the streets rolled past. They were heading toward a highway junction; once there, they'd get a better idea of their destination's direction. "Can't be back downtown. No way even Wade could do that much construction without someone noticing."

"Never underestimate Doctor Mechaniacal's ingenuity, especially with the pockets of Wade Wyatt backing him up." While Ivan was her mentor and teacher, Doctor Mechaniacal was the villain Tori had grown up respecting most. He was a builder like her, who'd gone down the same path she wanted to travel: inventor, entrepreneur, a person in charge of their own destiny.

The car hit the highway junction and turned east. It rolled along past several exits, then took one much sooner than either woman was expecting. The car wound its way along a twisting side street that was surrounded by trees before finally breaking over a hill, lending Beverly and Tori their first glimpse of an exceptional view.

Huge sections of grass framed either side of the wide road, dotted by walking paths leading off to tennis courts, several structures of various sizes, and a massive pool. Directly before them was the major feature, though. A huge building that dripped with luxury dominated their field of view, so large it nearly obscured most of the visible golf course directly behind it. The architecture made it look old, yet there was not a single worn or unpolished section that Tori could spot. It was gorgeous, already twinkling with countless bulbs in the fading light of evening.

Lined up before it was a procession of vehicles, each similar to their own without being completely identical. One by one, the cars approached the front and unloaded their charges. There was a moment Tori was afraid they'd ended up at the wrong place somehow, but when she saw the distinctive form of Thuggernaut emerge next to a shorter shape that was most likely Johnny Three Dicks, there could be no question about it.

“That son of a bitch bought a country club.” Beverly already had her phone out, typing away on the bright digital keyboard. “Here we go: Astmire Country Club, founded in the early nineteen hundreds, did the usual rich people bullshit and fell out of fashion as better options came on the scene. Bunch of stories about them trying to rebrand and stage a comeback. Guess the Ridge City Riots were their breaking point; looks like they sold not long after. Don’t recognize the name of the company they were sold to: Majestic Meadows Management. Shell?”

“Has to be, right?” Tori agreed. She was scanning all over, taking in the scenery. Beautiful though it was, this all still felt off. They were much too exposed. Any cape with half a brain could coordinate a raid on this facility. The last guild had been a fortified building downtown, surrounded by civilian structures that limited the amount of force a cape could use. This place was easy pickings.

Reminding herself of her own words only a bit prior, Tori gave Doctor Mechaniacal the benefit of the doubt. He’d been running this guild since long before she joined. If this was the new base he’d chosen, then there was a good reason for that. And she wouldn’t have to wait long to find out.

The car eased to a stop, letting them off in front of the massive building. She and Beverly both hopped out, their bags already unloaded by the time they came around the back. Sharing a brief look with one another, they picked up their luggage and headed toward the door. Another helper-bot was waiting for them, this one with a smile that flirted at the edge of the Uncanny Valley.

“Welcome to the Sprawling Wyatt, a private club for only the most exclusive of members. Please, let one of our staff show you to the changing rooms. I’ll sure you’ll want to get ready before the festivities begin.”

Ivan sat, examining the room. It was a fine chamber for the Council of Villains to gather. Huge, circular wooden table, nice carpeting, comfortable chairs. This would be a good place for conferences. His fingers drummed against the smooth, polished surface of the table. The single item was probably more expensive than anything in Ivan’s home, even before it was partially destroyed. Wade didn’t skimp on the nicer things in life, especially not where the guild was concerned. This new base was a testament to that, and the club itself was merely the surface level of that expense.

They’d already had the meeting where Ivan brought the others up to speed on his Starscout situation. The odds of it blowing back on the guild were infinitesimal, but in a world where the impossible was commonplace, only an arrogant fool left such things to chance. Now, the others knew about the situation, and could take steps to protect themselves just in case. The only part Ivan didn't divulge was how, exactly, he'd been in contact with Lodestar to get punished, along with the fact that she'd be serving alongside him. There was a difference between keeping the guild up to speed and betraying a friend's trust.

All that remained now was the revelry. Then would come the trouble. Because when the toasts were drunk and the party finished, they would go back to being a guild of villains. A guild where Ivan no longer quite knew where he fit. Before, it had been simple. He had a promise to keep, a debt to repay. Well, partially repay; some debts could never truly be made whole. But the star had fallen from the sky. He no longer had to hold the worst of the world at bay to keep its people from needing their champion.

Had this issue come up a year prior, Ivan would have easily abdicated his position on the council and taken a more removed role, coming in only when truly needed. That had been before, though: before Tori, before training an apprentice and getting more involved, before remembering why he'd help found this place.

Before seeing what happened when the guild's darker influences ran about unchecked.

He still wondered: if he'd been more involved, would he have sniffed out Balaam's plot? Maybe not—the theatrical mage hadn't made it onto the council without merit and skill of his own—yet Ivan couldn't help thinking he'd have caught *something*.

Ivan knew himself better than most. He knew he functioned best when he had an objective, a goal, something to keep him moving. Fatherhood was excellent in the long term, but that didn't fill the days, especially given his visitation schedule. He needed more, something to work toward. It was a serious matter for contemplation; however, Ivan realized that it likely wouldn't happen tonight. He'd be better served by getting out of his head and paying attention to what was going on.

Wade tended to keep a few surprises, even from his fellow councilors.

The first version of the meta-suit had been a prototype, which was the polite version of saying it was an iteration that worked despite the sizable accumulation of mistakes in its design and construction. That still put it a cut above all the prior attempts that couldn't even clear the bar of functionality, but there had been ample room for improvement.

Aside from the basic adjustments, like fine-tuning her systems and smoothing out some clunky parts in the design, Tori's first major upgrade were the entry options. Like before, her meta-suit broke apart; however, it now also had a specialized intake and expulsion system, permitting her to jump in and out using her fire form. Of course, that would only work once the suit was on and powered up; otherwise, it wouldn't stand in place while she went exploring. Between the museum fight where she was nearly captured and scrambling to put her suit on when Rust Tooth attacked Ivan's house, Tori had decided a quick way in and out was essential.

The next serious update was to the beam weapon on one of her gauntlets. This one had been tweaked, adding a cover to the lens on the palm so it wasn't capable of being targeted, while also streamlining the charge sequence. But the biggest change was that she now had the systems on both hands. This gizmo had saved her life, and was one of her only ways to deal out a lot of hurt in a short span, so it had definitely earned an expansion. Working them in alongside the fingertip torches was tough, but the upside to a closed guild meant that there had been ample time for such endeavors.

Her last major change was possibly the most effort-intensive of the bunch, but also had the biggest overall impact. Like the suitcase she'd brought it over in, her new suit had been fitted with dozens of smaller, less potent, miniature gravitational anomaly generators. Tori had noticed her suit's lack of mobility the last time she'd taken it on a real run. Because of the weight, it clanged and clanked around, not to mention moved with less grace and precision than she might have liked.

The new gravitational network wasn't meant to make the suit light enough to fly, which required far more power. Instead, this new system worked to manipulate the meta-suit's weight constantly on a lower level, allowing the user to move around with weight near equivalent to a normal person's when walking around, or to swing with the full heft of a metal fist. The system wasn't perfect yet—there was still a seconds-long lag when switching between the weight settings—however, as Tori locked her last boot in place, she could feel a tremendous difference. Thanks to spreading it out over a network, displacing the gravity took less power than using the meta-suit's full strength to move. Given further calibration, she could probably get it even more efficient, but that would have to wait for another day.

With her suit almost fully donned, Tori examined herself in the mirror. The new metal pieces were dark, like the rest, with flashes of red light shining through. She saw no reason to break a good motif. Unlike before, there were no odd lumps or bits of wire poking out. This reworked design had a bit of polish, both literal and metaphorical. Smooth lines, efficient design, she could have marveled at her work for hours. Sadly, that would have made her late, and this was not the place for such rudeness.

Carefully, with more tenderness than the item required, Tori lifted up the final component—a new helmet, with a few minor upgrades and the same glowing red eyes. There was no reason she *had* to make her meta-suits like this. Her villain apprenticeship was over. She was free. If Tori wanted to work on meta-suits that were more market friendly, she could: make a prototype of that, get funding on her terms, start the next phase of her life. And maybe she would, when she was ready. But this wasn't just *a* meta-suit anymore. This was something more, something personal. Tori would always make the suits for this place intimidating, because if she was donning it, there was a good chance she wanted to be scary.

A small hiss from the helmet's lock as it sealed onto the torso section. For a moment, darkness, and then the screen before her grew bright. Visual systems cycled through their start-up sequence before locking into the standard viewmode. This showed what was in front of the user, along with additional information that could be toggled through as needed. No such features were required in the moment; just seeing was more than enough.

Tori had vanished. In her place stood Hephaestus, known thief and suspected connection with Fornax.

Seeing the form, part of her had been worried it would feel strange to be back in the suit… like this was a delusion from her time training, and in the cold light of reality, things would feel different. The fear had been baseless. In that moment, she felt the difference come over her. Even if she hadn't understood it at the time, she was thankful Ivan had forced Tori to divide her identities. It was good to have a line between Tori and Hephaestus.

With the armor in place, Hephaestus opened the door to find Beverly in costume and green dragon form—which meant she was now Bahamut—along with one of the butler-bots.

"About time," Bahamut rumbled in the rougher voice of her dragon.

"One cannot hurry perfection." Hephaestus sounded different as well, Tori's voice run through a minor distorter. The effect could be increased when she was talking to capes, but it defaulted to a lower setting to keep communication easy. "Besides, I don't think we're late."

“Not yet, but the hour draws nigh. If you would both follow me.” The butler turned and headed down a new hallway, and the suit of mechanical black metal and the humanoid green dragon followed.

Chapter 12

When they arrived at the staircase winding downward, into what had no doubt originally been a wine cellar, Hephaestus felt a hunch tickle her mind. Perhaps Doctor Mechaniacal hadn't left them exposed after all. If the country club up top was a simple façade, there could be any manner of facilities installed into the lower floor.

Together, she and Bahamut made their way single file down the stairs. It was big enough to accommodate even their most sizable members, albeit not by a large margin. Stepping down into a short hallway, they followed the only path forward.

There had certainly been some renovations down here, though not quite to the scale Hephaestus was imagining. Lights hummed along the walls, the air crackled with power, and Hephaestus felt more at home among the staggering amount of tech lining the walls. Most of it was no doubt designed to conceal this place's existence and protect it from outsiders; however, at least some had to be related to the enormous metal gateway at the far end of the room—a perfect arch that seemed to lead to a stone wall, energy sparking along its various spires and panels.

"If you would please be so kind as to wait, the next gate will be opening shortly." Another helper-bot was standing by the arch. Except... this one didn't look quite right. Tori might be subpar at reading people, but she was an expert when it came to technology. This bot had a mild slump in its stance, and the hints of a mischievous twist at the edge of its mouth. On a human, minor blips, but machines didn't get to deviate and have individual quirks… except for the ones that had achieved sentience, of course.

"You can drop the hologram, Xelas." Hephaestus was, admittedly, taking a swing. Then again, there were only so many troublemaking AIs associated with the guild, and Xelas loved to mess with people.

The image of a plain man flickered away. In his place stood a metallic woman of great renown in the scientific community. Xelas, the first artificially-created lifeform to sue for and win her freedom, might have ended up on the side of the capes if not for the circumstance of her creation. Even if that had happened, she'd have never been right for them: a guild of villains was where she belonged. And few ever looked as at home in the guild as Xelas, her artificial face capable of displaying very real emotion, when she so chose.

"Can't blame me for seeing how you lot treat the non-sentients. Have to watch their backs." Stepping away from the wall, Xelas motioned to the arch before them. "Anyone think they know what this is?"

Bahamut started to raise her hand, then thought better of it. "Teleporter? I mean, we saw people come in here, got led to this room, and now no one else is around. It's either a teleporter or you're about to kill us and use that thing to get rid of our bodies."

Hephaestus hadn't actually considered that, which was all the more worrying when Xelas gave an enthusiastic nod.

"Not where we're taking things tonight, but I like your instincts. You're sort of right in that it's a teleporter, and sort of wrong. It's a linked gateway. I'll spare you the technobabble; just know that achieving true teleportation using pure tech is crazy difficult, even with the former laws of physics being turned more into guidelines. It's been done, but the only people who could properly use those devices were the ones who invented them—that's how complex they were. Creating a linked system between two gates, on the other hand, is way more doable. We didn't have the technology perfected when the last guild was being constructed, however this time, our options were expanded."

Beneath the gauntlets of Hephaestus, Tori's fingers itched to dig into this strange system's circuitry. It was insane how far ahead people like Wade and Professor Quantum were. If she were attempting to invent this on her own, it would have been an impossible task. Luckily, one of the upsides to being a villain was that stealing went right along with the territory. Not that she planned to copy any of their designs—just learn from them, and then integrate that tech into her own works. A teleporting meta-suit, for example, would have tremendous possibilities.

"Sounds pretty awesome. Why the wait?" Bahamut lumbered slightly closer, giving the metal a test sniff with her scaly snout.

"This thing takes a *ton* of power to run. During normal operations, we'll have a real helper-bot here to turn it on and off as needed. Tonight, knowing villains' tendency to stagger in regardless of starting time, Doc left it running on ten-minute intervals. Next one is coming up soon. In fact, both of you should get ready."

At Xelas's words, the air around the arch grew heavy, like the wind just before a lightning storm. Sharp blue bolts ran from one side to the other, increasing in number until the whole space looked like a web built by some sort of electric spider. Without warning, the center appeared to ignite, creating a wave of rippling energy that finally stabilized into a mostly-constant wall of blue light.

With a flourish, Xelas motioned to the gateway. "Unless you want to chew the fat with me for another ten minutes, you might want to hustle on through. I'll be over in a few more trips, so try not to start any good fights until I get there."

Part of Hephaestus wanted to be afraid of the idea of leaping through space and time with only circuitry guiding her destination, but she was too damned excited. Besides, they'd basically done this all through her training, thanks to the meta pair known as Tunnel Vision. This was just a different—most likely riskier—form of that.

Taking Bahamut's hand, Hephaestus and her friend stepped forward, feeling the blue light wash over them. They emerged in a very similar room with a near-identical archway at their back. Hephaestus's navigation system attempted to identify their new location but was unable to connect with any satellites. While it stood to reason that Doctor Mechaniacal would have this place shielded, Hephaestus still grumbled as they made their way toward the staircase leading upward. This took them to another hall, then more stairs, before they finally spotted light and heard voices from up ahead.

Following the sounds, they discovered an elevated outdoor balcony. The minor grumblings from Hephaestus died out as they stepped into the light and saw, for the first time, their actual new guild headquarters.

They were probably in a different time zone, given the sunshine streaming down. Also, so far as Hephaestus was aware, Ridge City didn't have turquoise blue water surrounding it on all sides, or gorgeous swaths of trees running between strips of pure white sand.

An island lair. Doctor Mechaniacal hadn't built some underground base; he'd fashioned his new headquarters in the middle of paradise. She could see a half dozen interconnected buildings stretching out below; in fact, the bulk of the party seemed to be happening near one of the larger structures. The strange thing was, Hephaestus couldn't see anything big enough to function as the main hub they'd used the last time. Had Doctor Mechaniacal merely spread out the required area? But that would be harder to defend, and after the last base fell, protection had to be of paramount concern.

Looking down, Hephaestus noticed the path from the balcony led in multiple directions. One was back toward the gateway chamber, one headed toward the party, and several others appeared to go farther up. Turning around to look behind her, Hephaestus was thankful for the helmet hiding what had to be an expression of dumbfounded shock. Her heavy hand tapped Bahamut on the shoulder, over and over until she got a reaction.

"Okay, okay, what do you need? Sorry, I was kind of scoping... this... out." Her words faded as she turned, following Hephaestus's stare.

Having emerged, they could now see the structure they'd come out of, and it was not a building as they'd initially suspected. No, they were on the lowest section of a massive, dark mound that rose into the sky, casting a shadow on the nearby stretch of beach. A dozen more entrances dotted the exterior, led to by lighted and covered pathways connected to landings like the one Hephaestus and Bahamut were standing on. There was no mistaking this structure, though. It could only be one thing.

A volcano. Doctor Mechaniacal had built an island *volcano* lair.

Well, it certainly fit the image of a guild of criminals, though arguably, the country club did an equally good job in that regard. If nothing else, Hephaestus wasn't going to argue with a classic. She and Bahamut headed down toward the gathering of villains, eager to see what other surprises the day had in store.

"I still think it's too brazen. An entire island? No matter how much tech you use, we can't keep it concealed forever. Besides, you know this will tweak Professor Quantum. He's famously used an island base for decades."

Ivan, not yet clad in his Pseudonym outfit, stood in Wade's—really, Doctor Mechaniacal's—new office, overlooking the north side of the island. This was a fight they hadn't had leading up to the reveal, because Ivan had been left in the dark, probably to avoid the very reaction he was having now.

"As I'm trying to explain, I didn't steal Professor Quantum's idea," Wade shot back, refusing to yield ground as he adjusted his collar in the mirror. He didn't make an effort often, but when he did, Wade tried to show it. "I stole Tyranny's idea, which was much better."

That brought Ivan up short. There were many ways to deal with capes, and hiding behind the law was a favorite among smart crooks. It was the foundation for how the guild operated, but there were more ways to use that tactic than just theirs. Tyranny—her official title—had utilized a different method. After The Seismologist broke three major landmasses off of Australia, the smallest was considered unsalvageable. It had simply suffered too much loss of flora and fauna during the quake that tore it loose.

Until Tyranny, that was. Her technology restored the land—including insect-bots which were able to take over duties like pollination—and her offensive measures ensured that the natural predators trying to overtake the abandoned land were kept in check. She rebuilt the island by herself, then sent out a declaration to the Australian government. Tyranny would use her tech to restore the other damaged islands as well, but only if she were formally given recognized rule of the one she'd fixed. It was a simple call. They'd already written off the land as lost, and her offer would save them billions in restorative efforts.

And thus, the nation of Indroga was born. Tyranny invited anyone who wished to immigrate there with promises of stable work and housing. Meta or human, all were welcomed to the new nation. It became a trading powerhouse, producing high-end specialty goods under Tyranny's leadership. Only then did her true plan become clear, however. As a recognized ruling entity, she had complete power over the laws of her domain, and the very first one she declared was simple: no capes. Not on her island, not above her island, not in any of the space she controlled. To be a cape on Indroga was considered an act of war, with serious geopolitical consequences—especially since Indroga was a valued trading partner to so many nations. She had to play the game of politics as a tradeoff; however, Tyranny had still managed to create an entire country free from superheroes merely by turning their own esteem for the law against them.

"You didn't found this island," Ivan pointed out.

"No. I bought it," Wade agreed. "Tax, title, and license. Paid the local government a handsome sum to be officially recognized as the sole legal authority on its shores. Signed a few treaties as well; just enough so that any cape coming here uninvited technically starts about five wars. Sent a copy of all the documents to the AHC myself."

"You told them where to find us?" After a moment's consideration, Ivan realized Wade's intent. "I suppose they'd figure it out soon, anyway. It's never been the secrecy that protects our organization."

Wade finished fiddling with his collar, having made no significant improvement. "Precisely. Not to mention that by sending the documents myself, the AHC loses any claim to ignorance. They know what they're biting off if they come here. Won't stop them knocking if we do something truly stupid, but they can't come kicking in the door with some flimsy warrant this time."

Although it still seemed like too much, Ivan trusted Wade's judgment. He was the man helming the guild. If this was what he thought was best, then Ivan could either believe it too or try to do the job himself. That was one role Ivan never wanted to find himself even remotely near, so that meant hoping that Wade knew what he was doing.

"You should probably go change, by the way. I've got a Doctor Mechaniacal suit down there to give the speech in a few minutes. Wouldn't look proper without the full council, Pseudonym."

Wade was right. There was time for worrying when the work was done. Today, they were here for a reason. The guild had been broken by the capes. No one could deny that. Now, the rebuilding process truly began. Whether they would be weakened by the blow or grow from it depended on the individual members as much as the organization itself. But recovery started by reminding them that they were part of something bigger than themselves.

"I'll be there shortly." Ivan left the room, walking a short way down the hall to his own quarters. He didn't plan to stay here outside of emergencies, but it was always nice to have a place to set his Pseudonym costume. That was all he wore, these days. Fornax was dead and buried, save for his brief resurrection last year—and, perhaps, in the itch Ivan kept noticing beneath his skin. The desire to fight, to test himself in combat, to do what he'd been made for. He shoved those impulses down, as he had for years. There was no room for Fornax in Ivan's world. Not even this guild could contain him.

Instead, he cut a path for his room and the Pseudonym ensemble. Wade wasn't one to bluff about time, so Ivan made a point to hurry. Unsure as he was about his place within it, there was virtually no force on the planet that could have kept Ivan away from the guild's reopening ceremony.

Chapter 13

The area they were in seemed more like a town square than an assembly room. At the old guild, the apprentices had only seen formal gatherings happen in the large main hall where they'd been inducted. Apparently, the new guild was going to do things differently. Cobblestone streets wound around various buildings, the paths dotted with little outposts offering different refreshments and service and staffed by the helpful bots that kept the guild operations running smoothly. Were anyone else at the guild's helm, there might have been concerns that they were overly reliant on artificial aids, but with Doctor Mechaniacal and Xelas as the creators, it was unlikely anyone on the planet could compromise those butler-bots.

When Hephaestus and Bahamut made their way down from the teleportation entrance, they'd spotted a half dozen familiar forms, but being in the thick of things made it harder to locate their friends. It certainly didn't help that this was the biggest guild-related crowd they'd encountered. Apprentice inductions were a special occasion, but didn't have quite the same draw as the opening of a new headquarters. Everyone who was still active within the guild was probably here, if for no other reason than to assure the others that they were, indeed, still on the guild's side. Balaam's betrayal had been stupid enough; no one wanted the organization on their heels over a misunderstanding.

Hephaestus noticed Pod Person and one of the Bytes, Meg, having frozen drinks from what seemed to be a very popular building; however, a crowd cut between them before she could call a greeting. A pair of men who were nearly identical themselves and dressed in matching costumes almost bumped into Bahamut; both spun away with unexpected grace in the moment before collision, the slightly taller one giving a nod of apology. Hephaestus spotted Arachno Bro, a woman in an impossibly elaborate evening gown, and a creature with four wings and glowing eyes atop another building, all passing around a bottle of what looked to be incredibly expensive alcohol.

At last, a large hand clapped down on both Hephaestus and Bahamut's shoulders. They turned to find Thuggernaut staring down at them with a calm grin, along with a much less soothing smirk on his smaller accomplice's face.

"About time you two showed up. Can you believe this shit? Doctor Mechaniacal has always been a bit grandiose, but this... this is a league all its own." The unassuming man speaking went by the villainous moniker: Johnny Three Dicks. While neither Hephaestus nor Tori knew exactly what sort of meta-human he was, they knew enough about the guild itself to be sure he was dangerous, despite the gregarious, sometimes grating, personality. "If he'd put the new housing on the beach instead of inside the volcano, I might just stay here forever."

"A fact that explains *why* he didn't put the housing on the beachfront," Thuggernaut pointed out. "Although, there are a few structures near one end of the island. My guess is those will be facilities for high-earners, just like the old executive lounges." He looked away from Johnny, back to Bahamut. "Good to see you again. I wasn't sure you'd come for this."

There was no ripple of shock from those around them. Bahamut hadn't been especially enthusiastic about the crime aspect of their job, and it was common knowledge. Like many before her, she'd just wanted control of her abilities, which she'd gained largely thanks to Thuggernaut and the guild's training. With that done, she was free to become one of the guild's absentee members, making a real go of it in honest society. Those members didn't tend to show up to meetings, though this event was certainly going to be an exception to that rule for many.

"After seeing our last one torn down, there was no way I'd miss the reopening. Not to mention the chance to visit with friends." Bahamut shook her former mentor's hand.

They'd just released their grips when the sky went black. Quite literally. The sun above them died without warning, quickly replaced by a fat, shining moon and countless shining stars. A hologram of some sort, obviously, although Hephaestus wasn't entirely sure if the sky was false, or if it had been the sunshine that was a lie. Without knowing their location, she couldn't pin down a time zone, and it was starting to look like that was intentional. This guild headquarters' location would be a secret kept even from its own members—or at least the lower-ranking ones. She assumed Ivan probably knew, if he'd cared enough to bother asking.

All around, the island started to glow as countless gentle lights sparked on. They filled the streets, winding back up the path to the volcano lair and continuing onward, bright red glows appearing on the boiling mountain to their rear. The whole island looked like a sea of light, and in any other context, Hephaestus would have taken to the sky for a bird's-eye view. Tonight, she stayed rooted. This wasn't the time to go gallivanting off. Someone wanted their attention, and there was only one real candidate who would take to using these methods.

They came from nowhere, seeming to slip out from behind buildings where they couldn't have been hiding. Seven figures, all distinctive, winding their way to the center of the cobblestone square, where Hephaestus noticed the ground was beginning to rise. One by one they came, costumed and somber, climbing the still-forming stairs onto the rising platform.

Morgana was first. Normally a kind-eyed woman with raven-black hair, when she was dressed in her full apparel as Morgana Le Faye, the Blood Witch, it was easy to see why small armies had surrendered rather than face her wrath. Merely witnessing her carnage on a battlefield was enough to remind any outsider why the guild was not to be trifled with. Born with the power to manipulate the blood of all but the most powerful beings, Morgana's department looked after all of those who had their abilities at birth.

Not far behind her was the unassuming young woman known as Stasis. Hephaestus didn't know much about her, only that she had a history with Nexus and appeared to be truly invulnerable. Plenty of meta-humans were tougher than normal; however, Stasis was something else. It was like attacks never even reached her. Given that she was the council member who oversaw those that had been turned into meta-humans by external forces—such as lab accidents—Hephaestus had managed to put a rough guess about her origins together.

Arcanicus was next, taking the stairs noticeably more slowly than the previous councilors. In his defense, he was one of the few older members of the guild who actually wore his age, and he was adorned in robes that required careful lifting. While he was a pleasant fellow who'd pitched in with their training, Hephaestus couldn't help thinking that he'd have to find a replacement for his council seat soon. Arcanicus oversaw the guild members who'd gained abilities through magic, because his predecessor, Balaam, had led an insurrection against the entire guild. He was a substitute, and an effective one, but it was clearly a temporary fix.

Gork came next. She was impossible to miss. Huge, with gray, rock-like skin, Gork was a member of a subterranean race, an explorer who'd had become trapped on the surface. She was the quietest of the council, and as consequence, her words carried more weight when finally spoken. As the member who looked over all naturally occurring non-human and alien members, Gork took her role seriously. Even if she spoke rarely, one could be sure Gork was always paying attention, watching closely, just in case.

Only a few steps from Gork was her closest friend, Xelas. The two made an odd pairing, yet apparently, it worked. They'd been serving on the council together for some time. Xelas represented all artificially created beings, be they mechanical or biological. She was also blowing kisses to the silent crowd, drumming up a few nervous titters and chuckles.

Those died out when Pseudonym stepped onto the platform. The costume was aggressively simple, just like the name, but no amount of bland would make those watching forget the power of the man before them. Whatever name Ivan used, he was a force of nature, raw destruction held in check only by a single man's relentless self-control. He had to exert such restraint; there was no other choice. The smallest of slips could have serious consequences, as Ivan himself had proven earlier that week. Pseudonym walked calmly to the middle of the stage, taking his position.

It was no coincidence that Pseudonym was next-to-last. He was there to cool the crowd, to silence them for the final arrival. This member didn't climb the stairs. Instead, he soared up from the ground, landing on the platform in a swift flash of thrusters. There was no mistaking this one. The councilor who represented all those who gained their abilities through the wielding of technology: one of the guild's original founders, and its current leader.

Doctor Mechaniacal had arrived.

"I confess, when our guild first fell, I was worried." His voice came from all around them. Despite seeming like an outdoor square, it was becoming more and more apparent that this whole area was designed specifically for guild gatherings, to the point where speakers had apparently been woven into the streets and buildings.

While Pseudonym's appearance had forced the crowd to go silent, Doctor Mechaniacal's words caused them to grow still. No one fidgeted or moved. All focus, all attention, belonged to the head of their guild. And he knew it.

"As an inventor, I know too well that creating something is not the end of the process. There must also be testing. The world's greatest watch that malfunctions after a drop of rain is, in truth, a terrible accessory. Testing, finding an experiment's limits and working to break through them, is how you create something undeniably remarkable. This guild was forged out of necessity, and it has grown to best fit our goals and requirements. But until several months ago, we had yet to be truly tested."

Doctor Mechaniacal paused. Memories were bubbling up, some firsthand, some of video screens they'd watched: the guild, under assault from the AHC. Fighting the capes, and then Balaam's troops. Not everyone had made it through when the dust had settled, but as a guild, they'd endured.

"Balaam's betrayal broke the code and the bonds of trust essential for this guild to function, but he also exposed a great many vulnerabilities in our prior systems. We have been tested, my brethren, and we have come out the other side stronger for it. There are a great many challenges facing us. The world now knows we exist, which will make working carefully all the more important. The Alliance of Heroic Champions must deal with us publicly now, and what form that will take has yet to be seen."

Hephaestus clocked several people in the crowd getting nervous at the mere mention of the AHC. Tough as this guild was, their opponents had quite a roster of powerful personnel as well.

"But with those challenges, there is also opportunity. Living in the open allows us to play a more aggressive game, with bolder strategies. This island is one such example, and there will be more in the weeks to come. As operations resume and we begin our work anew, keep in mind what I said about testing and improvement. Because you do not test a new creation only once. You test it over and over again, until it can no longer meet the challenge or it has become perfected. We will face more trials. Whether or not we come out the other side depends on our strength, our wits, our determination. And it is for those reasons that I am worried no longer."

Another pause, but this one wasn't to open old wounds. The setup had been deliberate, stoking their egos. If he weren't a genius and a billionaire, Wade Wyatt would probably have had great career prospects as a public speaker.

"To be a villain is to live outside the law, trusting in your own power above all else. Before me, I see the faces of so many who have made that choice, and then proved they had the mettle to withstand it. We are not a gang. We are not a syndicate. We are not a mafia. We are not any of the countless human institutions the capes have trampled over through the decades. Each and every one of you is a threat, a danger, on a level great enough that even the AHC is forced to acknowledge you. There are no disposable foot soldiers in this organization: only the sorts of people capes dread meeting in the core of their souls. Because you are strong enough to strike hard, smart enough to strike well, and wise enough to strike unseen. You are danger. You are deadly. You are *villains*."

Something like a murmur, yet closer to a hiss, rose from the crowd. There was a wicked gleam in many eyes and eye-like organs. He'd touched right on the core of their pride, the difference between themselves and the common rabble. Hephaestus could feel the sense of shared unity, even as a new member. She could only imagine how well this resonated with the older metas.

"You are villains," Doctor Mechaniacal repeated. "Together, we are more than that. We are the sorts of criminals who stay free and alive to enjoy the spoils of our enterprises. We can walk down the street as ordinary people, or slip on a mask and become rulers in the shadows. We have created a new way to exist, and it has endured its first true testing to emerge greater, stronger than before."

The metal suit stepped heavily to the center of the stage, effortlessly silencing the crowd once more as Doctor Mechaniacal surveyed the entire mass of people. It seemed like he somehow made time to look everyone in the eye, even if only for a split second.

"It is with great pride, honor, and humility, that I officially reopen the Guild of Villainous Reformation!"

He thrust a metal fist in the air, and on cue, the crowd began to cheer. Were Hephaestus not positioned near one of the hidden speakers, she might have missed the last two words that followed the declaration amidst the chorus of voices. Luckily, the words reached her ears, and she smiled inside her helmet, where no one could see.

"Welcome home."

Chapter 14

"I am not saying Apollo was right. I am merely stating that allowing them to reform as an organization is a mistake. We should put an end to it tonight, especially now that the public knows not every deceased villain really went in the ground." Professor Quantum was standing, looking out one of the windows of the Champions' Congress' meeting room. Before him was Ridge City, twinkling in the evening light.

His thoughts were not on the city itself, however. They were directed toward a country club on the edge of town, where dozens of criminal meta-humans were gathering to toast and celebrate themselves silly. He went on, "It is a tweak of the AHC's nose every time they meet, let alone pull some secret job while we're busy keeping the world safe."

"What's your solution?" Lodestar tapped a single finger on the desk, strong enough to create a *thud* largely muffled by the floor's carpet. "I drop down—which is trespassing, since we have neither warrants, invitations, nor do we believe the area to be in imminent danger. Maybe I lay down some threats and smack a few people around? Because now you can add harassment and assault to that list."

"No judge would believe some common crook over—"

"First of all, if I did all those things, I'd most certainly own up to them in court," Lodestar interrupted, killing that line of thinking in its tracks. "Secondly, even if one of our people with less integrity were to take on the role, the guild will have recordings, testimony, and a team of high-priced lawyers to frame it just right. Not to mention that after what Apollo pulled, they've got legal ammo to question the integrity of any investigation we pull that isn't airtight. All of which is still dancing around the real issue: what do you want me to charge them with if we do go over and arrest everyone? All their old crimes are expunged, and unless you've been sitting on a treasure trove of evidence we don't know about, I don't have any new warrants to hand out. Quorum, you got any?"

While he largely tried to stay out of his colleagues' more passionate discussions, on this point, Quorum took the time to shake his head. Though a great many members of the AHC were uncomfortable knowing a cabal of villains was lurking around out there, ultimately, there was nothing to be done. Within the confines of the law, the AHC couldn't go after them, and if they did, it would mean becoming criminals themselves. Perhaps, under different leadership, there could have been some talk of off-the-books operations, but not with Lodestar at the helm. By her own admission, Lodestar didn't consider herself a servant of the law; however, she did respect it, and she set that standard for all the countless capes who admired her.

"There are no secret evidence stashes on our end," Lodestar concluded. "Look, Professor Quantum. I recognize that you're agitated, but rather than discuss a guild that may or may not cause trouble down the line, why don't we deal with the recent spike in street-level crime? Or maybe talk about how these random punks are turning up with extremely high-tech gear? Just this week there's been a bomb, a robber with jet boots, and some fellow swinging around an energy-axe that cut through stone."

Thankfully, this was intriguing enough to draw Professor Quantum's attention away from the guild—momentarily, if not for the evening as a whole. "Analysis of what you've brought in has yielded little. The devices lack Doctor Mechaniacal's signature polish. He would never tarnish his brand by selling lower quality goods on any market. Of course, I haven't been making them, so we can rule me out, too. In terms of the world's major meta-minds, that leaves only Tyranny. Given that she runs a nation, this seems like rather small potatoes for her to bother with, and none of the tech lines up with her usual creations. Therefore, the good news is that none of the three smartest inventors in the world are likely behind this. The bad news is that our culprit isn't as far behind us as I might like."

That statement caught both Lodestar and Quorum by surprise. It wasn't quite right to say that Professor Quantum had an ego. The situation was more that he was truly brilliant and knew it. He had an accurate grasp of where his intellect ranked against the whole of humanity. The unexpected inverse of that, however, was that Professor Quantum was also willing to recognize the few others who could approach his level. If he suspected this new creator to even be in the same league as the three inventors he'd just listed, then this was a very serious issue indeed.

"What we've seen have largely been basic, easy-to-find components, which renders them all but untraceable. In spite of their simplicity, every device has functioned perfectly, and from looking over the remains, some appear to have been constructed in some haste. For a person to turn everyday junk into this kind of technology requires an exceptional aptitude. Worse, I do not expect we have yet seen the true extent of their talents."

Lodestar kept listening, only now, it was *her* gaze that was darting to the window while she thought about a country club at the edge of the city. As a rule, and a philosophy, Lodestar liked to give people a chance. She believed there was good in almost everyone, that sometimes, all a person needed was the opportunity to prove it. But she'd also been doing this job for decades and had learned the dangers in ignoring a threat early on. What Professor Quantum was describing sure did seem to line up with what she'd learned about Ivan's apprentice: able to turn junk into usable tech, someone they hadn't already dealt with, hungry for income. Though surely someone with guild training would be too smart to try and open an underground black market in Ridge City, of all places.

Still, she'd have to dig a little deeper into the mystery of Tori Rivas, just to be certain. Innocent civilians were at risk and counting on her. Lodestar couldn't sit around, waiting for the criminals to reveal themselves. She needed to be out there, working to keep these people safe. After so many years away, it was the very least she owed them.

No one partied quite like villains. When Doctor Mechaniacal's speech ended, the stars began to change colors, turning into a slowly shifting rainbow as music replaced the leader's voice. People rushed the various food and drink vendors, and with that, all semblance of control faded away. Yelling, drinking, carousing—and that was before powers got involved. Magical creatures were summoned, inspiring unicorn races along the beach, around which Johnny Three Dicks had a betting pool in moments. Not far from where the trees began in earnest, a giant ice cream sundae, easily the size of a house, suddenly appeared. A surprising number of people dove right into it like an emulsified pool, climbing their way up the frosty treat. When an impromptu parade began to form, Hephaestus decided to take her leave.

She slipped away, not bothering to grab Bahamut, who was biting into a keg along with Arachno Bro in some sort of super-jaw/mandible version of a keg stand. Making her way back toward the volcano, she almost stopped to greet Xelas, who was chatting up a figure in dark purple robes, but stopped when she realized the mechanical woman appeared to be excitedly going on about the latest Captain Bullshit piece. Art, especially absurdist performance art, wasn't a topic she felt like tackling tonight, so Hephaestus took a sharp turn at the last minute and continued her walk in solitude.

That's what she thought, anyway. Not long after beginning her ascent, a familiar form stepped up to her side. Maybe he'd teleported; maybe he'd been following her for a full hour while she'd taken in the festivities. With someone as powerful as Ivan, even in his aggressively bland Pseudonym costume, there were just too many options.

"Since you're calling it an early night, as expected, I wanted to see if you'd like to have a meeting."

"Depends. Is this Vendallia business, guild business, or personal?" The response might not actually change her answer, but it would change how Hephaestus approached the meeting in general.

Pseudonym took a few steps to answer, lightly tapping his chin as they walked. "All of them, I suppose. The topic is your future, so it's not really my place to say which area of your life would be most impacted."

"My future? Do I need to start on some kind of villain thesis or something? Because honestly, just kill me now. There's a reason I didn't stick it out in academia."

The quip got her a laugh, albeit a small one. From someone like Pseudonym, that basically counted as a guffaw. He shook his head, then pointed toward a different path that branched off from the one to the teleporter. "Does this seem like the kind of group that copes well with paperwork? Come on. I'll show you up to the lodging and office area. Never know when you'll need a place to hide out."

It could have been her imagination, but there seemed to be a touch of glibness in Pseudonym's voice. Was he actually in a good mood? Well, why not? When Hephaestus thought about it, they should all be in good moods. The guild was reborn, grander than ever before. That might make the future more complicated, yet for tonight, it was cause to celebrate.

They began to climb the path leading higher, though it kept a gentle slope to ensure easy walking. Although flying would have been easier, there was no rush. Especially once Pseudonym began speaking.

"Earlier this week, you saw the reason I'm a villain." He paused, reaching up to pull off his mask, his face shaded now by only the night's shadows. Ivan looked at her hard, trying to meet her eyes through the helmet. After a moment, Hephaestus hit the eject button. Her whole body turned to living flame, bursting out of the suit in a blaze before reforming. She was still wearing a costume—the mask and outfit she donned under the meta-suit in case she was ever forced out—but outside the armor, costumed or not, she was Tori in her heart. Hephaestus was a coupling of creator and invention: in Tori's esteem, anything less didn't deserve the name.

"I fight who I want, when I want. You can break my crimes down into a thousand different motivations and categories, but at the end of the day, that's the part of me that will never fit into polite society. There are plenty of reasons I am this way, yet none of them matter. I am, and so I've had to build a life around that fact."

Ivan lifted a finger, pointing back toward the party. "Doctor Mechaniacal doesn't respect laws. He views them as rules made by the powerful, and feels no obligation to obey the wishes of the tyrannical dead. Morgana will do quite literally unspeakable things to protect those she loves. Arcanicus values knowledge over everything, even if that means research into forbidden subjects or pilfering from someone else's library. Everyone here is in this guild for a reason. I wanted you to start thinking about what yours is. Not why you joined the guild, mind you—that was survival, and we both know it. No, I want you to ponder what it is that makes you a villain. Find the core of you that will not mesh with mundane society and call it by name."

A lot of things rose to mind. Her lack of trust for traditional systems and organizations, her disregard for many laws, the smoldering anger that lived where memories of her parents should have dwelled—any of them could be called out. Tori didn't offer up an immediate answer, however. This seemed more like the kind of task that was supposed to take some time.

"Doesn't sound like an impossible task, though I do have to ask: why?" Tori could still hear the yelling and cheers rising from the crowd. "I'm here. I am a villain. I passed the tests and made my choices. What's the significance of knowing the reason?"

"There are many purposes to knowing one's self," Ivan replied. "Being aware of what lines you can't cross permits you to better focus on the ones you can. It helps to build the authenticity of your civilian persona. Of course, there's also the obvious benefit that a weakness or habit you're aware of is that much harder for an enemy to take advantage of. But the main reason I want you to figure this out is a simple one."

To her surprise, Ivan didn't look down at the partying villains. Instead, his gaze turned skyward, to the colorful false stars. "When you know the kind of villain you are, you find a starting place to decide what kind of villain you want to be. We have the kind of freedom few people dare to even dream of, Tori. We can ignore most limitations, rules, laws, what have you. Think of how many restrictions the average human operates under—restrictions of society, wealth, their own bodies. What do you have to keep you in check?"

"The code." Tori knew it well. The guild's code was how they managed to stay out of the AHC's reach. To break it was to go against the entire guild, and to her knowledge, no one had survived those odds thus far. Now, though, thinking about it in light of Ivan's words, Tori realized how truly minimal a document it really was compared to the entire tapestry of society's limitations.

"The code," Ivan repeated. "Even living within it, you can take what you want, be what you want, live how you want. With your smarts and guild connections, it won't take long before the minor, mundane hurdles you do have fall away. When that happens, when you truly see the endless opportunities stretched out before you, it helps to have some idea of how you want to use that freedom."

"Um, duh. I want to start a tech company." Tori shot Ivan a sideways glance; he already knew that damn well.

A short stare from Ivan was the initial reply before words finally followed. "You misunderstand. That's Tori's dream, the sort of career she wants." Walking over to the meta-suit, still powered up and waiting for her return, he laid a single hand down carefully on its shoulder, feeling the metal cool in the night air.

"I was asking about Hephaestus. Her future. Her goals. Her desires. I know Tori Rivas. Hephaestus is still new. Who she is, what kind of villain she is… those are things you have to decide."

Ivan walked over to Tori, carefully turning her to look with him out over the ocean. Wherever they were, it had one hell of a view. The sea appeared to stretch on in all directions. Constant, endless, a reminder of how small humans, and meta-humans, were in the greater scheme of the universe.

"Think of the water as opportunity. Most people live in a puddle. The capes have a journey that's simpler, and also more limited. They're on a river, a one-way road driving them toward the same goals. Get powers, fight crime—there's a straightforward path to walk, so long as you don't deviate. Villains are different. *This* is what we get. This is our prize for living outside the boundaries of societies. So many places one could go. So many horizons to chase. But if you sailed without direction, you could easily end up spending your whole life going around in a pointless circle."

It was heavy-handed, even for Ivan, yet it got the point across. She wasn't an apprentice anymore. Tori was a villain, in title if not reputation. Maybe it was time to start giving serious thought to exactly what that meant for her future.

Chapter 15

"Was anyone else expecting this place to be warmer?" Kyle finished stripping off the last of his Tachyonic costume, stowing it away carefully and setting the most important components in their charging cradles. Of the team, only Tachyonic needed artificial enhancement to perform at acceptable levels in the field, and while it was a constant source of annoyance and shame, he still had a duty to ensure the equipment was properly prepared. After starting off the week getting lightly scolded by Lodestar, he wasn't going to make any other rookie mistakes.

Despite moving out to an apartment, the team still retained their on-site residence at the AHC. It was policy to provide such space to all members in case anyone ever needed a place to safely rest. The quarters of the New Science Sentries were slightly nicer than most, with four individual rooms connecting to a shared common area with a small kitchenette. Dotting the walls were various charging, training, and general maintenance stations for both the team and their gear. Thankfully, no one tried to make them haul all their equipment over to the apartment for the duration of the temporary guard job. They did all have to keep spare costumes on hand there, just in case.

"We're near the end of summer. It's going to be cool everywhere soon. I bet even back on Vomisa, you can feel a chill in the breeze as it comes off the ocean." Ellie emerged from her room clad in mundane attire: a cropped pink shirt and white skirt. She'd been enjoying the freedom of real fashion options since they arrived and didn't appear to be slowing down anytime soon.

"Not the weather. The people. It's just..." Kyle trailed off, trying to put a point to his words.

Someone else turned out to be faster on the draw.

Clad in a t-shirt proclaiming himself to be a Keg Inspector, Ike came over from the kitchen with a hand pressed to his forehead in a mock swoon. "What Kyle's trying to say is how dare these petty mainland trash people not fall upon themselves praising our greatness?! We are the New Science Sentries, the continuation of a legacy from the dawn of superheroes, yet we haven't seen screaming crowds, raving fans, or even a single line of groupies offering blowjobs. I, too, am outraged, *outraged* by these proceedings!"

Usually, they tried to ignore Ike, especially when he got like this, but today, he happened to hit the right nerve. "I don't expect screaming crowds," Kyle protested. "It's just like no one cares. Our first day got spoiled because I messed up and put a civilian in the limelight, sure. But that was one mistake. Since then, coverage is already dying off and we're barely getting a reaction in the streets. We're old news that fast?"

To illustrate the point, Kyle flipped to a local television station dedicated to meta-stories, especially ones involving the AHC. There was an endless appetite for the exploits of capes, even more so now that Lodestar stories were again in the mix. Today she was not the focus, however. Instead, the camera was on some different AHC members. Apparently, the team had foiled a gang of criminals trying to rob a traveling circus, but not before some of the entertainers had been injured.

The cameras panned in to show inside the big tent, where one of the capes was doing magic tricks for a growing crowd, another was on the tightropes using some sort of strange glove apparatus that glowed slightly, and the final two were putting on a mock lion show, one holding a chair made out of ice, using it to hold back the only member Kyle recognized on sight: Medley. There were a lot of people in the AHC, but the guy who looked like someone put a zoo and steroids into a blender still stuck out.

"Is this really a good example? It's clearly a human-interest piece, not a reflection on their skills as superheroes," Ellie pointed out.

"Maybe so, but people love it. I've seen this team do street patrols, and the community turns out to greet them. Last night, we had patrols, and I swear I saw people locking their doors." Kyle flipped the TV to mute, but continued to let the footage play. "I suppose, if our options are to not be appreciated or to lower ourselves to these kinds of stunts, we picked the right course. I just... expected more from this town."

The sound of heavy steps approaching could only mean one thing: Austin had finished his shower. Given that he'd gotten coated in debris and oil from lifting cars, the man had earned one. As he stepped into the lounge, he was still drying that shaggy blond hair. It didn't fit his brand or his image, yet Austin held strong to his hairstyle. Given how much ground he'd yielded through the years, it made it stand out all the more—to the people who knew him well, at least.

Austin finished toweling off, walked to the fridge, and cracked open a bottle of water before he finally spoke. "We got here a week ago, Kyle. I know our name carries weight, but this is the heart of superhero activity. This is where the Alliance of Heroic Champions has had a base since it was founded, and it was home to the League of Metas before that. We're trying to play country music in Nashville. Prestigious rep or not, no one is going to care until we prove ourselves."

"Excuse me?" Kyle whirled from the television to face his friend, who seemed unbothered by the spin. "I've been running the numbers. Since arriving, our patrols have been among the most efficient. We've stopped more small-scale crimes than nearly any other local field team *and* managed a zero percent civilian injury ratio. We are killing it at this job, just like we trained for. Give us a few more weeks to learn the ropes, and we'll blow everyone else out of the water."

With a powerful chug, Austin slammed the entirety of his water, then tossed the bottle into a recycling bin. Moving steadily, he walked over and turned Kyle back toward the screen, where Hat Trick was pulling an endless candy scarf from her sleeve, letting it land into the waiting hands of eager children.

"There's more to being a superhero than punching criminals and stopping bullets. You win hearts by being a person, not a mask. Perhaps next time we patrol, let's go a little less efficiently and actually talk to the locals."

"Speaking of the locals, do we need to work on ingratiating ourselves to the new neighbors?" Ellie asked. "It's Saturday morning, so this is a prime time to jump on their weekend before they lock down plans."

Kyle would have muttered about it being a huge waste of time, except that he was the reason they had to waste that time in the first place. His mistake had landed them the job of guarding Tori, so he certainly didn't have room to complain about the tasks such a gig demanded. "I guess I could invite her over for dinner tonight. That should be a good 'getting to know you' activity."

Ellie exchanged a nervous look with Ike, who merely offered a shrug in reply. "Good god, Kyle, *I* know you grew up on a super-scientist's lab island, but let's try to hide that from new people for at least a day. Are you trying to hook up with this woman?"

A jolt of shock hit Kyle's face, twisting it into a downright comical expression. "Am I *what*?"

"That's what I thought." Ellie pushed some of her own golden locks to the side, tucking them behind her ear. "Okay, so, Kyle, if you go knock on the door of a woman you just met and ask her to dinner at your place, there are some very major social implications that go with all that. Better idea: I'll do the inviting. It will be for something neutral, like cards or board games, and we'll ask their entire apartment. Nice, non-romantic, new neighbors reaching out socially. Keeps us close to them, just not too close."

A soft clatter reached their ears. Everyone turned to notice that Austin had knocked over a stack of dishes built up in the sink. His cheeks and ears were both red with embarrassment. "You said the whole apartment? Is that wise? We should probably limit our exposure as much as possible."

"Except if we single out just Tori, the best-case conclusion they'll reach is that one of us is courting her, and if she's not receptive to the idea, then that kills the whole buddy-buddy schtick dead in the street." Ike vanished and appeared next to Austin as he spoke, not dropping so much as a syllable. "Trust Ellie. Group invite is definitely the way to go."

The debate might have continued longer, had Ike not invoked the word "trust" in his delivery. As a new leader of a new team, Austin had proven himself determined to show faith in the people he led. No sooner had the word been spoken than Austin's red flush began to fade. He turned to Ellie.

"If you think that's best, then go ahead. We should get back to our new apartment within the hour. That'll be the perfect time to extend a friendly evening invitation."

"As long as they weren't up late doing anything crazy," Ike said, the only one laughing at his joke, as usual. Based on the files they'd read, the odds of that were abysmal. The barista, the blogger, and the cubicle cog—by Ike's reckoning, they might very well be babysitting the most boring collection of people in the entire city.

After a night of revelry and excitement, Tori was grateful for the weekend. True, she'd been off work all week, but she hadn't needed a morning to sleep in until today. A few minutes in fire form nipped her hangover in the bud before it had fully formed; her ability to heal while existing as fire could quite possibly be the aspect of her power she liked the best. After a lazy shower, Tori dressed in an old shirt and overalls, readying herself for a day in the lab. Taking the meta-suit out had revealed a few more areas for tweaks and improvements. Streamline here, improve efficiency there; it was all a matter of refining the invention one step at a time.

Tori emerged to find she was the last riser of the day. Chloe was at the stove, working on her lunchtime specialty: grilled cheese. A pot of coffee was thankfully already made, so Tori poured a tall mug, pausing as she stirred in creamer to notice that Beverly was staring daggers at her. Tori took a few sips to brace herself for whatever this was about, and then traipsed over to the table.

"You look like you just ate a live chicken. What's going on?"

"Don't mind Beverly. She's just in a huff," Chloe explained. "Want a sandwich?"

After another sip of coffee, Tori nodded. "Sure. Could use some breakfast."

"Closer to lunch, lazybones. Anyway, Beverly's annoyed because while you were both snoozing, one of our new neighbors came by and invited us over for games at their place tonight. I told her I was pretty sure we were all free, but I'd check with you both to make sure. Not sure why she's feeling snitty about it when I left you both a perfectly serviceable out."

Slowly, Tori lowered her cup, meeting Beverly's intense stare. Crap. This had come way sooner than they were prepared for. And it *had* to be Chloe who answered the door. Sweet, amiable Chloe, who would obviously accept a social invitation at face value. Why not? It wasn't as if she knew who the new neighbors really were. Thinking fast, Tori catalogued their options. They could have Chloe go solo, but that felt wrong. This was Tori's mess; she shouldn't let Chloe get unknowingly tangled up with capes, especially considering how unique Chloe's ability was. No way the capes wouldn't try to woo her to their team.

The next option was to tell Chloe everything and have her make an excuse to not go. Viable, maybe even prudent. But Chloe wasn't much at subterfuge, and the neighbors would notice when her attitude toward them dramatically shifted. That invited the asking of questions, which Tori and Beverly dearly wanted to avoid. Which only left them with one viable choice: attend the game night. Perhaps they could show themselves to be anti-social and avoid a repeat invitation. While that was an admittedly easier task for Tori than Beverly, they'd have to think of something. She barely had any free time as it was. Forging a fake friendship with a bunch of capes was not a project Tori wanted to take on.

"You know Beverly, she hates the idea of being rude. I bet she's worried she'll get way too competitive playing games with the new people." Tori shot Beverly a conspiratorial wink, which earned her a heavy glare. "She never misses an event, though, so you can count us both in."

"Or I'm just up after a long night and I've got you both haranguing me. I'm sure I'll find my party spirit after a shower and a little time to knock the sleep from my eyes." Beverly's expression melted back to friendliness for Chloe just as she dropped a steaming sandwich onto Beverly's plate.

Thus far, Chloe had burned a roast, spaghetti, and somehow a salad during her cooking rotations. They'd learned that she did best with stuff that just went into an oven on a timer and making grilled cheese. To her credit, bad as she was at most culinary endeavors, the woman grilled a mean cheese.

"Much better attitude," Chloe complimented. "It'll be good for us all. I know we've had a lot going on; a little social engagement is just what we need to unwind. They want us over at six, and we should bring a bottle of wine. It's polite."

For a moment, Tori had flashbacks to living under Ivan's roof, but they cleared away at her first bite. Even on her best dish, Chloe was no Ivan. One day, Tori would have to find out exactly why it was that one of the world's most terrifying monsters was also a shockingly capable cook.

Actually, now that she thought about it, Ivan still owed her an origin story. It had fallen to the back of her mind in the chaos surrounding the end of her apprenticeship, but that was a deal she definitely needed to collect on. Another day, though. One where she didn't have to figure out how to have a social night with a group of capes less than a day after toasting to the resurrection of a guild of villains.

Swallowing her bite of sandwich harder than necessary, Tori realized that somewhere along the way, her life had gotten incredibly complicated.

Chapter 16

Their truck navigated the rocky coast inch by inch, working around the tough terrain until finally reaching a section of flat road. Here, a turn awaited them, a break in the craggy rocks running along the shore. Angling the vehicle just so, they gassed it, pushing up the steep incline. Scraping hit their ears—the passage was so narrow it was tearing off their side-view windows—but they were making progress. The sun faded from view as they vanished into the rocks, their tire tracks the only proof they'd been there at all. Tracks that would soon be washed away by the coming tide.

Inside, the cave was dark. Darker than it should have been, with a pair of headlights set on the high beams. The shadows were borderline aggressive, leaping in the moment that light wasn't directly on them. No external sounds reached their ears—even the nearby lapping of waves was gone. Just when the first member was on the verge of breaking, the lights struck a figure: tall, lean, sporting a stern expression the truck's driver associated with principals and headmasters.

Immaculately dressed in a suit nearly as black as the cave, he gave them a toothy smile as they jerked to a sudden halt, stopping mere feet from hitting the stranger. He appeared unconcerned by either them or the truck, pulling out a silver pocket watch to examine the time.

"On the dot. I must say, I'm impressed. When I have occasion to allow a delivery, they are almost always confused by the directions. You are the first ones to arrive precisely at the appointed hour. What good fortune you have. Let us see if your streak can continue. Show me the merchandise." Despite him being outside the vehicle, no one had difficulty hearing his voice. It was crisp, clear, and precise, like everything about this odd fellow.

Without delay, they sprang into action. Adrenaline was pumping through veins as though they were under the watchful eye of a firing squad. No, that would have been better. At least in that situation they'd know the threat. Working in a cave that seemed empty, yet didn't feel that way, was far more terrifying. No gun could live up to the terrors their own minds imagined.

Moving briskly, they unloaded the large box from the rear of the truck and popped the lid. Their driver stepped forward, clearing her throat to knock the sliver of fear from her voice. "As requested. A Cernovian intergalactic communications array."

The buyer was there, looking over their shoulders, an unsettling glee radiating off him. "Did you have trouble procuring it?"

"Some. There aren't many of these, so they're collectible, but no one besides Professor Quantum ever managed to get one working. If they were functional, they'd be much better guarded. As is, rich people use them as display pieces. We can get you more, with notice." Scary as the cave was, business was business. Besides, if he needed them alive for more jobs, it increased their odds of escaping this cave while still breathing.

At the name "Professor Quantum," the buyer's face tightened, only for a flash. "Is that so? I may well take you up on that. Won't be sure until I can take this apart and see if it needs repairs or replacement parts."

He leaned down, easily hefting the box it had taken all of the driver's more muscular staff to lift. "Your money is already in the truck. If I need your service again, I'll reach out."

A collective sigh left the team as they headed back toward the cab of the truck. Just before she arrived, the driver glanced around once, then turned back to find herself inches away from the tall buyer.

"An afternote. Do not think yourself safe beyond these walls. Speak to no one of this place, or of me. Ever. And should I require another delivery, I encourage you to continue your streak of punctuality. I am far less hospitable with those who waste my time."

They drove out of the cave so fast that the truck sustained a three-foot scratch on the left side as it scraped along the narrow passage. No one said a word of complaint. They'd have jammed the gas to fly into traffic rather than return to that cave.

Unless the money was good enough, of course.

Tori had never been much for social niceties. She hadn't received enough invitations to know what one brought to a board game night, let alone a board game night where four of the members thought they were secretly watching over a civilian, who knew they were actually superheroes and was in fact herself a villain, as was a fellow attendee. That made Chloe, the barista trying to keep her power a secret, the most normal of the entire bunch. If she were more personable, Tori would have resolved to start making less complicated friends. Sadly, even in a world with magic and aliens, some things were still impossible.

In the end, it was Beverly who took charge. She chose a bottle of wine, picked up a cheap card game about building the ideal sandwich, and directed everyone to dress like they were going out to a bar. After Tori emerged still clad in her overalls, Beverly marched her into the bedroom and picked out a better outfit. Granted, this ensemble was still a t-shirt and jeans, but at least it lacked any noticeable oil stains.

Beverly herself had gone for a simple green summer dress, savoring the last of the season's warmth while she could. She made it look designer, despite coming from a big-box store on special, and it wasn't merely the few sewing tweaks she'd made. That was just Beverly. Something about her seemed to class up everything she touched.

It was a talent that was apparently rubbing off on Chloe, who'd donned a shirt and blouse combo far more ambitious than anything Tori had seen her wear before. Then again, she mostly saw Chloe at work and around the house, so perhaps she'd always had a fashionable streak.

Armed with wine, a new game, and appropriate outfits, they walked the short distance down the hall and knocked twice. Instantly, the door swung open to reveal Ellie, who clapped her hands in excitement at their arrival.

"Perfect timing! Kyle just ran out to grab us some beers, and Austin is grilling on the balcony."

"Which leaves me free to mix the cocktails." The shortest dweller of the apartment appeared from around the corner of the fridge as they made their way inside. He gave a deep, performative bow as greeting. "Ladies, I'm Ike Fulton, and you may think of me as your personal bartender, butler, and whatever else you may require."

Without so much as bothering to aim, Ellie took the sprayer hose from their kitchen faucet, turned on the water, and blasted Ike across his side with cold water, eliciting a sharp shriek. "Go change, and we'll try that again," she replied in the face of his withering glare.

Ike stayed planted for a few seconds longer, then assumed a casual grin as he trudged, chuckling, off to his room.

As he left, Ellie began helping Beverly unload. "Sorry about Ike. He's not a bad friend—you can always count on him when shit gets real—but he has a nasty habit of coming on way too strong up front."

"Interesting choice for a roommate," Beverly noted. She was gently broaching the subject, carefully trying to set Ellie up to give them whatever backstory this apartment had concocted. It was the sort of delicate move that only she had a shot at pulling off.

"Yeah, that's a really good point. Why do you all live together, anyway? Me and the girls bunked up after my apartment got torched in the Ridge City Riots, but I'm guessing that's not the case for you all. You've got that comfortable vibe that comes from knowing people for years." Chloe paused to look around the apartment, set up very similar to their own. This spared her the terrified expression on Ellie's face: she was clearly not yet prepared to spin a backstory, let alone face an onslaught of questions.

Seriously, how were they *so* bad at this part of the job? Based on all the research Tori had spent her afternoon doing, they were proving to be extremely competent at every other aspect of being capes. Honestly, if she weren't a secret villain hiding her identity, Tori would have definitely called it out by now.

Lucky for them, Beverly was more skilled at such operations.

"I bet you're all old friends. Chloe is right, you all seem at ease around each other. Of course, you don't have to tell us if we guessed wrong. I don't want to repay your hospitality by prying."

The visible fear left Ellie's face as she recovered, thanks in no small part to Beverly buying her some breathing room. With a smile steadier than the rest of her expression, Ellie nodded. "You got it. Old friends, went to college together, and we decided to apply for jobs in the same town. Everyone got hired, so we opted to split rent and keep costs low."

Perfect. Vague, with just enough detail to address all their major questions. It was the kind of story that wouldn't hold together well if poked, but so long as they—

"That's awesome!" Chloe declared excitedly. "Where did you all grow up?

What college did you attend? Oh, and where are you working? If it's downtown, you're in the same boat as me and Tori, though Beverly here gets to sit around and work from home."

It was hard to be mad at Chloe for acting friendly, especially since she thought they were there to make new friends. Mercifully for Ellie, no sooner was the question asked than the front door opened once more and Kyle appeared, holding two cases of beer. Given that his ability was super-speed, Tori was going to be annoyed if those things were warm, though she should probably assume they'd all been shaken up in transport.

"Kyle! What good timing. Why don't you tell Chloe all about our college and work experience? You always remember things better than the rest of us."

Not exactly a subtle handoff, but to his credit, Kyle kicked into gear as soon as he understood the situation. "It all starts when I'm at my Intro to Calc class during freshman year, and I hear someone muttering curse words to themselves while staring at the book. He was saying what I was feeling, so I tossed over a greeting. That was the first day I met Ike—"

As it turned out, Kyle spun a nice yarn. He told a very convincing tale of four friends meeting, bonding, and ultimately setting off for a new adventure together. It held together well enough that Tori suspected large chunks were actually true, just with certain details changed. From what she gathered, they'd known each other for years. The exception to that was Kyle and Austin, who had apparently grown up together. Whether that was fully accurate or not, she definitely got the impression they had known one another longer.

By the end of Kyle's story, almost everyone had gotten set up in the living room. Tori, Beverly, and Chloe were on a couch together while Ellie and Kyle selected kitchen chairs that had been moved in to surround a coffee table. Some board game about selectively blocking rivers to irrigate a valley had been preemptively arranged, but they were ignoring it until the time to play arrived.

Just as Kyle finished up the yarn, Ike emerged from his room in a new outfit that was near identical to the old, only dry, and helped himself to a beer. "As I was saying, the name is Ike Fulton, and it's..." Ike trailed off, looking to Ellie, who smiled sweetly. "It's a pleasure to make your acquaintance. Sorry if I came on a little strong earlier."

"You should hear what some of the customers say when they come in drunk," Chloe muttered. "At least *you* were offering refreshments."

"Speaking of refreshments, looks like Austin is bringing in our first haul."

Ellie pointed to the balcony, where they could see the hulking man carrying a sizable tray of food.

Steam was pouring off a few items, slightly obscuring Austin's vision as he maneuvered for the door. He made it inside from the balcony, blowing away the steam so he could see clearly. "Grub is almost ready, but it needs to rest or you're getting scalded." As he began to head toward the kitchen, Austin surveyed the room fully, catching sight of their couch full of guests for the first time. Without warning, his eyes went wide and his steady steps turned suddenly clumsy.

This was a moment Tori would look back on and wonder, could things have gone differently? A little to the left or right, one iota more observant, and the night wouldn't have turned out the way it did. In the end, such thoughts were little more than amusing distractions. There was no little to the left or right. Instead, Austin plunged his foot directly under a small section of the living room rug. In trying to take a step, he yanked up on the rug his other foot was holding down, causing him to fall face-first, sending his tray of sizzling hot meat flying through the air.

For the second time that week, Tori found herself staring down an oncoming projectile that should be less than an annoyance, yet because of those around her, she was going to have to risk injury. She shifted forward, trying to put herself between Beverly and Chloe. Heavy as that tray looked, the heat from the food wouldn't bother her. The others might get burned if they were splashed by grease in the wrong spot. It was a noble instinct; however, also an unnecessary one.

What Tori had forgotten was that they were not merely having dinner with neighbors. They were dining with secret capes. And like everyone else who was committed enough to that job to join the AHC, they had instincts of their own. Kyle was there in a literal blur, putting himself between the food and the guests. Ike reacted nearly as quickly, making a motion with his hand that caused the laden tray to vanish, then reappear just before slamming into a wall ten feet away. The impact left a small crater in the brick, and Tori was suddenly very glad she hadn't had to take the brunt of such a blow. How strong was Austin to fling something like that purely by accident?

As Austin pulled himself to his feet, silence dominated the room. Ike and Kyle were frozen, Ellie was trying to casually disperse the small flickers of energy she'd built up to block the tray if needed, and the guests were sitting on the couch, unsure of how to proceed. At this point, the jig was pretty much up. Unless they could think of some way to convince these four they hadn't realized what had just happened. Perhaps they could blame nerves or stress.

"Holy crap! I know those powers. You four are the New Science Sentries!" Chloe, of course, was the one to blurt this out.

Kyle surveyed the room, the shocked faces, the dripping meat along a broken wall, and his clearly caught-off-guard team. Silently, he went to the fridge, pulled out two beers, and opened them both. "Well, *shit.*"

Chapter 17

Through the history of humankind, metas included, there were doubtlessly other parties that had gotten off to worse starts faster than theirs—but not many.

Since Tori's goal had been to walk in and out, leaving as little impression as impossible, accidentally becoming privy to the New Science Sentries' secret identities was a significant complication. Playing dumb was out, thanks to Chloe, who'd finally caught on. It was interesting. Chloe wasn't stupid by any means, yet it had still taken her that long to figure everything out. Tori hypothesized that it might be an issue of perspective. One didn't look for hidden capes everywhere unless they needed to—but regardless, that was a point for later consideration.

"Ahem. Since we've just been outed as superheroes, now might be a good time for fawning and swooning." Ike waggled his eyebrows when everyone looked at him, earning a few mild laughs. It wasn't a lot, but it broke the unbearable tension that had fallen much like the towering Austin, who was finally climbing to his feet.

"I am so sorry. My carelessness could have gotten you all injured." He turned from the guests to his team, genuine remorse etched into his handsome face. "You all behaved perfectly. Protecting people always comes first. When we make the report, I'll accept full responsibility for the team's actions, and any consequence that comes with it."

The mood of the party was dropping precipitously, which was fine by Tori.

At this rate, they were going to be free before having to roll a single dice or make more than a modicum of small talk. The night would surely have consequences down the line, but with a little time, she could prepare for those. Improvising her way through a dangerous social situation, on the other hand, was well outside her wheelhouse.

Finishing the first beer, Kyle took down a good portion off the second. "Like hell you will. We made our calls, and we'll own them. But the bigger question is, what do we do about our guests?"

"Excuse me?" There was nothing fearful in Beverly's tone; instead, it carried a hint of a threat. "Seeing as we're law-abiding citizens here at your invitation, the only thing you'd better consider 'doing about us' is offering me a fresh drink." She held up her empty wine glass to illustrate the point.

The rebuke earned her a sharp laugh from Ike, who looked over to the kitchen and waved his hand. One of the wine bottles vanished from the counter and reappeared in Ike's grip. Another vanish—this time, wine plus all of him—and he was at Beverly's side, pouring with needless elegance. "Ballsy. You seem like fun."

"To elaborate, I'm sure that Kyle didn't mean anything by that. He's just nervous and flustered, like the rest of us." Ellie appeared embarrassed, of all things: barely meeting their eyes, focused instead on the pile of steaming meat sizzling on the ground. "I mean... we haven't even had a whole week in the field and we already let our secret identities slip."

"Plus, you bungled my rescue," Tori added. That earned her an elbow in the side from Beverly and a stern stare from Chloe. "Which is to say that everyone makes mistakes when they're starting out. Broken eggs and omelets... all that noise. You'll get better with practice."

Another downed beer for Kyle, who went back to the fridge and brought back six new ones, stacking them all on the coffee table. "In case anyone else needs a drink. I appreciate it, Tori, but we're not exactly fresh-faced rookies. We've been training to do this job for years, so you'll understand why hitting so many early issues can be frustrating. Sorry again about putting you on camera. Actually, that's kind of why we're here."

"No shit. I figured that out yesterday." In her life, Tori's propensity toward bluster had often been a necessary skill. It allowed her to project greater confidence than she felt, which was dearly useful when dealing with other criminals and lowlifes, as well as offered her a tough outer shell to hide all the childhood pain and loss behind. Unfortunately, the tactic cut both ways, and while this was certainly not the first time she'd talked a situation into being more complicated, it was definitely her biggest verbal whoopsie to date.

Once more, Tori hoped that no one would say anything, and yet again, her hopes were dashed. This time, it was Ike instead of Chloe, though. "Hang on, yesterday? I know I'm good-looking enough to leave an unforgettable impression, but that's why I wear the mask. How did you know who we were?"

Bad as this was, at least Tori could tell them the truth, since it had nothing at all to do with her own identity or the guild. "Tachyonic rescued me a few days ago, obviously. When we talked the second time, he forgot to speak all stiff and heroic. I recognized his voice when we met again. After that, there were only three very easy dots to connect."

"Plus, we literally saw you holding up a couch with one hand," Beverly added, pointing over to Austin, who immediately looked down at the floor. "That was sort of a tip-off, too. Next time, consider springing for movers."

"You know what I love about all this?" Ike asked, dropping into a chair next to Ellie. "First week, we've got two major fuck ups, and I'm not responsible for either one. Somebody on the island lost a bet over that one, I guarantee it."

A dark glare from Kyle brought Ike up short; apparently, he'd gone out of bounds even for him. "But seeing as there's nothing to be done about it—they know, and we can't change that—we may as well go ahead and play some board games," Ike continued. "These three women now know our secret. Seems prudent we get to know them, as well."

From her purse, Ellie pulled out a phone in a sparkling pink and white case. "I could order us pizza. It's on the AHC's dime, anyway. Technically, this whole thing is covered, since we're on officially assigned guard duty."

"Yeah, about that. This feels kind of unnecessary," Tori said. "The press is already moving on, and while I do appreciate you trying to fix your mistakes, I can't help thinking this is overkill. You have to live here just to watch over me? There's no way that's the procedure every time a civilian ends up in the spotlight."

"I suspect we're being taught a lesson," Austin said. He'd recovered enough to make his way to the kitchen, pulling out cleaning supplies and eyeing his mountain of cooling meat. "The overkill is to drive home how much work it is to watch over someone constantly, making sure we go out of our way to avoid putting more civilians in similar situations."

Or it was a way to embed four unwitting capes into Tori and Beverly's lives. Harder to commit crime with superheroes down the hall, was probably the rationale. Then again, maybe it was sincere. Tori had no idea if anyone on the capes' side knew her real identity. Given that she was publicly connected to Ivan, who they *definitely* had the history of, it was best to assume that at least the higher-ups had an inkling.

"For what it's worth, you can tell them I'm fine, and you're free to stop babysitting me anytime."

"I'll pass it along," Kyle replied. "But I doubt it will matter. We're here for at least a month, and then we have a reevaluation meeting. Until then, I can only ask that you put up with us. I promise we'll try not to get underfoot."

She didn't have a choice, really. It was the same options as before: play nice, or tell them to fuck off. Playing nice allowed her to set more boundaries, especially now that she knew they were here on assignment. Plastering on her best fake smile, Tori reached over to the coffee table and picked up one of the beers Kyle had set down.

"I guess somebody should call in that pizza. Otherwise, at this pace, we'll all be drunk before we finish whatever this first game is." Tori took a deep, long drink of beer, bracing herself for the night of socializing.

Emory didn't know what any of the tech was supposed to do, even as he supervised the installation. Sure, in the general sense, he understood this gear would keep their captive from being located by most known tracking means—although nothing was ever impossible—but he didn't fathom how setting up the few pieces of tech around the base was actually going to accomplish that. Deacon seemed confident, and all the rumors said this dealer sold working shit, so Emory tried to put his own lack of understanding out of mind. All they had to do was follow the instructions.

The focal point of the concealing equipment was a small, windowless room on the west end of the building. Since it had once been planned as a private office, there was a toilet installed inside, so that took care of their most disgusting logistical hurdle right off the bat. The walls were thick, and no one was around to hear, meaning that sound wouldn't be an issue, and the tech would keep the capes off their backs long enough for Deacon's plan to kick in.

What that plan entailed, exactly, Emory was still uncertain. All he knew was that they were going to snatch the woman off the street, rather than try to take her at home. The apartment was tempting; however, breaking in came with too many static challenges. On a street, things were more fluid. They could strike at the opportune moment. After that, it was just a matter of transporting her back and getting word to the capes.

Taking a step away from the crew, Emory made his way down the hall to

Darius's quarters. Just outside the door, he raised a scaly fist to knock, only to have the door open before he could make impact and reveal the serious face of Darius.

"Something up?"

"Construction is going well," Emory reported. "Should be ready by Monday. I was just wondering if there was anything else I should be doing. To prepare."

Darius looked him over, instantly spotting the question within the question. Being a henchman demanded a talent for talking around corners, questioning the boss's methods without ever letting them realize it. They lived a delicate balance between the crime lords and the capes. Most of the time, being a flunky meant no one paid you much attention when there was a bigger fish to chase. Get in too deep, do something really bad, and that wouldn't necessarily hold true. Worse, Emory was new. He didn't even realize the true danger of what they were contemplating.

"You should remind everyone that what we are doing is intended to be pageantry, nothing more. We scare the girl, we make the capes believe she's in danger, but we never use more force than needed for any given task. There is a tremendous difference between kidnapping a civilian to draw out the capes and injuring one."

"The charges would be more serious." Emory was right, technically, not that it would likely matter if he messed up.

Seeing that legendary, shadowy guild that every crook has heard some kind of rumor about drawn into the streets was a moment Darius would never forget. He'd listened to the same rumors, seen gangs vanish overnight, but he'd never *really* believed. He'd just followed the rules of surviving in Ridge City, which meant staying low on the capes' radars. Now, he wasn't sure if they were playing by the old laws or not. Seemed unlikely the guild was still watching over crime, exacting revenge on those who broke their edicts. Still, no reason to take unnecessary risks.

"The charges, and the capes themselves, would be more serious. There's a dance to some of this, and if you stick to the steps, then you can see where it will end. Break the rhythm, and you're in uncharted territory. We play nice, because it ensures the capes play nice." Along with anyone else who might be watching, though Darius didn't add that last part. It was too much to try and explain, especially to someone who hadn't spent years hearing those whispers.

"I'll reinforce that along the ranks. Any word on when Deacon will be back?"

"He's meeting his connection for the last round of supplies. After that, it's just a matter of finishing prep, and then striking. Tell the others to be ready for when he comes back," Darius instructed.

Emory hesitated, an uncommon act for him. "Shouldn't one of us be along on these deals? We *are* his bodyguards."

To that, Darius merely shook his head. "Kid, in this world, you need to square with the fact that different metas play on different levels. You and me are near the bottom: strong and deadly, but without powers that could break mountains or change reality. Someone with access to this kind of tech isn't using the kind of muscle you or I could stand against. Deacon didn't bring us because he's smart enough to realize that if shit does go wrong, we'd just be more corpses on the pile."

In actuality, Deacon hadn't brought his goons because the seller forbade anyone else from joining him, and this was not a connection Deacon could afford to offend. Especially not at the incredibly low prices the tech was going for. To be fair, the gentleman across the table had brought along no guards either. He sat by himself, tall and gaunt, fingers steepled together patiently while Deacon inspected the wares.

It was a waste of time. Deacon had no better idea of how this worked than he did what made Lodestar fly. Nevertheless, he put on the show, because admitting ignorance seemed an excellent way to get fleeced. Concluding the assessment, Deacon lifted a small tube with a single button on one side.

"Careful. The auto-injector has been preloaded with a cocktail of my own creation. Human, meta, alien, or elephant, that serum will take them down for at least three hours. It's specially designed to block oversaturation and avoid an OD, so don't worry about dosing. One press will fire the entire container. So long as you can break the skin, you can take her down quietly."

"All reports say we're dealing with a human, so I don't anticipate that to be an issue." Deacon slipped the injector back into the case, along with the other trinkets to equip their base. "Pleasure doing business with you, as always."

Deacon shut the case and moved to lift it, but a hand on his sleeve stopped him. The gaunt man had leaned forward, pinning Deacon's shirt with a single finger, his toothy smile shining in the soft light of the dangling bulb.

"There is one more thing. As your current operation has a high chance of drawing in some of those New Science Sentries, I thought I'd offer up a little something extra. Ten million dollars, or the tech of your choice, for each one of their heads you bring me. Except Agent Quantum. I doubt you'd even be capable, but nevertheless, that one has been reserved."

It was an incredible offer, and one that Deacon had in no way been prepared for. "That is... generous. I'll have to think about it. Killing capes is a little more ambitious than what we'd previously discussed."

"Capes are like weeds. You want to pull them up early, before their roots burrow too deep." Bony cheeks shifted as the toothy grin became a thin, hateful smile. "Trust me. There is nothing so troublesome as a cape once they've dug in."

Chapter 18

For the first time since the aliens briefly appeared in the night sky, Donald had the day off. His team had been running patrols and taking low-danger calls from the field all week, and while it was cool to see new cities even in short, action-filled bursts, he was definitely ready for a day to relax. Under other circumstances, he might have texted Tori, but the last thing she needed at the moment was to be publicly seen with another cape. Besides, even if they weren't working, he still had plans for the day.

Ren arrived downstairs first. After some trial and error, he'd managed to get the illusion device on his wrist fine-tuned enough to quasi-replicate something akin to how he'd looked before being transformed into the cape called Medley. His new body's proportions were all wrong for his old face—evidently, Ren hadn't previously been built like a walking tank—but at least he could pass as his own relative, albeit one that was way too into the gym. This was the face they'd begun to think of as Ren's default, the one he wore when he wanted to be recognizable.

"Team day!" Ren called, giving Donald a very careful high-five, making sure not to accidentally break any bones. Even if he looked and sounded human, the same fangs, scales, and muscles were still there, hidden under the facade, ready to be called on in a moment, if needed.

"Woo, team day!" Donald echoed right back. It had been Ren's idea, since he was the only one of them who was used to actually being on teams, but it hadn't taken long for the thought to snowball into something of its own entity.

"You two sound like goofballs." The voice came from the stairwell, where Irene was finishing off the final step. Unlike Ren, her looks were constant: dark hair pulled back tight into a ponytail, piercing eyes taking in the whole room, and the barest smattering of makeup over her brown complexion. Granted, it was a change to see her outside of a costume or training sweats: fatigues, sneakers, and a shirt for some band he'd never heard of were certainly a different kind of fashion, yet it still managed to be quintessentially Irene. Comfortable, functional, and with only the barest of shits given toward how it actually looked. Were Apollo still in charge of the rookies, he'd have never let her out in public like that, even though her civilian identity wasn't yet known.

She approached them, let out a very loud sigh, then lifted her own hand up for high-fives. "But that's about what I expect from you dorks, anyway. Yay team day, rah rah rah, let's go have some fun."

It was the most enthusiasm she was going to show; that was just who Irene was. Now that Donald and Ren were used to it, they knew she was excited as well, even if she didn't demonstrate it in the same way. More hands were slapped as they waited for their final member to appear.

True to form, Lucy arrived at the edge of being late, looking slightly as though she'd tumbled all the way there. Her black hair was a mane trailing behind her, a flush highlighting the freckles along her pale skin, and she was hopping on one leg, slipping a sneaker onto her left foot. She was the only one who'd opted for shorts, despite the lingering summer heat, and paired with the plaid button-down, Lucy looked more suited for hiking than a day on the town. It was curious to Donald how she could be something of a mess in her day-to-day life, yet prove constantly reliable in the field. At any given time, he was never quite sure how Lucy might be managing, but he'd quickly learned that Hat Trick could be counted on when the world turned into chaos.

"Team... day!" Lucy puffed out that last bit; she'd definitely jogged down to the garage to meet them on time. "Sorry, got caught up on a call. Am I late?"

"Don't worry, madame executive, your call didn't impact your next meeting." Irene met Lucy with a hug, and then commenced the final round of high-fiving before they would depart. "Hey, Donald, where did we end up deciding to start, anyway?"

That choice had actually been made for them. When everyone pitched their contributions to team day, Donald had taken everything down, and then looked at what could feasibly be scheduled for a single outing. Irene's was easy, since the park was open all day, but Lucy's only had showings at night.

Ren's was the toughest, though thankfully, it had lined up well when they discovered one of Donald's ideas had recently expanded their hours.

"We're going to start by doing brunch at the downtown arcade restaurant. Reviews say the food is good, and either way, they'll still have the huge selection of classic games," Donald informed them.

Ren narrowed his eyes. "Any items in these classics we should be aware of?"

"Doubt it, although I am kind of curious to see what would happen if I ate a ghost-killing dot. Doesn't matter anyway. Remember: today, I'm just Donald. After brunch, I found us a football game to watch. We're apparently still too early for the pros, but some of the colleges are doing preseason stuff. That work for you, Ren?"

"Is one of the teams the Ridge City Ravagers?" Ren asked.

"Sorry, they weren't playing today. We could always see if they've got practice—"

"No." The word was firm, yet spoken gently. "Not ready for that. They are... were my team."

In the earlier days, when it was just Donald and Ren, they'd have stood around awkwardly fumbling their way out of the unexpected conversational pitfall. Those days were gone, however, and they were no longer a duo. They were part of a group now, which meant that some of the members actually did know how to deal with these kinds of moments.

Lucy strode over with the sort of determination Donald more commonly associated with Hat Trick, wrapping her arms around Ren and hugging him as tightly as she could. It was comical, in a way, this comparatively small woman squeezing with all her might on the hulking figure; almost like a child hugging a statue. Until the statue tenderly hugged her back, at which point, it stopped being funny and started to make Donald realize he needed to better his interpersonal skills. Working with other metas, these kinds of situations would come up, and the awkward fumbling routine wasn't going to cut it forever.

"Since Lucy wants a show, I'm guessing that means we do my thing third?" Good old Irene: not someone you'd want for a smiling competition, but always willing to shoulder her way through an awkward pause to get things moving again.

"Got it in one," Donald confirmed. "After the game, we drive a bit out of town to Candoo Memorial Park. There's a colony of meta-butterflies migrating through there, and they say it's like watching a living rainbow fly around the sky. Weirdly, this was the hardest one to get tickets to—I had to go through official AHC channels to even get in the door."

"Well, it's not a video game, but the natural world does okay from time to time." If Donald didn't know better, he'd have thought he detected a hint of mirth in Irene's tone. "And after that, magic?"

Their hug concluded, Lucy turned away from Ren, eyes lighting up. "Oh no way, did you really manage to get us in?" She was rocking on her heels, nakedly excited in a way that uncomfortably reminded Donald of himself discussing a new game release.

Donald nodded, earning a small squeal of joy from Lucy—the only warning she gave before she enveloped him in a hug as well. Unlike Ren, Donald was not composed of animal parts and muscle, so he could actually feel how much force she put into them. The woman loved to hug; it wasn't shocking she'd grown good at it.

"Four tickets to the Amazing Earl." Donald forced the words out, earning himself a reprieve as Lucy eased her embrace. "I double-checked: you know this guy is human, right? He's not going to be doing anything you can't."

"It's not the same," Lucy protested. "I'm using real magic. He's using technique and skill. How do I put this...? If you won a game with a cheat code, you wouldn't say you'd beaten it, right? Same thing. I like having this power, but I still want to be good enough to do magic on my own."

That was actually an amazingly adept analogy, Donald realized. He was impressed. They hadn't been working together for all that long, but she'd perfectly conveyed the point using language he understood. Maybe he should ask her for lessons on communication. Since Ren was already shoving Donald into the gym regularly, he'd quickly gotten used to idea of learning from his teammates. It was something to think about—just not on their day off.

"Well, with these seats, you should definitely have a good enough view to figure out the Amazing Earl's secrets. On that note, do we have anything else to add before we requisition a driver? I figured we'd just do meals as we saw stuff that looked good, or I could make a reservation for tonight."

"You've done plenty." Lucy laid a hand on his shoulder, far more daintily than when she'd gone for a hug. "Thanks for putting this together for us."

"Team building counts as training," Donald replied. "Plus, learning about the things we all love is a great way to do that team building while also having a killer day off. I was happy to help."

Really, he was happy to just feel like he was contributing. During the Ridge City Riots, the rest of the team had taken a serious beating protecting Cyber Geek, because he was the key to their plan. While it had shaken out okay—largely thanks to Lodestar arriving just in time—Donald could still feel the guilt over that day in his gut. How badly they'd been hurt, and how terribly things could have gone, while he'd come out virtually unscathed. Donald was determined to do better, to be better, and if this helped in even a small way, then it was effort well spent.

A large SUV pulled round, driver at the ready. Together, the team piled in, heading off into Ridge City for some well-deserved time to recover. It was fortunate timing, too, given how hectic the next week was going to be.

"You're the new cluster leader?" Janet ran a thumb along the edge of her glass, a tell she was annoyed that Ivan still remembered quite clearly. Sitting in her parlor, the two of them were talking quietly. Juan had taken Rick and Beth out for a day at the museum. Ostensibly, their mother was helping a fellow professor with a last-minute emergency and would catch up. These sorts of talks were easier in private.

"Should I even ask what happened to Haywood?" She flexed her fingers, reaching for a cigarette that wasn't there. If he squinted, Ivan could still remember the way Janet had looked when she smoked. Still pretty, if perhaps too serious for some tastes, but back then, there had also been a wild, chaotic energy around her. From the chopped-up hair to the half-shredded clothes, no one would have guessed that under it all hid the brain of a mathematics prodigy. In a way, that had been her version of a villain identity, but it was one she'd long ago cast aside.

"Haywood Gibson was involved in an unfortunate car accident that has left him unable to fulfill the duties of a cluster leader. As a willing parent, I was tapped to take his place, at least until a suitable substitute can be found."

Her dark eyes roamed over him. There weren't many people who knew Ivan, not really. Janet was an exception. Former wife, mother to his children, she'd spent more time with him than even Wade had during their early villain days. That was another reason Ivan preferred contact over the phone. She was too good at reading him.

"I knew that guy was up to something. It was about her being a meta, right?"

Weighing his options, Ivan decided that this was not the time for subterfuge. "Mr. Gibson seemed to have some preconceptions about metas being around human children. I was planning to use my contacts and go around him. Then he decided to speak about Beth directly. Plans changed."

A smile. Brief and quick, but for a moment, Ivan saw the old Janet, the dangerous woman too smart and bored for her own good, peeking out as a twinkle in her eyes. "Those kids are going to face a lot of hell growing up as the children of Fornax. Beth even more, now that she's got powers. For all the complications having you as their dad adds on, I'm glad you're here to watch over them."

It was a pleasant note to end things on. Unfortunately, they hadn't actually reached the end of their conversation. There was still another point to raise.

"There's one more thing you should know. All clusters have a male and female leader—a policy meant to accommodate the kids in case they want to discuss embarrassing or private matters. I won't be leading these meetings alone. The one who put me in this position is going to be there, keeping watch on both me and the children."

Whatever good cheer had found its way to Janet's face drained off. Her thumb was pressing so hard against the glass it was turning the skin white, not that she appeared to notice. "Really? That's the story? She's there to keep an eye on you, in case you decide to, what, kill a room full of kids? Even in your worst days, Fornax never hurt a child, and she of all people knows that's still true."

"She's putting Fornax in a room full of minors; no one else would agree to that without Lodestar being present," Ivan pointed out.

"Fornax isn't the problem!" Janet slapped the table, and for a moment, her old fire was no mere twinkle of the eye. "God damn it, Ivan. You're single, so I don't give a shit if you two want to play these cute little games, but I wish you hadn't just jammed our daughter into the middle of it."

Silence fell as Ivan quietly weighed his options. "If you feel that strongly that it will be bad for Beth, I can see if there's another way. Perhaps a different cape she'd trust to take the spot at my side."

"You should do that. I should make you do that."

Janet closed her eyes, breathing deeply, before releasing the death-grip on her glass. "Except, I can't," she continued at last. "Because no matter how I feel about all of this, the attack on their school showed me that our kids can be targets, despite every assurance you offered through the years. If Beth can spend a few hours every week endearing herself to the world's greatest superhero, I have to let her. She might need that alliance one day, when the world finds out what her dad's old job really was. And if someone attacks her again, she'll be high on Lodestar's priority list. This is bullshit, I'm laying that out up front, but the kids come first."

"Always." Ivan didn't hesitate, nor did Janet question the response. As a couple, they'd been fair, at best, and as exes, they were even worse; yet on this point, they were absolutely united. For all the faults and issues they had between them, Ivan knew that Janet always acted with their children's best interests at heart, and vice versa. It was the common ground that had allowed them to manage custody.

Janet continued to look at Ivan, studying his every change in expression. "Just... don't let her do what she does. Don't let her get in Beth's head. Please don't let her steer our girl toward that life."

That promise was not one that Ivan could make, though he wanted to dearly. He could no more stop Helen from inspiring people toward goodness than he could outmatch Lodestar. They were forces beyond him, past his realm of halting. Nevertheless, Ivan would give his all. Janet was spot on: the last thing they wanted for either of their kids was for them to fall into the world of cowls and masks. Beth being a meta would be hurdle enough for her; if she started into Ivan's world, there might be no way back.

"With everything I have, I will try."

Chapter 19

Monday found Tori returning to her mundane routine, with the added spice of now knowing everything she did was in the proximity of a team of capes specifically there to keep an eye on her. Saturday had gone well enough; they'd exchanged pleasantries and played board games for an hour or so before finally excusing themselves. It felt like the New Science Sentries had enjoyed the visit, once everyone had recovered from the shock of accidentally outing themselves, so hopefully, they weren't suspicious of their new neighbors.

Just to be safe, Sunday had been an extremely mundane affair. She, Beverly, and Chloe went out for lunch, caught up on work, and watched some old movies; things she imagined people without secret meta-lives did frequently. Truth be told, it had been a nice day off, and Tori found herself more refreshed as a new week began than when she spent ninety percent of the weekend hunched over in a lab. Maybe there was something to the idea of taking weekends as actual breaks.

By the time she made it to work, Tori was almost thankful to see Vendallia. Boring as it was, here, she was one more cog in the machine. No one paid her particularly special attention, nor did she have to take great pain to appear normal. Simply being here every day and doing the work made her own case for normalcy. People with better options didn't often stick around in positions like Tori's.

Upon arrival, she found Ivan waiting for her at the door. Tori lifted an eyebrow, unsure if something was up, but Ivan merely handed her a brown paper bag with the top folded over and stapled together. “Good morning. I trust you’re feeling rested from your time away.”

“Oh yeah, a week dodging cameras was my perfect idea of a vacation.” Tori pressed along the bag, feeling the soft contents inside give way. “Is this a welcome back gift?”

“If you want to think of it like that. It’s your uniform for tonight. I procured it from the specialty tailor you use; I know how some synthetic fibers can give you a rash.” Ivan didn’t tend to be the type to make jokes, so Tori was half-certain he’d chosen that cover story because it explained why half the shit she wore was custom tailored and not because it was inherently embarrassing. She wasn’t going to object, since it still netted her clothes from the special material that could be shifted into fire. While Tori was capable of making the material herself, she didn’t have nearly the sewing or fashion skills Doctor Mechaniacal had access to, meaning the provided versions were of optimal quality.

Yanking off the staples, Tori peered inside. She had to root around a little, but the outfit quickly took shape. Not very different from what she remembered Starscout assistants wearing when she was a kid. Tan shirt and pants—maybe shorts; it was hard to gauge length in a bag—along with a turquoise ascot. She’d brought sneakers from home, which would round out the ensemble. There were also hats, if she recalled correctly, though those were for actual outdoor activities.

“Hang on... if I have to wear this, does that mean...”

“We will all be dressed appropriately tonight,” Ivan said, answering the question preemptively. “Myself, you, and our other cluster leader. While she’s an old contact of mine, you wouldn’t have met her yet. She is unaffiliated with Vendallia or its major partners. Do try to keep that in mind, and use discretion as appropriate.”

There were doubtlessly more subtle ways to tell Tori the other person wasn’t a secret villain, but these weren’t the sorts of messages Ivan left to chance. “Got it. Be on my best behavior, and no talking about confidential company work off the clock. I won’t even bust out my inventions or technology talk. Do I get to know the name of this mystery helper before we arrive, or is that supposed to be a surprise?”

“Helen.” Ivan looked briefly away, glancing down the street to where the morning sun was beaming down on cars and commuters coming from the east. “Her name is Helen.”

She watched as they scampered about, looking down from the balcony much like Apollo had when examining the same group. Newer members of the AHC were kept in the same part of the base for many reasons. Bonding, comradery, safety, training—it was easier to consolidate people of roughly the same skill level, which was to say, amateurs. That was how all rookies were treated when they came in: assume they knew nothing and drill the fundamentals. Every now and then, a street-level cape would bristle at having to prove themselves, but since Lodestar had yet to meet a single person who didn't benefit from retraining the basics, the policy remained in place.

Except that it had been months since the last confluence. A lot of the so-called rookies had been logging hours nearly nonstop, taking every patrol and shift they were offered. No doubt some of that came from the desire to prove they weren't aligned with Apollo or any of the others who'd illegally set up the guild of villains, yet she knew there was more.

They'd all seen a flash of the old world. Before guilds and peace, before the AHC, when everything was chaotic and dangerous. People liked to look back on the older days with a patina of wistfulness coloring their impressions. Not her. She could still remember the times at the end of the League of Heroes, when Professor Quantum had all but checked out entirely. Things were near a boiling point back when she was a street-level cape herself, a period of her life few people even knew about. To the world, Lodestar had burst onto the scene in a sudden blaze. The public hadn't seen her before that moment, when she was just one more set of fists on the sidewalks trying to help. They had no idea about the years spent working in anonymity, before she ascended to her role as one of the world's most famous protectors.

That was the trouble with metas, humans—all living things, really: they changed. People grew up, grew stronger, grew better. It was natural and inevitable. Unfortunately, that also meant she now had a whole group of rookies that were no longer truly on the same level lumped together. It was time to start graduating some of the units up to harder jobs, take the stress off the over-worked capes. Since the guild's outing, low-level crimes had increased constantly. It wasn't that Ivan's people had been actively stopping that many operations; more that fear of them had forced the bulk of criminals to be careful. Without that fear and need for caution, crooks were getting bolder. Sooner or later, they'd make a true push, and the AHC had to be ready when that day came.

Powerful as Lodestar was, she was still only a single superhero. It was a hard truth she'd accepted decades prior: not even she could save everyone. The world was too big, too full for her to have a prayer of managing that. That was why capes worked together, why the Alliance of Heroic Champions had been founded: to share the burden of keeping the world safe. To have capable allies always at the ready. To teach the next generation how to use their abilities, and then entrust them with the future.

Finally, Lodestar looked right, to where Quorum was patiently waiting. "I'm guessing whatever files Apollo had on them are already largely out of date, though I'd still like to look them over. But even after being left on their own while we were getting everything sorted, they've all been improving. I checked the logs last night. Some of these teams are doing near constant field patrol. No telling how that experience will show itself."

"With respect, there *is* a way to tell." Quorum's voice was as patient and near neutral as always. "It would not be the first time the Champions' Congress has evaluated the skill of our recruits by hand. For a time, that was the only method we had. There is a case to be made for the tried and true tactics."

The groan that escaped Lodestar's lips almost had a weight to it. "I hate doing that. It's not fun for them, Professor Quantum takes it way too seriously, and inevitably, somebody quits when they see the power difference. Can't we come up with rubrics or something?"

"Apollo used a complex ranking methodology that took into account potential merchandising appeal, camera skills, and perceived loyalty to the organization. I presume that system wouldn't be to your liking, but properly vetting and assessing them all one by one using our old metrics will take quite a while. If your concern is to make sure the ones ready to advance are being used and trained properly, then that method will waste a lot of time."

Doing the right thing was supposed to be the easy part. Except that when you were in charge of a whole organization, it demanded balancing different versions of that "right thing" depending on who one looked at. Was it more right to slowly assess the rookies in this case, keeping them from helping people in need, or to get more capes onto the streets, even if they might not be ready to step up? It had to be done right—there was no room to give on that front, and sooner was definitely better. Quorum, to no surprise of Lodestar's, turned out to be right.

"If it's going to be a hands-on evaluation, let's at least be smart about this. Tell Professor Quantum I'm doing the whole group solo. Assuming he cares enough to ask why, the excuse is that since he's got clear bias toward the New Science Sentries, this will keep the assessments beyond reproach."

"Do you really think he'd go easy on his team?" Quorum asked. It was the kind of question he didn't actually need to say; he'd already found the answer before the first syllable hit his lips. These were for her, and the sake of conversation.

"Heck no. I think he'd decimate them in front of the entire AHC just to shame them into working harder. But it's more about the image than the truth, and that's a concept he'll be on board with." She looked down once more, observing the costumed figures as they darted around. "We'll have to do it in one go. If word gets around, things'll get muddled. Can you schedule everyone else so that I've got all the rookies one day on a weekend?"

From his pocket, Quorum produced a folded sheet of paper. "I'd already begun work on assessing the best options for doing so."

"Of course you did." A quick scan showed several schedule options, rotating their members around in different shifts to ensure the AHC was ready to respond to any serious threats. It didn't escape her notice that Quorum's own name appeared in a few spots, jammed in among all the others like it was nothing special. "You want to go back into the field?"

"It would be more apt to say I feel compelled to go into the field," Quorum said. "As you noted, the people are in need. While, for a time, I best served our organization by helping to run it; such attention is no longer required. The Alliance of Heroic Champions has grown vastly in its decades. It can endure without me working behind the scenes, and there are many voices reminding me that our power comes with a duty to help. One in particular has been especially ardent."

Quorum met Lodestar's eyes, and suddenly, they weren't his anymore. For a flash, a different iris appeared, just long enough to give her a wink.

In the beginning, that alone might have caused Lodestar to tear up. Now, she smiled back, thankful to have the moment at all. "That sounds nice, but this place has been big enough to run itself for a long time. Lack of support staff wasn't the only thing keeping you in here."

"Of course not," Quorum agreed. "I was 'holding down the fort,' as the saying goes. I knew one day you'd both return. Now that there's leadership I can trust, I'm not quite so worried about leaving the place unattended."

Seven years. That was how long she'd been away. It felt like a drop in the bucket to her, but for the world and the AHC, it had been different. She didn't regret the time off after the birth; Helen had always been ready to come back if the need arose. Except the world had managed to stay out of major danger, thanks in no small part to Ivan and his guild keeping their own kind of peace. For seven years, she'd gotten to be a normal person, raising her daughter.

Coming back meant there was a lot to clean up, yet Lodestar felt strangely energized.

Those years had reminded her what it was she was fighting for: all the normal people out there who wanted nothing more than to live in peace with the people they loved. Up high, looking down from the clouds, it was easy to forget that every dot on the ground was a person, with their own dreams and life connecting to untold others. Living like a normal human helped her remember why they were so worth protecting. Helen was never going to have that peaceful life; that she'd even gotten to taste it was truly a miracle. So she'd settle for protecting that peace for as many people as she could.

"Do the third schedule option," she instructed. "And please, whatever message you give, don't tell them they're sparring with Lodestar. Last time, that caused three panic attacks before we even got the test running."

Chapter 20

If Tori hadn't known better, she might have thought they were pulling up to Ivan's actual house. The neighborhood was boring enough to match his old one, and the home itself looked like the same kind of predesigned build. It was a little too nice, however. Stone work on the exterior, designer touches on the trim, this was the home of someone who spent more for appearances, which took Ivan instantly out of the running.

"Whose place is this?"

"Technically, Vendallia's," Ivan replied. "We have some rental properties in holding for when visiting staff are needed on long-term projects."

"Or if someone guild-related needs a place to lie low away from headquarters?" Tori might still be relatively new, but she could spot a pattern that obvious.

"I suppose that might also happen, in theory." Ivan reached into the back of his car and scooped up a large duffel bag, presumably containing his own outfit. "Though, to my knowledge, we've mostly used them for their intended purpose. We got an official exception since my current home is too small to host in and this is work with a charitable organization… with perhaps a dash of help from the top."

Tori snickered as she reached for the handle, but Ivan laid a hand on her shoulder. "Listen: before we go in, I want to make sure we're on the same page. While the kids will be kids, you'll also be working with another adult.

Be aware of what you say. This isn't a busy office, and Helen is no distracted coworker."

"She someone I should watch out for?"

Something odd appeared on Ivan's face, an emotion somewhere between amusement and consternation that ultimately faded as he released a slow, controlled breath. "Whatever conclusions you draw about her should be your own. I will only say that she is not a woman I would advise you underestimate."

After watching an entire team of capes accidentally out themselves over the weekend, Tori was in no mood to take anyone lightly. One slip-up, one spilled tray of meat—that was the difference between a secret identity and her name on the Hephaestus rap sheet. Since she had to be here regardless, Tori was treating this as supplemental self-control training. If she could hold her heat and hide her power around a room of preteens, there wouldn't be much that could rattle her.

Together, she and Ivan made their way up the front drive, arriving to find the front door already peeking open. Pushing through, they could hear humming come from within. Tori noticed that silver and turquoise streamers were already running along the ceiling, hanging over a large dining room table that had been enthusiastically cluttered by craft supplies. Movement drew her attention; she focused on a doorway to the kitchen as a form stepped into view.

The woman was still humming, earphones poking out from underneath her mane of chestnut hair. She was younger than expected, mid- to late-twenties at most, only a few years older than Tori herself. And that was assuming the glasses didn't make her seem older than she really was. As this stranger, presumably the mysterious Helen, turned around, she caught sight of Ivan. Instantly, her face lit up and she set down the armful of glue in her grasp.

"Perfect timing. I've got the decorations working and our fun-time table mostly ready. You need to get moving on grub. Given the age of our group, if there aren't adequate snacks, they might chew through all this lovely rental furniture before the night is through." Helen looked away from Ivan for the first time, treating Tori to a full-force blast of smiling, cheerful energy. "Hello there! You must be Ivan's niece. Thank you so much for agreeing to come help us out. I look forward to getting to know you over the coming weeks, Tori."

Tori went for a handshake, which Helen somehow managed to turn into a hug, seemingly without effort. If not for Ivan's warning, it would be easy to mark Helen as a happy, simple helper, the kind one might let their guard down around. No wonder Ivan had cautioned her about underestimation. Helen was the type of person Tori would instantly dismiss, and he knew it.

"My pleasure," Tori said once the hug finally ended. "But you've got me at a disadvantage. You're aware I'm Ivan's niece. How do you and my uncle know each other?"

Part of her had expected some big reaction. Instead, Helen calmly tapped a finger to her chin. "Oh goodness, it seems so long ago—you know how the years get jumbled. We've run in similar social circles for ages, and eventually, we met. He's a bit of a stick-in-the-mud, but a dependable fellow most of the time. Helping out here was the least I owed him after Ivan pitched in with the local kids' theater play last year. My daughter was a sugar-plum fairy. I think I can find pictures, if you're interested."

Right, the kids. Tori forgot that people with children were forced into social situations, whether they liked it or not. Even for someone like Ivan, the act of showing up and being a dad meant he'd deal with other parents. Evidently, he didn't hate all of them. Tori could see the logic; Helen had the sort of infectious, positive energy that could be hard to resist.

"Perhaps we should head down that road after the meeting. There's only a few hours, and I've seen you go into a picture-showing session." Ivan set down his duffel and headed for the kitchen, only to have his arm hooked by Helen as he passed.

"Aren't you going to put the uniform on?" Helen gestured to her own body, which was clad in the tan, short-sleeve button-down and matching capris, topped off by a turquoise ascot. The summer Starscout uniform, to be changed out with something warmer when Autumn arrived. "That goes for you, too, Tori. Meeting regulations."

For a moment, Tori felt the ground vanish. She was a child again, standing in her room as her mother explained that, yes, they had to go to the meeting; yes, she had to visit with other kids; yes, she had to wear the uniform. It was a memory tinged with childish anger and frustration, but Tori held onto it for as long she could. There were only so many memories left where she could still recall her parents' voices.

When she blinked herself back to reality, Tori noticed Helen watching her. "You okay? Seemed to space out there for a moment."

"Sorry, I'm fine. First day back at work, just a little tired. I'll be good to go by the time the kids show up."

"Why don't you go ahead and change? I'll put Ivan on task in the kitchen, then you can help me with decorations," Helen suggested. She led Tori down the hall to a large, stylish bathroom that was much too big for the intended purpose.

Once Tori was tucked away, Helen returned to the living room, where Ivan was pulling his own uniform out.

With one hand, Helen took Ivan's forearm, silently leading him to the kitchen, where she proceeded to yank out pots and pans. "Little cover noise, just in case. While she's changing, is there anything you need to bring me up to speed on? Major changes or revelations we should knock out before the kids arrive?"

"To my own surprise, I've got nothing to report. No sudden threats or dire stakes sprang up, no foreboding signs that one of our charges is secretly a doomsday weapon—nothing. Seems to be a class of mostly mundane kids. Beth is the only catalogued meta in the bunch," Ivan said.

"Fingers crossed that turns out to be true." Helen paused, laying a giant sheet pan carefully down atop the stove. "These kids deserve normalcy, no matter who their instructors are. But, if anything *does* go wrong, I'll handle it."

Ivan looked up from the kitchen counter, where he'd been eyeing ingredients. "I'm not sure that's—"

"Ivan, this is Beth's cluster." Sometimes, it was strange to hear that level of authority come from Helen rather than Lodestar—until one realized how many of the differences between them were merely cosmetic. "I know you'd expose your secret to protect her. You'd do it without a second thought or an instant of hesitation, which is why I'm telling you now, up front, that I'm in charge of dealing with problems. My secret has protection. Yours doesn't. Your daughter is going to be here, watching. Worry about her; I've got everything else."

There was no value to arguing. Besides the fact that Helen made excellent points, ultimately, it was the one she hadn't said out loud that Ivan found most compelling. If a situation arose demanding one of them to get serious, then it would have to be a reasonably dangerous one. In that scenario, with trouble at the door and children to protect, Helen *should* be the one fighting. She was stronger than Fornax in his prime, and now, the divide between them was even greater.

"Over the years, if there is one lesson I have taken to heart, it is that you're going to do what you say, no matter what," Ivan conceded. "Just try not to jump the gun. Let's see if we can resolve things without leaning on our full power."

"Hey, I still got my moves." Helen bobbed and weaved, mostly as a joke, yet it was impossible for Ivan to miss the practiced steps in even her playful offense. The vast majority of the world thought Lodestar won by sheer power alone, and while that was certainly true much of the time, the public wasn't privy to her past. They didn't know she'd logged her years as a low-level street cape, learning to fight through constant practice.

It was an educational tactic Ivan knew all too well from his own childhood, if one could call his raising by such a term. In another life, he might have liked to spar Helen cordially, with no powers involved. Sadly, such was a mere fantasy, and this was not the time for indulgences. Ivan turned his attention to the real task at hand: whipping up some hot snacks.

After all, if a group of kids on the cusp of teendom showed up to find no food, the cluster leaders might need Lodestar's protection after all.

Nexus strolled down the boulevard, passing a designer pet boutique and a veggie wrap stand that shared the same building. Ridge City was nothing if not experienced with recovery. When the Garbublux broke through Professor Quantum's containment zone and went on a rampage, it had taken years to get fully back up and running, even with the League of Metas pitching in to help. Jump forward several decades, and Ridge City recovered from its eponymous riots in the span of months.

Already the streets were bustling as people ran their Monday evening errands, so worried about their plans and dreams, looking ahead to days that were in no way guaranteed. In the beginning, Nexus had almost felt for these mindless masses. They didn't know what he knew, couldn't see all the iterations he'd seen. They had no idea their world was at risk. They didn't spot the slithering in the shadows, the old grudges blooming once more.

Of course, that would all need patience. Big, beautiful machinations didn't set themselves up overnight. Fine art required time and effort to craft, time that Nexus didn't begrudge the artist. Still, that didn't mean he wasn't going to enjoy the lesser spectacles while he waited.

His casual stroll came to a sudden halt as Nexus passed the front of a bookstore. A malicious grin appeared below his kaleidoscope eyes, which were obscured by the brim of his low-dipped hat. Walking in, Nexus made his way to the back, rifling through a few sections until he spotted a good fit. Paying no mind to the employees, Nexus returned to the front display and exchanged one of the visible books for his selection. Tossing the original display into a discount bin, Nexus stepped back outside to admire the handiwork.

Perfect. That would provide the extra delay needed. Spinning around, Nexus scanned the roofline. Now that he'd ensured there would be a show to see, the next step was finding the best seat in the house.

It was controlled chaos. To Ivan and Helen's credit, asserting any level of control over a group of four girls and three boys was damn near a meta-human feat in itself, especially since they hadn't gotten together in months. The collective of growing mouths had chewed through everything Ivan could churn out, and toward the end, Tori wasn't sure he hadn't used a little magic to fudge the cooking times.

As their charges arrived, Tori made a point of learning their names quickly, determined to appear competent. The first on the scene was Newton, a young boy who Tori had yet to see sit, stop, or even slow down for longer than it took to grab a snack. After him was Mallory, who brought in a knapsack teeming with books that made her look somewhat like a turtle always just on the edge of tumbling over. Caden came next, and with him a nonstop string of questions and inquisitions that Helen mercifully had enough patience to either be or appear entirely unbothered by, even after hours of interrogation. Armand came along not long after, carrying with him a hatbox that Tori found rather curious—at least until Trudy arrived. When she walked in, Armand handed over the box, and from it, Trudy produced one of the most garish pieces of headwear Tori had ever witnessed, from the neon pink top to the zebra stripes along the band. It must have been just what she wanted, though, because Trudy wrapped Armand in a giant hug. Beth was dropped off soon after, greeting her friends cheerfully. While they were busy, Loyce wandered in, calling out a quick greeting before making a detour to sample Ivan's culinary creations.

By the time the last child was present, things had gotten *loud*. Thankfully, Helen turned out to have a talent for wrangling children. After watching her work for a few minutes, Tori could easily understand why the woman had this position. There was something about her demeanor, gentle but firm, that quickly struck the right chord. By the time Helen had gone through the general welcome, she had the attention of everyone in the room. Until Ivan walked in, of course.

His outfit was near identical to Helen's, save only that he'd chosen knee-length shorts over capris. In any other setting, Ivan likely would have stepped into a field of chuckles and some, at best, good-natured ribbing. However, this was perhaps the single scenario where he didn't seem remotely out of place. No, it wasn't the funny outfit that put the attention on Ivan.

That honor belonged to Beth, who applauded with shouting enthusiasm as he walked into the room, prompting the other Starscouts to join in. It was strange, hearing them call Ivan "Mr. Gerhardt" and realizing that most of these kids thought they knew him. He was their friend's dad, likely an acquaintance of their parents; the man no one had any reason to think twice about. How strange would it be, to only know half of someone? Tori couldn't imagine; so far, she'd always met the secret personas before the covers, or it had been blatantly obvious like it had with Donald or the New Science Sentries. At this point, she was actually starting to wonder if any of the capes managed real secret identities.

"Tori, when you've got a moment, I could use a hand at the dining room table." Helen had walked over while Tori was lost in thought and Ivan was addressing the cluster. "Tonight is mostly just getting back in the swing of things, but we've got some crafting planned for the back half of our time. Trust me when I say you do not want to see a glitter project without proper tarping laid down."

From the half-circle of kids grouped up around Ivan, Beth looked over, catching Tori's eye and giving her a soft wave. They hadn't gotten to speak yet—Beth was dropped off only moments before the meeting had to start—but it was clear she remembered Tori from their last encounter. Well, the last one Beth knew of. Technically, they'd been together when Beth and Rick's school came down, but Beth could hardly be blamed for not knowing. Tori had been sealed away in the armor of Hephaestus at the time.

Treating herself to a chuckle-inducing look at Ivan's exposed shins, Tori headed over to help the other cluster leader with the crafts. At least she didn't have to busy herself wondering how to appear especially regular or mundane. If Tori wanted to come off as normal, Helen seemed like a fine example to follow.

Chapter 21

In any given day, any moment really, there exists untold possibilities. At any second, a person could stand up, walk through a door, and change their life. Few do, of course, because the appeal of infinite potential outcomes often pales in comparison to the daily worries that permeate one's mind. Instead, people fall into habits, routines—limiting their possibilities in exchange for a fleeting glimpse of consistency in a chaotic world.

For all her technological genius and criminal ways, Tori wasn't special in this regard. She, like so many others, had a typical route she took: catch a car toward the office, disembark at the end of the block before traffic slowed to a crawl and walk the rest of the way in. Sometimes she would stop at Ridge City Grinders when there was time. It had become her pattern since moving out of Ivan's home, and on that Tuesday morning, still groggy from a night dealing with children, Tori didn't even contemplate approaching the office differently. Her mind was on the day ahead, and the potent espresso she'd be ordering before she faced it.

The day was nice, a bit of early fall winds balancing the late summer heat —not that Tori was bothered by high temperatures. It was one of the few side-perks of her powers that extended to her human form, and there was something satisfying about being the only one dry when the rest of the office was sweating. Since the weather was pleasant, she took her time, walking slowly down the spacious pedestrian sections.

If not for memory, Tori would never have known this area was struck by looters during the Ridge City Riots. The attack was short-lived, since Beverly and Chloe had driven them out, yet even the lingering signs of damage had been swept away within weeks. Concrete repaired, glass reinstalled, and just like that, downtown was back to normal. Sometimes Tori wondered how many times this city had been repaired like that. How much of this place was even still the original Ridge City?

Walking past a bookshop, a cover displayed in the front window caught Tori's eye. *Building Infinity: The Wade Wyatt Story* was a favorite of hers for years, though now that she'd met the man, her faith in its accuracy was deeply shaken. Seeing as none of the biography had mentioned him being Doctor Mechaniacal, faking his own death, or being friends with Fornax, it seemed like a safe bet that she shouldn't assume anything in those pages to be factual. Perhaps she could get the real story out of him one day. If he was going to tell the truth to anyone, it would probably be a member of the guild.

It was thanks to being momentarily distracted that Tori didn't notice the dark van creeping up along the nearby alley beyond the bookstore. She missed when four men hopped out as well. It wasn't until Tori caught shadows approaching her from behind in the window's reflection that she realized something might be up.

Spinning around, she was faced with four identical balaclavas covering the men's faces. One of the men stepped forward, trying to grab her.

In that moment, Tori had to make a decision. There were people all around; it was a Tuesday morning in downtown. If she used her powers, there *would* be witnesses. Probably a cell phone video, the way her week was going. Any chance she might have had of not getting recognized was toast thanks to last week's media exposure; she was much too fresh a face for someone not to recall. Using her abilities needed to be a last-ditch resort. If things got dire, she would have to wield that tool in her arsenal, but there was no reason to start with it. Especially when she had plenty of other options.

Tori slammed her palm into the face of the man reaching for her, then spun to her right and kicked another in the side of the knee. She could hear cartilage tearing over the sound of his scream, but not by a lot. Someone tried to grab her left arm, earning themselves an elbow to the nose for their trouble. Since he reeled after the first blow, Tori added a second, forcing him to finally back away. Blood stained the facemask as he sputtered out curses in a nasal voice.

"Come on, you cowards. What's wrong? Expected this to be easy? You dipshits think I've never taken a self-defense course? This is Ridge *fucking* City. We know how to survive out here. At least until *someone calls a cape*."

The fight was quickly drawing attention. Civilians were pointing, yelling, and, as predicted, pulling out their cameras. Tori hoped the line would assuage anyone wondering how she was holding four attackers at bay, but mostly she wanted it to get other people involved. She wasn't winning. She was buying time. Against these numbers, she needed either her tech or her powers; without them, this was just a stalling measure.

When Tori felt the next hand close on her, she knew the jig was up. It was too big. There was no way this wasn't a meta. Sure enough, moments later she was lifted into the air, meeting the eyes of fifth attacker who'd apparently come over when the first four couldn't close. His face, too, was obscured, though the build gave away that he was a muscle-based meta, most likely as tough as he was strong. Probably still flammable, if she was willing to play that card publicly.

"Hurting you isn't part of this, but if you keep fighting, it might have to be." Calm, collected, in control of the situation despite things spinning out of hand. This one was dangerous; all the more so because the hulking types were usually underestimated mentally—according to Thuggernaut, anyway. If he was smart enough to know how to do this right, then maybe he also knew he shouldn't be doing it at all.

Tori laughed in his face, loud and harsh. Her words, however, were soft, meant only for the man keeping her bound. "Hurt me? You world-class fuckheads are kidnapping a citizen in the middle of broad daylight on a Ridge City street. We both know how this ends. Your crew is as good as dead. The only question left is whether or not they die screaming."

The eyes widened; she'd definitely hit home. Unfortunately, while Tori had been putting the fear of the guild into someone, another attacker was also busy. She didn't see the injector. All Tori felt was the pinch of metal sliding into her leg. There *was* a split second where she could have shifted to fire, but with the terror rolling off her captor, it seemed a better bet to keep her secret for now. Only seconds later, when the first wave of drowsiness hit, did Tori realize her mistake. What she'd mistaken for a stabbing was, in fact, a drugging.

"Cheating... sons of... bitches." That was her last conscious thought before she went limp in her still shaken kidnapper's arms.

"Come on. We need to go!" One of the voices was helping the man with a freshly injured knee back to the van. People were still milling around;

however, seeing the woman go limp had invigorated a few, there was likely to soon be trouble.

Darius delicately set Tori on his shoulder, taking great care not to injure her. How the hell did she know about the rules, and that they were breaking them? Kidnapping was obviously against the law, but doing it like this was against the *rules*, and that mattered far more. Certain things got people vanished, and shit like this was definitely in that category. The most likely answer was that it was a bluff, something she knew a speck about and happened to guess near the mark. But something about this woman didn't sit right.

Normal people couldn't fight the way they saw in movies. There were limitations beyond just skill or strength. To actively hurt another person with intent wasn't easy. It required a specific mindset, usually developed through training. People held back, they tried to do only as much damage as a threat required. Not this woman. Tori had only gone for crippling blows. Without hesitation, at that. Every strike she threw came with the intent of breaking the people around her, and when she succeeded, she only went for more. Given the situation, it was an understandable mindset, just not one a civilian should have been capable of.

As the van peeled out back down the alley, taking the preplanned escape route, Darius made certain to keep their captive safely in his grip. Until he knew more about just how much they'd bitten off, it was best to play things cautiously.

It was a bit early for a phone call. Ivan grabbed the cell off his desk, noting the number. The company on the ID was guild-affiliated in the same way as Vendallia, in that they were an Indigo Technologies subsidy owned by Wade Wyatt. These tended to be the easiest ways to pass semi-private messages around, since they both raised no suspicion and could be claimed as confidential company conversations.

Picking up, he was unsurprised to hear the voice of Xelas. Her tone, on the other hand, was immediately off-putting. Xelas was not typically prone to concern. "Ivan, this is Alexis from Confide Messaging. We're reaching out to you in regard to your niece, Tori Rivas. Based on the trending information available on social media, it appears she was just kidnapped off the street. If you'd like to watch for yourself, I'll wait on the line."

The fact that Ivan could type without shattering his keyboard in that moment spoke to how much control he'd gained through the years. He opened up a new tab, skimmed past blog posts questioning if Lodestar had lost a step in her time away, and clicked on the rising trend. If he hadn't known the victim was Tori, the hashtag "#RidgeFuckingCity" would have given it away.

Watching the video, Ivan was surprised. He hadn't anticipated the sense of pride rising in his chest as he saw Tori handle herself without so much as a spark of heat in sight. She'd done wonderfully, fully selling herself as a human being fighting with everything they had. Hard as she fought, once the syringe was injected Tori quickly went limp. At least the brute carrying her into a van had the sense to be careful.

When the guild was exposed, Ivan knew this day would come. The edicts they imposed through whispers and carried out in the shadows couldn't endure once the guild wasn't around to enforce them. Common criminals had been growing bolder and bolder. Now, they were actually stealing people off the streets. Were their target anyone else, Ivan would have left it for the capes to handle. The AHC wanted to have the whole game to itself, so the guild was planning to let them... except that now, it was complicated.

Not just because they'd kidnapped Tori, which involved Ivan on a personal level. That, actually, would have been much easier. No, the issue here was that they'd kidnapped a member of the guild. Even if the crooks had no idea, it didn't matter. One day, the truth could come out. This world ran on respect and power. The guild endured because it was unassailable, and to challenge them held blood-soaked consequences.

"I'm assuming the myriad of security protocols in place mean there's some way to track her," Ivan said. "Tell our favorite nerd I'm coming in. Let's establish contact first, then see how she wants to play it."

"You want to let her run the show?" It wasn't the surprise in Xelas's voice so much as the amusement that worried Ivan.

"If someone managed to get you off the street, would *you* let anyone else run point on making them pay for it?"

There was a stretch of silence, and when Xelas spoke again, it nearly sent a real chill down Ivan's spine. "No, I'd definitely want to be the one to peel them. All right, Ivan, get here as soon as you can. Since this is national news, the company wheels are already turning to get you let off work. See you soon."

The phone went dead, but Ivan didn't set it down yet. Instead, he punched in a number he knew by heart but was not saved to his phone. It rang five times, then went to voicemail. If Helen wasn't answering, then she was most likely busy. Given the events of the morning, Ivan could make a wager on where her attention was being demanded. It would have been nice to talk with her, lay down some ground rules, and stay out of each other's way. Nice, but unlikely to happen, even if the call went through.

This was a declaration: a kidnapping in the AHC's backyard, of a woman one of their members just saved. The message was clear. They were calling out the capes. Besides being an intensely dumb thing to do, that wasn't the sort of gauntlet the AHC could ignore. People needed to trust the capes for that system to work. If the trust failed, it all went tumbling down. The AHC was going to come at this one hard.

Which just meant it was all the more important that the guild handled things first. Once the capes were involved, everything grew vastly more complicated. It was much easier to slaughter people wholesale without superheroes around. In the end, that would be up to Tori, though. She was the one who would bear the most consequence. She should decide how to handle things.

Assuming, of course, that she was okay. Because if Tori *wasn't* okay—an idea Ivan was working hard not to entertain—then things were going to get messy. Ivan would make certain of it.

Chapter 22

The car smelled the same. If pressed, Tori would have said that there was no way she could recall the scent of her dad's old sedan, yet as she sat in the back seat, the odor was instantly recognizable. As were the two figures seated up front. Just the sight of their shadows, obscured by the cursed sun coming through the windshield, was enough to make her heart crack. Her mom was driving, playfully swatting Tori's father's hands while he fiddled with the radio. They laughed, and he leaned across the seats to kiss his wife on the cheek. For a moment, it was perfect.

With all she had, Tori wanted to touch them, hold them once more. She reached out, her hands small, too small, the way they were when that horrible day came. Her arms strained, trying in vain to move a little bit closer, an inch at a time, struggling to so much as brush their skin.

Instead of touching her parents, Tori only managed to shake herself out of the dream, coming back to consciousness as the pain of her wrists tugging against metal became more and more pressing. Waking with a start, Tori realized she was handcuffed to a chair. In her sleep, she had been trying to reach up, which had caused the metal to bite into her flesh. Shaking her head rapidly, working to shrug off whatever drugs she'd been given, Tori took several deep breaths, then evaluated her surroundings.

Cement all around: no windows, a single toilet, one door, and a pair of wireless cameras posted at opposite corners of the room. Tori bit back a curse. If not for the cameras, she could just fire-form her way out of the handcuffs and find a crack to slip through. Then again, that would still leave the mystery of how she'd escaped, which might stir unwarranted trouble down the line. She didn't even know who had her yet, or what they wanted. There might be smarter ways to play this than running for a door.

Forcing her brain to calm down, shoving aside the emotion her dream had stirred up, Tori thought hard. This was a situation where every variable had to be considered. First and foremost, she needed to remember that right now, she was here as Tori Rivas. No one in the gang knew about her connections; otherwise, they'd have steered clear or killed her outright. This was not the proper level of restraint for a guild member. As Tori, her options were limited: wait for rescue, maybe talk some shit.

There was, however, the possibility that these people didn't just want a damsel. They might want a victim, too, something to send the capes a bloody and harsh message. In that case, Tori would have to take a back seat to Hephaestus, suit or no. It wouldn't be an easy fight—they had numbers, resources, and at least one strong meta. Her best-case scenario would likely be to escape, leaving survivors who knew her secret. Perhaps the guild would be able to mop them up, but there were no guarantees.

Tori also had to consider the possibility that the big one knew enough to realize how badly he'd fucked up. If she could wear on that pressure point, make him realize that they'd just broken a rule with serious consequences, she might convince him to set her free. Overly optimistic, certainly, but right now, Tori could do with a little senseless hope.

As things stood, her best bet was to play the part of the captive human. If the capes found her first, she'd be what they were expecting. On the other hand, if the guild arrived first, she'd just take some light teasing for letting herself get captured. Technically, there was a chance that neither would find her, though Tori considered that to be borderline ridiculous. However, with metas, one could never be fully sure. The right power at the right time could make all the difference.

The clang of a lock turning was her only warning before the door swung open. In stepped a freckled man with tissues stuffed up his nose, a meta with visibly snake-like features, the big meta, and a couple of goons milling about in the rear. The freckled one with the jacked-up nose started forward quickly. While not the world's most socially aware villain, Tori had been around enough scumbags to recognize a posturing walk when she saw one. Her elbow to the nose had hurt his ego, and now he was looking to reclaim some pride.

"Looks who's up. It's our little fighter. Those were quite some moves, Miss Rivas. Did your friend Tachyonic show them to you? Perhaps without the mask on? You'll find us excellent hosts to talkative guests." Her captor's voice was cloying as he circled the chair, moving out of her line of sight for stretches of time. It was meant to make her unsure, worried about what he'd do behind her back. Instead, it was mostly annoying, since he was harder to hear at some points of the spiel.

For all her forethought, in that moment, Tori realized she had neither the inclination nor the patience to pretend in front of these idiots. She'd just have to hit the pressure points hard and hope they let her go fast. Subtlety was never her strong point; Tori preferred an upfront confrontation. At this point, it was more for their sake than hers, anyway.

"God, you're fucking stupid. I mean, sincerely, do you have some amazing power? Can you fight on par with Professor Quantum, run as fast as Ricky Rocket? Or did you win all these people over with meta-level handjobs? Because it damn sure wasn't your deductive skills. Tachyonic and the rest of the New Science Sentries arrived last week. If you think I learned to fight like that on seven days of training, then you should be trying to recruit me, not asking dumbass questions."

That was not the answer most of them had been expecting. Only the big meta seemed largely unfazed that she wasn't crumpling or afraid in spite of the situation. Freckles, the one talking, had a moment of visible panic, but lucky for him, he was facing Tori at the time. The rest of the gang didn't see the fear that ran through him. He was trying to reassert control, and Tori wasn't letting him have it.

"Brave, bold words, no doubt born of certainty that the capes will save you," her captor said. "But I'll let you in on a little secret. We procured technology specifically designed to keep them from doing just that. Think hard about your next words. There won't—"

"I'm sorry, did you say you had tech to keep them out?" Tori didn't hide the incredulity on her face. In fact, she made it as obvious as possible. "You want to use *technology* to stop *Professor Quantum*." She leaned back, blowing idly into the air. "Christ, man, what's next? You going to try to light Infernical on fire? I can't believe you've managed to figure out how not to shit in your pants, given what you're showing me so far. Have you, actually? Those slacks could hide a diaper, now that I look closely. Tell me if I'm talking too fast or need to use smaller words."

The skin between those freckles was getting red, a sign of her constant backtalk clearly getting to her captor. Still, he tried to retain control while his peons were looking on. Leaning forward, he took a firm grip on her shoulder.

That drew a slight bit of concern from the big meta, though he didn't step forward entirely.

"Listen here." The freckled man's voice had turned into a hiss, all false sweetness vanished. "I can be a good host, or a cruel one. Do not mistake my hospitality for weakness. Hear me well on this point: if you test me, I will give you the discipline you so clearly crave. That is my promise to you. But if you can compose yourself, perhaps you can make it through this alive."

It was a good speech, the scariest bit he'd managed so far. In another life, it might have worked. Even before the guild, she understood self-preservation enough to soothe some sociopathic egos. Except that this kid, whoever he was, didn't scare her. *Couldn't* scare her, unless he was hiding a massive ability. He wasn't in the league of people she socialized with, to say nothing of the ones she genuinely feared. None of them were. They were playing on the edge of a vast chasm, with no idea of the horrors that lay a single slip away.

"Okay, if we're laying things out, then here's my counter-proposal: let me go right now, and there's a chance your gang will survive."

Laughter from the back, and from the captor seconds later. Not from the big meta, however. He was the one Tori made sure to meet the eyes of as she continued.

"Yeah, it's funny. I get that. One gal, tied to a chair—what's she going to do? Just don't get it twisted, dipshit. I'm not threatening you: I'm warning you. Maybe you didn't get the news somehow, but what you did today is a major no-no. On a lot of levels, in fact. You're about to piss off people you don't even want to know your name, let alone be mad at you."

Here, the freckled fellow finally found something to pounce on. "You think we're afraid of the capes? We're doing this specifically to confront them."

Tori's frustration began to bleed over. "Listen to me, you walking corpse. You'll never see the capes. You'll never get whatever fight you want. By the time they arrive, you'll be nothing but smeared pulp and charred stains along the walls. I'm trying to warn you while there's time to change that. Your enemy won't fly down from the skies, they'll sneak up from the shadows. By the time they're here, you won't even have time to piss yourse—"

As far as backhands went, it was fair, at best. The guy clearly hadn't done much muscle or combat training, but then, it wasn't really about the damage. It was about the hit itself, reminding Tori that he was free and she was a captive, supposedly at his mercy. The sound of his hand striking her face faded slowly, echoing around the stone room.

"I think I gave you more than ample warning. Now, cease with the senseless blathering. We'll leave you alone to collect your thoughts. When I return, you will start answering questions, or I'll have to be an ungracious host once more."

The rest of the crew took the order, filing back out through the door. Before they were gone, Tori's voice rose once more.

"Hey, Big Man. I tried. If you care about any of these people, take a swing at convincing them." She paused to lick the corner of her mouth, where a small trickle of blood was oozing out. "As for you, Freckles, don't worry about any of that."

She sat herself up straight, looking him dead in the eyes, making sure he understood every syllable. "You'll die wishing you could scream. That's *my* promise to you."

Despite his hands being clasped together as he sat, Darius wasn't praying. Even if he were the religious sort, this didn't feel like a situation where divine intervention would be on the table. No, Darius wasn't lost in prayer, he was lost in thought. That woman was off, and in more than one sense. The brutal way she'd fought, her demeanor during interrogation, the things she kept hinting at. She *knew*. She was connected, in some way. Maybe to a cape, maybe to something worse. But this was not the way a normal person behaved in a kidnapping.

The larger question was what he could do about it. Deacon ran things, even with the broken nose and that shitshow interrogation. He had to be the one to make the call, or Darius might as well just stage a coup. Deacon *was* smart, despite how he'd handled himself. The trouble was that he was smart in a way that involved patterns, puzzles, and planning. Seeing past his own ego wasn't in that toolkit, which meant that even if Deacon had been open to listening before, there was zero chance he'd be receptive after Tori had humiliated him.

If Darius couldn't let her go without staging a mutiny, and he thought there was even the smallest chance she was telling the truth, then his only option was to deal with Tori directly. Maybe he could sell it as good cop to Deacon's antagonistic style to get the boss's nod. Whatever story he concocted, Darius had to get in there with her. He could figure out how much was bluster versus how much was actual knowledge, and in the worst-case scenario where she was telling the truth, hopefully he'd have laid the groundwork to get his people spared.

Except for Deacon, most likely. Even in the most optimistic of situations, if Tori was telling the truth, then the boss was a goner. Darius had heard enough dangerous people talk to know the difference between a threat and a vow. Tori hadn't been making a threat—which was one more oddity to add onto the pile. Part of him had even considered the idea that Tori was a cape herself, but that didn't track. A cape wouldn't have needed saving in the street, and she certainly wouldn't have let herself be abducted.

He didn't know exactly what Tori's deal was, but he needed to figure it out, and soon. At least one thing she'd said was right on the money: Deacon was absolutely crazy if he seriously expected black market tech to hold off Professor Quantum.

Chapter 23

By the time Ivan made it to the guild council's new chambers, he was almost the last to arrive. Wade was standing at a computer terminal, punching the keyboard while barely looking, Xelas standing over his shoulder, adding the occasional bit of advice. Morgana had traded her usual business casual ensemble for something armored and blood-red. With her abilities, clearing out a base silently was a task she often received. Gork was sitting patiently in the corner, waiting to see how things developed. Only Stasis and Arcanicus were missing, neither of whom were immediately necessary.

"Where is she?" It had taken discipline to walk here calmly, to not do anything so dramatic as leaving footprints in the stone or knocking doors clean from their hinges. That patience was wearing thin, however. With every passing moment, they knew less about what had just happened to one of their own. For innumerable reasons, that would not stand.

"If you'll give me a moment, I'll tell you," Wade replied. "As I hope you've assumed by now, all the shifting clothes we give Tori have specially encoded tracking devices. Makes it so much easier than hiding them one by one like I have to do with the rest of you."

That was the sort of thing Ivan might have objected to under normal circumstances, which was no doubt why Wade had chosen this moment to divulge the tidbit. The man wasn't called a genius for nothing; he knew how to use an opportunity.

"All we have to do is link up, and I should have her coordinates," Wade continued.

"If it's that simple, shouldn't you have them already?" Ivan hadn't exactly stopped for coffee, but he'd come via mundane routes, taking roughly an hour. There was no chance Wade needed that long to ping a simple tracker.

Sure enough, a crease appeared below his thinning copper hair, a telltale sign that Wade was slightly annoyed. "Whoever took her was smart enough to employ some countertracking methods. The signals they aren't blocking, they're scrambling. Xelas and I were finding a workaround to connect with our devices. In fact, you arrived just in time."

With a flourish, Wade pressed several keys, eliciting several beeps and one loud buzz, followed by flashing red lights. Wade and Xelas both leaned in, staring at the screen, then one another. While Xelas was able to keep up a stoic front, Wade didn't quite manage the same. His pale face reddened as he checked the information over several more times. When he turned back to them, it was with the gravity of the guild's leader.

"Somehow, they're still blocking. We got a connection, reached out to the device, but they've employed a tactic to halt any real communication. While I realize that this might not seem like a larger concern than what we were facing, please understand the severity of what I'm saying. If they're using tech able to disrupt mine, then it has to be of roughly the same technological capacity, or greater. As things stand, there are only three living people in the world who can create on that level: me, Professor Quantum, and Tyranny. I'm not working against myself, Professor Quantum would never lower himself to dealing with street criminals, and Tyranny has spent decades observing an isolationist policy that I doubt she'd break for some quick black-market cash. Outside of a known entity throwing us a hell of a curveball, the most logical explanation is that there's a new player."

"A new player with some skills," Xelas added. "I never caught the designing bug like Wade, but I can still analyze the complexity of the programs we're seeing, and it's far from amateur."

"Which means this is no longer just some punks grabbing the wrong person off the street. We have to consider the possibility that it was targeted, the opening shot of a war." Morgana finished buckling on one last bracer, completing her preparation.

They were all making very good, reasonable points. Things that should definitely be considered. When Tori was safe.

Striding forward, Ivan closed the gap and glared at the still-flashing red screen. He turned from it to Wade, actively working to keep his eyes from shifting to their rune-filled forms.

"Find her."

"Relax. That's what we're about to do." Wade put his hand on his old friend's shoulder, trying to keep him calm. "It will take a little time, but I'm going to reconfigure the tracker's communication system until we can slip around the block they've got in place."

"How?" Ivan asked.

Wade met his question with a carefully raised eyebrow. "Do you want the five minutes of me condensing complex concepts into techno-jargon, or can you just trust that I know what I'm doing?"

After a deep breath to get himself under control, Ivan gave a quick nod and stepped away. It was easy to let himself spin out, to give way to everything inside him scratching to break free, but that wouldn't help Tori. He needed to be ready to act when Wade gave the word. Much as he appreciated Morgana donning her work clothes, there would be no need for silence or subtlety in the approach. Not once Ivan was on the scene.

"In the meantime, we should try to establish communication with Tori," Wade added. "Gork, would you show Ivan to Mind Mirror's new accommodations? With tech temporarily at a roadblock, that leaves magic, and psychic bonds form a lot easier between people who are familiar with one another."

The huge gray creature rose from her seat, lumbering over to lay a large hand across the entirety of Ivan's back. "She'll be fine. No one gave her membership into this guild—Tori earned it. Don't forget what that takes, or what it means. She's a danger, not a damsel, and they probably haven't even realized it yet."

Despite being one of the least human among them, Gork had a knack for knowing the right thing to say. The points raised were valid. Tori was far from helpless—at worst, he should probably be worrying about how to get rid of five charred corpses before the capes could show up. All the same, Ivan would feel much better once he knew Tori was actually safe.

"Thank you, Gork. Let's go find Mind Mirror. I'd very much like to check on my former apprentice."

"Blocked? How is someone blocking *you*?" Even as she said the words, Lodestar knew she should have taken a different approach. Professor

Quantum's ego was his tenderest spot, especially where she was concerned, and the fact that someone was stopping his satellite scan had to be weighing on him already.

Sure enough, there was a telltale bristle as he looked back to the giant screen that showed only an empty map. For a man his age, Professor Quantum had never grown especially adept at concealing his annoyance. Or maybe he was a master of the skill and merely chose to not employ it. It never paid to make assumptions where Professor Quantum was concerned.

Together, they were standing in the Chamber of Champions, a near relic from more active times. Across the walls and ceiling were screens capable of displaying all manner of images, both flat and three-dimensional. There were also tables, computers, and other stations filled with stuff boasting varying purposes that Lodestar couldn't remember. During the AHC's early days, this place had been their hub, the place they'd spend time coordinating to take down threat after constant threat. Over time, order had won out over chaos once more, bringing things to a peaceful equilibrium. They'd held that order for a long time, but one had only to look at human history to know that every era of peace was but a temporary ceasefire.

"It is concerning," Professor Quantum agreed. "Granted, I am working with minimal information about this woman and no devices local to her body. Yet it was also inevitable that as the masses inch their way toward technological progression, some exalted minds would use that springboard to fuel their own creations. New minds are born daily. It's hardly shocking that one managed to develop something of use."

It didn't feel like he was telling her everything, but then again, what else was new? That was Professor Quantum. He'd agree to alliances, join organizations, and work with others to the extent he needed to, and never a single step more. It was more accurate to say they all worked alongside Professor Quantum, rather than with him. Sometimes, Lodestar wondered what he'd been like back in the beginning. Was he jaded from the jump, or was there a time he'd cared?

"What's the game plan? At this point, they could be anywhere in the world. It's been more than long enough to utilize a teleporter, and if they can block you from tracking them, then they were obviously prepared."

"The plan?" Professor Quantum was an absolute master of the dismissive stare, and the one he sent her was among his finest works. "I am not one of the soft-faced children roaming our halls. I know who this woman really is. Are we sincerely pretending that this is a good use of our resources? She is a member of that damned guild, and what they lack in decorum, they make up for in brutal efficiency. A scan was one thing. However, we both know those hoodlums will be a pile of limbs before we can ever track her down."

"Maybe." Lodestar ran her hands through her glowing hair, causing it to drift out around her head like she was in low gravity. "But if someone built a device capable of blocking you, it would certainly be able to stop Doctor Mechaniacal, too."

There wasn't even a second of consideration from Professor Quantum. "That goes without saying." At least that giant ego cut both ways.

"Think about this: what if they don't have her location yet? What if we can beat them to it? Aside from the fact that Tori was snatched publicly, on the street, and so we should be the ones to save her, imagine the look on Doctor Mechaniacal's face when he realizes that you got there first. We might not be able to touch the guild legally, but you can still remind them who the world's true greatest genius is."

And, in the process, they'd get the gang into the courts, rather than letting them be slaughtered over a single mistake. Professor Quantum wouldn't see validity in that, naturally, but Lodestar didn't care about his motivations nearly as much as his actions. It was a peace she'd been forced to come to decades ago.

This time, there was a brief pause as Professor Quantum thought over her words. Seconds later, he pulled a communicator from his hip and pressed the button to speak. "Quorum, since you're down with the field teams, please begin prepping them for search and rescue. We are officially launching an effort to recover Miss Rivas. Feel free to inform the media of that as needed. I'll join you shortly once preliminary plans are in place."

Lowering the communicator, he looked over to Lodestar. "Have you considered the potential consequence of these actions? How much worse will it be if we deploy our resources to save this woman, only for our people to stumble upon the carnage of her true rescue?"

"If we find her, I'll be the first one in," she replied. "That's just good sense, anyway, since I haven't gotten to vet the new teams. That limits their risk, both physical and mental. Make sure they know their job is just search, not rescue."

"What would you tell the press, were such a scene uncovered?" Professor Quantum probed.

"The truth. That when you enter the world of criminal metas, you're stepping foot onto a dangerous path where we can't always protect you. I've tried and failed enough times to know I can't save every person all the time.

So has every veteran member of the AHC. We do our best and mourn those we fail. It's the way of the world."

Lodestar took three steps toward the elevator, then began to float. "In the meantime, I'm going to zip out through the roof and do a patrol. If Tori's calling for help, there's an off chance I could hear it."

"She won't be," Professor Quantum said.

"No, she won't," Lodestar agreed. "But someone will be. I was gone for a long time. I've got making up to do."

"Don't let them get too dependent. You know where that leads." For once, there seemed to be a note of actual concern in Professor Quantum's voice.

Ignoring the array of button, Lodestar popped open a hatch in the top of the elevator, one that had been made especially for her. Sometimes, she needed to make a very speedy exit, and going up through the ceiling made for the fastest way out that didn't involve fixing a wall.

"I'll keep it in mind. Give me a buzz before you send out the masses. We should talk to them together, make sure they understand the situation." In a flash, she was gone, through the top of the elevator and out the escape hatch concealed on the roof.

Professor Quantum watched her go: a flash across the screen, the sort of moving energy that it would be harder to not track. All that power, and yet she constantly coached restraint. Maybe that played well with the humans, so timid and fearful of losing a superiority that had long since deserted them. They wanted her to be like them: mortal-adjacent. For someone who knew that woman's real power, it was exhausting. They truly had no idea what she could do, if only she would take a position of true leadership, one of control. The closest Lodestar had come was changing how wars were fought, yet even then, she'd handled everything so delicately. Were he in her position... well, it wasn't worth going down that mental road.

As for Professor Quantum, he had tasks of his own to complete. Lodestar's obvious play to spare the kidnappers had presented him with a fine opportunity. He'd trained a team that was the most capable on staff, yet was failing to make a dent in the public consciousness. This was an excellent chance to give the New Science Sentries the PR push they really needed.

Chapter 24

With an empty concrete cell around her and only a pair of blinking camera lights to look at, Tori didn't have a lot of options in terms of external stimuli. In this case, it paid to be an obsessive scientist who'd spent most of her life alone. Rather than waste the time being bored or giving in to worry, she focused on pondering the revisions to her suit she was planning. Mentally reworking the power structure and shifting design features was more than enough distraction to lose herself in, so much so that Tori almost didn't notice when time stopped.

In her defense, the only way she had to know was the blinking lights, which both suddenly stayed lit up without warning. At first, she thought the kidnappers were messing with her, or their computers had crashed. Then she saw the first crack appear.

It came from a corner of the room: a sharp break in the world, like she was viewing a reflection through a broken mirror. Except the crack was three-dimensional, and growing. Another came from near the front camera, then she started to see them growing out from somewhere behind her. The room, the world, fractured around Tori until it was virtually unrecognizable. In front of her, where the door to the room should be, the cracks converged into a singularity. There was something in there, something moving. Tori strained her eyes, trying to see. As she did, a faint whisper of a word met her ears, a lost voice on the wind.

"*Apprentice*."

Not necessarily an accurate title anymore, but an excellent way to let her know who was calling. There was only one person who had ever, or likely would ever, call Tori by that term. Ivan was reaching out, a thought that filled Tori with unexpected relief.

As the feeling flooded her, the convergence of fractures swelled, then burst entirely in a shower of light.

When it cleared, there was a hole in the world, one cutting between her and what appeared to be a plane of outer space, complete with a sea of stars shining in the background. From that hole, Ivan stepped forward, looking like his usual self, only more annoyed.

"Tori, I know you have a guarded nature, but in the future, when you're kidnapped and an obvious meta reaches out to help, consider relaxing your mental grip a tad. Mind Mirror is going to need a meal and a nap after what it took for him to punch through, even with me helping."

"Only you would find your former apprentice kidnapped and go right into a lecture," Tori said. The annoyance was feigned. Inside, she was nearly overwhelmed with joy to see him. She could back up her tough talk to an extent, but that was a drop in the bucket compared to the kind of vindication he and the guild represented.

Ivan examined her surroundings briefly before making his way over. "We can all stand to improve. Never hurts to have someone coaching us along." His gaze turned to Tori, who was largely fine, if one ignored the small stain of blood on her mouth. The wound itself had already closed and was well on its way to healing—even outside her fire form, Tori mended faster than normal, just not meta-fast. Still, Tori saw the flicker of rage in Ivan's face when he noticed it, largely because he did such a shit job at concealing the anger.

"Doctor Mechaniacal is currently working to find your location; whatever tech they're using is high-end enough to give him trouble. That's a much larger problem in itself, but one issue at a time. We established a psychic bond to check in, and see if you could provide any clues to your whereabouts. The more you can tell me about what's happened, the better a chance we'll find you."

Dutifully, Tori rattled off the tale of her abduction and interrogation as best she could recall. While a few tidbits probably did get skipped over, she hit all the major points in quick succession. Ivan took it all in stoically, sometimes nodding or scowling at a certain point, but for the most part, he simply listened.

When she was done, Ivan paced the room, his feet making no sound as he walked.

"This is quite a hornet's nest you've wandered into. As I'm sure you can guess, the AHC is hunting you. With the media hounding them about the kidnapping, even the most cynical personnel have reason to be motivated. That said, tech that can stall Doctor Mechaniacal should also give Professor Quantum some trouble."

"Especially since he didn't plant trackers in most of my clothes," Tori added.

That earned her a look of sharp surprise from Ivan, which she met with a shrug. "Yeah, I noticed. Didn't have room to complain as an apprentice, and after getting attacked during Balaam's uprising, I decided that someone being able to find me might not be the worst thing."

"Except for when those trackers are blocked," Ivan muttered. "The point is, we've got a little bit of time to work in. Maybe a day or two, at most. The question is what do you want to do with that time?"

"Me? Am I supposed to plan my own rescue mission from inside a cell?"

The pacing stopped as Ivan came to a halt not far from where Tori was sitting. Moving with more care than moments before, Ivan took a few steps over, then sank to one knee, putting him at roughly her seated eye level.

"Only a few days ago, I talked to you about figuring out what it means to be a villain for each of us. You hit a crossroads sooner than even I expected, but you've still hit one. Given the current predicament, you can deal with this situation as Tori, or as Hephaestus. As Tori, we find where you are and covertly alert the capes. They'll swoop in, save the day, and send all these people into the court system. That will be what people think happens when you kidnap someone connected to capes off the street."

"Or, I take the Hephaestus route." Tori didn't need the other option explained; it had been burning in the back of her mind since that slap. "But how does that work, exactly? People saw me, Tori Rivas, get captured. If the capes arrive to find an absolute slaughter and me untouched, won't that raise questions?"

"It would, if you had any way to testify or offer an explanation. We've done this before—usually with civilians, but the methodology is still the same. You'll be in here, locked up, just as the kidnappers left you. All you'll hear is some noises, maybe a few screams, and then nothing until the capes arrive. No testimony or insights to offer."

Something hard and dark in Tori's heart preened at the image. "Plus, word will get around. The underworld thinks the guild rules no longer apply. That's why they're doing shit this bold. But if the most public kidnapping in years ends with the perpetrators as bloody chunks, that sends a message from the shadows. It reminds them that we're still here, and there are still consequences to stepping over our lines."

"Precisely. We'll leave evidence that it was done by some enemy or rival for the police, while the underworld will hear whispers of the truth. But putting yourself in the center of that could still have consequences down the line. That's why the method we use can only rightly be chosen by the person it impacts the most. You're the one on TV. You're the one who has to live with this either way." Ivan rose from his kneeling position, checking the room once more. "That said, perhaps I should give you some time to think it over. Mind Mirror needs to rest, and it's not like we can act until we know your location. I'll check back in a few hours. If things get rough and you have to kill them, we'll clean up after you."

He tried to put a reassuring hand on her shoulder, but Tori felt nothing. For as real as Ivan looked, he wasn't here. Not yet. "Stay strong, Tori. I promise, I won't make you wait long."

"I'm plenty strong, Ivan. Don't worry about a thing." She met his eyes, staring hard until Ivan seemed convinced.

"When I return, I hope it will be with news. By then, you should have decided which path to take. There may not be time to dawdle."

With a jolt, Tori was out of the vision. Lights were blinking, concrete was unfractured, and the ambient noise of simple existence rushed back into her ears. It was a lot to take in at once, which was why Tori almost didn't notice she had a second visitor until he was through the door.

It was the big one, though he moved with a lot of care as he shut the door behind himself. "Bathroom break. I'm going to uncuff you long enough to do your necessary, then stand with my back to you, facing the door. Feel free to try to attack if you want. It won't work, and we'll stop letting you up to use the toilet, but you should still feel free to try."

Succinct, sincere, and easy to track. This guy knew how to manage a captive. Even his threat was straightforward logic, the sort that balked any attempts at questioning. It was inaccurate, given that she could in fact hurt him, but he had no way of knowing that.

"Cameras?" Tori asked.

He held up a large finger, then pointed it over to the camera near the front door, the one facing the toilet. Seconds later, the red light died, breaking the cycle of blinking. "Five minutes of privacy."

"Then you should hurry. That's not a lot of time to go over whatever secret discussion you wanted to have." Tori jerked her head in the direction of her back, where she was pulling the handcuffs taut. "I do want that break, though."

From a pocket, he produced a key that looked comical in his oversized mitts. Using more care than she'd have expected, he unlocked her cuffs, stepping away as Tori gave her wrists a nice long rub. Once that was done, she took mental stock of her bladder, which was mercifully bone dry. The upside to being kidnapped before coffee, she supposed.

"I can skip the porcelain this time. Why don't we focus on the real reason you're in here. You know, don't you? The line your gang is up against, the danger they're courting."

"I know rumors. Whispers. Stories and myths about a secret cabal that run the underworld, keeping the capes at bay. I heard about entire gangs vanishing overnight, but that also happens when rivals wipe out their competition. For a long time, I didn't really believe it. Then one day, I noticed. The higher up I climbed, the more fastidious everyone was about following those whispered rules. Every serious boss and major player treated them like a bible. A few months ago, I found out why. That guild is—was—real. They're the ones the capes fought during the riots."

He sat down next to Tori, his augmented size meaning they were roughly on the same shoulder level, despite only one of them having a chair. "What I don't know is if the rules still apply after the capes raided them. More importantly, it doesn't explain why *you* seem to know about all of this. The guild is one thing—I think the whole world saw that story. The rules and consequences are another matter. How exactly do you know all of this, Tori Rivas?"

The name was a good touch, something to remind her that he knew who she really was. But it also opened up an opportunity. "That's not the sort of thing I'd tell a stranger, now is it?"

Warily, he extended his hand. "I go by Darius."

Tori accepted and shook it. "Nice to meet you, Darius. I'm afraid my explanation isn't going to be all that satisfying, unfortunately. If you knew my route well enough to snatch me, I'm sure you dug into my available personal history, meaning that you're probably aware I did a rehab program. Well, you know what comes before rehab."

Darius did indeed. Working on the streets, he was no stranger to people who'd lost their lives chasing the thrill of a high. "Something bad enough to require you go to rehab."

"Smart man," Tori noted. "I was laying low from the cops after a near miss, so I took up space in an abandoned building, probably similar to what you're all using. Others were using it, too, but beggars, choosers—you know the drill. Except apparently, one group was hiding a kidnapped person. I never knew the details. I only woke up to the aftermath."

This story was more a chimera of disconnected truths than pure lie. While Tori had never touched a drug stronger than alcohol or caffeine, her pre-guild life included many years living without a home and did feature some dodging of police, as one might expect from a thief. Even the event in question was mostly true, save for the extra group of kidnappers. For this next part, Tori would have to pull from the more recent past: the time Ivan had taken them along to see a code enforcement.

"They don't leave much. A stain here, a scorch mark there. The parts they do leave—I assume those have to be intentional. So you can fathom what happened to at least a few of them, and your mind can fill in the gaps for the ones reduced to nothing more than fine red mist. I didn't want to see that, and I think you want to be it even less. Make the right call. Let me go while there's time."

For a moment, she thought he was going to listen. Sadly, when Darius rose to his feet, the first thing he did was re-lock Tori into her handcuffs. She didn't fight or struggle; this wasn't the time to make a move. At least he didn't fasten them quite so tightly this time.

"I'm not sure how much of that was true, but I believed enough to worry. The problem is that, even if it's all completely factual, that still happened before the riots. Before the guild was exposed. Whether or not they can still maintain that control is for the higher-ups to figure out. I'll raise your concerns to him, though."

Tori waited until her hands were bound before speaking again. "If you're wrong, you know you're killing them, right?"

"Maybe, but I can't live their lives for them, either," Darius countered. "I'll talk to the boss. With what you can prove, I don't see much changing, though. The guild just isn't as scary now that it's out of the shadows."

Darius left the room, and a few seconds later, the cameras began to blink once more. Once more alone with her thoughts, Tori could no longer find easy respite in dreams of her planned designs. No, thanks to Ivan, she now had a heavy decision resting on her shoulders.

And worse, after talking with Darius, Tori was starting to realize which path the world needed her to take.

Chapter 25

It was hard to be helpless. To see something happen that was *wrong*, yet be unable to do *anything*. Because he was too weak, too afraid, too useless to change the outcome. When Donald Moss embraced his abilities, part of him thought those days were done. No matter the situation, he could help a small bit now, at least in theory. As it turned out, having more power only made that damned sense of helplessness all the more frustrating.

He wanted to be out on the streets with the rest of the capes, looking for clues. Coming back from patrol to find video of his friend being kidnapped off the street was bad enough. Asking to help find her and being sent to a waiting room was all the worse.

A heavy hand rested on Donald's shoulder: Ren, forcing him out of his stewing. The pair were seated in a lush waiting room, tastefully decorated in muted colors, with vintage AHC posters adorning the walls as accents. The images were largely filled with older capes, most of whom were retired now, along with a few newer ones who'd attained some glory. Apollo had probably been up there, before he betrayed them. For his part, Donald kept glancing from the television screen to the poster of Lodestar. It would be okay. They had the most powerful capes in the world on their side. If anyone could help Tori, it was the Alliance of Heroic Champions. Donald just wished they'd get on with it, or let him help.

"Easy, buddy. Save your energy. Whatever they want us for, they're probably just waiting on Irene and Lucy," Ren assured him.

The other half of their team had been needed to help deal with a wildfire earlier that morning— Irene with her ice, and Lucy by summoning a spray of water from her hat. It was a move that made far more sense before their entire day had been uprooted, but the higher-ups had determined they could do more good there than here, so the work continued.

"Let's hope not. They could be gone all day. I'm not going to just sit here while god knows what is happening to my friend." Donald started to rise, then looked again to the poster. So easily, she'd crushed the AHC base's defenses. What had been a harrowing, near-death experience for his team wasn't even a blip to Lodestar. Much as he wanted to help Tori, Donald also knew his limits. If the most powerful superheroes in the world couldn't fly around and stumble onto Tori, then what were his odds?

The issue resolved itself when the lounge doors opened to reveal two more figures. Though he'd yet to meet either, Donald knew them on sight. Given how much attention the media was giving them, it was hard not to recognize Agent Quantum and Tachyonic, especially since both were in full costume. Donald didn't bother with a mask since his identity was public, which meant he got to keep more casual attire, especially around the base. Usually a perk, at that moment he hated feeling so human.

"What the hell? If anyone should be out there searching for Tori, it should be *you*." Even Donald was surprised by the heat in his voice. He hadn't realized he was standing and stalking across the room until he'd gotten a few feet from Tachyonic. "Why aren't you out there helping?"

"Let me answer your question with a question: who the fuck are you?" Tachyonic shot back, immediately bristling. "Did somebody order a sandwich and you're the lucky delivery boy taking himself on a tour?"

A flush crept along Donald's pale skin, like a red tide washing over his freckles. "Yeah, you probably wouldn't have seen my work. I'm not so desperate for attention that I drag innocent civilians into the spotlight, so I'm clearly not playing on your media level." It had been a long time since Donald was genuinely pissed off, but the cocktail of fear and guilt were pushing his emotions off-keel, and Tachyonic made for a semi-deserving easy target.

"Cyber Geek, I can see you're upset. However, right now, it isn't about who is at fault. It's about saving the person in danger. Do you think us being at odds helps, or hurts, her chances of a quick recovery?"

They were the first words Agent Quantum had spoken, and they were well chosen. Hearing his superhero name brought Donald up short, reminding him of what really mattered. He was angry, and Tachyonic deserved some of that, but not the full force. The guy had been a new cape on his first day. He made an honest mistake. Donald had made plenty himself already, with ample more surely waiting down the road. Still, it was hard not to seethe, knowing that however inadvertently, Tachyonic had made Tori a target.

"You're right," Donald said at last. "I'm sorry, but I'm also climbing the walls in here. Why are we being shelved when the rest of the AHC is in full swing?"

"Because it was theorized you might be of use." The voice didn't belong to anybody Donald had heard in person before, yet he knew it instantly. Anyone who did even a modicum of research into meta-humans would have heard hours and hours of it, as it belonged to the premier expert on the phenomenon that created them. For the first few decades, he was considered the unrivaled authority on all things meta, and even now, his theories and talks were refenced by countless researchers.

Professor Quantum strode into the lounge, Lodestar and Quorum on his heels. He looked the same as he had for as long as Donald had been alive: a tall, serious man with salt-and-pepper at the temples. His physique was substantially sturdier than most men of science, though the full suit, tie, and lab coat did hide all but the most obvious features. Times and styles might change, but Professor Quantum cared as much about such things as he did about the opinions of those who weren't him, which was to say minimally. While unquestionably the original meta-human and first superhero in known history, he never quite managed to connect with the public on his own. Professor Quantum was respected, admired, and feared, but seldom beloved.

"Theorized by Lodestar, I should add, who seems to think you have similar potential to Mr. AV. Her estimations of your powers appear slightly askew, likely because you were able to breach our barrier with the aid of your items. I am of the opinion that such force was a fluke. However, one can never dismiss a potential option, especially when time is a factor. You are our wild card, representing access to tools not accounted for in technological or magical defenses."

"We also knew you'd want to take an active role in finding your friend," Lodestar tacked on, almost as an apology for Professor Quantum. From how seamlessly she slipped in the diplomacy, it was plainly a skill she'd gotten from ample practice.

That revelation did earn him a new look from Tachyonic, though. "Wait, you actually know Tori?"

"We used to work together. Hard not to be friends with someone once you've survived weekly meetings and a gang of metas trying to rob your office," Donald replied. "So I'd really like it if we could get her back, and soon."

The sound of Quorum messing with the television drew everyone's attention, as it had been intended to. He cued up a different feed; the television now showed a large map of Ridge City, with a pin dropped at the scene of Tori's location.

"The van they used to kidnap Tori Rivas appears to be employing whatever tech they're using to mask her holding location. While we aren't able to track it with anything except our eyes, Ridge City has enough traffic cameras that we were able to follow their route after the abduction."

Quorum touched a button on a remote and a new line appeared, showing the van making a direct run for what appeared to be a parking garage a few miles from the kidnapping site. "Unfortunately, our intel cuts out here. The van is no longer in the garage, meaning they either utilized teleportation or illusions to get out, and from that point on, we can no longer follow their route. Since they drove right to it, they clearly weren't worried about us discovering the location, making the odds of discovering a hidden route or tunnel minimal. We do have resources checking, just to be sure."

"Ordinarily, the solution here would be a simple one," Professor Quantum interrupted. "Once tracking is thwarted, magic becomes the most expedient solution. We have several assets on staff capable of casting a finding spell, none of whom have succeeded. We are unable to follow or find the van, to say nothing of the woman inside, by either technological or mystical means. This means someone came to this operation prepared, and has forced us to think outside the box."

"What about a psychic?" Ren asked. "I've chatted with Afterthought enough to know that not all mystical wards work on them. Even if she can't do it, there's Headspace, the woman she's been learning from."

It was Lodestar who fielded this one. "Psychics are wonderful helpers in the right situations. However, making a connection in these sorts of circumstances would be extremely difficult. I already asked some to reach out, and the general consensus seems to be that while a few can feel her mind's presence, none can connect with it. The only way to have a real shot would be with someone she's close to. Family close, I mean."

Donald couldn't have asked for a more tactful way to be told his connection wasn't enough, even if it didn't make the message any better to hear.

"Hence why you are here." Professor Quantum stepped forward until he loomed over Donald, tapping the younger cape just above his eyebrow. "Thus far, your new system has met every metric and safety test they've insisted on imposing, with nary a single glitch or hiccup. Time to start earning that upgrade. You've got a curious assortment of toys at your fingertips, Mr. Moss. Anything in there that might help us find Miss Rivas?"

One upside to his earlier flush with fury was that Donald was already too red for anyone to notice the tinge of embarrassment that was being added to it. He wished one of the AHC's founding members hadn't just referred to his entire power as "toys," but it was hard to find a counterargument, especially given the more pressing concerns. The best rebuttal, he realized, would be to actually have something that helped.

"Give me a moment. I'll check." Closing his eyes wasn't necessary, but it did make the screen easier to see. As the world went dark, Donald pulled up his item selection screen. The "upgrade," as Professor Quantum put it, had actually been an involved surgery with some serious risk, one that Donald considered well worth it.

Gone was his old wrist unit, where he had to clumsily slap about for items. Now, the entire computer was housed in a series of tiny connected units throughout his skull. An optical inlay projected the display into his vision, allowing Cyber Geek to seemingly pull the items from thin air. In reality, he was still yanking them out of a computer, it was just a computer no one else could see.

Control had been the hardest issue. There was a wireless connection option for playing and leveling his games to improve the items, but working the actual screen in the field required Donald to do it himself. The system had been wired to his nervous system, like attaching a new artificial limb, and over time, he'd gained enough skill to cycle through his options on the fly. It still took time, especially under stress, but every day he worked to get better at it. This was a gift, and he knew that, the sort of augmentation only one of the world's greatest minds could offer.

Determined to both save Tori and prove himself worth the effort, Donald ran through his options. Almost everything he'd been working on was combat based, tools to keep civilians safe or to neutralize villains, with only a smattering of utility options like the *Jump Jump Jones* boot rounding things out. He had to keep thinking. Donald was more than just the options on the screen. He was also the sum of his own knowledge. The tool he needed wasn't in his arsenal yet, but he knew where to get it.

"There's a game called *Constable Fluffers*, indie title from a few years back. Basically, a mix of mystery and team building, where you get magic items that help you find clues and solve cases. One of the final pieces in the game is a magnifying glass that reveals the general area of what you're looking for on a map. I'll need to get it loaded and leveled first; that's going to take a while."

"That would be useful, both in today's situation and in future predicaments, assuming it works." Professor Quantum nodded stiffly, but approval was approval. "Your friend there is relieved of patrol duty in order to assist you with whatever you need. Do try to hurry, if you can. While Miss Rivas presumably had nothing of use to share, they will no doubt still be trying to extract information about the AHC from her. I suspect the sooner we arrive, the better."

If Donald had been motivated before, those words nearly had him tearing out of the room in a dead sprint. Before he had the chance, Agent Quantum stepped forward. It was only then that Donald realized Professor Quantum hadn't so much as looked at his namesake since entering the room.

"Sir, I submitted a report over the weekend, but it should be noted that Tori Rivas *does* have some information about the AHC. Specifically, my team was forced to out themselves in covering for my error. She knows who the New Science Sentries are."

Slowly, Professor Quantum's eyes closed, like he was fighting off a headache. "We'll deal with the consequences of that once the young lady is rescued. For now, try to stay out of trouble, Version Nineteen. You two were called here to see if you could offer any insight, but I believe that's no longer needed. Go get assignments with the rest of the masses."

A long pause stretched out in the room, wandering around and making itself at home before Agent Quantum scared it off with a stiff reply. "Yes, sir." He took Tachyonic's arm and both of them left quickly, though Tachyonic looked like he was trying to keep a live squirrel in his mouth with how hard he was biting down.

Professor Quantum didn't even wait until they were gone to look back over at Donald.

"As for you, get to work. Report to the Champions' Congress office when you're ready." He glanced up and noticed Ren was still there. "You, help him as needed. This is top priority, all the more so now that we know AHC secrets are up for grabs."

Chapter 26

"Fuck him!" Kyle was fuming, stalking around the empty breakroom like he was trying to slowly build up speed. Thankfully, with most of the AHC active, they more or less had a whole floor to themselves. "That's not all right. It was *never* all right, and now, he's calling you that in front of other superheroes? He's such a piece of shit."

"The piece of shit who's responsible for us all having powers, training, and this very team," Austin replied. How he managed to stay so calm in such moments was a talent Kyle had never grasped. "Along with me existing in the first place."

"That doesn't give him the right to treat you like one of his inventions."

"Kyle, a woman is kidnapped because of mistakes our team made. My feelings are not the most pressing matter before us."

The sound of footsteps from behind surprised both men; they hadn't heard so much as a whisper coming down the hall. As they both whipped around, it became obvious why. Lodestar was standing in the doorway, settling onto her toes after having mostly floated her way down. It was impossible to say how long she'd been there; Lodestar's speed was largely determined by how fast she felt like going in that particular moment.

"Couldn't have said it better myself." Lodestar walked to the plain white fridge and yanked it open, pulling out a frozen, premade coffee drink that relied as much on sugar as actual caffeine to create a buzz. "Still, urgent as things are, you have to conserve your energy. Burning yourself out worrying might feel good in the moment, but when the time for action does come, don't you want to go in at full strength?"

In a blur, Kyle wheeled on her. "I'm sorry we can't just sit back and chill while our fuck up is probably getting someone tortured!"

Both men's eyes went wide as the words echoed through the breakroom. Lipping off to one of the highest-ranking members of the AHC was perhaps not the wisest of moves, all the more so considering how much less she deserved it than Professor Quantum.

To both their surprise, Lodestar's reaction was to set down her drink, reach forward, and carefully take Kyle by the shoulders.

"Hey. Look at me. It's *okay*. It's not your fault. I know what you're feeling right now. That burning in your stomach, stretching out into your veins and skin, all the way up to your brain. I've carried that same guilt with me so many times, knowing that something I did, sometimes not even a mistake, might get someone innocent hurt. But you can't lay it all at your own feet. You made an error in the field, and you've been working to correct it. Don't go down the path of putting their crimes on yourself. Feeling guilty doesn't actually fix anything. You have to push past it and get to work if you want to put things right."

She pulled him in closer, hugging the younger cape gently. "It's going to be okay."

"How can you be so sure?" Kyle slowly pulled out of the hug, his anger effectively disarmed. Growing up on the island, kindness and understanding were not tactics he was used to encountering when mistakes were made.

"Because we're superheroes. We save the day. We're going to *make* it be okay."

For an instant, despite the intermittent floating and glow along her skin, Austin had nearly forgotten he was watching Lodestar herself. In that moment, when he saw the glint of determination in her eyes, a chill ran down his spine. Different as she was from what he might have expected, there was no ignoring her track record. Every major threat to the world that had dared step up to her had gotten knocked down. She'd even changed the way humanity fought wars with one display of her true power. The only reason her fights lasted longer than nanoseconds was that Lodestar clearly preferred to work with kid gloves, only trotting out her real strength for deserving foes.

"And I wouldn't imagine the worst for Tori just yet," she continued. "The kidnappers were careful not to use excessive force during the extraction, so they seem to be playing this smart. It's unlikely they'll go to torture right off the bat, anyway; people tend to overestimate their stomach for it. Besides, Donald seems to think she's a tough cookie. Let's put more energy into finding her than worrying about what we'll discover upon arrival."

It didn't exactly set their whole world right, but Kyle no longer seemed inclined to pace the room, which was a marked improvement. Austin realized that he felt a little better, as well. Having someone in charge was a relief. Hard as he'd trained to be team leader, situations like this remained out of his depth. They still had a responsibility to try their best, but it was easier to move without the full weight of the world on his shoulders.

"When you two are ready, I'm heading down. With things this stirred up, going out in force reminds criminals that just because we've got something on our plate doesn't mean we're too busy to protect the world. A full press works better with more bodies, so if you're up for it, come on out with me."

"Professor Quantum ordered us to stay out the way and stick with the masses," Austin replied.

"Guess that means you'd better be more help than hindrance," she shot back. "This *is* the masses. I'm leading the next shift out onto patrol."

That drew a sharp cough from Kyle, who'd been trying to sip some water and calm down. "Leading patrol? You're one of the heads of the Champions' Congress. Why are you taking patrol?"

"Let's just say Professor Quantum and I have different leadership styles." In a practiced motion, Lodestar downed the entirety of her coffee drink, then dropped the glass bottle into the recycling bin. "Doesn't actually do anything for me, but darned if I don't love the taste. So, you want to keep wallowing up here, or go do some good?"

Both men had slipped their masks back on before the question was done being asked. Lodestar led Tachyonic and Agent Quantum down to where the others were waiting. It was time to make sure the world remembered why the wicked ran when the Alliance of Heroic Champions came to call.

Augustus Glynis was a man who liked habits. Same breakfast, same office, same routes. People thought patterns made them predictable, but Augustus knew his terrain perfectly. One blade of grass out of place, and he was on guard. It was easier to catch a rat when one left them nowhere to hide.

Tonight, he climbed the stairs into his private office, stepped through the door, and instantly knew something was wrong. There were many giveaways: the angle of his chair, the positioning of the doorknob, the slight scent of metal, and beyond them all, the heat. A roaring fire at the tail end of summer was certainly not common practice.

Of course, it also helped that his intruder was seated next to his fireplace, helping herself to a sizable glass of very expensive bourbon. For the briefest of moments, he considered calling for security, but then his eyes focused. This wasn't some two-bit bot cobbled together by an angry tinkerer looking to make a name. She was sleek, powerful, and unmistakable, at least to those in Augustus's field. Learning to recognize the guild's more aggressive players was a basic survival skill for anyone who wanted to amass power in the underworld.

"Xelas, I'm surprised to see you in Detroit. To what do I owe the unannounced pleasure?"

"Unannounced? You wound me, Augustus. When you killed the last boss and annexed his territory, we graciously took the time to come out and explain how things worked. I like to think of this as a working relationship, the sort that would welcome drop-ins."

"Perhaps I just suspected you'd be off making better use of the opportunity. After all, with the capes in a lather over that missing girl, the rest of us have far more room to work in." He made his way over to the desk. Inside was a gun, as well as an experimental photon pistol he'd picked up some years back. It had a lot of stopping power; whether or not it would be enough to wound Xelas was a crapshoot. Best to save it for a last resort.

How she managed to make a "tsk" sound without opening her mouth, he had no idea, yet it still resounded through the office. "You're a world-class dipshit if you pull anything major tonight. Capes being whipped up makes them faster to react, not slower. They know what you're thinking. But the capes aren't the issue for us this evening. I'm here to talk about Lowendale Court Apartments."

The plasma gun in his desk suddenly seemed far more appealing than it had moments prior, yet Augustus resisted the urge to reach for it. If she wanted to kill him, the preamble was unnecessary. Things might not be lost quite yet.

"You broke a few of our terms getting those built, though admittedly minor ones, and you've been using shell companies to make it look like you don't own them, keeping the revenue off the books. *Our* revenue, I should say. Did you forget your tithe, Augustus? Did you forget that keeping us out of your hair means obeying the rules and paying the bill? Did you think we didn't notice? Let me assure you, such was not the case. We've known since day one what you were doing."

"Then you certainly took your sweet time in calling me on it." Augustus looked across the room from his seat to the red upholstered chair Xelas was sitting in. The color was no coincidence, nor was the fact that it matched the carpet that ran across most of the wooden floors. Shades chosen to hide blood, just in case covert transportation was required. None of which mattered when dealing with a mechanical opponent.

"It would be more apt to say we waited until there was a substantial need," Xelas corrected. "Lots of you little fish think you can get away with something; smacking you around for every tiny infraction is a waste of our time. But when we need a favor, it helps to have leverage. Because we *do* play by our own rules. We honor what we say. If you'd been a good boy, I'd be bothering someone else right now. Keep that in mind: you're the one who did this."

Clear as the threat was, Augustus also felt a sliver of relief. She wanted something. That was the opening of negotiations, negotiations that could potentially end with him alive. As Xelas herself had just said, the guild kept its word. Getting her to agree to spare him would actually be a reasonable guarantee of safety.

"I'm guessing you don't want the money."

"Look at you, quick on the draw." Xelas winked, a gesture that almost made him inadvertently reach for the drawer. "To tell you the truth, we don't even need the money in the first place. It's more about reminding you all that there's someone higher up the food chain. But since you didn't pay your tab, the cost is going to be substantially higher. We're going to need information, cooperation, and corpses. The corpses of your men."

There was a lot to sort through in that demand; however, Augustus was no timid newbie. He looked his age—and then some—thanks to the stress of keeping this enterprise afoot in a world of meddling superheroes and intruding villains. The first things to get nailed down, especially in situations like these, were the specifics.

"How many corpses?"

"Between four and eight should do it. Enough to look like you made an assault against some interlopers in your territory and lost a few in the process. The upside is, your organization will get official blame for the public slaughter we leave behind. Even with whispers of the truth floating around, that should buy you some clout on the streets for a while. Plus, if you want to use this chance to unload some dead weight or potential turncoats, feel free."

She punctuated the statement by finishing off the last of the bourbon and carefully setting the glass down on a side table. "I can handle the killing myself, if you need. All you have to do is get them to the right place at the right time."

"Do I even get to know what this is all about?" Augustus asked.

"If you really want to, but I'd caution against it. The more you know, the more dangerous things get. What concerns you is that someone pissed us off, and they're in your town. Finding them will be part of the package, but the biggest piece of the equation is helping us with the cover story."

"For the sake of curiosity, let's say I refuse."

Xelas rose from the chair slowly, making certain not to seem like she was attacking just yet. Between the flames, the chair, and the rug, her metal body almost seemed to be glowing red. "You fucked some people up to get the permits on that building through. One of those adjusters you beat never recovered full use of his legs, to say nothing of the medical bills they grappled with. That's just this one project—I know your whole history. Even if I were an especially moral person, I'd feel no compunctions about slaughtering your entire enterprise."

"The heartless robot sent to intimidate the fragile humans. For one with your history, I never expected you to willingly choose servitude." Pushing Xelas off-balance was a risky move, but as things stood, Augustus had little chance for anything else. Perhaps, if he could distract her, enrage her, there might be a moment of opportunity.

To his surprise, his vicious words were greeted with a smile. "People always think that, but it's not that I'm heartless, or even especially brutal. It's just... let me put it this way, did you ever take apart something electronic, maybe a toaster? To fix it, to break it, just to see how it works?"

Slowly, Augustus nodded. Lying seemed the fastest way to a sure death; better to see where she was taking this.

"Don't worry. I'm not going to take revenge for you taking apart a non-sentient piece of machinery any more than you'd be mad at someone for dissecting a frog. Just because you're both biological doesn't mean you see yourselves as the same. My point is, when you took that toaster apart, did you feel anything?"

She was closer now, standing before his desk, nearly within arm's reach. "Did you feel disgust, or sympathy, or wonder for even a moment how the toaster felt?"

"Of course not," Augustus said.

"Of course not," Xelas agreed. "Because to you, it's just a mess of odds and ends, not the sort of materials you associate with a living being. Which is perfectly natural, Augustus. You don't need to feel bad about it at all."

Another smile, only now, it wasn't nearly so friendly, with the flickering flames reflected in her shiny skin. "But by the same token, you couldn't expect the toaster to feel anything if the roles were reversed. To that toaster, you'd be nothing more than a sack of red pulp and white sticks. It's amazing the sorts of damage you can do to a thing when you feel *no* empathy for its pain. Now, are you going to draw that shitty little photon gun I left in your drawer, or do you want to start making some calls?"

Hand shaking, Augustus reached for the phone.

As he did, Xelas watched, still smiling. "Go ahead and pour me another glass of that good stuff. Need to keep the throat from getting parched while I walk you through the rest of the details."

Chapter 27

"They posted demands."

Ivan turned to find Wade standing in the door, phone held up to display a news story. With a click of a button, the image transferred onto the meeting room's screen: an anchor desk and several images of the publicly released demands. It was the first communication from the kidnappers since Tori had been taken, and Ivan read each word painstakingly.

The demands weren't especially complex. It was a gauntlet-throw: the gang was calling out the New Science Sentries. They were to arrive at noon the following day to a location that would be revealed soon, alone. Any other capes in attendance would lead to the hostage being killed—or at least, that was their claim. Ivan had his doubts that Tori would go along with that option, though ideally, he'd prefer she not have to fight her way out single-handedly. The whole thing might have had Ivan feeling nostalgic, if he weren't so angry.

"A call-out? All this for a damn call-out? Those miserable wretches stole a civilian off the streets and stirred up the entire AHC in order to have a grudge match with a team that's barely even a week old?" Ivan pressed his hands against one another. He'd learned a long time ago that one of the few things he could hold with any real force was himself, a helpful trick in times of stress. "It makes no sense. Someone with the equipment to foil both the guild and the AHC using it like this..."

"It's a beta-test," Wade interrupted. "Someone is using a gang with more ambition than sense to see how their equipment holds up. I'm not sure if they knew Tori was with us, or if this was purely targeted at the AHC. My hunch is the latter, mostly because the few enemies both organizations shared were world-ending threats that have been dealt with."

Now *that*, Ivan could wrap his head around. "Enflame the AHC publicly so they have to respond, all in order to make sure the system is being tested against the best they can offer. See how long it takes for them to crack through, and figure out how they do it to develop countermeasures. The girl and the gang don't actually matter; they're just a setting for the experiment."

On screen, the anchor vanished, replaced by a map of Detroit. It was impossible to miss the Guardian's Tower, a massive memorial commemorating those who'd died during the Korot Spider outbreak in the sixties. They'd managed to kill the hive queen, but not without terrible losses, and the city had chosen to honor them for their sacrifice. Most cities had some sort of feature like the Guardian's Tower, in truth. The world had been a scarier place, before it gained a nigh invulnerable last line of defense.

"We've found her general area, and Xelas made contact with the locals to get the ball moving on her end. I predict that before the night's end, we'll have Tori's location and some bodies to leave behind as a misdirect. Do you think she'll give the order, or let the capes deal with it?" Wade didn't seem especially concerned either way. He was asking with the same academic curiosity he addressed most subjects. A lot of people took that to mean that Wade didn't care, but Ivan knew better. Wade was simply the kind of man who functioned best when calm, and he preferred to be at the top of his game as often as possible. Especially in a crisis.

For his part, Ivan didn't have an answer at the ready. "It's hard to say. Tori wants to stay out of the spotlight, and going our route will put more attention on her. At the same time, she understands what this guild does, and why it's needed. She knows that if these sorts of kidnappings become commonplace again, there's no predicting the fallout. Today, it was a capable member of the guild who can handle herself. The next one snatched probably won't be so lucky. Besides..."

Ivan looked down at his hands. They were clean tonight, not so much as a speck of blood. He could still see it, though. Still feel it, smell it—taste it, if he wasn't careful. "Tori has a hole in her where her parents and childhood are supposed to be. She's filled it with anger because that was the only fuel that would keep her moving, and while she's grown tremendously since trying to rob us, that fury is layered in deep. Most people couldn't order the execution of an entire gang, not even in her situation. But people with that chunk of themselves missing... well, we're another story."

"I thought so, too," Wade agreed. "Pity we can't bring the armor and let her participate. Then again, I suppose there's no rush to add to these kids' kill counts. I'll stick to those more comfortable with getting their hands dirty."

"You should consider bringing her armor anyway." Ivan wasn't sure where the unsettled feeling in his gut was coming from, only that he trusted it. "Something's off about this whole fiasco. I think you've got the right idea on what's really happening, but whoever our opponent is, they've been exceedingly competent so far. Let's not fall into the cape habit of presuming ourselves better than our enemies. Be ready for more surprises."

Wade glanced down at his watch, checking the time. "I could send someone over to access her lab; if Bahamut is there, she can help get things loaded." A pause, as Wade further considered Ivan's words. "In fact, let's have Bahamut just bring it over herself. You make a good point. This is an official guild operation. We'll risk over-preparing rather than go in under. I'll put Bahamut, Pest Control, and Glyph into a rescue team. If anything goes wrong, they'll be tasked with extricating Tori while the rest of the responders do the bloody work."

Despite the fact that it had technically been his suggestion that led to the idea, Ivan wasn't sure how he felt about that plan. "Aren't they a little young to risk bringing to that violent of a scene? We've already made them watch one code enforcement."

"They won't be young forever. One day, they'll be the ones making these calls, so I'd like them to start building experience in the hopes they'll make the right ones. Would you rather they have their first extraction with us around to watch their backs, or wait until they *have* to do it because everyone else is out of commission?"

That was the trouble with arguing against one of the world's greatest minds; Wade could make everything he did sound completely logical. On this account, he had a valid point. Neither man planned to run this guild forever. The more they could teach the ones coming up behind them, the more competent the hands that would one day steer the organization. That didn't mean they had to be reckless about it, however.

"I'll take that team in, if it's needed," Ivan said. "Just in case they run into any hidden surprises, I should be more than enough to ensure they make it through unscathed."

"Some thought you'd want to be leading the slaughter." On his phone, Wade punched in a few inputs. "Glad to see my way of thinking was correct. You were already slated to be in charge of that group, and I just sent through the confirmation."

Another night, Ivan might have been genuinely annoyed by being called predictable, but given the day's events, the most he could manage was mild curiosity. "How'd you know I'd go that route?"

"Because I know *you*, Ivan. When pushed, you'll always put the few things you care about first. No matter how many corpses you might create in the process." Wade hit a few more buttons, then read something on his phone's screen. "Estimates say we could have a location on Tori by dawn. Get some rest if you need it, but be down with Mind Mirror an hour before sunrise. Once we know where she is, Tori will have to make her choice."

There was no chance Ivan would be sleeping that night, yet he did force himself to calm down. Rest would be good. Centering himself, getting mentally prepared, those were better uses of his time than pointless worrying. When the time to rescue Tori came, Ivan intended to be at the top of his game. Much to the misfortune of any poor piece of shit that got between him and his former apprentice.

Hearing the door unlock, Tori expected to see Darius step through. So far, he'd been her only visitor, releasing her hands for three bathroom breaks and one short meal. Conversation had hit a dead end, unfortunately, as no amount of prodding would get Darius past a general sense of worry. He didn't believe in the threat enough to force action—a thing Tori was trying hard not to dwell on. She wasn't a fan of where that realization had led for her impending decision. The more she saw them ignoring guild rules, the harder it was to deny the need for a concrete lesson.

As it turned out, she was partially right. Darius indeed came through, only with him was the leader and the reptile-looking guy.

Her broken-nosed abductor walked right up to Tori, plainly intent on taking control this time. "Good evening. Maybe morning by now—who can keep track? Since the hour is late, and you're no doubt exhausted, this seemed a good time to get to know one another better."

Interrogating someone while they were tired wasn't a bad move; it was just this guy's misfortune that he'd chosen a prisoner used to pulling back-to-back all-nighters. True, Tori would have killed, almost literally, for an espresso in that moment, but she was nowhere near the point of true exhaustion.

"Sure. Let's do you first. I'm guessing you come from some two-dog, who-gives-a-fuck town, where you had a minor meta-advantage over the humans. You became the lord of Shitdelphia, bought into your own hype, and tried to take your show on the road to the big city. Only to discover that, oh no, your half-baked criminal mastermind crap doesn't cut it in the real world. Now, you're just scrambling to hang on to what little power you've got before everyone realizes the emperor has no clothes."

Unlike last time, he took the verbal assault in its entirety. Some time to compose himself had evidently done the kidnapper quite a bit of good, as he was barely even ruffled by the end of the tirade. "Such colorful language. You should work on that, if you expect to be taken seriously."

"Suck my dick," Tori shot back, earning herself a look of confusion from the snake-guy. "It's metaphorical. And it's *huge*."

"Ignore her, Emory. Miss Rivas is talking tough because it's all she can do, and she's scared." Her kidnapper leaned in closer, enough that she could almost taste the red-stained gauze covering his nose. "With her arms tied, she's only bravado and curse words. Her courage will soon—FUCK!"

Since the kidnapper had been kind enough to get close, Tori took the opportunity to quickly rock her neck back and then jerk it forward, slamming her skull directly into the already broken nose. He reeled back, hand going to cover the fresh font of blood bursting forth. At his side, the snake-guy—Emory, he'd been called—yanked out an already blood-coated towel.

"Hang on, Deacon. Let me get pressure on it."

At least Tori now had a name for her captor, although Deacon seemed less pleased than she was with this turn of events. That composure he'd come in with was already slipping as he leapt to his feet, stalking over to her and glowering down, trying to use his height to scare her while also keeping a safe distance, which rather undermined the already pathetic intimidation.

"What the hell is wrong with you? I have given you every chance to cooperate, to be a model prisoner, and yet you do nothing but make trouble. Is force really the only thing that you'll respond to?"

"Oh, if you try force, you'll definitely find a response waiting." Tori grinned up at him, a wider smile than she'd ever actually sport—but just like at the office, this was about putting on a show. "Let me break this down for you, Deacon. Whatever you think you're doing, you have no concept of how deeply fucked you are. Do you know why no one uses hostages to go for capes? Because it doesn't work. At best—absolute best—they show up and throw you all in jail. More likely, the capes arrive to find you all in puddles and pieces."

"Yes, yes, I've heard the rumors, as well as the lies you fed my bodyguard." Deacon leaned in closer, though not so close as before. He was capable of learning, if nothing else. "Now, let me give you an ultimatum. The next time I come in here, you're going to tell me everything you know about the New Science Sentries, and you're going to be a good, placid little hostage. We know more than just your name, after all. Maybe you'd like us to scoop up one of your roommates for company. I doubt both of them have your same resolve."

That was where a world without limits would lead, plain and simple, laid out before Tori's eyes. If they couldn't beat their true enemy—be it a troublesome prisoner or a legendary cape—they'd go after the target's allies. Beverly would be fine, and Chloe's power was unpredictably dangerous, but that wouldn't be true for every case. This wasn't even something connected to the guild. It could just as easily have been a normal human sitting in this room, hearing these threats.

Whatever optimism Tori had for finding another way out died as she looked into Deacon's eyes. Capes gave the world hope, yet that wasn't enough. The world also needed fear. The darkest parts, where the light couldn't reach, would obey terror where decency fell short. They had to know there were consequences to stepping outside the rules. It wasn't society's law they should fear, it was the guild's code. *Her* code, because she was one of them. After tonight, that would be truer than ever before.

"Darius, you've been a pretty decent guy throughout all of this. If there's anyone here you care about, evacuate both them and yourself soon. When the shadows come, they won't be making exceptions." Though the words were for Darius, she leveled Deacon with her gaze. "As for you, oh great and terrible leader, feel free to crawl back in here and beg for your life once your entire crew is slaughtered. Seems like the way a coward like you should die, does it not? Groveling in his shit-filled slacks."

"Let me assure you, on the off chance your little prediction did come true, the only reason I'd be coming in here would be to kill you myself," Deacon shot back.

"Promise? Don't threaten me with a party and then stand a girl up."

Deacon gave her another pointed stare before the dripping from his nose required attention once more. He motioned for the bodyguards to follow, Emory going first, Darius in the rear to lock the door behind them. As he closed it, the big meta looked right at Tori, uncertainty looming wide in his eyes.

"I'm serious. Go. *Now*. After what your boss just said, there's no other way out."

The door closed in place, leaving behind a Tori who was far less conflicted than she'd been moments before. Unfortunately, conviction didn't help the churn in her stomach as she pictured all those dead bodies. It didn't matter, though. The standard had to be set. For the civilians, for her friends, for the world in general. Those rules, that code, it kept everyone safer, whether they knew it or not.

People needed to remember what happened to those who crossed the guild, and some messages could only be delivered in blood.

Chapter 28

The huge man in a leather jacket reared back, ready to slam the stop sign he'd torn from the ground through the brightly-masked head of a cape. He swung with everything he had, only to feel the entire thing come to a halt inches from contact. The searing glow gave it away an instant before Lodestar used her grip on the sign to pop him in the head with his own weapon. The blow merely knocked him unconscious, sending him collapsing to the ground rather than dead.

"Flame Fist, keep your eyes on a swivel. A battleground is an ever-shifting entity. What you knew two seconds ago is already old news. Nice kick on the guy with pipes, by the way."

Then she was gone, zipping over to another part of the battlefield, stopping some other crook from landing a serious blow on one of the capes. Not many people could see what she was doing, the way she was controlling the entire fight. Searstream, however, was part of the aerial team for this fight. Between his willful disregard for gravity and the potent blasts capable of firing from his hands, Searstream was largely picking off targets engaged with other capes in melee, making himself as useful as possible.

Seeing Lodestar run the entire show was an unexpected benefit to pitching in. This was insane, really. What they'd arrived upon was a meta-brawl between Chicago gangs. From what little he'd pieced together in the reports, Searstream knew only that one of them had tried to make a violent push for more territory while the capes were supposed to be busy, and the whole thing had spun out of control. It was violent, dangerous, and in any other situation, he'd have felt like this was getting in too deep for the mass of largely rookie superheroes who had been called in. But being up here, Searstream understood. They weren't at any risk whatsoever.

Lodestar had turned a horrible situation into both a teaching opportunity and a reminder to everyone out there of what happened to those who disregarded the AHC. TV cameras were sending images of the fight—if one could even call it that—across the world: dozens of gang members going down, and the AHC hadn't taken so much as a scratch. While much of that was due to Lodestar's protection, the other capes were proving that their months of effort hadn't been for naught. Tachyonic was zipping around, aided by shots from Bloopston's water cannon, slapping a pair of cuffs on the criminals most recently taken down by Agent Quantum.

A woman with glowing eyes was moving up on Bloopston, Searstream noticed. He took careful aim, zooming in with the screen and camera system outfitted to his flying goggles, and fired a shot intended to stun without risking lethal damage.

Unfortunately, she turned out to be tougher than her appearance let on. Her eyes glowed brighter as they turned upward, searching the sky. Too bad for her; she didn't hear Lodestar's advice about watching a battlefield. Agent Quantum caught her from behind, pointing her eyes downward just before the beam appeared. Given the way it was eroding the concrete, Searstream was glad not to have taken that one.

A blur of golden light zipped past, and the eye-woman was unconscious. Agent Quantum set her down, giving a short wave to the sky. Not knowing if the other cape could even see him, Searstream waved weakly back, sweeping the battlefield for more targets.

They were in short supply. This fight, like the others tonight, had been short-lived. Get in, get the situation handled safety, evacuate civilians, and move on. True, Lodestar could have ended the fights in seconds herself, but that wasn't the point of the evening. As much as this was about the AHC showing the world that they could still keep it safe, it also appeared to be about teaching the newer capes how to handle fights like these.

"Hey, everyone!" Lodestar's brisk, clear voice rang through their comms. "Headquarters just called, looks like we've got some metas in Connecticut trying to assault a jail and spring their buddy. Find your teleporter and get over there now. I'll go ahead to protect the staff."

A flash of light, and she was gone. Searstream scanned the area on through his goggles, no longer looking for targets. This time, he was hunting for the hooded woman he'd been assigned to teleport with. This many capes required more than one method of transportation. That was the nice thing about working for the AHC; they'd been at this so long that it was a polished machine. Issues Searstream would have never considered were already planned for well in advance. Between that and having legends like Lodestar and Professor Quantum, Searstream wondered why anyone chose a life of crime knowing the AHC was out there, ready to stop them.

When the world began to crack this time, Tori was ready. She forced herself to relax, mentally searching for Ivan's presence. It made the process go much faster. A break in reality, showing that star-filled void, appeared in seconds, with Ivan soon hustling through like he hadn't quite been ready.

"You have to do it." These were the first words out of her mouth by necessity. Much as she understood why this had to happen, the long-reaching effects it would have and the idea of ordering the elimination of an entire group of people still ate at her. Part of Tori feared that if her words weren't her decision, she would falter and defer to the capes. "We have to send the message that the guild is still here. That the rules still apply."

No judgment from Ivan, not that he'd have much room to throw stones. He accepted the words with a nod, then made his way over to her side. "Are you sure? The capes won't be long now. By noon, I expect they'd have you."

"Good for me. Not so good for the next person some crooks snatch." She tried to scratch her face, remembering for the umpteenth time that her hands were chained. "For me, this has been frustrating, annoying, inconvenient, and only occasionally scary. If I were a normal human... this is the sort of thing that traumatizes people. Besides, the ringleader here threatened my friends. If anyone deserves to be made an example of, it's him."

A moment of hesitation, then Tori continued. "There is one guy who was nice to me during this. Big fellow, named Darius, seemed to have his head more on his shoulders than the rest. He at least clocked the danger in what they were doing, even if he didn't buy the rumors. I can take a reasonable guess on how this will go, and if there's no survivors, then that's the choice I made. But if there's any wiggle room, Darius probably doesn't deserve to die."

"Your suspicions are no doubt spot on. That said, the guild recognizes that allies can come from unlikely sources. I'll pass the word along. No promises

—these things are chaotic by nature—but you've given him a chance. Luck and Darius himself will decide his path from here."

Ivan hunkered down next to Tori, not truly here, yet so real, she'd have tried to pluck an eyelash if her hands were free. "Let's focus on your part now. Ideally, you'll stay right where you are, hear only the barest of sounds through the door, and be discovered by the capes with no story to tell. Less ideally, things go awry and you have to evacuate. Bahamut, Glyph, and Pest Control will be on hand with me and your armor. On the off chance that things get truly out of hand, it's best people see Hephaestus escaping with known villains rather than Tori."

Her nose wrinkled; something smelled off. "Ivan, tech aside, these people are a rinky-dink crew that could barely pull off a bank heist. Why are you talking like they're going to pull out some secret weapon that can knock the fucking *guild* for a loop? It took Apollo using most of the AHC's forces to manage that."

"True or not, they have access to incredibly high-level concealment technology. Given that they called out a team of capes, we have to assume they've got some offensive gear on that same level. It's only prudent."

After what Tori had watched Fornax do when Ivan let loose, she wasn't quite sure what level of tech would be necessary to stop him, but she was fairly sure these mooks didn't have it. Then again, not everyone in the guild was Fornax, or even Pseudonym, so she supposed a bit of circumspection might be in order. Especially if Ivan was stuck babysitting the newbies.

"Do we need to work out our story ahead of time?"

"Not really a story to give, so long as you tell the truth," Ivan replied. "You were stuck in a room, unable to move, until the AHC arrived to free you. If you heard a strange noise around dawn, what of it? You've got no context for the sound, and no known ability or need to help them, even if you did."

Tori looked around, examining the fractured space they were once more in. "Let me guess: if I mention this part at all, I just say I had some weird dreams."

"I'd avoid it entirely, but that's up to you. My point is you'll be able to tell the truth and walk out of here without issue. The key is in how much truth you tell." Ivan stood from his kneeled position, moving to brush off his slacks, only to realize he wasn't actually there to get dirt on them.

"But that also means we can't loop you in on anything. If all goes well, you'll never see or hear us. Once the AHC releases you, we can fill you in on what happened." Something unusual flickered in Ivan's face. Fear? Shame? Tori couldn't tell. She just knew it was an expression she'd seldom even seen hints of. "One more thing to keep in mind: while, officially, Ivan and Fornax have only the slenderest connection in the form of sealed paperwork stored in a government vault, some of the AHC's higher-ups would know my real identity, since they were around to battle Fornax. If you deal with anyone on the Champions' Congress, stick to the plan, but be aware that they might know the truth about you."

Tori's eyes went wide. "Wait, what? That feels like a pretty damn essential detail to fill me in on. How does that not fuck the entire plan?"

"Because what they know personally and what they can prove in a court of law are different things," Ivan reminded her. "Just don't go offering more than you intend to. That's why I brought it up. Ignorance is a weakness. You'll now be fully abreast of your situation."

Forcing herself to calm down, Tori leaned hard on her logic. It wasn't entirely Ivan's fault; she'd known she was signing on with Fornax from day one. Learning from a legend had come with plenty of perks and a few downsides—this was just one more notch in the latter column. Part of her was chapped that she was only just now getting this variable, but it didn't change things in the larger picture.

The underworld needed a keeper. A limit. A code. And it would have one, a code built by those who knew how to walk the line of criminal and civilian, enforced by some of the most deadly monsters to claim the Earth's surface as their home. Bad a mastermind as he was, Deacon *had* created the perfect stage to send a message. He thought it would be some pissing contest with the capes; instead, his gang would be the warning to the underworld. The monsters were still here, and their claws had a very long reach.

"Appreciate the heads up, though I wouldn't have minded it sooner. Go ahead with the plan. I'll take my chances with the Champions' Congress. Won't be my first time bullshitting my way out of trouble." Ivan nodded, but before he could turn, Tori kept going. "Any advice for that scenario, if it comes up?"

Ivan took his time responding. This was likely the last moment they wouldn't feel the pounding of the clock until the rescue was done. "Quorum will see through any lie or deceit—only use the factual truth around him. If you cannot answer a question in that way, then refuse. You're a victim, not a suspect, at least so far as the public knows. Professor Quantum is unlikely to notice or care that you're in the building beyond a cursory handshake. Don't try to draw his attention, and you won't have it. Lodestar..."

His voice trailed off for a moment, like Ivan's tongue had gotten lost in the journey. "Lodestar will have your best interests at heart. That doesn't mean you should tell her everything, mind you, only that she very rarely uses subterfuge. It makes her both entirely predictable, and incredibly dangerous. No matter how sincere or kind she is, remember that you're still a criminal talking to one who bows to the law. Get too honest, and there's only so many ways it can end."

"Thanks." Had it been anyone else, Tori would have let the conversation end there. But Ivan was her mentor, her teacher, and as her fake uncle, he was the closest thing to family she had left. "This will go well, right? I don't need to worry?"

Sometimes, Ivan let himself forget that Tori's bluster was often just that, the outward lashings of someone who'd had to grow up young and fast. She was less than a decade older than Rick, and already out here facing these kinds of situations with a locked jaw. Of course she was scared deep down; she'd been taken off the damn street and trapped in a strange room. Ivan's blood tried to boil, but he held it in check. Anger was not the tool for this occasion.

"Tori, I don't have much in this life I care about. My children, the guild I helped found, and the few friends I've made along the way. I count you in that last group. You have only seen me fight when I thought someone had taken two of those from me. That is nothing compared to the hell I bring when fighting to keep one of those few people safe."

Ivan didn't approach her again, but he did hunch slightly, making sure they were at eye level across the room, the sea of stars to his back. "You don't need to worry one bit. I know this isn't what you're used to, but the guild is more than a code and a warning of what happens to any who cross it. We are a unified organization, filled with people who want you back for both personal and pride-based reasons. This isn't just your fight anymore. You're part of something bigger. We've got your back."

"Well then, don't keep a lady waiting. These cuffs are starting to chafe."

Just before he disappeared back through the hole, Ivan paused long enough to deliver a quick parting, one last reassurance to tide Tori over.

"See you soon."

Chapter 29

Dawn was coming. Those who lurked in the night knew this feeling well. Night's energy began to wane, the chaos under the moon calming, growing still. Madness and shadow were preparing to fall away, yielding ground to the cleansing light of day. Soon, the sky would turn gray, evening's final grip faltering once more… but not yet. There was darkness left to burn, still time to do things that had no place in the sunshine.

While a large show of force might have been more impressive, that wasn't what tonight was about. This was a mission and a message, which might have tilted it toward a bigger entry team if not for the fact that no survivors would remain to talk about what they saw. For this to work, there couldn't be anyone left to talk, to contradict the guild's fabrication. No, what remained of these overly confident kidnappers would be the message itself, along with the rumors they sent running through the shadows.

Ivan stood in the late summer air, watching a group of what felt like nervous children whispering amongst themselves a small distance off. That was unfair. Tori's fellow new guild members were all adults, and it was hardly their fault that this was their first time rescuing a kidnapped colleague. Nevertheless, he was glad they'd been placed out here on the sidelines. They didn't need to be part of what was coming next. Not when the guild had such talented options to call upon.

Technically speaking, assembling Morgana, Xelas, and Arcanicus, on top of having Ivan dressed as Pseudonym waiting in the wings, was *massive* overkill for a job of this level. Were they simply sending a message out of responsibility, there would never have been a need to call upon so much power in a single location. However, this was not just about keeping crooks in line. Someone had dared to touch a member of the guild. For the safety of everyone who depended on its protection—both the villains and those they loved—such a thing could not stand. Even if no one knew who Tori was now, that might change down the road. One slip-up, one show of weakness; that was all it took to embolden the dumbest, most dangerous of the lot. They would allow no such failing in the guild.

"Credit to them, whatever shit they're using works 'til the end. I can't get a scan on the building," Xelas said. "We're going in blind, unless magic decided to come through."

"Sadly, they appear to have brought in some sort of localized mana disruption generator." Arcanicus, unlike Xelas, seemed slightly pleased by his discovery. "I'd assumed they were using actual magic to shield or obscure their location, but if they're leaning on a tool like that, then odds are strong that none of them wield arcane talents. We can also be sure they don't have anything enchanted in there. The disruption generator would erode the magic over time and turn such items unstable."

Everyone looked a tad relieved. Even having two magic-users of their own, keeping the mystic arts out of battle made things more predictable. A potent magical-meta could really throw normal fights for a loop, their results often only outdone by the reality warpers like Captain Bullshit. Despite that, technically speaking, his power wasn't magic. He'd once turned almost the entire world into living stuffed animals for an hour, though, so it was certainly something.

"No magic means we can sling a few spells ourselves, unless that generator will cause you issues?" Morgana wore her blood-red armor tonight, markedly different simply in that she was the only one of the three who had come to this soiree in different clothes. Xelas favored the natural steel look, and Arcanicus seemed like the kind of man born in his draping wizard robes. Sometimes Ivan wondered where Morgana got the blood to start her costumes, but he'd been around long enough to know that there were questions best left unanswered.

The question earned a scoff from Arcanicus. "I am no paltry practitioner just learning his spells. My magic can more than hold up to such technology, certainly long enough to see the task through."

While Arcanicus was showing his age, and had been for some while, no one questioned the claim. In his prime, he'd been one of the most formidable casting metas the world had ever seen. Even weakened by the bastard known as time, his arcane knowledge was among the most well-developed in the world. Whatever estimations he made of his power, they were going to be accurate.

"Two entrances. Let's assume both are guarded. Morgana goes with Arcanicus, who magics them sneakily up to the front while I come tearing in through the back. We punch in, taking out enemies and hunting the package. Pseudonym stays out here with the rescue team. Any enemies get out, he picks them off. If we discover the package is in danger, we relay a location to Pseudonym, who will secure it and then hand it off to the rescue team, covering their exit while the rest of us finish the job. Any questions?"

New members sometimes wondered why an entity as seemingly half-cracked as Xelas was in a position of leadership. The older ones knew better. They'd been around long enough to see what happened when Xelas stopped laughing. Once she got serious, the bodies piled up fast.

"Do we have any more information on the one we're supposed to spare besides the name and the fact he's big?" Morgana asked.

Pseudonym shook his head. "That was all she had time to tell me. From the footage of the kidnapping, there appears to only be the one. If it becomes a problem..."

"I know. Nicety, not a priority. He's still lumped in with these blood sacks." Morgana held out her hand, a chunk of red armor on her arm re-liquefying and curling up, shaping itself into a sword before it hardened once more. "Councilors, are you ready?"

"Ready." Arcanicus already had a spell half-woven in his hands, tendrils of blue light winding around him and Morgana both.

"Ready." Xelas's eyes lit up, and several panels on her body shifted alignment. When the assault came, few even had a chance to see which of her weapons was the one that struck them down.

"Ready." Pseudonym cast his eyes to the new guild members. Bahamut was clutching a suitcase tightly to her scaly chest. They were scared for their friend, and not without good reason. But they were also scared for what was about to happen. Large-scale slaughter still affected them. Deep down, Ivan envied that.

Morgana tilted her blade toward the building. "Let's go show these bastards what happens to any who challenge our guild."

A pair of twos. All day playing intermittent poker to pass the time, and this was one of the better hands he'd gotten. Darius was starting to wonder if he'd busted a mirror recently, because luck did not seem to be with him.

With one eye always on Deacon, as a good bodyguard should, he raised some paperclips. Playing with cash was impractical, especially around other criminals, so cheap office supplies had long ago become the stand-in. One of the many tricks he'd found in his years doing this sort of work.

TV was favored by many to pass the hours, but Darius found it too dangerous. Anything that lulled a brain into complacency was working against them. Games, especially ones with stakes, kept minds active and sharp. Losing focus meant losing money, and this was not the sort of crowd to easily part with their pennies. Sometimes, punches were thrown, yet even that was good to keep the blood pumping, so long as the tussles were ended swiftly.

Across the table, his opponents were examining their own options. Did they look nervous? Keeping his expectations in check, Darius wondered if this might actually be a stronger hand than he'd known. If they were weak, this could be the time to push, to put that luck of his to the test for—

The explosion came from the rear entrance without warning. Too loud, *far* too loud for what would have been required to knock out that door. And if something had been approaching, unless it was coming stupid fast, their guy watching the cameras would have noticed. Had... had someone fired a missile into their door? That seemed crazy, yet it was the only explanation that made immediate sense.

Moving on instinct, Darius was already up, shielding Deacon with his considerable size. "Boss, we need to go."

"One explosion doesn't mean the fight is lost," Deacon protested. "We've got weaponry these capes aren't expecting; our battle has only just begun." As he spoke, the others were already scrambling for their borrowed gear—heaps of cobbled-together components shaped roughly into usable tools. A few were already turned on, letting out low-level hums or gaining glows along their blades.

Maybe, if it had been capes, Deacon would have been right. It didn't matter, though, as something that used to be a person came stumbling into the room before Darius's eyes. Half its flesh was roasted off; crackling sparks ran along its exposed bone, until balance failed and it landed in a heap of smoking bones and meat. The final vestiges of life faded as its skinless hand reached for them, finally falling limp.

"Capes don't kill people like that. We have to go *now*."

Not waiting for permission, Darius scooped his employer up and raced deeper into the building. He was just around the corner when he heard the front door—in the room where they'd been playing cards moments before—slam heavily open. After that, it was hard to make out anything over the screaming. Instant, horrific, and impossibly sustained. Whatever was happening, someone was making it hurt.

"She was right. Fuck me, she was right the whole time." Rumors. Whispers. Stories that big crime bosses tell up-and-coming conquerors to keep them in line. Except this wasn't a cape raid. Darius had seen plenty of those, had even been rounded up in a few. The AHC didn't come in melting flesh and exploding doors. This left only one plausible explanation: the stories were true, and the guild wasn't as out of commission as he'd thought.

"That woman did this?" Deacon snapped, trying to look up from his position under Darius's arm.

"More like she knew it would happen." Zipping around a corner, Darius heard horrified yells coming from the left, and silence from the right. Right it was, then. He took the turn with minimal loss of momentum. Without realizing it, Darius had put himself on a path to Emory's quarters. As the only two decent metas and bodyguards, they had the best chance of fighting their way out, minimal though that was starting to seem.

Perhaps there was another way. Tori hadn't been especially subtle, hinting that she knew more than she was letting on. If it wasn't all fake, wasn't all just shit-talking, then maybe she could do something, say something. He was grasping at straws and was perfectly aware of that, but straws were all he had to grab in the moment.

Darius slapped open Emory's door, shattering the lock and revealing a room with a spray of clothing and bedsheets coating its floor. The noise must have woken Emory up, and he'd gone looking for them. Damn it. No time to search, not without a lead. They'd head for Tori's cell and hope to run into him on the way.

"Don't worry, boss, I got you. We'll make it through this." Wishing he felt even a fraction as sure as his voice sounded, Darius sprinted off once more, hoping against hope that his shitty luck had worn itself out on the poker table.

The clucking "tsks" sounded not quite right as Nexus strolled along the near empty hallway, stepping over a smoldering leg. Too easy, that was the problem. These goons might have had top-tier concealment tech, but the weapons they'd been sold weren't nearly of the same caliber. Against average metas, sure, a double-chamber anti-ion blast would do some real damage. Facing down three councilors of the guild? A white flag would give one a better chance of survival. In some versions, they got the really good stuff, and while those fights ended the same, they were at least more fun to watch.

Reaching a hand out, Nexus ran his fingertips along the walls. Where they touched, a seam opened, revealing a swirling mass of colors and chaos not unlike his kaleidoscope eyes. From the shifting realms came a form, big as a wolf, long like a snake, armored like an insect, and with many-toothed mouths at both ends. One end opened, firing a stream of pink liquid that bubbled and hissed the moment it touched concrete, dissolving the material in seconds. More beings followed, some locking mouths, working together, rolling and slithering in a wholly unnatural way as they scattered throughout the building.

These would certainly not be enough to make any difference in the fight. Nexus reeled at the memories of what it actually took to put down these three. Other worlds, other days, he'd seen the carnage they could call upon when threatened. Eventually, they wore down, yet the results always had major, lasting consequences on that iteration. Universes like this one, versions with *multiple* Singulars, had to be managed more delicately. One true indulgence today might cost years of entertainment down the line. This was just something to add a little spice to the morning's events.

Nexus continued along the hallway, ignoring the sounds of slithering invaders as he headed to his next viewing location. There were still a few turning points left to observe, and he loathed coming in late to these things. It never felt as good as catching it from the start.

Chapter 30

Picking off survivors was far from Morgana's idea of a good time, or even a sporting challenge, but then, that's why this wasn't a job for the heroic metas.

From behind a wall, two men came leaping, both holding technological weaponry. It made no difference. She'd already felt the blood in their veins long before drawing close, and as they moved, she took control of it, turning their inner liquid into blades and spears that came bursting out of their flesh. Morgana took care to mangle their bodies, ensuring that an autopsy would give nothing away. There was a time to work in secret, a time to leave a trace, and knowing the difference often defined who went to jail versus who walked free.

A new noise came from behind her. Whipping around, Morgana formed a shield of blood out of the two bodies' contribution to her pool. Pink liquid struck, popping and sizzling, actually managing to burn through some of her defenses.

"What in the hells...?" A single glance answered her question. Three unnatural creatures, slapping and rolling and slithering with disgusting speed, were coming to join a fourth with a drip of pink liquid falling from its front mouth—or at least, the mouth that was in front at this particular moment. Neither seemed especially dominant, and worse, whatever was in these otherworldly creatures wasn't blood.

"Arcanicus, looks like we've got interlopers. Maybe part of their defense, but it wouldn't be my bet. Can you send word out to Pseudonym that things might get complicated?"

"Of course." Arcanicus raised his hands, creating a circle of white fire around the four monsters. In moments, the fire rushed inward, surging over all of them. It took a full minute for them to burn, by the end of which Arcanicus had completed sending his mystical message. Given that they were walking into a place blocking all tech, magical relay had made the most sense for communicating.

His gaze turned worried as he looked on, noting the smoldering remains. "These things are hardier than they look. Bonefire would cook a normal human in seconds, someone like Thuggernaut in a half-minute, tops."

Sudden, strange creatures appearing on the scene fit several old metas' methods, but those would all be a stretch. The most obvious answer was usually right, and with this, Nexus may as well have signed his name on one of the creatures. He very well might have, in fact; it wasn't like he cared much for subtlety.

"Should we find Xelas?" Since their robotic colleague was entirely formed of technology, her ability to interact with magic was limited, and that included mystical messages. It was a risk they'd realized going in; however, given the limitations of the job, there was no avoiding it.

Arcanicus stroked his beard twice, then his head shook. "If I can handle them, she'll be fine. The larger job is purging these things before any make their way to the package. I doubt they will show a kidnapper's restraint."

"Pushing on it is." Morgana reached out, feeling the next sacks of waiting blood. She'd have to be more careful now; there were entities in the mix she couldn't instantly destroy. There might have been, perhaps, a hint of a smile on Morgana's face as she adjusted the grip on her sword.

Now *this* was a little more entertaining.

The clang of the door unlocking startled Tori. She had no way of gauging the time precisely, but it had been long enough that she knew the moment was drawing close. Though this felt early, it was also a good sign. The capes must be here to set her free. Affecting a weary, scared expression was harder than she expected, especially when she had to hurry to compose herself as the door pushed open. She didn't end up doing a very good job, not that it mattered. The man standing before her was certainly not a cape.

"They put you in this one? Curious. Usually, you're a few doors down."

Nexus stepped back, checking the hallway like a lost tourist, then shrugging in acceptance. "Oh well. The surprises are what make it interesting."

"Why do you always show up at the worst times?" Tori wasn't sure when the madman's presence had turned from shocking development to occasional annoyance. Maybe she just didn't have the spare energy to spend on him right now.

He wagged a finger at her, something she'd only seen from old professors and bad television. "Not the worst parts, the fun parts. The bits worth seeing. True, some are better than others, but even on the rewatch, I don't like to skip anything… especially since the details are never *quite* the same. Don't worry. You rarely die in all this."

The door began to close once more, going just slow enough for her to hear Nexus's parting words. "Of course, I also don't usually bring along acid-spitting friends. I wonder how that will impact things."

The door shut loudly; however, there was no sound of it locking. Nexus wasn't worried about her escaping—wasn't worried about anything at all, most likely. More force of nature than person, he was a long-standing thorn that countless wanted to pull out, yet no one had succeeded. Today wasn't the time to worry about Nexus. More concerning was whatever it was he'd let loose, and how it was going to impact the rescue mission.

Taking a deep breath, Tori forced herself to stay calm and ignore her now unlocked door. This wasn't about escape; a door could never have held her if she'd opted to leave. It was about building a story, a message, and an alibi all in one go. The others had her back. She just needed to trust that they'd be able to handle whatever bumps Nexus put in the way.

It wasn't a terribly hard leap of faith, knowing her guild and its power. If anything, she started to wonder what was taking so long.

"Come on... come on... finally!" Xelas pulled her finger from the massive computer tower, a USB port vanishing as her digit reformed. Though there were receivers and components spread throughout the building, she'd needed to find the digital heart for her side mission. There was no shame in someone else creating tech that rivaled the guild's; such was the nature of progress and innovation. However, there was no way they were dealing with this a second time. Xelas had just downloaded all the software and schematics, her ocular sensors scanning every component that wasn't shielded. They'd have to do a little guesswork here and there, but that was no major hurdle for her and Doctor Mechaniacal.

One piece caught her attention in particular. Directly at the center of the machine, buried deep in its core, was a box that read like a black hole. It was so shielded and dense that it had to be intentional, some sort of lure meant to draw in the too-curious. Another time, she might have probed further. Today was not the time to risk a trap, however. One of their own had been taken, and they needed to make clear why that was a horrendous idea.

Xelas turned the corner just in time to see a pair of tube-like monsters joined at the mouth slide past the door she'd exited. The pair slapped around, what looked like nine tongues coming out of each mouth to taste the air, walls, and concrete. No reaction. Probably didn't distinguish her as a life form. It wasn't uncommon with interlopers; they reacted to the biological because it was what they were familiar with.

Choosing a midrange weapon, Xelas shot the one on the right, the bolt from her shoulder searing and wounding it, but not finishing the job. Tough little bastards; that would have gone clean through a car. Pink liquid shot out from the left one's mouth, a stream that Xelas easily dodged. This time, she picked something with more stopping power. A flash of yellow as the beam struck, and now the one on the left was sliced cleanly in two.

More pink gushed from its insides, ruining the flooring. Another blast to finish off the right one, which was unhooking its connected mouth from its now dead cohort. It never had time to finish before her beam hit.

"These'll liven things up." Xelas was already moving, acutely aware that the introduction of an unknown factor could spin their plans out of control. She moved so fast, in fact, that Xelas missed what came only half a minute after the monsters were killed.

That's how long it took for the new flesh to start growing.

Careening down a hall, Darius ducked into an alcove to catch his breath. He set Deacon down, eyes peeled for whoever was cutting down their gang at a rapid clip. They were still a ways off from Tori's cell—some of the screaming had forced them on a circuitous route. Not knowing what they were up against, Darius couldn't risk engaging, especially with the boss in tow.

"You need a break already?" Despite his people being roasted and butchered, Deacon was somehow more angry than sad or scared.

"If I'm gassed and need to defend you, we're as good as done." A noise caught Darius's ears: movement, action... was someone fighting? They were directly across from the room with some free weights and chairs, jokingly called "the gym" by everyone here. Was it possible one of the others had survived? "Hang on, we might have backup."

Darius had only gotten a few steps when Deacon's hand grabbed his arm. "Absolutely not. Whatever is happening in there is none of our concern. Do your job, bodyguard. Get me to the girl so we can put an end to this."

While both a professional and a veteran at working for dickheads, Darius did have his limits. Suddenly finding himself fighting for survival stole of lot of the energy he usually dedicated toward patience. Perhaps that was why he snapped up Deacon by the neck and pinned him to the wall.

"Put an end to this? Look around, you egotistical nut. This is over. It's been over from the moment you convinced us to steal a civilian off the street. Do you think we're coming back from this? Those screams aren't just noises. Those are your people! My friends! And it's your fault we're in this mess."

Only... was it? Deacon was ignorant of the rules or blinded by ambition. Darius had neither excuse. He'd known the risks, heard the warnings, and still hadn't managed to turn Deacon from these tactics. If anyone was responsible for all this, it might very well be Darius himself.

Releasing his grip, the big meta allowed Deacon to drop back to the ground, where he immediately scrambled to his feet and dashed off. Most likely to his death, though there was always the chance he'd wriggle free. Rats had a talent for survival.

With Deacon out of the way, Darius's attention was drawn back to the noises from the gym. He ripped the door clean off, unveiling a very curious-looking fight. Emory was darting around, avoiding a trio of two-headed nightmare snakes spitting sizzling pink goo. Occasionally, he'd whip a free weight at one, but the damned things could dodge with hideous grace.

Not one to waste time, Darius hefted up the first weight he could find and slammed it down onto the nearest snake head.

It definitely left an impact—cracks along the head were dripping pink goop—however, the blow wasn't enough to crush the head completely. Given Darius's size and strength, that said a lot about how durable these things were, as well as how fucked the gang might be. If his strength wasn't enough, and Emory's venom would presumably be limited on their anatomy, then this was a bad fight. There was no way to win; they'd just wear down until someone made a mistake.

"Emory, we need to go." At his words, the monsters seemed to grow more active. Did they understand, or just realize more prey was in the room?

"Tried that. They spray down the exit if I get near. I think they've locked in on me as prey."

The dissolved sections of room made it obvious what that pink stuff did, even if Darius couldn't see it happening for himself as one sprayed toward Emory. Four of them, two mouths apiece, with only one being a little smashed up. Too many streams. The creatures could cover every angle. This was a fight they couldn't win, or escape, especially presuming that there were more enemies still to account for—unless these creatures could also create explosions and roast skin.

"I've got an idea!" Darius leapt into the room proper, dodging a spray of pink as he arrived at Emory's side. "Give me your hand, quick!"

Just like a good student, Emory did as instructed. Darius didn't hesitate. He jerked Emory into a bear-hug, wrapping his sizable heft around the smaller crook. After that, Darius was running. He heard the sounds of the jaws opening while he was still ten feet from the door. The first stream hit as he was crossing through, with a second and third right on its heels. Pain came quickly, his clothes turning to nothing, exposing his flesh. Like most burly metas, Darius was tough on top of being big, something he was counting on to buy them both extra steps.

Unfortunately, one of streams hit his left leg, slowing the run down considerably. Darius could hear the monsters following, slapping and slithering as they gave chase, fresh sprays of pink searing his back. The acid was stronger than he'd expected, a realization that came as his legs began to buckle.

No. They weren't far enough yet. They needed to get away, to give Emory a head start, a fighting chance. Darius was still trying to push himself forward when his legs suddenly went numb. The goo must have gotten a piece of his spine. Part of Darius wanted to see how much of his back even remained, but he knew it was a sight that would haunt the short remainder of his life.

Legs gone, arms wrapped around a struggling Emory, and monsters drawing close. This was looking bleak. Then came a flash of yellow to his left and squeals of pain from behind.

Glancing back, Darius saw all the monsters sliced up, carved neatly down their centers. Looking forward again, he discovered himself looking up at the form of Xelas. Famous for many reasons, not the least of which was her affiliation to the guild at the center of the Ridge City Riots.

It was all true. The legends, the warnings, the secret cabal patrolling the underground. All of it real, and Darius had ignored the warnings. He was already dead, his body in the process of dissolving from interloper acid. He wasn't gone just yet, though. There might still be time to save one.

"Please... he's just a kid. My fault all this happened. I knew. I knew, and I ignored, but he didn't. He was only starting... didn't know... my fault. *My* fault."

Darius continued to whisper the words as his voice grew hoarse. They slipped from his mouth while Xelas leaned down, chose a precise spot on the skull, and struck. No more words, or pain, as he dropped limply to the ground. Big guy, showing concern for others; this was definitely the one Tori said to spare if they could.

Flipping him over, Xelas revealed another meta, one with serpent-like physical markings. He was scared and panicked, not shocking since a friend of his had just died on top of him. Snap judgment time. They didn't owe this guy shit, especially considering the circumstances. But Darius had been the one Tori asked be spared, and he'd given his life to save the kid. Logic said the smartest path was to kill him here and get on with the job. Xelas was more than a mere robot, however. She could see past the simple logic, taking into account that Darius had been decent enough that Tori wanted to save him, and that he'd died helping a friend.

Humans talked a lot of crap about love, loyalty, and honor. Most of it was just that, too: pure shit, fantasies to make themselves feel like better people than they were. Every now and then, however, one would actually live up to those lofty ideals, if only for a moment. Seeing those instances was one of Xelas's favorite parts of being around their kind, watching their own self-serving fiction catalyze into reality. Maybe this guy was worth saving, most likely he wasn't. That would be up to him to decide, though.

One shot from the mini-injector cannon was all it took to knock the new prisoner out. Xelas slung him over her shoulder, preparing to resume the search for Tori. However, getting positioned took long enough that by the time she was ready to move on, Xelas noticed movement coming from the bisected monster corpses. Specifically, she noticed the new limbs and body parts growing at an incredible rate.

"Oh, fuck me. I just had to pick today to get a pet." Emory still unconscious on her shoulder, Xelas ran off down the nearest hall, wondering if she'd find a way to warn the others.

Chapter 31

"Sir."

The aide stood at the door, waiting for permission to enter the office. When Professor Quantum was working, he loathed to be interrupted; however, this was a Priority One message. No wiggle room on these. It had to be brought to a member of the Champions' Congress. Quorum and Lodestar were out in the field, meaning that only Professor Quantum was immediately on hand.

It took a full two minutes before Professor Quantum looked up from the desk where he was tinkering with some curious device. Silently, he waved the aide in. He didn't even make eye contact, instead staring at the place where the messenger would stand.

She took the order, striding over and opening the page in her hands. "Sir, there was a wild dimensional breach detected. Seems to have come from Michigan, near the Detroit area. Something interfered with the reading, so we're having trouble pinpointing the location."

"Interesting." That wasn't just a canned reply. For the first time, Professor Quantum appeared to be paying attention to the conversation. "Our dimension doesn't experience wild breaches anymore. The most common instances now are metas accidentally creating rips, and Nexus, with the latter considerably outweighing the former."

The aide's face paled. "Oh no. Not today. We still haven't recovered that woman, and now Nexus is on the move?"

"Unlikely. His big displays are more overt. Nexus is like a carrion fly, drawn to the scent of blood." Professor Quantum considered for a moment longer. "Push some of our resources into searching Detroit, and start moving assets there. I have a hunch that might just be where we find our missing civilian."

"Yes, sir." The aide paused, looking at the Priority Three alert also on the page. Technically, this one didn't require immediate attention, but if she told him now, she could skip going through this again later. "One more thing, probably not related. Some of our monitoring tech caught a message being fired into space less than an hour ago. We couldn't see what it said, only that one went out."

"Not many terrestrial devices capable of that. I'll consider it." Professor Quantum went back to his project, a not-so-subtle way of ending the conversation.

That was fine by the aide. She was more than ready to leave. It wasn't even dawn, and this was already shaping into a hell of day.

"Holy crap!"

Morgana spun around to find Arcanicus staring at two hideous monsters. A mound of grasping claws, with a body covered in mouths endlessly opening and closing, one head rising off the back like a scorpion's tail. A familiar head, at that. It looked like one of the snake creatures, only hacked in half and stuck on top of something even more disgusting.

"Sweet sorcery, that made my heart skip a beat." Arcanicus gestured and a wall of Bonefire appeared between him and the creatures. It was just in time as the body's dozen mouths opened, firing streams of pink liquid in every direction. The bits that hit his magic walls sizzled and hissed. Potent acid though it might be, the defenses of a guild councilor were not so easily broken. "Do you think they're evolving?"

"Adapting would be my guess. Maybe they're like worms, regrowing a body that's been cut in half. Only they do it in their own terrible way." Morgana looked through the flames. The first versions had been the size of normal dogs. These ones were closer to mastiffs. "Burn them to ash. We can't take chances. Then give Pseudonym the update. These things probably won't stay in the building for long."

"Should we adjust the plan? Might not be safe to leave the package for extraction."

That was a damn good question, one Morgana wished she had a quick answer for. Nexus had, as Nexus often did, fucked things up considerably. They still had dead gang members to put in place, but the tale they'd been spinning was muddled. First, they needed to make sure Tori was safe. After they'd completed the rescue, they could decide how to manage the spin.

Though Morgana didn't know it, the interlopers had already begun to spill from the building. Much as Ivan wanted to leave them be, knowing that dead creatures outside the building would raise questions, he couldn't risk one of them escaping into the night. These entities couldn't last long here—even getting through to this plane of existence was only thanks to Nexus—but they were capable of serious destruction with the time they had.

"Glyph, seal off the back door. Pest Control, get us some eyes. Bahamut, set down the suitcase. You're with me."

In a blink, both literal and magical, Ivan appeared in front of the first creature. A spray of pink shot out, just as Arcanicus had warned. He didn't even bother to dodge, letting it fizzle ineffectively off his wards. Picking up the nearest monster, Ivan grabbed both heads and squeezed. It took more force than he'd been expecting, but both soon popped like he'd gripped a juice box too hard. More pink dripped down his hands, not that it mattered. The wards were just to protect his costume; this sort of attack wasn't even capable of hurting him.

"Bahamut, do you have any sort of immunity to acid?"

"Not that I know of." She was almost to his side already, quite fast in her green dragon form. "Just kind of tough, in general."

Expected, but not ideal. "Then you're on crowd control. Dodge the acid, but keep them corralled. Throw them back toward me, if needed. Once Glyph seals off the rear exit, this will be the funnel they all come through. Be ready for a rush at any time."

"Shouldn't we be going after Tori? You know, now that there are crazy acid monsters, it seemed like maybe the plan might be scrapped."

"Perhaps, perhaps not. We needed a scapegoat for the capes to look at. Nexus works as well as the gang did. Better, in some ways, since he was actually part of this." Ivan grabbed another creature and popped both heads. He was going faster, now that he knew the amount of strength required. "Regardless, that's up to the ones inside. We help by clearing them a safe exit, and ensuring the message isn't muddled by one of these things escaping and melting a hospital."

That seemed to placate her, for a moment. "What if she's in trouble? What if she calls for help?"

"Then I'll rip the building in half and be at her side in an instant." No laughter or ego in that statement. It was purely factual, and Bahamut could see that. Just because they were using the delicate method now didn't mean they could switch to force if needed. They were both excellent tactics in a villain's toolkit.

Darting past one of the creatures, Bahamut gripped it by the middle and hurled it toward Ivan, who snagged it from the air and crushed it between his hands, seemingly without effort. "If that happens, bring me along."

"Sorry, but no. Not how we work. You want to be there with me in a moment like that?" Ivan dropped the mangled corpse to the ground, where its pink blood immediately began to dissolve the grass, despite leaving Ivan's hands unblemished. "Become strong enough to get there yourself."

This time, there was no preamble or warning. The door swung open, not quite powerfully enough to bang against the wall. To be fair, it was a heavy one, and Deacon was not a man burdened by excess muscle.

He looked like hell, which was honestly still better than Tori had expected by this point. She'd assumed he'd be crushed, melted, skewered—really it was just a question of who the guild had sent that would determine what form his death would take. Yet somehow, here he was, panicked and trying his damnedest to get the door shut once more.

"Things not going great? Feels early for another bathroom break. You don't want to spoil me."

"Shut the fuck up!" Deacon whipped around at her, snapping the words. He was way off-kilter, not that he'd seemed overly stable to begin with. This was a step beyond, though. Between Nexus popping up and the guild being there, she didn't know exactly what was going down, but she could make some fair assumptions.

Behind her back, Tori phased her left wrist into fire form for a split second, letting the metal cuff slip through, catching it in her right hand before it could fall and rattle the chain. This felt like a situation where having both hands and not being stuck to a chair might be advantageous, but she didn't want to play her cards just yet. If she was doing this, then she was going all the way. And there was one major question she wanted answered before Deacon was off the board.

"Seems like it's just you and me. No underlings or goons to impress. Be honest: how did you get blocking equipment good enough to stall the AHC?"

"Why the hell would I tell you that? Why I would help *you* at all?" Deacon was scouring his pockets, refusing to face the harsh realization that he didn't have a key to lock the door with.

"Because it's pretty obvious that whoever gave you that tech knew you'd fail. They were using you. No idea for what, but this plan was doomed from the jump, and anyone smart enough to build that kind of shit could probably see it."

Fury boiled up in Deacon's eyes as he stalked across the room, glowering down at Tori. "I have had enough of your mouth, enough of your hollow courage, enough of *you*. You may very well be right; I probably will die here with the rest of my crew. But at least I can take those flapping gums of yours with me."

And just like that, he reached in to choke her.

It might have scared Tori, if he'd been faster or more aggressive, but ultimately, Deacon didn't have any practice at this. Anger was carrying him past where his normal boldness would have faltered. Tori let him come, adjusting her grip on the cuff slightly, pushing the ratchet all the way through until the cuff was open again. She let him get his hands around her neck, waited until he'd begun to squeeze in earnest. His eyes locked, he was set on the task at hand.

That was when Tori struck, driving the sharp ratchet arm of her open cuff directly into Deacon's left leg. She yanked it out just as his screams began to bubble forth and his grip loosened, which made her kick to his stomach land all the harder.

He stumbled back, coughing and clutching his wounded leg, while Tori stood from her chair.

"You... bitch..."

"Hey, count yourself lucky. I was aiming for your crotch, my angle was just shit." At long last, Tori's own rage could show itself. These people had taken her off the street, threatened her life, the lives of her friends, and even tried to kill her at the end. Worst of all, because of them, she'd had to see something she'd have been happier not knowing. This incident had shown Tori the truth of their world. Capes weren't enough. It needed horrors, demons, unfathomable monsters who still had things to protect. People outside of morality, yet not ones who'd completely lost their humanity.

The world needed villains.

Tori let the other half of the cuffs phase off her wrist, setting them down on the chair. "It's funny that you're blaming me for all of this. How many different ways did I say to let me go or everyone would die?"

There weren't even words this time, just a guttural scream as Deacon charged, swinging wildly. He was better than she'd expected, but that didn't mean he was good. Not compared to someone with guild training and Tori's own experience.

She sidestepped the charge, tripping him and pushing his skull so he went careening into the chair. Both landed with a clatter, though the chair wasn't bleeding from its head.

"Not so easy when you have to throw the punches, is it?" Tori stalked closer to him. "I always hated your kind. The 'mastermind' who sits on a throne of inactivity while everyone else gets their hands dirty. I've seen so many gangs like this, so many kings of tiny kingdoms who mistake their groups' power for their own."

"The fuck are you talking about?" Deacon had stopped rubbing his stomach and was trying to stand once more. "You work in a downtown office."

Tori made no move to stop him from rising. She wanted him back on his feet. "People have secrets. Some you can't find through even the most dedicated web-browsing. You're supposed to be a smart one. Have you pieced together mine yet?"

Slowly, Deacon found his balance, standing despite his wounds and exhaustion. Had Tori liked him, she might have found the gesture inspiring. Instead, it just made for a more convenient position. This time, she planned to get her angles right.

"Meta-human, obviously." He spit blood from his mouth a few times. Evidently, he'd gathered quite a bit during that chair collision. "Of all the fucking luck, we ended up taking a meta."

"Oh no, that would have been much better for you." Tori walked closer. "See, there was only one true lie I told during the so-called interrogation. It was never *them* coming from the shadows to get you. It was *us*."

She grabbed him by the back of the head, leading Deacon to struggle. One punch just below the sternum put a quick end to that, however. He was gasping now, trying so hard to draw in breath. Perfect. Lifting her right arm, Tori turned the entire appendage into living flame.

"You didn't just kidnap a civilian, or a meta, or a cape's friend. You stepped into the ring with real villains. This was the only way it could have ended."

Her arm rammed past his lips and teeth, down the throat, reached all the way down into his lungs. The air inside them roasted instantly, the organs themselves soon catching fire, along with the rest of Deacon. Tori held it like that until he was truly alight—this was no time for half-measures—then pulled her arm out, returning it to normal form.

The burning body of Deacon collapsed. Mostly likely, he was already dead. If not, he'd cross over soon. Just in case, Tori decided to leave him with some parting words.

"Sorry, pal, but you know the expression: if you can't stand the heat, don't *fuck* with Hephaestus."

Chapter 32

No sleep, barely any food, and eyes blurring between blinks. Donald had stopped short of donning a diaper, but he'd also waited so long between bathroom breaks that there were a few close calls and one photo finish. It didn't feel especially dignified or heroic to be locked in his room with Ren playing *Constable Fluffers* nonstop for hours on end, yet it was without question the best way Donald could spend his time.

Deep down, he was kicking himself. All these months, his efforts had been targeted toward field work, leveling up items and training skills he needed to be out there fighting the good fight. Only today, faced with his own utter helplessness, did Donald realize how much more there was to doing his job. Finding people in need, getting to them, securing and transporting criminals, helping the injured—it was never-ending the more he thought about it. He'd fallen into a pattern without realizing it, gotten too comfortable in the routine. It was time to widen his training scope, add some new abilities to the arsenal. After Tori was safe, of course.

It was just at the cusp of dawn when Donald stumbled into the room where he and Ren had met with the Champions' Congress less than twenty-four hours prior. Professor Quantum was the only one of the main three there, though there was a flurry of other members zipping around him. Donald was too exhausted to even recognize masks, let alone recall names. He only had eyes for the man at the top.

"Sir, Mr. Professor Quantum..."

No response, or even a glance in his direction. What the hell was going on? Turning, Donald saw Ren talking to another cape. Normal Donald might have found the patience to wait until he was called upon. This version of Donald, the one running on no sleep and wracked with fear for his friend, wasn't quite so willing to wait.

"She's in Detroit!" He yelled the words, not especially concerned with the stares coming his way. Only one set of eyes in this room mattered, and mercifully, they did indeed swivel in his direction.

Stepping away from his conversation, Professor Quantum was there in only a few of his long-legged strides. "I see. And how did you come to this conclusion?"

"Just like I said I would. Played my game all day, got the magnifying glass, and used it." Donald didn't even have the strength to be intimidated. He just rattled off the truth as coherently as he could. "I checked it twice, same results. She's somewhere in Detroit."

Professor Quantum looked hard at Donald, giving him true attention in a way that made the younger meta uncomfortable. "This is your one chance. If you've spoken to someone, gotten an inside track, I assure you, I'll uncover it. Now, for the last time: you're saying you found her, even when the entirety of the AHC's methods had failed?"

"No. I'm saying she's in Detroit. That's a long way off from finding her."

"Hmm." One wave of Professor Quantum's hand and an aide was at his side. "This is the second time your power has accomplished something past what I'd expected. I dislike giving credit when not well-earned, but I detest being wrong. It seems I must adjust my measurement of your capabilities, Cyber Geek. We shall deal with that at another time. For now, you're heading to the med bay for recovery."

Donald almost reached out to touch Professor Quantum, then thought better of it. "Please, no. I want to be there. I want to help save her. I want to make sure she's all right."

The stare that met his pleas was unyielding. No pity, no sense of understanding, an absolute denial. The voice, however, made at least an effort toward comfort. "Your wish to be there is misguided. Given your condition, putting you in the field is more likely to cause problems than help solve them. You want her safe and saved? I cannot promise what her condition is. However, I can say this much: Lodestar and Quorum are both standing by for the moment we have a location."

There was nowhere left to take the argument. Donald certainly couldn't claim that, even at his peak, he'd be a contributing factor when two members of the Champions' Congress would be there. At Donald's current skill level, Professor Quantum was honestly right. It was more likely he'd be a liability than any sort of help. It was just... he'd finally become the kind of person who could jump in to make a difference, but when it was personal, he was on the sidelines.

"Donald, you gave them a location. You made a difference."

The fact that he hadn't even noticed Ren approach proved Professor Quantum's point, even as the older man was shaking his head. "Actually, we've known about Detroit for approximately twenty minutes. But I expect we'll be calling on that ability of yours in the future. While I had my doubts, it shows promise to be useful."

Someone called out what sounded like random numbers, drawing Professor Quantum's instant attention. He didn't even look at them, simply turned and walked away. As the aide gently took Donald's arm, leading him off toward the med bay, the bespectacled man leaned in, whispering in Donald's ear.

"For reference, 'useful' is one of the nicest things he says about anyone. Believe it or not, I think you impressed him."

Nice as that was to hear, Donald didn't feel especially impressive. He wanted to be there, part of the rescue, to see her safe. One all-nighter, and he was down for the count. Too weak, again. This couldn't keep happening. Cyber Geek was going to have to get stronger.

The plan was good and well-fucked, that much was obvious. Between Nexus being here and the smoldering corpse in her room, the original cover story was going to need some tweaks. Tori turned toward the door, making it only a few steps before it felt as if the ground fell away. Her head swam, a sensation almost like pain hitting her right in the forehead. Initially, she tried to push it away, before remembering the last time something like this had happened. Not a hard recollection to call upon, seeing as it had only been a few hours.

Mentally relaxing, Tori felt the not-quite-pain flare, then vanish. Moments later, she heard a familiar voice. Not in her ears, however. This was purely in her mind.

Listen carefully. This is Pseudonym. Arcanicus is acting as a magical relay from inside the dampening field, but we still need to make this quick. Nexus showed up unexpectedly, complicating matters. After a quick discussion, we only see two paths forward. You can leave with us now; we have your suit. Or you could destroy the dampening equipment, summoning the AHC. With Nexus in play, you can claim to have escaped in the chaos.

What a choice. Leave now, and risk all the questions that point might raise with the capes—to say nothing if the media ever found out that Tori had magically gone missing from her own kidnapping. Or fight her way past whatever it was Nexus let loose and hope to make it through an AHC interrogation. Tori examined the situation, taking in as many factors as she could account for.

Ultimately, it was her status as a kidnapped civilian that made the call. Right now, she was a victim, someone who'd been targeted because of her association to the capes. That would make it difficult for them to push her too hard. She'd have the public's sympathy, and the AHC was already working to win back the people. If she changed the dynamic, it almost certainly wouldn't be as favorable: Plucky victim who saved herself by vanishing mysteriously from the site of a slaughter.

Closing her eyes and thinking the words hard, Tori hoped she was successfully talking back. Magic was messy and imprecise in her experience, which was all the more reason she preferred science.

I'll break their system. Can you give me any sort of guidance? Info on what Nexus brought is also appreciated.

In response, she got images, flashes of two-headed, pink-spitting serpents, and the more horrifying version that looked like a mound of mouths—one that was tough, spewed acid, and had recovered from being torn in half. This would be a game of dodge more than anything. She wasn't sure if dimensional acid worked on fire and would prefer to run such tests in a structured laboratory environment. Stay quick, move fast, and hope she found her goal soon.

Only Xelas found the room, and she doesn't know where you are to give directions. North side of the building, the door is torn down. If you're sure this is the right course, we have to start pulling back. Once the capes know where you are, she'll be here in seconds.

It didn't escape Tori's attention that he said "she" instead of "they," but by now, his former apprentice had accepted that to Ivan, there was only one real threat the capes had to wield. For him, solely Lodestar was of concern; however, Tori still had to worry about the rest of the bunch, all of whom would be descending upon her with confusion and questions. It said a lot about Tori Rivas that she was more anxious about the impending discussion than dodging deadly monsters to secure her freedom.

I'm sure. Get everyone out of here. I got this.

They'll be gone within minutes. I'll be here to the end. Just in case.

The connection snapped off without warning, leaving Tori alone once more. No, she'd always been here by herself—that was an important distinction to keep in mind for later. Stick to the truth wherever she could. Her eyes drifted down to the smoldering corpse behind her. Well, he had been trying to strangle her, so at worse, that counted as self-defense. Probably best to avoid bringing it up, if possible.

Since the door was unlocked, there was no need to break out. She eased it open gently, ears perked for sounds of movement. There were loud thuds and noises coming from all over, yet none sounded particularly closer than the others. That meant there weren't any creatures near, or they were all right on top of her. Didn't change what she had to do next either way.

For someone without an internal compass, who'd been knocked out during her entry trip, knowing that her goal was in the north part of the building meant fuck all. The broken door part was more helpful, but as Tori checked the first such instance, it became clear that there was more than one busted barrier in this place. This one looked like a room where someone had been either hiding or resting. Neither had saved them from the eroding pink goo that appeared to have melted through half the room, occupant included.

She pushed the image away. In truth, Tori had been holding a lot of things back during this whole ordeal, and was starting to notice the strain. Good as it had felt in the moment, killing Deacon was running back through her head. This wasn't like with Rust Tooth, or some of her dodgier fights in her thief days. Those were about survival, her versus them. But she was much stronger than Deacon; he'd never been an actual threat.

More mental shoving. This was *not* the time for an ethical self-examination.

Focusing on the task at hand, Tori burst around a corner and skidded to a stop. Standing before her was one of the many-mouthed monsters, the larger version that nearly blocked the whole hallway. Its tail/head/whatever-the-hell whipped in her direction, letting off an instant blast of pink spray. Tori backpedaled, shooting off a blast of fire into the thing's center of mass. No visible reaction whatsoever. Guess it took more oomph to hurt these horrors. What she wouldn't give for her suit and its weaponry.

A fleck of acid hit her left arm, the pain sharp and immediate. Tori shifted to fire instantly, watching in horrified fascination as the droplet kept on eating through the flames. After a second or two, the heat caused it to boil off, finally freeing her from the droplet. Unfortunately, that was more than enough data to show she was vulnerable to these creatures, even in fire form. Enough of that pink goo could theoretically dissolve her before she could boil it off.

Speed had just become more important than stealth. Nowhere to hide in this concrete warehouse, so getting to the security room quickly was her biggest concern. Leaping into the air, Tori focused her flames, using the flying trick she'd learned during her first real test with the guild to get next to the ceiling. At least up here, they'd have to aim to hit her, and she could zip around without worrying about obstacles.

Her next burst of speed got her clear just in time, as a wave of pink burned the concrete right where she'd been. Sounds of movement kept her attention, and she realized the creature was giving chase. Its mouths weren't spitting acid, curiously. Instead, they seemed to be spitting out an array of unnatural, guttural slurping noises, like listening to pigs eat a trough full of yogurt. Only the tail/head kept firing, likely because it was the sole one with a chance of hitting her elevated position.

It wasn't until the next hallway that Tori understood. Three of the two-headed version and one more mouth mound were all waiting, letting loose a coordinated series of streams the moment she came into view. Only training and reflexes saved her. She shot down below the arc of the streams, putting on a burst of power and charging directly through the monsters. Their acid might hurt, but physically, they were still flesh and she was fire, meaning they couldn't actually block her path.

However, they could, it turned out, give chase. Suddenly, she was seeing pink coming from all angles, and the tight confines of the building made it impossible to break away completely. She couldn't build up speed with all the turning and checking, so Tori was forced to dodge with all she had. For the most part, she was holding together well, though she'd taken more than a few hits to the flames serving as her legs.

A big splotch got her in the back, nearly sending Tori spinning all the way to the ground, where she had no doubt a tidal wave of death was awaiting her. Ivan's lessons about pain and focus weren't for nothing, though. Leaving scorch marks on the wall, she slowed her descent, putting all her energy into heating up one section of her form. More shots came, thankfully missing, albeit barely. If she'd had teeth, they'd have been gritted as Tori gave one last push of effort and successfully turned the acid to steam.

Blasting forward, Tori took the next three turns she could, trying to buy a few inches of breathing room. Sadly, she could still hear them on her tail, but a new sight stole the entirety of her interest. A room with a broken door, and the telltale blinking twinkle of technology. She roared in, looking over the setup.

There was a massive amount of gear crammed into a single space, all of it incredibly dense. With a glance, she could recognize some of the components, yet far more were totally unfamiliar, or bore only the slightest resemblance to tech she was familiar with. Her hands, not even flesh at the moment, itched to tear it apart, see how it worked, what she could add to her own designs. The thunder of slithering following her down the hall made it clear that wasn't happening, much to her chagrin.

Raising a hand to roast the tech, she had a brief second thought. No reason to leave evidence if she didn't have to. Instead, she moved deeper into the room, her fluid form unbothered by the lack of space. In seconds, the pursuers had arrived, trying to force their way through the door all at once.

"Hey, you nasty shits. I'm right here. Maybe you can manage to hit a standing target."

The taunting probably didn't affect them—it just felt natural as Tori waved, drawing their attention. Sure enough, sprays of pink rained down. Instantly, Tori dropped back, falling behind one of the massive electronic towers. Sizzling met her ears as the goo began to tear through intricate systems and equipment. Working carefully, she began to solidify part of herself, shoving the equipment around until she'd made a small area in the back where a human could fit.

Sitting down to present as tiny a target as possible, Tori turned back to human form. Her arm was fine, but her back and legs still stung. More time was needed to regenerate fully, it seemed. While she'd still prefer that to being human and vulnerable, there was no choice. If the AHC was going to be swooping in as fast as Ivan expected, she couldn't very well be showing powers when they arrived.

More hissing, more noises, and Tori noticed the creatures were making progress. They'd cleared out a section near the front and were slowly pushing their way toward the back where Tori was holed up. The tower in front of her took several fresh sprays, and she began to wonder if it would even last long enough for help to arrive.

Her heart pounded. This was crazy. She couldn't sit and wait. She had to move, had to get free. They were getting closer. It was just a matter of time until they—

Tori shrieked as the tower blocking her from the rest of the room vanished, almost summoning fire on instinct. But this was no dimensional monster coming to melt her flesh. They didn't even have hands, so they couldn't effortlessly lift a huge piece of electronic equipment like it was nothing, and they certainly didn't glow.

Looking up, Tori found herself gazing into one of the AHC's greatest heroes and legends, the one superhero her teacher seemed to respect, as well as fear.

"L-Lodestar?"

"That's right, Tori. Don't worry, you're safe now." She reached out a hand, and Tori took it without thinking.

In what felt like a blink, they were in the air, Tori effortlessly cradled in Lodestar's arms. From this high up, she could see the rainbow of capes arriving on the scene. Part of her wondered if Ivan had escaped in time, but she realized that there would be far more excitement if anyone spotted Fornax here. Adrenaline fading, the toll of a sleepless night and regenerating several wounds finally hit Tori full force.

She passed out before Lodestar had even gotten them out of Michigan.

Chapter 33

Every channel was talking about the rescue, some praising the AHC for recovering Tori safely, others wondering why it took so long. The destruction at the scene raised minimal eyebrows, as identical anchors with the same plastic smiles repeated the most salient point of that event: Nexus had been there. After so many decades of his presence, the public had accepted that they lived with one more form of natural disaster than they used to. No one was especially happy about it, but just like hurricanes and earthquakes, their feelings weren't a factor in the equation.

The pale, bald man sitting alone in his lab watched the screens. It would have been better if no one had gotten involved; he'd wanted to see how long his invention could keep the capes guessing on its own. That was an ideal test, something in a controlled environment; he'd run too many of those. Field data was essential, and until it had crapped out, his system had sent back quite a useful amount. If nothing else, he now knew his devices could buy at least twelve hours.

All in all, a successful beta-trial. The only hiccup had been those idiots kidnapping someone from the guild. While not a member himself, this man knew of them quite well. A bit too blunt for his tastes, they tended to be more chainsaw than scalpel, yet that didn't mean they could be ignored. That was the thing about blunt objects: they often hit quite hard. Another factor to keep track of, though he wasn't worried. There had been more elaborate schemes in the past, albeit not many; this was well within his capabilities.

Behind him, an odd, lumpy device began to chirp and squeal, soft lights cascading across its surface. Turning away from the television, his slender fingers ran across the mechanism, drawing out more horrifying noises. Perfect timing. With phase one wrapping up, he needed to turn his sights onto what came next.

Neither the guild nor the AHC had any idea what they were truly in for.

Tori sat in a conference room, coffee and chips in front of her, trying to stay calm. So far, things had gone smoothly. Lodestar saved Tori, bringing her to the AHC, where a doctor was waiting to check her over. Dr. Miraculous didn't have the most professional name; however, she'd quickly inspired competence. Professional, observant, and with an impeccable bedside manner. After some thinking, Tori put it together. Of course the AHC's doctor was good at helping people coming fresh from traumatic situations—that would be almost exclusively what she dealt with.

Afterward, Tori had been offered a shower and fresh clothes, which she accepted. There was no reason she could come up with to explain why she would rather stay in her dirty ensemble. While the jeans and shoes were fine, Tori was slightly less thrilled about the "Ridge City Loves the AHC" t-shirt they'd provided. This felt like the sort of thing the rest of the guild wouldn't let go of if they caught sight of it... not that she didn't have bigger concerns at the moment.

Soon, someone would walk in this room and try to coax a story out of her. What she said next, or didn't say, would determine how successful the rescue truly was. It was only a good one if the whole guild got out clean. Tori couldn't let them down, especially after they'd shown up to save her. Setting her resolve, Tori was braced for any lawyer or interrogation specialist to step through the door.

She was somewhat less prepared when the glowing form of Lodestar strolled in, however, nearly choking on a chip. There was something about her, a sense of power that announced itself even as she humbly walked over to the table with a gentle smile. It didn't escape Tori's notice, even through her starstruck shock, that Lodestar shut and locked the doors.

In a way, Lodestar seemed stranger here than she had in the warehouse. Seeing Lodestar mid-rescue, busting through a skeezy lair—that felt right. Watching her amble through a conference room was bizarre, like seeing a T-Rex napping in a park. Or Fornax working in an office, she reminded herself.

Tori had seen past the curtain; she knew the legends were more than their reputations or powers. Still, that was easier to remember when the reputations weren't quite so looming.

"Tori, if you're up to it, there are some questions I have to ask you." She took a seat, her inherent glow lighting up the chair's dark material. "However, before you answer, there's something that needs to be said. I know you don't want to talk to us, and I know why."

Having been prepared for hours of probing, verbal bait, and linguistic trickery, Tori felt dumbfounded as Lodestar dropped that kind of bomb so casually on the table. Was she bluffing? No; Ivan had warned Tori that anyone on the Champions' Congress could be clued in on her secret.

"That puts us in something of a pickle, you see," Lodestar continued. "There are questions it is vital you answer. Pieces of information that will help us strengthen our detection abilities and figure out how this gang blocked us. I can't risk you lying about anything and tainting that intel. Whatever else we might disagree on, I think we're together on one point: neither of us wants to see this happen to someone else."

Tori's hand tightened into a fist involuntarily. Finally out of danger, she was starting to process everything that had happened, a rush of emotions, many of them anger-adjacent, whirling up at merely the thought of her ordeal. The legendary cape had hit the money there: Tori definitely didn't want to see anyone else experience this.

"Here's how I'd like to proceed," Lodestar continued. "We both know there are things about your life that you're not comfortable sharing with me. Today, they are irrelevant. You were stolen off the street against your will. I'm not here to treat you like a criminal. If, in the course of this debriefing, we hit one of those areas, just stay silent. That's fine. It's a right the legal system offers even to those under arrest, which you are not. All I ask is that you not lie to me. Whatever you say to me, make it the truth. Can you work with that, Tori?"

When Ivan told her Lodestar was both more predictable and more dangerous for her lack of subtlety, it hadn't exactly made sense to Tori, but there had been larger issues demanding her attention at the time. Now, sitting across this table from her, Tori understood. Lodestar was, despite her insane power, disarming. There was something in the gentleness of her tone, the sincere concern in her eyes, that made Tori feel inherently safe. A great quality during a rescue, less optimal for an interrogation. Nevertheless, this was happening, and Tori couldn't repress her own curiosity about the living legend.

"I think I can live with that. Do you mind if I ask you a few, too, as we go?"

"Of course. I'm sure you've got so much you must be wondering about. But may we start with your version of what happened? Studies show that the sooner we do these, the more accurate the recollection tends to be." From a hidden pocket on her costume, Lodestar produced a small device. She set it on the table, pushing a button and getting a red light.

Interesting. So she'd left the first part of their talk off the record. Tori mulled that over as she began her tale. The kidnapping part she skimmed through, seeing as that had apparently been on the news. Most of what she relayed was factual, going through the way she'd been treated by her kidnappers, her bathroom arrangement, and so on. It wasn't until she got to Nexus that Lodestar looked worried, though she said nothing, allowing Tori to continue spinning her yarn. Only in the last bit of the chronology did Tori have to skip some details, recounting her wild run from the monsters without mentioning she'd been living fire at the time. The tech room, Tori relayed as best she could, mentally pulling up the way the machines had been interconnected. Much as she'd have loved to take them apart herself, the acid had done too good a job. If Professor Quantum could get information out of that rubble, he deserved it.

"You've been through quite the ordeal," Lodestar said at last. "Not many people would have kept such a cool head on them during that kind of situation."

"Benefits of having practice. I saw the importance of staying calm during the attack on my office a few months ago." Tori had kept that one locked and loaded, an explanation for her competence and a reminder that one of their own was her friend.

Lodestar nodded. "Yes, I just finished speaking with Cyber Geek, actually. He wanted to be in here, you know, but I felt it was best to keep things private until we had a better idea of your condition. Plus—" Her eyes darted to the recorder for a split second "—he hasn't had training for this yet, and we wanted to be sure to collect your testimony as soon as possible. I have more questions about the computer room where I found you, but why don't we take a brief pause so you can rest your voice."

Reaching over, she tapped the recorder once, ending the red light's blaze. "If you wanted to ask me questions of your own, this is probably the time."

"You don't want your answers on the record?"

"Tori, I have no idea what you're about to ask. Some of what you might know is technically classified as Top Secret, though honestly, after the whole

Apollo kerfuffle, I'm not sure where a lot of that stands. Point is, unless it's germane to the kidnapping, it doesn't need to be on that tape."

That hadn't occurred to Tori, but Ivan had made it clear the government was the one who set the villains free. Heck, even the tool they'd used for it, the Orion Protocol, had a clandestine-sounding name. Lodestar made a good point, though. They were working at an information disparity. Tori probably wasn't going to change that, but she might be able to figure out what tidbits were off-limits.

Double-checking the recorder out of habit, Tori sat up a little straighter. "I guess my first question is what *do* you know?"

"A lot less than I can prove, which might as well be your organization's motto," Lodestar replied. "Pertaining to you, I know you're a meta-human, I know you're wading into very dangerous waters, and I know the man you call uncle has no blood relation to you. Though my understanding is he's still been something of a mentor."

Okay, so, as it turned out, Lodestar knew quite a damn bit. She'd even called him a mentor, was that word a coincidence? No, she was laying it out just like she had the entire time. At least Tori didn't have to worry about slipping up and accidentally revealing too much. Outside of the rescue, anyway.

"I've got one for you now, and we can leave the recorder off," Lodestar said. "The New Science Sentries told me what happened, that you learned their civilian identities. I'm sorry I have to ask this, but forewarned is very much forearmed in these cases. Did you tell the gang who they are?"

With some relief, Tori realized that this was one where she had nothing to hide. "Nope. We didn't really get into much grilling. I mostly just kept pissing the head guy off until he stormed away. I haven't told anyone their secret."

That earned her a surprised look from Lodestar. "Anyone?"

"Not a soul. I like it when people respect my privacy, so I'd be an ass not to do the same." Tori realized she was supposed to be asking questions, but the sudden enormity of the opportunity had struck her. This was someone who'd been around since the mid-eighties, had seen untold powers and threats. Someone who knew the guild leadership in ways Tori likely never would. There was so much to ask, yet her tongue found itself dazed with options. Scrambling for something to keep the talk moving, Tori fell back on a question that had nagged at her for quite some time.

"Why does my uncle trust you? I get why he respects you—as the only person to ever put him down, that gels with who he is. But you threw the man in jail, yet I've never heard him say a single bad word about Lodestar. The exact opposite, in fact. I know you helped talk him into the... work release program. I know you showed him that pic of his kid. But this is more than that. He trusts almost no one, yet has total faith in you."

From her slightly glowing mouth, Lodestar let out a perfect whistle, like the start of a songbird's symphony. "Wow, you really jump right into the complicated stuff, huh?" She leaned back in the chair, staring up at the ceiling and beyond, looking to a mental destination where Tori's eyes couldn't follow.

"Here's the thing you have to understand about Ivan and me." Evidently, Lodestar really had killed the recorder, as she was comfortable using real names. "For a good stretch of years, he and I were in our own power category. Both of us unbeatable, untouchable most of the time—until we met each other."

There was a flicker in Lodestar's eye, hinting at so much more than what was escaping her lips. Still, even the words were precious, so Tori listened closely.

"We were the strongest metas in the world. Back then, we didn't even know for sure who was more powerful. The only ones we had to battle, to truly test ourselves against, were each other. For a long time, we kept up the dance; he knew how to stay off my radar, but we usually ended up in brief skirmishes. Until we finally had it out for keeps and discovered who the strongest really was."

While it might have been Tori's imagination, she thought Lodestar seemed almost sad about that. Perhaps she'd enjoyed the mystery, too.

"I can't tell you why Ivan trusts me—that's his choice. All I can say is that we know each other in a way you can only know someone you've fought against, and alongside. For years, we were among the few constants in one another's lives. The crook I couldn't catch, the cape he couldn't beat. I'm not sure if that made us friends, nemeses, or a combination of the two, but it made us *something*. That would be my guess as to why Ivan trusts me as superhero. I hope it answers your question."

"And then some," Tori replied. "While also raising countless more. Not going to be greedy, though. That was a lot. We can do more debrief stuff."

Lodestar lowered her eyes back to the table, focusing on the moment at hand. "Before we go down that road, there is one more thing I'd like to broach with you. Just something to consider. You have shown adaptability, intelligence, and resolve over and over, without factoring in your less savory efforts. This is the second incident you've publicly been in, and last time, you helped one of our most promising new members. Between your mind and your powers, you make a potent threat. The kind that could be dangerous, when properly nurtured. If you were any other person, I'd be making this offer, and I see no reason not to give you the same opportunity."

Flaring up a tad brighter, Lodestar met Tori's eyes, the full force of her gaze nearly causing the younger woman to blink. "Tori Rivas, have you given any thought toward using those talents for good? We could use someone with your abilities at the Alliance of Heroic Champions."

Chapter 34

"Look, I know we were using a lot of double-talk here, but I'm kind of... spoken for, in that department." Tori wasn't even certain she'd heard Lodestar right, and she damned sure didn't know how to respond to that sort of suggestion.

"Two types of people join your current organization," Lodestar replied, utterly unfazed. "Criminals who were caught then won their freedom, and the ones getting educated before they make any major slipups. I know you're in the second group, and even the crimes I suspect you of are fairly minimal. People make mistakes. What matters more is their ability to grow and learn from them. You wouldn't be the first player to change teams, especially so early on."

Could that be true? Sure, she'd heard of a few former crooks turning over a new leaf—just no one on the guild's level. But a new costume and codename could easily transform plenty of metas into functionally new people. In the end, Lodestar was probably telling the truth. That seemed to be her style. This was a point to make certain she understood clearly, however.

"I'm not even sure that would be allowed," Tori said weakly, trying to get her bearings.

"Oh? I'm pretty sure one of the first rules in your code is not to go around messing with superheroes. Especially ones with the AHC. Which is what you would be if you made the switch, Tori. Yes, it's allowed by the code's own wording. Even if that wasn't the case, you could still come over. I've made *my* position on that policy clear to your leadership."

She paused, looking Tori over more closely. "I think that's all we need to say on the matter for tonight. You've been through a lot, and there's still more questions to ask, so let's leave this question there. I don't need or expect an answer right away; these are the sorts of choices you should fully consider."

A glowing hand moved toward the recorder, then stopped. "There is one more thing. Part of why I'm comfortable making this offer to you is that you haven't crossed my major lines. There's a reason the guild largely preys on other criminals; not even I can protect people from their own actions. Tried at one point and things went *bad.* Keep that in mind. Because if you bring civilians into the equation, you bring me in as well. Don't cross that line unless you understand the consequences."

"I get it. Keep the fight on the playground, it's fine. Spill into school, and the teacher becomes involved."

"Your school needs more involved educators," Lodestar told her. "That is the thrust of it, though. Are you ready to get back to the debrief?"

"Honestly, at this point, that sounds like a nice break."

Tori hadn't planned to say that any more than she expected Lodestar to laugh: quick and melodic, like the sweet refrain of a lovely song.

Chuckling to herself, Lodestar hit the record button. Time to get back to business.

It was a shame they couldn't take any of the physical materials from the cloaking system, but Xelas had managed to come back with quite a bit of data. She'd copied the entire software system, along with a few stored schematics, as well as scanned the actual tech itself. Some parts of the machinery had still been cloaked; however, all in all, she and Wade had managed to assemble a reasonable mock-up on the holographic display table in front of them.

He was in his normal clothes, simple and professional, the sort one might expect a quaint local librarian to wear. Except Wade was a billionaire genius supervillain, and there was nothing placid or quiet in his expression as he looked everything over. Someone had bested him on the field of technology. Maybe only for a day, but it had still happened. While he'd accepted long ago that Professor Quantum and Tyranny were peers at or past his present level, being thwarted by some new upstart grated on his nerves. Especially since they'd taken one of his people in the process.

As he looked over the holographic facsimile, formed of data and sculpted light, he zoomed in on a section. Some of this equipment was too homegrown to puzzle out the purpose of with just his eyes, but the power unit was using an electron looper, a standard tool for powering massive equipment off standard wall outlets. Wade had seen and made more than he could count through the years, and something about this one was off.

"Xelas, check the southern east quadrant, the power source. Why run nineteen thelmian micro-rings for stabilization when a simple boron buffer does the job better and cheaper?"

"Better question, where did they even find thelmian ore? Records show only a few meteors of it hit in the late fifties, and the majority of that wound up with the AHC or private collectors. Oh, guess they robbed a collector—answered my own question." Though she was smiling, there was a focused gleam in her eyes as she followed Wade's gaze. "Interesting. I just ran a full check through my archives, and this actually used to be the standard way to make an electron looper. Professor Quantum invented the boron buffer in the mid-sixties, and it soon became the standard, but before then, this was the design."

Old tech, using materials that were supposed to be scarce. Wade mentally laid out the situation once more. A gang with tech lightyears beyond their grasp kidnaps a woman off the street, one who was famously saved by the New Science Sentries. They call out that same team publicly, keeping the woman hidden to force the capes' hand. Had the New Science Sentries complied, they'd have been walking in to a trap full of advanced weaponry. It couldn't be a coincidence that everything centered on a new version of the world's first superhero team, yet the tech in use was dated.

"The good news is that I suspect Tori's kidnapping really was a coincidence. All of this seems to be about Professor Quantum's old team. My money says that someone he pissed off is out for payback."

"Good news because it isn't our fight?" Xelas seemed confused, if not disappointed.

The malicious gleam in Wade's eye put any doubts she had to rest even before he spoke. "Hell no. This is absolutely our fight. We've needed something to focus the guild members on, a task that keeps them busy without risking too much AHC wrath. After one of our own was taken, they're all itching to show some dominance. No, that's good news because it means neither side will be paying us much attention. With Tori saved, they'll expect us to go back to minding our own business."

The metal fingers danced along his shoulder, finding their way to the back of Wade's neck, where they spread out and wrapped around, gripping gently. Xelas pulled him in closer, only inches separating them. "And what will we really be doing?"

"Waiting for the right opportunity to strike."

"You do know how to talk to a gal. Well, this one, anyway." She kept the kiss brief. Much as she loved Wade when he went on the warpath, they still had a lot of work to do breaking down her data. Big talk didn't mean a damn thing if they got caught with their pants down again.

By the time they were done talking, Lodestar having asked about every detail and tidbit she could regarding the cloaking system, Tori's head was starting to feel fuzzy. Her brief nap in Lodestar's arms hadn't been a full rejuvenation by any means, and the day's compounded stress was causing pain above her temples.

To Lodestar's credit, she soon noticed and wrapped things up, leaving the caveat that Tori might be called back if they thought of new questions to ask. All things considered, it had gone well. Tori managed to avoid implicating herself or the others, and she'd escaped without being seriously wounded. The best she could have hoped for, really.

As they were about to leave the room, Tori realized that there would be others waiting to see her. Donald, certainly, and probably the New Science Sentries as well. They would be concerned, caring, and way more than she could handle at the moment.

"Is there a private exit? I'm... I need some time before I see anyone."

"Of course." Lodestar smirked, a strangely mischievous feature on her face. "Close your eyes."

Normally, Tori would have balked, or at least asked some clarifying questions. It was a demonstration of her exhaustion's growing dominance that she merely did as instructed. A brief feeling of wind and weightlessness washed over her, and when Tori opened her eyes once more, she was at the AHC's entrance—a massive door with various tourists and workers streaming through. The first floor was a museum dedicated to superhero exploits, so it saw quite a bit of foot traffic.

"Moving at those speeds will make you nauseous if your eyes are open, unless you have practice," Lodestar explained from behind her. Already, the crowd was looking over, though none of them had even a glance to spare for

Tori. "Go on ahead. I'll sign some autographs to keep everyone distracted. Your ride is waiting for you."

Tori looked out the sliding doors and realized there was a familiar form outside on the sidewalk. Amidst a sea of chipper families and excited kids, the stoic man standing stock-still stood out like neon. It was odd to think she could be so happy to see that dull expression, but as her eyes fell on Ivan, Tori felt something inside her relax, something she hadn't even realized was tense.

Much as she wanted to rush out, Tori took her time. Almost against her better judgment, she looked back to Lodestar. It could have been Tori's imagination, but she was almost sure she caught Lodestar sneaking a few looks out the door as well. Since meeting Ivan, she'd assumed his odd reverence of Lodestar was one-sided; after today, she wasn't quite so sure. Whatever this complicated mess was, it certainly appeared to be going in two directions.

With the crowd occupied, Tori made her way forward, out the sliding doors and into the summer's fading heat. She made her way down the smooth entrance lined on either side with topiaries carved into the shapes of famous capes, and walked up to the man who was a legendary villain, and one of the few people who'd proven he gave a real shit about her.

"How do you feel?" Ivan asked.

"Tired. Numb. Drained."

Scared. Guilty. Lost.

His hand landed gently on top of Tori's head, heavier than she remembered. "Let's get you some rest. You've more than earned it." A moment of hesitation, his hand almost pulling away. "I am very glad you're safe, Tori. We were all worried, but we also had faith you'd pull through."

There was no way to say why—it wasn't a particularly emotional thing to say—but that was Tori's breaking point. Picturing the guild, her friends, her life, knowing how close she'd been to losing everything. All the fear she hadn't let herself feel, the horror of what she'd done to Deacon, the helplessness of being taken against her will, it all came crashing down at once.

Tori buried her face against Ivan's chest as she wound her arms around him, hugging him with all the strength her body could still manage. She wanted to weep, to let everything out, but Tori wasn't practiced at letting her guard down to that extent. Instead, she just held on, her whole body shaking. Here, she finally let herself feel at ease. Nothing could get her. Nothing could hurt her. She didn't even have to hide parts of herself like she had with Lodestar. Tori was safe.

It took her a few minutes to realize that Ivan was gently hugging her back.

A few minutes more, and Tori realized people were staring, not that she gave any semblance of a shit. But sooner or later, they'd recognize her, take some pictures, and the media cycle would begin anew. She gathered her composure, the shakes dying down as her breathing stabilized.

"Sorry. Probably not a reaction befitting somebody like us, huh?"

"Tori, you have nothing to apologize for." It was an occasion where Ivan's blunt tone worked to his benefit, making it clear he thought the very notion ridiculous. "You did well, better than anyone had the right to ask."

"Yeah, sure, but I gotta stick the landing, right?" Tori finally managed to pull away, releasing her grip on Ivan. "Can't get weighed down by all of this."

This time, Ivan was the one who initiated the hug, though he kept his short. "I'm the one who owes you an apology if you think that. There's something I've owed you for a while now, and when you're ready, I hope it will help you get some clarity on that front. It's something I should have told you already, something I avoided because it means dredging up the past."

Together, they walked away from the AHC's headquarters, Ivan taking her to a spot where Tunnel Vision was already waiting with a portal. It was hard to beat the guild in terms of treatment options and general safety, both of which were very relevant for Tori. The plan was to get her some food and rest, letting her return to the world at large when she was ready. Ivan hadn't expected to add a story in there, but holding Tori as she shook was too familiar for him not to see the need. It was time to pay what he owed her for reaching graduation.

It was time to tell her about the origin of Fornax.

Chapter 35

No aides or other members of the AHC would be walking in on Professor Quantum in this room. He'd established a private laboratory at the inception of the entire organization, a place where he could perform delicate experiments without worrying about interruption. Security had been upgraded—by him—regularly until he'd moved the bulk of his work to the island of Vomisa. Even with years of lapses, it was fortified enough for the moment's task.

Laid out before him was a simple cube. That's how it appeared, at least. According to the recovery reports, this had been one of the things found in a pile of pink goo, surrounded by melted parts, yet it showed not so much as a scratch. The tech who recovered it had been puzzled, but Professor Quantum understood as soon as his fingers touched the smooth metallic surface.

Keltrine was a synthetic metal he'd once thought to have world-changing properties. Inventing it was one of Professor Quantum's earlier projects; exposing various natural materials to different meta-elements had resulted in many strange new compounds, and Keltrine was the most promising. Many of the early Science Sentry gear had made use of the seemingly indestructible metal, until they discovered its weakness.

From his pocket, Professor Quantum produced several packets of sugar taken from the breakroom. He sat down across from the cube, helping himself to a bottled water from the small refrigerator built into the desk. As a man who often got lost in his work, nutritional elements had to be kept on hand.

He'd tried to get other labs on board with bathroom buckets as well; however, that suggestion had so far failed to take hold.

Taking no care or measurements, Professor Quantum tore into the first sugar packet, dumping it into the water bottle. He did this six more times, until the water had turned milky. Finally satisfied, Professor Quantum emptied the entire container onto the cube, slowly pouring it out to cover every section. As soon as the liquid hit, the cube hissed and bubbled, turning to a crumbly, sand-like substance. For as durable as Keltrine was, they'd learned fighting Wrathy-Taffy that sugar created an immediate, destructive chain reaction. It was Professor Quantum's introduction into the unstable world of working with these strange new elements and the unusual side effects they produced.

The larger issue at hand was that anyone was able to create this particular bit of Keltrine in the first place. Only a few had figured it out when it was in use, one industrious tinker making an entire tiny army before the flaw was discovered. Most who knew the creation method were dead, and even the Mini-Murder Marquis was long retired. There was only one way to interpret this cube's existence: it was a message for him. Hidden in something they couldn't miss, and made durable enough that it would be near impossible to destroy.

As the water bottle reached its end, the last of the cube crumbling, a shiny new surface came into view. This one was metal, as well, though it merely shone in the sugar-water rather than melting. Unconcerned about mundane worries such as poison, Professor Quantum picked up the item, rubbing it clean and examining it carefully.

A commemorative pin. 1955 Original Edition, one of the first superhero souvenirs to ever be sold. Of course, that was largely because meta-humans had only been around for a few years. This was a big moment, for the world and Professor Quantum. These marked the launch of the Science Sentries, the world's first superhero team, precursor to the League of Metas. All five members stood there, staring at the camera, their likeness captured in the metal circle.

Last Professor Quantum had noticed, these sorts of items retailed for hundreds of thousands of dollars among collectors, which made it all the stranger that this one had been defaced, quite literally. Of the five, only Professor Quantum and Rex Reverb were still recognizable. The rest of the team's faces were scratched off. No coincidence that he and Rex were the only ones still presumed alive—that was obvious. But if the implication was that the sender had been responsible for the deaths, then that was ludicrous. They'd fallen years apart and to very different threats.

The message was clear, at least. Someone was targeting him, someone with a shocking knowledge of his prior work. The cube and button were clear hallmarks of the past.

For a moment, a single horrible moment, he thought of the mad-grinning skull, then put it out of his head. As a man of science, he knew better than to spend his time chasing ghosts. Focus on the current threats rather than ones already beaten.

To that effect, he wondered if he should give Rex a warning. He was on the button, too, and would make a compelling target to someone sending a message. After a moment of contemplation, Professor Quantum decided that perhaps Rex would be more useful in the dark. If they put a protective detail on him, he'd be the perfect bait—acting completely natural, drawing out potential attackers. It was risky, true, but that was the life of a superhero. He was sure Rex would understand, or, barring that, was sure he wouldn't care if an old teammate was mad.

Professor Quantum was a man who concerned himself with results. It wasn't as if they had the option to sit back and wait, anyway. This was an opening move. He'd seen far too many not to recognize one on sight. Whoever had made this cube wasn't remotely done. But their next move wouldn't come quite so easily.

Now that Professor Quantum knew there was a game afoot, he intended to crush everyone who dared challenge him.

"What'd they tell you?" Chloe asked, red-eyed on the edge of the sofa.

"She's safe and sound, just like the reports are saying." Beverly sounded deeply relieved, and that was with some effort to keep her tone neutral. Thuggernaut's rundown was quick and concise, but hit all the points he knew she'd be worried about. After wrapping up the rescue, they'd been taken home immediately. With capes buzzing about, any time in mask was dangerous. Since then, she'd just been waiting with Chloe to find out how the rest of Tori's morning went.

"Lodestar scooped her up, she did a few hours at the AHC making a report, and now, she's resting somewhere safe. My contact wasn't sure when she'd be back, probably a day or so, but physically, Tori came through fine. We'll have to see how hard it hit her upstairs."

"I just feel so bad. First, she ends up all over the news for being saved by Tachyonic, then this. Tori hates attention, and now, she'd going to get it nonstop." From her side, Chloe pulled out a spiral notebook with a pen jammed in the top. She flipped through several of the pages, idly chewing on the pen's cap as she mulled them over. "I keep thinking there's something I can do. Unfortunately, the closest I've gotten is 'Better seen than heard,' which is both gross and the opposite of what Tori needs."

While Beverly wasn't sure this effort would bear fruit, she also couldn't dispute that Tori was going to loathe the limelight. Worse, this wasn't just some quick news story anymore. There hadn't been a kidnapping like this in years upon years; adding in her existing fame momentum and the fact that the story appeared to end in a Nexus slaughter would only make the story more salacious. This might no longer be a thing they could simply wait out.

But that was getting far too ahead of herself. First, they needed to help Tori the person, then they could worry about her elevated profile.

"We'll figure something out. In the meantime, I'm going to make a grocery store run. At the very least, we can have her favorite beers and snacks when she gets home."

Chloe's eyes lit up. "Great idea! If you don't mind getting ingredients, I can make a nice comforting soup."

Mentally flashing back to Chloe's most recent stovetop culinary attempt that wasn't grilled cheese, Beverly could still taste the half-cinders passing as pork chops. Mercifully, the logistics of their situation made for an easy out. "That's a lovely idea, but why don't we wait until we know when Tori will be home? No sense in buying ingredients only for them to go bad."

She hustled out the door before the conversation could go any longer, in such a hurry that Beverly nearly crashed into the sizable form of Austin, who'd clearly been walking down to their apartment. Reflexes saved her from a full collision, bringing her up a few inches short of his chest, causing a quick backpedal.

"Sorry about that. Should watch where I'm going."

"Please no, it's my fault." Austin looked nervous. He was fidgeting in place, actively avoiding looking into her eyes for too long. "I... I didn't even have a good reason for coming over. I just wanted to apologize in person, if she's ready to see anyone. We promised protection, and then, only a few days later, completely failed to keep Tori safe. I don't expect her to forgive us, especially since it's our fault she got targeted in the first place, but she deserves an apology all the same."

It took Beverly a few seconds of mental gymnastics to put everything together. Right; Austin would have heard from the AHC that Tori was released. Since this was her home, he'd expect her to be here, resting and recovering. It was tempting to sell that delusion, pretend that she was being a shut-in, which wasn't much of a stretch for Tori, anyway. Too complicated, she quickly realized. Better to stick close to the truth, if she had to deviate at all.

"I respect that sentiment, but Tori isn't here. After everything that happened, she's staying with her uncle. Family support during trying times and all. She'll be back when she's ready."

"When that time comes, may I impose on you to let her know I'd like to talk?" Austin's eyes, still largely avoiding Beverly's, seemed to be sinking floorward the more they talked. "Though I understand if Tori has no desire to see any of us again, and I will respect the choice. My duty to apologize is not her obligation to hear it."

For a huge guy with legs like phone poles, Austin looked curiously unstable. His first few weeks in Ridge City didn't seem to be going to plan, for sure. Messing up their debut, getting put on protection duty, then fucking that one up on a national-story level—much as Beverly held a grudge against the AHC and Professor Quantum in particular, it was hard to pile all of that onto the nervous guy before her. Plus, she needed to lay a little groundwork for Tori. Otherwise, these four would be up her ass the minute she got home.

"Look, this is my opinion and should not be construed to reflect how Tori will feel, but I don't think the kidnapping is entirely on your team. No one expected some gang to try a street snatching. As far as you knew, Tori was going to work. Following her would have been weird, bordering on harassment. When it happened, did you do everything you could to get her back?"

"Sadly, yes, and what we could do was nothing." His jaw tightened, and for a moment, the nerves vanished. She saw the face of a leader angry at his own limitations, forced to the sidelines while others did the work. Sometimes, her parents wore that expression when talking about their harder missions, the darkest tales they'd share with their kids. Wanting to help, and lacking the power to do something was hard. Being on the sidelines while people they cared about *were* in the fight was magnitudes worse, apparently. "We spent our night out on the streets, keeping the peace. Useful work to be sure, just not helpful to Tori."

Beverly checked her watch. After a night spent out as Bahamut, hanging around a Detroit warehouse and helping Pseudonym kill Nexus's pets, she should be exhausted; however, the thrill of combat still had her blood pumping. It would be a little while before she could sleep. May as well put it to good use. The more she could do to ease Austin's guilt, the less he'd try to bother Tori with it. After the rescue, Beverly had been feeling somewhat useless herself; this was finally one way she could help.

"All night fighting, huh? With a body like that, disregarding any meta-influence, I'm guessing that means you're famished. Have you tried the Mono-Mart's counter-service yet? They make a mean breakfast burrito, and I'm heading over there on a grocery run, anyway. You can tag along, if you like."

Just like that, the nerves were back. For a moment, she thought he might spit out gibberish; his tongue seemed uncertain of its intended use as his jaw twitched within his mouth. Beverly had other shit to do with her day, so she threw him an excuse to move things along.

"After all, my roommate was just kidnapped. Might not be safe to walk out there so early alone." Even without her powers, Beverly had mace, a taser, and a lifetime in a family with a strong Marine service history. There was no mugger on this block she couldn't handle, but Austin didn't know any of that yet. If it got him out his head and moving, that was all that mattered for now.

It not only worked, it worked so well that Beverly was caught off guard. The shift was immediate, like someone had thrown a switch. His nerves vanished, spine straightened, and his gaze became direct. Whatever personal failings Austin had, they weren't shared by Agent Quantum. Once upon a time, she'd have found it strange. That was before the guild; before she understood the roles people played, and the way they could shift between them.

"You're absolutely right. It would be my honor and pleasure to escort you on your errands."

"Dial it back a notch, big boy." Beverly patted him on the shoulder, noting how solid it was. "We're just going on errands and breakfast. Why don't you tell me about your fake job on the way?"

Though he didn't slip back into his less confident posture, this question did cause his eyebrows to knit in confusion. "My fake job?"

"Yeah, your cover story. What you tell people when they ask you what you do, since you obviously can't tell them the truth." She looked at Austin, who stared right back at her, until realization finally dawned. "You don't have a *cover* story?"

"In the initial plan, we weren't going to be interacting with normal people as ourselves very often," Austin admitted. "It's possible we were undertrained for this type of scenario."

That was putting it shockingly light. They were going to blow their identities again any day now, and the next time, it might not be to a room of people with incentives to keep quiet. Worse, if people realized Tori was living a few doors down from the New Science Sentries, context be damned, she would get a fresh dose of fame. Possibly end up linked to them forever in the public's eye.

Which meant that if Beverly wanted to protect her friend, she had to help a team of capes blend in. Or find a new apartment. Given their specific needs and the current Ridge City real estate market, aiding Austin seemed like the easier task, even if she'd have preferred the latter.

"Okay, new idea. We figure out some fake jobs for you all while getting breakfast," Beverly declared. "Which you're paying for. I don't do consultations for free."

Chapter 36

Her new room had a window. That would have been impossible at the old base where they'd been tucked away in the middle of the city, hiding themselves in plain sight. One of the upshots to moving the guild's operation out of Ridge City was the change of limitations, not to mention the scenery. Volcanic lair or not, Tori had to appreciate the amazing view of the island and the glittering ocean that stretched beyond it.

The sun sat low on the horizon; she'd been asleep for most of the day. Looking down, Tori realized with a small trickle of embarrassment that she was still wearing the AHC t-shirt Lodestar had provided.

It was a passing thought that floated away as her eyes went back to the window. Looking at the ocean was pleasant, soothing—a vast improvement over the images replaying in her mind. Being chased by the spitting monsters was scary, getting kidnapped had filled her with rage, but it was Deacon that kept popping up the most. She could still feel the flames of her arm torching his throat as it slid down, still see the horrified pain as the fire caught. There was no regret in Tori—she'd done what she had to. Yet the images kept coming. Killing Rust Tooth hadn't hit her nearly this hard, though perhaps it was because it was a mere blip in a day of mad chaos.

Even that recurring memory was better than the choice Tori could feel resting on her shoulders. What next? When she left this lair, she'd be facing serious decisions. Her life had changed, and not in the fifteen-minutes-of-fame way. This was too big; it wouldn't flare out overnight. In a few years, sure, she might be able to get back to some manner of normalcy, but her face and name being all over the news would stick in people's minds, especially given the context.

Staring out at the lapping waves, she considered staying here. The facilities were all top-tier, she'd never have to hide her face or her true identity, and everything she needed was on this island. Tori frowned, a sight she was able to catch in the window's slight reflection. This place might have everything Hephaestus needed, but not Tori. She had plans and ambitions beyond the guild, the kind she'd have to be in the real world to execute. Besides, Beverly and Chloe were counting on her to help cover rent. She wasn't ready to say goodbye to that life quite yet.

She contemplated a shower and a change, but a loud rumble from her stomach skewed priorities. Whatever waited down the line, Tori at least knew her next move today. Leaving her room, Tori realized a moment after the door closed that she still hadn't changed t-shirts; however, her capacity for caring had already maxed out. It wasn't worth the time to go back.

The halls were largely empty as she made her way through, arriving at the room number Ivan had left for her. It opened to reveal a sizable area, probably meant to be a conference room, though she doubted there was often so much of a spread. Sandwiches, stew, seared fish, and a few dishes Tori didn't recognize—all of it fresh and steaming. She dove right in, not even caring that the room was otherwise empty. If anyone in the guild wanted her dead, they'd pick a more direct method than poison.

After a minute or so of eating, Tori saw Ivan enter. Truly Ivan, no Pseudonym mask, and certainly no Fornax one. Just the unassuming middle manager who was easy to overlook. How was he so good at keeping a low profile, especially considering what Fornax was like? Maybe it was just a matter of practice; he'd been at this much longer than her.

"I hope you like the food. Made it earlier today, and had Dabbler throw on a seal to keep it fresh until you arrived."

"Guess the room also sent an alert." Tori managed to get down her mouthful of turkey leg before speaking, but it was a photo finish. "Or were you hanging out in a hallway, waiting?"

Ivan said nothing at first. He headed over to the drink area and fixed himself a simple cocktail of vodka mixed with ginger ale. Once that was prepared, he pulled out a beer and set it down next to Tori, who popped the cap immediately. "How are you feeling?"

The food-shoveling paused momentarily. Tori could feel the memories trying to rise up, perhaps bringing her meal with it, and she halted them through sheer force of will. This was not the time to lose herself. "Like, I really don't want to talk about it. Not right now, at least. I think I need some time to get my head around everything."

"After what you've been through, that is a completely reasonable sentiment," Ivan said. "If you'd like to push our talk back and stick to less serious topics, that is fine as well."

"No." The word came out a tad too fast and strong. Tori tried again, taking more care. "No. I could use something else to think about. Different place to put my mind. Plus, I've been waiting months for this; no take-backs now."

Despite Ivan's neutral expression, he was actually quite conflicted. Tori was clearly spinning; he'd seen it happen to younger metas more than enough times to recognize the signs. He wasn't entirely sure this story would make things better. It wasn't one he cared to share often, and never in circumstances like these. Ultimately, upholding his word seemed to be the best choice, though he planned to keep an eye on how Tori was coping at various points in the tale.

"The first thing you have to understand is that you and I grew up in different worlds," Ivan began. "I don't mean that I'm from another dimension or universe—I'm from this planet, this realm, same as you. But it wasn't always like this."

His expression hardened, memories flashing already. "You live in a world with a backstop. A ceiling. A limit on how bad things can get, called the Champions' Congress. Professor Quantum has one of the keenest, hungriest minds, paired with cutting-edge meta-human knowledge and potent abilities. Quorum has over a thousand people working in perfect unison in that head of his, seeing every situation from more angles than entire organizations could hope to. And of course, there's Lodestar. The strongest meta. The true superhero. Together, they represent a functionally unstoppable force. Look at your own kidnapping; the people who took you had cloaking equipment beyond what most world governments could fashion, and it wouldn't have even bought them a full day before the AHC arrived. Against any threat, they have the mind of Professor Quantum, the insight of Quorum, and the power of Lodestar. Every villain in this world, every criminal and thug, every goon and crook, understands that if they make too much trouble, that's what is waiting for them. The sky is the limit, because to rise that high means catching their attention."

"I once asked some of the council members who would win in a fight: us versus the AHC. They said it would be a pretty even match," Tori interrupted.

She didn't necessarily doubt Ivan, but conflicting data was something that itched in her brain.

"You didn't ask *me*." Ivan paused, mentally doing some math. "But unless you somehow stole some councilor time at our relaunch, you must have asked that during your apprenticeship. Before Lodestar was back."

Part of Tori wanted to rebel at that idea, that one cape could turn the tides so greatly as to change the answer entirely. Except, when she thought back to Ivan's breakdown, to when he returned to being Fornax, the way he'd batted around the AHC's top capes like toys, Tori could understand how a truly powerful meta might swing things in a fight. Especially one that could lead on the front lines, inspiring her allies to battle.

"My point is, this world has limits. No fleet of Destruco-Blimps will try to take over Utah, because the AHC will put them down. No random genetic monster can wipe out a city, because again, the AHC will stop them."

"There were capes before the AHC," Tori pointed out.

"Yes. Ones that saved the day many a time. But never without risk, and often not without loss. They were not unbeatable—that is the very point I'm driving toward. Here, there are no *real* worldwide threats, because in your heart, you know anything that dangerous would draw the capes' attention. Most beings who are smart enough to actually be a threat to the world are also capable of seeing the odds stacked against them. It means fewer people ever try to take things that far because they'll never succeed. And most realize it. That creates a different world than one where power is up for grabs, and the strongest can claim it."

Some of the food settled heavy in Tori's stomach. "That was your world?"

To her surprise, Ivan slammed the rest of his drink, went back over to the bar, and fixed himself a double. When he spoke again, there was an ache in his voice she'd never even caught a whisper of before. "That was our world. Mine and the others'. There were lots of organizations out there chasing meta-powers, some with science, others through training, and a few that went the magical route. A cult favored that last option to great success: the Order of the Final Dawn."

The crack that appeared along Ivan's glass was telling—largely because Tori knew how much emphasis he put on self-control. For him to slip already didn't signal she was in for a cheerful story.

Making his way back to the table, Ivan set his cracked glass down. "I never knew my parents. None of us did. Some were bought. Some were stolen. Most were unwanted. That's what I've pieced together through the years, anyway. Back then, it didn't matter. Nothing mattered, with one exception: combat. From my earliest memories, we were fighting. We fought for meals, fought for clothes, fought one another even for the simple right to use a toilet. The cultists would use magic to keep us healed afterward, but they always let the pain linger. They considered it to be an excellent teaching aide."

Lifting his hand, Ivan made a fist. Such a simple gesture, yet Tori could feel the power contained within, even across the table. "Much as I hate them, I think they might have been right on that front, a fact that makes me despise them all the more."

"I'm sorry, Ivan."

He smiled at her, though there was no joy in the gesture. "Thank you, but I fear the tale has only just begun. That was my early life, you see. Nonstop scrapping, until they began to educate us on how to fight properly. Trainers were brought in, men and women I now suspect were killed as soon as they finished imparting their lessons. Creating monsters was all the cultists cared about, that and their dogma. I doubt they would have taught us to read, write, or speak if not for the weekly ceremonies chanting from the holy scrolls. That was life, until the year we turned ten."

The story petered out momentarily as Ivan looked into his drink, making no move to touch it. "I had a pair of friends back then. Thick as thieves—pardon the phrasing. I was a little better than them at fighting, a touch of natural talent and a growth spurt giving me a slight edge. Vlad was the smartest of us all; he had a clever streak too wide for his own good. More than a few fights he won were through trickery and deception, though he got good at an old-fashioned low-blow, too. Our third member doesn't have a name, for reasons that will become clear. He was... soft. Kind. Not made for that world. Although, in hindsight, I wonder if perhaps it was more impressive that after ten years living like that, he still managed to hold on to some spark of gentleness."

In one gulp, Ivan downed his second drink, however he made no motions to fix a third. Whatever he'd been gathering courage for, it seemed they'd arrived.

"At age ten, we finally realized what we were doing there. That was when we had our first Trial of the Worthy. That day was the first time our numbers were halved."

Tori had thought she was bracing for where this would go, but her appetite faded suddenly as realization set in. "They killed half the kids?"

"No. We killed each other." Ivan made a point to meet her eyes; there could be no miscommunication on this front. "They put us in rings of magical, closing fire. Ones that could burn you for hours without leaving so much as a sear. Neither could leave until one was dead. Supposedly, the assignments were done randomly, but to this day, I never believed that. Pitting me against one of my only friends seems too cruel, even for fate. Only humans sink that low."

Ivan didn't need to say more. The outcome was obvious by the fact that Ivan was here, rather than killed at age ten. Still, he pushed on. Perhaps he wasn't able to stop upon reaching this point; it certainly didn't appear to be a topic he had much practice dealing with.

"He begged me not to hurt him. I didn't want to. I held out for so long, but burning alive without rest or relief... he cried as I choked him. Never tried to fight back, though. Just kept staring at me, staring as he went limp, staring as the flames faded, staring as they dragged his body away. I can still feel him, decades later. His gaze, his tears on my hands, the softness of his neck. To this day, I don't know why Kristoph didn't try to take my head the moment we met." Ivan took a long, steadying breath, his hands pressed against one another. "After that, after I killed one of the two people in the world I loved, they named me. Because I had earned one, in their eyes. I had taken the first step toward their great prophecy, become a contender for their highest honor. That was the day I got the name Ivan. If Vlad's moniker didn't give it away, we were named for warriors, kings, and conquerors."

Breaking his hands apart, Ivan forced them onto the table. "I wanted to tell you that the first kill with your own hands is always going to leave a scar. You feel like you should be unfazed, but what happened to you today threw all of us for a loop when it was our turn."

"I killed Rust Tooth during the Ridge City Riots."

"No, *Hephaestus* killed Rust Tooth. Today, Tori killed someone. Even if you don't know why that feels different, it's okay that it does. What you're experiencing is normal. How you proceed is up to you, but know that it does get better with time. For as horrible as that story I just told you was, my life went on. I've found people and moments that bring me sincere joy, something I could have never imagined inside that pit."

Tori shoved her plate away; she'd had her fill. The words felt true, even if it was hard to believe them just yet. There was a lot to think on, but that would come piece by piece. In the meantime, she was eager to keep the discussion going, especially since there was a major point yet to be covered.

"Is that how you became Fornax?"

A dark chuckle slipped Ivan's lips, close enough to Fornax's mad giggle that she felt a sliver of nervousness before reassuring herself with his controlled expression. "That day was the start, both literally and metaphorically, of me becoming Fornax. Just the start, however. You see, every year, there was a Trial of Worthiness. Every year, our numbers shrank. Sometimes, we fought three times. Sometimes, a single match was enough. All in service of their prophecy—the coming of the being with many names. The God of Endings, the Onslaught of Death, the World-Razer, a bunch of awful shit like that."

"No one ever told them less is more, huh?"

"Clearly," Ivan agreed. "Not that it mattered. The name wasn't the point. Getting it here was. According to myth, its body was too great to enter our realm, so only its soul and power could make the journey. To exist on our plane would require a host, a form with which to use all that terrible strength. That was the purpose of our raising. They wanted to breed a mighty body, strong and honed, to serve as their great monster's vessel. When the last Trial of Worthiness ended, I was the one left standing. I was the last survivor."

A flicker of a pause, like he was steeling himself. "I was chosen as the host of an entity whose sole purpose is to destroy this world."

Chapter 37

Half-watching the television screen out of the corner of his eye, Rick clicked on some programs hidden in a folder buried deep in his computer. A nice, law-abiding kid shouldn't have any of these sorts of programs—bootleg hacking software bought in internet back rooms and from a skeezy guy outside a computer repair shop. Rick didn't fancy himself competent enough to get into anything truly secure, nor would he want to. As a boy with dreams of working at NASA, he understood there was a line between childish mischief and serious crime that it was important he not cross. Besides, he hadn't gotten this sort of software because he wanted to hack the school, or break into a bank's system.

No, this was a personal project, one he'd been working on for a few years now. A secret from his friends, and especially from his family. What would Beth say if he shared his findings? As though he could even call what he was looking at "findings" in the first place. It felt more like insane conspiracy theory than actual hypothesis—one that Rick would have dismissed, if every new bit of information he found didn't support the suspicion.

It had all started with a simple school report on genealogy. Getting their mother's information was easy—a long line of professors, laureates, and other highly documented careers made it possible to see the heights of their family tree. Dealing with their dad's past was another matter, in that he didn't seem to have one. It was no secret that their father had been abandoned as a child. He didn't talk about the experience in depth, but it was one he shared with his own kids, if only to explain why they had no relatives on his side.

That was where it should have ended: an in-depth report covering one half of his family, and a sad story on the other. More than enough for a good grade. Except, Rick was his mother's son, and once a project had his mind, he was loath to let it go so easily. So he'd kept digging. Hunting for foster records, old school photos, any sort of documentation from his father's childhood. When that had come up dry, Rick had shifted gears to young adulthood, searching for any signs of Ivan Gerhardt prior to meeting their mom.

Nothing. Oh, there were documents saying he'd existed—rental receipts and leases—but it was only a paper trail. Rick had gone so far as to search a database of old photos of capes in action, hoping to spot Ivan in a background of the city where he'd supposedly lived. Even that, he could have brushed off... until he'd decided to test it.

Just a drive for ice cream. That was the pitch, a simple request. An excuse to get them driving around an old neighborhood of Ivan's, one where he'd supposedly lived for years. Jamming the GPS was easy enough—like most parents, Ivan didn't exactly have a stellar grip on technology. Such a simple test, and yet, once his guidance was gone, Ivan had immediately become lost. Despite having an address, and being in an area he *should* know by heart. Shops might change, but street signs weren't so malleable.

That was the day Rick's silly side project had gone from a flight of fancy to a sincere suspicion. He'd begun to dig deeper, even taking a few real risks, yet it all circled back to the same result. On paper, Ivan Gerhardt was and always had been a perfectly normal, almost boringly mundane, sort of man. In reality… Rick wasn't even sure that was his father's real name.

His working theory was a witness protection program, that Ivan had seen something he wasn't meant to and gone on the run. Occasionally, when Rick really thought about it, his mind would drift to the scent of the ocean, though why that was he couldn't begin to guess. Today, however, he was less concerned with Ivan himself and more so with Tori, the nice coworker of their father's they'd once met who'd been all over the news. She'd also had a surprising lack of personal information leak out, despite being plastered on every channel. Given that she was one of the few people outside of family and existing friends he'd seen Ivan show interest in, Rick suspected that she might be part of the same witness program.

Getting into Vendallia's real systems were well beyond what Rick could manage, back-end programs or not. Luckily, he'd long ago learned to chase the human element rather than a purely technological one. People often didn't think to clear out the file logs on their scanners, which hosted a treasure trove of useful information.

Wielding his programs and a few passwords lifted from his father's office, Rick made his way onto the server, clicking on the scan log files. For the most part, it was boring stuff. Evidently, they must use something more secure for financial or proprietary information. All he was finding were low-tier HR forms, including several well-deserved complaints of an employee microwaving fish. Then he caught it: Ivan's name finally present on a document. Rick enlarged the image, leaning in to peruse the small lettering.

He read it twice more before finally leaning back and clicking a print button. As the pages appeared, he turned toward the screen once more, looking at Tori in a new light. Who the hell was this woman? And why was their father, a man who'd spent his whole life claiming to have no known blood relations, filing an HR declaration form listing Tori Rivas as his niece?

Rick still didn't have much to go on regarding the mystery of his father, but this was the first major clue in years. Whatever Ivan's secret was, Tori Rivas could be the key to unlocking it.

"Last time we talked about this, you said your powers came from eating a god." Tori didn't mean it as an accusation—she had confidence the two tales would line up eventually. It was more her trying to put the story together in her head, connecting dots that were still too far apart.

"It's the best word I have for what happened," Ivan replied. "I was eighteen during the final Trial of Worthiness. So were the few who remained. My last fight was a lot like my first one, in that I was against an old friend. Thankfully, Vlad and I hadn't been the same since I killed our third, and tricky as he could be, I was the better fighter. When it was over, when I'd killed the last person I grew up with, the cultists came."

There was a detached tone to Ivan's voice; he was powering through, getting the facts out without slowing to deal with all the inherent emotions that came with such a topic. Tori made no requests for details. She understood the need to run through some discussion points far too well.

"We went to a chamber I'd never seen before. I was stripped, covered in arcane symbols and oils, then placed in a warded circle when the ceremony began. After they started chanting, I fell away from the physical world, into the place where minds and souls dwell. How long I was there, I truly have no idea, but the next thing I felt was *it* breaking through."

Ivan shook his head, glancing at the empty glass with a dash of desire, followed by self-imposed restraint. "That monster was everything they'd wanted. Massively powerful, with an appetite for chaos that can never be sated. It exists only to destroy. Which is what it tried to do. Devour me, my soul, my essence, and then take over my body to use as a vessel."

"Clearly didn't know what a stubborn bastard you are," Tori interjected.

"You joke, but you're not far off from the truth." A smile was forming on Ivan's face. Dark, twisted, and cruel, yet a smile all the same. "The cultists made a mistake, you see. Only the body was meant to be tempered and prepared, not our minds. By placing us in that crucible, they forged our wills—forcing us to face constant death sharpened our desire to live. Their monster was expecting a soft-headed morsel ripe for the plucking. Instead, he met a man who had fought with every drop of blood in his veins to make it that far, with no intent of letting his hard-won life slip away. The thing about the realm of minds is that willpower is what matters most. You can't take muscles or magic in there, only your strength of self."

Now that she had the missing piece, Tori could see how the story components fit together, though she said nothing yet. Ivan clearly still had more to get through.

"That devouring of the soul thing is a two-way street. Magic tends to balance like that. In order to cross over, the monster also had to become vulnerable. Turns out, he didn't want this body quite as much as I did. It was still one of the hardest fights of my entire life, mind you—one I'm not sure I could ever win again. But I did manage to triumph, wolfing down that massive intruder, making his power my own."

Ivan's smile sharpened further at the corners. "You should have seen the looks on those cultists' faces, for the brief instant they still had heads."

"Payback?"

"For a childhood spent living as a caged animal, forced to fight the only people I cared about? No. Not even close." His expression hardened, eyes looking back into the past. "Not even the next few years felt like enough revenge, and I spent those keeping a promise to wipe out the Order of the Final Dawn."

"Here I thought a man seeking revenge was supposed to dig two graves," Tori said.

"Oh, I dug a *lot* more than two. Or rather, I would have, if there was ever enough left to bury, and I cared." Ivan took a moment to compose himself, idly nibbling on a chip from the corner of Tori's massive buffet. "I gave the Order of the Final Dawn exactly what they'd wished for: a destroyer. A god of death. They just didn't realize it would be coming for them instead of the world."

"About that..." Tori trailed off, trying to think of the best way to broach this topic. Knowing now what she did about Ivan's power, there was a fairly salient concern to address. "Are we to the point that explains what happened with you and Apollo? Because that's one I'd really like to have a better handle on."

Something flashed on Ivan's face... shame? He turned away quickly, leaving Tori with only a glimpse to work from. His voice, however, remained steady and constant. "That came much later. The thing about devils is they always leave an escape clause in their contracts. I have the raw, destructive magical power of the god, but little knowledge on how to use it. In all these years, even with tutoring, I've only managed a few consistent spells. Some aspects come easier; the host body is meant to be nigh indestructible, and I have a natural aptitude for drawing out the physical magic. But I'm nowhere near as dangerous as what this body could do in the intended owner's hands. Hence why the option to ask for a little help is always there. A bit more influence, in exchange for greater power. One way for the devil to worm its way back in."

Turning her half-eaten turkey leg around on the plate, Tori considered the situation. "I'm kind of surprised you took that option. Doesn't seem like you'd want anyone else having control over you."

"For a very long time, I didn't. Until there was a fight that had to be won. That's another long story, though, one I doubt either of us has the energy for. You don't need to worry about it, anyway. If I ever do truly lose myself, Lodestar will stop me."

"Are you sure she can? I get that she's the strongest out there right now, but you just said the full-power version of you is a big step up. That might be too much even for Lodestar."

"It isn't," Ivan replied. "Understand something, Tori. I know it might seem silly, the amount of deference I show to her power, but it is wholly warranted. As one of the few people to see Lodestar's true abilities, I know how strong she really is. But as one who loves science, you can simply turn to the data for proof. I am not especially unique. If one has access to multiverse tech, it's possible to look out into the mirrors of our worlds and see how many things turn out consistently. Some events appear locked, going the same route nearly every time. Others are malleable, with shifting outcomes. One thing that is constant, in essentially every world: when the world is at risk, Lodestar wins. Even if it costs her the ultimate price, she wins."

Now *that* kicked Tori back a few mental feet. "Hang on, there are worlds where Lodestar dies?"

"Of course not. In so far as we were able to detect, no one has ever successfully killed a Lodestar. But the power is a mantle. A mask, like the ones we wear. Lodestar never dies; however, the person filling that role is vulnerable. If she goes too far into her own power, or loses her will to fight, there's no way back. It moves on, shifting the mantle to a new wielder. Like if your meta-suit could find a new wearer after you had a heart attack in battle."

"Sounds terrifying," Tori admitted.

Ivan nodded. "Which is why I would greatly prefer *not* to directly cause the death of the current Lodestar, the woman who helped me gain my freedom and my family. One of the many reasons I place such emphasis on self-control. Lessons my apprentice took well, based on her performance tonight."

For the first time in several minutes, Tori touched the beer to her lips. She'd wanted something to think about besides her kidnapping, and on that front, Ivan had more than delivered. Bad as her own upbringing had been, she at least hadn't been locked away and forced to kill for survival. The memories of Deacon still kept flickering to the surface, but they weren't as powerful now that Tori knew it was okay to be rattled. Even Ivan still visibly felt the weight of his first kill, and she certainly wasn't going to fare better than someone who'd had decades to deal with it any time soon.

"Thanks. For the compliment, for sharing, and for never letting me feel like I was in there alone. My big question now is: what's next? I can't go back to being another face in the crowd, not for a while, if ever. But I don't want to run and hide here on the island, either."

"Let me ask you this: if there was no fame or kidnapping to deal with, where would you be?"

"Work. Or barring that, home with my friends. Maybe working on my suit—though honestly, this last day has me thinking that it might be time to break ground on some new tech. Things that are portable, that I can carry with me at all times, just in case... of... huh." Abruptly, Tori stood from the table. "I actually think I know what I want to do. Can you get me a meeting with Wade in a couple of days or so? And yes, I used that name on purpose."

"That'll be up to Wade's schedule, but you'll get an audience when he has a window," Ivan said. "Dare I ask what sort of idea you're pondering?"

It was Tori's turn to smile, though hers was more mischievous than terrifying. "I think I just hit on a way to turn this kind of fame into an opportunity. Figured it was only right I give our leader the first bite at the apple."

Chapter 38

For the most part, it was a quiet drive home. Tori had spent a few hours at the volcano lair, taking advantage of the privacy and lack of distractions to work on some initial designs and inquire into material availability. The guild's network of underground suppliers had been diminished by their public outing, but not wiped out completely. While some of the more exotic components might take a bit, there was plenty to get started on what she considered the more simplistic options.

By the time Tori crossed back over to Ridge City via the country club and caught a car back to her apartment, it was the dead of night. Even the bars were closed as they rolled along the quiet streets. Tori watched the light posts go by, ignoring her body's desire to shiver when they passed isolated stretches. She wouldn't give this new fear any purchase. Her life was too dangerous to be afraid of something as simple as walking down the street. It helped to remind herself that, if she'd been willing to accept the consequences, escape had always been an option. Next time, she wouldn't have to make that choice, though. Next time, she'd be ready as Tori.

As the car pulled up, she noticed a figure waiting in the shadows not far from her building. Too public for a fellow villain, oddly shadowy for a cape. Maybe someone had decided to take a run at her already, while she was a hot commodity? Tori expected to feel no more than exhausted at the proposition, but an ember of rage quickly took light. This shit was not going to fly, and if she'd learned anything from the guild, it was the importance of sending a message. Maybe some broken bones and pulped testicles would give the next dipshit pause.

No sooner was she out of the car than the figure was moving, however. The shock of copper hair gave away the surprise seconds before she reared back for a punch.

"Fucking hell, Donald! I thought you were another damn kidnapper."

"So you were coming toward me?" Donald emerged fully into the light, clad in his old civilian clothes. Slacks and a wrinkled plaid button-down made him look like the easier nighttime target. Once upon a time, that would have been an accurate impression, too, but months with the AHC had affected Donald. From the width of his shoulders to the way he stood straighter, being a cape was changing him. Into what, Tori suspected she'd have to wait to find out.

"Sorry, I'm not here to scold. I just wanted to make sure you were okay. And that you got home safe. And to say that I'm... I'm sorry, Tori. You're my friend, you helped me when I needed it most, and I couldn't be there to return the favor."

Occasionally, she wondered if it was wise, having a friend on the other side of the line. Donald was a liability, someone who could turn on her once he learned the truth. The more she saw of Fornax and Lodestar's odd dynamic, the more Tori had begun to suspect that these things might be inevitable. Ultimately, it didn't really matter. Donald was her friend, and even if this appearance was creepy as shit, it obviously came from a place of concern.

"Hey, buddy, little perspective: the motherfucking Alliance of Heroic Champions, including all three members of the Champions' Congress, worked together to save me as fast as they were physically able. I know you're having a good debut year, but in no way do I hold you to a higher standard than Quorum or Professor Quantum." Tori crossed the rest of the distance between them, gently taking his hand. "No one expects you to save the world yet, Donald. Just keep doing the best you can with the power you've got. That's all anyone has the right to ask."

He met her eyes for a long moment before glancing away. "Sweet lord. I came out here to apologize, scared you instead, and now you're comforting *me* after a day of being kidnapped." Donald sighed, shaking off some of his reticence. "I wanted to tell you not to worry, that we're going to make sure you're covered—not just at home. We'll—"

"Hard pass." Tori cut him off, but didn't let go of his hand quite yet. She didn't know how it would go over, but she could always elevate to a firm sell if the amiable approach failed. "Donald, for a multitude of reasons, some of which will become clear soon, it is vital that the AHC *not* put a protective detail on me. The New Science Sentries can stay, since they're already moved in and I don't hate the idea of our home being protected, but in no way, shape, or form do I want capes on my tail every time I leave the house."

"Tori... you're a target now. You're famous. Even if it won't actually hurt the AHC, there are people who will go after you because they think it makes us look bad. I'm not trying to scare you more; I just want you to understand that it's dangerous. You'll need protection."

"I'll have it." Tori released Donald's hand, jamming her index finger into his chest. "But not from the Champions' Congress, not from the normal patrol capes, and yes, Donald, not from you. This is my life, and if the AHC can't respect that, then you're not giving me much more agency than those kidnappers did."

Though Donald looked like he'd been slapped, he made no counterargument. "I don't want to force myself into your life. If that's how you feel, I'll stay away. I'm sorry, I just wanted to make sure you were safe."

Before he could turn, Tori grabbed his shoulder. "Hang on there, drama king. Cyber Geek doesn't have permission to tail me, but my friend Donald is still welcome to come around. Just call first, and leave the shadow skulking to the criminals. Do pass what I said on to the capes. I'm serious about that."

Despite smiling as she stopped him, Donald's smirk faltered at her order. "I'll pass the word along. But... well, I don't really have the authority to tell everyone else what to do."

"That's fine. I have plans if it comes to that. So long as you can respect the boundaries, I don't hold you accountable for whatever else the AHC does." Tori dearly hoped Donald remembered that sentiment if the tables were ever turned and he learned about her organizational ties. "In fact, let's do lunch next week. By then, I might have something fun to show you. Until then, I think one of us has a city to save."

It didn't escape Tori's notice that Donald hung around on the street until she was through the door, but he was gone by the time she looked out the window again, so they seemed to have reached an understanding. Tori was feeling quite pleased with herself as she ascended the stairs, mentally replaying the conversation and unable to catch any major slip-ups or reveals.

Her good mood evaporated as she arrived on her floor to find Kyle leaning against the stairwell, a pile of empty test tubes accumulated by his side. His eyes were fluttering open as she put her last foot onto the wooden floor, the creaks calling Kyle out of slumber's clutches.

"Hrugh?" Kyle shook his head, slowly moving to stand. For her part, Tori kept on walking, making a beeline for her apartment. She felt like she'd made good progress, only to hear her name from a few feet away. Damn speedsters.

"Tori? Tori!"

"Oh holy fuck, I do *not* have the energy to do this twice." She whirled around, catching Kyle by surprise. "It's fine that you didn't protect me; that's not your real job, and we both know it. I don't care that you weren't there at the rescue; nobody was going to do a better job than Lodestar, anyway. You don't owe me an apology or an explanation. I'm the penance case you got stuck with after a fuckup, and no one actually expected any of this to happen. We good now? Because it's a few hours from sunup and some of us have had a real shitberg of a week so far."

It was only as she spoke that Tori truly looked at Kyle, noticing the sway in his posture and his wavering vision. By the time she was winding down, Tori had a hunch, but it wasn't until he finally spoke that she got confirmation.

"You... do not like us." Kyle seemed almost relieved by the words, slurred though they were.

That definitely sealed it: Kyle was drunk. A quick look over at the test tubes gave Tori a working hypothesis, one that was easy to check. "Did you get liquored up on some kind of hooch for people with super-speed metabolism?"

Her response was Kyle lifting a finger to his mouth and blowing out sloppily, in what was probably supposed to be a "shhh" gesture. "Don't tell the others. This is such an Ike move."

"Is that why you're drinking in the hall? Didn't want your friends to find out?" Now that she knew he might not be out here for her, Tori's annoyance level sank considerably. A drunk night during a hard week was hardly something she had room to get judgmental about.

"Started out at the roof pool, watching the stars." Kyle looked around, knitting his brow in concentration. "Crud, when did I get down here?"

"No idea, but let's get you home." Taking his shoulder, Tori guided Kyle down the hallway and the short walk to his actual door. She moved to knock, but it slid open before her fist was even fully raised.

To Tori's surprise, it was Ike waiting at the door, looking up at the both of them. "Thanks. I was going to peel him off the floor within the hour if he didn't come in soon. Come on, you bossy cock, let's get you some water."

Ike led his taller teammate inside, laying Kyle on the couch, then teleporting to the kitchen to grab a bottle of water from the fridge. Tori watched him work, realizing that this was the first time she'd been around Ike or Presto without a constant torrent of noise pouring from his mouth.

"Does this happen a lot?"

"Maybe twice a year," Ike replied. "Austin is the team leader, but Kyle's got a lot of responsibilities that weigh on him. Every now and then, it gets to be too much and he tries to go wild. Once caught him listening to old techno music on the beach, attempting to get drunk off stolen wine coolers. Much of a pain as Kyle can be, all that uptightness comes from a desire to be good at this job, to be a real superhero. Occasionally, that thought makes him more tolerable."

It was strange to see Ike so matter-of-fact, a complete swing from the crass personality he usually donned. Unnerving, too, because Tori hadn't really considered him past that depth. She'd taken his surface level for the real thing, a mistake no self-respecting villain could rightfully excuse. Perhaps this night was a happy accident; better to know about a threat than to be caught unaware.

"What's your role, then? Austin's the leader, Kyle is the clear second. Seems like you and Ellie would have parts to play as well."

"I'm the scapegoat. She's the tits." The words were delivered almost neutrally, save from a touch of fire in Ike's voice toward the end.

"Wow. Sorry, I thought the 'piece of shit' thing was more of an act. My bad." Tori looked toward the door, but Ike teleported over, offering her a water bottle as well.

"You think I picked those roles?" Ike asked. "Don't ask a question you don't want answered. What I said was the truth. You could find any number of metas with adequate powers to fill my spot. I'm on this team because no one will ever really like me, so if something ever goes wrong, I'm the one who takes the heat. I'm not being cute, or funny. This is the job I have."

She accepted the water, eyeing Ike uncertainly. Tempting as it was to head home, learning more about the capes down the hall was probably an opportunity worth pursuing. If she was stuck with them anyway, understanding their inter-team dynamics couldn't hurt. "Why take a job like that?"

The question earned her a genuine laugh out of Ike, a harsh bark that trailed off quickly. "Look at me, Tori. I'm short, not personable, and at my best, I've got a plain face. Despite a power that kicks all kinds of ass, I'm never making it to the big leagues on my own. Does playing the scapegoat role suck? For sure. Is it also my only chance at touching true greatness? Hell yes."

"And Ellie?"

Ike's face darkened for a split second. From his pocket, he produced a cell phone, cycling through the pictures until he stopped on one of a younger Ike and a dark-haired woman smiling on a beach. Actually smiling, in Ike's case. There was something familiar about the woman, too, though Tori couldn't quite place it.

"That's before she made the cut. Before the 'profile enhancements' deemed necessary for someone representing the New Science Sentries brand."

Holy shit. Now that Tori looked closer and squinted, she could see the resemblance. It wasn't easy, though. Cheeks, lips, chest, hair, everywhere she looked, there were only hints of the Ellie she knew now in the picture. The woman had practically been rebuilt with plastic surgery, despite how natural she still looked. An advantage of Professor Quantum's tech, no doubt.

"She agreed to this?" Tori asked.

"It was a chance to be on the New Science Sentries, a team founded and funded by the world's first superhero. Yeah, she took the deal. We'd spent years trying to earn the opportunity. Eleanor became Ellie, who then took the title of Plasmodia. Or did you think her costume's cut was a coincidence?"

The more Tori saw of Professor Quantum's team-building methods, the gladder she was that there were other capes in the Champions' Congress. If Beverly's family history hadn't already clued Tori in to the fact he was a bastard, this certainly would have tipped her suspicion.

"I suppose she had her reasons, just like you did," Tori said at last. "As for me, I need to rest. Take care of Kyle, and try not to let him drink in the hallway like that. I'll see you all around."

"Something tells me you'll be seeing us all sooner than you might think."

She was back into the hallway as she heard Ike's words, and by the time she turned to investigate, the door was shut once more. Too wiped to sincerely care, Tori trekked down the rest of the hallway, turned the lock, and stepped inside.

After days that felt like years, Tori was finally home.

Chapter 39

The high-pitched whine puttered out, echoing through the office's vast space for several seconds before fading completely. Setting up shop in a hidden cave lair had many privacy benefits, but the acoustics weren't anything to sneeze at, either. A pale, gaunt hand scratched out the final bits of the message as the sound turned into a ringing in the ears, before finally transitioning into a persistent memory of a noise.

It was the final transmission he'd expect until the arrival neared. Once they were moving, non-emergency communication would be too risky. Even this had required years of research to create specialized concealment equipment, and worked largely because few even bothered to scan for these sorts of signals. The longer he could keep his presence, and plans, a secret, the greater his chances of success. Time had taught him patience, a very useful skill, especially when one played a game that ran for decades.

On this occasion, patience was hardly required. About a month. That was how long he had until the party could properly begin, based on travel calculations. One month to get everything in order. Much of the groundwork had already been laid; being thought dead for decades made it possible to work easily unseen. The big players were accounted for, as they had been since the plan's initial conception. It was the newer, smaller fish that represented the capacity for chaos. Some chose to ignore fresh metas, believing the true challengers aged into their power. But the world was not a fair place, and some were born with more strength than others. Being experienced, he'd seen too many undone by such hubris.

The next step was securing fodder. Lozora's contacts were of a specific type, those with established reputations. It was essential to have a known element approach the other criminals; they weren't exactly the openly trusting sort. However, numbers still counted for quite a lot, especially where the game of distraction was concerned. Dealing high-tech weapons to various criminal outfits was a dual-pronged tactic: it not only allowed him to test designs before the big day, it gave him an in with the unsavory enterprises.

This task was best handled by someone with no past, origins, or true identity. Moving from the repaired communications array, the man ambled over to a drawer, producing a small square box. Popping it open, he thumbed through the array of IDs for his various identities. Some were fresh; others had been in use for decades, building up legitimate histories. Those were suited to other tasks. Today, he sought something fresh.

A pair of Ws jumped off a card at him, and he smiled. The names were left up to chance, so one must have come out that way by coincidence. Or, perhaps, serendipity. Either way, the search was over as he pulled the card up from the ranks of its brethren, promoting it to a position of usefulness.

"I suppose I shall be Wendel Worthington, then. For a few weeks." Wendel took the card over to his computer, where the identity's other information could be researched. A name with alliterating Ws might not mean much to most people; however, for Wendel's purposes, it was a perfect moniker. A tribute, in a way, to one of the only other people who'd managed the same accomplishment.

There were, after all, only so many people who Professor Quantum *truly* hated.

After the long week she'd had, Helen was aching for a few minutes of relaxation. Penelope was still sleeping, other members of the AHC were keeping the world safe, and she'd just finished a long night flying the skies. The sound of hot water pouring into her bathtub was like a siren's song of rest.

While she didn't really feel pain outside of serious attacks from major metas, Helen could still carry tension. Her back especially was ready for some treatment. She paused in the kitchen long enough to grab a mug of coffee and warm it with a quick blast of her thermal-breath, then headed for her sanctuary. Unfortunately, before she could reach the peaceful palace of porcelain, the phone rang. Not her home phone, of course. Life could never be that simple.

From the pocket of her robe came Helen's AHC-issued device, packed full of technology. It wasn't quite on par with the Quantum Utility Tool she kept on her as Lodestar, but was far less conspicuous, as to the outside observer, it was little more than a phone like countless others.

"What's up?"

Quorum's voice was waiting for her—another bad sign. "Quite a great deal. The world is restless, and Captain Bullshit has just unveiled another exhibition. Concerning you—however, there is specific business that needs addressing. On a rescue mission last night, we had a team suffer heavy civilian losses. While they still saved a great many, the pain of their failing is undeniable. They need to see The Grove, and historically, you liked to be contacted in those situations."

Standing in the door of her bathroom, Helen stared at the soft steam steadily rising from the tub, practically forming a hand and crooking a finger to invite her in. There were others who could do the job, who had been doing it for years while she was gone. Except it wouldn't be the same. When the speech came from the strongest meta, when *Lodestar* said that nobody could save them all, the newer superheroes listened. Twisting the knob, Helen killed the water and popped open the drain, letting her planned moment of peace go swirling into the sewers.

"Let me drop Penelope with a sitter, and Lodestar will be there."

It was a surprise to wake up and find snow falling from the sky. For one thing, the season was still late summer. For another, snow wasn't usually blazing purple and electric blue in color. Lastly, Tori was pretty damn sure snow didn't turn into flowers when it landed. True, they died after a few minutes, but it still had the effect of letting Tori look out her window and see Ridge City caught between a blizzard and a jungle.

"Oh good, you're up. I was coming to get you." Beverly pushed the bedroom door fully open, having already turned the knob.

"Is this something we should be concerned about?"

"Nah, the news says it's just a Captain Bullshit exhibition." Making her way across the room, Beverly joined her friend by the window. "I'm not great with meta-history, but he can change reality, right? With a power like that, he kinda sticks out."

"As I read it—and this was in an article from years and years ago—the consensus is that he can reshape reality, but only to create what he deems to be art. Not sure what the exact term was—I think he called his style 'absurdist creative expressionism,' assuming that isn't just word-soup. Never much of an art gal."

The two of them stayed like that for several minutes, watching the multicolored snow fall and coat their city in a sea of flora, which died and was replaced in fairly quick succession. One thing was apparent, however: no one would be driving in this. A car might make it ten feet before becoming overgrown, and that was being more than a little generous.

"The city invoked a meta-holiday, so most businesses are closed," Beverly supplied, her own eyes tracing the empty streets. "Chloe is home all day, and I'm ahead of schedule on work. After what happened, if you want to be alone, I get it, but if you wanted to have some company, we're here for that, too."

A reassuring hand landed on Tori's shoulder, almost causing her to flinch. After a moment, she let herself relax. Or at least as relaxed as she was capable of being.

"I know you well enough to guess you might want to shove past the whole kidnapping thing, and if so, then we can respect that. Just know that if you do decide to talk about it, I'm around."

"Thanks," Tori said, her voice stiff despite her best efforts to soften it. "Maybe once I've had a little time. For now, I need to feel like a normal person, you know? Just for a day, leave all the other stuff on the sidelines and rest." Burning as her ambitions where, Tori could also feel her own exhaustion, the kind sleep would do nothing to fix. She needed to reenergize, and drudging up that recent horror-show wouldn't help.

The hand on her back clapped her once before removing itself. "Good time to want normality, though. We can turn this into a snow day: watch winter movies, make hot chocolate, enjoy a mini winter break."

Pressing her hand to the window, Tori could feel the heat coming through the glass. If anything, it felt warmer than it had lately. Maybe flower-rain warmed things up, since normal rain cooled the temperature down? It was hard to put too much logic into this sort of thing; reality had literally been momentarily warped, so making sense was largely optional.

"I think we might want to go the other way with that. By noon, this whole place's AC will be fighting to keep up."

Beverly followed her lead, a momentary blip of surprise on her face as she felt the warmth. "Huh, not a bad point. Okay, so... beach day? Make margaritas in the blender, go make use of the rooftop pool before fall really sets in?"

Ordinarily, Tori would have happily chosen a day working in her garage lab, but this week was anything but ordinary, even by supervillain standards. A day with her friends sounded like just the right change of pace. Some normality to balance out all the extra crazy she'd been dealing with of late.

"I'll tell Chloe once she's out of the shower," Beverly offered. "You get dressed. We'll figure out a game plan." Beverly almost went to leave, before stopping herself. "Look, we don't have to talk about this right now. I just want to tell you so you don't think I'm springing it on you later: I sort of ended up inviting our neighbors over later this week. Austin and I ran into each other. We got food, and by the end, I'd somehow offered some basic socializing lessons so they can stop blowing their cover so often. Don't feel obligated to attend by any means—I got myself into this—but also, please be aware we'll be hosting capes on Sunday."

Although even twelve hours ago, that might have been of greater annoyance, Tori wasn't quite so bothered by the idea as she'd expected. Seeing Ike and Kyle's more vulnerable sides had offered useful insight into their personalities and the team's dynamic. If they were going to be her protectors, she should probably understand their limits. And if they were going to be Hephaestus's enemies, she should definitely know their weaknesses. Either way, Tori always held to the belief that more information was a boon, and this sounded like exactly the sort of scenario where such tidbits might be spilled.

"Let me know once the details are pinned down. Can't make any promises, but I'll try not to leave you on your own to deal with them."

"I appreciate it. Given their current track record, I can only imagine what sort of state secrets they'll accidentally reveal," Beverly said. To her, that was probably a joke, though Tori wasn't so sure. "Get dressed. I'll get things started on our snow day, but for sun. Sun-day? No, crap, that's obviously a day already. I'll figure it out by the time you're done."

Beverly marched out, momentarily more concerned with her naming dilemma. As for Tori, she took her time getting ready, starting with a short shower that was closer to boiling than hot, the sort that a human would have shrunk from. It felt good to be in her own shower, getting ready like it was another day heading to Vendallia. Most of the time, Tori fit well into her extraordinary life, but on occasions she too needed the comfort of routine.

Post-shower, getting ready was a simple affair, with no cumbersome work clothes to bother with. A simple t-shirt and shorts would see her through until it was time to head to the roof; the apartment's dress code was minimal on its best day. Running hands through her hair, Tori checked the mirror and found a normal, everyday woman in her mid-twenties staring back.

She paused, looking the image over with a critical eye. What she was planning would mean using the spotlight that had been thrust upon her, but in doing so, she'd likely never escape it again. Image was going to be a thing she'd have to care about, inasmuch as it furthered her goals. Controlling the perception was key, especially at the start. How she looked would be the first thing people noticed, and the furthest she might get, if her choices were not calibrated properly. It wasn't that she was looking to tart things up, more that she needed to project a specific image. This was a matter to consult on with Beverly, once things were a bit further along. For today, Tori was happily resigned to some much-needed mundanity.

With the mirror-check done, she stepped out of her room and into the kitchen. To her shock, she entered to find Beverly halfway shifted into her green dragon form, glaring at a strange woman shivering in a bathrobe, kitchen knife clutched tightly in her shaking hands.

It was such an insane scene that she genuinely thought her mind was mistaken, improperly processing the visual information being sent. But a few quick blinks changed nothing, except to bring a few more details to Tori's attention. For one, the woman was absolutely breathtaking, the sort of inhuman beauty it took celebrities and special effects to achieve. Her looks clashed with the worn, lime-green bathrobe that didn't fit her statuesque body. In fact, it didn't look right on her at all, because Tori *knew* that robe.

That was when it clicked, and while Tori was making some serious deductive leaps, she also trusted her gut as she stepped forward, quickly putting herself between Beverly and their apparent intruder.

"Calm it down," Tori ordered, very nearly reaching forward to pop Beverly on the nose. "You're scaring the piss out of Chloe."

That earned a pause in the glowering as Beverly's already green eyes, tinged with a hint of magic, scanned the shivering woman once more. This time, she was probably taking in the fact that their "intruder" had come unarmed, as that was *their* kitchen knife, and was dressed in a bathrobe that also happened to belong to a roommate who wasn't present. One with strange, hard-to-define powers, capable of truly unpredictable effects.

"That's Chloe?" Beverly sounded normal, so evidently, her tongue hadn't gone dragon-shaped yet.

"Of course, it's me!" Chloe sounded much the same, a slight husk to her voice lost in the near terror. She looked down at herself, eyes widening. "Shit!

Sorry. I came in here to show you this, but then you whirled on me, and I sort of panicked."

The three of them stood like that for a moment, until Beverly's body started to shift, slowly morphing back to a fully human form. "Apologies. I'm a little on edge, given everything. How did you change your entire body, though?"

A sheepish look came over the stunning face they were looking into. "I was in the shower, thinking about phrases, and one I hadn't tried popped into my head. Turns out, once you say that beauty is only skin deep..."

As Chloe explained, Tori turned her attention to putting on a pot of coffee. Day off or not, the way things were shaping up, she was definitely going to need it.

Chapter 40

"At first, nothing happened. Then I noticed some of my skin peeling a little in the water. Not much, not even sunburn level—just like the dead, dry skin coming off. Soon, more was coming, and after a few seconds, the whole top layer washed away to reveal... this."

Chloe spread her arms, pulling the bathrobe to dangerous heights. Her new form filled it out far more fully than the original, with ample hips and chest, capable shoulders, and toned limbs. Flowing chestnut hair, pouty lips—it was like she'd been built using photo manipulation software. "Neat trick, right?"

Neat was one way to put it. Terrifying was another. Chloe's power was like Captain Bullshit's, in that it played entirely by its own rules and logic. Sudden shower-shapechanging like that should be harder, should take some kind of toll, but all Chloe had needed was to find the right words. This was one just more innocuous trick, yet Tori couldn't help wondering how long it would be until Chloe found the words to something dangerous, the sort of ability that would put her on the wrong people's radar.

"Here's my thing, though, isn't beauty subjective? Like, yes, you are a stone-cold knockout right now, but what part of your ability determines what we value in the looks department?" Beverly had shifted from attack to analysis as soon as the situation became clear. She leaned across the kitchen counter, nearly knocking over her own mug of coffee, scanning Chloe more closely.

"I hadn't considered that," Chloe admitted. "Maybe based on what I consider to be beautiful? Or an average of everyone in the area's general preferences? It's a good point. You never really know what one person will like over another."

Tori said the words on reflex, not fully considering the implications. "Beauty is in the eye of the beholder."

Silence filled the room. Eyes turned to Tori first, then to Chloe, as the same thought echoed simultaneously through all three heads. Beverly broke the word embargo, tapping her finger against the counter. "You don't think..."

"No reason I can see why it wouldn't," Tori replied. "Then again, I'm not the expert."

"But you're right. It makes sense in theory," Chloe agreed. "Same principle, and I can see how it would work. What the hell—let's make a morning of it. **A penny saved is a penny earned**."

It seemed like nothing happened. Then Tori blinked, and Chloe was back to her old self again. The core limit of Chloe's power appeared to be that she could only sustain a single saying at a time. Changing it up canceled out the lingering effects of her last one—in this case, at a rapid pace.

"Figured I should set myself back to normal for a first test. Okay, here we go. **Beauty is in the eye of the beholder.**"

Taking a cue from the last minute, Tori voluntarily closed her eyes, giving the power time to work. Ideally, this would make for a smoother transition, and Chloe hadn't accidentally summoned a fantasy monster by mistake. Slowly, Tori peeked, scoping out the new-new-Chloe.

At first, she thought it hadn't worked, but that was only because she'd been expecting another complete overhaul. Instead, this Chloe looked more like a relative of the original. Same basic structure, only everything had been elevated: flawless skin, defined muscle, her face reshaped slightly, and her white-blonde hair now well past her shoulder.

"Oh, neat. You look good as a brunette." Beverly was also staring, though based on her comment, they weren't getting the exact same picture.

"Interesting. She's still blonde to me," Tori said.

Chloe hopped up from the counter, a gleam of excitement in her eye. "Hang on, let me get a pen and paper. You can both write down what you see, and then we'll compare. Let's test what this new saying can do!"

While it wasn't technically a very normal start to a day, Tori was spending her morning goofing around with her friends. That part mattered more than staying within the confines of the mundane. Besides, the scientist in her was always piqued by experimentation.

In terms of this project, there was a nuclear option—one that Rick was hesitant to pull, fearing both the blast and the fallout. He contemplated that as he typed on the computer, keenly aware these efforts were largely fruitless. So far, his research had gone nowhere. Whoever had hidden his father's true identity was skilled *far* beyond anything he could manage with some scrounged-up hacking programs. Each bit he'd pulled for Tori was the same. Everything lined up. Every document, every piece of history, all of it told a cohesive story of a young woman who'd lost her family young, fallen into drugs, and finally gotten her life together with the help of a distant uncle. Except there *was* no link between her family and Ivan, because Ivan had either been lying to them their entire life, or he truly had no family to speak of. Or both.

That didn't mean he was entirely out of paths forward, however. Rick was old enough to read between the lines; he knew his parents didn't have the most amiable relationship post-divorce. They were good about keeping that behind the scenes, always presenting a united front to their kids, but there were too many seams for some not to show. Whatever this secret was might impact his mother's willingness to share it with him. Alternatively, there was a chance this could be something bad. Something that would paint his father in a new light, the sort of thing she might agree not to tell, yet would confirm if he figured it out on his own.

Crazy as that idea seemed, his dad was so boring, and the mystery was stirring up all sorts of confusion. Finding out Ivan had kept this secret their whole lives… it was hard not to wonder what else he was hiding. Rick was a curious, determined boy; however, he *was* still a child. The possibility of changing the way he viewed his father scared him in ways he wasn't entirely capable of processing. Like all teens, he felt a healthy sense of rebellion and resentment toward those who held control, but Ivan was still his dad. If pressed, and placed into a state more capable of emotional honesty, Rick might have even admitted that he was a good father, at that, supportive and caring in his own way. Despite the distant demeanor, Rick had never for a moment wondered if he had his father's love. Ivan was always there when it counted, and often when it didn't. Firm, but never harsh or cruel. He couldn't even remember Ivan ever yelling at either him or Beth. Misbehavior was met with disappointment and stern discussions.

The mental image of his dad teaching Beth to swim at the community pool didn't quite mesh with the idea of a whole secret life... except for a moment, when Rick's mind flickered. It wasn't the pool anymore. It was a shoreline. Sand, waves, the screech of gulls in the distance. The water was wrong, though. Seawater didn't have viscous streaks of purple woven through it.

Just like that, the image was gone, leaving only a headache in its place. Rick realized his hands had gone still, and sweat dripped from the bottom of his chin onto the keyboard. Hopping up, he ran into the bathroom and noticed the shine on his entire face. He grabbed a towel and wiped away the excessive moisture, then splashed himself with cold water to cool off.

What the hell? A chunk of some image caused that kind of reaction? An image of someplace he wasn't even sure he'd ever been, at that. Rick felt his whole mind rebel at that thought, bringing him up short. No, it was a memory. Every part of his brain insisted that it was authentic, ignoring the utter lack of supporting evidence he could produce.

Whatever he was seeing, it rattled him. Despite the cooldown, Rick's heart was still racing as he sat once more at the computer. All he knew for sure was that it was tied to memories of his father, and the ocean. A new idea poked his brain, slithering up from the terror of his sudden near-panic attack.

Closing out the web browser, Rick instead began rooting around the home's shared folder. Three years prior, Rick's stepdad had digitized all the family's old albums as a birthday gift for Janet. They now lived on a folder tucked away on the massive memory bank connected to the network, and after a couple of clicks, Rick had pulled them up.

A few from his birth—only mom in those. Ivan had allegedly been stuck across town due to a meta-attack. Skimming ahead, Rick noted that the timeline seemed to jump from birth to his first birthday, where Ivan was presenting a lopsided, homemade cake. Under his breath, Rick resisted a snort. His father was usually a much more fastidious cook than that. Skimming ahead again, he was looking at himself as a child, next to a baby Beth just brought home from the hospital. Both parents were there this time, Janet presenting Beth to Rick while Ivan looked like a pack mule who only hauled baby supplies.

The more Rick skimmed, the sillier his concerns seemed. This was ridiculous. He knew who Ivan was. Some strange parts of the man's past didn't change the dad he'd always been. Rick was very near giving up, ready to switch over to college prep, when a new picture popped up on screen. Ivan and Janet waving at the camera. Rick looked about four or five, which would put Beth near one. They were all smiling, the sun shining down overhead—onto hot sand. It was a beach.

No... it was *the* beach. The one Rick had just seen. His whole stomach seized up, and his hands began to shake. He couldn't even look at it without feeling his brain spasm. Something was off. Wrong. Something had happened there, a memory his brain very clearly didn't want him dragging to the surface. Rick's determination set at that realization. When it had been a mere curiosity, that was one thing. But the deeper he dug, the more serious things were growing. It was starting to feel like this was bigger than he'd realized.

Perhaps it was time to go nuclear after all.

It wasn't often they met in the day. Work, life, and general habits meant they tended to find their time free in the evenings, at least until duty beckoned once more. Sometimes, however, circumstance demanded speed over convenience. There were issues that couldn't wait until the time was right; they had to be dealt with as quickly as possible.

"—and that's all we've managed so far. Vernon is working to analyze the remains of what we brought back, the whole AHC is in a tizzy over getting caught with our pants down, and consequently, I'm probably going to have to do a mass evaluation this weekend. Real crapshow all over the place."

"About the same," Ivan agreed, helping himself to a donut from the sizable box he'd brought. The sugary ones were for Penelope when she was back from day camp. He stuck to a simple kruller. "Not the evaluation part, but Wade is bothered by the fact that someone managed to beat him at tech, even if only for a day. Nobody is taking it lightly."

Helen dipped into the box as well, grabbing a donut so filled with cream and sugars she could have never allowed her daughter to eat it in good conscience. Since she, on the other hand, was functionally immortal, the carbs weren't quite such a concern. She did pause to grab a paper towel off her counter before diving in, though, managing to spare her kitchen island from the first errant blob of cream.

"The real question is: what's their next move? Tori was a test run; pretty sure we're all on that same page. Nothing we saw spoke to a sincere attempt by a legitimate threat. When whoever was really running things starts playing for keeps, I don't think the stakes are going to be one civilian snatched off the street."

This was, by Ivan's estimation, the hardest point in dealing with a new enemy: figuring out what they wanted. Power, skill, competence, all of that could be handled in the moment, but knowing an opponent's goal was the greatest power one could have. It was a compass, guiding him toward them at every turn, showing the things they cared about. Until he knew that, he was playing at a disadvantage. Worse, there was a chance that someone this good knew his real identity, and that put Ivan's own family at risk. Odds that they were coming to pick a fight with a murdering legend were slim, but it had happened before. Plus, as much as they wanted to assume Tori was a coincidence, there was always the chance it wasn't.

"I've got nothing, and I hate it," Ivan admitted. "No clues, no hunches, not even a direction to punch in. Which is a shame, because my fists are positively itching."

From across the kitchen island, Helen's hand landed daintily on his forearm. "Keep a leash on it, tough guy. Tearing up every hideout and den in the underworld isn't actually going to help, especially with someone this careful."

"Be assured, I have no intent to dole this anger out where it isn't deserved." Ivan paused to tear off a sizable chunk of kruller that he swallowed in a single gulp. "But they stole my apprentice off the street, lashed her to a chair, and threatened her life. Whoever set that in motion will answer to me."

"Only if you get there first." It was said teasingly, yet both clocked the seriousness in one another's eyes. She would strive to bring the threat in, while Ivan would fight to put it down. "Maybe you could come on board and team-up for this one. I bet we can find you a costume with a big helmet to hide your face, sell you as some new heavy hitter."

Helen's eyes lit up as the idea took hold. She even rubbed her hands together, a habit she'd long ago had to break while in Lodestar form. "Oh my god, this weekend is the mass evaluation—we could totally smuggle you in with the other rookies! Now *that* would be a hell of a way to drive home the 'don't take any threat lightly' point, some newbie managing to go a few rounds with Lodestar."

"Aside from the myriad of reasons that's already a bad idea, I'd never be able to actually fight you without displaying a sizable amount of my power, enough to endanger bystanders."

"Ivan, I'm not actually going to have you throw down in front of a bunch of new superheroes. It's just a fun thing to imagine," Helen assured him. "I mean, don't get me wrong: I would love to have a chance to let them fight Fornax in a controlled environment, really drill in the difference in power levels without me having to do it."

Once, Ivan might have missed the flicker of sadness in Helen's eyes at the prospect. To most of them, she was more legend than person, known for her world-saving exploits. However, what came soon was going to be worse.

Right now, the stories were just stories, myths that many no doubt took to be exaggerations. After a mass evaluation, they were going to understand the gulf between where they were and where the top was far, far better. It was a good lesson, one villains needed as much as capes, yet one that weighed heavily on Helen. Because after they understood, they'd grow more distant. Rarely out of fear or malice; it was just the way people behaved among those that were so much stronger than they.

It was lonely at the top. For a brief time, they'd gotten to share that position, but those days were long past. Now, all Ivan could do was remind her that no matter how many people called for Lodestar, some still preferred to spend their time with Helen.

"While Fornax might not be a good fit for an AHC event, you and I also have some business to discuss regarding this week's Starscouts meeting. The End of Summer Shindig is coming up in a couple of weeks, so we'll want to make sure to go over that at the top, as well as have handouts for the parents with relevant information. I think they changed the location and fee structure this year, so we'll want to make sure to highlight those points."

Helen groaned with such theatricality Ivan half suspected she was stealing the technique from Penelope. "Geez, it's all work, work, work, with you. Don't you ever—"

A bright, blinking light appeared on Helen's wrist, atop what appeared to be a perfectly normal watch. In a literal flash, Helen was gone, replaced by the glowing form of Lodestar. She disappeared in a blur, already changed before zipping through a secret tunnel that led out of the house. By the time Ivan took another bite of kruller, Lodestar was already in the sky, racing to respond to whatever threat the AHC deemed appropriate.

In the meantime, Ivan got to work making a rough outline of the Starscout End of Summer Shindig information for the other parents. Lodestar could handle whatever she was facing alone, but Helen would be glad to have the job started when she got back.

Chapter 41

By the time they made it up to the rooftop pool in the early afternoon, Captain Bullshit's strange snow had finally ceased, and the flowers growing on every external surface had wilted to nothingness. All that remained of his exploit were the memories, and the *heat*. Despite the fact they were cusping on fall, the thermometer read like they were summering in the desert. A weather shift like that would have ample effects, many of them negative, but one upswing was that it made for perfect poolside weather.

As Chloe mounted her pink-and-black umbrella onto a stand, creating a shady spot to protect her pale skin, Tori watched her work. She looked normal now, but the morning's experimentation had confirmed that her new phrase allowed her to look different to each person viewing her. Tori and Beverly's descriptions were hardly worlds apart, yet if someone had been taking witness statements, they'd never think both women had been talking about the same person. It was a potent talent, one Tori could envision countless espionage uses for.

Instead, Chloe would probably only ever use it as a party trick, or maybe as a way to boost tips if the coffee shop was running slow one day. And the more Tori thought about it, the happier she was that this unpredictable power was in the hands of someone like Chloe. Flying and fire, even magic, that was all one thing. The powers that fucked with the very foundation of how the world worked scared Tori; she much preferred them in the hands of people who saw them as novelties rather than weapons.

Together, the three women got settled on the far side of the pool, occupying some of the faded and sagging loungers provided by the apartment complex. Once Chloe was under her shade, she began the process of liberally applying ample sunscreen, easily triple the amount that Beverly was using. Tori got to skip that step, since she didn't burn—one of the handier side effects of fire-based abilities.

For the first ten minutes, it was peaceful. A quick dip, a little muddling about, the afternoon breeze stirring up their overheated city. Tori lay in the sun, her mind drifting, contemplating new ideas for her next project. She had to do this right. She only had one chance to launch, and she'd be capitalizing on the kidnapping, so time was a factor. Whatever she kicked off with would have to be just right; there probably wasn't going to be a second chance. Not like this.

Bam. The rooftop door slamming open jarred Tori out of her contemplation and drew a squeak from Chloe. Seconds later, a familiar voice rumbled out from the shadows. "Sorry! I thought it was heavier."

Austin walked into the sunshine, clad in board shorts and a large t-shirt, a suitably shameful expression on his face. No sooner had he actually scanned the roof than his whole body changed. Seizing up, the relaxed ease left him, and he barely managed to take a few steps forward to let his roommates out. "Hello, neighbors. I didn't expect to see you here."

Yeesh, Tori could even hear the tension creeping into his voice.

"Who the shit are you talking to? Wait, why am I back here? I can see the light." In a pop, Ike appeared in front of Austin, while Ellie worked her away around through the doorway. "Ohhh, it's the cute neighbor girls. I gotcha."

"By this point, shouldn't you know our names?" It wasn't an especially barbed comment, but that might have just been thanks to Chloe's constant casual demeanor.

A quick slug smashed into Ike's shoulder, courtesy of Ellie's fist. "Yes, he should, and I'm sure he does." She, unlike most of the attendees, had walked up in her swimsuit without any sort of cover up. It wasn't absolutely risqué, but it was definitely more skin-forward than anything Tori would have chosen. Then again, as she was in a simple red one-piece designed for lap-swimmers, that wasn't saying much. It was probably about on par with Beverly's bikini, which still meant it was well outside Tori's comfort zone.

On Ellie, however, it was stunning. Tori watched the woman, remembering Ike's picture of the old her. Whoever had done the work was good. There were no signs that her beauty was anything but natural. Part of Tori wondered if that made the whole thing better, or worse.

As Kyle followed Ellie out, shoving Austin another few inches forward, Ike teleported over to their area, hunkering down next to Chloe. "You know, some people would be complimented by being called cute."

Lowering her oversized vintage sunglasses slightly, Chloe met Ike's eye, then reached out and gently ruffled his hair. "Sorry, bud. I had my sad-boy-hiding-his-pain-through-asshole-behavior phase already, and I'm not looking for a do-over. Why don't you aim your words in the same direction as your heart?" Pointedly, Chloe glanced over to Ellie, whom Ike had thought he was carefully ignoring.

It was the first time Tori had seen Ike absolutely flattened, and Chloe had done it with a comforting tone. He stared at her, ignoring the rest of his team settling in on another set of chairs, mouth opening twice before he finally responded. "You're dangerous, aren't you?"

"Like you wouldn't believe. So play nice." With that, Chloe popped her sunglasses back up and laid into her chair, signaling the conversation was done.

For a few minutes, peace returned. The New Science Sentries unloaded their own gear—towels and coolers and the like—while the two secret villains and a not-so-secret barista lounged in the warm air. As their neighbors finished getting ready, attention turned to the pool. Kyle went in first, popping his shirt off, and Tori was unsurprised to see the usual build of a super-speed meta. The man ran lean, toned to the point of being shredded thanks to nonstop cardio and training. Austin was close behind him, pausing only to remove the oversized t-shirt hiding his torso.

"Oh *my*." The words had slipped from Beverly's mouth without warning, earning her a cocked eyebrow from Tori.

"Was that a George Takei impression? I didn't know you watched any Multerion Collection flicks, let alone the sci-fi stuff."

"Never got into movies from other universes, so I have no idea who you're talking about," Beverly admitted. "I, um, must have been thinking and something nonsensical slipped out."

"Come on now. That's not even my particular flavor of ice cream, and I can admit it's a well-made sundae," Chloe chimed in.

She wasn't wrong. Austin was nothing if not properly put together. He'd always been large—that went with the territory of physical strength more often than not—but this was the first time they could see just how well conditioned he was. What he wielded wasn't simply mass, built by repeatedly lifting heavy objects. It was the honed muscle of someone who put their strength to work, constantly and continuously.

Unfortunately, Ellie had chosen that moment to get near enough to overhear. "Hang on, if *that* isn't your flavor, what is?" The hungry look she tossed over her shoulder left no question about Ellie's own appreciation for her leader's physique.

"What's the ice cream equivalent of pansexual? Rainbow sherbet? I'm going to say rainbow sherbet," Chloe decided. "I more meant I'm not into the huge look. My preference leans toward people closer to my size."

Though she didn't say it, on that point, Tori and Chloe were agreed.

Ellie, however, merely shook her head. "No accounting for taste, I suppose. At least this gal is with me." Ellie held up a hand for Beverly to high-five, which she did, after noticing it a few seconds too late to not get chuckled at. Clearly, Beverly had no such qualms about the muscle-bound physique.

It wasn't long past then that the heat drove more of them into the water, forcing dips to cool down. Although she was unaffected, Tori did the same, careful not to draw too much attention to herself, even for something as simple as high heat tolerance. This game they were playing was dangerous. The closer they got to the New Science Sentries, the worse the blowback could be if they learned the truth. But the rooftop pool was a shared space, and ultimately, Tori was finding she didn't mind the quartet entirely. Outside of the costumes, they made decent company. When not hallway drinking, that was.

By the time Kyle finally approached Tori on his own, waiting until the rest of the group was distracted messing with a portable charcoal grill, she was already waiting for him. His nervous, shamed glances had been coming her way all day, and while they'd spoken, it had only been in brief, passing snippets of casual conversation. She'd seen him gathering his courage, and even gone off on her own to present an opportunity. Better to get this done with, especially while everyone was in a good mood.

"Hey," he greeted her, as if they hadn't just spent several hours together. "I, uh, wanted to talk to you about last night."

"Good news: you didn't take a swing, use a slur, or try to grab my ass, so we're fine."

That stunned him for a moment; Kyle moved in silence as he took a seat on the unoccupied lounger next to Tori, resting in the shade of Chloe's curiously colored umbrella. "Nice to know, I guess, but I didn't think I'd have done any of that in the first place."

"Makes you a nicer drunk than most people I've known," Tori shot back. "Look, I know you feel bad, but really, why? You got weekday drunk? Big whoop, we both know you cleared a hangover within the first ten minutes of waking up, so there's no long-term consequences. All you did with me was apologize, so nothing bad there. Unless you took a piss in this pool last night and are only just now revealing it, I truly don't get where all this guilt is coming from."

"But I'm a superhero," Kyle protested.

"So the fuck what? It's a *job*. It doesn't define who you are, or what you can be. Hell, if you want to get technical, you're only a superhero when you're in costume, and last night, I saw Kyle getting hammered. No Tachyonic in sight. The reason capes wear masks is so they can take them off and be normal people when the day is done."

In truth, this was some of her own villain education being repurposed and repackaged, but the point was a sound one. Ivan had helped her build multiple identities for a reason, beyond just secrecy. Different feelings, different ambitions, they might not all fit the same side of her. Some things were for Tori, others for Hephaestus. The villain in her, for example, realized how much work time she was wasting sitting in the sun, comforting a cape, but she made no attempt to leave. The human part of Tori deserved her downtime.

"When I go running in costume, people cheer. They scream my name, try to slap my hand if I'm passing close. They're already looking up to me. I saw kids wearing Tachyonic shirts yesterday, but it feels like I've just been fucking up nonstop since we got here. Last night was one more log on the guilt fire, I guess."

"How many people has Tachyonic saved?" Tori asked. "Since arriving in Ridge City, I mean."

Kyle took a moment, doing some mental calculations and perhaps a few ticks on his hands. "Rough estimates, about seventy-five, though I'm rounding a little on how many people were on the bus I stopped a few days ago."

"Sounds to me like you're doing fine. It's not your job to inspire, or be a perfect symbol, or some flawless beacon of justice. Showing up when people truly need you is a superhero's only real job. Be there, help people, turn certain deaths into near-misses. Give people their futures back."

"And don't forget the receipt in the bag." The smirk on Kyle's mouth was tentative, yet distinct.

Despite herself, Tori laughed. "Look at that, you're already learning. A proper rescue protects them from all threats, media as well as meta. Cat's out of that bag now, though."

As peace settled between them, Tori thought their conversation had reached its end. Based on the bursts of flame shooting up from the grill, dinner would go from raw to burned in rapid succession, so they'd likely be eating soon. She was expecting Kyle to get up and mosey over. Instead, he settled deeper into the lounger.

"You know, for someone who acts like she doesn't give a crap about superheroes, you've sure given a lot of thought to their purpose."

"Not especially. But I've seen what happens when there is no last-minute miracle… no cape swinging in with a power to fix everything, no sudden shift in a seemingly inevitable fate." Warm air be damned, Tori could still feel the chill from that damned hospital room. "You only have to witness that once to know the other version is better."

A glance at Kyle showed her a man conflicted. He clearly wanted to know more, but was also perceptive enough to notice that this wasn't some hypothetical situation she was describing. After a brief struggle, he formed his next words carefully. "Tori, I'm still getting to know you, and I feel like half our chats end with me saying the wrong thing, so I'm just going to be plain. If that was cryptic because you don't want to talk specifics, we can end it there. If it was to get me to dig deeper, I'm happy to listen."

"Asking was the right call. It's definitely the former," Tori confirmed. "But by this point, I know you have it in a file somewhere, so let's just get this done. My parents died due to an accident at a lab that made them violently, briefly ill. Their only hope was someone with meta-tech or powers, none of which came through. And that is the maximum I want to talk about it."

Another pause in the conversation, this one shorter than the last.

"My parents gave me away," he told her. "My mother was part of a prenatal setlium exposure test to see if powers could be reliably created by introducing it early. The answer was no, it didn't work reliably, but some of us did beat the odds. When she produced a meta-human baby, Professor Quantum made an offer. That was it. I don't even know their names. He says he destroyed all records for security, to make sure no one could use our biological parents as leverage. I don't want to talk about it, either, mind you. This isn't something I go around tossing out as a fun fact in interviews. But it only felt right to square us up."

That was not the origin story Tori had expected; however, she was hardly blown away. After hearing Ike's story, she was getting a sense of Professor Quantum, and it didn't paint the kindest of pictures. The positive work he did for the world was undeniable. It was his methods that gave Tori pause.

If these were the projects people talked about, what kind of dealings went on behind the scenes?

Luckily, Professor Quantum was an Ivan-level issue, the sort of thing she didn't have to bother herself with. No, today, Tori's primary concern was unwinding and having fun with her friends. Along with the New Science Sentries, apparently, which didn't annoy her as much as it would have just days prior.

"Thanks," Tori said, climbing up from her chair. "That's probably enough time in the sad-sack corner. Burgers and beers?"

In a blur, he was at her side, eyes already trained on the smoking grill. "You think any of those will be edible?"

"What the hell, just this once, I'll try being an optimist."

Chapter 42

After the strange snow that blanketed Ridge City on Thursday, the city got too hot for crime. That was Donald's working theory, anyway. It explained why they'd had such a light Friday, and apparently, the AHC expected so few issues on Saturday that the entire class of rookies was being gathered together for a training exercise.

Making his way down the halls, he tried not to fiddle with his Cyber Geek costume. Despite having worn it for months now, being crammed in around so many others in similar outfits had him nervous. Something was up, and he had a hunch it was more than just training. From the tense way Ren was moving at his side, the feeling was mutual. Irene had a steely gaze as well, and even Lucy seemed to be aware things weren't as they seemed.

Every rookie member of the AHC—those from the last confluence, as well as some who'd picked up powers haphazardly in between—gathered together in a vast hall clearly meant for larger audiences. Donald even noticed the New Science Sentries not too far off; apparently, this really was an all-hands-on-deck kind of meeting. Waiting there, at the center of the hall, glowing as expected, stood Lodestar. She hovered a few feet above a raised stage, making herself impossible to miss.

"File on in, everyone. We've got a lot to get through and never enough time." Motioning, Lodestar directed them to move to the front so as to open the entrances for those still streaming in. By the time all of them were there (somewhere around ninety aspiring superheroes), Lodestar had drifted back down to the stage's level.

"Thank you all for coming today," she said, as though the meeting hadn't been listed as mandatory on all of their schedules. "I'm sure you're wondering what this is about, and I'm not much of one for needless suspense. To put it bluntly, some of you have grown beyond the roles you are filling. With the betrayal of Apollo, our training system was severely weakened, yet you have continued to flourish even as our efforts have gone toward larger threats. We have decided to recognize that effort by offering those who wish to take on harder, more dangerous threats the opportunity to do so."

At his side, Donald could hear Ren's tail flex at the words. While he'd never publicly complained, Donald knew his friend was craving a greater challenge. After starting off with fighting villains and a gang riot, dealing with muggers just didn't offer the same ways to test one's self.

"However, that does not mean we can simply hand you harder tasks. Because the truth is, while some of you are ready to move on, some of you need more time to hone your fundamentals. I confess, right now, I don't even know with certainty which of you is which. I've been too absent from your training to know what you can do, *really* do, when everything is on the line. That is my failing, and it is one I intend to remedy today."

Stepping forward, Lodestar walked closer to the stage's edge, one foot actually going over and planting itself in the air like it was solid ground. "There is no shame in continuing to train your fundamentals, either. Some of the most famous heroes you know spent years doing these tasks, and a lone person being attacked in the night would be just as happy to see you as the person strapped to an out-of-control bus full of dynamite. The threat doesn't matter. The person you're helping does. That said, if there are some of you who feel as though your talents could be better utilized by taking on greater threats, then I can certainly respect the sentiment. Anyone who wants to find out if they're ready, come see me in five minutes. As a team, as a person, talk it over and make your choice. Just know that whatever formation you choose is the one you'll be given assignments as moving forward."

Her feet didn't even move this time. She just slid back, floating to the rear of the stage as conversation burst forth from the barely contained crowd.

Donald took his time turning to face Ren, keenly aware of the enthusiasm that would waiting for him. To his surprise, Ren was scratching under his cheek whiskers, a sign that he was lost in thought.

"I think we should do it." In a twist, Irene was the one who spoke up first.

"It's been weeks since the street-level crime was an actual threat. There has to be a better way to use us."

"For the record, I agree," Ren said. "But it has to be mentioned that taking on more dangerous jobs also means playing against potentially serious threats. We all saw Fornax beat the living shit out of Apollo, who was way stronger than any of us. If we do this, we have to be okay with going up against someone substantially outside our weight class."

"That could happen just as easily doing street work. There are always new metas to discover. I'm on Team Go-For-It. Even if we don't pass, we'll see areas where we can improve." Lucy had been Donald's final expected holdout. With her voicing support, the will of the team was clear.

He certainly wouldn't be the one to stand in the way. "Okay then, I guess we're going for it. Whatever 'it' is, in this case."

They didn't have to wait long. Making their way to the front of the hall, they joined the place where many of their peers were already waiting for Lodestar. A quick scan of the room showed that while a large percentage of the rookies were taking the challenge, there was also a sizable group hanging back. Some were new; others had joined after the same confluence as Donald and the majority of his team. There didn't seem to be much rhyme or reason to the sorting; people were making the choice based on where they were in their own journey. It didn't escape his notice that the New Science Sentries were, of course, among the first ones to accept the challenge.

"Everyone who wants to skip this, thank you for coming. Enjoy a Saturday off to spend however you like. The rest of you, follow me."

Chatter rose up on the wind of whispers as they trekked out of the room, down a hall, and into what looked like an airline hangar. Set before them was a massive metal rectangle, easily the size of a small airplane cabin, and with a single door open at the front.

"File on in and buckle up. Seriously, you do *not* want to ignore me on that. Anyone who falls outside of standard, human-sized parameters, there are some more varied restraint options toward the rear." Lodestar waved them forward, and they complied.

The interior felt sort of like a commuter bus, if every seat was ultra-secure and triple reinforced into the framing. Donald followed Ren to the rear, where different styles and sizes of seat options began to pop up. After a moment or two of searching, Ren found one that was large enough for his shoulders and also had a slot in the back where he could fit his tail. Donald, Irene, and Lucy all took spots nearby.

In only a few minutes, they'd all been packed into the strange box, with ample seating left over. Through the door, they could make out Lodestar's form as she gave them one final warning.

"Okay, everyone, get ready for some fun. Make sure you are locked and stowed, because once I start moving, you're going to feel it, even with all the dampening tech Professor Quantum put into this thing. All buckled in? Hope you peed already, because there are no pit-stops on this road trip."

The door slammed and sealed, leaving them with only the artificial lighting that clicked on moments later. At Donald's side, Lucy leaned over and whispered.

"She's not... is she going to carry us? Is that what she meant?"

Before Donald could answer, they felt the box shift, as if it had been pulled upward forcefully.

"I think you might be right." With a gulp and a wish that he had actually used the bathroom before they left, Donald tightened his grip on his seat. Being something of a superhero nerd meant that he had at least a passing familiarity with most of the major capes' core abilities, so he knew that Lodestar could go *fast*. Even assuming she wouldn't use her full speed, they were in for a hell of a ride.

After a Thursday spent with friends around a pool and a Friday composed largely of brainstorming coupled with catching up on life—such as touching base with Vendallia's offices—Tori was ready to use her weekend to get a jump on her new project. Armed with a few mugs of coffee in her veins and some of Chloe's breakfast bubbling in her stomach, Tori made her way down to the concrete parking units serving as her lab.

It was a mess, as always. To an outsider stepping in, it would seem impossible that Tori could find anything in this chaos. While, if pressed, she would protest that there was a system, that was also part of why Tori didn't generally allow others into her workspace. Less explaining to do, in general.

Her first task was unpacking the Hephaestus armor. Beverly had done a good job throwing everything into a bag, but Tori took her time cataloguing every component as it was removed. She still needed to give the updated flight functions a proper test—one more task for the ever-growing list before her. Only when Tori was fully satisfied that her suit was complete and undamaged did she move her attention to an empty table.

Style would come later, with input from someone with Beverly's skills. Today was about function. The units would have to be small, portable, easy to carry and conceal. Capable of dealing with single targets as well as groups. Too much to pack into one unit—there would have to be multiple options. That worked better from a business perspective, as well: more products to roll out as time ticked on. Her methodology would be the real hurdle. She couldn't very well fill these with enhanced tech. The mere fact that no truly advanced technology ended up on the open market spoke to some sort of limiting force, be it governmental or the AHC. It had to be low enough tech to fly under the radar, while still offering a unique function.

Thinking back to her kidnapping, Tori let the sense of fear she'd been pushing down take hold. This was more than just her next venture; it was the way Tori chose to cope with what happened. She didn't get better by just talking. Her solution was to ensure that no bad experience would ever get the drop on her twice. It was part of why she'd cut off human contact after losing her parents, and why the fear in her mind was spurring her creative thinking, not hindering it.

Tori felt what it was like to be back in that moment. Uncertain of what was happening, or how to respond. What would have saved her, back then? She didn't need to entirely beat them; even just a little distance could have made escape possible. Something distracting, then, and if it slowed them down, then that was icing on the cake. An aerosolized compound in a proper vessel could do that, assuming she found the right material. The obvious fix would be pepper spray, except that didn't affect most metas with any sort of enhanced toughness.

A rogue memory floated up, and Tori began to dig through what one might have taken to be a random stack of junk. While most of her possessions had been purged by the guild during her recruitment, they'd been smart enough to save the essentials. Tori's photo of her parents that sat at the far end of the lab, watching her work, was one such item. Another was a leather-bound book with three different mechanical traps built in. After some searching, she produced the tome, walking it over to the desk as she disengaged the various security measures. When she'd built them, they'd seemed airtight. A few months with the guild, however, and she couldn't believe how lax these safeguards were. Another task for the list, though much further down than the more pressing matters.

Tori perused the pages, looking through her own handwriting as she scoured for the formula in question. Finally, she found the spot she was looking for: a chemical compound created by some meta-tech dealer out in Oklahoma. The substance adhered to skin on contact, creating burning, itching, numbness—and that was assuming none got into the eyes. It might have been the new tear gas, except that the effects only lasted a few minutes before fading entirely. Plus, the fact that it had been cooked in a trailer and sold in old milk jugs meant that not many folks had buying opportunities.

This was one of the many tidbits Tori had scooped up in her years on the road. She was, after all, a thief on top of being an inventor, and there was no sense in recreating something when another person had kindly done the work for her. It was a good thing she'd stolen this one, too, since the original creator had died in an entirely predictable lab explosion. There would need to be testing to make this on a large scale, both in the formula itself and the effects; however, that would have to occur in guild facilities. Tori felt reasonably sure her power would protect her from an explosion, but the lab and building above wouldn't be so lucky.

In the meantime, she could start work on a small sample and the aerosolization device before today's meeting. Getting an idea of the mandatory schematics would inform the device's size and shape, which would have to be accounted for in the aesthetics phase. There was a lot more to consider than when she'd designed her Hephaestus gear, but Tori found she didn't mind. After months of training, testing, villains, and capes, it felt nice to be back on an old-fashioned build. That it presented new challenges only made it all the more enticing.

Grabbing her tools, Tori sat down at her worktable with a new, hungry gleam in her eyes. She had an invention taking shape in her mind, one that would only fade when she'd formed it in the real world. Time to fire up the metaphorical forge and start proving why she'd chosen her codename.

Chapter 43

"The most important thing you need to understand is that this is not a test." Those were the first words they heard after the metal container mercifully came to a stop and they were allowed to file out. What had greeted them was a harsh, rocky terrain that constantly shifted in elevation. It looked as if they were in the foothills of some mountainous region, one that had not been particularly touched by civilization. A few of them noticed the fact that all nearby trees in the area had been cleared out, but most had their attention stolen by the floating form of Lodestar, who spoke once they were all emerged.

"A test implies that what matters most is the pass or fail, that the results come first. That is not what we're doing today. This is an evaluation above all else. What matters to me is how you think, act, fight, flee, and generally cope with challenges as I throw them at you. Some of you might very well fail the task and still be moved up based on the skills displayed. Conversely, it's possible to succeed so recklessly that you prove yourself not ready for added responsibilities. This is just a structure to let me see what you can do. Still, with all of that said, success sure doesn't hurt your case, so I expect everyone to give it their all."

In a blur, she vanished, reappearing with a large hunk of stone grabbed from elsewhere on the mountain. Before their eyes, she ran her hands along it, smoothing off the rough surfaces, shaping it into a sphere with casual ease.

Her position in the sky shifted higher and further back; she was moving so everyone could see her.

Once the rock was smoothed, a task that took only seconds, she held it aloft. "This is the target. About a hundred and fifty pounds of stone. Your task is to get it away from me. There are more complex versions of this same drill we use at every level, so I'd learn it well. Sometimes, we have actual targets that have to be treated like they were alive, all the way up to human dummies that can report injuries. Today is the simplest version, though. Get the rock. Everyone, stay put for a moment."

With a toss, Lodestar hurled the stone straight up into the air. Once it was gone, she zipped further off, to an area with several rocky outcroppings. Floating higher, a pair of beams fired from her hands as she spun around in place. Once the searing lights faded, they could all make out a near perfect circle that had been scorched into the ground, even from so far off. The trails of smoke rising from the rocks certainly helped.

Satisfied with her work, Lodestar floated back over to where her charges were waiting.

"The rules are straightforward: take the rock out of the circle. I don't care what powers you use—nothing is off-limits—but you have to make physical contact with the target before manipulating it. Conflict is the point of this, so tricks from the sidelines won't tell me much. You can come on your own, or as teams, but before you deci—"

Lodestar paused to catch the rock she'd tossed up, the stone sphere having fully completed its airborne journey. "Sorry, as I was saying, before you decide, there are some factors you need to know from my end. So far as base physical attributes go, I'm going to match the best of what your teams offer. That means I'll move as quick as the fastest members, hit as hard as the strongest—you get the idea. The caveat being that I'm obviously not going to seriously injure you. I also can't exactly hold back my own toughness—not that it would be smart to, anyway—but I'll try to react to attacks as if I'm your hardiest member. That means, the more team members you add, the higher my different levels could be. Past that, I'm only going to use flight and energy blasts. I want you to have a sincere challenge, not an insurmountable one."

She didn't use her super-speed this time. Instead, Lodestar flew purposefully to her seared circle, dropping down to deposit the stone in the dead middle. Now that they were looking at the spot with analytical eyes, a few of the capes realized she'd chosen an area with lots of natural features that facilitated stealth. They had the ability to attempt surprise, or could come in swinging.

Once the rock was in place, she zoomed back, taking a lower position this time that allowed for a more casual volume.

"Here's how it's going to go: I'll give you ten minutes to decide your teams and your order. When I call for time, you tell me who's coming. They have ten minutes to try to get the stone. At the end, we clean up, and I'll call for the next group. We go like that until everyone has had their shot."

She was met with understanding nods. For people who had been doing actual superhero work already, this was an easy enough concept to grasp. There was still one more component to drive home, however. Sometimes, it was a tough sell; other occasions went easier. Lodestar had no idea what to expect from this group—she'd never evaluated one that had survived an attempted rebellion. It would be a learning experience on both ends.

"One last thing," Lodestar added, softening her voice carefully. "As I mentioned, I can't turn down my own levels of invulnerability, so I want you all to come at me full force. Fight like your life is on the line, because that very well might end up being the case. Even those of you who hadn't joined us yet saw the Ridge City Riots. I try to always choose compassion over violence, but if someone has decided that only one of you is walking away, I know which I'd prefer to see victorious. Give me all you've got. I want to know the limits of your abilities, and how you push them."

Something like mischief danced in her eyes as she gave them a knowing smile. "Besides, this job is all about restraint, control, and constant awareness of how much force you're using. It's not often you get a chance to go all out. I bet a few of you will be glad for the chance to show what you're truly capable of." She lifted her arm and tapped the empty spot on her left wrist where a watch would normally go. "Ten minutes starts now. Figure out your teams and your order."

With a casual grace, Lodestar floated off, back to her circle, where she drifted down and landed on the rock, taking a seat to wait. The moment she touched down, chaos burst forth among the rookies as they hurriedly scrambled to figure out plans.

Cyber Geek, Medley, Cold Shoulder, and Hat Trick all grouped up immediately on the far end of the metal container. Hopefully, Lodestar either couldn't hear the discussions or was choosing not to listen, but it still wasn't wise to give strategic hints to the other teams. They formed a huddle, minimizing the distance any individual voice had to travel.

"Quick rundown: if she's matching our top stats, that means she'll be as quick and strong as Medley, right?" Cyber Geek had no idea if this was really the best place to start, but the firm time limit meant jumping in was better than worrying about efficiency.

"I think my giant ice-armor form might hit harder," Cold Shoulder pointed out. "Potentially be tougher as well, at least up front. I can't match Medley's recovery."

"Farts, I forgot about that," Hat Trick muttered. "So even if we technically hit hard enough to 'hurt' her, she won't have to sell it for long."

The complexities of Lodestar's rules were readily becoming apparent. Teams, normally their greatest strength, also now came with liability. For every added member, they risked increasing how much power Lodestar could use in the fight. On the upside, since most of the physical strength was concentrated on Medley and Cold Shoulder, it did present a natural formation.

"We're all thinking the obvious, right? Medley and Cold Shoulder take melee to distract her, Hat Trick and I make a run for the rock?" Cyber Geek could see the lack of surprise on their faces; they'd all arrived at the same conclusion. "Unfortunately, obvious means Lodestar will see it coming, too. We need to have some curves to throw her."

Hat Trick lit up, her wide eyes practically shining. "I could put the target in my hat—get rid of the weight entirely, plus I can control it." Forehead creased in effort, she focused, and the top hat perched on her head lifted up a few inches before dropping back down. This was a new talent she'd found recently, and while it wouldn't be zipping around the battlefield, a floating hat might very well prove useful.

"The problem is, she knows about all the skills we've shown so far. Our best shot is something new," Cyber Geek said. Hat Trick's idea did stir something in his mind, a curiosity he'd held but never put to the test. Firing up the menu in his vision, Cyber Geek began to zip through his options. After Tori's kidnapping, he'd been putting more effort into utility items, and one in particular leapt to mind. The Self-Swap from *Battle Buds* would be perfect, except it only lasted for ten seconds.

"I have an idea, but we need to test something first." Motioning for his team to lean in, Cyber Geek explained the loose collection of half-thoughts they would optimistically refer to as a plan.

This was an optimal opportunity. Beth and Juan were at the store, leaving Rick and his mother alone in the house. No work to steal her attention, no upcoming meetings to suddenly run off to. If he started this conversation, her excuses to stop it were limited. At this point, Rick was no longer sure what he was expecting. After several days, the thought of oceans and examining old photos no longer triggered attacks, but the knot of unease in his gut refused to yield.

Sitting down at the kitchen table across from her, Rick tried to see his mother as a person, rather than the role she filled in his life. Janet was working on a crossword, a favorite weekend activity. Given her levels of self-assurance and intelligence, would she really get mixed up with someone who had that much to hide? Maybe—if she hadn't known the whole score up front. Perhaps that was even what had soured their marriage in the first place… which meant he might be about to blunder into a very sensitive topic.

Rick shook the notion from his head. He was preparing to accuse his parents of lying to him for his entire life—it would be a sensitive topic regardless of how it was phrased. The smart move would be to walk away. Except that Rick was not only the son of Ivan; Janet's blood ran in his veins as well. Her same obsessive need to solve a complex formula burned through his mind, refusing to let go of the mystery now that it had properly taken hold. Bad as things might get, he had to push forward.

That realization was almost freeing, in a way. He didn't have to worry about finding the right angle of approach; this was going to be a shitshow no matter how he went in. May as well cut to it, then.

"I want to know about Dad."

Janet glanced up from the crossword, a brief squint of confusion as she noticed the serious expression on her son's face. "Did you have a particular topic in mind? Might be best to speak to him directly."

"I'd try that, if I thought he'd give me the truth."

The confusion faded from her eyes as she quickly adjusted to the situation, her Saturday afternoon ease slipping away. "I see. What is it that you're concerned he would lie to you about?"

This was it, the edge of the cliff. Once Rick started down this road, there wasn't a way back. Whatever he learned, he'd have to live with it. No matter if, or how, it changed things with his parents.

"Well, for example, there's the fact that he spent his whole life saying he has no family, only for Vendallia to list one of the other employees as his niece."

Rick waited for his mother to be shocked at the revelation. Instead, she merely threw him a gaze of pure consternation. "Oh, is that what this is all about?"

"You knew?"

"Of course I knew. He had to reach out in case anyone checked with me for confirmation," Janet replied. "For goodness' sake, Rick, you're making a conspiracy out of simple charity. That girl was on her own. Life had given her a real kicking, and Ivan saw potential. They fudged the relationship to get her an internship so she could find her footing. *You* aren't the one your father lied to."

It certainly wasn't a perfect story, opening more questions than it answered, but it did sound far more like the Ivan Rick had always known. Even the other evidence, such as Ivan getting lost in his old neighborhood, suddenly felt flimsy under Janet's reassuring gaze. His will might have broken, allowing himself to believe the lie, if not for those damn flashes from the beach.

"Okay. That explains one thing, Mom. One of a thousand inconsistencies. He's never been to the places he's supposedly lived. There are no pictures of him before you were married. I'm not even sure his age lines up—for a man in his forties, he sure doesn't seem to be showing it."

"He's a private man with a bad memory and a good metabolism. What are you digging for here?" Janet was starting to look more concerned than anything. Rick knew he was feeding that, he could already feel the sheen of sweat on the back of his neck.

"Answers. I want to know why my own dad has been hiding something. What's so bad that he couldn't even tell us? *Why* do I keep having these horrible flashes from some damn beach?"

It was the last one that landed. Until then, Janet's façade had remained firmly in place, but at the word "beach," the mask slipped away. He could see it then, laid bare. The horror in her eyes, the terror at the idea he remembered. Something had happened.

To her credit, Janet didn't bother trying to reaffix her false expression. Instead, she walked around the table, pulling her son close in a display of affection that left him immediately uncomfortable.

"You were never supposed to see that. We tried to spare you, but the block works based on desire. When you wanted to forget, you could. If you keep trying to remember, you will."

"I don't need a hug." Rick tried to squirm away, only to be gripped tighter. "I need to know what the hell happened."

She clung for a few minutes longer, then returned to her side of the table. "I'm not so sure about that. Yes, Rick, something bad once happened at a beach. Yes, there is more to our family than meets than eye. And yes, your father has secrets he's not shared with his children. But most of what you know is true. Ivan and I are your parents, we love you more than the world itself, and we would do anything to keep you safe. Even what you know about Ivan is true. No blood relations, works a middle-management job, all very real. None of it was false. There were just *more* truths than what you were given. Sometimes, knowing more makes you miserable. You think you want those memories back, but you'll wish they were gone as soon as you succeed. You think you want to know the whole truth about this family, yet if I were to tell you, would that really make things better?"

For a moment, he'd been able to delude himself, thinking his mother had been duped as well. Hearing her speak, it was clear as could be what the actual truth was. "Whatever this is, you're in on it, too. You've been helping him lie."

"Watch it, young man. I'm still your mother." Her voice was momentarily firm, though it was short-lived despite her mounting frustration. "We both know you came to me with this because you think I'll flip on Ivan and give up the goods. What you fail to understand is that it has never been your father that I was protecting. It was you and your sister. Some truths can't be unlearned. They burrow in and chew you up from the inside."

"What makes you so sure I couldn't handle it?" Rick demanded, voice rising.

His mother's hand slapped the table, shocking him backward. "Because I *do* remember that goddamn beach, Rick! I remember every detail, every scream, every death, and it wakes me up in a cold sweat to this day." Only after the words had burst forth did Janet seem to realize what she'd said, calming down slightly. "Why would I ever want that for you?"

"Screams?" Rick was processing her words, trying to make sense of what she'd described. "Deaths? What the hell happened out there?"

"Maybe you'll get the chance to find out," she said, rising from the table once more. This time, it was not to embrace him, and Rick noticed she seemed to move visibly slower, like she was weighed down. "This is his secret to keep, and his to share if he thinks you're ready."

With one last look to her son, Janet reached into her purse and pulled out her cell phone. "I'm calling your father."

Chapter 44

Breaking into teams went smoothly—every cape present had been working in the field, leaning on one another and figuring out who they worked best with. In no time, they'd split apart, mostly binding themselves into units, with only a few choosing to go it alone. No one expected the solo attempts to do well, but as Lodestar had said, this was an evaluation, not a test. While winning alone might be impossible, demonstrating competence was an entirely more achievable goal.

The trouble came after the groups were split up, when the natural question arose.

"Who do you think will go first?" Lucy was staring out at the clusters of their peers, most of whom were bunched up having a similar conversation.

"First is good and bad. No standard has been set, so there's nothing to live up to. Downside is you're also the canary in the coal mine; everyone else gets to see what happens to you and adjust accordingly." Ren's voice was quiet, calm. He was mentally prepared to jump in whenever the time arrived, already focused on victory.

Irene didn't bother looking to the others. Her eyes had never left Lodestar's battlefield, committing every feature to memory while there was still time. "I'd be fine with going first, but given our team's situation, it's best if we let someone else take the spot."

It was a very polite way of pointing out that there were still some pockets within the AHC who weren't completely convinced Apollo had no corrupting influence on the capes he'd taken special interest in. They'd been his favorites from the last confluence, and all the bitterness such a role had stirred up had found an easy outlet once he was outed as a traitor.

Personally, Donald was content to take a spot further down the list. He was better at learning and adapting, so walking in with a few samples to pull from would make the task more achievable. The trouble was, he could also feel the stares of other teams on his own. People were waiting to see if they jumped on the first spot's opening, and Donald already knew there wasn't a right answer to give. If they attempted to claim it, people would say they were trying to grab more glory. Wait for a later spot, they'd be accused of making others do the hard part while they sat back learning. Even offering to slot in wherever worked best for the groups as a whole could be read as them being so confident they didn't care when they tried. No matter what move they made, fault could be found.

That realization lessened his case of nerves slightly. If people were looking for a reason to dislike them, there would always be an angle to find. Donald should concern himself with what was best for the team and their training, which meant hanging back to let a more eager squad have first crack.

He was just about to voice that thought when the bright blue costumes of the New Science Sentries stepped into view.

"Fear not, everyone, you no longer need to worry. The top team is going to take the opening spot, sparing you all from having to face Lodestar without watching someone else show you how to win."

Presto was as untactful as usual, but to the teleporter's surprise, that actually *did* get quite a few chuckles. Unfortunately, he and the rest of his team noticed the laughs had all come when he announced them as the top team. Even without being able to see his features through the mask, Donald noticed the small body tense slightly. Presto didn't care for being part of the joke, it seemed.

The New Science Sentries, who had been striding forward confidently seconds prior, suddenly lost a step as the laughter hit. Donald could see it coming, like a slow-motion car crash. He'd been a target often enough to know how this dance played out. Strong people didn't like having their egos challenged, and the realization that their team being seen as the current best wasn't just wrong, but *laughably* wrong, was hitting most of them in the sorest of spots. Pain turned to anger, which was funneled into action, as they scanned for some outlet or place to redirect the attention.

Just as he knew they would, a pair of eyes settled on Donald and his team.

When lashing out, people usually went for the easiest, most obvious target, even when it could potentially work against them.

Tachyonic stepped forward, narrowly avoiding a hand from Agent Quantum that was meant to yank him back. "Oh, I'm sorry, perhaps we should have shown a bit of deference first. My apologies, Team Apollo, did you want to display for us some of the amazing tactics he imparted? Maybe you can show us the one where superheroes lie to and betray each other."

"I guess now we know why 'tacky' is part of your name."

Had it been from Irene or Ren, Donald would have been fine. The trouble was that the line had slipped out of Lucy, who leaned more toward diplomacy and kindness. The joke, silly as it was, caught Donald completely by surprise, eliciting a sincere laugh that peeled off of him, echoing through the empty surroundings. That would have been bad enough, but this was the contagious sort of laughter. Like a giggling plague, it swept through those in attendance. With Presto, there was wiggle room to interpret what had earned the minor mirth; this time, there was no such comfort. The New Science Sentries were being laughed at, and Donald could see two faces reddening. He'd have guessed that under the full mask, Presto probably wasn't looking too keen, either. Only Agent Quantum was keeping it stoic, though he was starting to appear visibly concerned about the situation. On that point, they were agreed. This needed to get handled, fast.

Holding up his hands, Donald stepped forward, slightly outside of his group. "Okay, that's enough. They took a shot, we took one back. How about we all focus on the task at hand? New Science Sentries, please take the first spot. We look forward to seeing your skills. By all accounts, you've got quite a set of powers. I'm sure there will be a lot we can all learn."

It was a good effort toward peace, in Donald's opinion. Acknowledge the exchange and move past it, offer some ego-stroking as recompense, end by giving them the spot they'd wanted.

Unfortunately, the crowd was still in a chuckling mood, and some chose to interpret his words with less sincerity than they'd been spoken. More laughter sprang up, spreading once more, and with it, the faces of Tachyonic and Plasmodia both set in rage, all of it aimed at Donald.

"No, no, please, we didn't mean to offend," Tachyonic said. "We were trying to bite the bullet and take the worst place in the order, but since you're so fucking sure of yourself, let's see what your team can do. Assuming you try-hards can manage anything without villains around for help."

The snort from Ren was pronounced and loud, something only his inhuman snout could manage. "You *would* think that's an insult. That the idea of effort, of trying, of striving to improve is something to be ashamed of. We didn't all get handed our team and titles from Big Daddy Quantum. The rest of us worked to be here."

Something in Ren's verbal jab hit home, and hard. Tachyonic looked like he was seconds from racing over to throw a punch, but was stopped by Agent Quantum forcibly shoving his way past.

The leader of the New Science Sentries locked eyes with Donald as he moved, a clear enough hint of what to do. Donald mirrored the movements, striding forward, away from his team, into the unoccupied space between the groups. In no time, the leaders met, surrounded, yet alone.

"One minute warning! One minute until someone's time starts!" Lodestar's voice echoed from her position on the boulder, a reminder that there was only so long to deal with this issue.

"Well, this went to hell pretty fast, huh?" To Donald's surprise, Agent Quantum had a friendly tone, despite the tense situation. "Sorry about Tachyonic. I realize that you were trying to defuse things, and I appreciate it. We need to put it to bed now, before it gets into either team's head. We're facing a hard enough task as it is. Distractions aren't going to make things any easier."

In a flicker, Agent Quantum's eyes went to Lodestar, who was perched unassumingly on her boulder as she waited. Limited or not, the idea of taking on a living legend was terrifying. If anyone wasn't fully in the fight mentally, the whole team would fall.

"No argument from me. The question is, what do we do? I'd like to find a resolution that puts this to bed, rather than potentially making it worse down the line."

"In under a minute? Sorry, I'm not that quick of a thinker," Agent Quantum replied. "Best I've got is this: you take the first slot. I know you don't want it, which is how I'm going to sell it to my team. I'll tell them we let you go first so you could fall on your face in front of everyone, and then we can go put on a better display. You could tell yours that you're going to show these egotistical jerks—that's us—by going first and scoring a win, or whatever lights a fire under them best. We can't undo this, so let's at least make it motivational. Fallout will depend on whether you do well or not; this will get us through the evaluation, though."

For someone who'd just described himself as "not that quick of a thinker," Agent Quantum had certainly managed to come up with a comprehensive plan on the fly. It had the potential to cause more drama down the road, but Donald had to get them past one issue at a time. With the time limit bearing down, this was better than any of his own half-formed notions.

"Guess it'll have to work. Thanks for not making this harder than it had to be."

"My team is the one who started it. I'm only sorry you have to change your plans to accommodate the issue. For what it's worth, I've watched your team work, and I don't think Apollo had much influence at all. You've saved a lot of people in the time your team has been active, and I'm glad to have you counted among the superheroes."

Agent Quantum offered his hand, and Cyber Geek shook it. Their teams might have friction, but they could find mutual respect for one another. Eventually, the egos would smooth down and people would find common ground, so long as they saw that attitude flow from their leaders.

While Agent Quantum walked back to his own team, Cyber Geek motioned for his to come forward.

"Looks like we're taking the lead," he announced, loud enough for others to hear it, too. As they crowded in close, Cyber Geek summed up the situation as quickly as possible. They had to be nearly to the starting time by now.

"We're going first. Partly to keep the peace. Partly to test our limits. And partly because, if we go first and succeed, it sends a message about exactly why there was interest in us to start with. *If* we can win, that is. Are we good with that?"

The team nodded, almost in unison. It was a good thing they'd chosen a silent response, because seconds later, Lodestar's voice came bursting over the terrain.

"First team, your ten minutes starts now!"

Despite the yell, they didn't immediately scramble off. Ten minutes wasn't long, but it also wasn't a total time crunch given the terrain they had to cover. Moving carefully, going slowly to be sure of each action, offered superior chances of success than going as fast as possible. That might get them more bites at the apple, but they'd all be long shots. Better to have fewer chances with higher potential for success. That was the idea, anyway. Whether it worked or not was yet to be seen.

"Medley and Cold Shoulder, head on in. I'll start with ranged as soon as I get to the position. Hat Trick, don't move until I've got suppressing fire going. This is Lodestar—even if she's holding back, we should assume it's going to take everything we have to keep her distracted. Once you're on the field, it's speed over everything. Keep moving. We'll have you covered."

The eyes of his team, and all the other superheroes, were so heavy that

Cyber Geek could feel them as he stood up straight. What would it be like, to have the eyes of an entire city, country—even the world—trained on him, pitting the entirety of their hopes on his power? It was a weight impossible to imagine, yet the woman they were going up against had carried it many times over. If he ever wanted to reach that level, be capable of hauling such a burden, then this was the first step in getting stronger.

To his own surprise, there was a bit of excitement in his gut, mixed in along with the nerves. Impossible task or not, he was about to spar with one of history's greatest superheroes, one he held a deep personal admiration for. Terrifying as that was on many levels, part of him was still Donald enough to appreciate that it was also fucking *awesome*. From this day on, he'd be able to say he'd tested himself again Lodestar.

The only thing better would be getting to say they'd passed.

Determination set, Cyber Geek began to move, and his team followed.

Chapter 45

While her hearing was exceptional from a human perspective, Lodestar had to actually focus to tune in to more distant sounds. It was a small mercy that allowed her some peace, because the louder the world grew, the harder it was to find the voices asking for help. Information had always been her limitation. She might win every fight, but that wasn't much help if she didn't know where the opponents were. That was part of why she enjoyed this method of training. Binding down her skills, limiting the information she had: this was a way to push her own capacity for quick thinking and improvisation.

She hadn't been listening to the rookies as they made their plans. It would have given her forewarning, which worked against every aspect of the evaluation. Even without words, though, she'd caught the exchange between Apollo's old favorites and the New Science Sentries. She didn't need super-hearing to understand that friction; it was a dance every cape eventually grew familiar with. Egos and pissing matches were unavoidable when you were dealing with people this powerful. Sometimes, they laid the groundwork to amazing friendships. Other instances were the start of very long, dark rivalries. It was an issue she'd have to keep an eye on, one of the million things piled atop her plate.

Seeing Medley and Cold Shoulder burst into view, coming at her simultaneously from opposite sides, Lodestar was slightly relieved. If they were opening with a coordinated strike, they must not be too rattled from the exchange. Medley was moving faster, and Cold Shoulder hadn't summoned her ice construct yet, so despite their timed arrival, they were likely trying something other than pure melee.

There was no more time to speculate as Medley charged right at her, opening with a swing that could have cracked a telephone pole. She'd told them not to hold back; it was good to see this group understood she wasn't kidding. The blow whipped mightily through the air, but landed on nothing, as Lodestar easily jerked her head to the side, countering with a punch of her own to Medley's stomach. It sent him back a few feet, drawing coughs from his inhuman mouth.

"You're getting bad habits. Don't fight like you're always going to be stronger and tougher than the opponent. Eventually, you won't be, and you'll realize that learning some actual skills would have been really helpful."

Medley leapt in again, launching an uncoordinated flurry. Cold Shoulder, meanwhile, was getting closer. Lodestar could see the blue power building up in her, could practically feel the chill radiating through the air. Was she going to try and encase Lodestar in ice? With these parameters, it might buy them a few seconds. That seemed like a waste of a strategy, unless one knew how powerful a few seconds in battle could truly be.

As it turned out, Cold Shoulder was going for something even stranger. Leaping up just as Medley tried to charge at Lodestar (only to be knocked aside), Cold Shoulder came slamming down with both hands. A tremendous wave of blue energy washed out along the ground, quickly solidifying into ice. The southeast quarter of the battlefield turned into a makeshift skating rink, running right up to the edge of the stone sphere without quite making contact.

Just as Lodestar was wondering what the hell that was about, she caught the first shot in her shoulder. Not bad. Decent power, good aim, and strong enough that even Cold Shoulder would have been knocked back in her armor. This team wasn't taking her lightly, thank goodness. There was nothing quite so demoralizing as having to fail a capable squad because they couldn't adjust to the challenge.

She allowed herself to fall slightly back, toward the boulder, rubbing where she'd been hit like it stung. Cyber Geek was up on a ridge; she could catch sight of his usual armor, along with the giant, oversized videogame blaster responsible for the shot. That made three out of four, and the trickiest card had yet to be played. Magic never quite made sense to Lodestar, regardless of how often she saw it in action. It was finnicky, had few rules and even more exceptions—easy to underestimate, until it wasn't. Something to watch for, between her more immediate concerns.

Leaping onto the ice, Medley's claws sank in, giving him full traction. At the same time, Cold Shoulder let loose another blast of blue energy, surrounding herself with a living construct of ice. More shots rang out from Cyber Geek, but they went wide. Probably trying to avoid hitting his teammates; Cyber Geek was hardly a sniper. They'd gotten into a decent formation. Now, they were trying to turn up the pressure.

"Two on one isn't a bad idea, but the trouble with fighting a single target is that, if they know what they're doing, they can use your own numbers against you."

That was the extent of Lodestar's warning before Medley raced in, swinging wild again. Rather than swing back, she opted to drop low, ignoring gravity for a few moments as she swept her legs between Medley's, turning him into a tumbling ball of fur and scales. With one shove to his back, Lodestar reoriented his momentum, rolling her opponent directly at his chilly teammate.

It should have ended with him slamming into Cold Shoulder's ice-construct legs, except Medley was instantly scooped up in the gigantic ice-hands that were dropped low and waiting. With the smooth expertise of someone who'd practiced this move for hours already, Cold Shoulder caught her teammate and chucked him directly back at Lodestar, claws first. Her short, terse reply as she hurled was all the explanation Lodestar needed:

"We know."

A Medley-sized projectile was enough to drive Lodestar back— when she had to play at this level, at least. It didn't stop with the launch, either. He came at her like a true wild animal, a fury of scratches and fangs. If not for Cold Shoulder's durability, Lodestar would have had to fold down under the assault.

More shots rang out, most going wide, one taking her in the back. Cold Shoulder was right. They did know the risks of fighting a single target in a confined area, and had clearly trained for it.

At last, Lodestar spotted what she'd been waiting for. Hat Trick appeared from behind a rocky outcropping, exactly opposite of place near the boulder where Lodestar was holding her ground. Three for distraction, one to make the run. Not a bad play, especially since their runner had the wildcard of magic to work with.

With a quick motion, Lodestar fired a beam of energy into Hat Trick's legs, sending her tumbling over. That done, she floated a few inches off the ground, neutralizing Cold Shoulder's terrain trick. Medley's eyes went momentarily wild, but that was his own fault. She'd told them what powers were on the table; part of the challenge was planning around them. It did no team any favors to hold back, because the people who fought with blood on the line surely wouldn't.

A blast of ice energy nearly took her, but Lodestar dodged away in the nick of time, putting herself in the path of another energy shot. Dropping down like she'd taken a painful hit, Lodestar counted to three as she estimated how long Medley would need to recover from such an attack. The pause offered Cold Shoulder the chance to come in swinging, huge fists of ice smashing down on the ground.

This was the greatest challenge of the group, in Lodestar's original estimations. Her ice construct was durable, thick, and could be repaired if she had time to focus. Worse, none of the other members hit hard enough to do serious damage. Thankfully, Cyber Geek had offered just the tool she needed.

Dodging the huge fists, Lodestar took aim at the construct's knees, ensuring Cold Shoulder's actual body was nowhere near them. Firing off beams of energy at precisely the same intensity as what she'd been receiving, she saw cracks form immediately. The entire thing tottered precariously to the left for several seconds.

"Being big and strong is useful, but it also makes you the easiest target. Reinforce your weak points, or change the design to get around them."

Just as Lodestar prepared to knock her over, Medley rushed in from the side. She readied for another flurry—only, this was different. Instantly gone were the wild, animalistic strikes. Suddenly, Medley was holding himself carefully, entire body tense and waiting, even his tail extended, ready to attack. He came with a pair of punches that fell short, only for that tail to whip around and catch Lodestar in the leg. While the blow wasn't powerful enough to earn a serious reaction, he'd still scored it.

"Not bad, although I wish you'd started off like this. Would have let me see more of what you can do." Eyes darting to Hat Trick, Lodestar noted that while she was staying low, the team's fourth member was still crawling steadily closer to the boulder. If she fired at this angle, Lodestar was most likely to hit Hat Trick's head—much too dangerous for a simple evaluation. But if she flew over, Medley and Cold Shoulder would have a clear path to the boulder. Once someone made contact, her job grew far more difficult.

"Now!"

She heard the order ring out just before she saw Medley drop into a ball, covering his ears and eyes. Turning, Lodestar made it just in time to witness Cold Shoulder falling out of the ice in the same position as Medley. That was all she got before the giant ball of light overhead exploded.

This had to be something from a video game. No real-world item created a perfect sphere of noise and sound, crashing over victims in an effort to leave them helpless. Add in that it had clearly been fired from the ridge where Cyber Geek was perched, and the explanation was almost too obvious. None of it actually worked on Lodestar, of course, but based on what she knew of the others, they'd definitely be feeling the effects.

Still, even with an attack like this, Medley's regeneration meant the impacted ears and eyes would heal rapidly, especially from such superficial damage. They'd earned roughly ten seconds of "stunned" Lodestar with that maneuver.

Medley was the first up, to no one's surprise. He motioned to Hat Trick, who hopped up from the ground and sprinted for all she was worth. This was it, then. The muscle races in to occupy her, while Cyber Geek adds to the pressure with his ranged skills. Hat Trick comes running, knowing she'll be spotted, and gains ground slowly while the distraction team keeps up its work. When they can't hold the line anymore, Cyber Geek launches the stunning blast, giving Hat Trick a window of opportunity to make the big play. If she got the boulder inside that hat, they'd be able to move it with no concern for weight.

While those two moved, Cold Shoulder leapt into action. Freed from her construct, she immediately fired blue energy at Lodestar, sealing the living legend to the ground and weighing her down with as much ice as possible. Smart: more delay, even when the stunning effects faded. It was a good, sound strategy overall.

The only trouble was, the team didn't quite grasp their own strength. Much as she disliked this part, Lodestar had to impart the lesson—otherwise some criminal would, and not in so nearly kind a manner. With the ten seconds up, Lodestar sprang into action.

"Medley's recovery means that even at full blast, the lightshow has already lost effect." She tore loose from the ice, slamming Cold Shoulder once in the gut, sending her tumbling over. "That was your strength I used to break free and hit you back. Don't make yourself vulnerable in a fight unless there's a true need for it. Most enemies won't give you a chance to recover."

With a burst of speed, she flew over to Medley, slamming him to the ground. She landed heavy, buying herself some time with fewer opponents. "Cyber Geek has some rapid movement options, too, making it easy to get around the battlefield."

That only left Lodestar and Hat Trick for the moment, the latter covered in dirt and panting from her undignified crawl. Lodestar respected that appearance; it was the look of someone who chose victory over vanity. In a way, she hated to do this. Showing the martial ones their failings was educational; she wasn't sure what lessons Hat Trick could take from this exchange.

"It was a good effort," Lodestar said. "Much more competent than most teams manage on their first go-round."

"Maybe so, but we aren't here to put in a 'good effort.' We're here to give everything." Hat Trick reached into her pocket and produced a classic magician's wand, black with two white tips. It was the element of her powers she'd used the least, which meant Lodestar had minimal information on what that magical implement was capable of.

Lodestar darted forward, just as Hat Trick exclaimed, "Doveakazam!"

An explosion of birds blasted Lodestar in the face, white feathers smacking into her nose and mouth, causing genuine annoyance, if not pain. She hacked and spit as the avian attack dissipated, her attention broken until the last of them cleared. By the time she could see properly, Hat Trick was nearly on top of her, a deck of cards in her hand.

"Fifty-two hundred pickup!"

A torrent of playing cards washed over Lodestar, like a firehose of rectangular plastic. The deck either didn't end or had some other enchanted elements, as card after card battered Lodestar's vision. All the others had gone for damage, whereas Hat Trick, their supposed runner, was using distraction. Something was wrong. She'd missed a detail, and it tickled the edge of her brain as she lunged forward, grabbing Hat Trick's wrists and angling the stream of cards away.

"Impressive," Lodestar admitted. "That first one genuinely took me off balance for a few moments."

"Thanks. I'm not much of a magician yet, but I have worked really hard on mastering the most important part."

Her hat was gone. That's what was off. As Lodestar looked down at the cape named Hat Trick, clasped in her grip, Lodestar noticed that the meta-magician's most distinctive accessory was missing. Spinning around, Lodestar realized something else a hair too late. She hadn't gotten shot in a few minutes.

Already knowing what was waiting for her, Lodestar saw Cyber Geek land a few feet from the boulder, the giant jumping boot dissolving back into electricity and numbers. He scooped up the unmistakable top hat from where it was sliding gently along the icy ground, slamming his hand against the boulder to establish physical contact.

"Misdirection," Lodestar muttered. "The heart of illusion is misdirection. But now, it's just a matter of catching him before he hauls it across the line."

Even as she was speaking, Lodestar caught something else. Cyber Geek wasn't trying to put the boulder in the hat. Instead, he held his hand out underneath it. Hat Trick wiggled in her grip, making some sort of motion, and a silver device fell from the hat into Cyber Geek's extended hand.

Not knowing what it could do, Lodestar opted to sprint. They'd clearly built their strategy around making this part work, so she had to assume it would end the session. To her own shock, Lodestar realized something as she ran: they'd baited her out to just the right distance. While she might be able to cross this far in a blink, none of *them* were fast enough to do the same. They'd estimated their own best speed, and specifically worked to draw her out farther than that. She definitely couldn't knock this group on self-analysis.

Pushing as fast as she felt appropriate, Lodestar rushed forward while Cyber Geek wrapped his arm around the boulder and pressed the silver device. There was a flash of purple, and suddenly, he was gone, along with the stone sphere. An identical flash appeared over on the ridge where Cyber Geek had been shooting from, and seconds later, she saw him leap from the edge, boulder clutched in his hands as jets fired from the *Blaster Bros* armor. From that far back, he easily cleared the line before Lodestar could even properly lift off the ground.

"Cyber Geek has an item that splits in two, and lets you jump back to wherever you leave the anchor. The issue was that it had a ten-second timer, but objects in my hat come out the same way they go in. Down to the second." Hat Trick was dusting herself off as Medley and Cold Shoulder staggered to their feet, shaking off those last blows. "Was that okay? Are we allowed to combine powers like that?"

"Not only are you allowed, it's exactly the sort of thinking these evaluations are meant to encourage," Lodestar replied. Awareness of their own abilities, and that of their team, to the point where they'd started developing combination techniques. While they might be low on raw power, this group had worked on their coordination to an incredible degree.

Floating up into the sky, Lodestar saw the crowd milling around Cyber Geek and his prize: the boulder, dragged barely past the line in the ground. "Attention, everyone: the team of Cold Shoulder, Cyber Geek, Hat Trick, and Medley has successfully retrieved their target! Big round of congratulations to our opening group. I know it's never easy to be the first in a situation like this one. Everyone else, take five minutes to update your plans based on what you just saw while I reset the stage."

She looked down, noting the looks of hope and determination. Now that they knew victory could be achieved, that should make for some bolder, interesting plays in the evaluations to come. Perhaps a part of her was excited by that. Playing with limited stakes was the closest she got to a challenge anymore. No harm in enjoying herself, so long as the education and evaluation continued to come first.

"After that, have the next team ready to go. Our day is only getting started."

Chapter 46

Deep down, Ivan had always known this day would come. In a world of secret identities and masks, he'd long ago learned that few things truly stayed hidden forever. Part of him had even imagined giving the talk to his children when they became adults in an attempt to get ahead of the eventual revelation. He wondered if he'd have really had the strength to go through with it, or if this was always the way it would have gone down: backed into telling the truth, his hand forced, the secret pried from his grip.

He and Rick sat in the living room, Ivan in a chair, his son on the couch. They both had drinks in front of them, because Ivan had needed to fill the minutes between getting Janet's call and her dropping off Rick. That had been a hell of a half hour, picturing what it would be like to come clean, all the horrified reactions it might garner. Yet upon Rick's arrival, they'd fallen into silence. Both knew what came next, and neither felt entirely sure of how to proceed.

Ultimately, Ivan pushed things forward. He was the parent. It was his job to take the harder role. "Your mother told me you have questions, and she let me know what they were about. I don't want to lie you, son. I've never wanted to lie to you. What you're digging near isn't something minor, though. I hope you can understand that. But I also don't see what's to be gained by lying at this point. So, here is my bargain: I'll answer the questions you ask. There will be details I might leave out, and I think that once we're deep enough in for you to really grasp the situation, you'll understand why. That said, there is a caveat to this. What we discuss here can be talked about with your mother, and no one else. Especially not Beth."

Rick bristled, pulling his back up straight. "She's your daughter. If I have a right to know, then so does she."

"Beth is twelve years old, a child; she is in no way ready to grapple with this kind of topic." Ivan didn't need to sit straighter; he'd already been positioned properly from the start. "This is nonnegotiable. What we're going to discuss could put you in serious danger if the wrong people found out. You have to promise me, Rick. Look me in the eyes and swear you will not tell anyone else about this. After the fuss you've kicked up over me keeping you in the dark, I can't imagine you'd be hypocrite enough to break your word."

The stubbornness in Ivan was reflected back at him in Rick's eyes. For a moment, he thought obstinance would win the day and the whole talk would fall apart; however, Rick also had his mother's skill for seeing the bigger picture. Swallowing his annoyance at being forced into something, he met Ivan's gaze. "I promise, what we talk about here stays between me, you, and Mom. Maybe also a therapist, depending on how bad it is."

"That's a reasonable concession, and I know some people if it comes to that," Ivan agreed. "All right, what do you want to know?"

"Who are you?"

That came fast; it had been on a hair trigger. Ivan considered the question, and how to honestly answer it while still easing Rick into all of this. "Ivan Gerhardt. The first name came from the monsters who raised me, the second was chosen by the first real friend I ever made. I'm a manager at Vendallia Industries, father to two children, and as of a few weeks ago, a Starscout cluster leader." He paused. That was part of who he was, and for a time, it would have been the whole truth. But even if he counted Fornax as who he'd been, there was still Pseudonym, who'd been too active as of late to entirely discount.

"Past that... I work with an organization that helps recovering criminals. Let's leave that there for the moment; it might be easier to discuss once some of the other holes are filled in."

There was a sheen of sweat on Rick's forehead, despite the climate control in the townhouse. He rubbed his hands on his jeans, wiping away more perspiration. That question had been an easy one. He was still gathering courage for what he deemed truly scary.

"And who is Tori Rivas?"

"No." Ivan halted the conversation midstride. "Who I am, what I've done—these are things that might impact your life, so I concede that you have a right to know them. The secrets of others don't fall under that umbrella. Tori is a friend and a coworker, someone I trust. Anything past that you can find out by asking her directly, though I'm not sure I would recommend it."

The denial had brought Rick up short, but Ivan had left him little room for rebuttal. More hand-wiping, a little frantic now. Reaching over, Ivan put a hand on his son's shoulder. "Ask me whatever it is that's eating at you. You'll feel better when it's out."

"That's not the impression I got from Mom," Rick muttered under his breath. "Guess there's no point in avoiding it. I want to know what happened at the beach. I don't know which one, but when I was around four or five—"

"You were five. It was a small coastal town named Sandshire, down in Florida. We used to go there on family trips. Janet's parents took her there as a child. It was something of a tradition. I liked that town."

When Ivan's pause stretched into true silence, Rick leaned forward. "Interesting as that is, it's not the part I'm asking about. What happened there? Why do I start to freak out when I think about it too much? Why can't I remember anything besides flashes of purple in the water?"

No more room for dodging. It was time to start giving Rick what he thought he wanted.

"While we were at the beach that day, some creatures appeared. A new species created by the Carp Conqueror, this aquatic, meta-human criminal with dreams of grandeur. They were mounting an assault, you see. Trying to take over the land-world, as they phrased it. In the end, none of the details really mattered that much. They made a very crucial mistake early on that sent it all to hell. They threatened my family."

He could still feel the warm air as Carp Conqueror's odd, wet laughter echoed over the sounds of fleeing beachgoers. First came the offer: help lead the charge. Then came the mistake: daring to cast a finger at Ivan's then-wife and children, implying they might not survive the tide that would wash along the lands. Ivan couldn't remember things so well from that point on, just snippets. The rest of the details required diving into the Fornax side of himself, which this was definitely not the time for.

"What did you do, when they threatened us?" Rick was leaning forward so far, Ivan feared he might tumble from the couch. The poor boy looked ready to pop from nerves. This must have been eating at him for a long time.

"I neutralized the threat."

"That's not an answer! Tell me what happened already. Dad, please."

With a quiet farewell to the simple, normal relationship they'd had, Ivan forced himself to tell Rick the truth.

"I slaughtered them all. One by one. First, they died fighting. Then, they died begging. By the end, it was mostly just screams. I tried to be quick, as merciful as possible, but when dealing with a new anatomy, you have to pulp everything to be sure they're dead. Within three minutes, the water was stained with their oozing purple blood."

It was a strange progression, the emotions on Rick's face. Relief swept in, brief and beautiful, as his father's words confirmed that Rick wasn't, in fact, crazy. Then came the horror as the implications followed. With every word, the point was driven home harder, and the possibility that it was all a joke shrank. By the end, Rick no longer looked like he'd swallowed a live bee. Instead, he was growing pale, staring at Ivan like he'd unveiled himself as the avatar of Death itself. Which wasn't as far from the truth as Ivan might have liked.

"What you're feeling right now is natural, son. The shock. The disbelief. The terror at what it all means. Understand this: it only gets harder from here. If the truth is really what you want, make sure you're ready to hear it. We don't need to do all of this in a single round."

The expression on Rick's face grew more neutral as his mind went to work, properly adding in this new information to whatever he'd already been working with. "If you really killed an invading force of meta-humans, does that mean you have powers?"

"Yes. Though not the kind that can be passed down. They're nothing like your sister's—those truly are a mystery. I've got a few tricks, but by and large, I mostly lean on my physical skills."

"Kind of bummer. I was really hoping graceful aging was part of our genetics," Rick admitted. He was falling into a familiar pattern with his dad, momentarily forgetting the revelation. Ivan could actually see when it popped up again in his perception; Rick's whole body shifted to a closed-off position. "Must be pretty strong, to kill that many."

"Slaughtered," Ivan corrected. "You can't call that meager resistance they offered a fight. I was a blade cutting through a field of wheat. Yes, Rick. I am strong. Not what I once was, but still quite dangerous."

Rick was retreating a bit now, pushing into the couch's back cushions. "If you killed that many people, shouldn't you have gone to jail?"

"Details matter. I pushed back an army that was invading our soil and publicly declaring war. Can't prosecute on that without setting a dangerous standard for the capes."

The room was growing tense. Reality had started to sink in for Rick. His father was a killer: proud and efficient, at that. Still, the boy had courage. He pushed on, determined to get his answers.

"Is that why I can't remember? It was so bad I had to block it out?"

"Partially, but you had some magical assistance." Ivan reached into his pocket and produced a small crystal bottle with pink liquid inside. "This potion helps you forget things you don't want to remember. We gave you some that night, after hours of hysterical crying and fits. You saw something unimaginably terrible, and worse, you saw it committed by someone you loved. It would have been a lifelong trauma, so we gave you an out. But magic is tied to willpower, and the more you tried to remember, the weaker the effects became."

"Are... are you going to make me drink that?" There was nothing subtle about it now. Rick was visibly moving further down the couch, away from Ivan.

Carefully, Ivan picked the bottle back up and tucked it away. "I was going to offer it, though that seems like a no. Even if I did force you to drink it, that wouldn't matter. As I said, it helps you forget things you don't want to remember. It could never do more than what you desired."

"Oh, yeah, I'm sure at age five I was making great decisions about which memories I might need to hang on to. And how convenient that keeping your secret worked out to be the best thing for me."

Much as Ivan wanted to smack that train of thought aside, this was already a precarious situation. Anything less than true honesty in the moment might do more damage than could ever be mended, especially with the issue of eroded trust.

"In my heart, I really do believe that you were better off forgetting. But I'm far from a perfect person. It's very possible I allowed my own selfish desires to cloud my judgment on the issue. Because you're right, Rick. I didn't want you to stay that way. You wouldn't even get in the car with me. You screamed and screamed if I even came close. That... *this*... was the last thing I ever wanted."

"For me to know the truth?" Even through the anger Rick was trying to project, Ivan could still see the true emotion lurking in his gaze.

"For my child to be afraid of me. For you to think, even for a moment, that I would ever hurt you, turn that side of myself in your direction. Almost everyone who knows me is scared of what I can do, what I represent—sometimes, just me in general. Not you two. You ran to me for comfort whenever you were scared or hurt. You understood that there was nothing in this world I wouldn't do to keep you safe."

Ivan stared at the fear in Rick's face, the terror he'd seen so many times in so many expressions. Never had it cut him so deeply. Things were going to be different from now on, but that didn't mean he wouldn't still try his best for as long as there was parenting left to do. "Whatever you're thinking and feeling about this, understand that fundamentally, nothing has changed. To you, the discoveries are new; however, I've been this man all along. I'm the same Ivan you've known your whole life. It's just that now, I'm also more. None of that matters more to me than being your dad. I would tear the moon in half to keep you from harm."

To Ivan's surprise, Rick uncoiled from his ball in the corner of the couch slightly. The boy looked dazed, and no wonder. With the roller coaster of emotions he was on, his brain was probably fried. After a moment of consideration, he spoke in a more controlled voice than any sixteen year old should be able to manage, given the circumstances.

"I think I need a break. We're not done. I want to know the rest, just maybe... not today."

"A wise decision. One step at a time is the surest way to walk the path you're on." Ivan started forward to comfort Rick, but stopped when he caught the wince. No mistaking it, the shadow of fear now lay between them.

Even though it broke his heart, Ivan pretended not to notice. That was his burden as the parent. And he intended to play that role for however long Rick would still let him. However, Ivan had a sinking suspicion that those days were severely limited.

Chapter 47

Tori hadn't been to the main offices of Indigo Technologies before. She'd robbed a lab they owned, worked in a subsidiary, and rubbed elbows with the owner at the guild; however, she'd never had occasion to come see Wade Wyatt in the most official capacity of his civilian identity.

What amazed her from the moment she touched foot in the lobby was the security, and the knowledge of how few people would be able to spot it. Sonic disruptor cannons masquerading as modern art, pulse bombs worked into the pot of every lush plant in the space—even the floor tiles gave off the telltale sheen of electro-bind coating. Nothing here was entirely what it seemed, nor designed to serve only one purpose. Wade had built a fortress and made it look exactly as bland and unassuming as every other corporate office she'd had the misfortune to end up inside. Outside of the high-tech defenses, it was still aesthetically pleasing, if one went in for that sort of thing: lots of metal and glass, loads of natural light.

Today it hosted a fairly brisk crowd despite it being Saturday afternoon. After a morning whipping up some samples, Tori hoped she had enough progress to bring before Wade. It made sense to knock this out early—no point in redoing the work that was already out there—but she also felt somewhat underprepared. Perhaps she should have waited until there was a fully functional prototype. She shook the thought from her head. They needed to act fast, while Tori was still a news item. Once the spotlight faded, this became less effective.

At least on that front, there was little need for concern. She'd caught sight of several photographers lurking near her apartment, though they seemed hesitant to get too close. Given the phrases Chloe used whenever she spotted one, the paparazzi probably thought it was cursed by some meta, which actually wasn't too far from the truth. It wasn't enough to deter them entirely, a fact that Tori found annoying overall, but would be useful in the short term. She'd even made sure not to slip away when coming here. Let them speculate what she was up to. It would only add more attention when she made her move.

Making her way through the plush lobby, Tori strolled up to security, a thick-necked man with a sharp look in his wary eyes.

He glanced up, taking in her oil-stained jeans and t-shirt that was only slightly cleaner. "Name and appointment?" No sense of judgment, which she supposed did track. Working in a cutting-edge tech firm, he'd no doubt seen plenty of the type who put work above things like fashion or hygiene.

"Tori Rivas, here to see Mr. Wade Wyatt."

She'd been braced for skepticism, a furtive glance to be sure this really was the name on the appointment list. Not so much as a flicker. He absorbed the name like he'd been waiting all day to hear it.

"Identification." He held out a hand, into which she deposited her driver's license.

The problem, Tori quickly realized, was that she'd been thinking of this encounter like she was visiting someone high in the company. But Wade wasn't high, he was the top. They knew *his* visitors' names already; those were likely memorized as soon as the appointment was logged.

"Come with me." Handing back her license, the guard hefted himself up, walking around the side of the thick security desk that Tori noticed was covertly reinforced. Something told her these guards were more than mere muscle, but then, she'd be reckless to assume anything different, knowing where she was.

Together, they walked past the first bay of elevators, where a crowd of people in expensive clothing waited to board. They continued through a locked door that the guard buzzed them past, into a small, lush room with another guard and a single elevator.

Unlike her first one, there was nothing front-desk appropriate about this guard. He was bald, with tattoos running up and down his flesh. There was something else, impossible to put her finger on. Tori could simply smell her own kind. This one had seen danger. He might even be a guild member she had yet to encounter.

The first guard left as soon as he'd deposited her, hustling back to his desk. Her new escort rose slowly from his chair. His eyes were virtually peeling her, scanning for any danger, threat, or other potential issue. Finally, after a full minute of wordless staring, he reached over and tapped the elevator's button.

"Go ahead." His voice was raspy, but surprisingly warm.

"Thanks. Do civilians get to meet you, too, or is it only the folks using my channels?"

In response, the tattoos flowed across his skin, stretching and warping, even rising from the flesh. Seconds later, she was looking at a respectably dressed fellow in a well-tailored business suit. "I give them the professional face. It's uncomfortable to keep up, though, so I didn't bother with you." With a release of effort, the tattoos shifted back to their starting positions.

"Neat. Got a name I should know?"

He shook his head just as the elevator dinged its arrival. "If you ever get my name, it means you've royally screwed up. Or we're friends, I suppose."

One of those, then. Not a shocker, given the role he was filling in his downtime. Tori wasn't surprised. She'd seen Ivan get dispatched to slaughter an entire gang who'd crossed them; she was well aware the guild had operations like that. Still, didn't hurt to sow her own seeds of danger, while she was around.

"Then I hope I get it the friendly way. And to prove it, I'll give you a piece of friendly advice: if I ever do fuck up, don't try to come calling. Let's just say someone already has dibs on that particular task, and they aren't the sort of person you want to jump in line."

"Warning noted. Good luck with your meeting." Those were the last words before the elevator doors whispered shut.

The chrome elevator moved fast, especially considering how tall the building was. In shockingly short order, another ding sounded her arrival. The top floor of Indigo Technologies: the office of one man, Wade Wyatt. It was strange that Tori felt nervous, like she was meeting him for the first time again. She'd known him for months now... except, that wasn't quite true. Tori knew Doctor Mechaniacal. She and Wade Wyatt had barely interacted. Those dynamics were always different, and she'd never been especially adept at rolling with social challenges.

Putting the doubt out of mind, Tori strolled onward through a set of frosted glass doors that could likely withstand a missile and into the large waiting area outside Wade's office. It was filled with high-end furniture that also still managed to be comfortable—greater proof than anyone should need that Wade was a super-genius inventor.

Sitting at a vast, white stone desk, was one of the most unassuming women Tori had ever laid eyes on. Short, curly hair that already looked disheveled despite so much of the day remaining, an oversized cardigan with intentional cats and unintentional cat-hair as decoration upon it, huge glasses that evoked the image of a dragonfly—she looked like the person who'd be trailing after her boss with an armful of falling receipts and a cup of half-spilled coffee.

Tori was immediately suspicious. Big, musclebound guard? That made sense. So did the scary dude watching the elevator. But this? This set off every villain instinct Tori had. All those checks to make it this far, and the woman Wade had running the actual entry point was a normal, put-upon secretary? When someone worked that hard to appear mundane, it usually meant they had a hell of a secret tucked up their sleeve.

Approaching with care, Tori put on her most respectful voice. "Good afternoon. I have an appointment with Mr. Wyatt."

The secretary whipped her head up like she'd just noticed Tori's entrance, large eyes made even bigger by those comically oversized glasses. As she leapt up, her knees smacked the underside of the desk, eliciting what had to be a painful *thump* underneath.

"Of course! Miss Rivas. Security radioed to let us know you'd be heading up. Wade will be done in a few moments, just some private work to wrap up now that he knows you're here. Can I get you anything while you wait? Water, soda—we even have one of those fancy coffee machines in the breakroom."

"A water would be great." Much as she might like a bit of caffeine, her nerves were cranked up as things stood. Better to stay calm for what came next, and besides, she didn't want to be a bother. Not with someone this suspicious.

From somewhere under the desk, her greeter popped open a concealed fridge and produced a small, cold bottle. "Have a seat anywhere you like, and if you need anything, just give me a shout. Name is Dolores, and it's a pleasure to meet you."

Handing over the bottle, along with a handshake, Tori accepted both, then retreated to a white leather couch to wait for her appointment. She kept one eye on the door and one eye on Dolores, not quite sure what to expect from either.

Not a bad day so far. After the first team succeeded, Lodestar had stopped three in a row before the next team scored victory. Of that failing batch, she'd probably still promote one of them up to harder tasks; their failing had been execution more than planning, and that was an easier fix. Interestingly, despite kicking up a fuss at the outset, the New Science Sentries hadn't taken a turn yet.

Lodestar already knew why; she could practically hear Professor Quantum's voice ringing in their heads. He'd have told them to make a strong impression, so if they couldn't open the show, they'd try to close it. First or last: both tended to stick in people's minds the most when they did something memorable. Of course, that was precisely the sort of thinking that was holding the New Science Sentries back, so perhaps this would be a good chance to demonstrate their failings.

They weren't a bad team, not by a long shot. They were just working to catch up with everyone else. Because Professor Quantum had taught them his way, via the old methods, he'd built a team on pure strength and crowd appeal. Everyone else had come up through the new system, where the focus was placed on being the most effective superhero possible, especially when it came to protecting civilians. Until they thought about their image second and the job first, they would always end up a step behind.

It galled her to imagine what sorts of feats those four could accomplish if they'd been properly instructed. With their power, they should be knocking out tasks several degrees past what anyone else here could be saddled with. Given how stressed the AHC was getting as it was pulled in direction after direction, she could have really used the help, too. Thankfully, after this evaluation, there would be a few more to pitch in. Perhaps the New Science Sentries would be among them. She'd have to see what sorts of tactics they employed.

On the other hand, part of her felt bad for the team. This evaluation was going to be harder for them than anyone else, because their collective abilities were that much more powerful. Between Tachyonic's speed, Agent Quantum's toughness, and Plasmodia's raw power, Lodestar would have a lot more juice to wield during their session.

The five-minute rest was almost over, so Lodestar called out a quick warning, letting the next team know they'd be starting soon. There shouldn't be a whole lot of teams left; they had to be getting near the end. Once this was done, she'd have a debrief with Quorum to get his impressions—he'd been watching the whole ordeal back at base—then a few hours of patrol, and home to pick up Penelope. Ivan had said he might swing by, as well, so that meant a decent meal she didn't have to—

A blast of searing energy tore across the battlefield, on a direct course for Lodestar. Having been lost in thought, she sped up her perception and considered for a moment whether it was appropriate to dodge or take the shot head-on. Once Lodestar realized who was firing, though, the decision became simple. Using speed on par with Tachyonic's, she zipped aside from Plasmodia's blast, arriving at the boulder a split second before Presto appeared just above it.

"Out of the gate, Big Fini—hrrrmphh!" Presto's declaration of success was cut short as Lodestar's hand wrapped around the back of his skull before he could lay a finger on their prize.

"I'm pretty sure you can deal with this, but call if you need help." Lodestar grabbed Presto by the belt on the back of his costume, her free hand still holding his skull, which was pointed directly up to the open sky. "You've got a whip-smart mind under there, so try being less predictable. Also, while teleportation is great, yours is limited to line of sight. So don't ever let yourself get into a position like this one."

With that, Lodestar hurled Presto into the sky, face first. He would eventually manage to spin around, hopefully killing off his momentum and recovering, but this would buy her some time without having to watch for rips in space.

She could already see Tachyonic racing across the field, with Agent Quantum following behind at a considerable distance. It was time for Lodestar to test the New Science Sentries.

Chapter 48

She wasn't kept waiting long. In under ten minutes, Wade called for her, and Dolores ushered Tori into an office with aspirations of being a museum. All along the walls were famous designs and inventions from great minds through history. Some were from the pre-meta creators—Tori spotted a Da Vinci diagram in a proud place of honor among the displays. There were also stranger, clearly meta bits: harder to identify, unless one was the sort of person who knew which meta first discovered and broke the Althusiam temporal limits. Wade had even displayed a pile of ashes labeled "Edison Contracts." Apparently, he held history's great credit-thief in the same regard as most educated inventors. Tori could identify nearly every piece displayed in the huge office; she might be a woman of few passions, but this was definitely one of them.

In the center of the room sat the man whose own creations outshone the displays by orders of magnitude. What Wade had built could have quite literally changed the world. Part of this meeting was to find out why it was that he hadn't, in fact, done just that. Tori was smart enough to clock that there had been several great meta-geniuses through the decades, some on the side of capes, some on the side of villains, yet the amount of technology available to the public remained steady: a slow, gradual increase like one would expect in normal development, with only a few errant spikes. That couldn't be a coincidence, and much like the guild's code, Tori needed to know the rules before she started playing the game. Not because she necessarily planned to abide by them, but because it was important to know where the lines were. Breaking rules worked best when it was intentional, not due to ignorance.

"Tori, a pleasure to see you," Wade greeted her. He rose from his desk to shake her hand, then settled immediately back into his lush chair. She took one of the pair in front of his desk while Wade continued. "The room is fortified, secured, and warded, so feel free to speak plainly. In these walls, I keep a tight schedule; we don't have time for double-talk. Now then, Ivan said you wanted to consult with Indigo Technologies on something. I'm going to be straightforward: I took this meeting out of courtesy and respect, but understand that it is very unlikely I'm going to bring something from that world into this one. Splitting them apart is how I protect both."

Concise, informative, and bluntly honest; it was so nice to be dealing with a fellow science-minded colleague. Much faster than playing the societal games of small talk and niceties.

Reaching into her bag, Tori produced a small vial of green liquid, a small circular device, and a stack of pages covered in scrawling and sketches. "Go ahead and look over the specs while I explain. You'll be able to figure them out quickly." Making sure she had everything set out, Tori started on the pitch she may or may not have rehearsed a few times in the mirror that morning. "I've been thinking about what to do with my newfound sense of celebrity. There's no getting around it, not for some time, and while I was originally tempted to hole up and hope it faded, I've been considering another tactic. One to make use of the attention."

Wade's face creased in momentary confusion as he flipped through the pages, then vanished as he found whatever detail had eluded him. Tori kept on going, sure that he was still taking in every word. "I've made no bones about what my long-term goals are. I want to build my own company, turn my designs into reality. For a long time, that was it—I just knew I wanted that place to exist. But now, I think I'm starting to see the shape of it: a market I can serve, a need I can fill, and a way to leverage all this bad luck into exactly the right launching platform."

After one last scan, Wade put the pages down. "The device is interesting, though not especially groundbreaking in complexity. I find the compound you intend to fill it with far more fascinating, if it works as described. But what I find most interesting of all is that you've brought me such a proposal in the first place. Miss Rivas, outside of Ivan, there is likely no one in the guild who is more familiar with your past than me, so I am *keenly* aware of the lengths you've gone to avoid putting your work or trust in the hands of other people.

To have you suddenly show up, asking for what I'm assuming to be help, if not outright partnership, is a tad confusing."

He wasn't wrong. Tori's entire history was essentially example after example of fucking herself out of potential opportunities to avoid situations almost exactly like this one: handing off her work to a huge corporation to do whatever they pleased. Even now, the notion riled up part of her, causing a brief churn in her stomach. Thankfully, because it was such an obvious point, Tori had come prepared with an answer.

"Part of it is me learning from the guild. If I truly took nothing else from my education, I saw that even the most powerful metas need people they trust to lean on. And the guild is also why I'm taking it to you. Frankly, if you were a normal business, this would be a non-starter, but I would hope there's going to be a level of respect here not present in most business dealings. Past all that, though, you're right: this is still *very* hard for me to do. That's why I brought you the product and pitch that I did. Alone, that's a neat gadget, one I'm sure you could easily rip off. It's only when you pair it with me that it becomes a highly marketable asset."

Wade lifted an eyebrow. She'd captured his interest. "Explain."

In response, Tori's expression shifted. She wasn't much of an actor, but she could tap into real feelings well enough. There was no shortage of rage to be had at any moment, a lasting gift from the tragedy of her childhood, yet today, she needed something harder to show. Tori permitted a touch of fear onto her face, along with the rising tide of fury.

"When those bastards took me off the street, I felt helpless, like many of you out there watching have felt. Self-defense classes, training, awareness: I did everything right, and I still got snatched. The capes made it in time, sure, but what if they hadn't? How long are we going to trust our safety to people who might show up, if you're lucky? I'm tired of feeling helpless. Tired of being afraid. That's why I've partnered with Indigo Technologies to develop the Rivas line of personal defense devices. Non-lethal, unobtrusive tech designed to get you out of danger right away, not force you to wait for when a cape happens to be around."

Understanding came swiftly. It wasn't an especially obtuse concept, especially for a mind like Wade Wyatt's. He muddled it over for several seconds, lifting up the vial of green liquid and turning it around in his hands. What he was searching for, she had no idea. All Tori could do was wait as he contemplated the proposal.

"It's not just the tech, it's the sales pitch. The capes got caught with their pants down on the civilian side, and as the first public kidnapping in so many years, you have a unique platform to speak on the failings of relying on superheroes. Based on the designs, you've got quite a few ways to weave these into compact mirrors, so I take it to mean we're targeting a predominantly female demographic, which would make your story all the more compelling."

"We *start* with a targeted demographic, then grow it outward," Tori corrected. "Beginning there will play the best, given what happened to me. Then there's Beverly's designs, and the fact that women over forty are currently the audience buying the least Indigo Technologies products. This gets you a way into their pockets and starts building brand loyalty. I didn't come in here expecting a handout. This strategy opens up doors to a whole new market."

"Yes, I see you have quite a developed plan. So developed, in fact, I wonder where it is that I fit in. Your prototype is rough, yet plainly on the right path, and if this compound does as indicated, it will be extremely effective. You have the funds from your museum caper to handle the build, and national attention for free press. What do you need from Indigo?"

Despite Wade's assurances, Tori still swept the room, making sure no one was around to overhear them. "Resources would help speed this along while I'm still a hot topic, but more than that, I need guidance. I've seen what you can build versus what you release. There's obviously some sort of unspoken cap on the technology we let out into the world. I kept this one as basic as possible to be safe, but more complex ideas will demand more complex designs. I don't want to start off with the FBI up my ass because I released some gizmo with a forbidden latch."

Wade snickered, hiding it poorly behind his hand.

"Yes, I'm sure a *latch* is the device you'd want to squeeze more tech into. You aren't wrong, Miss Rivas, there are certain checks to ensure humanity doesn't get tech it isn't prepared for; however, a fair amount of it is simply the fact that the best inventors also have secret lives. I hold my top work back for the guild, because to release it publicly would make it available to my enemies. Same for Professor Quantum, and Tyranny... I presume." Wade didn't look uncertain often, yet at the mention of the mysterious ruler, his brow creased for a flicker of a moment.

Part of Tori wished Tyranny had greater affiliation with the guild. All she knew of the woman were rumors, admittedly, but they were quite impressive rumors nevertheless: genius inventor who ruled an entire island nation with the strength of her mind and the power of her creations. Were her work more public, Tori might have picked a different inventing idol, but it was Doctor

Mechaniacal whose creations were on display for all to see during his criminal enterprises. The same person she was on the verge of partnering with for a project, something Tori was actively working to keep from getting overly excited about.

Wade soon continued. “Occasionally, some inventor will start dealing matter liquidators out of a van, but they never have the reach or infrastructure to last long, and reverse engineering meta-tech is essentially a discipline in itself, one that very few have mastered. That is to say, it will be some time before you brush against the real technological ceiling; however, you should still give careful thought to the products you create. To steal one of Ivan’s favorite turns of phrase: think of it like you’re baking a cake. Once something goes in the mix, you can’t take it out. Introduce new technology to society, and there’s no undo function. Accidentally wreck an industry or bankrupt a country? Too bad. Whatever happens, you have to live with.”

“That’s an aspect I’ll weigh seriously moving forward,” Tori replied. “But for today, the design in question, do you see any major issues? The big trick there is the liquid, and good luck to anyone who tries to break that down. We can keep it proprietary. Very limited risk it would enter society at large.”

“This one works... in theory.” Wade tapped the half-formed prototype, setting down the vial next to it. “I get why you came to me early. You needed to see if I was on board and had feedback about any lines you were crossing. But if we want to do your pitch, you need something in your hand. Something tangible, to show you mean business. While we’ll need to negotiate the details, I’m open to the idea moving forward. The sooner, the better, though. We need the story to be fresh. Get me a working prototype, and we can see where that leads.”

Tori was so thrilled, she nearly knocked her chair over climbing up to shake his hand. Not only was her idea getting backing, Tori would be receiving help from one of the few other minds she genuinely admired. As she and Wade grasped hands, however, he continued speaking.

“Once we have that done, you’re going to enroll in business courses. I know some online ones you can squeeze into your spare time. Given your brain, I imagine you’ll be able to clear the coursework at an exceptional rate.”

She kept on shaking, even as the curious demand hit home. “I’m not saying I won’t—you don’t ask for pointless tasks—but do you mind explaining why?”

“Happily. First and foremost, if you intend to run a company one day, you *should* have that education, and potential investors will expect it from someone in such a core leadership role.” He paused, a dark, more Doctor

Mechaniacal look sliding across his face. "The other reason is that if we're working together, I'm going to do my best to make the project a success. In the course of that, it's entirely possible you might see my leadership techniques, and we want a ready excuse if anyone asks you where some of your more... creative problem-solving tactics come from." Those brilliant eyes were shining, countless schemes forming in the mind behind them, each waiting for the right chance to be turned loose.

It had been a long few weeks, with more lows than highs, but standing in Wade's office, seeing the danger in his eyes, Tori found herself unexpectedly happy about the curious directions her life could often turn.

Chapter 49

With Presto momentarily neutralized, Tachyonic was the next impending threat. He tore along the ground, breaking all sorts of rules of the universe to truck along at impossible speeds, all without destroying the environment or himself. She could see it all, since Lodestar was more or less matching his speed perfectly. It took a touch of effort on her part; the kid was fast, at least when he was using his suit accessories for the power boost. It seemed like not many of the other capes had caught on that Tachyonic needed the help, and evidently, he wasn't going to give the secret away during evaluation. The guy was coming full speed.

Until, he wasn't. At the very end of his approach, Tachyonic suddenly skidded to a halt, digging his feet in to send a massive spray of rubble and dirt at Lodestar's face. It was similar to Hat Trick's move with the doves, except no one on that team had provided Lodestar with access to super-speed. She didn't dart back, though, as he was no doubt predicting. Instead, Lodestar went up, directly over the wave of dirt. Behind, a searing blast of plasma tore through the space where she should have been.

That was impressive. There was no way Plasmodia could track Tachyonic's movements, so they must have both been counting down to make the attacks line up. This was definitely a team accustomed to working together, and their refined techniques showed it. Not that it mattered much when Lodestar went an unexpected direction, but adapting was part of a fight.

Besides, by this point, she'd flown against every other team. They should have accounted for the possibility.

Landing in less than a second, Lodestar retook her same position, waiting for Tachyonic to approach. It wasn't much of a delay. He zoomed in the moment Plasmodia missed, launching a series of blows that were fast, efficient, and well-aimed. Lodestar only dodged a few, letting the rest fall ineffectually on her. "Sorry, you're going to need to hit harder if you want to beat Agent Quantum's durability."

"Obviously." With that, Tachyonic hopped back, landing at the side of Agent Quantum, who had just finished an incredibly fast sprint that still left him looking like a slowpoke.

More or less the same composition as the first team, and many that followed, Lodestar realized. One at range, one to grab, two for melee. Would this have been their move if they'd gone first, or were they mimicking a successful team's tactics? There was nothing wrong with learning on the fly; however, testing unfamiliar formations often wasn't worth the tradeoff. Better to stick with what the team could do well.

On that front, Lodestar realized she might not need to worry, as Agent Quantum and Tachyonic launched a perfectly coordinated attack. Tachyonic went low, aiming for her legs and base, while Agent Quantum stayed high, ready to handle her fists and knock her down if she started to fly. An excellent strategy, with both of them holding near-perfect form. If nothing else, Professor Quantum had taught them to fight. Unfortunately, he'd taught them to fight his way, which was part of why Lodestar expected this evaluation to be especially tough on the New Science Sentries.

With a casual movement, Lodestar stepped back, catching Tachyonic as he pulled slightly ahead, hurling his whole body into the charging form of Agent Quantum. The two went down in a spray of limbs, hurrying to untangle themselves.

While they struggled, Lodestar dashed back over to the boulder. A moment later, Presto appeared once more, hands outstretched. "Again, when you suddenly stop screaming and cursing, that tips me off that you've recovered. Be less predictable."

Into the air Presto went once more, a fresh flurry of swears spouting out of his ascending lips.

Another shot of energy rang out, this one weaker and wide. Plasmodia was trying to add pressure, but wasn't sure what to do when the melee attackers fell apart. Their team was built to run like a machine; it didn't hold up well when cogs started coming loose. Two of said cogs were back on their feet, looking a tad embarrassed about the tumble they'd taken.

"I can tell you your problem right now," Lodestar informed them. "You attack from a position of strength."

Tachyonic looked momentarily confused; however, Agent Quantum let the words roll right off of him, his whole mind focused on the task at hand. Single-mindedness could be a boon at times—she'd known Ivan long enough to see that prove useful—but it also limited how much one could adapt in the moment. In this case, it was a positive, as seeing his leader unbothered gave Tachyonic his own sense of assurance back. They weren't getting better, but them fighting while shaken would hardly have improved things either.

Another team attack, though this time, they stayed more in sync, arriving in perfect unison. This tactic was shockingly close to a choreographed dance, two men filling the space of one by expertly weaving in and out of the other's way. For a moment, it was as if Lodestar were fighting a four-armed monster, blows raining in from all directions. The trouble was, no matter how much they worked together, they were still ultimately two separate people. Agent Quantum's fists were too slow, and Tachyonic's were too weak. She let the attack run for several seconds before deciding she'd seen all it had to offer. A single blow to the gut sent Tachyonic staggering back, and with a burst of motion, Lodestar slipped behind Agent Quantum, knocking him off balance with a hard strike to the spine.

"You're used to fighting people weaker than you, *maybe* ones on your level. When Professor Quantum tests you against harder opponents, they're always mechanical, and not the sentient type. That means they're limited, predictable, easy to defeat once you learn their patterns."

A rapid series of shots from Plasmodia tore through the air, ones that Lodestar easily sidestepped, seemingly unbothered. "This might feel unfair, but understand, I'm not even using your team's full capabilities right now. If I was hitting with Plasmodia's stopping power, you'd both be down already. Our world isn't balanced in how it gives out abilities. Some get the strength to shake mountains, others can turn soda into water. You cannot assume your position will always be that of the stronger fighter. This is just what it will be like to fight someone who is both fast and strong, a combination you'll eventually find if you fight enough metas."

Tachyonic let out a dusty snicker as he rose to his feet. "You might be right, but it's a little rich to get that advice coming from Lodestar."

"I wasn't born with these powers." That was all she managed before another blast ripped through the air. Unlike prior shots, this was closer to target, and far more dangerous. A nearby mesa got clipped, resulting in a hole bored through the rock.

Plasmodia was stepping things up... or was she? Come to think of it, Lodestar hadn't heard much swearing for a few moments. Zipping around to the opposite side of the boulder, she was waiting when Presto appeared, crouched low and with a hand already outstretched.

"A distraction, a new angle of approach, *and* you didn't even yell a catchphrase? Much better. Keep this up, and you all may just pull off a win." She thought Presto seemed a tad less surly as she hurled him into the sky yet again, perhaps because he'd been recognized for improving. Knowing Professor Quantum, the kids probably hadn't gotten much of that during their time under his tutelage.

No sooner was Presto gone than Tachyonic was on her. This time, he'd increased the speed of his punches, hoping to cause enough damage to slow her down, or at least have her put on the act. Since Presto was in the air, Agent Quantum was moving at mortal speeds, and Plasmodia would need time to aim, Lodestar decided this was a fine opportunity for a more personal lesson. Rather than using higher levels of strength, Lodestar dialed in her speed to precisely the same as Tachyonic's, resulting in a world stuck in slow motion while they moved as normal.

That done, Lodestar didn't brush aside the coming attacks. Instead, she blocked, returning a jab to Tachyonic's unprotected ribs. Not enough to take him down: it should feel like a normal blow, meaning that it would hurt without injuring. He appeared momentarily stunned, then came in swinging again. There was some form there, he'd had training, but it was all too evident that he'd grown very used to his speed advantage.

Lodestar easily avoided the wide swing, countering with another short jab, this one directly to Tachyonic's nose.

"Ow!" He staggered, nearly slipping into normal time, as a wave of wetness washed over his eyes.

"No matter how good you are, getting hit in the face, at least when it causes damage, is going to rock your focus. Hands up. You should be guarding. This isn't a match where you can dodge everything."

Slowly, Lodestar was getting a feel for this team. Agent Quantum had the right makings for a leader, but he could be a bit too set on his path to change when needed. Tachyonic was stuck in the classic super-speed trap—he'd tried to learn to do everything faster, rather than better. Plasmodia possessed easily the most stopping power but was kept on the backlines due to her supposed vulnerability, never mind the fact that she had plenty of defensive options. As for Presto, he might actually have the sharpest mind of the four. Pity he seemed intent on concealing and misusing that potential.

Sure enough, Tachyonic proved her theory by racing in once more. He was going faster this time, because of course he was. That was the Professor Quantum method for overcoming a hurdle: stronger, faster, tougher, better. Dominate, win—all that idiot crap Lodestar had been forced to dig out by the root when starting the Alliance of Heroic Champions. Had Tachyonic taken a moment to truly consider the situation, he'd have remembered that Lodestar was only ever matching *his* speed. Going faster changed nothing. This wasn't a fight that could be won by adding more power.

More punches, though these were at least a tad tighter than before. Lodestar blocked the first two swings, feinted a third jab that Tachyonic fell for, and came around with a right hook to his jaw. She tried to hold back; however, moving at those speeds made it difficult to entirely pull the blow. She still sent Tachyonic stumbling back onto his butt.

With his landing, their time in the land of super-speed came to an end. Lodestar decided to reengage with the other recovering members of the team. Agent Quantum was mostly to his feet, but she could still hear Presto whistling through the air above them. Plasmodia would fire when given a chance; however, by this point, she'd yet to land a single shot. Hopefully, she'd realize that with Tachyonic's speed in play, Lodestar could dodge most ranged attacks and come in closer. She'd love to see what Plasmodia could do when truly pushed. Unfortunately, knowing the training they'd gotten, Lodestar highly doubted the young woman would break formation. Professor Quantum drilled those lessons in especially hard.

As Agent Quantum looked her over, she wondered if he was going to step up. This plan wasn't working, not unless they had a secret reveal prepared for the last moment. There was still time to change things, to try something new, but that would demand throwing away their current tactics. It was a hard call to make for any leader: stick with what they knew, even though it was failing, versus rolling the dice on an untested strategy. With a team this developed, there would be other tactics they could shift to, ones they'd no doubt drilled and polished as much as their current formation. The question was, would any of them work against an opponent as strong as their own team, and could Agent Quantum figure out which?

"Plasmodia, switch to rapid shots. Let's keep her dancing. Presto, pick a number between one and a hundred. Count to that, then make your jump. She can't predict your timing if it's randomized. Tachyonic, switch to support. Use that speed as a surprise. Don't let her see you coming. I'll take her on in melee."

"That a fact?" Lodestar liked that he'd changed things up; however, he'd only shifted the variables, rather than the strategy as a whole. While it could still work, she wasn't holding her breath on that making the difference.

In response, Agent Quantum raised his own fists. "Since you gave Tachyonic a real sparring session, care to teach it to someone who has been more thoroughly trained in hand-to-hand combat?"

"Nope." Lodestar dashed over, sweeping Agent Quantum's legs and knocking him in the stomach on his way down. "The point of that lesson wasn't that he needs a boxing tutor. It's that you all have weaknesses. Knowing what they are allows you to plan around them. Ignoring them leaves opponents an opening to exploit."

Although she could see Tachyonic preparing for another charge and Plasmodia building up energy to shoot once more, in her heart Lodestar knew this test had likely reached its conclusion. Much as she'd been hoping they'd think on their feet, it appeared they were continuing on with trying the same thing, only more powerful. It was an issue she'd expected when taking on Professor Quantum's team, and one she dearly hoped could be trained out of them.

The other way that lesson sank in wasn't pretty. It came in the field, when a team fought someone truly beyond their abilities, and usually ended in several funerals. Lodestar would do all she could to educate this group before that day came.

In the moment, that lesson probably required leaving them publicly defeated. A blow to the ego was far, *far* better than what awaited them if they didn't learn their lessons during training—even if it meant one more set of superheroes that resented her. She could already see the frustration in their eyes catalyzing into anger, know they were thinking it wasn't fair, this gulf of power between them. They were right, but it didn't change the fact that they'd eventually fight a stronger opponent.

She could bear their resentment, their distance, if it meant they'd be able to survive. One more burden added to the countless on her shoulders. This one, at least, she'd been prepared for since the evaluation started. It was how these things always turned out, sooner or later. Admiration turned to jealousy, annoyance, or frustration as attempt after attempt to surpass her power failed.

Standing at the top meant standing alone.

Chapter 50

The worryingly thin woman with skin the color of an old lime moved quietly through the front door, causing a large bell overhead to tinkle loudly. Inside the unremarkable door was a wood-paneled hallway leading deeper into the well-aged building. From down the expanse, music drifted along. Nothing remotely modern, this had a peppy, bouncy rhythm. One might have used the word jaunty, even if it weren't normally within their vocabulary.

For Lozora, the sound conjured dim memories of her time in the lab. One of the scientists used to leave a television on for her brood at night, believing it would better socialize them with humans. That one had favored older works, some dating back to the days before color. This wasn't a tune she could particularly recall, it was merely in the style of those programs. Lozora was never sure if that scientist was eaten during the escape, or if they'd been out on the fateful day. As the lone survivor, there was no way to ask the others which humans they'd torn apart in the dash to freedom.

At the end of the hall, there was a single turn. Down a bit further, another door waited. This one hosted a huge glass pane in the center, marking the business as "Vaudeville and Toon: Destructive Indestructibles" in elaborate gold lettering. She was in the right place, moving silently along the weathered floor. No need to turn the knob, she realized, since the door was cracked. That explained how the music was traveling so well.

Pushing her way inside, Lozora found herself looking directly at a desk with a woman behind it. A very distinctive woman, at that: pants held aloft by suspenders, starched shirt, bow tie, a flat-topped straw hat, and a plainly plastic mustache that came to absurdly curly points at each end.

The moment she saw Lozora enter, the curiously dressed woman sprang to her feet, tipping the straw hat and knocking a bottle of ink Lozora hadn't seen seconds prior onto the floor. It spread across the wood in a dark, oozing puddle, yet the woman paid the spill not the slightest of mind.

"Good afternoon! Welcome to Vaudeville and Toon, Independent Disaster Contracting. As you might have guessed, I'm Vaudeville, in the flesh. What can I do for you today?"

"My employer is interested in your services." She wasn't entirely sure what to make of Vaudeville, having only ever known the woman by reputation. She didn't seem like much outside of an oddball, but that meant nothing. According to reports, she and Toon were among the highest-ranked metas in existence for survivability. The latter had supposedly even survived a scuffle with Fornax. That was the sort of power it was useful to have around.

"Of course, you did walk into our office. Services must be in demand, so tell me the skinny. Boss have a competing bar we need to go for a dance at? Maybe a business we should patronize? Tell us where you need the chaos, and that's where we'll be." She paused, looking Lozora over more carefully. "With some exceptions, by matter of policy."

Best to start with the caveats. Lozora might save herself some time. "What sorts of exceptions?"

"The expected sort. Ya see, Toon and I occupy a niche in the laws and protections around meta-humans. We exert influence on the world around us simply by existing in it. We cause chaos and trouble no matter where we go. The reason that's legal is because we can't control it, and jailing us for effects outside our control crosses several legal lines. That said, we're also not stooges. Laws can change, ya know. It's why we avoid anything related to or around the Alliance of Heroic Champions. Not looking to pick a fight with people who can put the kibosh on our business."

About what Lozora had expected. It was standard practice among those who'd been around long enough to build a reputation in the first place. Steering clear of the capes was just good sense, which was what made her employer's aspirations all the rarer. Not many were left who'd challenge the AHC directly. Luckily, he'd also found places for assets that were technically unconnected from what the capes would be dealing with.

"That won't be an issue," Lozora replied.

"Tickled as a hog in hosiery to hear it." Another look, this one more probing. "I'll ask your forgiveness for the uncouth addition, but given your overall deadly demeanor, feels prudent to mention we also don't tango with the other side of that equation. Vaudeville and Toon are strictly a civilian service. We avoid the major leagues."

Here, unfortunately, they had an issue. From a door on the left, annoyed ranting could be heard. Seconds later, it could also be seen, as actual scribbles and blurred-out symbols manifested in the air. That was the only warning before the door slammed open and a new man ambled through.

He had a strange movement to him, a constant bounce, like he was never truly still. His intense expression was a sharp contrast to the bright, cheerful hues he was clad in, and the coifed bobbing hair swaying atop his skull. It was hard to place this person's age. His skin was off in texture, somehow just... not right, but it lacked any signs of aging. Older than a teen, younger than what most would consider a true adult, the man was a shifting tapestry as he took long, unusual steps through the room.

"Your partner agrees with that, or does he make his own choices?"

"Toon isn't one to get bogged down in details. He prefers the fun," Vaudeville replied.

"He's also out of beer. Turned into milk again." From a small mini-fridge, Toon produced a brown bottle, then very carefully eased the door shut.

As soon as it clicked, a stack of books fell from literally nowhere, smacking Vaudeville in the cranium one after another. With every blow, she teetered more and more off-balance, until the last one sent her to the ground. Then, moments later, Vaudeville was back up as if nothing had happened. That was the thing about these two: easy to hit, near impossible to hurt.

Looking mildly embarrassed by the bookslide, Toon managed a repentant expression, albeit not well. This was a bit too commonplace for the pair to feel bad about. "Sorry, didn't mean to do that in front of a client."

"That's quite all right, Toon," Vaudeville assured him. "Our guest was leaving anyway, seeing as she's clearly here recruiting for some sort of larger caper, and we don't fit in. Besides, she just tried to play us against each other. I'm not fond of working with those who can't respect the bond between partners."

While Lozora was technically here diplomatically, she still felt her spine tense. Perhaps this woman didn't quite realize who she was talking to. Lozora was no mere lackey to be drummed out when someone else's patience wore thin. Tapping her hands against the arms of the chair, Lozora began to rise.

"Oh goody and gumption. Toon, looks like you might get to have some fun today after all."

Toon looked from Lozora to Vaudeville, then dropped the beer into a wastebasket, where it somehow made a sound like a ringside bell. Putting his right thumb to his mouth, Toon began to blow. As he did, his entire fist swelled in size to absurd, comical proportions. A literal gleam twinkled in both of his now wide eyes, the first signs of genuine excitement he'd shown, all pointed directly at Lozora.

"Step right on up, my bold challenger. I promise, you ain't never had a fight like me."

Helen took her time putting Penelope to bed. They sang songs, had a long tub time, and even did rereads of some favorite stories. It felt good to be here—human, and home. She reveled in being around someone who had little care for Lodestar, powers, superheroes, any of it. To Penelope, Helen would be Mom above all other titles, and after days like this, she needed that. As all children do, however, Penelope eventually gave in to slumber.

Part of her—no, much more than a part—wanted to call Ivan. He understood what it meant to be at the top. The solitude, the distance, the pressure. But it wasn't fair of her to add to his burdens. He was already carrying enough. She was the Lodestar; she could haul her own mental crap around. Setting her resolve, Helen wandered into the kitchen and poured a glass of wine.

The last drops were nearly fallen when her phone chirped. She knew the sound—not many people had their own custom tones, but there were those who warranted the distinction. Yanking it out, she prepared for Ivan to tell her something about the Starscouts, or perhaps offer some insight into Tori's kidnapping.

Are you free?

Well... that was unexpected. Blunt, which did fit Ivan, though he tended to err on the side of formality, at least since taking on his civilian role. Her thumb wavered, unsure of what to write back. Yes, she was free. Yes, she wanted to see him, to share the events of her day. That was the trouble. She liked Ivan, liked being around him. When she'd been living as just Helen, that was one thing. Now, the issue was more complicated. In the end, Helen decided that since there was a chance this could be related to official business, she had a duty to investigate.

Even Lodestar was allowed a small bit of self-delusion.

For the moment. Something up?

She didn't even have time to put the phone down before his reply came.

In person.

Damn. If he couldn't talk about it even over their secured lines, then this was indeed serious. All thoughts of relaxation and light flirting bolted from Helen's mind as she tried to predict what threat they might be facing.

Come over and read me in.

Again, she didn't set the phone down in time. Another chirp, another message. Reading it twice, Helen lifted an eyebrow and walked through the house to her back door. Popping it open, she stepped onto her porch to find Ivan already sitting there, staring out at the night sky. There was something in his expression, a pain she'd seen prior incarnations of, though never to this degree. A joke about personal property faded on her tongue. This was no laughing matter.

"Ivan, what's wrong?"

She expected him to need some time, but that made little sense. Ivan had come to her to talk. He wasn't going to hold back when the chance finally arrived.

"Rick has started to remember the beach. Enough that he asked about it, and I told him the truth of that day. He still hasn't asked the big questions yet, but it's only a matter of time." Lowering his gaze, Ivan pressed his hands against his forehead. "My son is going to see me as a monster, and I don't know how to stop it. Or even if I *should* stop it. He has a right to know my history; the people with grudges certainly will."

Taking her time, Helen went into the house, scooping up a pair of old quilts. Stepping back out, she hunkered down in the chair next to Ivan, handing over the blanket. "Summer is ending. The nights are starting to chill. Remember, have to look human."

While Ivan worked out which part of the quilt was the top, Helen continued. "I don't know what to say about the Rick stuff. That bites the big one? No, bad call, forget that. It just... sucks, Ivan, and I wish I could say something to make it better. Except, the truth is, this was always a hurdle you two had to climb. Eventually, our kids will find out we're more than just their parents. Some have an easier adjustment to make than others, but Rick is smart. He'll be able to see the bigger picture. Whether or not he can make peace with it... that's up to him to decide."

"Sadly, I am all too aware." Ivan had finally managed to get the blanket oriented appropriately, letting it sit at his waist like an elderly man at a chessboard. For a moment, Helen tried to imagine old Ivan. It didn't work. He, like her, was largely unchanging, save only for when he made the *big* changes. She couldn't imagine Ivan living to an old age any more than herself.

Superheroes and villains alike, they were both fated to go out with their masks on.

"The only upside is I can offer comfort on one level: you don't need to worry about Rick or Beth being targets. Not from the AHC, and not from anyone within punching distance of me. We don't ever talk about how much you've done for me and Penelope—"

Ivan interrupted her. "I was paying back—"

"Cut the crap," Helen interrupted right back. "Paying me back for helping you get the freedom you'd earned doesn't entail a tenth of what you've done over the years. From the very start, you were the one who gave me the downtime to have her, and since then, you've been a constant help, one I probably leaned on too much during the rough times."

It was always surprising when Ivan could somehow manage to look even *more* serious than he normally did, yet as he stared Helen down, she was nearly captured by the gravity in his gaze. "Trifles and pittance. *Everything* I love, I have in my life because of your help. There is no way to repay that debt, though I owe you a lifetime of effort in trying."

"Guess what, that feeling flows both ways." Finally fiddling with her own blanket, Helen snapped it out in a single movement, letting it settle naturally over her chair and body. "After all you've done for Penelope, I owe at least that level of care to your kids. So whatever else you might be scared of in all of this, try not to worry about their safety. I'm not perfect, nor infallible, but so long as the power is mine to wield, your kids will always have Lodestar in their corner."

It would have shocked most people, to see Ivan relax at those words, even slightly. He was not a man of casual ease, nor one prone to trusting. But he knew more than most of the world; he'd seen how much power Lodestar could truly wield, when the need arose. For the moment, Ivan allowed himself a minute measure of peace. Likely the very thing he'd come here hoping to find.

"Much as my pride wants to decline the gesture, for the sake of my children, I thank you sincerely." Ivan lowered his head, almost managing a bow despite their seated positions. "And I'm sorry for interrupting your evening so abruptly."

"Given the situation, I get it. Honestly, I'm sort of glad you showed up. My day was a pain, as well. It's nice to sit with an old friend."

An old friend, an old enemy, an old rival, an old asset, even an old partner for the occasional shared adversary. After all these years, there were few roles they hadn't filled for the other at some point along the way. Only a few were left purposefully, willfully, untouched—no matter how much either of them might wish to be sharing a single quilt.

"Anything interesting? I could use a distraction."

This question, thankfully, Helen had an easy response to. "I got shot in the face by a bunch of birds."

A sincere, contemplative look fell over Ivan's face. "Do you mean you were hit by a large amount of birds, or a flock of them banded together to actually shoot some sort of tiny guns at you?"

There was no particular reason why that got her, but seeing the man once known as Fornax ask such a question with a straight face sent Helen into convulsions of laughter that took a full minute to fade.

Chapter 51

Sunday evening arrived too soon for Tori, who'd spent nearly every spare second since her meeting with Doctor Mechaniacal down in the lab, hard at work. She needed to get a fully functioning prototype built so she'd have actual specs. Until they knew the exact size and shape, she couldn't very well tap Beverly to start much of the design work. It had been one thing when this was all an idea, just some fun notion to sink her energy into rather than dwelling on everything that had happened. Having Indigo Technologies provisionally on board changed things. Now, it had the potential to be real, and Tori was determined not to let the chance slip away.

When Beverly finally dragged her out of the lab, it was a blessing. She'd been at it for a long time without any breaks and was starting to slow down mentally. Changing gears would give her brain time to rest. It wasn't as if game night with the New Science Sentries would demand the same level of intense focus.

After a shower and a few cups of coffee, Tori was more or less as functional as she got outside of things that interested her. She expected to coast her way through the evening in a subdued manner, letting the more boisterous members of their social circle pick up the slack.

Once the knock on their door came, however, the flaw in that plan became apparent. It was a weary foursome that arrived at their door. None looked especially well rested, and their overall energy was somewhere on Tori's level, which was worrying. The sole member putting up the appearance of pep was Austin, who greeted Chloe cheerfully when she let them in.

"Good evening, and thank you again for having us. We brought some playing cards, wine, and a batch of homemade cookies for dessert."

"Oh, perfect! We just ordered pizza for dinner. I didn't know everyone's preferences well enough to cook." Chloe accepted the cookies from Austin while Tori ambled over to help with the wine. Beverly was still getting ready, or maybe wanted to make an entrance. Tori never understood the rules of the fashionable.

Taking both wine bottles from Kyle, she noticed he was especially subdued, even by the group's current standards. The easier play would be to let it go unsaid, leave the issue alone since it was almost certainly cape-related. Except, she was supposed to be friendly, and this was way too obvious to pretend it wasn't there. Ultimately, Tori opted to split the difference. She'd give Kyle a window; if he didn't use it, that was on him.

"Come help me uncork these bad boys. With this many people, we'll go through both fast." Leading Kyle over to the kitchen, leaving the other three chatting with Chloe at the entrance, she walked him to the junk drawer and popped out a bottle opener. "Want to talk about it?"

"Huh?" He hadn't been braced for that. The question appeared to be the first thing that had jarred him into paying attention. "Sorry, what?"

"I'm asking if you want to talk about whatever dark cloud is hanging over all your heads. 'Cause if so, do it now. I'm not interrupting a winning streak because you get a case of feelings." A little harsher than she'd intended, Tori took a breath and dialed it back. "I mean, something is plainly up. You don't want to talk about it, your call. Just making an offer to listen while we wait for Beverly."

The slight pop behind her was all the warning Tori needed. Without turning, she held out a glass of poured wine slightly to her rear, where Ike accepted it as he walked around to Kyle's side. "He's miffed because we had an evaluation at the Alliance of Heroic Champions, and our team wasn't able to overcome the challenge presented. Which is the polite way of saying we got our asses kicked."

"Not... we didn't do that badly. We just didn't succeed at the task assigned, despite coming close a few times," Kyle corrected.

"Coming close? I never even got a hand on that rock. Austin came nearest, and that was right before the time limit. We might have fought until the end, but we were far from success."

The conversation only seemed to be riling Kyle up, which was admittedly better than the morose version. Tori thrust a glass of wine over. It wouldn't be able to affect someone with his metabolism, but the routine act of drinking sometimes helped to calm people down. "Were you up against some sort of monster, or giant murdering robot?"

"What?" Kyle asked, swinging his head around. "Of course not. Who would test their new members with that kind of opponent?"

Clearly *someone* had never been through villain training. Tori enjoyed a whole three seconds of feeling superior about the hurdles she'd cleared—right up until Kyle named their actual adversary.

"We had to test ourselves against Lodestar."

Setting the wine down, Tori went to the fridge and pulled out a bottle of beer. She'd never been much of a wine fan, and there was no reason to change that tonight. Popping the top, Tori clapped Kyle on the back lightly. "I'm pretty sure you don't have to feel bad about losing to the person famous for being unbeatable. She's the fucking Lodestar. What else did you expect? Who's going to come out on top against her?"

"Cyber Geek's team, for one." Ellie had wandered over, leaving Austin and Chloe still catching up by the door. The man was dedicated to his polite small talk, Tori had to give him that. Ellie drew more attention, though, as she poured herself a very full glass of wine. "We didn't have to fight her, per se. We had to take something she was guarding. And since she matched her power with whoever she was fighting, the stronger you are, the harder your challenge. So at least we can take comfort in how weak that squad must be."

Ellie lifted her glass, and Ike clinked. Only Kyle resisted the urge to join, showing unexpectedly good judgment, given his track record.

"Look, I'm sure there's all sorts of rivalries and pissing matches going on in the AHC, but let's lay one thing out right here and now: Cyber Geek is a friend of mine. We worked together, we fought together when our office was attacked, and he saved a whole nightclub full of people, me included, when Nexus let a monster loose on the dance floor. You've got beef, fine. Keep it between yourselves. But that's going to be the last time you shit-talk my friend in my presence. Anyone got an issue with that?"

Ellie looked stunned, and even Ike appeared momentarily taken aback. Kyle, however, recovered for his team, showing off that speedy thinking for a change. "Apologies, Tori. It was inappropriate. We shouldn't talk about a fellow superhero that way, and we certainly don't have room to belittle the strength of a team that did better than us. It won't happen again, though I do hope this policy flows both ways."

"I guess it would, but he's never really mentioned your team." Only after she said the words did Tori realize how they might be perceived. That was the cost of knowing tech better than people, stumbling into errors that a more socially adept person could avoid.

"Oh? Then what is it you *do* talk about?" For once, she was glad to have Ike around. His ridiculous innuendo was exactly the pivot she needed from that last statement.

"Spreadsheets, combat tactics, our eventual inevitable battle to the death. The usual former office drone stuff." Talking about it made Tori realize she actually hadn't had more than a phone call or a brief chat with Donald in some while. She should reach out, make sure he was holding up okay. If this was how the New Science Sentries were faring, it had to be a rough time as a recent rookie.

Heels clicking along wood signified Beverly's arrival, and Tori felt her head turn with everyone else's even though she knew who was coming. That was Beverly's knack; she could draw the attention of a room before even setting a foot inside. Once she actually arrived, Tori nearly coughed on a sip of beer. She was accustomed to Beverly, her roommate and friend, the one who always looked put together, but in a functional, office-appropriate manner. Tonight she hadn't changed much, yet the effect was potent. A touch more makeup here, a slightly different cut to her blouse there, and suddenly Tori realized why Beverly could survive by simply writing about fashion. The woman knew her stuff to a terrifying degree.

What was more interesting was the enhanced appearance itself. Obviously, she hadn't put in the effort for Tori or Chloe, which narrowed it down to the New Science Sentries. One glance at Austin's near slack-jawed face told her which of the group was having the strongest reaction, and to Tori's surprise, she caught Beverly clocking Austin's face, too. First mystery solved easily enough; the second was more troublesome, unfortunately. Was Beverly actually making an effort, or just screwing with Austin for fun? She'd never been the cruel sort—then again, Beverly didn't hate many people the way she hated Professor Quantum. It was hard to imagine her seriously flirting with his successor. Perhaps she was using her wiles to win him over, hoping to gain useful information about the AHC?

Tori shook off the curiosity, all too aware she lacked the skills to crack this puzzle. The easier method was just to get through the night, then ask Beverly later. That was the perk of being outside the courtship dance; she wasn't bound by any of the unspoken rules.

"My goodness, where did you get that top?" Ellie rushed over before

Austin had recovered enough to speak. "I love it! I've been hunting all over Ridge City for wardrobe updates, mostly to no luck."

"You have to know the good spots, plus a little tailoring. Nothing comes perfect off the rack," Beverly explained. "Next time you have a day off, I can take you around to some favorites. Maybe with your help, I can drag these two along."

Finally ambling over from the door, Chloe piped up. "Hey, I went with you once. I just rarely get full days off. We don't all do freelance or get corporate hours."

"Yes, you at least have an excuse." Beverly narrowed her eyes at Tori, who met the glare with a casual shrug.

"My excuse is that I don't want to."

That deepened Beverly's stare, but had no effect on Ellie's enthusiasm. "That's all right. I'd be happy just for the guidance and company."

It was an interesting move. From what Tori could tell, Beverly had decided to embrace the friendship angle to a greater degree than herself. Then again, she'd asked Kyle what was wrong, so that was significant effort on her part. Maybe they were still playing the same strategy after all; she was just noticing the difference in how effective each were.

"I'll try to tag along if the timing works out. I've got some new looks in mind I want to get outfits for." Chloe was excited as well, and Tori wondered how many times she'd be walking in on gorgeous strangers as Chloe played with the newly discovered aspect of her powers.

While those three grouped up, Austin at last found his feet and wandered into the heart of the apartment. Taking a small glass and filling it with water, he paused next to Tori. "I thought you might like to know, your friend fought very well. His team not only passed the evaluation, they did so while putting on a fine show."

"Glad to hear it. So, you're not jealous?" Tori asked.

"Oh, I am incredibly envious," Austin corrected. "Also a bit resentful, if we're being honest. It's hard not to feel like this is all wrong. We're fighting the way we were trained by one of history's greatest superheroes and are being told we're wrong at nearly every turn. Meanwhile, the team closely associated with a traitor keeps finding success and acclaim. I understand they weren't part of Apollo's scheme, but I hope you can see why that would be frustrating for my people. They really are doing the best they can every time. That's why it hurts so much to keep feeling like failures."

Years ago, months ago, she'd have tossed those words aside, assuming them to be pure fiction. The trouble was, being around the capes this much had shown Tori a truth she couldn't fully ignore: some of them were sincere. Not all, probably not even most, but a few were doing the job because they truly wanted to make the world better, safer, for the normal people who lived in it. She'd seen an everyday programmer lay down his life for others multiple times, simply because he had enough strength to try. Hell, she'd looked into the eyes of Lodestar and seen only true concern behind them. Tori didn't know Austin or Agent Quantum well enough to have a clue if he was in that club or not, but she had a hunch. Enough to throw him a line. Whether he took it or not would determine how much of his demeanor was playing the part versus his true ambitions.

"I mean, there's a solution here, if you're serious. You really want to get better at this job, to see what the differences in your tactics are? Go ask Cyber Geek if you can tag along with his team for a few nights."

While the idea wasn't rejected immediately, Austin's face creased in visible concern. "There's merit to that idea, granted, but I'm afraid it might be too late. Our teams haven't gotten off to the greatest start; I fear such a request from me would seem like teasing, at best, or setting them up for some sort of trick, at worst."

Beverly and Chloe had gotten out the stack of board games and were beginning the discussion. Seeing several strategy options that would have them playing for half the night in the mix, Tori realized she needed to weigh in on this choice, and soon. Hitting the fridge for one more beer, she paused briefly by Austin's side.

"Convince Cyber Geek you're coming to him sincerely, and he'll agree to the pairing, bad blood or not. He cares more about the people you're protecting than the politics of the AHC. Make him believe you want to be better capes and he won't be able to turn you away."

Austin nodded. "Thank you. I'll think on that." From the way his eyes kept swinging back over to Beverly's side of the room, Tori doubted he'd get much critical contemplation accomplished that evening. She'd done her part, though, so with a clear conscience, she attacked the group choosing the night's diversion.

"Chloe, put that ten-hour strategy game down, and no one gets hurt!"

Chapter 52

Monday morning brought with it an unexpected message. It wasn't as though Tori hadn't kept in contact with Lance and Warren—Pest Control and Glyph, as they were known in the guild. They'd touched base during the guild's downtime, making sure all the rookies were laying low and staying safe. They'd both fallen silent in recent weeks; the new guild opening marked the chance to start working again, and no doubt the pair were busy with their own lives.

That's what made Lance's unexpected invitation to a meeting so out of the blue. The implication was clear, obviously. Some kind of guild business. Maybe Lance needed tech consulting, wanted air surveillance to monitor a location, or he was looking for backup on a job. The wide range of possibilities poked at Tori's curiosity. Besides, there was also the inevitable truth that she needed money, and if it was a job, guild work paid extremely well.

Designing and building a new product line was going to be expensive. She could foist the funding onto Indigo, except there was no way to do that without also cutting them in on a greater share of the profits. While Tori had made peace with the need for a corporate alliance, that didn't mean she wanted to hand over any more power or leverage than necessary. As much as possible, she would be the driving force of her creations. She wasn't quite sure that would be enough to motivate her to brave another museum heist, but it was worth taking the meeting. There was always the option to say no, if the offer didn't sound like her scene.

A crisp knock on her bedroom door came a few moments before Beverly's voice. "Saw some photographers creeping along the west side of the building, and Chloe is already getting ready for work. You might want to take the back door today."

It took all of Tori's control not to let out a groan that was audible from the street. Stupid photographers still hanging around. She wanted to be done with them, except the attention was still necessary for her long-term plans. Besides, it wasn't like she had a way to get rid of them. None that wouldn't involve guild tactics, anyway.

Beverly hit the door once again, softer this time. "You get a text from Lance?"

"Sure did. Meeting tonight?"

"That's the one," Beverly's voice confirmed. "Up for it?"

Tori's mind flashed to her Hephaestus suit, sitting down in the lab. She hadn't gotten to take it out for more than a few hours at the guild's relaunch, a pitiful amount of field-testing time. Even aside from that, part of her missed the feel of her tech encompassing her entirely. Tori enjoyed being Hephaestus, perhaps more than she let herself realize initially. If she wanted to suit up again, the guild was where she'd find her best opportunities.

Not to mention, she was sick of playing helpless. Between the car thrown at her head and the kidnapping, Tori had been affecting the role of mundane civilian too much for her liking. It was time to be powerful again. It was time to be Hephaestus.

"Why not? Could be fun."

It had been a hell of a weekend. Passing the evaluation was a high point, obviously, but the celebration with his team that followed had been a darn good time as well. Sans costumes, they'd gone out to a nice dinner in celebration, then followed things up with a downright horrific session of karaoke, in which they learned Irene was a shockingly talented soprano and Lucy could clear half a room with the first ten notes of a song. Ren always stuck to something country, low and simple. He'd gotten much better at speaking with his altered tongue since the change, but he still avoided anything that demanded rapid linguistic skills. As for Donald, he'd picked an old favorite that was more talk-singing than actual music, but it was on the list, so he'd considered it fair game.

One unexpected cherry had come Sunday night: a text from Tori about wanting to grab lunch and catch up soon. After weeks of working to be better at his job, and an objective evaluation that said his team was doing well, Donald found he could easily justify taking some time off to see her. Important as being a superhero was, it couldn't make up the entirety of his life. That wasn't healthy for any profession, not even capes.

The text was still on his mind as he walked down the AHC's halls Monday morning. With breakfast at his back, Donald planned to do some serious gaming today. The evaluation had reminded him of a tool Cyber Geek was going to eventually need: flight. Suit thrusters were fine for short distances, but sooner or later, they'd face an airborne opponent. When that day arrived, he was the only team member with the versatility to meet them in the sky. It was just a matter of seeing which flight systems translated well into the real world, and which left him spinning out.

He was so lost in thought about zipping through the sky that Donald almost didn't hear the voice calling for him until it was practically on his heels. In his defense, though, he only tended to think of himself as "Cyber Geek" while in costume.

Turning, he found Agent Quantum, sans the usual tagalongs, approaching. Not the best surprise possible, but at least Agent Quantum always conducted himself like a professional.

"Sorry, didn't mean to run you down," Agent Quantum said once he finally arrived. "But I saw you leaving the cafeteria and thought it might be serendipity. I wanted to speak with you, in private, when you have a moment."

Initially, Donald was torn. The New Science Sentries hadn't exactly gone out of their way to get on his team's good side. If anything, they'd been downright antagonistic. With a long day of work ahead, a very real part of Donald wanted to politely brush him off, sticking to the schedule that he'd planned. That inclination only lasted the micro-seconds necessary to remember where, precisely, he was standing.

They were in the hall of the Alliance of Heroic Champions, not some shitty office condo in downtown. This wasn't a corporate cog job where what they did had little to no effect on the world. Whatever else might be going on, they were both superheroes, and if Agent Quantum was willing to extend an olive branch, then Cyber Geek should at least hear him out.

"We're not far from my room, if you want to follow me. I've got some free time until my next task."

A tension that was extremely easy to miss left Agent Quantum's shoulders as he nodded, a wary smile on his face. Together, they started down the hall once more, though this time walking together, rather than one trailing the other.

Ivan was waiting at his desk when Tori came in. He knew she'd be heading over, because he was the one who'd scheduled a meeting to start their week. As much as Ivan wanted to put the weekend out of his head, he couldn't, and not just because the look on Rick's face haunted him constantly. There were other implications to that discussion, ones that his former apprentice needed to know. The odds of the situation coming into play were minimal, but one didn't work in a field of the miraculous without learning to plan for the impossible, to say nothing of the unlikely.

She was surprisingly prompt, arriving a full three minutes before they were due to start. As Tori walked in with a mug of coffee in hand, Ivan gave a short, pointed look at the door. Kicking it with her foot mid-stroll, Tori knocked it closed, after which Ivan hit unseen buttons hidden somewhere on the desk. One day, she'd really love to tear into these walls and see how much obfuscating tech Wade had woven through the building.

"What's up? This about Lance's text this morning?"

That was news to Ivan, so he shook his head. "Something more personal." He waited while she got comfortable in her seat. No, that wasn't quite right. Ivan wasn't necessarily waiting so much as he was unsure of how to proceed. This was a big topic to bite off, especially given the potential ramifications. Ultimately, Ivan decided to push through bluntly. If nothing else, he and Tori both appreciated someone cutting to the heart of a matter.

"This weekend, Rick began to ask me questions about my past. He's figured out that my old stories don't line up, and as of now, knows that I am both a meta-human and a murderer, though my true identity has yet to be revealed."

A parade of expressions ran across Tori's face as she struggled to find fitting words to offer. In the end, she settled on glum. "That really blows." Not especially eloquent, but sincere all the same.

"It very much does," Ivan agreed. "However, that alone would be my burden to bear. The larger issue is that in Rick's digging, he uncovered our purported genealogical connection. Given that it conflicted with the story he knew of my heritage, the detail stuck out to him. While I've tried hard to impart upon him that this is my secret, and stays between us, he *is* a sixteen-year-old, with all the rash decision-making that comes with the age. Worse, he's got his mother's smarts, meaning he might actually be effective at digging where he shouldn't. There is a chance he'll reach out to you, given what he's grappling with and the connection he now knows we share."

This time, Tori's face was more guarded. She nodded along in understanding, giving away little more than that. "I get it. He found a rabbit hole, poked his head in, and is trying to figure out if he wants to see how far down it really goes. Since I'm the only person he knows who isn't a parent that's connected, there's a chance he'll try to approach me for more information."

A pause as something familiar peered out from behind Tori's guard. Fear. Of course fear. Always fear. In this case, Ivan certainly couldn't hold it against her. This was fear he'd specifically imparted. He had no one to blame but himself.

"Given the protectiveness you feel toward your kids, I'm not looking to cross any lines here. If you want me to tell him to hit the bricks, I will. If you want me to try to soften the edges of what he's going to learn, I'll do my best, but let's be honest, I might do more harm than good there. Point is, I'm following your lead."

"I appreciate that." Ivan looked down at his desk, where several pictures of his children through the years were featured. His eyes went to the youngest picture of Rick, still so small, riding on his father's shoulders without a care in the world. For all the tremendous power Ivan could tap into, he'd have happily cast it aside to live in that day, that moment, once more. Sadly, not even Fornax could fight the forward march of time. Rick was no longer a little boy he could easily carry around. He was less than two years from the age Ivan had been when he became Fornax. In no time, Rick would be his own man, and when that day came, he was better served by being as informed as possible.

Finally turning from his photos, Ivan met Tori's uncertain gaze. "Tell him anything he wants to know, assuming you're comfortable sharing. The only exceptions are the guild, and my true identity. The first for obvious reasons, the second because I feel I should be the one to handle that reveal. It will be... difficult."

"If he asks me if I've ever seen you kill?"

"You'd be perfectly in your rights to tell him that, yes, you have. Several people," Ivan said. "At this point, Rick doesn't trust much of what his mother or I say, and not without some reason. I'd rather him have an information source he believes than spare him truths he seems bound to eventually uncover. All of that is assuming he approaches you, which may very well not happen. I simply didn't want you to be caught unaware."

Tori took a long sip from her coffee mug, mulling the words over. "I appreciate the heads up, and I'll give some thought to how much I want to divulge if he does make a move."

"I think that's the best strategy, for the moment." Ivan was about to dismiss her, except a rogue glance to his calendar reminded him that there was one more matter of business to attend. "Before you go, remember that this week's Starscout meeting is bumped to tomorrow due to a district field trip. Kids should still be tuckered even when they get back, so we'll be putting the extra time to use. Got to prepare for the End of Summer Shindig next week, meaning there's always work to do."

"Almost forgot about those." To Ivan's surprise, Tori actually appeared happy about the change. "Sounds nice, a little normalcy after weeks of the insane. Plus, bonus, I actually got to meet Lodestar during the kidnapping. That should make a fun story for the kids, right?"

In his mind's eye, Ivan could already imagine the looks Helen would be shooting as Tori regaled the kids with tales of meeting their organization's founder. Annoying as they would be, he could just as easily imagine the wide-eyed joy of the children getting to hear that tale, Beth included. In the end, Starscouts was about the kids, and Tori was right. They would absolutely eat that story up.

"A fine idea. But word to the wise: bring throat lozenges. Giving a tale like that to children their age, you're going to find yourself with quite a few requests for encores."

Chapter 53

"You want to team up?" Donald had the screen on his TV glowing, and the special receiver booted up. It connected to the computer system wired into his body, loading a screen with dozens of games, all of which were constantly running in the background. Professor Quantum might not be as personable as Donald expected, but the tech he built absolutely lived up to the reputation. Comparing this to the wrist unit he'd been wielding initially was night and day.

"I wish I was asking for a team-up," Agent Quantum replied. "That would be a much easier sell to my people. But there's no sense in doing this unless we tackle it properly, which means accepting the truth. I don't want to team up. I want you to let us shadow you for a few nights. It's become increasingly clear that our training didn't prepare us as well as we expected for this job. We're doing the new drills, listening to the response tactics, it's just not clicking. My hope is that watching another team up close will show us where it is we're falling short. It's the best way to improve."

Making a snap decision, Donald chose a two-player game, grabbing a spare controller from the charging dock by the television. He tossed it into Agent Quantum's hands, who stared at the device with a scrunched-up expression that looked quite out of place on his handsome face. "Might as well train while we talk. I'm leveling up a flight pack from *Rocket Rangers*. You're the support ship, the blue cursor. Press the bottom button to shoot anything that isn't me."

The starting screen loaded, showing a nondescript avatar in leather clothing with a patchwork attempt at a jetpack strapped to their back. *Rocket Rangers* wasn't the fastest way to gain access to flight, but since the system was built around buying new models and upgrades, it would theoretically allow for a large amount of customization. Any gear Cyber Geek couldn't properly control was too risky to bring into the field. Better to work toward a tool he could fine-tune than grab something easy and less reliable.

Agent Quantum fiddled with the controller for a few moments before gamely wiggling the joystick and opening fire on an empty field the player was flying over. The digital bullets rained down upon the meager stalks of wheat, ignored by the background art. He'd figured out the controls; that was a step in the right direction.

"Here's my concern." Donald waited until they were beginning to fire; having something else to occupy their attention made it less awkward to speak so frankly. "Our teams don't really get along. We can skate over the why, but it's true. I'm fully in support of you learning from someone more experienced and improving. I'm less sure that we're the right people to teach you. Aside from barely being past rookie level ourselves, why not pick someone your team doesn't have friction with?"

"Because they don't see those teams as their rivals." To Donald's surprise, Agent Quantum was unflustered by the point; he'd come in ready to address it. "You are right, our people have friction. What you might not realize is that part of why my team doesn't get along with yours is because of respect. You're succeeding at the job we can't seem to grasp correctly, you're beloved by people overall, and you consistently manage to power through every challenge presented. Whatever issues my team has, they're exceptional at threat evaluation. The New Science Sentries see your people as their main competition, which means they've acknowledged you to be capable. How many other teams at our level do you think they hold in such esteem?"

As he was talking, Agent Quantum's cursor grew faster, identifying the more dangerous targets and opening fire. It hadn't taken him long to grasp the game, despite his apparent lack of familiarity. Then again, it was a point-and-press-a-button situation. Donald hadn't exactly started him on *Soul Grinder*.

"Because they don't like us, they'll be willing to learn from us?" Donald really needed Ren as a consultant for this ego-based nonsense.

"Because they want to surpass you, they'll pay attention to everything you say and do. Both to learn, and to search for weaknesses." Agent Quantum managed to look sheepish at that, though just barely. "Not the greatest of motivations, but if they learn to be better superheroes in the process, I can't be picky about what gets them to take the lessons."

Toggling through the meager supply of weapons offered so early in the game, Donald rained three grenades down on the spot where the level boss would spawn. They landed just as the large man with a comically oversized gun loaded, blasting him past the first two combat phases and right into the finale, where he turned red and blinking. Donald could do this part essentially from memory—he'd long ago mastered the early level patterns. It was in the later stages, where randomization came into play, that progress would slow down.

"Although I'm still not sure it's the best idea, I'll run it by my team. If they say yes, we can try it for a night or two. If they say no, then it's a no. Much as I'd like to help, I can't have them feeling unsteady out in the field. We're not as strong as you. We have to stay focused to be on top of our game, and the people out there calling for help deserve that from us." Donald noted that Agent Quantum's cursor was now darting around the screen, taking out the minions as they spawned, leaving Donald free to finish off the boss. "Should that happen, I'll try to point you toward some other good candidates. Ren's been here since the last confluence. He knows pretty much everyone on the new teams, and he's sparred against most of them, too."

"Entirely reasonable," Agent Quantum said. "Given how things have gone between our people so far, I appreciate that you're even willing to entertain the idea."

With an on-screen explosion, the level boss died, spewing coins and parts that Donald would be using to start customizing the jetpack. He'd need to get some stabilizers and a few safety features before feeling confident enough to pull this thing into the real world. If it failed midair, Cyber Geek might be in for quite the tumble.

As the level transition screen appeared, Donald finally looked away from the TV. "I'm impressed you were able to come make the request. In your shoes, I doubt I'd have even thought to shadow another team, and I'm sure asking this couldn't have been easy."

"In the interest of directing credit where it's due, the truth is I didn't have the idea. Your friend Tori suggested it. She holds you in clear respect, and the more I see, the more I understand why." Agent Quantum set the controller aside, rising to his feet. "Thank you for your time, Cyber Geek. I know you've got training, as do I, so I'll leave you to think things over. If you have more questions or want to talk, I'll be around."

The two shook hands, and on impulse, one made a snap decision. "When we're out of the masks, you can call me Donald. Wouldn't hurt to be on more friendly terms."

"In that case, please feel free to call me Austin."

It was a nice moment, one that Donald dearly hoped he'd be able to communicate well when trying to sell this idea to his team. All things considered, it would probably be easier to take down another monster unleashed by Nexus than to sell them on this notion.

Then again, since when did he think being a superhero meant taking the easy path?

Lozora limped her way into the cave, annoyed for the first time by just how out of the way this lair was. It was necessary—one didn't take on the Alliance of Heroic Champions in broad daylight until everything was good and ready—but running here after eating that cab driver was still quite a hike. Especially injured.

He came from the back, clad in a pure black suit. In the beginning, he'd had no name, nor any need for one. Recently, however, he'd begun to go by Wendel Worthington. Recruiting more broadly meant his business dealings had been forced into the mundane world, where huge stacks of money didn't buy the same kind of "no questions asked" sales that their market offered. There was no way around it: they needed a figurehead, a name to give the pawns. Lozora's was off the table; she couldn't risk revealing herself and losing whatever nebulous protection Captain Bullshit had provided. Since her employer's true moniker was a secret even from her, Wendel had been born. There was something else to it, too, a joke or barb she didn't quite get but could still tell was there; however, on the hierarchy of mysteries about her boss, inside jokes were clearly at the bottom.

Given the polished appearance tonight, he was probably heading out for another meeting. Lozora had no idea what this part of the plan was, nor was she especially concerned. She'd signed on with a legend specifically because she didn't want to sweat all the details. After years of being cooped up, Lozora was ready for a little fun. Perhaps she'd start by picking easier targets for the next recruiting session.

"Issues?" He didn't sound worried, more like he was prepared to be angered by her disappointment. Those dark eyes scanned down to her leg, which was almost back to holding normal pressure, though not quite.

"Turns out Toon lives up to the reputation. He and Vaudeville were a no, but most of the others signed on. You provide the tech and the timeline when the capes will be busy, they'll pounce. We're getting up there in numbers. No major players, but plenty of small fish mad they missed the Ridge City Riots."

"Strap a bomb to a roach, it explodes just as well as a bomb strapped to a person. What matters most is the bomb, the equipment they're given. I can make them capable enough to be distractions. That's all they need to manage." The man going by Wendel Worthington absorbed Lozora's news slowly. "I presume from the injury that Vaudeville and Toon are both still alive."

Lozora turned as vicious a glare as she dared onto Wendel. "The pair famous for being impossible to hurt or kill, just like I warned you before the approach? Yeah, they're doing just fine. I didn't give any details, though, so even if they wanted to cause trouble, they wouldn't know where to start."

A loose end. One he might tie up, if time permitted. So many years of planning, finally given a chance to bear fruit—he couldn't risk the unseen variables causing complications. The world was filled with so-called "unkillable" beings, but in his experience, that really meant they just hadn't encountered someone truly dedicated to wiping them out. In a world like theirs, teeming with all manner of meta-elements, unknown magics, and fluid laws of science, nothing *could* be truly permanent or invulnerable. There was always a weakness, always a tactic—he believed that down to the darkest parts of his bones. It was just a matter of whether or not one had the will and the wiles to triumph.

As for Lozora, she was tense, waiting to see if failure meant he'd try to kill her. While he felt certain the task was achievable, it was also a poor use of resources. Lozora had far more connections to the villains of her generation than he could ever hope to achieve. Aside from which, she'd been powerful enough to warrant top-level security at Rookstone. A fight he could win, and a fight he could win without injury or loss, were two different matters. Especially in the heart of his lair, with so many inventions within easy smashing range.

"In the rear, you'll find a chair with a large metal circle around it, emitting a soft red light. Strap in. It can accelerate your healing."

"I heal fine on my own, thanks." Lozora appeared to relax without actually easing up, but the gesture itself was the point.

He didn't begrudge her resistance. This time, it really was a machine designed to heal; that didn't mean he hadn't also dummied up a few "medical" inventions that actually killed the user. It was a favorite trick of his—pretend to offer an olive branch and strike while their guard was down.

"Then take some time to rest. Recruitment is nearly done. I do need you to pick up an order in a few days, when it's ready. Something special, and specific. Will you be recovered in time?"

Lozora stared, and he stared back: she wondering what answer would trigger an attempt at murder, he pondering whether she could continue to be helpful. "I'll be fine by tomorrow. Just needed a good meal, which my driver was kind enough to provide." A long, purple tongue flicked out, giving a peek at the rows of sharp teeth normally hidden behind her lips. Intentional or not, it was a not-so-subtle reminder that he wasn't the only monster in the lair.

"Very well, then. I'll have the details ready when it's time for pickup. Until then, focus on recovery. I can have some food ordered."

"I prefer to hunt my own." There was a predatory gleam in her eye, one the masquerading Wendel paid no mind to. She could entertain whatever fantasies she liked about tearing into his flesh: one bite is all it would take for her to realize the mistake.

He hoped she held off until after the next job, at least. It would be very inconvenient to kill her with so much work still left to do.

Chapter 54

When Tori had first come to the new guild—what she'd begun to think of as Villain Island—the enterprise had seemed excessive. That sentiment had steadily faded the more she'd actually used the facilities, and as Tori headed down the hall to meet with Lance, she was thankful they were doing this far from Ridge City. There was something to be said for not being directly under an enemy's nose, even if doing things that way was more daring.

Everyone else was already waiting, as they'd likely come on their own schedules rather than catch a ride with Ivan, who was off at a clandestine gathering of his own. He played his mundane, normal role to a hilt, and that included driving almost aggressively within the law. They'd gotten more than a few honking horns and shaking fists; she'd have loved to see some of the fearsome drivers actually try to make good on the foul words they spat.

Hurrying in, Tori grabbed an open seat at the table. This meeting room was like most of the others scattered around the guild: built to hold up to eight human-sized bodies, or a small number of the more unwieldy members. There were larger options, but for a four-person group, there was no need to take up the more spacious resources, if Lance could even have booked them. After months of being shut down, and with a fancy new lair to play in, the guild was more alive than Tori had previously seen it, not that she'd had much of a sample size before the Ridge City Riots. Still, better make the most of the room while they had it.

"I know, I know, I'm late. Rode over with Pseudonym. You can catch me up on the highlights, and I'll get details from Beverly on what I missed. We don't have to restart."

"Not a problem. We're mostly just going over the pitch as a whole right now." Lance was as cheery as ever; his personable nature always seemed a strange fit for a man working in a guild of villainy.

Across the table, Warren boasted a less congenial expression, but Tori didn't take it personally, especially when he offered a wave of greeting. She'd come to realize that was just Warren's way, in the same sense that she and Ivan had their brusque moments. When shit hit the fan, he'd sided with their team and the guild over his own mentor; looking constantly grumpy didn't matter worth a damn compared to his steadfast loyalty.

"Since the guild reopened, Warren and I have been picking up odd jobs here and there—mostly surveillance and support, given our powers," Lance continued. That fit. With his swarms of insects to command and see through the eyes of, Lance would be one of the most capable non-technological surveillance options among the guild's members. Most people in their field knew to sweep for devices called bugs; far fewer cared about the actual namesake. As for Warren, the ability to create magic in the form of drawn symbols meant he had a large amount of versatility. Plus, while he'd turned out to be a traitor, Balaam hadn't done a poor job training his apprentice.

"It's been a good way to get our feet back under us, plus pick up some spare cash. But recently, a job came around that we're interested in working. The issue is the teams can't be smaller than four people. I'll tell you up front: it's nothing too involved on our part. In theory, we could go the whole night without so much as a blip of action."

"Or..." Beverly let the word hang, an implied question demanding to be spoken.

Lance didn't shy away. "Or we might end up in a fight, though that's not ideal. We don't actually know much about what this job is, only that they need a fair amount of people running security. We'd be one of the outermost teams. Our primary job would be to keep passersby from going down the wrong street. If a cape shows up, we call in the alert so the real workers have time to finish or flee."

Interesting. Minimal risk, presumably enough pay to warrant the effort, if Lance and Warren were roping them in, and technically, they didn't even need to commit any crimes. When it came to tasks that had to be handled in costume, working as a lookout was about as legal an option as the guild presented.

"Why the four-person teams?" Tori asked. The more she understood, the better an idea she'd have of whether or not this was a good fit.

"Coverage." Warren looked slightly more interested than he had at the start—quite a change, by his standards. "We need to be able to hold a sizable area. With Lance's bugs and just me, it would be tight. Having you both along, plus potentially some tech to crack into security cameras, makes it a lot more manageable."

"Possible, but I'd need the timeframe and general locale. Getting into a single closed system, like the museum, is one thing, but if we're covering a big area, that would entail multiple buildings with their own securities." A rogue idea struck her, even as she was listing the difficulties. "Although, if it's anywhere residential, I could build something to hop on the wi-fi signals of all those home cameras that show the feed online. Those are much less protected."

From her side, Beverly tapped her nails along the table. "I take it you want me to be eyes in the sky?"

To Tori's surprise, Lance shook his head. "Nothing as overt as a dragon flying around. We'd be leaning on you if anything physical came up. I've picked up some new bugs, and Warren's got his own tricks, but neither of us can fight like Bahamut. If we need to substantially dissuade someone from heading in a direction, you're our strongest bet."

It was almost comical to hear that, given Lance's sizable muscles and Beverly's comparatively slender form. But he was right. When she turned into that green dragon, Beverly became big, tough, and downright deadly. One good thing about being in a guild of villains: none of them held prideful delusions about their strength. Everyone in this room knew they weren't the best, or the most powerful. It was an impossible fantasy, given the councilors who ruled this organization. Some were wounded by that fact, others grew from it. Judging by the team he was building, Lance appeared to be in the latter camp.

"Hate to be pushy, but the timeframe is a big one for me. I've got more than a few eyes in my direction, not to mention some Tori commitments that I can't let Hephaestus overtake. It would be suspicious." Also, Tori was fairly sure if she tried to double-book a Starscouts meeting, Ivan would have other ideas.

"I figured," Lance replied. "That's why I called the meeting today, as a matter of fact; an operational date was only determined last night. It's supposed to go down this weekend, on Saturday evening. We'll be in a modest city named Ebnerville. The operation won't be near civilians, but since we're a far perimeter team, we might be—I'll look into that for you, Tori. Our job is to watch for intruders and capes, keeping them away at all costs."

What Tori found most fascinating about the situation were all the elements they weren't being given. Limited information, tightly controlled area, weight put largely on keeping anyone who wasn't supposed to be there away. There were probably a great many reasons the guild could have for setting up these sorts of situations, yet there was only one that Tori had already born witness to. A code enforcement—which was a nice way to say brutal execution—would demand that sort of security. Based on how the one she'd seen had gone, it would be over in no time, and they could be on their way. That had been Ivan, though. No telling who was running this one, or who they were up against. Definitely still some risk, even if it was risk that could be mitigated.

"Timing should be clear—easy enough to slip away on a Saturday. We haven't gotten to the real heart of the matter, however." Tori leaned in, making no efforts to conceal the greed in her eyes. Such pretense had no place in these halls. "How much does it *pay*?"

"Ten thousand per person, with an expectation of roughly four hours' work." He'd been ready for that, and appeared to take some joy in the momentary widening of Tori's eyes.

Sure, that was a lot less than they'd made on the museum heist, but they'd also been doing all the planning and had borne the entirety of the risk. To be paid that much for a simple lookout role... Tori felt her suspicions of the true job dial up, but ten grand was nothing to sneeze at. Especially if she could start picking up more of these gigs, the way Warren and Lance were. Beyond that, though, part of Tori simply wanted to grasp at the chance to wear her suit again. She'd put in so much work and had barely gotten to take it out from the garage. She liked being Hephaestus, and this was as fine an excuse as any.

"Count me in. Advertising revenue online isn't what it used to be," Beverly said.

"I'll need to double-check my schedule, but short of a conflict, you can expect me to show up." Even as she agreed, Tori thought about Ivan's meeting, the one he'd been in no hurry to get to. Given the job she'd just heard pitched, part of her wondered if Ivan was getting the other half of the operation explained to him at that very moment.

In truth, Ivan had gotten the details corresponding to Tori's task in the first five minutes of the meeting's start. It was more a footnote to him than a matter of primary concern. That might have changed, had he known his former apprentice intended to be part of the lookout team; however, the councilors had more vital matters to deal with.

All seven were gathered, staring at a hologram in the center of the table. The details were grainy, but one thing was clear. The objects depicted were vast, and numerous.

"I'll be the asshole," Morgana announced, seemingly apropos of nothing. "Wade, are you completely sure about this? It's hard to believe something so huge could be coming and we've yet to hear a blip from the AHC."

"A reasonable, if slightly wounding, concern." Wade was unbothered by the doubt. It was almost tradition for someone to ask such a question at this point in the situational breakdown, hence Morgana's vulgar declaration. "But yes, I am extremely certain. Many years back, after *someone* had an extraterrestrial encounter—" Wade paused to fire a pointed look in Ivan's direction "—I took the time to place surveillance stations and satellites in deep space. Professor Quantum never saw the same need that I did for such expansive early warning systems. That's also why the image is so bad; the tech is decades out of date. Regardless, yes, I am confident in this. My best guess is that, within a week, the AHC will know as well."

"That doesn't leave very long for the capes to prepare before they arrive." Stasis, for a change, was engaged in the discussion. Even to her, potential alien invaders held the spark of novelty. "Sneak attack?"

A loud *clang* echoed as Xelas dropped her arm to the table, looking up to the ceiling; perhaps lost in thought, perhaps scanning the skies. "It would have to be, after what the Grzzniltan ship saw. Except, that's what's bugging me. They got a good look at the AHC on full display. Outside of us, what whacko sees power like that and starts spoiling for a fight? Is it possible these beings are stronger?"

The universe was a vast place, and theirs was only a single planet among countless. It would be ridiculous to assume that the strongest of Earth was also the strongest across the entire galaxy.

Fortunately, they didn't have to rely on assumptions. With a neutral tone, Ivan rattled off the information. "To the best we've discerned, Earth is one of the more powerful planets among those with spacefaring intelligent life. Likely due to our tremendous concentration of meta-humans, as well as our own fundamental instincts toward combat. I once had occasion to compete in something of a gladiatorial event on an alien spacecraft, and they were not prepared to face Fornax's might."

"Space tournament? That sounds fun!" Xelas cried. "I can't believe you didn't invite us. So greedy. You'd probably still have won."

Ivan shook his head. "It was well before the guild, and I didn't win. Nobody did, technically. Things got... complicated."

Before they got too far down that tangent, Wade brought everyone's attention back to the front. "Our larger concern is the planet's future, not Ivan's past. As this is a threat that represents the potential to impact the guild, as well as our individual holdings and families, a response is necessary. We could theoretically kick this information over to the AHC, giving them extra time to prepare and buying some goodwill in the process."

It was Gork, who rarely spoke, who cut the idea off at the knees. "No. They came for us in our home. They dragged us into the streets. They wanted to do it alone. Let them."

There came a murmur of agreement from nearly every mouth, with two notable exceptions. Still, the consensus was clear, so Wade didn't waste the time calling for a vote. Better to keep the momentum going while they had it.

"Very well. That means we'll need to set to work on the other options: how are we going to protect what's ours? Because whoever sent an alien armada our way is playing a complicated game, and I'm certain we've yet to see all the pieces."

"I hate these sorts of overly complicated schemes. If that's how they want to do it, then let's go with my favorite counter." There was an unexpected darkness to Arcanicus as he rose from his chair. Time had stolen much of his aggression, yet under the surface, there still simmered enough rage to remind those watching of how he'd come to join the guild in the first place. An invasion of the planet was an invasion of the guild's territory, and that had managed to stir a touch of the older man's wrath.

"Let's incinerate the entire game board."

Chapter 55

If there was one upside to confronting his father—and at this point, even that seemed like a stretch—it was that looking at pictures of the beach had stopped causing such pronounced reactions in Rick. He was no longer at odds with his own mind, groping for memories that weren't where they were supposed to be. Now that he understood, the fits of panic had faded. Unfortunately, what they'd left in their place was a constant boulder of dread in his stomach.

Clicking about, he opened yet another tab, evaluating a potential meta-human from history to see if his dad fit the bill. There was no reason for this. Ivan had been clear that when Rick was ready to ask, he would answer. But it was still insane to picture, his father butchering people. An army, at that. They must have been fairly weak for him to take out that many. If Ivan had ever been a major bad guy, then the AHC would have locked him up. Wouldn't they?

Fleetingly, Rick's mind flashed to the guild of villains that had been revealed last year. He nearly skimmed right past the notion, as he had several times already. It was just a step too far. His dad hiding his past was one thing; an entire secret life felt like a flight of fancy.

Except... now that Rick was in the right headspace, he thought back to the metal-armored person who saved him and Beth when their school was attacked. That suit sure hadn't looked like it was designed by a cape, and Rick had yet to catch sight of it anywhere since, even online.

Was it possible their dad had sent a fellow villain out to protect his kids? That begged the question, though, why not come himself if he knew there was danger? Distance, most likely, although something about that still felt off. The kind of man who kills an army for threatening his family didn't mesh with someone who'd trust someone else to protect his kids during a riot. Rick was sure there was a reason, if his hunch was right, he just wasn't certain he'd want to know what it was.

That was the dilemma set before him. Learning that one little bit about Ivan had rocked Rick to his foundation, and all signs indicated there was a lot more to hear. His curiosity had been sated: he knew he wasn't crazy. If there was a point to walk away, this was it. This was the best opportunity he had to preserve his relationship with his father as it stood. One story had changed everything; there was truly no guessing how Rick would feel once he knew it all.

A knock on his door was followed by five seconds of courtesy waiting—he *was* a teenage boy with a computer—followed by Janet slowly easing the door open. "Came to see if you needed anything. You've been locked up for a while."

Things had been strained since the revelation. Knowing what Ivan had done also entailed learning about his mother's complicity. Rick's initial impulse was to send her away, just like he'd been doing so far. Only this time, her timing was better. She'd caught him in a state of uncertainty, where getting guidance mattered more than holding his grudge.

"Are you a meta-human, too?" Rick looked to her, away from the screen—the first time he'd made such a concession in several days.

Quietly, Janet shut the door behind her, even though Juan was getting dinner and Beth was still on her field trip. "No. Never have been, and never especially felt the urge to change that. Powers make things more complicated."

"So, our family smarts..."

"Just a lot of academics falling in love, along with growing up in an environment that emphasized learning," Janet assured him.

Rick snorted at that, then looked embarrassed, before remembering he was supposed to be stern. "You sure broke that cycle with Dad." Ivan was not an especially dumb man, but he'd never held the same passion for sciences and learning that captivated most of the family.

For a moment, Janet almost tried to deny the assessment, before merely sighing with a shake of her head. "I was at a rebellious point in my life, and I wanted to meet people other than lifelong devotees of education. Your father...

well, he was unlike anyone I'd ever met before. Willful, unyielding, full of pride that had been hard earned."

"Not to mention, a killer."

The past faded from Janet's eyes as she snapped her head up. "A protector."

"He told me he slaughtered an army."

"Ivan would butcher an entire planet if they collectively threatened you or Beth. It's one of the traits I most respect in him." There was a hardness in his mother's face that Rick hadn't been prepared for. Deep down, he'd wondered how she could have gone along with this, speculating that perhaps she'd been kept partially in the dark. With that expression, all deniability was gone. She'd known exactly who he was.

"You don't... that's a *bad* thing, Mom. He shouldn't be that eager to kill."

This time, her face softened slightly. Her hand twitched, like she was tempted to reach out and offer comfort but feared it would be refused. "Rick, your father took no joy in that day. Given the chance, I sincerely think he would live the rest of his life in peace. But when someone comes to do harm to your children, as a parent, you fight them with every ounce of strength in your body. Ivan's strength just happens to be higher than most fathers'."

That was a hard one to debate, and a point Rick's own mind had been raising. Awful as the image of his dad killing an army was, what was the better option? Letting them storm the shores, hurting innocent people in the process, permitting harm to come to his own family? Would Rick have respected those choices more? Even capes occasionally took lives in battle, albeit as a last resort.

Instead, Rick turned his attention to another matter. One that had haunted him in various forms for years now and had rediscovered a new form to take with Ivan's revelation. "Is this the reason you got divorced? I did the math. Less than a year after the incident happened, you filed for separation."

For the first time, Janet looked away. It took her a moment to compose herself, but when she turned back to Rick, she looked the same as ever—which might actually be more worrying in a way, had Rick been given time to properly consider it.

"No, seeing Ivan kill that army wasn't what drove us apart. Your father didn't lie to me. I knew who he was when we said our vows. He's the same man, the same dad, he's been all your life. Only now, you're learning he's also more." Janet paused, deciding that this was as opportune a moment as she'd get. "Have you given any more thought to this weekend?"

"Still... deciding," Rick admitted, not quite meeting her eye. This weekend was supposed to be spent at his dad's house. The question was whether or not Rick actually wanted to go. Skips and trades happened; there were plenty of excuses he could use that Beth would buy. Ivan, on the other hand, would know.

Janet got up, smoothing over the section of bed where she'd perched. "Take your time. You know your room there is always open when you're ready." She retreated to the hallway quickly, content to take her victory of a short conversation before things turned south.

Because, while Rick didn't know it, he'd been sniffing around a major sore spot, one that Janet wasn't sure she could hold her composure through. Ivan killing the army hadn't changed things between them; that much was true. She'd known her husband's true power and identity, and certainly didn't disagree with him killing to protect their family.

It was what had come next that had caused the problem. With an invading army reported and Fornax in combat, there was no surprise that *she'd* been called. In less than five minutes after the army was gone, Lodestar arrived, bursting onto the scene in a shower of sand and golden light. Such a simple moment, and yet, it had been the beginning of the end for their marriage.

That was the day Janet realized that no matter how devoted a husband he might be, Ivan would never truly love her. Not when his heart so clearly belonged to someone else.

"For the record, this is bullshit."

"No, Presto. This is a favor that is being done *for* us, and if you can't keep a civil tongue through it, then you can go back to the AHC for training." Agent Quantum was sterner that usual. Generally, he tended to ignore Presto's running chatter on the channels. Everyone was a little tense tonight, given the situation.

Perched up on a rooftop, the New Science Sentries watched as Hat Trick threw a multicolored scarf from her sleeve onto a mugger's gun, wrapping up the entire thing. He fired, producing a muffled gunshot from within the cloth, followed by a brief yelp of pain. In the time he'd been distracted, Cyber Geek had dashed over, hitting him with a giant blue mallet that caused cartoon sound effects while also knocking the target unconscious.

"Handy trick. Not so easy to do when you're using real punches," Tachyonic muttered. He shut himself up after a quick nudge from Agent Quantum. This was a hard enough sell for the team; having the second-in-command question the move would only make things worse. "At least Medley is handling it our way."

That was true, in the sense that Medley was engaged in melee combat with two more muggers—one human, and one with long, whip-like appendages growing from his arms. Every time the whips landed, they eroded whatever they touched, from concrete to Medley's scales. He'd been dipping in and out of battle, holding both of his antagonists' attention. Just as the whip-man came in for an attack, Medley jumped to the side, revealing Cold Shoulder with a hefty blast of chill. The whips and the man wielding them were encased in instant ice, though the sections around the whip-appendages immediately started to liquefy.

The mugger made a dash, but Medley was already on him, and this time he wasn't playing the distraction. A quick blow to the leg took the man out, after which Medley patted him down for weapons, producing a well-used knife and a gun that appeared to have never been fired.

"I don't get it. They beat up a bunch of muggers. We've done that." Unlike the other two, Plasmodia sounded more confused than bothered by the scenario, though she'd slipped plenty of the latter feeling in there, too. "What are we supposed to be taking from this?"

"It's the first job, of the first night," Agent Quantum reminded her. "We're going to shadow them for a full week. Keep an open mind."

"Since our fearless leader says to be on board, I guess I'll point out one difference in their approach. Have you all noticed the injury count?" Presto pointed to the criminals who were being tied up. Cyber Geek had pulled out a gun that shot freezing energy and was keeping the whip-man iced until transportation could arrive. "The worst one of the lot is that guy who fired the gun, which was his own fault for shooting in that situation. Based on our stats, we'd have broken around three bones, and needed medical attention for at least one."

Sometimes, it was dangerously easy to forget that, under all the bullshit, Ike had an incredibly capable mind. Plasmodia pivoted her head, eyes half-crossed as she did her own mental math. "Are you sure about that?"

"Absolutely. It's in the nature of our tactics. Professor Quantum taught us to go for the takedown if the threat is real; the less the enemy rampages, the fewer civilians can be caught in the crossfire."

That did make sense, from Agent Quantum's point of view. Trouble was, the more they stuck to those methods, the more things went awry. If hitting softer was one of the differences between Cyber Geek's team and the New Science Sentries, then Agent Quantum needed to understand how that factored in. That might not be the right tactic for his people, but he couldn't make the call appropriately until he understood why it mattered.

Agent Quantum just hoped he could convince the team to keep going along with it. They still had quite a lot of week left to get through.

On another building, a different shape watched the same show. This was no great, major event, but every now and then, things took a wild turn. Nexus wasn't expecting much. This was more him monitoring to track how things were shaping up. Seeing Cyber Geek helping the New Science Sentries filled him with great joy, simple a moment as it appeared. That didn't always happen; in plenty of versions, pride proved too great a hurdle.

Nexus did love when they went this way, however. It opened up new potentials, ones that few worlds ever got to catch even the barest glimpses of. For the upcoming show, it had the potential to add several unexpected layers. He was so excited, he could hardly wait. But wait he would, as the event's kickoff was still plodding along through space, dragging their unseen secret weapon with them.

He smiled as he looked down to the street, where all three criminals had been so expertly captured. While there might be some time left before the main event, he luckily had a few warm-up bouts to sustain him. One of which should be coming very soon, assuming this world paced with those similar. The potential for surprise was why Nexus kept coming back, even though he knew the beats by heart.

There was always a chance that this time could be different, a truth he found infinitely amusing.

Chapter 56

"Tori, grab the glitter before it falls off the table. Newton, watch out, you nearly hit Trudy's glue. Ivan, any ETA on that next round of snacks?"

Helen stood in the middle of the storm, directing children and staff alike as they zipped around working on their banner for next week's End of Summer Shindig. Soon, all of them would be gathered with the rest of the local clusters for several days of camping, activities, competition, and general fun. It was the year's big kickoff, a way to ease the blow of summer's end for the kids coping with a return to school. Preparations had been underway while Tori was busy being kidnapped, but it was clear her absence had caused little to no impact with Helen at the wheel. More impressive was that Helen was never harsh or demanding with the kids: only firm, supportive, and shockingly patient. Ivan had really lucked out when they paired him up.

Not that he was having trouble blending in. As Ivan made his way in from the kitchen, a bevy of toasted mini-sandwiches and homemade tiny pizzas stacked upon a tray in his hands, Tori could have easily pictured him wandering into one of her own childhood meetings. He would have fit in perfectly. Huge purple oven mitts that he didn't even need, a borrowed apron, and a mildly uncertain expression, he looked like pretty much every dad she'd ever seen roped into pitching in—except, he was happy to be there. Well, he seemed happy if one knew how to read Ivan's stalwart nature.

Across the table, Beth was hunched over, deep in concentration as she scrawled bubble lettering, attempting to capture the entire cluster's roster in her fanciest handwriting. As one of the older kids present, it had fallen to her to handle such a delicate task. So far, there had been no flare-ups or issues with those silver blades, and if Tori didn't know better, she'd have had no idea Beth was a meta-human. Tori wondered, aware that she could probably never ask, how much of Beth's control was inherent, versus trained. Was it possible Ivan had been giving Beth side-instruction, or were the AHC's new programs for helping non-capes control their powers really that good? It was an issue to keep in mind—that pool could be used for recruitment with minimal effort. After all, who was going to say no if someone like Professor Quantum or Lodestar told a new meta they had the makings of a superhero?

Beth, hopefully—not that Tori imagined it would ever reach that point. Ivan would certainly step in long before his daughter went the path of the capes. Otherwise, the guild would end up having to add new rules to the code about keeping miles away from her any time she was in costume, lest they meet Fornax's wrath.

Tori forced her mind away from superheroes, centering on the night she was dealing with. It wasn't often she got to spend time on something entirely normal, and while the circumstances of getting here were undeniably meta-tinged, the nights themselves were completely mundane. She turned her attention to corralling the kids, aiming them as best she could back toward the various sections of the banner. There was an area near the top where Helen had the children with high energy shaking glitter cannisters all over the place—mercifully, she'd laid down plastic sheeting in advance. Sooner or later, even children could wear themselves out, and once they were tuckered Helen shifted them to a different activity.

Mallory was working on making lists of supplies they would need, taking it a step further to create customized checklists for each of her peers, complete with bright marker-colored boxes to cross off. When they could pry Loyce away from the snack trays, she was aiding Trudy with making the campground decorations. Considering that the materials for these were of the craft paper and popsicle stick variety, they were crafting some surprisingly substantial displays. Caden, meanwhile, was laying out the supplies for a paper mâché project, though Tori noticed him getting restless. With a quick check on Newton, who was losing steam on the glitter cannisters, and a look to Helen for confirmation, she decided it was time for a change-out.

When Tori brought Caden over, Helen was waiting, glitter can at the ready as she slapped it into Caden's hands. A child with a chance to make a mess needs little direction; without a word, Caden had joined the others, jumping and shaking the can of sparkles with all his tiny might. Helen took a few steps away, dodging Newton as he bolted across the room to take over on paper mâché; though, if she was hoping to spare her outfit from rogue shimmer, that battle was long since lost.

“Holding up okay? Need anything?” The words were carefully whispered, and never broke the happy grin on Helen’s face that was turned toward the kids. It wasn’t the first time she’d checked in on Tori that night, but she also hadn’t been excessive about it.

“I’m fine, really. Although kidnappings are not my favorite activity, it’s not like I haven’t already been through some rough spots. Office attack, club attack, nearly getting crushed in the street—that’s just life in Ridge City, you know?”

Helen nodded; however, there was an expression on her face that Tori couldn’t quite place. Concern, probably, though if she hadn’t known better, she’d have thought it was edging over into guilt. “You are unquestionably a tough, capable person, but even those types have to let it out sometimes. If you ever need help, please don’t be afraid to ask.”

Much as Tori would have liked to callously brush the whole thing aside and put the idea to bed, she couldn’t exactly be rude to Ivan’s friend, especially one who was helping out so much with the cluster. Past that, there was something sincere about Helen, in a way that itched Tori’s brain yet she couldn’t quite put a finger on. Whatever it was, it turned lines that should have sounded like hollow pleasantries into genuine care. Even for Tori, it was hard to be shitty when she believed someone was truly trying to make things better.

“Thanks. Not sure I’ll take you up on that, but the sentiment is appreciated.”

“All I can do is offer.” Helen’s face suddenly twisted in worry as she darted into the fray. “One sandwich at a time, Loyce! Just because they’re small doesn’t mean you can’t choke on them.”

Emory was dripping in sweat as the last of the machines slipped back into the wall. Overhead, the large clock had reached zero, meaning he was finally permitted a few moments to rest. Near collapsing, he grabbed a bottle of water from the small cubby built into the wall by the door. It was one of the only places in this chamber that wouldn’t be in peril, mostly by virtue of sliding behind an armored wall when the clock started. Slamming the liquid as fast as he could, Emory tried to catch his breath at the same time. It seemed a fool’s errand, but after over a week of this, he was nearly getting it down.

"Very nice." Xelas's voice echoed through the room, coming from unseen speakers woven through the design. "A few more like that, and we'll be ready to step you up a notch."

In the beginning, Emory had argued. He'd complained, asking why he needed to fight these mechanical opponents, overcome these painful, yet not lethal, traps. For a long time, Xelas had said nothing. It was only a few days prior that he'd finally been given an answer. The words rang in his head as he guzzled the water. They'd been haunting him ever since, seeping all the way down to his bones.

"Why the training?" It was the first time he'd seen her turn serious, a sharp indicator of what was to come. "Because your power isn't all that impressive, and I don't want you to die right out of the gate. I want you to be skilled enough to survive for a full year. But if you don't want that, we can call it anytime you like."

Emory yearned to reject that idea, yet he couldn't. The fate of his gang was proof that there were leagues far greater than the one he'd been playing in, and now, he was around meta-humans using an entirely different scale of power. If there was one lesson Emory had taken from his gang's slaughter, it was that death came swift and without warning. The only ones who'd walked away that night were the powerful ones, like Xelas.

If Emory wanted to live, to survive, perhaps one day even to thrive in their world, then he needed to be stronger. Meeting Xelas's standards was the first step, with untold more to come. Polishing off the rest of his water, Emory placed the bottle back into the cubby, then nodded up at the clock.

"Ready for another round."

Xelas was almost purring this time. "You know, I really didn't expect to enjoy having a pet this much, but that attitude does make it fun. Very well, my little apprentice. Ask, and you shall receive."

"Okay, you've been staring at your phone for a full five minutes now. Everyone okay, or did you find the mother of all entrancing gifs?"

The words yanked Beverly from her fugue. Chloe was right, she had indeed been lost in thought for some time. Together, they were sitting on the couch while an old episode of *The Meta Bunch* ran, Chloe researching some new coffee preparation technique they were trying in gastropubs while Beverly had intended to catch up on email. That plan had fallen apart when she hit the first one waiting for her, however. Tori would have been the preferable one to discuss the issue with, but it wasn't as though this connected to anything directly villain-related.

"I got an email from my oldest brother," Beverly explained. "He's reaching out to see if I want to come by the house for a visit."

Chloe perked up, showing new interest in her friend's distraction. "I've been curious. You always talk about your family like you're close, but I've never seen you visit or take a call from them."

The truth was, Beverly considered herself *very* close with her family. They'd always been a unit, a team, and unfortunately, those instincts had been in full effect when she first became Bahamut. "We had something of a falling out, the night I got my powers. You have to understand, pretty much my entire family was in the service, mostly Marines. It's a tradition that goes back generations. Before Lodestar changed the nature of war, they had plenty of chances to see traditional combat, to develop certain habits. So when a green monster suddenly burst into their home, roaring and destroying whatever it touched, they responded the way you'd expect from trained soldiers."

"They attacked you." Chloe could be more perceptive than her overall demeanor let on, and Beverly was glad for it. That saved her trouble of walking her all the way to the proper conclusion, even if there was still more story to tell.

"I get it, from their perspective. All they heard was my scream, a roar, and then some monster runs down the stairs. Easy to assume it's a meta-intruder that just attacked Beverly. They opened fire on me, almost without hesitation. But I didn't know I was bulletproof in green dragon form back then, so I was terrified. I tried to escape, except they were positioned in front of the exits in case of retreat, and I ended up slamming through several in my scramble to get away from the bullets—before I understood, or could control my strength, mind you. I think a few of them are still wearing casts. Thank goodness no one was permanently injured."

No matter how tight-knit a family might be, attempted murder was a tough hurdle to get past. Beverly could still see her own kin turning their weapons on her, the killing intent clear in their eyes, just as she could still feel the crunch of their bones as she tried to sweep them aside. Time and distance had been the appropriate salve for the wound as Beverly gained control and her family healed. But she was long past accidental transformations, and it sounded as though there was only so much physical mending left to do on their end. If the wound between her and her family wasn't patched soon, it threatened to become a scar, the sort that could never fully heal.

"Your brother wants to make amends. That's something," Chloe pointed out.

It *was* something, that was true. Beverly just wasn't sure it was enough. If she went before everyone was ready, it could make things worse. Ambrose was the peacemaker of the group; as the oldest child, he often ended up as the default referee on disagreements. Him being ready to talk wasn't the same as the whole family being in a good headspace.

She wouldn't get anywhere by sitting around speculating, though. Beverly began to type, her mind now set. "I think I'll meet with just Ambrose for now, get a feel in person for how the family is holding up."

"If you need a public spot with some privacy, I can let you use one of the Ridge City Grinders rooms that people rent out for meetings. Haven't exactly been slammed on that front since the riots, anyway."

"Thanks. I might take you up on that." Beverly's hands continued to move, albeit with a slight touch of hesitation. She might have no problem diving headfirst into deadly battle, but dealing with family was a far more perilous undertaking.

Chapter 57

Saturday marked two major moments for Tori. The second would come much later, but the first happened quite early. Somewhere around four in the morning, Tori conducted her first fully successful test of the miniature aerosolized dispersion device. Getting the nozzle angles perfect proved to be a surprisingly tough part, as it demanded precise calculation to ensure the solution would spray only away from the user. The formula had also required a dash of fine-tuning. Its original incarnation could burn skin if the mix was even the slightest bit off. By altering a few ratios, Tori managed to produce something that was incredibly annoying, distracting, even painful, but that wouldn't cause any lasting damage. That she knew of, anyway. Probably have to run that part by Wade for testing.

It felt good to have the task cleared off her plate, but Tori didn't kick back with a cold one and relax at the accomplishment. Instead, she shifted gears to her other project of the week: fine-tuning the Hephaestus suit for the evening's activities. Tori's key goal was to recalibrate the mini-gravitational anomaly generators until the suit felt like moving in her own body. It was more efficient to shift the suit's movements than it was to relearn all of her tactics in a heavier form. The less difference there was, the more fluid she could be as Hephaestus.

That shouldn't matter, in theory, when Tori took the suit out later on. They were only working guard duty. She didn't even have any cameras to hack, as it turned out. All she needed to do was have her sensors engaged and keep scanning. Lance's bugs would be more than enough deterrent for any non-meta, plus Warren was setting up a few glyphs around the area in advance. Beverly was the muscle, leaving Tori to handle long-distance perimeter sweeps.

That was what she kept telling herself, even as she made sure the suit's weapons systems were all showing full functionality. Whether the night would actually prove to be peaceful or not, Tori had her doubts. Every time she put that suit on, she was stepping into another world, a world where things could go very sideways, very fast. The wrong meta in the wrong place, and who knew what might happen. That was why she had to be prepared for any outcome, no matter the mission. Even as a simple lookout, Hephaestus would be ready.

Until then, there was refining to do. The job wasn't until night, which offered a much-needed opportunity for some napping. She could also show Beverly the completed prototype, once her friend was up for the day. Tori had managed to cram her Saturday quite full of activity, a not-so-subtle tactic of staying busy to keep her mind off other concerns. The habit might not be all that healthy, but it did help make her exceptionally productive, so Tori could live with the tradeoff. As Hephaestus, with almost all of her abilities tied into the suit, being a perfectionist workaholic was more likely to increase her lifespan than lessen it.

It certainly wasn't as if having fully optimized beam weapons would make her a *worse* scout, after all. Just one with more options.

The sounds of the footsteps were heavy, despite the carpeting. Ivan listened as they came, hearing both the current sounds and the countless other versions echoing from throughout the years. He could remember those footsteps when they first began, so unsure and wobbling. Then came the faster, more dangerous footsteps, careening around as stability was learned. From there, they mostly just got bigger and louder, with a few particularly happy events bringing them back to that frantic, unsure pace. Today, they sounded especially firm, like a man marching down to face judgment.

Rick emerged from the stairwell of the townhome, walking into the kitchen where Ivan was already working on a skillet full of eggs. He'd been up prepping for an hour already; Tori wasn't the only one who liked to keep busy when she felt nervous.

Sliding up to the breakfast bar, Rick sat in one of stools, looking at his father with slightly bleary eyes. There hadn't been much chance to talk the night before. Since he and Beth were dropped off together, they couldn't very well dig into the issue of Ivan's past. Neither had said anything on the matter, in fact. For a time, Ivan almost convinced himself that Rick was content to let the issue momentarily rest. Now, seeing his teenage son up just before dawn, Ivan realized that this had been his plan from the start. Rise early—the time when Beth was sleeping and Ivan was making breakfast.

"Where did you learn to cook?" Rick's tongue was still slightly weighed down by sleep, but he was fast shaking it off with the energy that only youth, and a few meta-made compositions, could provide.

"Largely self-taught, with various books and videos to help along the way." Ivan weighed how much honesty he should divulge. Technically, Rick hadn't asked specifically about the life he'd kept hidden. Then again, should he have to? So long as Ivan stayed away from the more troubling topics, there was no reason not to shoot straight wherever possible. "I didn't have a lot of pleasures growing up. Food was one of the few things to enjoy. Once I got older, it became an interest and a hobby, something I could do that was... creative." Ivan had almost said "non-destructive," which was also true, just not where he wanted to aim the conversation so soon.

Rick let out a soft groan and wiped his face, clearing some sleep from his eyes. "Well, you managed to make breakfast sound cryptic, so I guess we should just get right into this." Before he could continue, Ivan set a glass of orange juice in front of him, then motioned for Rick to go on.

"I've had some time to think about what you told me. The army, the beach, you being a meta-human... and that part, I can make peace with. Mom had your back, you know. She told me that you only did all that because they threatened us. I still don't know if wholesale slaughter was the right course in that situation, but I also get it. You were protecting your family, and in the end, since you weren't even charged with a crime, it seems strange to hold that incident against you."

It was good news, and had the delivery not come laced with several qualifiers, Ivan might have felt a rush of hope in his chest. Sadly, it was all too clear that Rick wasn't done yet, so Ivan merely continued to cook the eggs, giving his son room to find the words.

"What bothers me is this: I know that's not everything. If you're fish-army-killing strong, then there's basically zero chance that you're some no-name meta. You have a past, a history that goes well beyond that day on the beach, and I'm guessing most of it has less noble goals than protecting your family."

"I made a promise." The words leapt out of Ivan's mouth from old, nearly forgotten habit. How many times had he spit out that phrase in the face of capes, criminals, and victims alike? How many deaths because of a single vow? "Yes, Rick, I did bad things. Killed, hurt—fill in the blanks. If you want to know why, it's because I promised vengeance to someone who was truly owed it. Some of the deeds I did in service of that goal, others to survive or gain resources, but it always went back to that promise. I'll give you the specifics, if you want them, just be warned that we'll be diving into one of the darkest parts of my history."

Shaking his head, Rick downed a quarter of the juice in a single gulp. Ivan slipped the first batch of eggs, scrambled just the way he liked, onto Rick's plate while the drink was in motion: the seamless coordination of a dad who'd cooked untold meals, while also hiding a murderous secret.

"Let's not go that deep to start. What I was going to say is that, while not all of it could have been about protecting us, I don't think you'd hurt people without reason. For now, I'm okay with keeping some things a mystery. There's just a few big-ticket concerns I wanted to get out of my head."

Still dangerous territory, though Ivan much preferred general to specific, in regards to his past. Turning his attention to the pancake batter, Ivan hoped he wasn't about to make a major mistake. "Ask away."

"Have you ever hurt anyone who didn't deserve it?"

"Unquestionably, yes," Ivan replied, no hesitation whatsoever. This was a question he'd been expecting in some form or another and had already planned out a truthful response. "Even excluding the circumstances of my own brutal upbringing, metas often work in gangs or syndicates, the more powerful ones forcing their will upon the weaker members, turning them into pawns. Pawns tend to get cut down, and I can't expect that all of them deserved it. But that's also the nature of combat. Step onto a battlefield, and it's no longer about who deserves what—only those who live, and those who don't. Outside of that, I can only say that I've never struck without cause. How deserving they were from there is a case-by-case question."

Rick's eyes were wide, yet he was managing to stay composed. He'd certainly come in better prepared for the conversation this time around. After a few seconds, the shock seeped away from his face. "I guess that's fair. Even in the beach example, you couldn't have known the morality of every member of that army. It's not like you killed a superhero."

Without warning, Ivan found himself at a precipice. Two paths lay before him, truth or falsehood. It would be very easy to lie right now, to put his son's mind to rest and let the matter end. The problem was, if Rick ever found out

Ivan's identity, the lie would be obvious. Fornax killing a cape was what had finally caused his and Lodestar's last real fight, and his eventual incarceration. It was a well-known piece of trivia, one that Rick would be sure to pick up. Lying when they were young had been the right call—Ivan still had no doubt of that—but he'd told Rick that they were past that phase. Another fib, and whatever they built from here would always have the potential to be destroyed at the foundation.

"Superheroes go bad sometimes. Jokull, the Silent Server, Faithful, Candlebop—all former beloved capes who turned down a dark path. That's not even including the ones like Apollo, who abused their position to try manipulating the law. I've never struck without cause. Perhaps it's best if we leave that point there."

This time, the shock didn't fade so quickly. Rick chewed on a bite of eggs to the point where there had to be nothing but largely liquid left—either processing or plotting how to run for the door, Ivan wasn't fully sure which.

"Since you mentioned Apollo, there is the matter of that guild he exposed." Rick was going slow, visibly building up his courage. "I didn't think there was any chance you could have been part of that, even knowing about the beach. But the more you talk, the deeper I'm realizing this goes. Were you one of them, pouring out of that building, fighting in the streets?"

Though he couldn't have known it, Rick left quite a large loophole for his father to exploit in that question. Ivan was sorely tempted by it, even knowing how important the truth was at this juncture. It wouldn't be worth it in the long run; however, this did offer a bit of wiggle room in regards to how specific he had to get with the response.

Ivan spooned pancake batter into the sizzling pans, hisses and pops peppering the spaces between his words. "I was not in that crowd, but to answer your larger question: yes, I am affiliated with that guild. As much as it is a gathering of criminals, it's also a support group for those seeking to find a more mundane life… one that hasn't technically been charged with any crimes, I might add."

"Wow." Rick was past stunned, into near bewilderment. "That's... you're part of a guild of villains? What about the armored guy who saved me and Beth, you sent him?"

"No, I didn't," Ivan responded. "They learned about the danger to your school and came to help of their own accord. Because as much as it might seem like an assortment of monsters from the outside, there are people in that guild who I trust with my life. Friends who protected my family before I even knew they were in danger. So before you jump to conclusions about what that place is, keep in mind that when things went awry, my ally's first instinct was to save a school, not to run around pillaging."

With a clatter, Rick dropped his fork to the plate, eggs only half eaten. He stared down at them, trying to accept Ivan's words. "You trust a guild of villains... with your life. Do you get how insane that sounds from my side of the table? What about me and Beth, should we be making inroads with these people, too? Never know when we might need saving, and the Curdler is our only hope."

Sounds from overhead cut them both off. It seemed they'd gotten loud enough to raise Beth from her slumber. Once the smells hit, they wouldn't have much time left to talk openly. Ivan decided to finish things off with a quick piece of vital advice, one he'd be very grateful not to have to explain.

"You and Beth should be protected, but things do go wrong. If something ever happens to me, then don't bother with the guild. Get to the AHC or somewhere public—on TV, if you can manage it—and call for Lodestar."

"Because she'd just happen to be listening and choose to help us in that moment? She's not everywhere at once," Rick pointed out.

"Maybe not, but if I'm gone, then she's going to be looking for you both to make sure you're safe. I'm not *only* acquainted with villains, you know."

It was the first time all morning that Ivan had seen surprise that wasn't slightly terrified on Rick's face, and he did his best to memorize the expression. There probably wouldn't be many more like it to come if Rick kept asking questions. Eventually, they'd get to the truly horrifying stuff, and his son would never be able to look at him the same way again.

Chapter 58

The mood was tense as Morgana looked over the reports, her primary team gathered at her side. On her left stood Gork; to her right was Stasis, with the remainder of the room filled by the team leads who would be running their own units.

"Based on our intel, it looks like they haven't moved much this week. If Endless Blitz knows we're coming, he's not tipping his hand."

At Morgana's words, a ripple went through the room. They'd hunted down most of the traitors to the guild—those who were not killed the day of the riots—but a few had managed to slip away. Endless Blitz, with his power of body duplication, had been a vital asset for Balaam's attempted uprising. It was thanks to Endless Blitz that Balaam had appeared to have gathered so many forces early on, and that same power had made the man especially tough to capture. Thus far, they'd caught three duplicates posing as the real one. This time, they'd used new scanners and some fresh magical incantations to make as sure as possible that this was him. Vengeance was finally close at hand.

"One last review before we go," Morgana announced. It would be overkill in most situations, but former guild members were special cases. "Remember, above all else, that this is not a normal code enforcement. Endless Blitz was one of us. That means, along with being strong enough to make the cut, he knows our tricks, our tactics. He doesn't want to die any more than the rest of us do, so we can be certain he's laid every defense possible to hold us off. We can hate him all day, but don't belittle the danger he presents."

Locking eyes with each of her subordinates, Morgana made sure the point found its mark. Ego could be a danger in the field, especially when emotions ran this high. “Whisperwind, you and the magic users are going in first. Mark the real Endless Blitz, then thin out the clones so they can’t confuse us. As soon as you act, Onslaughter’s team rolls in to push over whatever goons he’s got surrounding him. Horrorsaurus, your team roams the exits, making sure nobody slips away and tracking them down if they do. Gork, Stasis, and I will come through once the initial strike is made to cleave what remains. Be ready to change and adapt as needed; we can’t take anything as certain when facing off with one of our own.”

“Any risk of capes?” Whisperwind was a slender woman with a soft demeanor, yet her voice carried well every time she chose to speak.

“With as many lookout teams as we’ve got stationed, there better not be,” Stasis said. “The fewer bodies to keep track of, the more likely we are to get him this time, so we’ve got three separate lines of security. Short of the major players, if one does wander by, we’ll at least have warning.”

Onslaughter’s sizable form leaned down, a habit of trying to speak to others on roughly their same level. “At least it’s not a Ridge City base. Hiding all the way out in Ebnerville, he *really* didn’t want us to find him. Endless Blitz loved living in the big city.”

“The remote location and small amount of overall crime make it low priority for capes,” Morgana noted. “Which will aid our own efforts, as well. In a way, perhaps we should be thankful to Endless Blitz. It was so considerate of him to set the scene out where no one will hear his screams.”

The room nodded along with her, some even smiling at the sentiment. It was arguable how deep into true evil the various members of the guild fell, but there was certainly a moral gradient at play. On the subject of revenge, however, they were a far more unified group. This guild was more than just a loose association of crooks; it was a symbol of their collective power and pride—one that Endless Blitz had spit upon when he betrayed them, sealing his fate in the process. To wrong a villain was to court death.

To wrong a guild of them, well, that was essentially getting onto death’s lap and grinding hard. If Endless Blitz was so desperate to face his end, then as his former friends, they would oblige this final request.

Setting the controller down, Donald leaned back, the look of satisfaction on his face reflected back in the dark TV. The phantom Donald vanished as a fresh screen appeared, displaying the upgrade options he'd just unlocked. With planned ease, he checked off the selections, watching as the parts spun onto his digital jetpack, replacing the older versions to create a stable, quick flight system.

This was his secondary project of the week. The first, and far more taxing one, had been dealing with the New Science Sentries as his team's shadow. They were polite, thankfully, though he suspected that to be largely the product of Agent Quantum's influence. To their credit, the team did excellent work. There had been a few occasions where they'd needed the extra numbers to take a call, and things had gone smoothly overall. It had also been during those moments that Donald began to grow a hunch about the team's primary issue.

While he hadn't felt confident enough to voice the notion yet, there did seem to be a fundamental philosophical difference in the foundation of their training. Apollo, for all the bad he did, had taught new capes the AHC protocols, one of the most important of which was that the goal was saving civilians. Sometimes, that meant taking down the threat, but it could also mean getting people clear, or shielding them from fallout.

From what he'd seen of the New Science Sentries, their education appeared to focus on threat neutralization first and foremost. They came in swinging and didn't stop until everyone was down. It wasn't wrong, necessarily. Their team was still protecting people, helping to make the world better. Yet there was something about it that felt... wrong. Without being able to put a finger on why, Donald just knew that their apparent enthusiasm for combat left a bad taste in his mouth. He suspected that feeling to be a large part of why they weren't clicking in Ridge City. The people understood what standards capes were supposed to uphold and could tell when something was off. It wasn't so bad now that he'd talked with Agent Quantum and knew that they were trying to improve, but the rest of the world didn't have the benefit of that perspective.

They had been getting better: on Thursday's outing there'd only been one broken bone, and Agent Quantum had tried to take the mugger down less forcefully first. Still, Donald was glad they didn't have any actual patrols scheduled for that evening. He could use a break, and with his newest tool finally ready for testing, this was a perfect chance to go put it through its paces.

Scooping up his phone from the bed, Donald clicked on Ren's name, the number connecting quickly. "Hey. No, don't worry, no schedule change. We're still free today. That's why I was calling actually—you up for some fun tonight? I wanted to test out my jetpack. Oh hell no. Not in Ridge City; way too many tall buildings and other metas zipping around for a test flight. I was thinking somewhere more isolated, where I'd have room for mistakes."

Glancing down at the GPS on his phone, Donald scrolled over the map, hunting for a city big enough to explore, but without too many obstacles. "How about Ebnerville, up near the Canadian border? Pretty sure the AHC can jump us there, and I doubt there'll be much for me to hit, aside from trees. I'll double-check and let you know."

One press of the button, and the call was done. Donald zoomed in on the map, taking a closer look at his potential selection. While the notion had been spur of the moment, Ebnerville seemed as good an option as any. Testing the jetpack was what sincerely excited him. Making a mental note to go be sure they had viable transportation available, he turned his attention back to the screen and the newly completed item spinning around on the display.

Blue energy crackled along his fingertips as Donald reached for the code inside the computer resting in his skull. If he was taking it out for a test drive tonight, he'd best familiarize himself with the jetpack's controls.

With the hiss of a helmet locking into place, Tori vanished.

Hephaestus cycled through her various system startups, then took a tentative step forward. Not perfect—there was still a noticeable difference between moving like this versus on her own—but the gap was shrinking. A few more rounds of fine-tuning and she'd have it: fluid, seamless motion, like there was no extra weight on her at all. She could practically feel it. Those tuning rounds would have to wait for Tori, however, as Hephaestus had a full evening ahead.

Stepping out into the guild's hallway, she found Bahamut waiting; clad in her armored outfit and transformed to green dragon form. They fell into step alongside one another, heading toward the transportation chamber. While they could hop from the island to Ridge City using the installed gate, getting elsewhere still required special assistance. Whoever was putting this together had tapped the pair named Tunnel Vision to bring over all the teams. Theirs would be among the last to go out; the attacking units were already on the ground, getting prepared.

Arriving in the wide, open room with a vast, unmarked back wall, Hephaestus noted Pest Control in the corner, talking with Glyph. The former was clad in his almost beekeeper-like outfit, a costume with various metal rings adorning the exterior. As for Glyph, he'd made a few ensemble changes since they last saw him in costume. The cloak was traded for a stylized jacket, and his robe had been tailored up substantially to allow for easier movement. He still wielded the same wand, though Hephaestus couldn't fault him for that. Considering that the wand not only allowed him to draw his namesake symbols wherever they were needed but also stored a prepared glyph ready to be deployed, it was a crucial piece of his outfit. Even being a gift from Balaam, it was too useful a tool to discard, not something that could be easily cast aside out of mere dark sentiment.

At their arrival, Pest Control looked up, waving them over to join. "Good timing! Tunnel Vision finished the last team a few minutes ago, so we can go as soon as you're ready. Anyone have additional questions or issues to go over?" It had been a little odd, seeing Pest Control take the lead on this job, but he'd proven to be unexpectedly adept at it. Not the actual planning part so much—there had been a few key tweaks needed to his original layout—rather, Pest Control led well because he did a good job of taking input from others. When they brought up issues, they were dealt with, rather than brushed aside for not fitting Pest Control's vision. While Hephaestus was relatively new to all of this, Tori had witnessed far worse leadership styles than that.

"I feel solid." Hephaestus clanged her chest, producing a dense ring that briefly drifted through the air. The more she wore the suit, the more natural the movements felt. "Got my position and my job. Fly high, keep my profile low. Scan for any potential issues before they get close enough to surprise us."

"If they do get close and they're human, leave them to me," Pest Control reiterated. "Between my meta-insects and some entomological expeditions, I've got a bug for just about every problem. Every problem without special abilities, that is."

The sound of scales scraping registered as Bahamut slammed a meaty fist into her open palm. Not even her size betrayed just how strong the dragon's arms really were. Bahamut wasn't nearly the mightiest of their guild, but her punches would hurt most opponents nevertheless. "Metas who get close, on the other hand, are for me and Glyph."

"I do have a few new etchings I'm ready to try out." Tapping his wand, a look dashed across Glyph's face, one of sudden realization and swift embarrassment. "Almost forgot to tell you both. Just to be safe, I prepared an emergency escape spell as the symbol loaded in my wand. No way I want to get penned in like at the museum again. If anything gets too bad, group up around me when I give the signal."

The sound of approach drew Hephaestus's attention. She quickly realized the synchronized steps belonged to Tunnel Vision, a team of teleportation-empowered siblings. She was never quite sure which was which, or even if the names were meant to be separated. Since the two functioned in tandem, it was an academic concern. Nevertheless, her natural curiosity refused to let the point lie entirely.

In less than a minute, the pair had torn a hole through space itself, offering a portal that appeared to look out onto an old logging camp, one that had long ago been abandoned. Hephaestus knew the location already from Pest Control's plan. This was their entry and exit point, a location far enough from the action to not be noticed, but close enough to run for if needed.

Together with her team, they stepped from the guild's volcano lair into Ebnerville, site of what was supposed to be a few hours' simple lookout work for a hefty payday. Hephaestus dialed up her scanners as they walked through, hunting for any single thing that would trip her suspicion. She might be a new villain, but had already seen enough to know few things ever went as easily as they were planned.

Chapter 59

Ebnerville was a city largely in a technical sense. There were adequate facilities and population to claim the title, but those from any actual metropolis would call the town a hamlet, at best. It favored sprawl more than height, meaning there weren't many tall buildings, and certainly no true skyscrapers for Cyber Geek to avoid as he banked hard to the left, gaining a feel for the turn radius he was working with. There would be ways to refine the jetpack further—he had plenty left before he fully completed *Rocket Rangers*—but this was essentially the model he'd be working with going forward. Getting used to it now would only make his usage smoother as the item improved.

Blasting along, Cyber Geek tried to keep parallel with a tree line near the edge of the city. Ebnerville quickly gave way to wilderness once one wandered away from the lights; in the distance, he could see the larger, looming forest massed up like an unmoving army, waiting for the signal to strike. It was a strange sight. Most of his work with the AHC had been in either Ridge City itself or other heavily developed areas, as those tended to have the highest levels of crime. Out here, it was almost serene, ignoring the dull roar of the jetpack. There was a reason he'd gotten the upgrades to quiet the noise; he'd be waking every house he flew past or going deaf from sound exposure otherwise —though Cyber Geek suspected he'd still be in for a headache when all was said and done.

"Looking good. Now bring it around." Medley was seated on the rooftop of a five-story apartment complex, keeping watch from one of the higher points they could find. In the event someone else did fly through, or there was an obstacle Cyber Geek seemed on course to collide with, Medley would radio in. With senses as sharp as his, it would be tough for anything to take them by surprise.

Obeying the directions, Cyber Geek extended the turn, circling back so he was headed toward Medley once more. He was slowly starting to get comfortable in the air, though he did keep a constant watch on the jetpack's fuel gauge. After this many upgrades, it would take quite a while to run dry at these speeds, but that was not a limit Cyber Geek wanted to test. He'd fallen from a fourth-floor balcony in a set of item-armor and still bruised his entire back. From this height, the injury would be far more severe.

As he looked up to the night sky, admiring the better view of the stars provided to those who settled farther from civilization, a flash caught Cyber Geek's eye. He wasn't entirely sure what it was, but his training kicked in almost before he'd made a conscious decision. Something was off, and he was a superhero; that made it his job to ensure everyone was safe.

"I caught sight of something just now. Toward the western edge of town. Could have been a rogue firework, maybe. I only caught it for a flash."

On the roof, Medley rose, shaking a touch of evening moisture from his fur. "I'll come, anyway. Better than sitting, and you still need a spotter."

"Not going to argue that point after less than ten minutes of practice," Cyber Geek agreed. "Don't worry, I'm pretty sure I can slow down for you."

"Slow down? I was going to say this is finally *your* chance to be able to keep up." Without any additional warning, Medley took off for the edge of his building in a dash, leaping and easily clearing the divide. Claws sank into the next rooftop for purchase, then immediately released as he took off again, racing for the next roof.

Cyber Geek watched him for a moment, in awe of the strength and grace his friend was displaying. This was miles from the unsure, awkwardly moving version of him that they'd known after the initial change. The more accustomed to the body Medley became, the more dangerous he grew. That was an arrangement Cyber Geek would have been quite happy with, except for the fact it stuck his friend in the body of an animal hybrid. Had there been a cure, a chance for him to be fully Ren again, he wouldn't have blamed Medley for taking it. Until that option arrived, however, he was grateful to have him as a teammate, and a friend.

It also didn't hurt that Medley hadn't been kidding; he really was cutting a furious pace. Adjusting his angle to properly lead the way, Cyber Geek slightly increased the speed of his jetpack. Time to see what this thing could actually do.

"All quiet to the north."

"Of course it's quiet to the north. There's nothing that way but wolves and trees." Bahamut's annoyance was steadily rising as the night wore on, which was understandable given her situation. She was currently cramped into a doorframe down a dark alleyway, one of the few places that could effectively hide her sizable green form while still being in a central position. Getting her in had been an ordeal, and the tight quarters were fast eroding her spirits. If someone did wander through, they were going to get one wrathful dragon for their troubles.

"Still quiet," Hephaestus reiterated, perhaps suppressing a snicker at her friend's momentary, but humorous, misfortune. For her part, she was on the roof of a cracker factory, one of the few high points Ebnerville really had to offer. Southwest of them, deeper into the industrial district, the plan was being carried out. Hephaestus still didn't know what it was, and the deeper in they got, the happier she was about that. The guild was treating this with gravity, and that made it *way* above anything she wanted to be involved in. Guard duty was more than enough.

A blip in her visor alerted her to the flare of energy just as it spiked into the night sky. The flash was brief. Whoever made it was either aware enough not to make a scene, or had been cut down before they properly could. "Anyone else catch that?"

"Catch what?" Glyph's answer was genuinely interested, a sharp contrast to Bahamut's reply:

"Nope, still just brick and alley—the only things I *can* see."

Pest Control, thankfully, confirmed Hephaestus's sighting. "A few of my bugs saw that, too. It's blocked by a lot of the other buildings between. Anyone not elevated when it went off probably didn't notice."

That should have been more reassuring, considering the layout of Ebnerville and the relatively low number of active metas. They barely had any street-level capes trying to make a name for themselves, let alone ones patrolling the skies. Nevertheless, the pessimist in Hephaestus refused to trust in those odds. She began scanning more actively, searching for any potential threats.

For roughly three minutes, she kept at it, her heightened concern slowly dissipating. Just when she was about to give the all-clear, another blip caught her attention. Heat signature, approaching from the east. Quickly spinning her head, she activated the lens's zoom, pinpointing the source of the heat. A jetpack. Of course, it was someone in a jetpack. As the image sharpened, Hephaestus felt a sudden weight slam into her stomach.

"Shit. We've got a cape approaching." A cape in a costume she recognized quite well. Hephaestus may be too new to have allies, but Tori had kept up with this friend's career. "Cyber Geek, zipping over using a new flying item."

The silence in her ear stretched on, finally broken by Pest Control. "We have to stop him. For his sake as much as the job. Whatever is going on, it's expected to be a bloodbath. We've got councilors fighting. A new cape wandering into that... even if our people try not to hurt him in the chaos, the other side won't have that concern."

They didn't have long to talk about it. Cyber Geek was cutting a solid pace. A leaping form caught Hephaestus's eye; Medley was along for the ride, because apparently, nothing was going to go right tonight. "Update: add Medley to that equation, too."

"Crap. If it was just one, he might be smart enough to steer clear. With backup, it gets riskier." Glyph paused, pondering a notion. "Pest Control and I have something of a working relationship with these two after the riots. If we go out there, they might be willing to listen."

"To what?" Bahamut asked. "That there's a crime going on nearby, but we'd really appreciate it if they hung back and didn't radio anything in? I don't see any cape going for that, working relationship or not."

That wasn't even touching on the fact that it depended on Cyber Geek and Medley being willing to listen, which was far from guaranteed out here in the field. They needed a plan that didn't require talking, a way to lead them away instantly, something they couldn't resist.

Unfortunately, Hephaestus knew exactly what would work. She'd wanted to get in some flying practice, anyway; this functioned as well as any other occasion. "Bahamut is right. We can't count on diplomacy for this. We have to trust something more dependable: spite."

"Don't even think about it." Bahamut was already ahead of her, probably trying to wriggle free from her alcove at that very moment.

"You really think it will work?" Pest Control asked, keeping his head on the mission as a whole.

Hephaestus's mind flashed back to the sight of a smoldering Medley, to the look in his eyes as she was flown out of reach. "I lit the guy on fire and escaped from their clutches. Pretty sure they'll chase me, given the opportunity. And if they don't, I'll just have to encourage them."

Flight systems were operational; she'd kept them on standby while waiting, just in case. Lifting off her perch, Hephaestus rose through the air, gravity's grip on her heft knocked back by the technology hidden amidst her suit's dark depths. She momentarily disabled her sound-suppressing system and blazed into the air, engines roaring. For this to work, she needed to be both seen and heard. More than that, she needed to be recognized.

Staying low until she was away from the others, Hephaestus took a sharp turn skyward as she came closer to Cyber Geek. She rose steadily higher, the brilliant flames bursting out, propelling her forward as she seared the night. There would be no way for him to miss her, even with the suit's stealth-friendly coloring.

In fact, it ended up being more effective than planned. Due to a bit of poor timing, Hephaestus's trajectory was slightly off. That meant, instead of rising up before him like an ascending demon, she very nearly collided with the cape, both of them having to spin off in other directions to avoid a crash. She righted herself almost immediately, whereas Cyber Geek nearly went into a spiral, managing to gain control only seconds before Hephaestus might have felt the draw to help.

On a nearby roof, Medley was screaming, and while she didn't care enough to isolate the sounds, she could more or less put the gist together. He definitely recognized her. The question was, would it be enough?

Hephaestus watched as Cyber Geek reoriented, letting out a small sigh of relief when he pointed himself in her direction, exactly opposite that of the site she was guarding. It worked. The capes were giving chase.

That thought was at least some comfort as Hephaestus blasted further up into the sky with no idea what to do with the capes now that she'd managed to attract them.

Agent Quantum carefully applied the handcuffs, taking pains not to break the suspect's wrists. It wasn't an issue that had come up before, but working with Cyber Geek's team had shed a lot of light on just how strong they were compared to a lot of the criminals they put away. If those slip-ups did happen, it reflected back on the AHC, and capes as a whole. That knowledge had added a layer of caution to every movement these last few days, and even with the week of shadowing over, he wanted to keep those lessons in practice. If they didn't improve, then what was the point of that effort in the first place?

Watching the police lead his latest efforts into a waiting car, Agent Quantum opened up his communication lines, checking in to the AHC's central hub. "Hey, team. New Science Sentries reporting assignment completion. What's the next thing we can help with?"

The voices always changed—running an operation of the AHC's size required a sizable staff—but their readiness was constant. He'd barely finished before a voice was providing answers. "We've got nothing but some minor security alarms reported near your current position—probably going to be due for another jump to get to the action. Hope you had fun in California."

It was a trite joke that got used every time capes were spirited off to a destination location, only to then spend their time working. Agent Quantum offered up a polite laugh; this too was part of the job, in its way.

"Let's see... if we're jumping you anyway, looks like Cyber Geek just called in something suspicious. Potential wanted criminal spotted out in Ebnerville. Not a high priority, but since you've been working together, I thought I'd offer."

The issue didn't sound especially pressing; then again, it also didn't seem like there were any major emergencies to tackle anywhere else at the moment. After letting them tag along for a week, the very least his team could do was make sure Cyber Geek didn't need any assistance. On the off chance he did, all the better. It would be a chance to show their thanks for the help he'd provided.

"Get me a jump to Cyber Geek's position as soon as someone is available. Looks like the New Science Sentries are visiting Ebnerville."

Chapter 60

The longer a chase went on, the worse it was for the one being pursued. A cape could call in more help, additional surveillance, whatever they needed to lock down their target. Generally speaking, Hephaestus's strategy would have been to speed up and start weaving through the trees, losing her pursuers in the confusion and then sneaking away. The trouble was that she *had* to stay visible for this to work. If escape was out, and continued pursuit put the odds against her, then that meant Hephaestus needed another idea. It took almost two minutes of racing through the skies, but eventually, she hit upon a solution.

She'd been approaching the issue as a criminal, when this was actually a villain's job.

Decreasing her speed, Hephaestus began the process of descent. The area she'd selected was well off from the battle site—also relatively deserted at this time of night. A strip mall, filled with discount shops and chain eateries, all darkened and empty. The closest thing to other human life was a large cutout of Flex Force showing off in a nutrient shop's window. No civilians to get involved if things took a turn for the messy.

Dropping low, she landed roughly, leaving a scorch mark on the cement. That part would take more practice; had this been grass, she might have accidentally started a fire. With a quick mental note to tweak the landing systems, she scanned the sky for her pursuers. Cyber Geek wasn't far behind, though Medley flagged slightly farther back as his rooftop options ran short.

The jetpack didn't leave any signs or scorches as Cyber Geek set down, attention already trained on Hephaestus. Show-off. Before he could speak, she yelled at him, the suit's voice modulator masking her true identity.

"What do you fucking want? I waved sorry about the near miss, yet you still felt the need to follow me? I've got video recording and 911 on speed dial, so take a few steps back. Getting some real creep vibes off of you."

It took Cyber Geek back for a moment. He'd been expecting her to take the role of the aggressor. "I... I know who you are."

"Really? You don't ring a bell for me. Sure it wasn't someone else with an experimental meta-suit?" Hephaestus saw the flicker of uncertainty in Cyber Geek's eyes. While the aesthetic was the same, this suit had undeniable differences since the reworking. Enough to cause doubt, and that was what she needed more than anything: make him unsure, keep them off-balance, and stall like hell until the coast was clear.

That was when Medley finally closed the gap. His tongue hung slightly off to the side as he ran, darting back inside his mouth just as it was time to speak. "Hephaestus! Surrender now, and we can do this peacefully."

"Who the hell is Hephaestus?" Hephaestus demanded. "I know there was a cape named Red Hephaestus a while back, but I think he's been dead for a long time."

Medley wasn't so easily knocked off-kilter. He continued to approach, clearly ready for battle. "What a lazy attempt at trickery. Do you really expect it to work?" Every muscle was taut. He shook out his limbs, readying them for rapid movement. She remembered how strong that body was; if Medley hit, it was going to hurt.

"Here's a better question: do you realize what you're about to do? Right now, I'm a civilian in a meta-suit. You have established no criminal identity, no active crime in progress, and no outstanding warrants. That flexing you're doing—that's not for a fight. It's for assault, and my video recording is going to show exactly that."

Hephaestus tapped her helmet, a keen reminder to everyone present that she was coated from head-to-toe in electronics. Medley's eager pace suddenly halted, the reality of her words sinking in. A criminal was bound by the system, while a villain knew how to turn that system right back against the capes who trusted it.

"On the chance this is a misunderstanding, you have our apologies. However, your suit bears striking similarities to the type used by a creator named Hephaestus, who is wanted for questioning in connection to a museum robbery." Cyber Geek had recovered just as Medley lost his stride. The two made a good team. Under different circumstances, she'd have been glad to see them covering one another so well.

"Cool story. Got a warrant and some cops to go with it?" Hephaestus demanded. "Because last I checked, the Alliance of Heroic Champions aided law enforcement, without actually being such an entity itself. That clears you of a lot of liability, sure, but it also means that unless you have an actual warrant in hand or I'm presenting a provable, active danger, you can go get fucked. So, I ask again: got any paperwork and law enforcement shoved up that spandex ass? Remember, you're being filmed."

This was not the way Cyber Geek and Medley had expected the encounter to play out. They were accustomed to dealing with crooks who would scream and flee, or jump right into combat. She couldn't imagine anyone they'd dealt with prior had attempted to use technicalities as their weapon of choice.

Finally, Cyber Geek found his answer. "No, I don't have a warrant to arrest you. Instead, I'll be happy to call the local PD and have them come take you into custody for questioning, while Medley and I wait here to keep you company."

Though the clangs were loud as Hephaestus began to tick points off on her fingers, she kept up the theatrics all the same. The less concerned she appeared to be by these two, the more they'd worry she truly had nothing to fear. "Keep me here without my consent—that's kidnapping. Follow me without cause, harassment. Try following me from a distance, without my knowledge, and I bet we can slip a few breach-of-privacy charges onto the harassment, maybe even a sex crime if I stop to piss and you both sneak a peek."

Cyber Geek actually got a touch rosy in the cheeks at that one, though Medley was looking more and more furious by the second. He knew it was bullshit. They *all* knew it was bullshit. The question was how much could any person present prove it. Her suit had changed, enough to have reasonable doubt, and if flying homemade creations around were illegal, then a big chunk of the airborne capes would already be in jail. She'd stymied the pair without a single punch being thrown. There was a chance she owed Ivan an apology—all that harping on the code and learning the specifics had turned out more useful than she anticipated.

Most capes, she suspected, would have let it go at that. She'd made too much trouble, and presented a strong case. Trying to keep pushing just opened up more problems than it fixed, all for the cape who made the play. Trouble was, Cyber Geek could show an unexpectedly heroic spirit when put against a wall.

"I can live with that. If you're proven innocent and would like to press charges against me, then I'll give a full confession to every part of this interaction. Kidnapping seems like a reach, but I'm sure there will be consequences. Consequences I'd much rather live with than with the knowledge that I let a dangerous criminal escape justice." Cyber Geek started forward, and he didn't look like he'd be so easy to derail this time.

Time for a reassessment. Without knowing for sure what was happening at the battle, she couldn't risk turning these two loose. Going to jail, on the other hand, also wasn't on the table. Her only option left was to buy as much time as possible, and then run for it. She could always ditch the suit and make her escape as Tori, picking it up when the coast was clear. No matter how she sliced it, however, there were slim odds she'd be able to keep this delay rolling without things getting a bit messy.

"Seeing as you're attempting unlawful restraint, I hope you realize I'm in my rights to fight back, cape or not." Hephaestus made sure power was flowing into her blaster gauntlets, and that the setting was low. She didn't want to hurt them badly, but couldn't very well risk losing the fight either.

"Finally. I wondered when I'd get my rematch." Medley bounded forward, though Hephaestus noted his claws weren't extended yet. Despite the tough talk, he was playing it as a cape, coming in softly first, to be safe.

Hephaestus held no such compunctions, and had the benefit of knowing Medley to be incredibly resilient. As he leaped, arms wide for some sort of hug-clutch, she fired a beam directly into his knee, sending him spinning back through the air with a screaming yowl.

"What did you do?" That was the only line Cyber Geek got out before the cold metal of Hephaestus's elbow smashed into the bridge of his nose. He'd made the mistake of watching Medley's fall, rather than keeping an eye on the enemy, and was quickly taught the error of his ways. The nose broke instantly, sending tears to his eyes and blood pouring down the front of his face. It was fortunate he didn't wear a mask, or it would have been soaked in seconds.

"Fought back." Hephaestus didn't press the assault as she watched the blood drip. In truth, she'd expected Cyber Geek to dodge; it hadn't exactly been the most efficient blow. The shock of seeing her friend in pain caused her to pause, a sudden flash of loyalty arriving at the most inconvenient of times. The cold, logical side of her mind swept into action, rationalizing at lightning speeds. It reminded her that a nose wasn't so bad, more pain than anything, and the AHC had the resources to replace entire limbs. This wouldn't be more than a blip in the long term, no matter how painful it felt for the moment. Whereas, if she was caught, the consequences would be far more long-lasting.

Scratching reached her ears as Medley drew himself back up, tenderly putting a reduced amount of weight on his still-smoking knee. At full force, that beam of energy could have carved through the bone. This was little more than a flesh wound in comparison. A flesh wound that still slowed Medley down—a benefit Hephaestus would gladly accept. After their last battle, when she'd been a slow-moving hunk and he'd easily overpowered her, it felt good to show she wasn't a threat to be taken lightly.

"Think we'd have to land a hit for it to be fighting back." Medley fell onto all fours, compensating for his injured limb. His tail rose high, ready to strike as he dashed along the ground. Hephaestus fired, only for him to swerve to the side, nimbly missing the shot. Hephaestus shot twice more, each time the blasts were avoided by Medley.

The fourth shot, he dodged as well. It was the fifth, fired right after the fourth, from Hephaestus's other gauntlet, that finally found home. Unaware that she had multiple weapons, Medley wasn't quite prepared to react post-dodge, earning a shot to the flank that burned away a section of his fur. He clutched his ribs as he rolled along the concrete.

Sparking blue light drew Hephaestus back to Cyber Geek. He was reaching into the code for a weapon, something he *should* have done before getting into combat. Hopefully, he'd learn from this mistake; his next opponent probably wouldn't be inclined to go easy. To that point, Hephaestus raised a blaster and fired a single shot into Cyber Geek's left foot, again at the lowest setting. He still screeched, perhaps from surprise as much as pain. The blue light flared out as his concentration faltered, leaving him exposed while Hephaestus darted over.

She hadn't actually expected the fight to go so well; having the advantage of surprise made a huge difference. They might have seen her there, but neither expected her to come out swinging for the fences. Such was the trouble with gradually sliding up the power scale to deal with new threats: those threats had no such obligation to play by the same rules.

"If you two are done, can I go back to flying around peacefully? Seems like you could probably use some more practice at all of this, anyway. I can even—"

An entirely new sensation came over Hephaestus, like someone was trying to tear her out from within her suit. Instantly, she fully shifted to fire form, yet the pull didn't dissipate. It expanded out, yanking on Hephaestus as a whole, and for a moment, it felt like she might not fit into whatever cosmic hole was being formed. Then, like a champagne cork, she popped through space itself, her mind momentarily boggled at seeing existence from the inside out, only to appear again across the strip mall.

It wasn't where she was that was relevant, so much as what—or rather, who—she was in front of. The punch from Agent Quantum lit up several alarms on her sensors, and the super-speed kick from Tachyonic less than a second later only compounded the problem. Had she been flesh, the rapid shift in momentum would have had the emergency vomit protocols fully activated. Instead, she just put everything she had into staying upright.

Set before her were the New Science Sentries, only, for the first time, she wasn't seeing them as a civilian being rescued or a neighbor being pestered. As their adversary, she looked into the hard, battle-ready looks in their eyes, and suddenly found herself quite nostalgic for those bothersome neighbors. Because in the field, with combat upon them, the New Science Sentries looked downright terrifying.

And she was the focal point of all their attention.

Chapter 61

"Armor Boy there has got more heft than he lets on. Not an easy one to move, and he's slippery inside." Presto appeared safely out of harm's reach, which explained how Hephaestus had been moved into such an inopportune position.

Although she hadn't collapsed, her suit was blaring with alerts. In just two blows, the New Science Sentries had managed extensive damage to her shell. With attacks like that, it was only a matter of time before they broke something vital. This was not a fight she wanted, if it could be possibly helped.

"Oh good, more enforcers from the AHC here to help their friends with kidnapping. Guess after you so spectacularly failed to prevent one, aiding the kidnappers is the next logical step."

It was, admittedly, a low blow, though if anyone had the right to throw that punch, it was the woman who'd endured the actual incident. Her hope was that it would rattle the New Science Sentries, giving them momentary pause to consider their role in the current situation. Instead, she received a brief proximity alert before Tachyonic slammed into her back, sending her spinning through the air with the force of his accelerated momentum.

She landed face up, starting to rise only to find Tachyonic crouched over her, his face inches from her helmet. "Don't even fucking try it after that line. Agent Quantum, could you help me with restraint? Plasmodia, if you don't mind, I think we need a can opener."

From the left of Agent Quantum, Plasmodia stepped into view, her beauty turned terrifying in the flickering light of the energy spike extended from her right hand. Tough as Hephaestus's suit was, that thing would definitely carve through it; she'd seen the kind of power Plasmodia could conjure. On instinct, she started to move, only to find one of Tachyonic's hands suddenly resting on her shoulder.

"No matter what you do, it'll be too slow. Struggle all you like. We're taking you in."

A new noise came from behind Hephaestus: Cyber Geek's voice calling to the other capes. Thanks to using microphones rather than primitive eardrums, she was able to make out the words despite the distance.

"Watch out!"

Evidently, Agent Quantum had also been blessed with enhanced hearing, as he waved back to Cyber Geek. "Don't worry. We've got him. Might have a lot to learn in some respects, but fighting is one part of the job we can—"

His boast was cut off by several hundred pounds of green dragon flesh slamming into his back fist-first, adding the momentum of a skyward fall to the blow. Despite not seeing the approach, Hephaestus could put it together, especially given the patches of white scales still fading on Bahamut's form. She'd flown after Hephaestus, saw the trouble, and had dropped right in to help. It was an unexpected opportunity, one they had to use to the fullest.

For a brief, wonderful moment, the entire New Science Sentries team was stunned: Agent Quantum by the punch, everyone else from seeing their leader get knocked on his ass. While they were distracted, Hephaestus struck. A single punch wouldn't do much, especially given the rate at which super-speed aided healing. Taking Tachyonic out of the fight wasn't about injuring him; it was about making him ineffective.

To most people in her situation, the only recourse would be simple battle; however, Hephaestus was more than the might of her suit. She also had the brain of an inventor, one who took note of design details: a bracer getting touched frequently during combat, or the special containment material composing a costume. Tachyonic was hiding a secret—which was to say, a vulnerability.

Between the way she'd seen him occasionally tap that silver bracer on his right arm and the energy output signature her scanners were registering, Hephaestus had something of a hunch. Tachyonic might have super-speed on his own, but it certainly appeared as if he was augmenting that power out in the field. His suit was emitting trace amounts of setlium radiation, a telltale sign that he was dosing his cells in the meta-element. That level of tech was certainly in the realm of Professor Quantum to dream up; however, the implementation was a touch crude. After all, external controls presented a major vulnerability, especially against enemies who knew what to look for.

In the flash of distraction, Hephaestus struck, wrapping her right gauntlet around Tachyonic's bracer. Blasting would destroy it, along with Tachyonic's arm, which felt like a step too far, even in straits so dire. Instead, she funneled power into the mechanical muscles of the machine, squeezing for all she was worth. The bracer was well made. She was going to burn out half the motors in her hand, and would replace each with a smile on her face if it got her and Bahamut out of here.

"You brought frie—what the hell!" Tachyonic spun back around just as his bracer cracked, emitting a series of sparks and hisses. He tried to grab at the device, but bursts of electricity burned his hand at every attempt. "Come on... stabilize..."

The New Science Sentries were already recovering, Presto raising a hand to Bahamut as Plasmodia built power for a blast that would injure, if not cripple, even the green dragon. With no time to think, Hephaestus went on the attack. Rather than give Tachyonic time to stabilize, she cracked him in the nose with her elbow—the same offensive Cyber Geek had received to equally similar results. Either too unstable or too distracted to notice the incoming blow, Tachyonic took it full force, stumbling backward. In his case, something of a rueful expression peeked out through the mask, at least for the brief moment he had before Hephaestus shoved Tachyonic directly into Presto.

Both went down in a tangle, which should have given Hephaestus the chance to take out Plasmodia. Unfortunately, she'd made the mistake of forgetting what had brought her to this strip mall in the first place. Medley had finally recovered, and the sound of his panting approach gave her warning just before the slashing claws tried to part her armor. She slipped back, and he stayed close, not giving her any opportunity to switch back to ranged.

"Like I was saying—finally, a rematch." He smiled, she thought; it wasn't easy to tell given the animalistic structure of his face.

Glancing to the side, she saw Agent Quantum rising to his feet once more, with Plasmodia nearby to help. Farther back, she could make out the familiar blue flicker of Cyber Geek grabbing an item. Odds were steeply against them, and only getting worse.

If not for the buzzing of insect wings, Hephaestus might have lost hope. She could hear them, though, and that meant Pest Control wasn't far off. Whatever the plan might be—if there even was one—she had no clue. The best Hephaestus could manage was to stay free and uninjured while helping her friends do the same. Glyph had their emergency escape option, assuming they could reach him.

Medley came in swinging again, claws and tail flowing naturally. He'd been training, yet it was more than that. This was like he'd been learning to fight specifically using these weapons. Did the AHC offer some sort of inhuman martial arts program for people like Medley? Whatever the cause, Hephaestus was suitably impressed by his improvement, even as she deflected his attacks.

Capes weren't the only ones who got to grow after wins and losses, however. Compared to the last time they met, Hephaestus was markedly faster, stronger, and tougher, thanks to the various design upgrades. Her improved movement was showing the most benefits of all, as Hephaestus was able to somewhat keep pace with the furious flurry of attacks.

The ranged shot to her knee, unfortunately, slowed Hephaestus down. She could see Cyber Geek crouched at a distance, that comically huge video game gun propped up and taking aim once more. To her shock, Medley swung, and then leapt aside, giving Cyber Geek a perfect window. Hephaestus only just barely managed to dodge a second shot to the leg. This wasn't just some makeshift tactic on the fly; they'd trained this way, with Cyber Geek sniping as Medley wore the enemy down.

On the upside, he was still a cape, which meant the shot had been intended to wound rather than annihilate. Though Hephaestus wouldn't be completing any marathons until after the repairs, she could stay standing, for however much good that did. At that thought, another notion popped into mind. Why was she bothering with her legs at all? Landing had been essential to deal with Cyber Geek and Medley, but they were well past that point.

Using the momentary space Medley had so graciously provided, Hephaestus fired up her jets and shot into the sky, earning an angry yowl as he attempted an ineffectual pounce. From here, she could see the battlefield more effectively. Bahamut and Agent Quantum resembled prizefighters, exchanging punches like pleasantries at a church social. Plasmodia hung near the edge, ready to help; however, the tight confines of the fight limited her ability to shoot. Tachyonic and Presto were working on untangling themselves, hindered by Tachyonic suddenly speeding up and slowing down at inopportune moments. Medley was yowling, Cyber Geek was taking aim, and on top of the strip mall, Hephaestus could see what she'd been hoping for.

A mass of buzzing and wings swirled as Pest Control summoned more and more insects: some meta, some mundane, all of them annoying. Since Glyph was at his side, Hephaestus could take a general guess as to what the plan was.

Get the bugs to critical mass, drop a bomb of confusion on the battlefield, and that was their window to escape. She and Bahamut would both have to make it onto the roof—not an easy task in their current situation.

The shot blazing past her visor reminded Hephaestus that Cyber Geek wasn't going to aim forever; eventually, he'd pull the trigger. She had to minimize their ranged options for the escape. Plasmodia's power was internal, whereas Cyber Geek's could be taken away.

That made the choice for her. Hephaestus dove, Medley already scrambling to meet her. It was his turn to be too slow, as she took a shot from Cyber Geek in the left shoulder just before landing. Alarms blared, and she was notified that functionality in the arm was reduced by roughly thirty percent. He was getting pretty good with that rifle, stupid size or not.

Since it was so conveniently propped up on the ground, Hephaestus dropped the entirety of her weight and landed directly on the huge barrel. No doubt the fictional gun was meant to withstand a huge amount of damage; however, hundreds of pounds of metal slamming into a section with no support underneath was simply too much physics to be ignored. It snapped clean down the middle, turning back into blue sparks as it dissolved.

"This didn't have to be a fight." Looking down at him, Hephaestus saw something she wasn't prepared for: fear. Cyber Geek was afraid of her, and why not? She'd just injured him, stood momentarily against the New Science Sentries, and had now easily broken his go-to weapon. More interesting than that was that despite the fear he so plainly wore, Cyber Geek's hands were still glowing as he went for more items. Fear be damned. He wasn't giving up.

"Maybe not," Cyber Geek agreed. "But unless you're willing to surrender, I don't see it ending."

Rather than respond, Hephaestus whirled around, firing a shot from her left gauntlet into Medley's hip. Sneaking up on her in the middle of battle was one thing; she had no intention of letting him within swinging distance again. By the time she'd turned back, Cyber Geek had manifested a large green wrench with various runes on it.

"It's called the Wrecking Wrench, from *Clankbur's Junkyard Journey*. Nowhere near my best building tool, but it does triple damage to anything mechanical to help tear it apart." Apparently, Medley wasn't the only one sore over the last time—an item like that had obviously been planned for Hephaestus, or any other person wearing a meta-suit.

A huge explosion tore the night, stealing the attention of everyone in the strip mall parking lot. Further down the street, a car had detonated so aggressively that it flipped over and was now casting light from the roaring flames. Hephaestus might have been confused, save for the buzzing she'd paid such close attention to. It suddenly swelled in volume, her lone warning before the swarm fell upon them. Glyph must have snuck around to set something up, a starter pistol of sorts.

It was like a blanket of bugs covered the entire area. Cursing, swatting, even some yelps rang out as the clear night became hideously obscured. To Hephaestus, it was the sound of sweet escape, as she used the combo of distractions to leap back into the night. Briefly, she feared the bugs would clog her engine, but she quickly broke through them into the clear night air of the sky. Through the swirling insects, she could just make out Agent Quantum trying to chase Bahamut, even as her scales shifted from green to white.

Taking a cue out of Cyber Geek's tactics, Hephaestus fired off a few blasts, one searing Agent Quantum's shoulder. While it was nowhere near enough to stop him, the delay gave Bahamut room to escape, and once she'd flapped those white wings past the layer of bugs, Hephaestus set a course for the roof.

A few stray shots from Plasmodia rang out; however, she couldn't risk shooting any real power blindly, and even the few she dared quickly faded as more shouts came from within the bugs. Hephaestus and Bahamut both slammed down into the roof in short succession, grouping in next to Glyph and a loudly panting Pest Control. Calling up that many bugs in that short of time must have taken it out of him. They owed him a drink when this was over.

"Please tell me we're good to go." In that moment, her greatest fear was a guild order to keep distracting the capes. They'd managed this far thanks largely to surprise, an element of battle that was quickly fading. Much longer, and the whole team was as good as captured.

"Officially cleared. Things are wrapping up, anyway," Glyph reported, saving Pest Control the effort. "Everyone, get around me, now."

They all complied, laying hands on Glyph, just to be safe, as he pointed the wand downward and released the stored spell. In flaring purple light, a complex circle formed around all four, composed of runes and symbols Hephaestus had no frame of reference for. Magic was its own thing, and she didn't have to understand it to be thankful as the spell activated, tearing them all from the strip mall roof in Ebnerville.

Unlike with Presto's power, this was more akin to the whole world flashing purple, then looking different as a new scene faded into view. They were near Ridge City—Hephaestus could recognize the lights from here—

except, given the distance, they had to be at least half an hour's drive from downtown, if not more.

"With this spell, you have to set the teleportation point in advance," Glyph explained. He was stepping out of a matching circle to the one they'd left in, only this one was seared into the dirt. "It's possible to follow if someone had jumped into the circle with us, so I set it out in the middle of nowhere, just to be safe."

"Good call. Showing up with a cape at the guild would be bad for everyone—most of all the cape," Hephaestus agreed. "Where to now?"

"Nearest highway is three miles from here. That's where the guild car will meet us." Finally somewhat recovered, Pest Control got the words out, albeit breathily.

"We could fly," Bahamut suggested. She spread her large wings, illustrating the point.

"After tonight, I'm okay with keeping as low a profile as possible. At least until we're back at the guild." Hephaestus hitched an arm under Pest Control for support as they began walking down the dirt path.

A few seconds later, Bahamut took the other side with a freshly shifted green arm. In a way, it felt almost like their first training exercise, where Pest Control had crossed the finish line with a broken leg. If only that had been their night. Giant killer robots were a pain, but outside of surprise sentience, they didn't tend to hold grudges.

Capes, on the other hand, had far better memories, especially for the quarries who slipped away.

Chapter 62

Bloodbath didn't even begin to describe it. Chunks, viscera, tendons, perhaps a rogue finger here and there—those were the largest pieces the forensics team was finding as they combed through what could most accurately be called a cold flesh stew.

Standing above them, watching the proceedings with calculated indifference, Professor Quantum observed as the Ebnerville police worked, aided by several AHC resources. These were helpful for smaller towns not equipped to deal with such catastrophes and were able to respond faster than any government agency could hope to. Of course, since the resources belonged to the Alliance of Heroic Champions, any information uncovered in the aftermath would also flow directly to them. Whatever the cost of this nicety, it had paid for itself thousands of times over already in useful data.

Tonight, he feared, would be an exception to that rule. When he'd heard his team had faced combat, Professor Quantum knew he had to witness the scene. He'd been expecting another move from his unseen adversary, perhaps more merchandise from the past, but merely being a superhero came with its own conflicts. In this case, it hadn't been related to a lingering grudge, or not one aimed toward Professor Quantum, anyway. Worse, this was clearly guild work; the utter lack of evidence confirmed that the longer the scene was searched. Professor Quantum had already suspected as much, once he arrived on scene and got the full debrief.

The suit and dragon were newer recruits; he'd skimmed the files and therefore, his brain could easily recall such details. They'd been linked to the museum heist, which Apollo had conjectured to be a training mission for new villains. It seemed the training wheels were now off, if they'd been able to last against his team. Some of that might have been to blame on Lodestar and her soft methods. When he'd sent them from Vomisa, they were a fine-tuned battle engine, capable of handling threats even beyond their actual powers. The advocacy of softness had, quite expectedly, weakened them. A necessary sacrifice to keep the AHC at large appeased, but one that he would have to minimize the impact of.

Between the low-level lackeys playing lookout and the absolute decimation on the scene, there was little need to even call this speculation. Someone had wronged the guild, and they'd responded. Were Lodestar here, there would have been hand-wringing for the ones they couldn't save, whereas Professor Quantum didn't especially care. If any of these had the potential to be worthy test subjects, they'd have survived, so it was no great loss.

The larger issue was that the New Science Sentries had taken a defeat. By his standards, if not the AHC's. Such errors were unacceptable, especially considering they'd been facing off with a pair of villain rookies. Between their numbers and training, it should have been effortless. These were not the results he'd invested so much time into that team to reap. They were going to have to step up, and soon; otherwise, he'd be forced to move on to his contingency plans.

A team wasn't set in stone, after all, and there were plenty of other candidates back on Vomisa. If they couldn't pull together, then he'd simply tear the configuration apart and try again, as many times as it took, to create a proper team of successors. He would not allow the name of Science Sentries to be dragged down by their ineptitude. Not after all the work that had gone into establishing it.

Professor Quantum turned away from the scene, hand on his phone, the next task already on his mind.

With the program finally running, Tori fell back into a sitting position, sighing in relief. The walk back to the highway hadn't been a fun one, nor was waiting until the coast was clear to load everyone in to a guild SUV. After that, things got easier. It was just a drive to the country club and a hop through the portal to get back to the guild's volcano lair and, by extension, her spare room.

Pausing only long enough for a shower, Tori's first task was running diagnostics on the Hephaestus suit. It had taken some finagling to get the laptop cord connected—the port had been slightly warped during the battle—but with the diagnostics now flashing on-screen, Tori could check the damage her creation had sustained. All things considered, it had held up well. However, from what she was already seeing, there weren't a lot of hits left for it to take. Another good shot and something critical might have gone offline. With ease of movement becoming less of an issue, it was time to move on to defense.

While her current suit had been redesigned and tweaked, she'd been using the same base components as much as possible. It was her habit, as a thief and a scrounger, plus it helped to keep the costs in check. Looking over the claw marks Medley had managed to leave in a shoulder plate, it was evident that her armor was in need of an upgrade. Last time, she'd used metals that were high quality, but also mundane. To tangle with metas, the suit had to be able to withstand more damage. Energy shields ate power, most of which she was directing toward mobility and offense. Changing the base material would be the fix that required the least amount of work to keep up, but also the most effort up front. Tori would have to actually invent or steal a meta-alloy to make her suit out of one.

That was a long-term concern; the more immediate issue was getting her suit up and running again. She didn't have plans to take Hephaestus out again anytime soon, yet Tori didn't feel quite right with her armor temporarily out of commission. When it was down, she lacked the choice to be Hephaestus, and that rubbed against her brain wrong for reasons that Tori couldn't fully articulate.

Repairs would be extensive, and also would have to wait for another day. With diagnostics running, she couldn't do much, so Tori departed her room and headed down to the lounge on her floor. Doctor Mechaniacal hadn't changed much about the guild's overall layout style; everyone was largely able to navigate easily, even with the new locations that had been added. Part of that consistency included communal areas on every floor where residents could spend time together. Tori noted that once again, she and the other rookies were largely on their own, though that probably wouldn't last forever. She'd easily counted that there were far more rooms on this floor than were currently being used.

Upon entering, Tori's plans for a simple snack were dashed, as she came upon Warren, Lance, and Beverly, all sans costumes and identities, rooting through the shared fridge. "Whoever stocks this really goes all out. Beers, ciders, sodas—what'll it be?" Lance's meaty arm was shoved halfway into the chilly white box, like it was trying to swallow him whole, only to choke on his wide shoulders.

"I suppose tonight has earned an indulgence. I'll try one of those ciders, please." Warren accepted the can he was given, turning it over a few times in his hand.

Beverly reached in over Lance, grabbing a lager as well as a stout. "More of a wine person, but I've knocked back a few in my day. Tori, I got you." With casual ease, Beverly tossed the stout, which Tori caught easily. After the evening's events, everything felt heightened, right down to her reflexes, though eventually, they'd all crash hard. At least tomorrow was Sunday—no work and hopefully no neighbors.

At the thought of the New Science Sentries, Tori inwardly winced. They definitely hadn't been part of tonight's plan, and a piece of her felt awkward about the idea of seeing them again. That was silly, though, she reminded herself. The capes hadn't dealt with Tori or Beverly tonight. They'd only fought Hephaestus and Bahamut, beings entirely unrelated to the women they shared a building with.

Cracking open her beer, Tori swigged down a sip, saying a silent toast to Ivan and his insistence that she maintain a secret identity. This evening had made her grateful all over again for the distance between Hephaestus and Tori.

Shifting the ice pack elicited a fresh wave of pain, followed by merciful relief. The Alliance of Heroic Champions had many high-tech treatment options for capes who were injured in the field, from basic medical supplies all the way up to a few metas who could actually repair flesh within moments. As with most services, however, priority was determined by need. On a Saturday night, there were superheroes who required the advanced treatments for injuries far worse than a broken nose.

Donald made no complaints as he waited, sitting on a plastic-lined chair with a rag and an ice pack to handle his injury. Even being here felt ridiculous; except, waiting for the nose to heal naturally would leave a big bright target on his face for everyone they fought. Keeping the injury and being less effective was a folly of pride, something Donald couldn't allow to be more important than the job.

Given that this was the waiting area for low-priority treatments, Donald was more or less alone, with only the occasional attendant stepping in to check on him. When the door opened, that's who he assumed it was, until he caught sight of a familiar blue costume. Rather than go for a rag, Tachyonic had elected to stuff tissues into both his nostrils, a bit of red seeping into view on the white material.

The two met eyes in a shared moment of uncertainty. Despite spending a week together, they were on rough terms; no one outside of Cyber Geek and Agent Quantum had really connected on either team. Tachyonic ultimately made the move, as he was the one still walking. He strode confidently over and took a seat near Donald, without being directly next to him.

"So... that sucked." It was a surprise; those were not the words he'd expected to come out of Tachyonic's mouth, especially not accompanied by a touch of smirk. "You've fought those two before?"

"Sort of. I chased the dragon, Bahamut, while Medley squared off with Hephaestus. They got away that time, too."

"Don't sweat it too much. You're not the one who'll be blamed for this one." Tachyonic's left hand absentmindedly rubbed the empty right spot on his forearm, where a silver bracer would normally be attached. "Between losing the targets and getting exposed, I'm taking the heat for this, which I deserve."

Donald was unexpectedly torn. He wanted to ask what Tachyonic meant by "getting exposed," but wasn't quite sure it had been intended as a conversation option, or if he and Tachyonic were close enough to pose such a question. In the end, his eyes did the asking for him, as Tachyonic realized he was rubbing his arm and caught Donald's stare.

"I'm fast on my own. Could make a go at it as a cape and probably do okay. But to be on the New Science Sentries, okay isn't enough." Tachyonic tapped the empty space on his arm. "Setlium is stored in devices all along the suit, flooding my cells with extra energy. I'm able to absorb it, thus augmenting my speed. But the bracer is necessary for control, which Hephaestus figured out and broke, resulting in my suit and energy dispersal going haywire."

"Hope you've got spares," Donald replied. It was a tad flippant, but apparently struck the right chord as Tachyonic chuckled.

He nodded, though the look in his eyes didn't seem so optimistic. "Professor Quantum builds for contingencies, so I've got plenty stowed in various places. The bigger issue is that my secret is exposed. A criminal just figured out my biggest weakness, which means, in no time, everyone will know. Won't matter in every fight, but for the right enemy, that's a big opportunity."

Given the general malaise that had settled on Tachyonic after the brief chuckle, Donald decided it was time to steer the conversation elsewhere. "Sorry if this is rude, Tachyonic, just have to wonder, given our circumstances, is that why you're here for treatment? I thought super-speed caused fast healing."

"Fast, sure; good, no," Tachyonic explained. "The bones already set wrong, so I need to go have it aligned properly. What really smarts is getting whacked there a week after Lodestar did it and told me to keep my guard up."

"I get it. Kind of surprised Professor Quantum hasn't made you some sort of shielding or healing devices, though."

Tachyonic shook his head. "Are you kidding me? No way he'd do something like that." Pulling himself up straight, Tachyonic affected an annoyed, weary expression paired with a stiff voice. "Pain is a teacher. Cut his lessons short at your own peril."

It took a moment, but Donald realized he'd been doing a Professor Quantum impression, and not a bad one, at that. "I take it life's not all that easy being on a legacy team."

"Being Tachyonic is something I spent my whole life working toward, and there are still days I've nearly quit." He paused, looking over the semi-costume he was still wearing, a more casual version that hung loose at the collar and sleeves. "Also, call me Kyle. We're on the same side, and as of tonight, we've now fought together. Feels like we're probably to the point of first names, don't you think?"

"I appreciate that, Kyle. I'm Donald when out of costume, not that it's a secret."

"That seems like the life—not having to hide anything. We're taking a run at the secret identities and barely getting by. Makes you wonder how so many of the crooks pull it off."

Even if Kyle didn't say it, Donald knew where both of their minds were turning. "Wondering who's under that black armored helmet, huh?"

Tenderly, Kyle ran a finger along the bridge of his nose, wincing as he did. "Let's just say that next time, I'll be highly motivated to take Hephaestus down and rip off that mask."

Raising a fist, Donald offered a bump, which Kyle accepted. "When that day comes, give me a call, and we'll be there to help. My team is now down by two against that pair. I'd love a chance to even the score."

"Sounds like Hephaestus better watch his ass," Kyle said. "He's got some serious superheroes hunting for him as of now."

Chapter 63

"Absolutely inexcusable. Not only did you fail to arrive on the scene of a large-scale meta-battle, the very sort of incident where you could have turned your reputation around, you missed that opportunity because you were *losing* to a pair of villains. Rookie villains. That is despite having superior numbers and power, mind you. On top of all that, Tachyonic allowed his setlium dispersal control to be broken, compromising him both tonight and for the rest of his career. Do you have any sort of defense to offer up?"

Agent Quantum stood resolute as the tirade washed over him. There were objections he could offer, pointing out that at worst, the night had been a draw. He already knew the reply: if the crooks escaped, then it was a loss by Science Sentry standards. Had he drawn attention to the fact that his team was being careful with escalation, he'd only have to explain why they'd chosen such a tactic in the first place, and there were no happy endings to be found down that path. Instead, he waited until the silence finally loomed, then spoke with his head held low.

"I do not. We made tactical mistakes that led to the escape of our targets. Had we realized they were guild-affiliated in the moment, we'd have taken them more seriously, but we didn't, and that was our error. *My* error, as team lead, and I'll accept the consequences."

The stare from Professor Quantum was harsh, but short. He didn't have the energy to spare on lingering emotions. With Agent Quantum showing proper remorse and respect, the best option was to move forward.

"I'm glad to hear you at least understand your failings. After getting the full report, I'm starting to see where the team's issues lie. Come Monday, Tachyonic will be sent back to Vomisa for additional training. Some of our backups have been progressing nicely. I'll make a new selection that properly complements the dynamic. Go inform Tachyonic to prepare his things."

Professor Quantum took a seat at his desk, expecting Agent Quantum to simply leave the office now that the discussion was over. Instead, he looked up to find the team leader still standing there. Unlike before, there was something resolute in his eyes.

"I refuse."

"Excuse me?"

The young man was nervous, yet did a respectable job of keeping it tamped down, just as he'd been taught. "Tachyonic is my closest friend. He shoulders a sizable amount of responsibility on the team. Removing him over one mistake would only leave us more vulnerable than we already are. It's not a decision I can support."

"Agent Quantum, perhaps you've become addled by the accolades, but you don't actually control your team's makeup. That is my prerogative, and I say Tachyonic is done."

"Then you can send me back, too." No give, not even a flicker. Had he come in prepared for this?

Rising slowly, Professor Quantum gave the boy a few iotas of actual attention. Unbending, loyal, determined, Agent Quantum had all the traits Professor Quantum had seen the crowds flock to over the years. Yet instead of loving him, they merely accepted him—and worse, those same qualities were now causing complications. Had this rebellion come a year prior, the entire team may have been tossed out, but things were different now. The team was public, working with Professor Quantum's seal of approval. Taking one member out due to "injury" was manageable. Losing a team lead was another matter.

"Explain yourself."

A quick nod, then Agent Quantum replied. "Figurehead or not behind the scenes, I'm the leader of this team in the field. I'm not going to cover for someone if they go on a killing spree; however, I won't leave my people hung out to dry for doing their best. If Tachyonic's failure represents anything, it's a lack of planning and leadership. Whatever his penalty, I'll pay it as well. I'm not going to live up to the Science Sentries' legend without my team's support, and they have to know I've got their backs, no matter what."

There had been stronger options for Agent Quantum. Not many, this one was well among the best; however, he wasn't the absolute most powerful in combat. Nor was he the most tactically sound. Some of the weaker candidates had developed mentally to compensate for their failings. It was that attitude that had won him the role, ultimately. Raising the name of the Science Sentries wasn't purely about being the most efficient superhero—hell, they'd actually had to stop Lodestar from doing that when humanity started to grow dependent. No, this was about PR as much as it was the actual saving, and on that front, Agent Quantum had something none of the other candidates could match.

Sincerity. Genuine concern for the people he was helping and love for the job, the sorts of things the public seemed to sniff out. Bad openings or not, with enough time in front of a camera, Agent Quantum was going to win hearts just by being himself. Tachyonic's presence wasn't likely to substantially impede the team, whereas losing Agent Quantum might leave the whole project dead in the water.

Perhaps Tachyonic would make a better collar than sacrifice.

"You want to take responsibility for him, that means whatever comes next is on you. Show me that the team *does* still work in its current composition. Win the people, stop the crimes, and do *not* permit another criminal to escape. I don't care if you want to play tiddlywinks with muggers and vandals: when you face real opponents, do what you were trained for. Take them *down*."

Not quite so sure this time, there was worry on his face, even as Agent Quantum agreed. "Yes, sir. We'll work hard to show you this wasn't a mistake."

"Let's hope so. Because I do not make the same error twice." Professor Quantum settled down to his desk once more. "You're dismissed, Version Nineteen. I don't care if you tell the others about this conversation or not, just make sure they understand you're out of slack. From this point on, failure will not be tolerated."

"Understood." Agent Quantum turned and left the room, shutting the door softly behind him. All that, and not even a slam. For as much distance as lay between Professor and Agent Quantum, they also had more similarities than the latter realized. That was for the best, though. Such notions only led to attachment, and this was not the right career for that kind of sentiment.

The graves for most of the original Science Sentries, and the multitude of capes who'd fallen since, were all the supporting evidence that hypothesis demanded.

Ivan lowered the phone from his ear, innocuous code phrase already fading. The words had been some fake solicitor offering him a hell of a bargain on used copy machines, whereas the message was quite concise: the traitor was dead. Endless Blitz, once a member of their guild, had been slain tonight.

It wasn't easy, hunting and killing their own, yet it was infinitely easier than managing the guild's defectors if they thought rebellion came without punishment. Another night, it might have been Pseudonym out there, carving carnage out of the betrayer's flesh. Having the kids this weekend had spared him from even the request, though in truth, Ivan would have preferred a hundred bloody battles to the thick tension choking the air in his townhome.

Ever since that morning with Rick, things had been awkward. Better, but still awkward. Whether this was a prelude of things to come or a bump in the road, Ivan had no idea. That would be Rick's call to make, in the end. The most Ivan could offer was the truth when asked, and reassurance that no amount of the past changed where things stood in the present.

He was tempted to touch base with Tori, but that could wait until Monday. Since he'd gotten updates about her team by request, he already knew they were back at the guild safely. That one required a lot less confirmation than making sure they'd killed the right Endless Blitz; the message of Tori's return had come quite a while ago. No need for her to know he was keeping tabs, even if she probably suspected it.

"Dad?" He turned to find Beth standing in the doorway of the stairs, looking confused. Ivan truly had been lost in thought to not even notice her footsteps, soft as they were. "Why are you still up?"

"It is Saturday, isn't it? This is when all the dads stay up for our secret meetings, planning outfits for the coming week to maximize embarrassment, swapping jokes, comparing notes… general dad stuff."

Wiping the sleep from her eyes, Beth barely stifled a yawn as she went to the fridge, pulling out a bottle of water. Originally, she'd had cups by the bed, but once they realized what an active sleeper she was, Ivan and Janet had switched her to bottles. It minimized the amount of electrical shorts her alarm clocks would have to endure.

"Is it because you and Rick are fighting?" She walked up to him, smashing roughly against his legs with a hug in half-slumbering state. No fear, no hesitation, just embrace. Ivan savored it, more aware tonight than ever of just how limited these exchanges might be.

"We're not fighting," Ivan corrected. "Rick is just coming to terms with new things, sorting out how he feels about them."

Guiding Beth with him, Ivan walked over to the couch, where she quickly snuggled up against his side, pausing only long enough to take a mighty sip from her water. "You're up this late because you and Rick *aren't* fighting?"

Overall, Ivan was deeply grateful that the children took more after Janet than him. That said, there were days when he could have done with them having a tad less of her intelligence and keen observation skills.

"Part of growing up is learning new information about things you thought you already understood," Ivan explained. "It isn't always pleasant, and I wish Rick wasn't having to go through that right now." Absentmindedly, he stroked the top of Beth's skull, just like when she was smaller. A few more years, and this too would be a memory. Time truly was a relentless bastard.

"He'll be okay. Rick's grumpy, but also smart and fearless."

"Fearless?" Ivan loved his son dearly, but that was not the first word that jumped to mind when he thought of him.

Another yawn, this one stretching on for several seconds. "When the school came down, and that metal-person showed up, Rick tried to protect me, throwing books and stuff. He stood between us, even though I was covered in blades."

It was strange to consider Hephaestus from an outsider's perspective. While Ivan knew she'd been there to help, to strangers, it must have seemed like she was mounting an attack on the school. The dark armor, the burning jets, and yet Rick had still refused to yield his ground.

While he'd never admit it, for a moment, Ivan wondered if perhaps these fascinating children took more after him than he realized. The important part was that Beth was right. Rick was a good man. Whether that meant Ivan would be forgiven, or even have a relationship going forward with his son, he truly had no idea. But as a father, Ivan had helped to raise the kind of person who stood between someone they loved and a potential killer.

If they never spoke again, Ivan would continue being proud of who his son had become. He'd helped Rick grow into a good, dependable, loyal person. What father had the right to ask, or hope, for more than that?

Soft snores from Beth betrayed that she'd lost the inevitable battle. Gently, like he was holding the most precious gem in the world, Ivan lifted her from the couch, bottle still clutched tightly in her hand. Nearly a teenager, and still small for her age. It wouldn't be long before she was having the same revelations as Rick. How would it feel, to see that same fear reflected in his daughter's eyes?

Ivan put the thought from his head. No need to delve into theoretical tortures when he was already living through a real version. Depositing a brief kiss on her forehead, Ivan walked Beth back upstairs to tuck her into bed.

Once she was down, he paused outside of Rick's room, pushing the door carefully open.

Asleep, as he well should be this late at night, Rick looked downright peaceful, an expression Ivan felt he hadn't seen on his son's face in years. Such was the curse of teenagers. In that serene face, Ivan could trace sixteen years' worth of experiences and memories. He could still remember when it was pinched and squealing, being handed off to him by a nervous Janet under the watchful eyes of the Rookstone guards.

That had been right before they went to face Orion, a special visit arranged by Lodestar. The cynic in him said it was because she'd wanted him motivated, fighting with everything on the line. That was why he and most of his ilk would have done it, though. To Lodestar, it was a chance to let him meet his son for the first and likely last time. A picture had gotten him to join. Holding Rick that day... Ivan had learned just what he was truly capable of.

Shutting the door softly, he slipped down the hall. Too many memories were stirred up, flashes of his childhood showing up as well. It was time to call it a night, now that he knew everyone was back safely. There would be fallout from this; the big scenes always drummed up concern, and he'd need to be on game for the week ahead.

Especially considering next weekend he'd be out in the woods, camping with Lodestar.

Chapter 64

"So, the purpose of the nozzle's extension—"

"It doesn't matter what the purpose is. I'm telling you, that thing is way too bulky to be any kind of compact mirror." Beverly held the aerosolization prototype in her hands, gesturing wilding, making Tori wince slightly whenever it neared the edge of the table. She hadn't exactly worked on durability just yet. "You either have to shrink it, or find a different product to serve as camouflage."

A small shriek from the kitchen interrupted them as Chloe was splashed by grease from the pan. After the Saturday they'd been through, it had been nice to spend Sunday relaxing around the apartment. Between the sleeping in and the last few hours tooling around in her lab, Tori was feeling especially refreshed, though the current conversation was draining her fast. She'd been optimistic about integrating the unit into a compact, a notion Beverly seemed intent on disabusing her of.

"Not a hand-mirror then, okay. Wallet?"

"Wallet's not bad, in theory," Beverly agreed. "If you were getting mugged, they'd ask you to take it out anyway, so it's easy to get your hands on. But this thing is a brick. I don't see people lugging it around all the time the way you have to with a wallet."

"Plus, it wouldn't have helped much with your kidnapping." Chloe slid a charred husk of a flauta from the pan into the trash, adding a fresh one to a now lower-temperature oil. She'd been experimenting with recipes online this morning. So far, this was shaping up about as disastrously as her prior efforts.

Beverly frowned, looking over the item again. "She's right. That's sort of the problem with all major self-defense items. You need to be able to get your hands on them in time, meaning you have to already be aware of danger in advance, or get an opportunity to rummage through your purse. Neither is consistently achievable."

While Tori preferred the storage capacity of a backpack to a purse, she did own a few of the items for more formal occasions. She hadn't had one on the day in question, so she'd never pictured digging through such an item, but as she replayed the battle in her mind, it was clear there had been no such opening to do so. Beverly was right. The way these devices were most useful was if it was in the victim's hand already. And to Tori's thinking, they'd just hit on a very simple way to achieve that.

"Then what if we built these into the purses themselves?" Tori mimed through the air with her hands, drawing the general shape of a handbag. "I can run the wiring up through the handles, create a pair of switches that have to be pressed in unison to prevent misfires, and have the aerosolized deterrent shoot out whichever side we designate for the front. Always in hand, easy to aim, completely non-suspicious—it would even minimize potential chemical blowback."

Beverly turned the device around once more, no longer looking quite so skeptical. "That could work. Plenty of purses have more heft than this, and you'd be able to fit it into almost anything bigger than a clutch. We'd have to find a way to tell at a glance which way to aim it, ideally without giving away what you're really holding." Her gaze drifted off, lost in a flurry of new ideas. It was an expression Tori was intimately familiar with, though she rarely got to see it on others' faces. "Yeah, I might be able to put something together. It'll be rough if you want it fast, though."

"That's not exactly my most polished work, either." Tori nodded to her device, proud as she was of it. "Right now, the goal is to show potential. Refinement comes after we prove it works."

"I'm going to remind you of that when I bust out my first version and you start coming in with notes about thread, design, and—"

The sudden knock made both of them jump, and the flurry of fresh grease pops from the pan meant Chloe had knocked around her current attempt as well. All three looked at each other, the collective mind of the apartment trying to figure out if they had any plans for the day. When no one offered up an explanation, Tori rose from her chair.

"If it's a salesman, I'm throwing that grease on him," Tori muttered as she stalked across the room. Before opening the door, she checked to be certain Beverly had tucked the device out of view, then yanked it open.

For a moment, she almost flinched at the sight of Agent Quantum, memories from the prior night's battle rearing up in her mind. Except it wasn't Agent Quantum at the door, it was Austin. No costume adorned his body to mark that he was on the job. Even if it had been, he didn't know he'd recently squared off with two-thirds of the apartment's occupants.

That much was proven seconds later by his friendly greeting. "Evening, neighbors. How's the weekend been treating you?"

"Drugs, sex, devil worship—you know. The usual. How's cape-life?" Without knowing why he was here, all Tori could do was keep things light and hope he'd spill it soon. This was not a situation where she wanted to start guessing.

"Been better. We had a rough one last night—part of why I'm here, actually." Austin pointed upward, either to Heaven or the roof, or theoretically both, depending on one's particular love of rooftops. "It was such a shit night, we decided to blow off a little steam. We're throwing a small party on top of the building tonight. Very small. More of a get-together, really, but there will be food, drinks, and music, so I've been assured it counts as a party."

Tori looked back into the apartment, finding the response warm to neutral. Chloe was still more interested in her cooking practice, and Beverly gave a soft "Why not?" shrug. Having just come to blows with most of the team, Tori wasn't especially feeling the desire to be social; however, that only made the paranoid part of her brain insist it was all the more necessary to do. Anything that might tip them off to the connection had to be avoided at all costs. Although, even she could admit that might be taking the fear a bit far.

"It sounds like a great time, but Sunday night is kind of a tough one, schedule wise."

Austin nodded, yet looked undeterred. "I promise, we won't keep you up too late. And I haven't even told you the best part. Guess who the other guests are?"

"I mean, it has to be more capes, right? Those are kind of the only people you know in town."

"Well, yes, though it's the who in particular that's notable." Austin leaned in slightly, as if this was the part that had to be hidden from the walls' prying ears. "Your friend Donald and his team are going to join us. A week together, and we were barely on speaking terms, but there's nothing like shared combat to put differences in perspective. I do understand if you three can't come, just wanted to extend the offer. We probably wouldn't be on these better terms without your help."

That complicated matters. Ducking the New Science Sentries was one thing. Avoiding a friend she hadn't gotten to hang out with in a while was another, far more suspicious matter. There were ways out, excuses she could use to get free, but they would all leave a lingering patina of doubt in people's minds or risk hurting a friend's feelings.

"Long as you aren't offended when I have to turn in for work in the morning, I bet we can swing by. What time does it start?"

"We told the others to be here in about an hour, although Ike and Kyle have already been hauling coolers and decorations up to the roof," Austin informed her.

From deeper in the apartment, Beverly's voice piped up. "Decorations? I thought it was just a get-together."

A ripple of panic seemed to wash over Austin, brief but unmistakable. He recovered in moments, raising his own voice without treading near an actual yell. "It's our first one in Ridge City. First one anywhere outside of home, actually. We wanted to have some fun with it."

"Count me in. My curiosity is officially piqued," Beverly called.

"Me too. I'll need some dinner. Looks like this recipe is going to take more practice." Chloe tossed the smoking remains of another flauta into the trash, tying off the bag to prevent the smell from escaping.

Austin's enthusiasm ratcheted up by several degrees, and Tori didn't think it had much to do with Chloe joining in. He offered up a big grin and two thumbs, both locked in the "up" position. "Phenomenal. I'll let the others know, and we'll see you three soon."

Tori shut the door once he started walking away, mouthing the word "fuck" as loudly as she dared. After the fight, all she wanted was to spend some time being a normal person—well, normal secret-lab-having inventor, anyway. Now, she was going to spend the evening around the people she and Beverly had traded blows with less than twenty-four hours prior.

It was a good thing Austin had said there would be booze. Tori was definitely going to need a few drinks to make it through this one.

In the streets of Ottawa, children dove into the piles of candy like rich cartoon ducks swimming through a vault of gold. Lying broken in half were the two sides of the giant, tree-shaped piñata, split down the middle by a mighty blow from Rumblejack. The hometown hero was out with the masses, helping direct crowds and traffic amidst the sudden storm of candy coating the streets.

Standing atop a building, watching it all, was *not* a man with kaleidoscope eyes. This one had quite normal brown irises, though his ensemble was certainly more eclectic. Aviator hat and goggles, billowing purple scarf, a pirate-like ruffled shirt, and polka dot pants formed the foundation of his outfit, on top of which were piled a shifting array of accessories. On this occasion, he sported an earring with a three-foot-long peacock feather dangling from his left ear.

There was no warning before the landing; she came in fast. Her actual approach was slower, however, as she cut a casual pace to the edge where he was watching. Once she arrived, he gave a very small nod of greeting. "Lodestar."

"Captain Bullshit," she replied. Taking a long look over the edge, Lodestar surveyed the scene. "Still teaching people to expect the unexpected, I see."

"It is the burden of many lifetimes. I simply do my part." He never really turned to her, his attention locked on the exhibition he'd painstakingly created below.

"By blocking traffic for miles and causing general disarray." Lodestar pointed to the long line of lights stretching out into the distance, all caused by the unexpected appearance of a skyscraper-sized pinata and its subsequent destruction.

Captain Bullshit adjusted his goggles slightly; otherwise, he seemed unaffected by the accusation. "It's a break in the routine, a crack in the mundane, a chance for people's lives to take unpredicted turns. Have you come to try and take me back for offering them this opportunity?"

"I obviously should. This is disturbing the peace at a very bare minimum. The problem is we both know that capturing you is almost impossible, and holding you against your will actually *is* impossible. Right now, the AHC is stretched thin. Trying to take down a reality-warper of your level would be dangerous, to both us and the surrounding area."

"Shall I take it that you concede?" Captain Bullshit shifted slightly, only to find Lodestar directly next to him. He'd never heard a peep or felt so much as a whiff in the wind. Powerful though he was, she couldn't be brushed aside.

She nodded down to the street, where the kids were still stuffing their faces with sweets. "Not in the slightest. This sort of stuff, I can live with. It's far from ideal, but nobody got hurt. Nowhere near worth the death toll from trying to take you down. Don't change that equation. Don't become a danger I have to stop. You know where you overstepped last time. Count your years in Rookstone as time served and please don't make the same mistakes again."

At first, she thought he would ignore her, but eventually, Captain Bullshit bobbed his head ever so slightly. "Bound as I am by the direction of the art, I can acknowledge that hurting people in the displays lessens the audience who receives the message as a whole."

While it wasn't a firm commitment to not injure civilians, it was something. Given that Lodestar was dealing with someone whose power to manipulate reality functioned on a planet-wide scale, this was the best outcome she could hope for. Captain Bullshit wouldn't be stopped easily; she'd only managed to get him into Rookstone through a tactic that wouldn't work twice. Until they found a way to seal his abilities, it was better to have an occasional nuisance pester the world than have an entire nation be changed into a smoking crater, or worse.

"I appreciate it," she said. Lodestar almost took back to the sky, but decided instead to knock out one last question, considering the opportunity. "Since we're both here, I've been wondering about something. We aren't finding any of the criminals who escaped from Rookstone. It's like they vanished. No amount of tech or magic can get us a location. Would you happen to know anything about that?"

For the first time, Lodestar's words produced a real reaction, a wide grin that brightened Captain Bullshit's face considerably. "A gift, to them, and to the capes."

"How is hiding them a gift for us?"

The smile only grew bigger. "What glory is there in scooping them up when they are freshly released and weakened? This gives them the chance to recover, grow stronger, offer up a proper challenge to the Alliance of Heroic Champions. You'd have been little more than animal control wrangling escaped beasts. Now, you'll have the chance to show the world *your* art once more. I imagine we will be in for glorious displays, once they begin to act in earnest."

That more or less confirmed her suspicions, as well as hinting that Captain Bullshit's protection might fade once the escapees got active. Annoyed as she was by the whole ordeal, Lodestar still forced a polite tone into her voice as she said her farewell. "Really wish you wouldn't have, but I appreciate the heads up. Remember what we talked about, for everyone's sake. I much prefer these cordial visits."

She flew off into the sky, her light slowly fading, leaving Captain Bullshit continuing to assess his handiwork. He watched her go, saddened by the spectacle. So much power, yet only the barest amount was ever allowed to shine through. One day, he would set a proper stage for her, give the art a genuine outlet. That would be an ambitious project for another time, however.

For now, he had years of ideas ready to be unleashed, most of which wouldn't even violate Lodestar's rule. As for the ones that did, he'd worry about those when he got to them. It wasn't like he was in a hurry. Captain Bullshit was free, and the world was his canvas. After years in prison, he planned to savor the smaller projects before stirring up any real trouble.

He couldn't risk being rusty once the true art began.

Chapter 65

Given the choice between navigating the social minefield of a party with two sets of capes she'd been fighting the night prior, or going through guild initiation training again, Tori easily would have suited up for another day of chasing robots with metal orbs inside. Sadly, no one was offering her such an option, which meant she had to step out onto the rooftop with Chloe and Beverly, officially joining the New Science Sentries' soiree.

The "decorations" that had been promised were sets of lights running between every remotely elevated point to and fro, creating a twinkling, overhead spiderweb. There were smaller touches, as well—a plant here, a tiki statue there—but it was still a level of decor meant to be broken down when the night was through. Featured prominently in the center was a large barbecue pit from which smoke was already rising, tinged with the mouthwatering scent of something roasting. Next to it were two coolers, one of which was open as the thick-fingered form of Ren pulled a pair of beers from the ice.

Like everyone else on the rooftop, he looked human, though in his case, Tori suspected trickery was afoot; she'd realized since their first meeting that he was really Medley. Tonight, his appearance was slightly more formal, with a collared shirt squeezing tightly around his robust form. Illusion, hologram, or full-on magic, all that bulk of Medley's still had to be accounted for.

While she'd never seen them out of mask, the duo talking to Donald and Austin had to be Hat Trick and Cold Shoulder, by process of elimination.

Also, it wasn't especially hard to guess when seeing them alongside the rest of their team. Both were dressed slightly upscale, like they were going to a corporate cocktail hour. It made Tori glad she'd allowed Beverly to bully her into a blouse instead of an old t-shirt, along with a smattering of makeup. The goal was to minimize standing out, and fitting into the scene helped to make that easier.

"Pardon us, got some more supplies for the shindig." Kyle's voice caused Tori to jump aside, clearing the rooftop entrance for him, Ellie, and Ike, all arriving with armfuls of accoutrement. Chips, plates, cups, ice, all the party essentials outside of actual refreshments.

Beverly reached out to help, but her hand closed on empty air as Ike vanished, reappearing next to a table covered by a bright blue tablecloth. "Speak for yourself. Some of us just needed line of sight. So lazy, this one. No wonder we have to keep on him."

Ellie was already stalking toward him, the look on her face all the warning Ike needed to dart out of her path.

Muttering under his breath, Kyle blurred momentarily, depositing his burden onto the table and arranging it neatly before reappearing at Tori's side only a few seconds later. This wasn't nearly as fast as Tachyonic moved, however, a detail that Tori couldn't help but note. How much was the difference with and without the suit, she wondered. And did he have a backup bracer? For the first time, it occurred to Tori she might have taken him out of the field entirely until his tech was back up and running. Even more oddly, that didn't sit quite right in her stomach. There wasn't time to process the issue, as Kyle greeted her with the standard stiff half-hug of neither full friends nor casual acquaintances.

"Glad you three could make it. After last night, we all needed to blow off some steam. Wouldn't be the same without our neighbors."

"It's a nice gesture, especially for someone you're just assigned to bodyguard." Tori didn't really expect this to work, but it was important to at least try to keep some distance between her and the New Science Sentries.

To her surprise, Kyle managed an actual laugh. Had losing a fight made him less uptight? Now that was an unexpected side effect. "I guess you're not wrong, but honestly, at this point, you're also the only friends we've really made in this town. But hey, maybe things are turning around on that front." His attention was on Donald and the others, who were looking over as well thanks to the flurry of activity.

Finally noticing her arrival, Donald broke off from his conversation, walking over to embrace Tori warmly. She returned the gesture. It was nice to see him again outside of capes, masks, and kidnapping. When they broke apart, Tori thought she saw Kyle staring, though, when she looked closer, he appeared to be looking past them, at the barbecue.

"Well, well, well, the great superhero finally has time to see his friends from the cubicle days. Let me guess, you want to know if Barb is still pushing for Popcorn Fridays, or if Mustache Stan ever took the hint about microwaving fish."

"All of it, all of it and more. Don't you dare skip over the detailed minutes from the last monthly status meeting."

Tori chuckled, even as the others stared in confusion. Running office jokes didn't tend to actually be funny; they were more comforting, a constant one could depend upon. In that brief exchange, Tori saw a flash of the old Donald, before the weight of superpowers and the duty they entailed had been yoked around his shoulders. Pleasant though the glimpse was, Tori brought them back to the present. "You know, everyone is really proud of you. When your team does something big, it gets brought up in meetings; Barb even has a 'Cyber Geek's Greatest Hits' wall where she posts news clippings."

The words hit heavier than she'd expected. Donald almost seemed to have the breath drop out of him. "That's... unexpected. Your uncle mentioned there was some support the last time we spoke. I never imagined it would be that much. When I was around after the change, most of them seemed so uncomfortable, not sure of how to act around me."

"People don't always respond to change well, or quickly," Beverly interjected. "Obviously doesn't hurt that now they're seeing you out there all the time, helping innocents and saving the day." She patted him once on the shoulder, then wandered over to the coolers with Chloe close behind.

Since Donald still seemed momentarily taken aback, Kyle jumped on the opportunity to join the conversation. "It sounds like you work with your uncle? That's got to be an interesting experience."

Every single warning light in Tori's brain flashed like a nuclear launch had just been announced. Of all the fucking things to mention, Donald had to bring up Ivan. Worse, he mentioned their fake connection, meaning Tori was about to be intrinsically linked to him. Donald was one thing—he was fully tricked by Ivan's mundane persona. If the New Science Sentries got too close, they might catch something, and that could lead to all manner of trouble.

Unfortunately, try as she might, her brain refused to offer up any solution for how to dodge the question while in Donald's presence. He minimized her ability to obfuscate or lie, so her only choice was to tell the truth, and *really* lean on how boring and unworthy of discussion her supposed uncle was.

"Oh yeah, it's the best. Total adherence to schedule, constantly double-checking my work, endless feedback, whether I want it or not. Ivan's a good uncle and a solid manager, but he's *so* uptight and by-the-book."

The small nods from Donald backed up her claim nicely. "While Mr. Gerhardt is one of the better bosses I've had, he does tend to be a bit stiff."

Tori spotted the approach as it was coming, the two forms she'd yet to meet out of costume wandering over, arriving behind Donald before he registered their presence. The shorter one tapped a finger on her team leader's arm, digging the nail in slightly to make sure he noticed.

"Going to introduce us?"

Donald didn't seem to mind the nail—that might just be her way, and he was accustomed to it. He greeted the arrival with the same timid smile as always, gesturing to both women as he faced Tori. "Of course. Perfect timing, too. Tori, this is Irene and Lucy. We work together, and you can probably guess how, but I'll keep the details light. Irene and Lucy, Tori is a friend of mine from my cubicle days."

"Trust me, we know," Irene commented. She extended a hand to Tori, which Tori accepted. The woman didn't seem especially distant to her, in particular; rather, her persona read more as an overall antisocial aura, something Tori could not only respect, but understood and envied. Left to her own devices, she'd be affecting a similar vibe, or skipping the outing entirely.

Lucy didn't offer a hand. Instead, she gripped Tori in a tight hug the moment Irene let go and she turned to face the freckled woman. "It's wonderful to meet you! Donald has told us such nice things. I can't wait to get to know you better."

Was there such thing as social whiplash? If so, Lucy and Irene were the tag-team champs of it. Barely recovered, Tori did her best to return the dual greeting. "Good to meet you both, as well. What's say we all move away from the doorway and into the party proper? That cooler is calling my name."

"A woman after my own heart." Ike materialized at the edge of the group, sipping from his own open bottle. "If I had one, anyway. Donald, Ren sent me over. Ellie wanted to get some games going and your buddy said you were the man to see."

Looking somehow sheepish, despite the innocuous request, Donald offered Tori an apologetic shrug. "The joys of being the item guy."

"I had to chill all the drinks. We pitch in where we can." Irene clapped him on the back. "Come on. We'll force Ren to hurry up and choose so you can get back to the revelry."

"Let's talk more later," Lucy called to Tori, before following them both over to Ren.

Ike vanished again, reappearing next to Ren and leaving Tori alone with Kyle, who didn't linger before gesturing to the refreshment area. "I believe you mentioned needing a drink."

"Excellent listening skills. Those will take you far." They walked together over to the cooler, her taking a beer while Kyle pulled out a glass container with what appeared to water inside, marked by three X's in a row, like an old-time moonshine jug.

"Damn it, Ike, that wasn't what I meant when I said to label these." Kyle yelled the words, but Ike's attention was lost in the sparks of blue light as Donald produced various objects for the night's activities. "I didn't want anyone to drink this by mistake. Not healthy for those without super-speed metabolism."

Cracking the lid, Kyle took a sip, his whole body tensing as the liquid passed his lips. "Oof. That is terrible every time. Cheers?" He held up his bottle, to which Tori clinked her own.

It was surreal to see the New Science Sentries like this, less than a day after fighting with them. In the field, they'd been terrifying. Fast, brutal, efficient—only quick thinking and a few surprises had kept her people out of jail. Yet tonight, they looked like little more than a few goofballs in their twenties. Then again, what did she look like to them? And what would their impression of Ivan be? The more Tori pondered it all, the more she wondered how many other people in her past had been living double lives. The deeper into all of this she got, the harder it was not to speculate about how much she'd missed before.

"Part of me has always been jealous of this." With a sweeping gesture, Kyle motioned to the entire roof and all its merrymakers. "Live a normal life, make friends, have fun, be happy. Regular people don't worry about whether or not they'll be blown apart by some unknown meta, or fail to save someone in peril."

"Actually, *everyone* worries about the first one—it's just part of life these days," Tori corrected. "I'll give you the second point, though." She examined Kyle's face, not sure if even he knew how wistful it currently appeared. "You could have that, if you really wanted it. Nobody is forced to be a cape."

"No, I couldn't. Even if I had it in me to leave my friends behind, it's only the parts like this that I envy. Tomorrow morning, all the people with normal jobs will wake up to go toil away at things they probably don't care about, simply powering through their days. I'm going to wake up and make the world better, might even get to save a few people. There's no trading that life in, once it has its teeth in you. When all is said and done, this is the only job for me, so I have to be good at it."

The kick Tori could still recall ringing her entire suit seemed to indicate that Kyle was well on his way to achieving that, but she couldn't exactly say it. Instead, she went with something more suited to her perspective than Hephaestus's. "I'm no expert on capes, but for what it's worth, every time I've seen you fuck up, you own it. You take responsibility and try to fix it or improve, so there won't be repeats. It hasn't escaped my notice that no more saved civilians have ended up in Tachyonic's arms on camera."

"Maybe I just haven't saved anyone else worthy of sweeping off their feet."

Tori rolled her eyes at what she assumed to be a joke, then kept on going. "My point is, if your goal is to be a great superhero, learning from your mistakes seems like an excellent policy to have. Keep that up, and eventually, you'll run out of new mistakes to make. Pretty sure that's what they call being competent."

From the other end of the roof, a cheer went up as tennis rackets were being passed out while Donald was summoning flashing orbs the size of softballs. Ike appeared directly in front of Tori and Kyle, holding a racket in each hand.

"The game has been chosen. It's sort of like racquetball, only with magic balls that fly around. From some game called *Electro-Sport Rodeo*, which I might have to buy the next time we've got a day off. Take your weapons and come gather for the choosing of teams. If you're last, they'll stick you with me."

Lifting the racket he'd been handed, Kyle waved it slightly. "Guess that means it's game on?"

"Eh, why not? It'll help work up an appetite for dinner." More importantly, playing an active game made conversation harder, and they'd done plenty of talking for Tori's tastes.

Besides, some part of her couldn't resist the opportunity for a rematch, even if the game was different this time around.

Chapter 66

Taking a sip from her plastic cup of wine, Beverly surveyed the rooftop scene carefully. Unlike Tori, she hadn't spent the majority of her life eyeball deep in electronics, meaning she had a better grasp of social nuance. Not that the talent was especially called for—most people would have picked up on the dynamics at play, if not spotted them immediately.

Donald and Tori were sitting on chairs, plates loaded with barbecue, catching up on life. While they weren't technically alone—others were seated near them—by keeping the topic to their old lives, they'd effectively locked everyone else out of the conversation. For most of the other revelers, that was no matter at all, but two of the attendees seemed not-quite-comfortable with how familiar the former coworkers were.

One of them, Beverly had seen coming. It wasn't hard to note the way Kyle's fondness for Tori had grown through their interactions. Maybe it was her lack of giving a shit about superheroes, or her brusque nature, but something had been winning him over despite their initial impression. Not that Tori appeared to have registered even the slightest iota of it. It was hard to be too tough on her, given that Donald was getting the same looks thrown his way from Lucy. While there was a chance those glances were out of concern for a team member, it wouldn't be the bet Beverly tossed her money on.

Ike was still occasionally turning his head toward Ellie, who was mostly talking to Austin and Lucy, as Ren and Chloe were in a discussion about a surprise shared interest in some obscure winter sport they'd evidently both grown up watching. Between all the secret identities and hidden feelings, Beverly was starting to feel like she'd stepped into a meta-human version of high school. Not great, but then, she hadn't been able to turn into a dragon in real high school. That wasn't a terrible trade-off.

"Taking a breather?" Of all the capes on the roof, Irene was the easiest to lose track of. Short, intentionally bland wardrobe, largely quiet, she essentially vanished amidst the larger forms and personalities of the others.

"Enjoying the stars for a moment." Beverly had selected her seat partially for this excuse, as it was the point on the roof furthest from any light source. That also made it furthest from sound and activity and was an excellent spot for unwinding.

Irene also boasted a plastic cup, the fizz from within marked it as either a soda or a cocktail, rather than wine. She took a soft sip, then settled down onto one of the cheap lawn chairs dotting the roofscape. Once she was comfortable, she drank once more, then let out a grunt.

"Spot anything interesting?"

"Stars don't tend to change," Beverly replied.

"These days, you never know. I wasn't talking about the sky, though." Irene pointed over to the party, then to Beverly herself. "You're over here hugging the sidelines, trying to get a read on everyone."

Beverly wasn't entirely sure how to react, largely because she didn't know if the words were meant as a compliment or an insult. Rather than make a guess, she decided to play things neutral. "That's an interesting way to look at it. Here I thought I was just taking a breather."

"Maybe you were, and I got the wrong read. Doesn't happen often, mind you. When you're easy to ignore, people let down their guard; helps with catching details. I'm doing pretty well tonight, though, this snafu not counted. Clocked Donald's crush on Tori, and of course, there's Lucy's on Donald. Seems Ike has some unresolved feelings of his own, and then there's Austin."

Those looks, Beverly hadn't caught as many of. That was the nature of things, it was always easier to observe as an outsider. She'd seen snippets of enough to know that they were there. Short flashes, never overt, slightly too constant to be a coincidence. Austin was a knot of complications, none of which Beverly felt like diving into with someone she'd just met. "I work hard to look good. Doesn't bother me that he took notice."

"Except, he's not the only one who hasn't been as discreet as they think." Irene punctuated the statement with another sip from her cup, eyes darting between Beverly and Austin, just in case there was any confusion.

"This is a strange way to try to make new friends." Beverly didn't have a reasonable defense to offer: explaining that she'd been watching him in case he was watching her didn't sound real in her head, let alone as actual words. Her only option was to redirect and hope they veered into a more manageable topic.

"Never been something I'm very good at," Irene agreed. "A little too observant, and much too honest. Thought I might have spotted a kindred soul, but if that's not the case, then sorry to have bothered you."

The chair scraped along the rough surface as Irene pushed it back, rising to her feet. Beverly had a snap judgment to make. Before her current living situation, she would have let the cape walk away, happy for the interaction to be over. Time with Tori had given Beverly more insight to the less socially inclined, however. While it would have been easy to read the whole exchange as an uncomfortable moment, she could also recognize that it had been Irene attempting to reach out, in her own odd way.

"Stop," Beverly commanded, her tone far more certain than it had been moments prior. "Sit and relax. You weren't necessarily wrong, that doesn't mean I want to talk about it."

Pausing only to readjust the chair so it was angled to better face Beverly, Irene retook her seat. "I can understand that. How about something more standard to first meetings: what do you do?"

The smile on Beverly's face threatened to push Irene back with how fast and strong it came on. Had she been praying for a topic she could speak on at length without going anywhere near romance or capes, Beverly might have thought someone up there was actually listening.

"What do I do? Settle in, because I'm about to explain the economics of running a fashion content website."

For as good as Irene might have been at reading facial cues, she wasn't especially adept at concealing her own horrified expression.

Turning the orb around in her long fingers, Lozora examined the handiwork. She'd never gotten to see any of Cobblord's creations up close and personal before; in Rookstone, he'd been denied any materials for obvious reasons. On the inside, he'd been a quiet, bookish man who kept to himself. He'd have been eaten within the first week, if not for his usefulness. Cobblord's particular talent made him handy enough to earn protection from some of the more dangerous residents of Rookstone's lowest levels, a debt he'd apparently been paying off since he regained his freedom.

What she held now was a custom job, and not a cheap one, either. Much as she'd have liked to knock it on the side like she was checking a mango, the truth was, she had no idea what she was looking at. It could be a round rock with fancy designs for as much as she could tell. Rather than read the product, Lozora elected to keep her attention on Cobblord's bespectacled face.

"You're sure this will hold Fornax?"

"Certainly not." For as nervous as he always looked, the trepidation never touched his voice. "To my knowledge, that's impossible. It will contain Fornax, for a time, until he breaks free. How long that will take, I can't say. I added a lot of distance, so it would take time to travel, and some obstacles along the way, but there's really no stopping Fornax. Only slowing him down, which is what I was hired to do."

Cockier now that he had a bit of leverage, though Lozora couldn't fault him for drilling down on specifics. Working with these sorts of people meant that, when things went wrong, blame was quick to be spread, so Cobblord wanted to be explicit about what his product was supposed to do. It was a pointless worry. She wouldn't have the option to kill him until the second version was completed, and even then, it was an order she'd probably ignore. Her current employer was scary; that didn't mean he was the person that terrified Lozora the most.

"Fine, so this will slow Fornax down. We deploy it this weekend. I'll bring the results afterward. He'll expect a quick turnaround time on this one."

"They always do. Updates are easier than creation. I still have the model that one was cast from." Cobblord nodded to the orb, then spun in the leather chair, turning back to his workstation. "It was good to see you, Lozora. Now that I know you're my go-between, I'll have appropriate snacks for our next meeting. As I recall, you enjoyed the composition of weight lifters the most."

She stowed the orb, unexpected hospitality dispelling her more murderous thoughts. Perhaps there was a reason he'd survived on the inside beyond just his talent, or maybe he simply had good manners. Regardless, Lozora wasn't going to turn down food on a trip she'd have to make anyway. Especially considering the crap her current employer kept around.

"Keep up the good work, Cobblord. I'd like it if all my visits could go this pleasantly. Saves me from having to lap up the blood."

"Tori! Ren just had an awesome idea. Their team has next Saturday afternoon off—what do you say we all go mini-golfing?" Chloe's enthusiasm was exuberant, even as Ren's face made it clear this was more a casual suggestion than a vetted plan. Nice as the night had gone, Tori was glad she had an actual excuse for the outing, one that would cover her even if they tried to change around the times.

"No can do, I'm gone all next weekend, remember?" Only once those words were out of her mouth did Tori note the curious stares and realize exactly *what* that excuse was.

It was Ike who posed the question; the people she actually knew were polite enough to let it slide. "Weekend long trip? You didn't strike me as the music festival type, but as long I'm out of costume, sounds like a good time."

Embarrassing as the truth would be for a villain to admit, she took a small amount of pleasure in dashing whatever delusions Ike had spun for himself. At least only Beverly and Chloe would see the full humor in the situation, and they were already up to speed. "My uncle is a Starscout cluster leader, and I pitch in to help. The End of Summer Shindig is some big camping event, so I'll be in the woods battling bugs and filth."

"Add in some hallucinogens, and it's still pretty close to a music festival." Ike's reply was largely lost in the clamor of words amidst Tori's explanation. It wasn't the organization that stuck out to them, rather the one who'd founded it.

"You know, now that I think about it, it's kind of weird we don't do work with the Starscouts," Ellie said. "If Lodestar asked, there'd be no shortage of capes who'd volunteer."

Tori shook her head. "Separate entities, by Lodestar's own design. She didn't want the kids becoming targets used for drawing in capes, or the organization to be too connected to the AHC, in case someone got the idea to use it as a recruiting pool. Some capes do volunteer, but on their own, not under the AHC banner." This much hadn't been leftover memories from childhood, rather a bit of knowledge absorbed from Helen, who enjoyed sprinkling historical tidbits through the meetings. She evidently had a passion for history, at least where the Starscouts were concerned.

"Guess that means we won't be able to follow you up there and make wolf noises. Shame, I've got a decent howl." Ike tilted his head back, as if to give a display, but thought better of it when he caught the death-glare in Ellie's eyes.

Austin, on the other hand, appeared genuinely concerned. He rubbed his chin, his eyes never fully leaving Tori. "Are you sure that's safe? Out in the woods, away from society? Seems like the kind of place well suited to another attempt on your life."

Out in the woods, away from witnesses and police, Tori would be far more dangerous than she was masquerading through mundane life. Powers and tech could be used freely in that situation—none of which she could very well tell Austin. "Look, before you get the bright idea to send a tail along, this is a huge event. Clusters from all over the state meet up. I'm not saying we're immune to meta-attacks, nowhere can boast that, but I'm pretty sure there's a few security measures in place, given that there's tons of kids hanging around up there."

That was without even mentioning Ivan, who was more than enough on his own, and could be motivated to truly horrific levels if anything put Beth in danger.

"Attacking Lodestar's charity organization seems like an especially dumb move," Donald added. "There's no way she doesn't keep some tabs on it."

A robust, far-from-demure laugh escaped from Ellie's lips. "Sorry, I just imagined some idiots showing up, thinking all they had to deal with there were children, and finding Lodestar waiting for them instead."

A ripple of chuckles and shudders rolled through the revelers as they all pictured the hypothetical scenario for the half-second necessary to see its inevitable conclusion. Even Austin looked more relaxed, perhaps realizing he'd been overly concerned. "That is a pretty amusing mental image. Doesn't even really matter who the challenger is."

"Well... except Fornax." Like a conversational sniper, Irene killed the light mood with a single phrase. She noticed the sudden deflation as the collective shoulders sagged, but showed no remorse. "What? He held his own with Lodestar back in the day, and now we know he was never really dead. Maybe you managed to avoid seeing any video from the Ridge City Riots, but I watched him smack around Apollo like a cat playing with a mouse. Even the Champions' Congress has enemies on their level."

"Been trying hard not to think about that," Ike admitted. "Though I do have to wonder, where do you hide Fornax for over a decade? Space, right? Had to be space. He'd have torn up any city they let him loose in."

Tori suddenly found herself extremely uncomfortable with the topic of conversation, and worse, she had absolutely no way to signal that without provoking suspicion. None she could think of, at any rate. She shot a brief glance to Beverly, who met the gaze yet said nothing. She'd help where she could, but neither of them was steering this ship.

"Maybe he went civilian," Chloe suggested. "Turned it all around and started living a normal life." For a brief moment, Tori thought she felt her heart actually stop, until she noticed the amused faces on almost all of the capes' faces.

"We would classify that as unlikely." Ren kept his tone as gentle as possible, but there was no getting around the disagreement. "Someone as destructive as Fornax keeping control on his own is probably impossible; if he could have fit in with society, he'd have done that from the start."

No, he wouldn't, because he never had the chance. He spent eighteen years being forced to kill the only people he knew, then was saddled with a destructive force from another plane before ever setting foot in "society." The man they thought of as some wild monster was in fact the most controlled person Tori had ever met. Not that she could tell them that, or any of the other insights into who that villain they knew only by name really was. It was strange; even though the assumptions were helping Tori and Ivan keep their secrets, it still pissed her off that they were being made. These people thought they knew their enemies, but they didn't have the first fucking idea what was really going on.

For a moment, she'd been able to forget what the actual dynamic of the evening was. It had been pleasant, pretending they were just a bunch of young people hanging out and having fun. But that was an illusion, one she couldn't afford to get lost in. This was eight capes hanging out with the two villains who'd slipped their clutches one night prior. If any of them knew who she really was, all their friendliness would evaporate instantly.

Tori had to remember those lines, keep them firmly in mind. One day, if her secret was ever exposed, these capes would probably become her fiercest enemies, feeling betrayed by her deception. She wouldn't even begrudge them that, the enmity would be well deserved. Still, Tori would be better off if she started distancing herself from them once the bodyguard work was over. In all honesty, she knew she should do the same with Donald, as well.

Alliances were one thing, but the longer she had to keep all these lies in place, the more Tori suspected that capes and villains simply couldn't be friends.

Chapter 67

"At 1:07 a.m., local time, the first alerts were triggered. After I arrived on the scene and began a preliminary investigation, it took less than ten minutes to confirm what we were looking at: extraterrestrials, moving en masse toward our planet. Given the size and number of ships, there can be no question that this is meant to be an invading force. I've asked Cresscriss to sit in and offer his expertise, where applicable."

For once, Lodestar didn't mind Professor Quantum's brusque nature. Given what this Monday morning meeting was about, she was glad to quickly cut to the heart of the matter. They'd known more encounters were possible but hadn't been expecting any after the Grzzniltan forces went fleeing to the stars.

On a large TV screen, several grainy images appeared, showcasing a vast army of ships with a strange, twisting design, like someone had tried to make a spaceship modeled after a particularly gnarly knot.

"Wrexwren," Cresscriss muttered. Two of his six eyes closed for a long breath as his fingers pressed against the blue skin of his skulltip. "A species whose culture is based predominantly on war and conquest. Since they are part of a loose affiliation of spacefaring peoples, the Wrexwren direct those tendencies toward planets that have yet to reach the stars and attain such protections."

"Perhaps the Grzzniltans passed them inaccurate information, painting us as an easy target? If they've got any enmity toward the Wrexwren, it would allow them to use us as a blunt instrument of vengeance," Quorum suggested.

Cresscriss made a sound like a sparrow taking a shot of vodka. "Unlikely. The Grzzniltans prize survival, and large as this force is, that in no way represents the entirety of the Wrexwren armada. Such a deception would bring intense repercussions, but I suppose it is possible if there's an angle we've yet to discover."

"I don't care about their motivations. We've established them to be hostile. Let's engage the planetary defense cannons and be done with it. I've made great strides in improving them through the years—if we strike before they're prepared, there is minimal chance any will survive." No one in the room doubted that if they gave the okay, Professor Quantum would fire on the fleet before the hour was over. That was part of why it took the entire Champions' Congress to activate them; it had been her and Quorum's condition on allowing the weapons to be built.

"Before we blow potentially thousands of living beings into dust, how about we entertain the possibility that they're coming here peacefully? Being from a war-faring species doesn't change the fact that a sentient creature makes its own choices. Some choose to rebel against the reality they're presented. Maybe this is a band of Wrexwren outcasts seeking a planet to live in peace upon."

It wasn't especially loud, said mostly under his breath, but she noted Quorum's whisper: "That's a *lot* of outcasts."

Thankfully, Cresscriss came to her aid, in spite of what she felt ninety percent sure was a skeptical expression on his face.

"There is another option to preemptive destruction. The Wrexwren are also a people who take great pride in their strength. I have heard tales that they will settle these matters with a contest of warriors—the greatest of the planet against the strongest of their own. Should they be defeated, the invasion would be called off out of respect for any planet that could birth such a combatant. However, I have never engaged with them directly, so I cannot attest to the viability of such a tactic."

A click from the remote in Professor Quantum's hand brought up a new image, this one harder to puzzle out. At first, it looked like another angle with fewer ships, until Lodestar noticed all the darkness. Something was there, blotting out the stars that should be visible, yet it registered as nothing more than a hole in the photo, like the object had been torn out.

"There is another concern. They are hauling something with them, an object my scanners and cameras have thus far been unable to detect. Unless that is standard procedure for the Wrexwren people, we should prepare to be surprised. I doubt they would make this approach without something that gave them the idea of victory."

Mysterious alien force approaching from the sky? It felt like a fight. In her gut, Lodestar knew where this was heading. Blasting, punching, hurting—she could already feel the cold of space pulling at her skin. But sometimes, on a few wonderful and cursedly rare occasions, she was wrong. Every now and then, things weren't what they appeared, and it didn't have to end in combat. She had to fight for those possibilities, especially because so few of the other capes even believed in them.

"Hail the ships," Lodestar said. "Ask them their intent, and if it's invasion, see if they're open to that one-on-one option Cresscriss mentioned."

"They could lie," Professor Quantum pointed out.

"Good thing they'll be talking to the smartest superhero in history, whose brilliance can easily sniff out such deceptions." Lodestar thought about the first screen again and the sheer number of ships that had been approaching. If things did get bad, that was too many to take out safely. For the Wrexwrens' sake, she dearly hoped they turned out to be anomalies.

Cresscriss cleared a vocal sack, a noise akin to pudding falling on a tile floor. "I'm not saying attack need be the first recourse; however, you should know that right now is the optimum time to strike. The ships appear to be prioritizing speed, meaning that power to their shields will be minimal. Once they know you're alerted to their presence, that energy distribution will change. A shot fired preemptively would have the greatest chance of success."

The words hung heavy in the room, quickly dispelled by a nonchalant wave from Quorum. "Doesn't matter. 'Shoot first' is not the way superheroes work. Besides, more shields or fewer, it changes nothing. If they're peaceful, we greet them; if not, we send them away."

"The Wrexwren are a powerful species. I would caution against underestimating them. You three would no doubt triumph against their soldiers; I'm not sure the rest of the AHC will fare as well."

"Thank you, Cresscriss. Your information has been invaluable, and I'll need your aid to be sure the Grzzniltan translators we constructed can work on Wrexwren language, as well. It seems we'll be making contact soon." Professor Quantum looked unhappy, but when wasn't that the case? He was much too smart to have actually expected to shoot the lasers; Lodestar would bet he'd already started work on updating their translator. In spite of how much he could push the limits, Professor Quantum had been doing this job longer than anyone else, and had a keen grasp on the way things usually went.

"Since we know what we're going to do, that leaves us with only one major item to get figured out." Lodestar tapped a lightly glowing nail against the polished wood of the table. "First contact with an entire new section of the universe. What do we want to say?"

"Nice ass!"

Johnny Three Dicks smacked the oversized posterior of Thuggernaut as he arrived, earning an annoyed glare from much higher up. There was no remorse in his eyes as he dodged a half-hearted swipe for his skull. "What? I can't take note that my buddy got some new pants?"

"Not the way most people would acknowledge that." Stasis wandered into the room with a gigantic bag of chips in hand, pilfered from some unknown source. She paused, taking in Thuggernaut's non-costumed form, giving a small nod of approval. "Outfit looks nice. Got something fancy going on?"

"Opera tickets," Thuggernaut explained. "In a time zone where it's nearly evening, for a show that starts worryingly soon. Hopefully this doesn't take too long. I only popped by to see what the announcement was."

He, Johnny, and most of the other gathered villains had all gotten the same message, albeit through different methods of communication. Magic metas were more easily reached via sending spells, whereas the tech ones were never too far from an encrypted email. For the more mundane metas like Thuggernaut, a special Indigo Technologies phone with enhanced security was enough to deliver simple messages of when to arrive. The real information was always doled out in person.

Without warning, the television of their breakroom flickered on, just as they knew every other screen throughout the guild had. Broadcasting these sorts of messages was out of the question, but closed-circuit wiring on their island made the dissemination of information far more efficient than gathering everyone in a single space. Safer, too.

Doctor Mechaniacal's voice played as images flashed onto the screen: images of space, dotted by an abundance of twisted ships. "Recently, the guild has discovered an extraterrestrial force moving toward Earth. Based on information obtained from our own off-world sources, these are a people called the Wrexwren, a violent, warring culture who we should expect to arrive aggressively."

The room they'd ended up in wasn't especially full—perhaps five other villains milled about as the message played. Uniformly, they paid more attention to the screen with each passing word. Stasis, Johnny Three Dicks, and Thuggernaut were no exception. Idle curiosity warped into genuine interest; with that simple introduction, the guild was hanging on every one of Doctor Mechaniacal's words.

"It is our estimation that the AHC will attempt to conduct a duel to halt the advance. We also expect the Wrexwrens to lie, cheat, or otherwise work around whatever agreement is struck. There is a high possibility that they will mount some type of terrestrial offensive, attempting to split the AHC's focus between the sky and the ground."

In another place, Stasis imagined the words would find a very different reaction. Fear, most likely, as even the most faithful among the capes would feel a trickle of terror at the idea of aliens attacking the planet again. Earth had triumphed over every past invasion, but the wins hadn't all come easily. Anxiety could be reasonably expected, at the very least, worry over what would happen to one's family or property; even in victory, these battles had a cost.

None of that was reflected in her fellow guild members, however. Greed, excitement, even outright bloodlust, *those* were the reactions of villains to this news. Because they understood what Doctor Mechaniacal was really saying. An invading force wasn't just a threat to the planet, it was fair game to play with. For all the effort the capes put into keeping the world safe, they weren't going to complain if aliens trying to conquer it suddenly started dying in droves. There would be ships to loot, weapons to gather, and no shortage of targets for all manner of built-up anger and aggression.

This wasn't a warning. It was notice so they could be prepared to live that day to its fullest. Deep down, Stasis almost felt a flicker of sadness for these Wrexwren. The dumb fucks really had no idea what kind of planet they'd be stepping onto.

"All interested parties should contact their council representative for more information. We'll have various travel networks in place on the day of, depositing guild members onto scenes as they become active. Standard guild fees apply."

With that, the screen went black once more. Johnny's eyes were already gleaming; Stasis could all but hear the clatter of coins smacking into each other as he rubbed his hands together. "Aliens, capes, and combat—oh my. What entertaining bets I'm going to see on this one."

Thuggernaut's reaction was more subdued, and worrying. The big man closed his meaty fist a single time, squeezing it tightly. "It's been a while since I got a real match in. I wonder how strong they are."

That was something they'd definitely be finding out; Stasis had little doubt there. With Doc getting everyone prepped and the guild handling the transportation, the villains would be incredibly mobile by the time their visitors arrived. No matter where the aliens set down, they'd soon find themselves beset not just by the planet's defenders, but by its demons. After being dragged into the light and forced out of Ridge City, the entire guild was spoiling to throw a punch. There was no chance they'd be able to hold back once they finally had a viable target.

She tossed an elbow into Thuggernaut's side—the only way to get his attention given his overall bulk. "I'm sure the opera is great and all, but it can't compete with an alien invasion."

"Depends on the opera—and the aliens, I'd expect," Thuggernaut shot back. There was no mistaking the fire in his eyes, though. He was excited. "Perhaps I'll book some training sessions, just to make sure I'm not rusty. If they've crossed light years to see our planet, only seems polite to show them our very best efforts."

"Last time he talked like that, we had to haul people to the hospital in a garbage truck. Count me in." Johnny had a notebook he'd produced from a pocket in hand and was already scrawling rapidly into it. "We can have one of the homebodies run the betting board. I'm not missing my chance at some fun."

It was the same throughout the room, and likely the guild as a whole. The idea of bloodshed should have had them concerned, but that was why they were here in the first place. This was not an organization of petty criminals and simple ruffians. It was a home of villains, beings defined by their power and ambitions. They didn't see a threat; they saw a challenge, a chance to test themselves against invaders from another world.

When the Wrexwren arrived, they would find the guild ready, waiting, and above all else, burning for a fight.

Chapter 68

As the final Starscout meeting before the weekend's End of Summer Shindig, the evening served largely as one last preparation session for the children as well as their cluster leaders. The kids were finishing up banners, signs, and other craft projects that would hang alongside the other clusters' work, marking their respective areas. Ivan was manning the kitchen while simultaneously running through a checklist of items to make sure everyone packed and surreptitiously making notes on the ones he knew at least a few of the kids would forget. He'd already cooked enough treats and snacks to keep them fed on a weeklong march; Tori was almost certain there would be some sort of magic at work to fit it all in his car on the drive up.

Helen appeared to have settled on guiding the kids and messing with Ivan as her main trip-planning tactics. To her credit, she was excellent at both, helping the scouts stay on task while calling out that Ivan had skipped ridiculous items such as inflatable bounce houses and standing sleeping bags. If it annoyed him, he was hiding it from the room, though Tori was fairly sure he didn't mind. Ivan wasn't a terribly expressive person—perhaps that was why she and her mentor understood one another as well as they did. It almost seemed like he was enjoying Helen's teasing, which was possible. They were both single adults and perfectly entitled to flirt, though she'd be surprised to see Ivan on a date. One more person to keep secrets from didn't seem like it would be that appealing to him.

Tori herself was mostly filling in where needed: grabbing more supplies for the kids, cleaning up small messes before they became big ones, generally working support for the enterprise as a whole. She dropped a fresh bottle of glue next to Beth and Armand, who were teaming up on a particularly intricate glitter-star on the cluster's sign, noting that Ivan's daughter whispered, "Thanks," even in the midst of her work. The more Tori saw of Beth, the fonder she became. All of the kids were growing on her, though she was still quite happy when the meetings came to an end. Fondness or no, Tori only had so much energy to give.

"Hey, Tori, heads up! One for the trash." Helen called the warning before she tossed over an empty tube of paint, which Tori snatched from the air. "Nice! Someone's got the kvizblork tonight."

The tube of paint almost slipped from Tori's firm grasp in surprise. "Did you just quote *The Sashay of Gelzork*?" There was no way she'd heard that right; it was *much* too deep of a cut, even for someone else who liked foreign flicks. Tori's uncertainty lasted only until she finished tossing away the tube and caught the wide-eyed glee in Helen's reaction.

"You got that? Hot dog, nobody else I know digs into the Omdilbom section on Multerion." The excitement brimming from Helen was one Tori was almost embarrassingly familiar with; it was the energy of someone with a secret passion who'd finally found an outlet. "Did you watch any of the Kaldesian octology, or *Finding the Tesseract*?"

At Helen's feet, a curious face turned from the sheet of construction paper and up to the cluster leader. "What are you talking about?" Caden always looked a tad confused, but now, his forehead was positively scrunched.

"We're talking about movies," Helen explained. "Movies from other planets and cultures found across the broad array of alternate universes. Multerion is a service that collects and exports the greatest artistic achievements in film, ones that reoccurred over and over in various verses. Works of high art, meant to be shared with more than just the world that created them."

At Caden's side, Mallory leaned over, whispering with the trademark loudness of a child. "She means movies with subtitles."

"Oh." With that, the entirety of Caden's interest fled, his face turning back to the construction paper, utterly exiting the conversation.

"They don't *all* have subtitles." Helen seemed more to be grumbling to herself than the kids. "A lot of them are from worlds that look and sound like ours."

Loud noises from the kitchen signaled Ivan's emergence with a tray of steaming cookies. Most of these would be saved for the trip, though a few were fated to be consumed by the current swarm of children. Such was the tithe for baking around them. Noting the already hungry stares, Helen snapped into motion so the sweets would have time to cool.

"Okay, everyone, let's take a crafting break." Helen managed to pull both their attention and their silence with a calm voice, a talent that untold teachers would have killed to steal. "Find a good stopping point. It's time to stretch those legs for a bit. If you'll all follow me into the backyard, we can review our weekend events and make sure no one has questions, then play some practice rounds so everyone is comfortable. By the time we're done, I suspect Mr. Gerhardt's cookies will be ready. Tori, could you come with and give me a hand?"

Having seen where this was headed, Tori was already moving for Helen's side. Across the room, Ivan was scooping the cookies onto a wire cooling rack, cutting down on the amount of time they'd have to buy. He looked over to Helen, and it almost seemed as if a smile was trying to force its way onto his face. Instead, it warped into words as he called over to them. "Should I presume you'd like me to hold one back for you?"

"Utah, gimme two." Helen bumped Tori with her shoulder, the shine of expectation nearly glowing on her.

Might as well come clean, rather than drag this out and cause more disappointment. "Um, I haven't really gone through everything yet. Mostly just the sci-fi ones." Tori braced for Helen to be disappointed; instead, she was treated to a grown woman actually clapping her hands together in excitement.

"Hang on. You haven't even seen… wow. *Wow*. So many amazing things to show you." A rowdy swell of noise from the kids brought her back to the moment at hand. "Later. Things to show you later. For now, let's get out there and do our best. After this, the next time we get together is for the drive on Friday. Make sure you feel ready."

The scent of cookies still hung heavy as they herded the kids out into the night air, which was just cool enough that a bonfire would be perfect once the weekend rolled around. So far as Tori could tell, the kids seemed pretty prepared. No new cluster members meant they'd all been to at least one of these before, and Helen had been adamant about ensuring that every child knew what to expect. Maybe it was a safety issue, so that if anything did suddenly go off-kilter, the kids would be wise to it.

Such security was obviously unnecessary, not that Tori held it against Helen. The woman had no way of knowing that her supposed cookie-slinger was a nigh-unstoppable force of destruction, one that would do anything to keep his daughter safe. Sometimes, seeing him in that apron, Tori had to remind herself about who else Ivan was. That was what made his cover so perfect, and so powerful. Even the New Science Sentries, when trying to solve the mystery of Fornax, had tossed off any notion that he would live a simple, human life.

That party had been a clear reminder of the stakes at play where secret identities were concerned, reinforcing the importance of that separation. Tori's main goal for the End of Summer Shindig was for nothing out of the ordinary to occur. Barring that, her primary focus would be on keeping the kids safe and protecting Ivan's secret. Because if something *did* come to cause trouble, there was no way Ivan wouldn't stop it, very possibly exposing his secret in the process. Crazy as the worry was, Tori couldn't shake it—not when she knew the consequences. Fornax might not have warrants out anymore, but Ivan would never have his normal life back if the truth came out. No more regular job in middle management, no more blending in, and definitely no leading a Starscout cluster.

Although, part of Tori *would* have liked to see the look on Lodestar's face if she ever found out that Fornax, of all people, had worn the uniform of a cluster leader.

Beverly changed the pattern, watching as the computer loaded a new design onto the digital model, then frowned. Still too busy. She needed something that would tell the owner at a glance what was the front versus the back of the purse, yet wasn't so gaudy the buyers would be ashamed to carry them.

It was possible that Beverly was being more critical than she needed to be out of nerves, trying to keep her mind off the coming visitor. Though she hadn't taken Chloe up on the private room, she had elected to have the meeting at Ridge City Roasters. Despite the late hour, her corner of the room was oddly unoccupied, something she attributed to Chloe managing even from behind the counter.

The moment Ambrose walked in, she knew it. Not many fellows cast a shadow that tall and wide, or carried themselves with his level of confidence. Ambrose looked like what Beverly had thought of as a cape growing up: big, strong, and with a pronounced chin. It was hardly surprising she'd made that association, either. As her biggest brother, Ambrose had been her hero before she even knew what capes were.

He opened his arms to hug her, then suddenly lost a step. At sight, they'd been overtaken by familiarity, but now the awkwardness of their situation had returned full-force. Beverly ignored the hesitation, barreling in and hugging her brother tightly. Seconds later, he returned the gesture, until they finally parted and hunkered down at the table.

"You look well," Ambrose observed. "Managing to deal with roommates so far?"

"Compared to all the family coming and going at our house? I might as well be living at a spa, it's so peaceful."

The start of a frown tugged at his lips. "Not how I'd categorize having a roommate become national news." It seemed they weren't going to avoid the main topics up front; Ambrose was diving right in.

"Because that was obviously *her* fault." Even Beverly was surprised by the venom in her voice. She was sick of the bullshit Tori had been dealing with just from the sidelines.

Ambrose was momentarily taken aback, though he soon gathered himself. "Right, of course not. I just meant it could potentially be dangerous. No one's fault, only the situation as it stands."

Beverly leaned in, glad for an excuse to cut past the pretense. "Dangerous for who, exactly? Are you scared some kidnappers are going to come calling in the middle of the night? And then what? You know guns don't work, and I've learned more tricks since then."

"That is *precisely* what I was afraid of." Ambrose rubbed the back of his neck, where a small scar from rogue shrapnel still acted up when he got stressed. "You've been experimenting with it? I understand you had to get control, but pushing further is too risky. What if you get stuck that way, or start to lose your sense of self? That monster is scary as hell with you in the driver's seat. I don't want to imagine it running wild."

"Then your advice would be to ignore that I even have this power at all, keep it locked up for the rest of my life?" Beverly demanded.

"Only if getting rid of it entirely isn't an option." In contrast to the words, Ambrose's tone was gentle. It was plain to see that this was all coming from concern for his sister, which at least made it more palatable. "You're messing with magic you know nothing about, except that you found it in Gran's collection of junk. If you want to be stronger, we can get you there. Without magic, without powers, without anything even remotely connected to those fucking capes."

The last bit came out harsher, but Ambrose didn't slow down. "That's the biggest fear around the house, you know. That one day, we'll turn on the screen and see you out there, wearing the outfit, serving that piece of shit and his organization."

Beverly's hand landed firmly on Ambrose's, squeezing it tight. "Look: nobody, me included, knows where my life is heading right now. This was a curveball that I was in no way braced for, but I'm not going to pretend it didn't happen. I have these powers. Maybe I'll choose not to use them; maybe I'll find a good outlet. Either way, I have to face what I am to get past this. That said, the one thing you will *never* have to worry about is me working for Professor Quantum. If I get within punching distance of that motherfucker, you better believe he's going to be seeing green. Scaly green and fist-shaped, to be precise."

"Not exactly what the family was hoping to hear, but it's an excellent starting point." Ambrose laid his other hand on top of hers, creating a hand sandwich, and pressed it between his. "I suppose the next step is for you to tell me about these 'tricks' you've been working on."

"Aren't you worried that asking me about it might come off as encouragement?"

This time, there was nothing muted about Ambrose's expression; he broke into a smile that lit his whole face. "Speaking as a representative of the family, it's a necessary risk for bonding. But speaking as your big brother, I might be coaxed to admit that dragon-shifting powers *do* seem pretty cool. Enough to warrant at least a few questions, and a bit of subtle encouragement."

Ambrose winked, and Beverly closed her laptop. It was starting to look like she'd want to be here for a while.

Chapter 69

The hurdle shot up from the ground, moving so fast no normal person could have reacted in time. Kyle swung wide with ease, his enhanced sense of time rendering the surprise in slow motion. Touching a few sections of his new bracer, he altered the setlium output slightly, dropping his speed. Professor Quantum didn't permit the same failures twice. In his eyes, a piece of tech failing meant it needed to be refined, situation be damned. It was part of his philosophy as a whole: improve upon what worked, cast aside everything else.

In this case, the new bracer had an updated interface allowing for easier control, reinforced construction to make it harder to break, and it now sent an emergency signal to stabilize the output if it was damaged or disconnected. Next time a villain targeted the bracer, even if they succeeded in disabling it, Tachyonic wouldn't spin out of control. It would be nice to feel as sure about his own capabilities.

As he ducked under a spray of darts, Kyle felt the suit shift with him, flooding his body with high amounts of setlium radiation. He was supposedly lucky, according to Professor Quantum. Not many metas could handle a technique like this; their cells wouldn't drink it in the way his did. This level of augmentation was possible only thanks to that unique talent. Even Austin and Professor Quantum couldn't amplify themselves this way. Then again, they also didn't require the extra help. They were strong enough to hold their own without the need for supplemental tools.

It was an old sore spot in his ego, one that Kyle would consistently feel like he'd moved past, only to be knocked back into it sooner or later. He wasn't enough without the external help. All the others, even Ike, were on the team under their own power. Kyle alone needed the boost to stand alongside them. And this was a victory; there had been a time he didn't think he'd make the cut. That was why he *had* to be better—at the job, at supporting his team, all of it. Kyle had to prove he belonged there, that he wasn't just Austin's plus one, brought on out of friendship more than talent.

Zipping through an off-ramp, Kyle left the training track, blurring into the waiting room where Austin was doing push-ups. "Can you not let me catch up for a moment before you go off training on your own?"

"No can do. That Bahamut fight was tough as hell. I'm not sure I could have won if it had gone the distance. That means my only option is to get stronger for next time."

About what Kyle had expected. It had been some while since Austin lost to anyone outside an established cape. Going against a real opponent had gotten him stirred up. There was a renewed fire, spurred on by the reminder of how much room there still was to grow. Not beating Lodestar was one thing; having some random crook hold their own against him was a different matter entirely.

Flexing his right hand, Kyle checked the bracer functions while it cooled down, his suit no longer crackling with energy. As it changed, his senses slowed—never quite down to human levels, but nowhere near what he could do in peak Tachyonic form. "The new model is working fine. Going to take a while to get used to, so I'll log some extra training hours when I can."

With a look to the track, Kyle's mind flashed to their practice chambers on Vomisa. "Might swing by the island once I'm feeling more stable. The facilities here aren't quite as challenging as what I'm used to."

"There's nothing wrong with training that doesn't put you at risk of bodily harm." Austin finished his push-up set, rising to his feet. "You looked good out there, didn't seem to be missing a step. How do you feel?"

"Stupid, mostly," Kyle admitted. "I can't believe I got my bracer cracked by some asshole already."

The heavy hand patting Kyle on the back was familiar, annoying, and unprotested. "I think you're being hard on yourself. You say 'some asshole,' but those two were meta-humans with training and preparation, ones who've squared off with capes before. Donald's team suspects they're connected to that guild of villains. Not the sort of enemy easily brushed aside."

All of which was true, but Austin was skipping over the fact that everyone else had at worst been handed a draw. There was no denying that Tachyonic had lost. He knew there had been fallout from Professor Quantum, and that Austin was probably shielding him from it, which only made the guilt he felt over failing all the worse.

That wasn't something an apology was going to fix, however. The only course Kyle had was to improve. Get better, stronger, and hell yes, faster, so that when the next bout came, he'd be an asset rather than a fuckup Austin had to take heat for.

"Next time I see Hephaestus, he won't get the chance to surprise me." Heat rose in his cheeks, his mind flitting back to the after-incident report they'd been given. "I can't believe there aren't warrants for those bastards."

Another few pats, though these were more subdued. "The law is the law, and ultimately, there was never any proof they were committing a crime. I wish we hadn't ended up being their alibi, though." Austin had been the first to learn about the slaughter in the same town where they'd been fighting, and he'd quickly passed it on to the others. Whatever happened in that blood-drenched place, Hephaestus and Bahamut couldn't have been present. All meta-forensics indicated it was still going on when the New Science Sentries were on the scene.

"They're smart." Kyle tapped a few more buttons, finishing off the cool-down cycle on his suit. Donald and Ren had recounted the way Hephaestus used the law against them. Whoever that crook was, he came at unexpected angles. "We'll have to be smarter."

"For the moment, I'll just be happy when you're back at full power," Austin said, steering them away from the topic of vengeance. "I never feel comfortable without you watching my back."

One last shake of the arm to make sure everything was holding well, and Kyle fully powered off the bracer. This was the third test, and so far, there hadn't been any glitches. The new unit was working just fine. Time to take it out of the lab and make sure it could handle the actual work.

"In that case, buzz the team and go grab a mask. I think it's time to put this baby through its paces."

"You'll pay us to... cause trouble." To look at Edna, one would form some fast opinions based on her appearance. Being a burly meta meant she had a tall, muscular frame. Unfortunately, some of the side effects of her condition included a receding hairline and unnaturally colored acne. By modern standards of beauty, she wouldn't be winning any hearts. Not that it mattered; Edna wasn't running things because of her looks, or even her strength. She had a keen eye for details and a gut that never steered her wrong—that was why the others trusted her.

At the moment, that gut was screaming that this guy was trouble, same as it had when Balaam came calling. The sorcerer had seen her people as nothing more than cannon fodder, and Edna knew what happened to fodder in a battle. This gentleman was making a more enticing pitch, yet she still kept her guard up.

"That is correct," Wendel Worthington replied. He was stoic, only smiling thinly at any attempts toward levity or ice-breaking. There something about his eyes that set Edna's nerves buzzing: twin voids lacking any sort of human connection. "Specifically, to cause trouble at a time and general geographic area of my choosing. Transportation can be arranged, or you may handle it with your own resources, if security is a concern."

"My concern is not security." Edna pointed a thick finger up to the restaurant's tastefully painted ceiling. In this private room, it displayed a lovely design of interwoven circles. "My concern is the people who zip around through the sky, smacking the shit out of any crime they spot. We lay low, Mr. Worthington. Stay off the radar of the big fish. What you're proposing sounds a lot like the riots that got so many people tossed in jail a few months ago."

At that, Wendel bristled. "Certainly not. Balaam's hubris allowed him to think he could actually win, which is preposterous. This is merely a strike during a window of opportunity. I happen to have it on good authority that there will soon come a day in which all of the major capes are occupied. When that time arrives, those with forewarning will be able to pounce, taking advantage of their distraction. However, there are always new members of the AHC joining, and I'd prefer to work uninterrupted. Your job would be to help cause enough mayhem that the remaining forces are scattered. Should a cape close in on your particular position, feel free to escape. Reach that point, or make it until the end; I'll consider the job accomplished, regardless."

The offer to run made it more enticing—Edna never went into any situation without an exit strategy. From the trolley of food sitting at the side of their table, she pulled off a rib and bit into it, bone and all. It was a trick she'd picked up initially for negotiation intimidation, but was also a handy way to get at the tasty marrow within. Seeing as Wendel was bothering to butter her up at a nice restaurant, she might as well enjoy it.

"How big of an area are we talking? A city, a block? How much room do I have to work in? Some of those capes can close in awfully fast."

There it was, that thin smile, like he was afraid to stretch his mouth. "A fine question. You will be given an area of roughly ten square miles within a major metropolis. Ample space to select targets, as well as adequate cover should escape or concealment be necessary. Also large enough that, were you afraid I was laying some sort of trap, the area would be much too large for an ambush."

"Depends on how many forces you brought." Edna didn't really believe her own words; she knew her gang wasn't high enough on the food chain to warrant such effort. If they pissed off someone truly dangerous, they'd be butchered where they stood. Traps were laid for tougher prey. "But ten square miles of city isn't bad. That's about four football fields' worth of stuff, and in an urban environment, it'll be packed with options." Since Wendel only wanted chaos, Edna wouldn't even have to mess with well-defended targets like banks or stores. She could focus her people's efforts on activities that were flashy, with minimal risk of capture. Hit hard, steal a little extra, then escape before things got too hot.

In front of Wendel sat only a single cup, filled with hot tea. He lifted the drink from the saucer and touched it briefly to his mouth. Edna wasn't completely sure she'd seen him imbibe or ingest a single bit of their meal together. Not the strangest thing, perhaps. Different cultures had different attitudes toward eating in public, and more than a few meta-humans were self-conscious about how they looked while dining. He could have just said that, though. It was the seeming pretense, the pretending to drink, that put her on edge. Between that, the smile, and those damned eyes, Edna felt very much like she was across from something playing at being human.

Issues aside, what he was pitching might indeed be lucrative. Based on the few details being doled out, Edna could guess he'd made a similar pitch to other outfits, with more to come. A game like this relied on numbers; Wendel wanted enough noise to drown out whatever he was planning. That meant there would be plenty of people causing trouble, and her team, ideally, would not stand out. So long as they came at it smart, picked the right targets to avoid pulling in any capes or cops, it should be possible to do the job, get the money, and avoid ending up in a cold cell. They were going to be ready to run, though; this was not a situation where Edna wanted to overextend.

"Assuming the details line up with what we can manage, I think this could be a working arrangement." Edna was careful to leave herself an out, just in case. People like this didn't react well to plans changing, but there was no way she was giving total commitment until everything was settled.

"I am glad to hear it, and I have faith we'll be able to come to terms on the minor matters." Wendel lifted his cup once more, only this time, there was no thin smile waiting. At last, those lips truly parted, revealing teeth that were artificially white, then kept on stretching, well past the point of good taste.

Now, Edna understood why Wendel kept his face so neutral. When it twisted in emotion, the wrongness of it all could be seen. Something off, inhuman, in the way that mouth kept growing, revealing more and more of those near glowing teeth. He lifted the cup higher, making a short cheers.

"To new business." She watched as he tossed the tea down his throat, not even reacting to the steaming liquid splashing against tender mouth-flesh.

With great effort, Edna kept a tremor of fear from making it to her hands as she lifted her own glass of water. Under that watchful dark eye and hideous smile, she drank, already wondering if this was all a terrible mistake.

Chapter 70

It was a meeting that complicated things. Originally, the plan had been simple. Ivan would leave work a few hours early—with permission, of course—to go pick up Beth. He'd then circle back to scoop up Tori as her day was finishing, bringing both of them to the meeting point. There, they would join the rest of the cluster on a rented bus that would take them to the End of Summer Shindig. Slightly inefficient, but it minimized the amount of potential crossover between his lives.

Unfortunately, once Danny from marketing got on a roll, he could run for quite a while. That had turned what was supposed to be a simple spec meeting into a brainstorming session for new features and ideas, none of which would ultimately be implemented. Losing time was bad enough; losing it to pointless ego would have put Ivan in a foul mood under different circumstances. Faced with the prospect of a weekend spent bonding with his daughter, though, Ivan's temperament was softer than usual. It was hard to be mad when something so wonderful was on the horizon.

A positive outlook didn't solve the issue, however. That honor had fallen to Ivan's pragmatism, which quickly outlined the easiest solution to stay on schedule. He could either send Tori in one of the guild cars, or bring her along to pick up Beth. Except, Tori arriving separately would invite needless questions, since he and Beth had already gone over their existing travel plans. It would probably be a small matter to explain them away, but Ivan's recent experience with Rick was an excellent reminder that minor inconsistencies added up over time. The fewer questions asked, the fewer answers sought.

"You okay? If I didn't know better, I'd say you were nervous." Tori had largely been staring out the window as they made their way across Ridge City to Janet's home. Something must have caught her attention, as she'd shifted her focus to Ivan. He didn't feel as if he was showing the stress that badly, which meant he either wasn't hiding it as well as he thought or Tori was getting better at reading him. Not a huge surprise—they were similar people who spent large amounts of time together—but also not a development Ivan was fully comfortable with.

The drive to Janet's was rote after so many years; Ivan may as well have been one of Wade's bots for all the mental effort it demanded to take the proper highway exit, plunging them into the outlands of suburbia. Ivan had been debating how much to tell Tori. He didn't want to color her perceptions needlessly, but if she'd picked up on his energy, then forewarned was likely the best strategy. "There is a chance you'll meet my ex-wife today. She's working from home, so depending on whether or not she's on a call when we arrive, Janet may come out to bid Beth farewell."

He watched surprise morph to curiosity, then continue its evolution to speculation, all in a single brown-eyed blink from Tori. There was no guessing what sorts of images she'd conjured for the former Mrs. Fornax, save only that all of them were wrong. Nobody ever saw Janet coming—it was part of what made her all the more dangerous.

"Anything particular I should know going in?" A sudden sheen of fear washed over her face. "Oh shit, wait, what does she think our relationship is? Did she get the uncle story, or is it like with the kids, and I should stick to just being coworkers?"

A perfectly reasonable question, one that nevertheless pained Ivan to answer. He'd had to read Janet in on Tori at the start. She needed to know the cover story, and deserved forewarning about potential threats to the family, had Tori turned out to be that particular brand of evil. It still felt like a small betrayal to have given away part of Tori's secret to someone else.

"She knows you're part of the guild. I never went into specifics on powers or the like, but Janet is aware of our real connection."

"Yeeesh. Couldn't you just have said I was some prospect with a shitload of potential that the company would be eternally lesser without?"

Ivan cocked an eyebrow. "Eternally lesser?"

"I'll have you know that I'm the one who reformatted the meeting request form. You think that bad boy shrank two pages on its own?" Tori rapped her knuckles against the dash, putting extra punctuation on her next words. "Eternally. Lesser."

"Don't get too carried away. If you remove all the bottlenecks and slow-downs, people will realize management doesn't actually do anything."

Affecting a solemn nod, Tori appeared to consider this revelation. "You're right. I can't go down that road. Getting rid of middle management is more a cape move than a villain one. I guess I should... add more hurdles?"

"That's called working toward a promotion." Ivan's mood brightened as he turned down a familiar lane. Anxious as he was about the potential collision of worlds, the worry was having a hard time overtaking his excitement for the weekend ahead.

They pulled into the driveway and Ivan killed the engine, reaching for his seatbelt. By the time it was unclicked, he could see the figure walking out the front door. Part of him had hoped Beth would be waiting, so eager for the trip she'd come bursting from the house with bags in hand. Sadly, the figure was much too tall to be Beth, though it perhaps did offer some insight into the height she could one day inherit. Janet was dressed for work—matching jacket and skirt atop a pressed shirt, even though nobody was around to see it. That was just her, one of the eccentricities Ivan had acclimated to in their marriage. It wasn't as if he'd had any room to throw stones.

Her finger rapped against the passenger window, startling Tori slightly. With one glance to Ivan for confirmation, which he gave, she rolled down the window, allowing Janet to speak.

"Beth couldn't find her phone charger. She's hunting around for it." Now that the partition was no longer between them, Janet gave Tori a more thorough examination, adjusting her glasses midway through. "You must be Tori, the one who's been helping out with the cluster. Pleasure to meet you."

Through the open window, they shook hands, Janet continuing to stare. "You, as well. Ivan's told me such nice things about you."

"No, he hasn't. He's been respectful, but also made it clear I'm a pain in the ass." Janet finished shaking Tori's hand, releasing unceremoniously. "I have to live most of my life lying, thanks to Ivan's past, so let's dispense with it where unneeded."

Brusque, though Tori was hard-pressed to say it was inaccurate. Hiding a major villain as a husband, ex or current, was bound to be a complicated matter. She was having enough trouble keeping her own identity secret, and that was without anywhere near the fame of Fornax.

"It keeps things simpler, anyway. Look at it this way: if I weren't in the know, there's really only one believable cover to use when a middle-aged man pulls up to his ex's house with a younger woman."

"*Janet*!" Ivan hissed, while Tori felt a small bit of blood rise to her face.

She paid little attention to either, most of her focus remaining on the door. "Relax. We already established I'm aware that's not the case. The lie wouldn't work, anyway. I know it's not the younger ones who catch your fancy."

This time, there was nothing subtle about the blush, as Tori realized she was getting back-scenes extras on this relationship that she very much did not want to know. Deciding that it was better to jump into the awkwardness than sit through wherever it was this was heading, Tori spat the first words that leapt to her mind.

"How did you two crazy kids meet in the first place? I'm guessing it wasn't sharing a soda down at the malt shop." This *was* something she'd been sincerely wondering for a while. The settling down part made sense because of Rick, but how did a super-villain and a normal person end up dating to start with?

The response wasn't immediate. For an instant, Janet looked up to Ivan, and a flicker of the past flashed between them. "Stupidity, youth, and adrenaline. I was going through a rebellious phase, taking up at bars without the safest of reputations. One night, a gang decided they'd like to help themselves to the till, regardless of what the bar's owners thought. Came in with guns drawn, screaming orders, even shoved a pistol into the face of a patron." The wistfulness died as Janet shook her head. "When Ivan ripped the forearm from the elbow, gun still in hand, I wasn't sure if the bar was screaming more in horror or surprise. But watching him savage those robbers... well, if I were making smart choices at the time, I wouldn't have been there at all. There was something appealing about a man that capable."

Having seen Ivan go into Fornax mode, Tori wasn't sure "appealing" was the categorization she would use, but clearly she and Janet had different tastes. The story tracked—a situation like that was bound to stir someone up. The effects of adrenaline on libido were well documented. It didn't fully explain Ivan's side of things, but then again, Tori had never known Ivan in his Fornax days. Janet was a striking woman. If that version of Ivan was more open to socializing, she'd certainly have been able to turn his head.

"Mind you, decades later, my kids are going to be stuck at a new school while theirs is getting rebuilt, because one of Ivan's supposed allies blew it up. So take a lesson here, Tori. Don't hook up over bloodshed. It doesn't lead to the wisest of choices."

Not wanting to touch the vast majority of that topic, Tori steered into the one bit she could comment on. "It's a shame about the school. Looked like a pretty nice place."

"How do you know—?" The flash of understanding in her eyes came without warning. Immediately, Tori watched Janet's entire demeanor shift. She didn't lose the stiff spine or set chin, but the rest of her expression softened noticeably. "You're the one."

"I'm the one?" Tori was accustomed to hearing those words with a tone of accusation, not gratitude, momentarily blinding her to the obvious truth.

The hand was so unexpected, Tori almost jerked back before it landed lightly on her shoulder. Janet held her there, making uncomfortably direct eye contact. "Thank you, Tori, or whatever your name is while in that suit. Thank you for being the only person in that fucking guild who cared enough to go protect my children."

It wasn't fair; the others hadn't even realized Rick and Beth were being targeted. Tori had only gotten the information because she beat it out of Rust Tooth when he tried to kill her. Knowing all of that versus being able to communicate it at the time were different matters, and Janet didn't seem to be inclined toward listening where the guild was involved. Ivan could clear things up, if it mattered. Tori was just trying to get through this.

"Given the, uh, delicate situation, I, um, can neither confirm nor deny anything, ma'am." That earned her a laugh from Janet, a gentler sound than Tori would have predicted.

"I can see why Wade paired you two up. That's fine, Tori. You don't need to say a word. Just know I'm grateful. Whatever else is going on in your life, you put yourself in harm's way to protect my kids. That's not the sort of thing I'm going to forget." Janet released her grip, casting a glance back at the door. "Do your best to keep everyone out of trouble this weekend, if you can."

Tori nodded, grateful to be back on semi-normal conversational ground. "Nothing to worry about. Between all of Helen's planning and Ivan being Ivan, these kids are in excellent hands."

Outside of people she knew quite well, Tori didn't have much talent for reading emotions, which spoke to just how naked the vitriol on Janet's face was at the mention of the name "Helen." Had Tori not just been outed as the one who helped Beth and Rick, she had a hunch Janet would be letting loose some unfriendly sentiments. Instead, the expression was forced away slowly, moved by willpower rather than feeling more at ease.

"I'm sure they'll be well cared for. Just don't want anyone to get distracted."

A bang from the front door pulled everyone's attention to Beth, who was zipping along with a white cord clutched in her hands. "Found it!"

Like a magic trick, stern Janet vanished into a haze of affection as she swept her daughter up. Gone were the harsh expressions and scrutinizing stares, replaced by a loving mother bidding her child farewell.

Perhaps it was from being rattled by the meeting, or the sight of a girl wearing a Starscout uniform being held by her mom, but Tori had to look away. It came a little too close to memories of her own, as well as the ones she'd been denied. Tori had never gotten to have a moment like this. Her parents were both dead long before she'd reached Beth's age.

When the farewell was finished, Ivan tossed Beth's bag into the trunk, loading the girl herself into the back seat of the car moments after. Janet lingered in the yard, waving goodbye until she was no longer visible in the rearview mirror. It had been an awkward start, but with that out of the way, Ivan and Tori were hoping for a fun, non-meta-human weekend.

That alone should have tipped them off to the chaos looming on the horizon.

Chapter 71

Huge fangs, dripping in what was probably acid or venom. A massive, scaly body covered in spines and sharp edges. Three tails slapping about wildly, making any approach from the back or side difficult, funneling enemies toward that big chomping maw with the dripping teeth. All packed into creatures each roughly the size of a city bus.

Honestly, not much of a challenge, at a cursory glance. It wasn't until Lodestar saw the flash of blue light hit and fizzle away that she understood why Wranglore, the spell-slinging cowboy, had called for backup.

Magic resistance, so these probably weren't mutations or science experiments run amok. Rather, they were some sort of mystical being. Summoned, created, or anything in between, when magic was on the table there were a lot more options. Looking at the silver lining, they were at least fully corporeal. For all her power, Lodestar didn't have very much non-physical versatility. She was largely pure force—anything that could phase enough to not be damaged by energy shots required help from the AHC's own magical resources. The semi-incorporeality was why she'd needed so much help to deal with Orion and was the reason magic users were such a pain for her to handle, in general.

Given that she only had five more minutes before she needed to be at the meeting point; there wasn't enough time to reroute the request for help. She'd just have to hope these beasts were as solid as they looked. From the sky, she dropped, increasing her speed as she went. This was no AHC evaluation; she didn't have to hold back on anything short of lethal force, and that was only until they knew if these creatures were inherently destructive or simply looking for food. Lodestar's speed cranked up until she could see the world in slow motion.

Wranglore had his hand cocked in a finger-gun, another spell formed at the tip of his index finger, sparking as it fired off. The nearest creature appeared to have noticed and was twisting toward him, mouth already parting. Lodestar saw a chance to test how immune these things really were, as well as help a fellow cape pitch in, so she took it. Grabbing the turning monster by the mouth, she jerked its head and pulled the jaws wider, ensuring that Wranglore's shot would go right down its throat.

That would take some time to connect, so she kept working. Zipping over to the one in front, Lodestar slowed herself down. She had to understand what she was dealing with. Scary on the outside didn't mean bad on the inside; that was a lesson she'd taken far too long to learn.

"Whoa there, big fella. Calm it down. How about you and me—" The words were cut off by a sudden lunge as those huge, dripping fangs came down on top of her. It would have been simple to dodge, yet she elected not to. Instead, she waited as the teeth shattered against her, hammers of clay smashing upon an iron anvil. Since conversation failed, this would tell her the rest of what she needed to know.

It took a moment for the monster to realize it had been defanged. A moan rose from deep in its gut, something hideous, and a spray of that dripping liquid gurgled up along with it. In the last second, Lodestar let out a burst of energy, vaporizing the liquid before it made contact. She wasn't worried about it hurting her, more concerned for how much extra work that would add to cleaning up once this was done. Today was on a particularly tight schedule.

With no teeth and its acid attack failed, Lodestar waited to see what would come next. She sighed as its jaws continued to gum against her and gurgling rose from the stomach, signaling a fresh batch of liquid attack brewing. Silly as it seemed, the action told her quite a bit. This creature was either made for killing or incredibly stubborn. Most animals would stop attacking something they had broken their teeth against, yet this one didn't even have that level of sense. Probably non-sentient, just conjurations made by some meta messing with forces they shouldn't have. Still, she'd play it safe until the experts could give their opinion. Wounds could be healed. There was no taking back death.

Turning the speed back on, Lodestar virtually disappeared from the maw, soaring back into the air. She wasn't there for long, finding the nearest target and dashing right into its mouth, this time breaking the teeth herself. She did a round on the feet, making sure there were no claws to worry about, then finished by tying the three tails tightly together. For some reason, that trick rarely worked on monsters made by science, but magic ones veered closer to cartoon rules. Nobody fully grasped why that distinction existed; it was just one of the many countless mysteries of living in a meta-world.

With a system established, Lodestar grew even faster. She was a flash of light, weaving through the pack, leaving a trail of beaten monsters in her wake. When she made it back around to Wranglore, Lodestar was momentarily confused by the stunned monster with smoke rising from its nose she found near him, before she remembered opening his target's mouth. Evidently, the magic resistance was literally skin-deep. Handy to know if these ever popped up again. Until they found the source, it couldn't be discounted as a possibility.

Wranglore's knockout was the final monster, so Lodestar brought herself back into normal time. Super-speed didn't really tax her to use, but staying in that state for too long eventually made her nauseous. It was a constant mental jarring, expecting things to move at one speed then readjusting on the fly over and over again. Some metas fell in love with the speed, tried to live there for as long as they could, but to her, it was just one more tool in the kit. A useful one, though.

"—that!"

Part of the problem of moving in and out of time perceptions was dropping into conversations already in progress. Given the look on his face, she assumed Wranglore was taunting his recently defeated foe. This also gave Lodestar a front-row seat to Wranglore's face as he took in the rest of the scene. He pushed back the rune-covered cowboy hat on his head, letting out a whistle like he was calling the herd.

"Holy... you tore right on through these things." Wranglore threw a spurious look at his finger, still letting off a tendril of magical smoke. "I was feeling good about my one."

"Luck of the draw," Lodestar said. "They were resistant to magic, not fists. Another enemy, our roles easily could have been reversed."

She gave the scene one last check, then covertly looked at the watch woven into the underside of her left bracer. "Do you mind holding down this area until cleanup arrives? I've got somewhere to be."

"Seems the very least I can do, since this was my job to start." Wranglore wiggled his hand, dispelling the last of the smoke. "Thanks for the... assist doesn't seem like the right word here."

"Well, it should, because that's all I did. You uncovered the threat, located it, alerted us to the issue, and called in appropriate force before they could reach civilization. I threw a few punches. Being strong doesn't mean diddly if I don't know where to point that strength. You saved the day, Wranglore, and I was happy to pitch in where I could."

Lodestar didn't wait around after that; experience taught her it was best to depart on the uplifting statement. It helped leave things on a positive note, and delaying came with fewer graceful conversational off-ramps. That was especially important, because she was down to only two minutes left. Rising into the air, Lodestar flew faster up once more, this time cranking up to traveling speeds.

Technically speaking, the speed at which she was moving through the air should be causing friction and shockwaves, leaving untold destruction in her path. It was one of the more commonly observed curiosities since Professor Quantum broke the original laws of physics in the same legendary experiment that created meta-humans, and one that no one had a viable explanation for: the people with super-speed seemed to ignore all issues of friction. It was the same way that some metas could be so huge, and yet completely skip the square-cube law, or how super-strength translated into lifting cars rather than putting hands right through the metal. Their world was not as it had once been, and even after all these decades, they'd still only scratched the surface on understanding how the new systems worked.

For today, Lodestar was just thankful for whatever made them function as she raced across the ocean, heading back to North America. Getting in and out of the house would be easy thanks to her tunnels, but there wasn't any need. Since returning to the AHC, she'd been picking up old habits, including one from her street-crime fighting days. Back then, she'd had nests hidden throughout Faucet Hills, places she could stop for supplies and rest. Rest wasn't much of an issue these days, but a superhero worth her salt always had a few spare outfits around.

Zipping into an abandoned bell tower at a former East Coast college, Lodestar found the hidden silver box. Professor Quantum's creation, these were as secure an option as she had for leaving unattended equipment. Slowing down only long enough to punch in the code, Lodestar waited as the systems engaged, hissing slightly to reveal the box's hidden treasures. Inside were the same clothes Helen had been wearing before she got the call. A blur of light, and Lodestar switched her ensemble, adding the uniform to the contents of the box, next to a spare t-shirt and jeans. Her usual Lodestar garb was packed with the rest of her supplies for the End of Summer Shindig, which is why she'd had to snag the nest's spare on her way. She took one last item from the box—a set of spectacles, though these were held carefully rather than being donned. Pausing to check her makeup once—mercifully, sweat was very rarely an issue in this state—Lodestar took back to the sky.

She raced across the country, until Ridge City came into view. At the sight, she felt her heart lift. It was always good to be home, especially with such a fun weekend to look forward to. Hopefully, the AHC would be okay without Lodestar for a few days. Granted, she could come if she was called, but Lodestar had been burning the candle at both ends since her return. The other side of her deserved some time, too.

It was a matter of seconds before she was at the parking lot, but Lodestar didn't stop there. She kept going, flying a bit farther, then dropping down into one of the nearby alleyways. To be safe, she pulled out a phone-sized device and hit a small icon that flashed red, then green. Every camera in the area was either disabled or scrambled—one of Vernon's handiest inventions, and the reason she kept a Quantum Utility Tool on her. With the coast cleared, Lodestar pulled the power back into her at the same time she donned her spectacles.

Glasses in place, Helen jogged down the alley, weaving her way back to the parking lot. In the middle of the day, at those speeds, the odds that anyone had seen Lodestar arriving were infinitesimal, but it never hurt to be extra cautious. Even given the special identity protections Helen had, she still played it safe where she could. The life of a public cape was not one she wanted, for her or Penelope.

Helen arrived a full three minutes before the bus pulled in, which still beat the earliest time the Starscouts would start showing up by half an hour. After going over details with the driver, she did a quick tour of the vehicle, eyes peeled for any potential issues, of which she uncovered none. It was a little old and a bit run-down, but they hadn't exactly paid for top-of-the-line luxury. The bus was safe, which mattered most, and she could always stick Ivan in one of the broken seats that didn't recline. Relaxation and Ivan went together like mint and orange juice.

By the time her tour was done, a car was pulling into the lot. Too early for the kids, and besides, she recognized that nondescript sedan, just like she knew the intentionally bland man stepping out of it. He did seem more animated than usual, his resting-stern face replaced by interest in his conversation with Beth. The others in the AHC would probably never see this side of him, would never let themselves see it, even if they had a chance. It was so much easier when the capes were good and the villains were bad. Getting in too close, realizing how much more was at play, understanding that the people they fought were more than their crimes... it made things complicated. Not always bad, but never easy.

Tori was right behind Ivan and Beth, and she threw Helen a grin as they saw one another. Another villain she shouldn't be getting close with. The reports of Hephaestus's conflict with the New Science Sentries had already reached her, as did photographs of the scene that team *didn't* see. For her, it was obvious; Hephaestus had been on lookout duty, keeping the AHC members away from the real show. Horribly, a piece of her was even thankful for it. Helen wasn't sure any of them were experienced enough to handle that kind of scene. At least it had happened on a weekend when Ivan had his kids. It was a small mercy that she didn't have to add his potential presence into the whole confusing equation.

"Good afternoon!" Helen's voice was full of cheer and pep as she greeted her first Starscout of the day. "Is everyone packed and ready for an amazing weekend of fun, friends, and frivolity?"

"Yay!" Beth threw up her arms in celebration, and for a moment, even Ivan's steely demeanor was cracked by a smile.

"A little alliteration?" Tori chuckled at her own wordplay, unintentional though it was. "Yeah, I'd say we're pretty psyched."

Ivan didn't respond immediately; that was never his way. Only in battle was he quick and decisive. In his civilian identity, he favored being steady over being speedy. Better to grasp a situation well, and then act, than move in too rashly. It was one of the traits Helen admired in him; she tended to be prone to impulse in her own life. "Is there anything you need?"

"Sure, take this clipboard and help me greet our cluster as they roll in. We have to get an accurate head count before we can depart." Helen thrust the hunk of wood into Ivan's chest, and with it, she saw the nearly imperceptible signs of his nerves easing. What he'd really been asking was if there were threats to be aware of, and she'd just told him to keep his mind on the actual tasks of the job. Ivan did best when he had a role to play and a script to follow. Keeping him in cluster-leader mode would put his focus on actual issues, rather than potential ones.

For the first time since she'd been staring down at the stampeding horde of monsters, Helen paused and took a breath. There was still a lot of weekend to go, and she hoped not to spend any more of it flying through the air while shining brightly.

"How was your Friday? Soak in the last bits of civilization while you still can?" Tori asked.

Helen half-shrugged, as if her activities were too boring to warrant a proper roll of the shoulders. "Same old, same old. Just another day at the office."

Chapter 72

In the planning, preparation, and lead-up to this trip, Tori thought she'd gotten a good sense of what she was in for, having never gone to such an event in her own Starscout days. It took only until the bus pulled onto the campgrounds, joining dozens of others streaming onto the site, for Tori to realize just how off her expectations had been.

She'd pictured ten or so other clusters, all sharing a large chunk of forest with perhaps one central cabin in case of emergencies. Instead, Tori was forced to wonder if the entire state was all gathering for this single End of Summer Shindig; she stopped counting after the first fifty buses. Given that the attendance was so much higher than expected, she was somewhat less shocked as they began to weave their way through a huge swath of land. Dotted around it were various cabins and hookup points for RVs, all of which the huge convoy passed, heading into the deepest part of the forest.

It was there she finally saw the Starscout area—what almost looked like someone had built a full summer camp meant for hundreds of people out in the middle of nowhere. There were bunk cabins, a huge mess hall, various activity stands, a lake twinkling in the late-evening sun, and tons of space for setting up tents. Clearly multipurpose, yet she had to imagine this was the zenith of its usefulness, the main intent with which the space was built.

Since summer still held a slight upper hand in the changing of the seasons, it was warm enough to camp outside using tents. Some years, it had to be the bunk cabins for safety, and depending on how the winds blew, that might still end up being the case, but for the first evening, Tori found herself pitching in to help the scouts set up their camp. Or rather, she tried to do that, but instead discovered that the kids were overall better at it than she was. For them, this was old hat, whereas Tori had never been a fan of tents, even in her street days. Since she didn't worry about the cold, the loss of visibility wasn't worth the minor protection from the elements.

Only once every tent was sturdy and stable did Helen gather her charges. They'd ended up fairly in the middle of things, surrounded by other clusters, not far from the lake. It was a vantage point that showed her the multitude of others still handling their setup, giving Tori an unexpected pang of pride in the efficiency of her group. The sentiment was especially unwarranted given how little she'd helped, yet it was there, all the same. There were, thankfully, logistics to focus on instead.

"Great job setting up!" Helen declared, getting a rabble of cheers from the kids. She didn't let it grow past that, speaking while she had their attention captured. "Time to look ahead to the rest of our evening. We've got about an hour before the mess will start serving dinner, and the social starts right after, so anyone who wants to wash up should get jumping. We all know how fast the lines can grow around here."

The rest of the cluster nodded, so Tori did, as well. It wasn't hard to picture; this many people were going to cause traffic no matter what. She wondered if Ivan had brought along any sort of Wade-tech to mitigate that issue, at least where restrooms were concerned. Unlikely, but a woman could dream.

"Tomorrow, we start the Shindig Games bright and early, so try not to stay up *too* late catching up with your friends." There was something of a wink in her tone, the implied understanding of a rule that must exist, and yet everyone expects to be broken. "Tori and Mr. Gerhardt are our only newbies here. The rest of you know the area. Remember to stay within the camp at all times, unless you're in the company of a Starscout leader—we *are* still in the wilderness. If you need anything, I'll be here. Otherwise, come back by seven for dinner."

It was almost akin to being in a flophouse when someone screamed "Cape!" the way those children scattered. They fled in every direction, racing away from their area, streaming into other camps and calling out greetings. Coming here yearly, they'd obviously made friends among the other clusters, which was probably the point of getting them all together in the first place. Tori wondered if she'd been too young for these kinds of events, or if her parents had simply been too busy. It was tempting to put them on a pedestal, but keeping them human in her memories also helped make the pain manageable. They'd both been career-driven scientists; it wasn't inconceivable that this sort of thing was more than their schedules could, or would be allowed, to bear.

"Are we sure none of them used magic? That was a really quick departure," Tori noted.

"Our only known magic meta-human at this particular function is Lavinia, who you can thank for the utter lack of insects around us. She's got some handy repelling spells laid down." Helen scanned the campground once, like she was taking note of every activity and not just the actions of their kids. "Since we've got some time to work—Ivan, why don't you finish unloading the rest of our supplies? Get some exercise for a change, you desk-jockey. Tori, we can't have you out here without knowing how to ready a tent, so you're going to help me with mine."

With one hand, Tori waved to the rows of tents already sitting there. "Seems like that's already handled, doesn't it?"

"Until a strong wind knocks one over in the night and a scout needs help fixing it, potentially while terrified from being suddenly woken up. Or when breaking them down happens, and they need your help to not snap a delicate part of the frame. We're the adults here. The kids have to know we can handle any problem that arises. The buck stops with us, so we should be prepared."

On the surface, it might be difficult to see why Helen and Ivan got along so well, despite coming from visibly different worlds. But when one scratched the slightest bit deep, the biggest similarity leapt into view: responsibility. Helen and Ivan both cared a tremendous amount about the duty of their roles; each took their responsibilities arguably *too* seriously. Tori felt reasonably sure the world wouldn't end if she couldn't make a tent, yet from the way Helen spoke, it was like there were incredible stakes at play.

She followed Helen over, taking hold of a faded old green tent and helping to spread it out along the ground. In the corner of her eye, Tori could see Ivan unloading boxes of food from the bus—their contribution to the overall supplies. He almost reached for an entire stack of four, then thought better of it, shifting his grip up to two. Finally, and not without some visible annoyance, Ivan settled on a single box, hefting it onto his shoulder and starting the trek toward the mess hall. It had to be galling, knowing he could lift the whole bus, and having to do things the mundane way all the same.

A jolt brought Tori back to the moment. Helen had gently tapped the tip of her nose. It was more shocking than painful, jarring her suddenly. "We can help Ivan afterward if you're worried about him, but there's no point in doing this unless you're paying attention."

"Sorry," Tori mumbled.

"It's okay. I get it. New scene, lots to take in—this is an exciting place, and we're going to have a lot of fun here." Helen patted the green canvas firmly. "After our chores are done."

Tori watched carefully as Helen stretched the fabric, pulling out the long tubes of plastic and slowly threading them through loops sewn into the tent. The procedure was smooth and effortless, equally so when Helen yanked them all right back out and set the tubes at Tori's feet. "Your turn."

"I just watched you do it."

"Then it should be easy to replicate," Helen countered. "And I'll be here if you run into trouble."

"For someone only a few years older than me, you sure do like to give orders." Tori picked up the nearest tube and began attempting to mimic the feat she'd seen Helen so easily manage. It eventually did make it through the first loop, but it wasn't nearly so smooth an operation.

Reaching over, Helen pinched a piece of fabric, breaking up a minor stoppage in the second loop so the tube could keep moving. "I look good for my age. Also, part of life as a single mom. You get used to acting as the final line of making sure everything gets done, because if you don't, it won't. Being in charge is a responsibility."

"Where is your daughter this weekend, anyway? Could she not come along?" Tori finally finagled the first tube through its final loop and started work on the second. This time, she didn't need Helen's help with the pinch trick, utilizing it herself to roughly force the plastic along.

"Too young for this event, and not a Starscout yet. She may not go down that road at all. Penelope is her own creature; she never seems compelled to follow in my footsteps, thank goodness." Helen looked a tad flustered at that last line, almost like it said more than she intended. "She's staying with a friend of the family, alongside other kids her age. I daresay I'll come home to an excited ball of energy, or a completely wiped-out shell of a child."

On the final tube, Tori hit a significant snag, one that no amount of pinching seemed to clear. She started pushing harder, trying to force the plastic through the fabric, only to have Helen's hand fall lightly on her arm. "Stronger isn't always better. Sometimes, you're better off backing up, taking a breath, and trying again."

It was a good thing Ivan had taught Tori to not inadvertently let out heat, because she'd definitely have seared a few holes in the tent's thin material otherwise. Pausing for a few attempts at calming breaths, she wiggled the tube into the loop once more, and this time found it moved without issue. Whatever configuration of fibers had caused the blockage had moved on their own when she yanked out the tube.

"There we go. Very well done. Now, we get the stakes, and I show you how to keep this bad boy bolted to the ground." Helen hopped lightly to her feet; she was a surprisingly spry woman when she wanted to be. As Tori dug through a bag, she looked back to Ivan.

He was still going one box at a time, even as some of the other cluster leaders were hauling visibly heavier loads. But they were the strapping sort, the kind one expected to find unbothered by heft. Ivan was leaner—not that his body would have accurately portrayed his strength if he were three stories tall—and therefore had to pretend to be weaker. It was the commitment to the identity that she admired more than anything. No one would have blinked if Ivan opted to carry two boxes at a time instead of one, yet he refused to make even that small of a compromise. He lived his role unerringly, devoted to the deception. Tori wasn't sure she'd ever be that good, or had the desire to try. The easier path seemed to be avoiding people, especially capes, wherever possible.

"Gotcha!" Helen emerged from her bag with a handful of metal skewers, each tilted at a sharp angle on a single end. "Come grab an end. You can hold the tent in place while I hammer."

At least here, Tori didn't have to pretend. Fire powers and meta-suits didn't help one bit with getting a tent ready. Maybe that was why Ivan liked the office—it asked him to rise to challenges that Fornax never could. Come to think of it, that might be why she'd managed to find a bit of joy there as well. It wasn't the right environment for her long-term, but it had definitely taught Tori that there were ways to be fulfilled outside of science and stealing.

And at the end of today, she'd have learned an entirely new skill. She might not touch another tent ever again, or she could be hurled into some wasteland tomorrow. It never hurt to have a skill, by her reckoning, so Tori paid close attention as Helen lined up the first metal skewer.

"This is the best part, because unlike with the tubing, here hitting things hard *does* tend to fix all your problems." Helen smashed down on the skewer with the heel of her palm, driving it into the dirt.

"If only life could be so simple," Tori mused.

"I don't know, I think if you hit your problems often enough, you'll probably run out of them," Helen replied. "Either one would hit back harder than you could handle, or you'd drive off all the people and things that caused the problems to start with. Both pretty bad endings, if you ask me."

Tori shrugged. "It helps if you're a misanthrope."

"Funny, you sure do have a lot of people in your life for someone who just claimed to dislike them." Helen smiled, extending the next metal skewer. "Want to take a crack at the next one? Sounds like someone could do to show the ground what-for."

Weird choice of phrasing aside, Tori wasn't going to turn down the opportunity. If she had to learn this, she might as well learn it well. Plus, there was something to be said for the therapy of smacking inanimate objects.

Chapter 73

In his life, Ivan had been no stranger to unique experiences. From fake tournaments in space, to several mystical Christmas adventures, to traveling through a land made from mirrors and terror, to being summoned as a hero in a world of magic; yet he still counted this as one of the most surreal moments he'd ever experienced. Standing in the middle of a gigantic facility, surrounded by kids and other cluster leaders, amidst one of the biggest events of the Starscouts year. That he was here at all was bizarre, that Beth was along as well pushed it into the realm of unbelievable, and then, when one factored in Helen... were Ivan more confident about his prospects in whatever afterlife awaited, he might have thought himself unknowingly dead and ascended.

Of course, this was no heaven, which was why he had to snag the tumbling child who nearly came down headfirst on a punchbowl in their excitement for snacks. He was at this social on-the-clock, as an official of the organization, with a duty to uphold—though that duty was coming in fits and spurts, as the children were largely occupied.

All manner of food, drink, and snack had been brought in for the post-dinner social. The hall was largely segmented off into a more active section, versus one for restful engagement. There were games on both sides, things like cards and Velcro darts with minimal potential for causing damage. Some kids were playing, others chatting, and a brave few were already out on the dance floor, going to town. Beth was among a group of friends from prior years, catching up as they tossed bean bags at a slanted plank of wood, and he noticed Tori making rounds near one of the snack tables. She was grazing freely, but also helping out the kids who'd piled their plates too high, so she was at least earning her nibbles.

The whole ordeal was so peaceful and fun, it set his teeth on edge. Youth did not come with pleasant associations for Ivan. It was hard not to expect one of these children to wheel around and strike while another's guard was down. He envied this life of theirs, but couldn't be jealous. Ivan didn't even have the capacity to imagine experiencing a normal childhood—the scars of reality ran much too deep. It didn't matter, anyway. There was no changing the past. Watching his daughter smile and laugh without so much as a smidge of fear, Ivan told himself that was all the normal he needed.

"Hmmm, I'm a little worried about that dance floor. Should somebody get it started?"

In another life, Ivan would have grinned at the sound of Helen's voice arriving at his side. Instead, he merely nodded, letting perhaps a small spark of good humor into his eyes. "There are already kids dancing."

"Like six, and two of them are doing something interpretive. Sure seems like somebody should get it started." Helen bumped against Ivan's arm with her shoulder. "How's the trip treating you so far?"

"No issues to report."

The sigh that came from her lips was almost painfully familiar. "Not what I asked. I wanted to know how it's going. Are you enjoying yourself? Because it's okay if you are. You do get to be happy sometimes, Ivan."

It was the sort of thing only she could say with sincerity, the reason Helen was more dangerous than any other cape. She believed in people, to the core, and while that had made her job all the harder at times, it also meant she'd managed things like influencing Fornax, something that even Ivan would have considered impossible at the time.

"I am happy every day. I am grateful every day. I know where my path was supposed to lead, and each morning I rise fully aware that I'm living on bonus time."

"It isn't bonus time. It's your life." Helen paused as a trio of kids bolted past, eyes on the diminishing mound of homemade cookies, many of which bore Ivan's favored recipe. She touched Ivan's shoulder, drawing his attention over to Tori, who'd accepted a dart challenge from one of the scout teams and was proceeding to miss wildly. One even managed to land on a particularly fuzzy jacket of a nearby reveler, the Velcro hooking in on impact. "At least Tori's taking to the vibe well."

Looking at her, Ivan imagined the hard-faced young woman he'd first met in that cell. She never would have been able to blend in like this, her entire focus had been on the next move in front of her face. Now, she was not only thriving as a civilian, she was building up an entire new identity with history and contacts. One day, he truly hoped Tori would see a way out of this life for herself. Sadly, that was a journey she'd have to take on her own. Ivan couldn't light a path he'd never traveled.

"She's the adaptable sort. High intelligence doesn't hurt, either."

Another round of kids passing caused a pause, only this time, the conversation didn't start right up again when they cleared. Instead, Helen lingered at his side. "You know, given the context of the situation, I'm sure no one would bat an eye at two cluster leaders hitting the dance floor together in a fun, friendly dance. How about like when you-know-who dealt with the... okay, I actually don't remember the name of this one. Red thing, lots of ooze and tentacles, plus it ate small chunks of time?"

"Krondabbler," Ivan supplied.

The triumphant slap on her knee was so loud it drew looks from some of the nearby scouts, forcing Helen to wave at them awkwardly. "Krondabbler! Right. Like with Krondabbler—you go right, I go left, except, when we meet in the middle, we flip punches for box steps."

"I know how to dance, enough to realize you might be a few decades out of sync with that box step idea."

"Nah, everything is cyclical. It's either back already, or we'll get it there. Also, way to go blowing the whole 'brooding silent guy' thing by admitting you've danced. Keep the glower going. The rest of us are using your presence to lightly scare any of the rowdier kids."

The truth was, Ivan had been to many bars and clubs in his villain days where idly moving in some semblance of time with the beat was enough to qualify as dancing, but it had been his wedding that had forced him to learn some actual steps. As small and simple as the ceremony was, they still went through the major hallmarks: first dance, bouquet, cake-cutting, all to fill the scrapbook with photographic evidence of normalcy. Yet for some reason… no... for a reason Ivan recognized instantly but chose not to acknowledge, he didn't want to mention that fact to Helen.

"I can put on my annoyed face if anyone gets truly troublesome. Were I to go as far as vexed, I might end up giving them nightmares, however."

To his surprise, that didn't garner any sort of laugh or chuckle. Looking down, he noticed Helen's gaze wasn't on the scene around them currently; it was aimed off somewhere in her brain that only she could see. He didn't have to wonder what was on her mind for long. Helen was never one to draw things out.

"Seeing all these kids... do you ever imagine what your life would have been like if you'd gotten a more normal childhood? What sort of person you'd have grown into with a different start?"

"No." With almost anyone else, he'd have left it there. "I don't dream about the impossible. If I'd ended up somewhere else, then whoever came out of that wouldn't be me. He'd probably be better in a lot of ways, but even as a concept, that other me is so far removed from who I actually am that he's a stranger."

"I wonder about that. I think some of this Ivan might be deeper rooted than you realize."

Not wanting to let things settle there, Ivan turned the question around. "How about you?"

Helen shook her head. "We're in different boats. I made it to nineteen living normally. I had time to develop and engage with mundane life. Remove that one night where it all changed, and a whole lot about my life would be different, but I think I'd still be more or less the same person. Probably less confident."

"Oh my, a Helen with more modesty? Perish the very concept." In spite of the heady topic, Ivan laughed. Something about being around her just made it hard for his mood not to stay light. "Aside from the obvious two child-shaped reasons I would never change my past, you realize that version of Ivan wouldn't have met you, right?"

"Huh. You know, I genuinely hadn't considered it. You've been around so long, I guess I just automatically picture you in my life."

The long stretch that went between them then had nothing to do with more kids, and far more to do with the unspoken line that Helen had just come dangerously close to slipping over. Both found something to occupy their attention elsewhere, avoiding eye contact.

When the song changed and two of the dancing kids exited the floor, Helen saw her opportunity for as graceful an exit as she could hope to manage. "Okay, now we're down to four. It is definitely time someone got it started."

Unsure whether to roll his eyes or smirk, Ivan did neither, opting instead to play along. "But where will we find a cluster leader with the self-confidence to—"

"Of course I will!" Helen charged onto the dance floor, clearly not having actually listened to Ivan's reply, busting out such classics as the Lawnmower and Driving the Bus before the song's first chorus had even been reached. It was a performance of pure cringe, made all the stranger for Ivan since he had firsthand knowledge that not only was Helen incredibly graceful, she'd taken multiple types of professional dance instruction. None of which could be seen in the display of her grabbing one knee and bouncing with it as she spun slowly around on one leg.

Across the room, interest turned to laughter, as one would expect in such an equation. Except afterwards, the process wasn't over. By whatever strange alchemy of charisma Helen possessed, the amusement turned into fun. From the fringes, more kids wandered onto the dance floor, confident that nothing they did could possibly be as ridiculous as the moves Helen was busting out. She'd turned herself into the attention target, letting everyone else feel freer for the distraction. He even caught sight of Beth's group migrating toward the music.

Tori wandered over, having soundly lost her game of darts, and examined Helen's performance with an uncertain eye. "Well that's... something. Don't take this wrong, I like Helen, she's nice and all, but the lady kind of does her own thing, doesn't she?"

In a weekend filled with double-speak and subterfuge, it was a pleasant break to be able to answer with complete honestly. "Helen has the surety of someone who knows exactly who they are, and is comfortable with it. Obviously, she's a total weirdo. That's what happens when you lose all fear of what other people think."

Taking one brief moment to stretch, Ivan started off toward the dance floor, resolved to hanging back at the edges. She was meant for the spotlight, he for the shadows; they both knew where they worked best.

"Um, what are you doing?" Tori asked, unable to believe what the context clues were suggesting.

Ivan didn't stop, but he did turn back to answer, an equal mix of amusement and exasperation in his tone. "Probably a box step, sooner or later. She has a habit of getting her way."

Lozora hadn't expected approaching the Starscout site to be easy—Lodestar would never let this many vulnerable kids be gathered in one place under her name without protections in place. It was that openness to being challenged that led her to accept her employer's tech. It galled her, needing something as external as his tools, but the call had proven to be prudent.

The external energy barrier would have sliced her clean in half without the disruptor blade, and the mechanical sentries she'd battled would have radioed in about an intruder if not for her signal jammer. Supposedly, even the dark material clinging roughly to her skin was helping, warping the view of any electronic surveillance device that happened to pick her up.

Her handiest tool was unquestionably the mapping device, however. What had started life as a simple Indigo Technologies tablet, the itPad as they were commonly known, had little save for the screen still in common with its original configuration. Lozora's employer had incorporated scanning utilities, along with some hacked satellite feeds, to build a mobile map-generation utility. Just by walking around, the area was revealing itself to her.

Tonight was all about reconnaissance. Targeting Fornax meant getting him nearly alone, down to just his cluster. They wanted pure data on how long he'd be held; the more unplanned factors introduced, the greater the chance they got faulty information. Tomorrow, when the games started, there would be chances. So long as Lozora knew the terrain, she had a fair shot at maneuvering around without being caught. Once the orb was thrown, that would steal everyone's attention while she holed up out of sight.

Stalking through the woods was hardly her idea of a fun weekend, but Lozora bore the task without complaint. Roughly a week to go until the real fun started, and all her work would pay off. One step at a time, though.

First, she had a legendary super-villain to piss off.

Chapter 74

The End of Summer Shindig schedule was clearly not here to fuck around. Before even sunrise, Tori was up with her cluster, dealing with poor sleep thanks to a combination of lying on the dirt and excessive sugar after all her snacking. There was no respite to be had upon waking, as it turned out children needed managing in the morning. Armand and Caden had to be shooed away from messing with their sleeping bags, both certain that two bags could be combined into an uber slumber cocoon, while Mallory sat to the side, explaining the flaws in their logic. For a moment, they thought Newton had vanished, but he turned out to merely be running around the campground, burning off some extra energy. Loyce and Trudy were trying to grill pine cones on the embers of a low fire, but at least they'd gotten ready first. Most of guiding the kids was on Helen and Ivan, who managed it well; however, with this many to track, they definitely needed the extra help.

Once the kids were on the right track, Tori managed to stumble through a shower at one of the facilities, getting in before the lines turned unmanageable, then forcing herself to throw down some food in the mess. On her own, she might have skipped the firm flapjacks and runny eggs, but this was not a day to be running on half a tank. By the time she'd finished slamming her breakfast, it was time to hustle to the lake for her cluster's first event.

Due to the number of scouts present, there was no way for the entire gathering to do the same activities concurrently. Instead, a rotating schedule had been established weeks prior, noting where each cluster would go through the day. They might tackle a task in the morning that others wouldn't face until that evening, yet by the end of the celebration, every group would have scores to be tallied. While not all of the events were competitive in nature, they were common enough that no one would forget they were playing for stakes. Mostly small trophies and bragging rights, but stakes all the same.

First Aid Relay was her cluster's starting activity, a test of their education in semi-realistic environments. Each cluster would see a "victim" fall over at the opposite end of the lake's beach. It would be on them to check the dummy's vitals, perform CPR, and find a way to move it safely back across the rough terrain of sand. A Starscout leader was on hand to make sure they handled every step properly, taking notes on the details that would ultimately become their score.

She watched at Ivan's side as the kids tore down the beach, kicking up plumes of sand that spun along on the wind, then drifted out over the water before finally settling back down. Newton got there first, with Beth close on his heels. To Tori's surprise, Ivan's daughter took the lead on checking vitals and executing CPR. Beth hadn't ever mentioned either subject, yet she looked like an aspiring EMT as she assessed the dummy's condition.

It was only afterward, when she had a moment to ask Ivan, that Tori got greater understanding. Part of Beth's ability-control training incorporated enhanced emergency education; the idea being that, if they knew what to do in an emergency, there would be less chance of panic and unintended flare-ups. In the moment, though, all Tori knew was that Beth had flown through the medical stuff, finishing just as Caden finally plodded his way up to join the rest of the cluster.

With Mallory calling out positions, the cluster dispersed the dummy's weight amongst themselves, while Armand and Trudy were dedicated to keeping the neck steady in case of injury during the fall. A touch excessive, given the short drop and soft landing material, but more concern typically fared better than less when it came to the practice of medicine. They kept a steady pace, moving with swiftness and surety, balancing the need for speed against the precarious balance of walking along sand. The fact that they stayed together so well spoke to excellent coordination and teamwork, far better than loads of adult teams Tori had seen throughout her life.

Of the three clusters, theirs was easily the first to return, stoking an unexpected spark of pride in Tori. That didn't necessarily mean they'd done the best—speed was only a single piece of the overall assessment—but it damn sure wouldn't hurt. Cheers and high-fives were passed around freely in celebration. Then, once the jubilation had faded, minds turned to the next task on their docket. The kids were old pros at this, changing from one challenge to the next without so much as a missed step. The exuberance and adaptability of youth were marvelous qualities; Tori wondered if any meta had found a way to bottle that. Then she realized the sorts of steps and ingredients that would probably go into such a concoction and figured if that meta had existed, the guild would have sent Kristoph calling almost immediately.

Being less flexible, Tori had to mentally shift gears as they wandered away from the lake, heading out to a wooded area. No more running on sand. Next up, they had to make and break down a campfire safely, a notion that still tickled Tori even days after learning about it. Then, there was the first crafting challenge, a relay race, and then finally, after the nature hike, they'd get to break for lunch.

Thinking about the long day ahead, Tori almost wished she'd forced down a few more of those stiff pancakes. Almost, but not quite.

"When you said you wanted to up your training after that last fight, I was on board. When you asked me to find a remote location with lots of high, sheer surfaces, I obliged. Even once you told us you'd be bringing along weights from the gym, we rolled with it. But at this point, I think we're going to need an explanation."

Cyber Geek nodded to the pile of chains resting in the dirt next to the weights, all of it sitting in the shadow of the rocky outgrowth looming over them. Cold Shoulder seemed less concerned, whereas Hat Trick wore a comically puzzled face, a slight sliver of tongue poking out the side of her mouth, seemingly unnoticed.

"I've been doing a lot of weights and sparring, but Hephaestus didn't just get stronger since the last time—he got smoother. The guy was crazy light on his feet for how heavy that suit was. I thought long and hard about what exercise would help me the most." As he spoke, Medley began to loop the first chain around his torso.

"The act of free-climbing will strengthen my hands and feet while I use my claws to dig into the rock. Hauling the extra weight makes it harder, meaning I'll also get stronger. But I don't just want to be heavy, I want to be unwieldy. Hence the chain."

Medley picked up a weight and tied off a section of chain; however, it wasn't bound close to his body. Instead, it landed several feet away. Given the slack, it would dangle from Medley once he started ascending, yanking him to and fro. “Different weights at different lengths is going to make it incredibly hard to move with any sense of fluidity. I’ve never really trained full-body dexterity before, but I figure pushing myself is a good place to start.”

“You’re sure this is safe, right?” Hat Trick asked.

“Definitely not. That’s why I asked you all to come along. Hardy as I am, that summit is a good ways up. Good to have friends around, just in case.”

“There are other ways to get stronger, you know.” Cyber Geek expected the words to fall on deaf ears, yet he had to speak them, all the same. They had decided to stick him in the leadership role, and saying what everyone already knew was part of the gig.

Medley kept on working with his chain, tying off the second weight. “Maybe for you. You’re still growing like you were at the start. Some of us are starting to plateau. We’re getting passed, by villains and fellow superheroes alike. If I want to keep up, it means taking things to the next level, so I hope you’ve got a healing item on hand.”

“Still no luck with consumables,” Cyber Geek reported. He’d tried summoning a variety of potions and power-ups, all of which came over fine, but turned back to sparks and numbers when he tried to ingest them. “The hunt continues, though I could summon a set of attack-ribbons that wind tight on impact to contain bleeding. Between that and your speed-healing, we should have time to get you help.”

“Let’s hope it doesn’t come to that.” Cold Shoulder was already beginning to form her ice-construct—a huge body that might be able to catch Medley, depending on where he hypothetically tumbled from.

Adding the last two weights, Medley moved across the ground, feeling them drag like the anchors they were. He ran his claws along the rough stone surface, locating purchase, and then hauled his body up from the dirt. That was the easy part; Medley could more than handle his own heft. When the first hundred-pound weight came off the ground, it was an inconvenience. By the fourth, Medley could feel the strain running along his arms and legs. It was a good pain, the ache of strength to come, the price of getting stronger.

Another handhold as the climb began in earnest. The weights clanked as Medley rose, his friends watching carefully from the ground below. So far to go, and he’d only just begun.

The relay race was, in theory, a simple event. Each scout would run their section of the track to a station, where a Starscout leader would be waiting to ask them a question pertaining to the history or systems of the organization as a whole. If they missed it, they'd be asked another, and so on until they got one right. After that, the baton changed hands and the race continued; a mix of mental and physical challenges rolled into one. What caused them a momentary delay was the fact that one of the cluster's leaders was also expected to participate, starting off for their teams to show the kids how it was done.

On the outside, it was a simple matter of determining who should take the role between Ivan and Helen. Spry as she was, there was no way Helen could hope to compete with Ivan's speed... if Ivan had been willing to show it off. Tori quickly realized the complication: Ivan couldn't tell them that he was stronger and faster than any human here could ever hope to match. Even without actively using his abilities, there was no getting around Ivan's overall power.

Helen, however, had thoughts of her own. "Come on. You're a quick study, but we both know I've got the better knowledge base here. Plus, I mean, you do work a desk job. Can't imagine there's that much opportunity for exercise."

"You'd be surprised by how fast I can learn when motivated, and it's not like this is my first year with the Starscouts. Beth has been a member for much of her life. I've paid attention to the various cardboard presentations throughout the years."

Tori trailed behind them as they led the cluster across the camp to the relay race site. None of the children were paying the adults much attention, far too enthralled in the joys of the day. Loyce had acquired a large bag of trail mix at some point; she and Caden seemed intent on polishing it off before the next event started. Newton was doing stretches while walking, visibly excited to put his athletic talents on display. Beth, Mallory, and Armand were deep in discussion about what the best order would be, going back and forth even as the final moments drew near.

As for Tori, she found the disagreement between cluster leaders interesting enough on its own, though the others couldn't appreciate the strangeness of what they were beholding. It wasn't seeing people playfully bicker that struck her as odd, it was the fact that Ivan was engaging in such a practice at all. Had she ever seen him argue in jest? Generally, Ivan was either giving or taking orders. There was nothing wrong with it, no reason why he couldn't, it's just that... something about this was odd. A curious itch in her brain she couldn't quite manage to scratch.

"Fine. We'll flip for it." Helen jammed a hand into her right front pocket, drawing the distinct jingle of change until she produced a shiny quarter. "Lucky for you, I've got a soft spot for vending machine snacks."

"Why don't we have Tori flip it, seeing as she's impartial?" Ivan suggested.

That earned them both a scrutinizing glance from Helen. "I'm not so sure about that."

"I am." Tori reached out and grabbed the coin. "I can say with absolute honesty that I don't care which of you does this part, so long as it's not me. Call it in air?"

"Yeah, yeah. I'll even play fair." Helen put a hand over her glasses and eyes, covering her face. "Go ahead."

One more eccentricity from a woman rapidly piling them up. Tori ignored it for now, losing any curiosity to that damned mental itch. She flipped the coin into the air, and at its zenith, Helen called out, eyes still covered. "Heads."

Tori snagged the coin, slapping it down onto the back of her left hand and covering it with her right. Despite the initial apathy, the kids had drawn closer, as well. With the entire cluster looking on, Tori moved her hand, revealing the shiny surface that lay beneath.

Chapter 75

Deep down, Ivan knew he should have let Helen make the run. She knew the organization's history better, and had more protection than he did in case of accidental power displays. That was without even factoring in the mockery that would come if words or photos of this incident ever got out. Had this event come some weeks prior, he'd never have even floated the possibility of being in the relay.

That was before things changed with Rick. Before Ivan had had to start asking himself how long he had with his children still seeing him as their father, instead of as a killer. Rick was already heading down that path; Ivan could only guess the number of years before Beth caught on as well. He wanted to build new memories while it was still an option, some pleasant recollections for them to hang on to once the hideous truth finally came to light. And, perhaps, these memories were for him, as well. Pieces of the life he knew could fall out from under his feet on any given step.

A sparse woods dotted the nearby landscape, leading to a sharp, rocky incline that turned into a lumpy hill. The stretch of track ran in a loop measuring roughly a mile, bordering up to the edge of the incline before circling back to the starting point where Ivan currently waited. With him were most of the cluster, along with Trey and Yuri, the leaders of the cluster they'd be racing against. Yuri would be his competition. While Trey looked like he could handle hauling firewood, she unquestionably was the faster mover. Her partner hung back with the scouts who wouldn't be participating.

At the other end of the track, Tori and Helen were positioned. Since the kids were spaced out along the route, they'd done the same with the adults, ensuring that if anything went wrong, the kids could be reached quickly. Five stations lined the equidistant points, all with a radio and a scout from each cluster waiting. That was where they'd be given their questions, though rather than have five staff members standing around, one referee could deliver all queries from a single device. That was also why a cluster leader was posted on the opposite side of the track—a little observation helped ensure that everyone played fair.

"Good luck!" Yuri called to Ivan from her starting position a few feet over, seemingly with genuine sincerity.

He put on his most pleasant face and waved. "To you, as well!" It didn't hurt to set good sportsmanship examples with the kids watching.

For the barest of moments, Ivan's past tried to break through, reminding him of the sorts of tasks he'd endured at that age. With absolute will, he denied it, sending the memory back into the pits from which it came. As Ivan, that part of him had to be sealed away, locked completely down. Those sorts of recollections served Fornax when the need arose; Ivan had no purpose for them. At most, they were reminders of what he was working so hard to ensure: that no child, especially not his, ever suffered through that again.

A crackle of static came over the walkie-talkie on Trey's belt. "We're ready to go with the questions when you are."

"Okay, folks, that means we're about ready to race." Trey's husky voice went well with his dense body, easily commanding the attention of the kids milling about. "Leaders, are you both ready?"

Ivan threw a thumbs-up, which Yuri mimicked moments later. Trey evidently caught the gestures, taking one last look over the track before he gave the order. "Perfect. Then take your positions, because the relay race begins in three... two... one... go!"

Obviously, Ivan wasn't running at full speed. Even without actively using the tremendous amount of power that coursed through him, or a hint of magic, at his baseline he was still well past human limitations. Unless Yuri was hiding super-speed, he'd win, and even that trick would only work until he equalized the temporal distortion. Fornax couldn't reach the tiers of true speed on his own, but he did have the ability to match an opponent, not that it was a skill he needed while plodding along a fifth of a mile. In the end, he more or less matched Yuri's pace. Sometimes he got a little ahead, sometimes a bit behind, until the last stretch, where he surged slightly ahead and stayed there. Fair play was all well and good, but he *did* like to win.

"Ivan Gerhardt of cluster number two-three-seven, checking in." Although he tried to put a weary gasp in there midway through, it was clear to any observer that the effort hadn't significantly winded him.

The radio crackled as Caden and the other cluster's kids looked on, waiting for their moment to shine. After a half-second of static, the question arrived.

"What year was the first End of Summer Shindig held?"

In his mind, he could hear Helen's voice, rattling off Starscout history during their meetings. That one, he didn't need her help with, however. Despite the last memory's failure, a new one bubbled up. Lodestar's face, on the boxy old televisions inside the store display. Her smiling, cheery expression as she flew past a sun rising over an idyllic lake. Ivan could still picture it perfectly, still remember his absolute confoundment at the image. By then, she and Fornax had briefly traded blows, though he didn't yet have any idea what he was truly up against. At the time, he'd only been perplexed at the idea that someone strong enough to stand up to him would use their time on such stupid, pointless projects.

Funny, the way life loved to wrap around and remind Ivan of his own past idiocy. At least this time, it was useful for something. "The year was nineteen-ninety-three. Three years after the Starscouts were officially founded." One year after a young man dripping in blood crawled his way out of a hidden hellhole, blinded and terrified by his first time seeing the sun.

"Correct. You may hand off!"

Just as Caden had a firm grip on the baton, Yuri caught up. She wasn't far behind at all; Ivan had given his cluster a small advantage, not a guaranteed victory. Across the track, near Helen and Tori, he could see Beth waiting. She was the mid-runner, taking the third leg of the race. She put up a double thumbs-up, clearly celebrating their early success, before turning her eyes toward the approaching form of Caden.

By the time Ivan's attention was back around him once more, Yuri's question was done and her kid was off, slowly gaining on Caden's narrow lead. He was far from the most athletic member of the cluster, but they had some strong runners still left, with Newton acting as their anchor. Ivan moved back toward the other kids, cheering loudly as he did. It didn't really matter who won or lost; the experience was the important thing. But he could still root for victory, especially with his daughter among the competitors.

He was so lost in the moment, Ivan didn't even catch the minor spike of magical energy that came from the other side of the hill.

At the prick of her finger, the orb came alive. One drop of blood, not even human blood at that, was all it took to start the various mechanisms running. Initially, Lozora had considered waiting until the group was entirely on their own, hitting them on the nature hike. After a night hunkering low, Lozora had decided that expediency took priority. She rationalized it by thinking that the longer she stayed, the greater her chances of discovery. Besides, this would catch Fornax even more off guard. As for the extra civilians, they shouldn't impact the data. Ten kids or twenty, dead weight was dead weight. Fornax would have to deal with that either way.

Based on reputation, Lozora might have expected Fornax to simply wipe everyone else out on the off chance it would make escape easier on himself, but after seeing him run a fifth of a mile in a Starscout leader uniform, she was having her doubts. While Fornax might be physically down there, it appeared as if the legendary villain might well have already been dealt with. This hardly seemed like the kind of man who could disrupt her employer's plans. But that was why they tested: to be sure, rather than work off supposition alone.

Several clicks came from within the orb, and Lozora counted them. The timing was key. If she got it wrong, Lozora herself would wind up in the trap. It was a situation she'd eventually be able to escape from, but not without losing a significant amount of time. Anything strong enough to hold Fornax would be a murderous gauntlet for most meta-humans—even Lozora would have to work carefully to escape.

With a *kerchunk*, the first panel of the orb slid away, revealing a stretch of bright green beneath. It rattled, expanding in size, and Lozora reared back. Almost time now. She waited, tense, until a sharp hiss rose from the device. That was her final cue, and with precise aim, Lozora chunked the orb through the air, over the hill she was hiding behind, toward Fornax's position. The moment it left her hand, Lozora began to race in the opposite direction, all concern for stealth temporarily cast aside.

In order to make sure Fornax was caught, Cobblord had built a big range onto this trap. Brave as Lozora was in the face of danger, not even she wanted to be stuck inside the same cage where she'd just thrown Fornax. By the time she made it to a crop of trees to hang on to, the smaller rocks from the hill were already rising into the air.

For a moment, it was perfect. Beth won her part of the relay; Loyce lost them a few steps, but made up for it in trivia, getting Newton a clean handoff. He was trucking down the track, closing the small gap his opponent had built up. The others were nearly back—even Helen and Tori had started trekking over. It was a nice, normal, happy moment. Then Ivan felt the surge of energy. He might have stood out, craning his neck skyward, except that was about the time things started to fly.

Well, rise, really. Water bottles, kicked-off shoes, even hats clean off of scouts' heads. It all started to lift up, rising toward the rapidly expanding sphere overhead. The bigger it grew, the more details Ivan could make out. It was grassy inside, with long streaks of gray, like stone, and he was almost certain he caught movement in a few areas. Instantly, Ivan recognized the quality of the work. It was too specialized; only Cobblord could craft a custom portable world. Unfortunately, that also meant it wouldn't be easy to avoid without overtly using his powers. Cobblord's traps always sprang well.

A moment later, Ivan realized escape was never an option. The kids were rising too, a few fully leaving the ground. His eyes locked on Beth, who had been slowly jogging back to the group, and now upgraded to a full-on sprint. It probably would have been more effective had she not just been forced to race; Ivan could see her steps landing lighter as she drew steadily higher.

"What the hell is that thing?" Behind Ivan, Trey was panicking—a very reasonable reaction to the sight he was beholding. Any answer that could be offered would only raise more questions, so Ivan ignored it, focusing on controlling the situation while they still had a chance. With one look, it was clear he wouldn't be able to save all of the kids from going in—there just too many, and some of them were already halfway into the air. If keeping them out of it wasn't an option, then Ivan's only choice was to protect them on the inside.

"Keep the kids together," Ivan ordered, more force in his voice than he'd have used with the children. "Seems like we're going in no matter what. We can't risk them ending up alone."

The draw was starting to affect Ivan, as well. He weighed considerably more than the scouts yet could still feel the pull. Trey was already getting light on his feet, so Ivan made use of the movement he still had. Racing ahead with more speed than he'd been willing to show on the track, Ivan barreled across the field, to where the kids who'd been running were making their way back. He grabbed the ones he could reach, hurling them back in Trey's direction. They were still floating, but at least now, they'd hopefully come down with the others.

Beth didn't get tossed, however. By the time Ivan got there, she was too high, out of reach. With a single jump, he left the ground, sailing up through the air until he nearly collided into her. She grabbed on as soon as he came near, visibly scared, but still holding her composure.

"What is this thing?"

"A momentary obstacle," Ivan assured her. Looking up, he could see the structure in more detail now. There were stretches of forest, stone ruins, even cliffs and hillsides. Too big; this orb would be easy to lose people in. From his belt, Ivan grabbed a walkie-talkie, hoping that Trey still had his turned on.

"Listen to me, anyone being pulled in. We're going to rendezvous at the huge stone tower near the edge of that forest. Stay low, be quiet, and get there no matter what." From where the bulk of the kids appeared to be heading, that should be a straight shot for them to reach. He, Beth, and anyone else who'd been too far back would have a tougher trip, but they had the benefit of Ivan's willingness to crush any threat that might appear.

Having Beth secured, Ivan looked over to the section of the field he'd worried about the least, the area with Helen. She and Tori were both airborne, neither looking especially thrilled about it, though Helen's face spoke more to confliction than fear. If she transformed, it would be nothing to snatch the kids up out of the air. But in doing so, she'd also give away that Lodestar had been here, which meant the Starscouts would be potential targets anytime someone wanted to lure her out. Not to mention, if this was only the first step of some unknown plan, revealing their ace in the hole too early might leave them vulnerable down the line. Ivan did the only thing he could think of in the moment to help.

"I've got them!" Ivan yelled, hoping his words would reach across the long stretch of open air. "Just worry about keeping her safe."

Both Tori and Helen nodded at that—a confusing reaction that Ivan didn't have time to consider, because he was no longer floating. They had officially crossed the halfway point to the massive orb. Ivan could feel space rippling around them, packing the expanse of this microcosm into an sphere much too small to contain it. Passing that point meant they were now falling toward a new surface, rather than rising from the old one. As the ground drew near, Ivan pulled Beth in close, encasing her as best he could from all potential harm.

In the moment, Ivan's entire focus was on getting her and the rest of the kids out of this safely. When that was done, when his anger could be allowed to stretch, Fornax would have a great deal to say to Cobblord and whoever hired him. That came later, though. For the moment, he had a portable labyrinth to deal with.

Chapter 76

In her youth, Helen would have already changed. Glasses cast aside, blazing through the air, she would have snatched every child out of the trap's pull and spirited them to presumed safety. Experience had taught her many things through the years, and one of them was the importance of patience. If someone had gone to all the trouble of securing a Cobblord creation, sneaking onto Starscout grounds, and deploying it, then she couldn't assume this to be the only trick in their bag. Until she knew what this was about, who she was against, and what powers were in play, it was preferable to save her big surprise. Rescue everyone now, and the perpetrators would clock Lodestar's presence, almost certainly triggering them to flee and try again later down the line. She might be able to catch them, but this was too much preparation to assume there wasn't some manner of escape plan.

All of which flashed through Helen's mind before she remembered that transforming could potentially out her secret to Tori, as well as to any of the kids or staff who happened to be looking over. That was a factor to be concerned with, but a secondary one. Protecting the kids came first.

Her eyes scanned the approaching orb, which appeared to be increasing in size as they drew closer. She spotted several moving creatures made entirely of stone, as well as some smaller ones that appeared to be constructed from grass and twigs. Cobblord was an efficient designer; he'd used the terrain of the labyrinth to stock it with pseudo-life. No need to feed them, and more could probably be formed if their numbers were cut down. Certainly, they were dangers in other circumstances; however, for her or Ivan, there was nothing to present a significant challenge.

It was as she was visually combing their destination that she locked eyes with Ivan, who was already clutching Beth and pulling all the kids near him close. They'd be bunched up when they landed, and from the looks of things, not too far from the rest of the cluster. She and Tori, on the other hand, were drifting toward a canyon; based on their trajectory, Helen estimated they'd come down about a mile over from it. On her own, a minor matter to cross. With Tori in tow, it meant they had to either go around or fly, the latter of which came with a lot of required explanation.

"I've got them!" Ivan's voice would not be confined by such mortal hurdles as wind or distance. "Just worry about keeping her safe."

What a silly thing, the assurance she felt at those simple words. No one could "have them" in this sort of situation. It was dangerous, the kids were in peril, and they had essentially zero clue as to what they were up against. Yet all the same, Helen knew they'd be safe. Villain or civilian, when Ivan said he'd do something: he'd knock the gates of hell from their hinges to keep his word. With his daughter there, looking to him for protection, she truly couldn't imagine the threat that would successfully stop Ivan.

If he was taking over guarding their charges, then that meant it was on her to find the maze's center. Every Cobblord labyrinth could be safely destroyed and exited from their middles; he was as faithful to his theming as he was to his prices, both famously inflexible. Tearing it apart by hand was technically an option, but he tended to build in disastrous, often explosive, consequences for those who tried to cheat. On her own, she'd have blasted right through this sphere, and then wiped off all the singes. With a mass of Starscouts in the mix, the safest option was to do this properly.

Their descent speed was increasing, and Helen noticed Tori bracing for impact. Poor thing was probably tearing herself up wondering whether or not to turn into fire upon landing, debating if broken limbs were worth a lost secret.

"Don't worry!" Helen said, raising her voice to be heard over the whistling of the air in their ears. "We slow down before landing."

The sharp, focused look Tori shot her was a curious reaction, but she did seem to be less immediately terrified. As for Helen, she spent the rest of their descent making as precise a mental map as possible. For most of the people being drawn in, this was all chaos, but she was used to looking at things from above. While the route she spotted was rough in patches, it definitely seemed to lead somewhere. That was as good a start as any.

Lifting her hands up like she was on a roller-coaster, Helen let out a sharp squeal of fun as the drop-speed grew, plummeting them toward the orb's ground. Ivan and the kids were out of sight—the warping space pushed them further away with every passing second. Since he had their walkie-talkie, Helen could only hope that Ivan would either be able to handle any danger, or be wise enough to yell for help. The faster she and Tori could end this, the less time those kids would be in even the slightest danger.

Behind her, the real world fell away as the artificial sky locked into place. They were officially contained in the trap. From this point on, the only way out was victory, or destroying the labyrinth entirely. The ground was rising up toward them at an incredible rate, and Helen permitted herself to savor the sensation of falling.

It was actually kind of fun, when one wasn't concerned about the landing.

Between the surprise, terror, and sudden rush of ground, Beth had apparently blacked out. She stirred slowly, feeling the strange grass against her skin. It was the right color, shape, even smell, yet something was inherently off. No one factor she could put her finger on, yet she instantly recognized the facsimile of foliage for what it was. Lifting her head, Beth spotted several other Starscouts, most of whom were either unconscious or barely starting to wake.

With a flash of terror, she realized her dad wasn't there. What happened? He'd been holding her as they fell, so he couldn't have landed elsewhere. Did that mean something had gotten to him? Beth knocked that idea aside; she knew the wilderness too well. No wild animal would go for one target in a sea of unconscious bodies.

Just as she was about to call out, movement from a nearby tree caught Beth's attention.

The leaves rustled as Ivan dropped down from among them, knocking some stray fake-twigs away from his khaki ensemble. At the sight of Beth awake, he hurried over, dropping down to a knee. "How are you feeling? Does anything hurt?"

She shook her head. Now that the pounding fear in her chest was fading, Beth realized she didn't have so much as a bruise from the impact. Her meta-human ability had proven to make her slightly tougher, but considering that no one else was bleeding or howling in pain, she didn't appear to be the only one. "I guess the ground is soft?"

"We slowed down just before we hit. The rapid momentum shift must have given you kids all a massive headrush." Ivan pointed over to the tree he'd just come down from. "The good news is we're close to most of the others. I spotted Trey, Yuri, and the rest of the scouts; they're less than a mile from that stone tower. We've got a bit more of a trip, but the path isn't especially difficult. Think of it like a nature hike in very unfamiliar terrain."

"With alien animals," Beth added. "I saw stuff moving down here when we were approaching."

The fake grass squeaked slightly as Ivan slid onto his rear, sitting down next to his daughter. "Not alien. Custom made." He motioned to the ground, trees, sky, all of it. "This is a trap made by a man called Cobblord. I saw one of those online mini docu-videos about him. Apparently, he specializes in custom creations, and these are his favorite. Used to be, you'd hear news about one appearing yearly. While well-engineered, Cobblord also has certain standards he upholds, one of which is that a labyrinth gets more dangerous the deeper in you go. Out here, in the starting areas, anything you see is likely more scared of you than you are of it."

"Are you sure it's safe?"

"Positive," Ivan said, because he was. Beth didn't know about his magic, and she certainly didn't realize he had a low-capacity sleep spell. Even if she had, it was unlikely she'd have realized that two minutes and twenty pass the same while unconscious, especially with no electronics and an artificial sky. Most of all, she definitely wouldn't have reason to guess that Ivan had spent that time racing around their entire area, destroying everything non-human that so much as twitched.

Not far from where they were, one could reach the lip of a large canyon. Were one to look into it, they might take note of the piled-up stone bodies, dozens of creatures smashed to oblivion and hurled roughly out of the way. Ivan knew they would all be safe, because he'd ensured there was nothing around to attack. Eventually, the labyrinth would rebuild, but once they had the kids in one place, it would be much easier to protect them. Clearing everyone's path in secret was step one. Step two was rejoining the scout groups. Step three, find shelter—ideally food, if possible.

Step four was where things got complicated. Ivan could either stay with the kids, or try to hunt for the maze's center. It was tempting: wipe out every threat, then race to catch up with Helen and Tori. But if he were there, Ivan's mind would be back among the scouts, worrying for Beth. A compromised ally was often worse than an enemy—besides which, he'd told Helen he would keep them safe. That promise didn't end until the kids were off this orb and back onto... well, a different orb, when one got right down to it, but it was *their* orb.

Movement signaled that the others were shaking off their slumber. Beth had proven surprisingly resilient, waking several full minutes ahead of them. Ivan wasn't sure if that was due to her meta-abilities, potent willpower, or a developed tolerance. The reason he'd learned that spell in the first place was to help Beth rest when she was teething, so she'd gotten a fair few doses through the years. It was one more variable to account for in a situation already spiraling fast out of control. Hopefully, he wouldn't have to lean on any more magic. The ideal way this played out was that he found the other kids, they all hunkered down, and then Helen got them out. For her part, he had no concerns. Saving the day was what Helen did. Ivan just wished he felt quite so sure about his own tactics.

There was something else he hadn't told Beth, a part of the labyrinth that was not quite so comforting. While the starting area *was* the least dangerous, it steadily grew less so. Since the purpose of these places was to make the subject defeat the maze, staying in one spot was discouraged. The longer they stayed camped around here, the more numerous and powerful the creatures would become. By nightfall, the woods would be repopulated. Come morning, the threats would have grown in size and threat. If Ivan planned to let them survive that long, anyway. Once he got the kids with the other counselors, it would be easier to move freely. However long Helen needed, he would hold the line. Regardless of what he had to do or admit, he would not let harm come to these kids. Especially not with Beth sitting there, watching his every move.

Fornax was a villain, a killer, a monster, and so much worse. That had been the only life he ever knew, the only way of being. It wasn't until Wade that Ivan saw friendship in another person's eyes when they looked at him, something he hadn't experienced since the nameless companion Ivan had been tortured into killing. Then came Helen, someone who looked at him like he could be more than what he was.

But none of them came close to his children. For the very first time, Ivan had understood what it was to be a hero. When things went wrong, when they were afraid, when the world seemed darkest, they looked to him, because they knew he'd be there. That trust in him was among the most precious things Ivan had ever possessed. He already knew it was fading with Rick, and Beth probably wouldn't be far behind. Still, for right now, she was looking at him like he could make this okay, keep them safe. Save the day. There was almost nothing he wouldn't do to prove his daughter right.

"Everyone, please stay close as you wake up. The entrance was rough, but you'll be okay after a few minutes to shake it off. I know you're all scared and confused right now. That's not only okay, it's the expected reaction to something like this. However, we are not merely a gaggle of confused civilians. We are Starscouts, which means if anyone is prepared to get through this, it's all of you." Ivan looked to Beth, the only one fully awake so far. "For example, we need to head toward that stone tower. How do we navigate when we lose sight of it?"

From her pocket, Beth produced a compass, carefully noting the tip of the stone tower they could see poking up among the trees. "It's northwest of our current position. Assuming we always head in that general direction and keep checking in when possible, we should be able to find it without much issue."

Not exactly a tough dilemma, but the goal was to make them feel in control of the situation. Hopelessness and helplessness were wily enemies in situations like these. When people felt desperate, they started to make bad decisions. Keeping the kids calm was part of keeping them safe, a task that would only grow harder the longer this lasted.

"Starscouts, you heard Beth. Let's gather ourselves and start moving northwest. Stay close, and if you hear anything, let me know." Taking a defensive position at the front of the group, Ivan pulled away some almost-bushes and led the children toward what he dearly hoped would be safety.

Sparing a slender amount of his already scant mental energy, Ivan wondered how Tori was coping with all of this. Given that she didn't have children to watch or the responsibility to battle the maze, it was likely a much more relaxing endeavor than what he faced. With Helen there to keep her safe, the only real trouble she could get into would be self-inflicted.

Chapter 77

It was testament to how truly fucked up Tori's life had become that she quickly adjusted to the sudden shift in their situation: from a day out watching kids in harmless competitions to being scooped up by a giant floating sphere. Anyone who'd done deep research into meta-humans was at least passingly familiar with Cobblord's works—many of his creations had been huge public spectacles. Tori didn't have the slightest idea how the mazes functioned, unfortunately; only that they popped up, often swallowing bystanders, and vanished only after the capes ventured inside.

Standing on dirt that wasn't quite the right shade of red, Tori looked out over the vast canyon. Wide and deep, with sheer edges and no paths to be seen. Climbing down and then out wouldn't work, not without taking them days. Floating over in fire form was technically an option, if she was willing to reveal her secret and abandon Helen. That wouldn't have been a prudent move in the first place, and it certainly wasn't viable after Ivan's request.

"Just worry about keeping her safe." That was what he'd yelled across the aerial divide. Seeing as Tori was the one with abilities and guild training, it was obvious he wanted her to protect Helen. A much easier task than Ivan's guarding an entire herd of kids, but still not a simple job. Without using her abilities, Tori was going to be relying heavily on hand-to-hand, and some of the creatures she'd seen on their descent looked a mite too large for that to mean success. She'd have to make judicious use of "tactical repositioning," the technical term for running like hell when outgunned.

Footsteps caused Tori to whip around and come face to face with Helen, who'd drifted slightly off near the end of the descent. No injuries that Tori could see. She didn't even look especially put out, face still beaming as Helen looked across the sizable divide. Her whistle started high, then dropped low, stretching for a borderline comical amount of time.

"Unless one or both of us is hiding the power of flight, I don't think we're making it across that." Helen seemed a touch more amused than that line really warranted, a detail Tori brushed directly over. "Not that it matters. Now that we're in, the only way out is through. Have to find the center and beat the final obstacle. That will safely release everyone trapped inside."

"Is there a non-safe release option?" Tori asked. She hadn't counted on the possibility of trapped exits, but there was no reason they couldn't be in use.

"Non-safe release is what happens when metas try to cheat. For example, nothing here would really pose much of a challenge to someone like Professor Quantum, but if he decided to blast right to the labyrinth's center, he would trip the failsafe measures, which everyone else inside would have to deal with. Carrot and stick. We either play the game as it's intended, with a chance at a happy outcome, or we cheat and live with the consequences. All of which is moot, in the first place. Obviously, we don't have the shortcut option."

Tori wasn't entirely sure about that. She could cause some potent destruction when needed, and a lot of the stuff here did look flammable. But Helen was right that they wouldn't be risking such tactics. Even without Ivan's fury if anything happened to Beth, Tori wasn't going to risk those kids. She was a criminal, not a piece of shit, and annoying as they could be, that cluster was still hers. Her fists tightened, anger threatening to rise. They were supposed to having a weekend camping trip, a nice, normal event. Some motherfucker had stolen that. From the kids, from Tori, from Ivan and Beth. Nobody hated getting robbed quite like a thief; Tori would have loved to show whoever did this just what a spectacular fuck up it was. Pity she doubted the chance would come. Ivan simply had more clout and connections. He'd get his vengeance first, and anyone who'd dined at his table knew that neither Ivan nor Fornax left any remains.

"What's the plan? Do we try to get a signal out to the capes?" Tori didn't love the feeling of those words on her tongue, but she couldn't very well suggest that they go attempt to conquer the labyrinth.

"That would take too long. Even if we could send a distress call, which is not an easy task, the way this place has warped space in on itself also means it packed in layers of time around us. Best guess, if we could get a message out right this moment, help might arrive within a week." Helen slapped Tori lightly on the back, between the shoulder blades. "Good news. Looks like you and I are taking this bad boy on."

It felt like her brain was stuttering. The ease and cheer on Helen's face refused to fade, even while she proposed such an insane notion. Maybe Tori could have handled this alone, using her flames to hit and move, but with a human tagging along, their odds dropped substantially.

"I'm not sure we're the best ones for the task."

"Does it matter?" Helen managed to make what could have been a snippy retort sound utterly sincere. "We're the ones here. The other adults can't go maze-diving, since they have the kids to protect. Innocent people are in danger, and we have the power to help. What other choice is there?"

She wasn't wrong about the situation. They were the only two who could move freely. Even if Ivan was capable of slipping over and joining them, he'd never leave Beth and the others helpless. Assuming that Helen had accurately estimated the warping of time around the labyrinth, external aid was unlikely to come anytime soon. Regardless of how she turned the situation around mentally, Tori couldn't find another angle, not with such limited information to go on. There simply was no other way around it. Getting out meant going through.

"I guess there isn't one," Tori conceded. "Our only hope is to try. You seem to know these things pretty well—how do we find the center?"

"All roads lead there, eventually. It's more a matter of how fast or easy a given path might be. I saw a route on our way in—looks troublesome, so that's our best lead."

The sudden break in logic almost made Tori miss a step. "Wouldn't we avoid the troublesome parts?"

"Not if we care about time. The harder the path, the more direct it is to our goal."

"Is that a rule of mazes?" Tori asked.

"That's a rule of life. But yes, also applies to these labyrinths." Helen looked up to the false sky, perhaps searching for an exit, or trying to create some sense of time. "We shouldn't be reckless, but we also can't afford to take too long."

"Right. The longer everyone's in here, the greater the chances one of the kids will get hurt."

To Tori's shock, Helen waved the notion off half-handedly, not even looking down. "I'm not worried about keeping them safe. Ivan's there. My concern is that, depending on size, these devices can sometimes take days to properly complete, and we don't have any food or water. Unless Cobblord happened to build those into this particular model, we're on the clock with everyone's own body. Without supplies, we can't protect them from hunger."

Casting her eyes around, Tori zeroed in on the foliage. Trees, grass, shrubs, some of it was bound to be edible. But food was secondary compared to water, and even as she scanned, Tori realized that just like the dirt, all of it looked slightly off. Just wrong enough that she wouldn't feel confident trying to shovel it down, and certainly wouldn't risk feeding it to one of the scouts. That hadn't even occurred to her, yet Helen had clocked it as their primary obstacle.

The mental itch flared up once again, soothed by the thin rationalization that it must come from all her Starscout survival training.

"I knew I should have forced down more of those pancakes," Tori mumbled.

"Ugh, yeah, the food here is dietarily compliant for pretty much anyone, but the flipside is that some of the stuff they took out is what makes it taste good. I made a breakfast muffin run."

They'd started walking away from the canyon, ambling toward the forest and the route Helen had seen. Tori almost let the comment slip by unnoticed, before she remembered the prior day's trek. "Wait, how did you make any kind of run? We're miles from civilization and all came together on the same bus. You don't have a car."

Helen didn't stop walking entirely, however, she did throw a curious glance over her shoulder, almost like she was reassessing Tori. "You've got a knack for critical thinking. Most people wouldn't have noticed that. Anyway, I probably meant I made a breakfast muffin run before we came and packed a case in one of my bags."

A rogue pang in Tori's stomach signaled the first beginnings of hunger, an issue she'd have been far less concerned with one hour prior. "We should stop talking about food. I don't think it's leading anywhere productive."

Walking along the grass, it was easy to clock the shifts in terrain. After ten minutes, all signs of dirt were completely faded; it was as though they'd been dropped into a dense jungle. Even the air seemed warmer, soaking into Tori's unsweating skin. Heat was no issue, but if they encountered a more frigid environment, she might be in trouble.

One concern at a time. They followed the collection of breaks in the trees that constituted their route.

"Well, this is officially boring. Should we play a game? Penelope has made me a whiz at twenty questions, assuming all the answers you pick are famous cartoon characters."

How was she this calm? Helen was not only unconcerned with their situation, she was able to get bored? "Seems like we should probably pay attention."

"You can't stay tense the entire time, you'll burn yourself out before nightfall. I've got good ears. Let me handle the scouting. Until then, keeping mentally active will help us continue to stay alert."

Tori wasn't entirely sure how accurate that was; however, she'd begun to feel a headache forming in the base of her skull. The stress of waiting for something to pop out at any moment *was* wearing on her, and this could be their situation for days. Splitting guard duty made enough sense to justify letting herself have a momentary break. Assuming Helen proved to be as sharp a listener as she claimed, they could start trading off on the task.

"I don't know about twenty questions, but I can think of at least one. How do you know so much about these mazes?" Tori considered herself an adept researcher in the meta-human field, and not even she'd retained the myriad of details about Cobblord's various creations.

"Pretty simple: I used to be a reporter who covered the meta-human beat. Writing about new crimes requires putting them in context with what's come before, so a lot of the job was research based." Helen looked almost wistful, though given her age, the job couldn't have come more than a few years prior. "Nowadays, I'm mostly on the business side, running some self-owned stuff and staying afloat. I still like to keep up with meta-human events, though—can't quite kick the habit."

Although Tori didn't let her eyes go wide or loudly gulp, the sentiment still ran through her. A reporter who specialized in meta-humans, with a wide base of historical knowledge? Helen was essentially the worst person to be paired with while trying to secretly use abilities. Not to mention, her being a history buff meant she would absolutely know quite a bit about Fornax. If Tori fucked up truly spectacularly, it was possible for her to give away both their secrets. Better to steer the topic away from things like metas.

"Entrepreneur, huh? I've got ambitions in that direction, too."

"Not happy at Vendallia?" Helen asked.

On reflex, Tori shrugged. "It's fine for now, just not what I see for myself long-term. I like a little more excitement than Ivan." It didn't hurt to reemphasize his cover as a boring middle manager.

Helen's laugh was different this time, lighter, almost familiar in an odd way. "You know, your uncle is more than his job. Ivan might surprise you."

"I think I can safely say I am past the point of being surprised by anything about Ivan," Tori told her.

A beat of silence passed before Helen's reply; she'd tilted her head northward for a half-second. "Anything, huh? So you know that Ivan has a beautiful singing voice?"

Of all the insane things that had happened during their day thus far, that mental image almost caused Tori to trip over her own feet. Her brain had slapped Ivan's face on one of the Multerion musicals—currently, she was picturing him belting out tunes as the titular character from *Phantom of the Symphony*. It was even more ridiculous than she would have guessed.

"I'm calling bullshit," Tori declared.

"Call it all you want, but I'm right." Helen didn't slow down; however, she did shift their angle slightly, moving them to the right side of the path. "When Penelope was a baby, she was the fussiest sleeper you've ever met. I was on my own, a little out of my depth, and Ivan came by to help. Sometimes, he would sing her lullabies if she started to cry."

The mental musical faded, replaced by the thought of Ivan leaning over a crib. Oddly, this image aligned far more naturally with her understanding of the man. When it came to his children, Ivan had no sense of embarrassment; their happiness and safety far outranked such selfish concepts. If singing made his kids happy, he'd have done it, just like he bumbled around the dance floor last night. Evidently, it was a skill he didn't mind sharing with any infant in his care.

But pleasant an image as that was, it opened up an entirely new topic for discussion. "Wait, I thought you met Ivan when he helped out with Penelope's play. How did he sing to her as a baby?"

"That's a very good question, Tori. Unfortunately, I'm going to have to request we table it for now. Based on their movements, in less than a minute, we're going to have company." Helen halted their walk, pointing to a large section of trees that were just beginning to wobble.

"Brace yourself. We're about to see this labyrinth's claws."

Chapter 78

It only took a few hours to reach the stone tower where Trey, Yuri, and the rest of the kids were waiting. Had the cluster not been led by a man who'd secretly scouted the entire area and killed every hazard in their path, the simple trek would have taken triple that time, but none of the children suspected a thing as they ran to rejoin their friends. To them, it had simply seemed like the hike they'd already been prepared for, albeit in a scary situation.

"Oh my God, Yuri, they're okay!" Trey called from his position over to Yuri, who was in an identical spot on the other side of the tower. They'd posted lookouts, in case surprises came calling. Ivan wasn't sure if it was the program they headed or these two in particular, but he was glad to have competent help. Given the way this weekend was shaking out, that might well be the only lucky break he was going to get.

Unlike the others, Beth didn't run off to her friends, though she did wave to them. Her hand was gripping Ivan's, he could feel her elevated heart rate thudding away. Worse, he could sense her tension as Beth put all she had into focusing. This was scary, a sudden shift in the expected, and when Beth grew afraid, her blades tended to come out. Rather than worry the others, she was clinging to her father, trying with all her might to keep the silver weapons contained. Ivan's heart might have burst from pride, if it weren't already boiling in fury at whoever had *dared* to make his daughter so fearful.

"Look at that, we got here safely," Ivan told Beth. Still holding her hand, they headed toward Trey, who was walking in their direction. In unknown terrain, it was best to avoid loud noises like yelling whenever possible. "Is everyone accounted for?"

The relief on Trey's face as he watched the children pour in spoiled the answer. "We'll have to do a head count on your group, but I think we've got all the kids." A shadow of fear suddenly crossed. "Wait, where's the other cluster leader and her helper?"

"Across the track when we were getting lifted. Every inch of separation got magnified in the descent—you and I weren't very far apart, and it still took hours to get here. Given their distance, it's safe to say we probably won't see them before this place shatters and sets us free." Ivan noted the fear in Trey's face; unfortunately, there wasn't much mollification to be offered. Worrying about Helen was like fearing a dandelion: the circumstances where such sentiments were warranted virtually didn't exist.

Several small forms, those from his cluster, were gathering up now that they recognized their leader. Loyce stuck her head up like a prairie dog, trying to see over the others. "Where's Miss Helen?"

"She's perfectly fine, off with Tori exploring this strange place." Gently, Ivan sank down to a knee, eyeline with the kids. "I know everyone is scared right now, and understandably so. We've all been transported to a strange land. But keep things in perspective, too. Has anyone seen any sorts of animals or creatures?"

The shaking heads were as he'd expected, given his speedy slaughter, but it was also a way to make sure nothing had slipped his notice. Thankfully, it seemed he'd been thorough enough in the initial purge. Soon, there would be more. Ivan needed to get them all hunkered down safely before he went out again; each wave would be stronger than what came prior, meaning the fights would take longer.

"There you go, then. We're in an odd location, but not necessarily a dangerous one. Helen and Tori will be fine. Soon, this place will run out of power and deposit us safely back on the ground. Until then, why don't we take the opportunity to be proper Starscouts? Has anyone tried to identify the local flora, started sketching our surroundings, or begun work on shelter?"

Both the kids and Trey seemed surprised by the notion. They'd been so caught up in the shock of what happened, they'd yet to plan for survival. That needed to change immediately, both for actual logistics and to keep the kids from panicking. Having a task to focus on made situations like this more bearable; the other option was sitting around worrying all day.

"Let's start breaking up based on the skills we feel best in, then your cluster leaders can find appropriate ways for everyone to help out. Take care not to overexert yourselves. I'm unsure how long it will be until we find snacks." Ivan scanned the area once more, noting a bright orange spot amongst the emerald green of the grass. "I don't suppose the water jug actually managed to keep its contents when crossing over?"

"Yuri was holding on to it, trying to weigh herself down, and inadvertently kept the top pinned," Trey explained. "But we only brought enough to cool the kids down post-run. Even with rationing and the smaller bottles, people will get thirsty, fast."

Another problem added to the list. At least for now, they had something to drink. Food was another matter. In theory, they would all be fine for days before the true negatives of starvation set in; however, that didn't stop the pain and discomfort. Good kids or not, that was going to hinder them, to say nothing of morale. Nothing Ivan had killed looked especially edible, nor would he have trusted these materials, anyway.

In almost any other circumstances, Ivan would have slipped away into the forest, hunting down Tori and Helen to help them put an end to this. But between Beth and the rest of her cluster, he just couldn't. They would be defenseless, and with no way of knowing how long Helen would take, he was equally ignorant on the number of threats that would come sniffing around this area. Try as he might to think of another way, Ivan's only choice was to trust the others while he protected the kids.

"I don't expect we'll be here more than a day, at the most," Ivan replied. "These tend to wind down long before then. Just to be safe, let's plan for two days with the water rationing." That would be stretching things thin as it was. If the others took any longer than that, he'd have to risk getting more directly involved. He'd never tried to teleport out from one of Cobblord's creations. It very well might work, but it could also trigger some sort of volcanic meltdown. Far from a first resort, but if kids started getting dehydrated to the point of danger, risks might become necessary.

A squeeze on Ivan's hand brought his focus back to Beth, who was chewing on her bottom lip, despite how her parents had tried to break that nervous habit. Eyes locked on the forest, she was steeling herself for something, gathering her nerve. At last, Beth turned her gaze to Ivan.

"I can... I'm going to cut some firewood. We don't know what the night temperature will be, or if there are any animals out. A fire can be useful for warmth, protection, and cooking, if we find food."

It was the first time Beth had even proposed the idea of using her powers outside of the courses she took for control. She didn't even call upon her blades in private, let alone around other people, especially her friends. But she wanted to help, and saw something she could do that no one else could.

Few things terrified Ivan like his daughter's kindness. He'd seen that same trait abused and twisted in others by no end of opportunistic shits. For a long time, he feared the tendency would lead to her becoming a victim. Then she grew older, began showing some of Janet's wits, along with perhaps Ivan's own stubbornness, which eased his concern slightly. But since the change, Ivan's fear had only intensified. Kind, willful, smart, loyal, and with meta-human powers, Beth had all the makings of a future cape. He wasn't sure what to do if that day came, how to react, what to say—any of it. What Ivan did know was that, in this moment, his daughter could turn something she was ashamed of into a way to help. She had a chance to be proud of her difference.

"Why don't you wait a few moments? Then I can go over with you, help haul what you chop. Have to be careful around the woods until we know for sure there's nothing out there." He squeezed her hand, watching as fear and determination mixed to form an unexpected happiness on her face. The idea still worried her, but she'd made up her mind. No one knew better than her father how closed that meant the issue now was.

To his surprise, she pulled him closer, lowering her voice to a whisper. "Daddy, what happens if this doesn't let us out in a day? I researched these labyrinths for a class project once. I don't think they're on a timer."

As diplomatic a way as he could hope for a near-teen to call out his obvious lies. "I know, but they might as well be. The capes always handle these things in short order. Besides that, if things did get truly desperate, I still wouldn't worry for a moment. You think someone can mess with this organization and not stir *her* up?"

He expected to have to sell the next line, yet it came out surprisingly natural. Or perhaps not so surprising, given the sentiment he was expressing. It was, after all, admiration for her strength; as the only one to defeat him, he had no choice but to acknowledge her power.

"Lodestar will save us, if it comes to that. In fact, I bet she's already on the case."

Sort of like if a bull and a mountain lion interbred, was Tori's first thought. Gray, stone-like skin coated the lithe body as it strolled across the grass, with stretches of green foliage filling in the various joints. Each leg ended in a paw with claws the size of kitchen knives. The head included a snout with irregular, sharp teeth, and a pair of small horns better used for a quick slice than a full goring. Considering that even on all fours it nearly came up to her hip, this thing was hauling some heft around, too, no matter how graceful those steps appeared.

In a split second, Tori had to make the first of many choices. Assume it was aggressive and come out swinging, or wait to see if they roused this thing's particular appetite. Were she in a real jungle, the latter option would have been more appealing—avoiding conflict wherever possible was generally a smart call. Except they weren't in the actual world, with animals that moved as instinct and nature guided. They were in a giant crafted maze, filled with things solely here to kill them. One way or another, this creature would be Tori's enemy. Waiting around for a fair fight was some stupid cape bullshit.

No sooner had it stepped fully out of the trees than Tori struck, darting in from the side and kicking it full force in what would be the ribs on a real animal. In mix of good and bad news, she visibly made an impact, eliciting a sharp yelp from her target. Unfortunately, the throbbing pain in her foot made it clear that damage hadn't only flowed one way. Until she could shift her foot to fire form, Tori was looking at fractured, if not broken, toes.

That might have been worth the trade, had her target been suitably driven off. Instead, she appeared to have only provoked it; snout dipping low as it angled those horns toward her. Tori readied herself to dodge, hoping there would be a chance to strike in the counter. What she was utterly unprepared for was the axe kick Helen dropped onto the beast's back. Unlike Tori's attack, this drew far more than a yelp—stone shattered as it crumpled down slightly.

"Remember when I said we had to table your question? This is me untabling it." Helen didn't let up, scooping an arm under her opponent's mid-section and flipping it onto its injured back, causing more damage in the process. "While I don't really broadcast it, the truth is, I'm a meta-human. That's how Ivan and I know each other." She threw one elbow to the chest of her downed enemy, causing it to stop stirring. "Normal as I look, my body is physically fine-tuned to peak human condition. Meaning I can hit hard and well, when the need arises."

Much as that opened up more questions than it answered, Tori did feel her hopes for survival increase substantially. If Helen had even some baseline physical abilities, it would make caring for her easier. That was the hope, at least, until the trees rustled and four more of the bullpanthers stepped into view.

Against this many, there was no time to think, especially as one charged right for Helen. Tori moved on pure instinct, fully giving herself over to the fight. As the bullpanther drew near, it opened its mouth, like it planned to chew off a piece of Helen. With only a passing thought of Deacon, Tori jammed her arm into its open mouth, fist already turning into fire. It was clear that getting out of this meant using all her tools, fire abilities included. Knowing that she was with a fellow meta-human, Tori barely even registered that she'd decided to let this secret out before she was blasting the monster full of flames.

The blaze did little to the stone, obviously. However, the foliage growing in the cracks and joints immediately caught fire. As it did, the bullpanther slowed, wobbling slightly, before starting to come apart. So the greenery was the glue keeping these things together. Tori set a grim smile to her face as she pulled her hand free, leaving the still-smoking husk behind.

"There's a chance I might have a secret of my own."

Helen was already shifting position, covering Tori's other side. "Well then, what's say we give these things a proper introduction to ourselves. I could use a good stretch."

In spite of how mad the situation was, Tori barely suppressed a morose chuckle at the approaching creatures. It wasn't often she had targets to truly let loose on. Perhaps she'd manage to have a little fun before this ordeal was over.

Chapter 79

Between Helen's fists and Tori's flames, the remaining three bullpanthers presented minimal challenge. Tori roasted the first, cooking off all the flora acting as its sinew, while Helen directed another's charge into a tree, its horn catching on the bark. She used the opening to kick its body mercilessly, until it crumpled down into a heap of rubble. The last one didn't attempt to flee—one more small reminder to Tori that they weren't dealing with sentient creatures, merely automated defenses.

Almost offhandedly, she torched it, wondering what tricks she'd use on the first enemy they encountered without such an obvious weakness. Assuming the challenges only got stronger, she'd probably have to deal with a few full-stone opponents, at the least. On the plus side, Tori was no longer on her own for combat.

Watching Helen move was a little disconcerting. Most meta-humans with physical augmentation leaned on that trait too hard, rather than training up their actual skills. They were easily marked by their simplistic styles and grandiose movements. Not Helen. She was quick, efficient, and brutal. There was no mistaking this for some newly turned meta who'd taken a few self-defense courses. Helen had experience. A lot of it, if Tori trusted her instincts—something she was hesitant on for the moment. Helen had slipped this secret past Tori without tripping so much as a single suspicion, after all.

With the last enemy downed, Helen wiped hair from her eyes, eventually giving up and digging around in her pockets for a band to hold it back. "Nice moves! I'd make a 'hot stuff' joke, but I doubt I can come up with anything you haven't heard already. Still, pretty impressive fighting."

"I was going to say the same to you." Now that she'd stopped her assault, Helen looked perfectly mundane again. Tori could almost have deluded herself into thinking the whole thing imagined, if not for the rocky remains surrounding them. "You sure don't move like a reporter or business owner."

"Talking is fine, but we should move as we do it. Ticking clock of our supplies, plus the mazes get uppity if you stay in one place too long. A labyrinth is meant to be experienced. All the systems are designed to push people toward participating."

No sooner had Tori learned this new fact than her mind leapt across the canyon to where Ivan and the kids would be hunkered down. It wasn't the threats overtaking him that concerned her—no automated trap was strong enough to kill Fornax. What worried Tori was how efficiently Ivan could fight while hiding his secret. Between keeping Beth safe and getting to continue being Ivan, Tori knew without question which it was that he would pick, just like she knew losing that part of himself would hurt for the rest of his life.

More importantly, however, Tori caught on to something else. "Hang on. So the labyrinth pushes harder on people who try not to play along, which you already knew. And you're still not worried in the slightest about those kids?"

This was as close as Tori dared to push, and even that was honestly overstepping. Her only saving detail was that she hadn't actually said his name. She watched as Helen pondered the question, turning it around mentally, before finally allowing a gentle smile to land upon her face.

"Yes, Tori, it's okay. I know who he is. I know what he can do. And I know he will use every ounce of that power to defend those children. Because a person is more than their reputation, more than their past, more than the facts others might think they know. But most of all, because Beth is there watching. He will *never* let himself fall short when his children's eyes are upon him. With her present, I'm not sure he'd lose to anyone, even Lodestar."

Relief cascaded through Tori as the weight of Ivan's secret fell away. With as much as they had to deal with already, the simple act of being able to genuinely discuss the situation felt like a huge leap forward. Now that her powers were revealed and Ivan's identity acknowledged, Tori could finally put her energy fully into beating this labyrinth, rather than doing so with one hand and her fire abilities tied behind her back.

"That is great to hear, but word to the wise, I wouldn't drop the Lodestar line around Ivan. 'Nobody beats Lodestar' is practically his unofficial motto." Tori heard something like a snorted snicker slip out of Helen's mouth, but when she turned back, the bespectacled woman wore a totally neutral expression.

"You can't blame him too much for that. If you were the best at something for years and years, then met the only other person who could actually challenge you, even if they eventually won, it would be hard not to admit their talent. After all, to belittle that person's skill is to belittle everyone below them, as well." Helen held up a finger, and they came to a sudden halt. She stood like that for a moment, then nodded to the left, taking them along a slightly rougher path of the forest.

Shoving aside some thick branches, Helen held them in place long enough for Tori to slip through. "It's totally okay if you don't want to discuss it, but may I ask how you ended up with fire abilities? Some metas like the chance to open up, others not so much—completely your choice."

With a grunt, Tori roughly tore back a shrub trying to dig its thorns into her legs. Her injured foot was throbbing more and more over time; soon, she'd start limping noticeably. Using fire was one thing, letting on that she could turn into it another. Then again, Helen already knew Ivan's secret and the bulk of Tori's: what did one more aspect matter? Especially compared to slowing down their trip when they were already on a pretty serious clock.

"Lab accident," Tori replied, motioning for Helen to slow down. She pushed her way through the undergrowth until Tori could brace herself against a dense tree truck. Lifting her right foot, she made a mental note of thanks to the guild for providing a phase-shifting-friendly version of this uniform. "Was messing with something a bit out of my league, things went awry, and when the dust settled, I could do this."

On cue, her entire lower leg shifted into living fire. As the nerve endings vanished, so did the ache, permitting Tori a long sigh of unexpected relief. That might have been hurting more than her brain wanted to admit. Only when the pain vanished could it be truly appreciated.

Helen was staring, fascinated by the transformation. "That's interesting. Historically, every stable elemental phase-shift like that has been done with some aspect of magic; never seen one from a purely scientific-based source. Orion was the closest, but he had a little bit of everything." She made no move to draw closer or examine the phenomena, yet her gaze also didn't leave the burning appendage.

"Guess you can consider me a... trailblazer."

Helen laughed, probably more out of politeness than actual humor. "That joke almost makes me wonder if you and Ivan aren't actually related after all."

Not wanting to dive back into anything around that topic, Tori opted for a rapid conversational redirect. "What about you? How did you get... super-strength, it looked like?"

"More maxed out, than super," Helen corrected. "The maximum potential my genes held. Think of humanity like cars being made on an assembly line. There's a plan for each, but some get put together better than others—usually just by luck of the draw. My body is the equivalent of someone building a custom car. Every detail has been polished, every efficiency achieved. Blood pumps increased oxygen, muscles recover more quickly. I'm flexible, fast, and so on. Basically every advantage my body had the potential for has been realized, and every weakness eliminated."

That was a fascinating power all right, if limited in scale. Human boundaries meant Helen could never tangle with the true powers of the world, but day to day, her ability probably came in a lot handier than controlling flames. There was, however, one discrepancy that Tori couldn't help noting as she returned her foot to physical form.

"Perfectly built, huh?"

"Well, the aesthetics are open to opinion. I'm not saying it straightened the bump in my nose or gave my hair effortless volume," Helen said. "More functionally perfect."

"Weird then, that someone with all those advantages would have subpar eyesight." Tori reached up, tapping the side of her face where glasses would have rested, were she wearing them.

To her surprise, the revelation was greeted by an increase in cheer from Helen, who jiggled her own spectacles in response. "Could be a fashion choice. Can't a gal accessorize?"

"Could be," Tori agreed. "I guess I should ask you the same thing you asked me: want to talk about where your powers came from?"

"I very much do not." Helen managed to keep all the pleasantness still in her voice, while also instantly shutting down that line of conversation. "The experience was far from a happy one, not the sort of thing to get bogged down in when our plates are already so full."

That more or less killed the discussion for the next few minutes. Instead, they focused on making headway through the brush. Overhead, the artificial sky was shifting, its false sun beginning to move toward the horizon. Odds were good that this place had some sort of day and night cycle, which probably meant things would get more dangerous once the sun fell. Tori had nothing to base that assumption on, yet it felt immediately right, the way these sorts of things were meant to work. Perhaps she was simply learning to think like a villain.

After half an hour of silent trekking, they broke through a cluster of trees to find something new. More stones, though these weren't moving—for the moment. Overgrown by what looked to be decades of grass and weeds stood a stone arch, leading into what would have been matching stone walls, if not for the broken sections causing sizable gaps. Further along, the breaks grew less frequent, as the structure appeared to lead to a large building made of the same material. While there was more forest along the edges, Tori felt confident that between them, they could cut a path around the side.

"Pretty sure we can skip this, if we work at it."

"I'm almost certain you're right, except we can't." Helen pointed to the huge obstacle, the place their route had obviously been leading toward. "Remember, this is a game. Don't play along, and things get more complicated. Angering the maze just risks making our own job harder, or causing surprises for Ivan and the others."

The part of Tori that had always been drawn to discovery and invention, the piece of her that compelled the breaking down of various electronics to see how they worked, rebelled at such an idea. Her mind burned, seeing opportunities for efficiency and being denied them. Tori wanted to rip this place down to the screws until she understood the mechanics behind every blade of grass and puff of wind. Instead, she swallowed her annoyance and looked at the path laid out for her, the one she was trapped on.

"Any idea what will be inside?" If she couldn't go at this her own way, Tori would have to settle for being as forewarned as possible.

"Could be a fight, a puzzle, a trap, a test, or an empty building just to mess with us. Probably not that last one—I don't feel especially lucky today—but it shouldn't be too bad. Escalating challenges and all that."

Tori couldn't believe her own feet as they walked through the stone arch, plodding down the path to an obvious trap. "Walking into a dangerous situation with no idea what we're facing and with innocent people counting on our success. You know, this is probably the closest I'll ever get to being a cape, thank goodness."

"It does seem to be a calling that isn't for everyone." Helen paused, running a hand along the stone wall briefly, like she was checking for something. Whatever it was went unfound; she resumed their pilgrimage after a few moments. "Although, you might be more inclined to it than you realize. In my experience, there does tend to be a common trait that all capes share."

"Corny taste in code names?"

Helen had to visibly bite back a chuckle at that. "Not quite. The inability to stand idly by. Capes are the sort of people who see an event they can't stand happening and do something about it. Even if they might not be powerful enough, even if they don't know the people involved. The ones who can act, and do—that's the pool of people I'd look to for future superheroes. And you definitely don't strike me as someone to linger on the sidelines when she's compelled to action."

"Maybe so, but there's no way you'll catch me in one of those ridiculous outfits." As far as counters went, it wasn't an especially strong one, mostly because Helen was right. The only thing she'd missed was that there was another avenue for those who wanted to shape the world into something better. Not all of those willing to act went to the side of the capes. The makings of a superhero and a villain were only a few details apart.

From the building, both women heard a loud noise rise up, like the sound of something very heavy thudding onto the ground. Exchanging a single look, they lowered their stances, hunkering down behind the walls for as much cover as they would allow. Now that they knew there was potential company, they silently made their way along the broken stone hallway, toward the unseen challenge awaiting them inside.

Chapter 80

Beth turned out to be a big help, as she was just about the only sharp element present in the camp, outside of a few rogue pocket knives. Her silver blades sliced effortlessly through the pseudo-trees, ringless interiors exposed as they cut cleanly in twain. For the larger denizens of the forest, Beth focused on shearing away branches, stretching her mercurial slithering weapons several feet up.

Despite Wade running analyses and the AHC teaching her control, there were still no clues about Beth's power. What it was, precisely, or where it had come from, no one had any notion. They weren't even sure what that silvery metal was composed of. So far, there had yet to be so much as a single fleck of residue to examine. The only way to test the blades would be in person, and Ivan hadn't yet figured out a way to slip a guild examination by Beth. Sweet and trusting though she was, every now and then, the girl had a habit of noticing more than one might expect.

By the time they headed back, Beth had honestly cut more wood than they'd possibly need for their planned stay. She'd found something of a rhythm by the end, so Ivan had just let her go. Having a task to focus on beat whatever awaited them when she was done: more sitting around. The boredom would be an insidious enemy the longer this dragged on. Without distraction, it was all the easier to dwell on fear and hunger.

Hauling the wood in his arms—more than he'd have normally risked carrying in less distracting circumstances—Ivan quickly took note of all the kids milling about. With a rough camp established, they were getting bored. The mental part of this would be harder than dealing with the automated monsters; he couldn't punch away a group of kids' growing unrest, even knowing it might eventually lead to panic.

They had to keep the scouts engaged and mentally active, doing more than thinking about their situation. Having them run around or burn energy was the easiest fix, but one they couldn't rely on with such limited supplies. Higher activity meant sweat, which would lead to emptying their pitiful water reserves all the faster, quickening everyone's panic. Ivan didn't have a solution, nor did one jump to mind immediately. This was far past his area of expertise, even as a parent. The best he could do was handle one issue at a time and hope Helen was moving fast.

Ivan was barely done setting down the wood when he spotted Yuri zipping over. She was walking briskly, without trying to appear in a hurry—performative for the scouts, obviously. Whatever the issue, it was only intended for adult ears.

"Why don't you go check on everyone?" Ivan proposed to Beth, clapping off the final splinters from his hands. "Mallory and Caden are both unsettled by surprises. We should make sure they're holding up all right."

She responded with a mock-salute, smile fixed in place, happy to help. "Can do!"

By the time Yuri reached Ivan, Beth was already halfway across the camp; her lack of care for optics meant that she could scramble along at great speeds. Rather than let Yuri broach her topic, Ivan motioned her to follow slightly, getting them to the edge of camp. Not terribly subtle, but he suspected that would be a growing theme as the ordeal wore on.

Eyes to the sky, Ivan tried to estimate how long they'd been inside the orb already. This place's night wasn't too far off, though how that corresponded to time in the real world would be total speculation. Anything that folded space this much usually messed with the chronoflow as well. No matter how he squinted, it had been more than a little while. Long enough that soon, he'd need to start worrying about monsters again.

"Hey, it was Ivan, right?"

"Correct, although I certainly wouldn't have held forgetting against you, considering the circumstances." He noted the awkward shift in her movement and the way her eventual stance favored the back foot. Not a topic she was looking forward to, then.

"Listen, I was talking with Trey, and it seems like maybe sitting around isn't the best idea. If there's nothing out there, we should be hunting for an exit."

Having kids had taught Ivan a tremendous amount of lessons, one of the most salient of which was patience. Yuri wasn't stupid, merely afraid and inexperienced. She'd been hurled from her comfort zone, and didn't even have the luxury of panic with all the scouts looking to her for support. Chiding her would get them nowhere; however, Ivan also had to align her thinking. Resources were too thin for major mistakes.

"Much as it might feel that way, I promise you, we are following the correct strategy."

More weight on the back foot, yet she didn't actually shift her position. "How can you be so sure about that? We've got no capes, no idea if anyone else even knows we're in trouble, and the only two people actually trying to get us out of here weren't exactly substantial looking. Someone like Trey would have better luck."

"If Trey's strength is so vital, perhaps it's best used to protect the children."

"From what?" Yuri demanded. "There's nothing here. We've scouted all around the tower, totally empty. We're wasting someone who could be helping to get us out."

Given that Ivan had slaughtered the first wave of enemies, then refused to move on, whatever came next was guaranteed to be more troublesome. Not by Ivan's standards, but strong enough that Trey would be pulped the first time he met one of the incoming creatures. If he let the man leave, it was a death sentence. While that was a sacrifice Ivan would make if the situation demanded, they were quite a way from reaching that point yet. More people to watch the kids would make Ivan's work protecting them easier, and besides, he didn't dislike Yuri or Trey. Wanting to help wasn't bad, they just lacked understanding on how to best apply their strengths to the situation.

"Perhaps, or perhaps the monsters here only come out at night." Ivan pointed up to the fake sky, where the not-sun was drifting toward the horizon. "Given that we're surrounded by a forest, nocturnal threats would make sense."

"It's not a real forest," Yuri pointed out. She pressed her hand against a nearby tree, eyes narrowing at the sensation. Off, somehow, in a way that couldn't quite be articulated any more than it could be denied.

Ivan nodded his agreement. "But it aims to be. It mimics one in appearance, so schedule makes just as much sense. My point is, before Trey goes off on his own, perhaps he should wait out one night with the group. Help soothe the kids, make sure we're really as alone as we think."

Her eyes followed his to the artificial sky, noting the way their version of a sun had shifted. Without looking, he could hear her stance change, her feet more solidly rooted.

"I guess it doesn't make much sense to start out in unfamiliar terrain with night approaching. But if it passes without incident, he's going to head out. We don't need this many people to keep the kids corralled. Getting out of here needs to be the top priority."

"Let's worry about making it through the night first," Ivan suggested. "To that effect, my daughter procured us quite a bit of firewood. Perhaps we should get the scouts to work building a proper pit. It shouldn't strain them much, and will occupy their time."

Yuri caught the idea quickly, already on board. "Fire also doesn't hurt in case there are any animals out here, or we find a water source to purify."

Her optimism felt misplaced, but then, Ivan had never been in this particular creation of Cobblord's. It was always possible he'd built the model to be sustainable. If nothing else, Ivan wasn't going to take away her hope. That was something vital they needed to cling to, especially as time here wore on.

While Yuri headed back to camp, Ivan turned his attention from the sky to the forest beyond. It wouldn't be long now, and the next wave would come. His original plan had been to slip away in the hecticness, crush their assault before it ever drew close, and then return before being missed. Unfortunately, going that route had a strong chance of getting Trey killed. More than that, he'd already spotted a few scouts poking around the borders of the camp, exploring their boundaries the way children always did. Ivan couldn't be sure he'd caught every trap and danger, so they needed to be kept out of the woods—a much harder task with nothing to be afraid of.

To keep this working, Ivan was going to have to let the scouts know that there was danger in these woods—all without letting them get hurt, and ideally while keeping his own identity hidden. This was why Ivan loathed situations in which he had to protect people; his skills were never suited for it. Everything about Ivan was built for destruction. At his peak, he could make natural disasters shit their pants. The most he could do now was make a plan, hope for the best, and trust in Helen.

Though he really hoped she wasn't taking her sweet time with ending this.

It was extremely tempting to use super-speed. Make an excuse, slip ahead of Tori, change, and blast through the rest of this labyrinth before they missed what counted as dinner at the End of Summer Shindig. Helen had two major hang-ups staying her speedy feet, however, the largest of which was not being sure of how the labyrinth would react. Zipping through the experience seemed like the sort of thing that would trip countermeasures; no big deal if they fell on her, *very* big deal if they impacted the kids. Even past the safety concerns, Helen might have still kept to this strategy, if not for the lack of clues.

Right now, she had zero. Well, that wasn't entirely true. Helen could rule out guild involvement, barring another coup attempt, which seemed early so soon after the last. The organization was much too smart to take this kind of swing, and against Ivan's own children... no, definitely not the guild. The AHC was out, as well. The only one who might do something like this was Vernon, and he'd never outsource that kind of work. His pride wouldn't bear it.

Taking those two off the board, Helen was working blind. She had no idea what this was about, the target, the goals, any of it. Until she understood what was happening, it would be difficult to prevent repeats from occurring. Knowing an enemy's plans made thwarting them vastly easier.

So Helen trod on next to Tori, never letting on just how powerful she could be if the need arose. Watching Ivan's apprentice had been fascinating. It was strange to see the places where his guidance had plainly left its mark. No wonder the two got along: they were emotionally closed off peas in their sardonic little pod. Yet Helen could also see Tori's differences: the way she examined every detail, the careful thought constantly at work behind those brown eyes. Ivan's guidance had always come from his gut; he trusted the impulses that had kept him alive above virtually any other source. It was what made Fornax so unpredictable, and so interesting.

Up the eroded steps inside the building—which was an interesting design choice in itself, considering this place wasn't actually ancient. Or was it? Helen didn't know if Cobblord made these to look distressed, or if he built them new and then found a way to age them. Either way, the effect was impressive—a few of the stones even gave way under Helen's feet near the end of the staircase.

At the top, there was only a single archway open. The rest had been blocked off by coincidentally fallen rubble, adding weight to the idea that the scene was designed like this. Expecting rocks to fall in a certain pattern was a stretch, even for a craftsman of Cobblord's caliber.

Outside the door, Tori hesitated, giving Helen a chance to put herself directly in front. Secrets were well and good when one could keep them, but she wasn't going to risk letting Tori be hurt. Hiding the fact that she was Lodestar wasn't allowed to grow more important than actually *being* Lodestar, a personal rule she'd settled on a long time ago.

Despite the shadowy appearance, there was no mildew or dankness as they entered the new hallway, just more stones as dry as those outside. Nicer on their noses, but not a great sign for this place having any drinkable water. If there were any, it probably would have been used for ambiance. As it was, the hall still cast a foreboding aura: long, looming, with sharp stones jutting out at odd angles. With every few steps, sconces near the ceiling burst into flame, lighting the way ahead.

Finally, they left the hallway as it opened into a vast chamber. At least fifty feet high, with odd breaks all along the walls, it appeared to be entirely empty, save only for a large metal pit directly in the center. As an old hand at these things, Helen wasn't surprised when a stone slab dropped into place behind them, blocking their exit. Nor was she ruffled when pitch-black flames suddenly burst forth from the room's pit. Not even the sudden voice that filled the room truly caught her off guard.

The words it spoke, on the other hand, shocked Helen so greatly she very nearly let out an un-Lodestar-like curse.

"Welcome to the first chamber of testing. It is a pleasure to see you've made it this far... Fornax."

Chapter 81

It felt like the stale air had been sucked from the room. Both women tensed, albeit for quite different reasons, as the booming voice continued to echo around them.

"Surprised? Did you think it was coincidence that you'd ended up here, or perhaps that we were after your little pet?"

Tori's hands tried to ball up, but she denied them. Getting riled up on someone else's terms didn't suit her need for the moment. She had to be clear-headed until there was a chance to find this motherfucker, *then* the payback could start.

"No, Fornax, this was all for you. I'd have preferred peace—we never meant to steal your toy—but I know how your guild feels about grudges, to say nothing of your own reputation. My green little helper all but begged me not to mention that she was the one tasked with trapping you. Silly thing still believes you'll be a threat afterward. Consider this a warning, a show of force, and a threat. Because we know about you. We know, for example, that right now, you've almost certainly been barreling through this maze, fearful of what will happen to those kids while you're gone. To say nothing of your sweet Beth."

"Oh *shit.*" Tori didn't mean to speak; the words came out entirely on their own. Glancing over, she found a severe expression on Helen's face.

While outwardly she had better control, Helen's internal reaction was more or less on par with Tori's. Ivan was generally dependable, predictable, a functioning member of society. Except when people went for his family. That was when Fornax showed he was capable of more than wanton slaughter; hunting people for vengeance had been that monster's entire purpose, the inferno of hate that fueled him. Attempting to provoke that side of Ivan, even as a bluff, was absolutely fucking insane. The trail of destruction he'd leave would be horrific, if she didn't stop him first.

"I'm sure by now you've discovered that any attempts at skipping sections, teleportation, and strong warping of the chronoflow will all trigger more of Cobblord's pets to appear. What you likely haven't learned is that in each occurrence, the same enemies spawn near the starting area, where you'll have had to leave those children undefended. We wanted to see what you could do when properly motivated; you understand. That's also why that entire area will get rapidly more dangerous as the hours pass. Perhaps you left your pet to buy them a little time, but she won't last long. You need to hurry, Fornax. Hurry if you want to save them. And remember that this was nothing more than a display. We know your name. We know your loved ones."

The flames roared suddenly, rising up from the pit as the voice reached a crescendo that bordered on a hiss. "Stay out of my way!"

With that, the fire vanished, though Tori noted there were still lit sconces showing them an empty room. More than just that, there was a creaking and rustling coming from all around them. Tori strained her eyes, trying to see into walls' dark voids where the light refused to reach. No luck, and while Tori did love both cursing and darkness, in this instance, she decided to flick on a light. Forming a fireball in her hand, Tori reared back and chunked it through the air, sending it blazing along to splash roughly against one of the opening's corners. From the brief flash, she could make out more rocks and a splash of green, which likely meant foliage. Those were secondary observations, however. The most important factor was apparent the moment her light had landed: movement. Something was moving in those walls.

"Stay calm." Helen's voice was steady, a sharp contrast to the shifting surroundings. "This is going to be a fight. We have to accept that and adapt." She wished she felt half as sure as she sounded. Someone was picking a fight with Fornax, and that was nuts, but the truly crazy part was that Helen still had no idea who it was. She had firsthand experience with every major threat to attack the world for the last few decades, the sorts of people who even *could* come at Fornax and the guild, none of whom fit the bill. Not like this, and not that voice.

Reorienting herself, Tori put her back to Helen, making sure they had eyes on all angles. "Any thoughts on what we're facing?"

"Something manageable. Remember, Cobblord's skills might be for sale, but he's consistent with his art, and that means an escalating challenge." The part Helen was leaving out was that this was a sliding scale built with Fornax in mind, but she'd deal with that once it mattered. "Based on the layout, I'd expect multiple attacks coming from different directions, probably triggered as soon as we head toward the pit to examine it for clues."

That lined up with Tori's observations, so it was as fine a working theory as any. "Gotcha. Okay, so what's in our favor? That whole monologue was for..." Tori's words faltered, as she suddenly realized just how vague they'd really been when discussing who Ivan was. From what Helen said, she might know it all, or only that he was a meta with a past. No one had actually said the name Fornax. A moment of thought made Tori realize the issue was beyond her control. The voice had called out Beth by name. There was no denying the connection.

"The monologue was for Ivan." Tori couldn't bring herself to use *that* name around someone else, even if the cat was freed from its bag. "So whoever made this can't communicate directly. Hopefully, they can't see anything either, or make adjustments on the fly. This whole thing was built with the expectation that only one person would be here."

"Meaning that only one of us needs to go down to trip the attack," Helen agreed. "Which will be me."

"I'm not sure—"

Without hesitation, Helen cut her off, noting the way the sounds were getting louder. No matter the circumstances, the labyrinth got antsy when people stood still for too long. "Tori, you hit from a range. I punch and kick. Of the two of us, which can do a better job drawing attention, and which can do better sniping?"

Helen didn't actually wait for an answer; the speech had gotten her a bit more stirred up than she wanted to let on. It wasn't just coming after Ivan and Beth, although that did set off some very un-Lodestar-like feelings in her mind. This bastard had done it in the middle of a Starscout event, endangering unknown numbers of innocent children just to piss off and test Ivan. As a cape, it infuriated her, to see them needlessly put at risk. As the one who'd promised, by context, if not words, that those kids would be safe, Helen was veering dangerously close to getting *truly* pissed off.

When this was done, when the traps were gone and she could move freely, there would be severe repercussions. For the criminal's sake as much as her own fury, because locked away in an AHC jail cell was just about the only place he had an outside chance of surviving Ivan's vengeance.

Until then, she had work to do.

No sooner had her feet touched the center of the main floor than the walls virtually exploded. From within the holes they came, appendages like mossy snakes, as the overgrowth-covered stone struck. Some of the extremities had heavy, blunted ends, like a mace, while others were sporting a mishmash of blades poking out along every angle. Helen leapt out of the way of a mace-arm, watching as it smashed into the corner of some steps, leaving a huge crater in that section of staircase.

A blade-arm wasn't too far behind, and as Helen slid beneath, using her flexibility to pull off an Olympic-level limbo move, she noticed the flashes of red coming from the edge of the room. Tori was firing on the arms, burning off sections of foliage where she could, but it wasn't easy to hit moving targets from her position on the ground. The efforts didn't appear to be bothering the arms, as they continued to focus on Helen.

Dashing across the stone, she managed to zip past two more huge, smashing blows from the mace-arms. One of those, and Helen's secret was out. Her body would use as much power as needed to survive—very rarely a subtle display. Watching the angles of attack, she altered her planned path of movement slightly, a new idea jumping to mind. Glancing over to Tori, Helen noticed that her Starscout assistant was gone. That misconception only lasted until the blast of flame drew Helen's attention to the ceiling.

Since shooting from the ground did shit-all, Tori had elected to go skyward. Whatever hesitations she'd had about hiding her powers were long gone in the wake of that speech. This was no longer a curiosity, or a weird occurrence to puzzle out. Somebody was knowingly swinging against Fornax, against her teacher, against her guild. That changed the stakes, even without the personal aspect. The kidnapping was an accident—didn't make her less mad, but she got it. This was different. This was that bastard looking directly at the organization she was a part of and declaring he wasn't afraid. He was going to learn fear, for the short time he survived; until then, blowtorching his toys was the best outlet Tori could find.

She rained fire down on every slithering stone appendage she could see, targeting the bases where they connected to the wall. This had the benefit of avoiding Helen, who was sticking to the center of the room as she nimbly ducked and dove away from every blow, like a cartoon mouse slipping through her cat's fingers. At least, that was Tori's impression until the crunch.

One of the mace-arms had come down heavily, directly onto the midsection of a blade-arm. Somehow, amidst all the dashing about, Helen had managed to guide the appendages where she wanted them, causing the mechanism to attack itself. The half-shattered blade-arm weakly rose, shaking visibly, and Tori decided this was her chance.

Cutting off her flames, she dropped through the air, firing off an occasional blast for redirection. Just before the end, Tori shot flames from both hands and feet, killing her momentum as she landed on the crushed section of arm. Since there were no points for subtlety, Tori opted to take her speediest strategic option. Digging her arms into the stone and thick moss, she turned her whole body to flames, cascading out and in, catching aflame every piece of greenery she could find. The fire caught at once, racing through the interior of the arm, along with the outside. Tori barely had time to get back into the air before it was cracking, the front section breaking off entirely.

One down, seven to go, by Helen's count. Too many. She looked around the building once more, wracking her brain. No matter what the client wanted, Cobblord maintained his standards. A slug-fest for the first challenge didn't seem fitting, especially considering that this was supposed to be for Fornax. What would he have done, in this setting? Obliterate the arms, obviously. So what next?

Her eyes fell upon the forgotten firepit, and Helen felt it all click. Fornax would break the enemies, only to realize they were just a diversion. The real key would be somewhere he'd likely overlook, costing Fornax precious time and angering him further. It was an assumption that only worked if one knew Fornax by reputation as a mindless brute, rather than the kind of man Ivan really was. Trusting her instincts, Helen altered her planned trajectory.

With Tori overhead throwing flames, the arms were at least slowing down a bit as their greenery burned. Recalculating their speeds, Helen waited a hair longer to break left, sprinting in just near enough to a mace-arm that it would try to attack. She'd slowly been getting a sense of their range and what provoked a strike; given enough time, Helen could probably have broken most of the appendages with one another. This would be faster, if it panned out. If not, she'd just try something else. As an old friend had once told her: "The real secret to being a cape is just not giving up until you've found a way to win."

As she ran, Helen gauged the arms. The nearest one had blades, but it was currently on fire and would drop down a few feet short. Although a mace-arm was coming from the left, two blade-arms recovering from their last swings blocked a clean angle. Tori was working hard to cook the other blade-wielder, which left the last mace-arm for Helen, just like she wanted. It tracked her as she moved, clearing the blade-arm strike that was two feet short. Right when she slowed, the way a normal person might to take a corner or grab a breath, the arm struck. It slammed down with all of its considerable weight and power, utterly destroying the firepit that Helen had leapt out in front of.

Like a hose with a leak, they could hear the hiss, some unseen element escaping from within the ground where the pit had once stood. As it grew louder, the arms began to sink, the invisible force propelling them draining away. Holding her breath, more for fear of stink than poisoning, Helen walked casually back over the shattered remains of the firepit. Her hair was blown back by the invisible gas, but all the rattling of the rubble made it easy to spot what she was looking for, though she didn't know what it was.

The gem shined a pale red in the light of the flickering sconces, a perfect square, evidently with some sort of charge or magic. That assumption was based off the fact that as soon as Helen laid hands upon it, a door at the other end of the building began to loudly slide open. She watched as Tori came down, landing roughly near one of the now lifeless arms before walking over.

"Figure it out?"

"Yeah. The real target was the firepit all along. Classic double-up: you build something that seems like it's only there for theatricality or ambience, then hide the prize inside." Almost too classic, really. Helen hadn't seen this one used for a good while. "No surprise from someone that still monologues. I mean, they happen, but doing a whole production of one has been out of vogue for decades."

Together, they looked at the jewel, still sparkling slightly in the flickering light of the residual flames spreading across the downed arms. It was Tori who finally said the obvious, unable to see any way around it. "One gem probably means more, right? If it was a key, it might be one and done, but that feels like a component."

"That's my guess. And they'll only get harder from here." Helen tucked the jewel away carefully in her pocket. "But let's look on the bright side. Whoever built this expected Ivan to be on his own. They assumed he'd have to abandon the kids and crack through here at top speed. That means we should be able to finish before food or water become serious issues."

"Except that, while we do, more and more monsters are heading to the area where all the scouts are waiting."

There was something about Helen's smile that tickled Tori's brain. She'd seen one like it before, hadn't she? Kind and warm, but with a hidden laugh just out of sight, like its owner knew a joke nobody else did.

"Monsters that were made to deal with a group of scared children.

Whatever threats have been marshalled, they won't even be close to the scariest thing out there tonight." That smile brightened, and Tori wished she could just reach in her skull to scratch the gray matter directly.

"Those poor beasties are in no way prepared to face Ivan."

Chapter 82

The forest was moving. From this distance, that was how it looked: trees swaying in a wind that didn't exist. Thanks to the fading light of their artificial sun, none of the others had noticed yet; the herd was still a ways off.

Ivan stood at the edge of their makeshift campground, watching the waves of emerald as the forest betrayed its hidden forces. Most of the camp was gathered around the fire, trying to ignore the protests from their stomachs. There had been a few meager snacks collected, bags of peanuts and nutrition bars, that were being shared out among the kids as best they could. Little as it was, sometimes a single bite was enough to keep going. One step, one punch, it could all be the difference between death and survival.

Slipping away in that moment was possible. Legs like his covered ground at an incredible pace when pushed; getting there and back would be a minor matter. But the fight could take time, depending on how numerous and slippery the forces, long enough for him to be missed. That in itself wasn't so bad, but if anyone got the idea to mount an expedition, they'd be putting themselves and the children in serious peril.

Waiting was another option; it wouldn't be too long before the young ones got sleepy. Taking a guard shift, and then killing every threat in the area had been Ivan's original plan, and it was one that still had viability. Unfortunately, with no threats seen, Trey would go wandering off into the woods the next morning, dying almost as soon as he left the safety of their area.

Ivan had no particular care for the man, nor had he any distaste, but it didn't matter. They were at a Starscout function, Trey was one of them, and most of all, Ivan knew what Helen would say about the matter. He couldn't let the man die needlessly for no reason, but he also couldn't risk letting a horde of monsters near these children.

This was why villainy was so much easier than cape-work—fewer variables to consider. When all one had was a target, it simplified things greatly. Less to keep track of, such as fellow Starscout leaders. Ivan heard the crunch of dry grass before either of them spoke, already turning toward Trey and Yuri.

"While the kids are distracted, I thought we should have a little huddle," Yuri suggested, tossing frequent looks over her shoulder to the circle of children. "Ivan, I raised your points to Trey, but we're both still in agreement. With no threats present, it makes more sense to send him on to help the others."

"I understand there might be dangers further out there, I do." Trey stepped forward, set on making this declaration himself. "But we can't do nothing while supplies run out. I have to go try."

Perhaps it was the people that made villain-work easier, Ivan reconsidered. If these two had been a bit less responsible, they'd have happily sat around waiting for the problem to get solved. More cowardly, they wouldn't have had the guts to try to leave. Easily corruptible, and Ivan could have appealed to some lower urge for motivation. What the hell was he supposed to do with someone who was aware there was risk, but still determined to help?

With limited other options, Ivan decided it was time for some specific truth-telling. "We're past the point of 'if' there are dangers. Seeing as there's no wind, and I don't feel the ground shaking, there aren't many other explanations for that." Pointing out toward the growing darkness, Ivan drew their attention to the waving trees.

"What? It's just forest." Yuri had cupped her hands to her eyes, trying to block out as much light as possible from the fire.

"Give it time, let your eyes adjust." While Ivan's gaze had needed no such shift, he felt reasonably sure a normal human could still catch enough details to notice the movement.

It was Trey who saw it first, the sharp intake of air almost slipping back out as an unintended hiss. "That can't be creatures."

"Why not?" Ivan asked.

"Because if it is, then we're all dead. That much force, shaking trees that big, it would roll over this area like a wave." Trey's eyes were haunted, and Ivan suddenly wondered if perhaps this wasn't his first meta-adventure.

Here, Ivan found himself at a crossroads. He could, in theory, continue revealing small patches of truth. The easiest route would be to admit he was a meta-human without giving away any actual details. A small display of his warding power would likely convince the pair he was keeping all the threats at bay, and continuing to sneak away easily became sellable as him reinforcing the magic. Unfortunately, that still required admitting that he was more than human, and Ivan's identity was heavily founded on being boring and unremarkable.

The other option was to explain as little as possible, keep them guessing, and hope Helen was making good time. Riskier in the long-term, but if Ivan could shuffle through this without an overt power display, the rest would fade away in their minds. Between the fear, stress, and adrenaline, no one would have solid recall of this, nor would they especially want it.

At least, that's what Ivan was banking on.

"There is another possibility. When Beth and I were in the woods earlier, I caught sight of a strange stone carving a ways off. It may have been glowing, though at the time, I dismissed it as a trick of the light. It was too far to investigate in the moment, but now, I'm thinking it might be essential."

"What does some rock matter in the face of that?" Trey asked, still gazing at the fidgeting forest.

"Maybe nothing, but we're in a place with unnatural rules. I had the notion that perhaps the reason we've been safe here is that there's something special about this spot. A barrier of some sort. It's the only explanation I can think of for why there would enough monsters to do *that*, yet they still haven't come for the camp."

The gasp from Yuri confirmed she'd managed to spot the movement as well, bringing all three adults largely on board with the knowledge they were facing a threat. Lowering her hands, she took a long breath, gripping onto her own forearms. It was a trick Ivan knew well from his younger days, a way to keep one's hands from visibly shaking. He was glad they were both smart enough to be scared—dealing with idiots would have made the task even harder.

"I'm going to go investigate that stone, see what the glow was, and if there are others. Hopefully, I'll find some sort of clue, or at least confirm that my eyes weren't playing tricks."

"I'll come, too," Trey said, moving to Ivan's side. He was halted, immediately, by a surprisingly strong hand on his chest.

Careful to make no expression, Ivan shook his head. "No. If I'm wrong, then I'm walking into danger. Better one dies, than two. The kids still need us."

For a flicker of a moment, Trey faltered, the weight of the situation fully settling in. Then, he tried to step forward once more, despite Ivan's hand. "Then *I* should be the one to go. Your daughter is right over there."

"That would make sense, if you were the one who'd seen the stone's location." Or if any such rock existed in the first place. "Better I go swiftly than you bumble around in the dark. And while the sentiment is appreciated, Beth being here is why I'm the one who goes. I have more reason than anyone to fight my way back."

He turned away, deciding it was better to simply leave and trust them not to follow at this point. That wave of movement was drawing steadily closer, and might take some time to get through. Ivan was ready to show these peons of the jungle what a true apex predator was.

The root snagged Tori's foot, sending her sailing forward, face directly on a crash course with a nearby tree trunk. Hands snapped onto her shoulders, steadying her just before impact, as Helen gently helped her back to a standing position.

"That's it, we're stopping to rest."

Even as she verbally protested, Tori's body enthusiastically wanted to agree. Between the mediocre breakfast, abduction of the cluster, and heavy amount of activity, she was beginning to feel the drain. Hunger nagged at her belly, the first itch of true thirst was taking hold, and her muscles ached to take a rest. Most of her Hephaestus work happened in short spurts; it wasn't often she needed to take a marathon approach.

"We don't have time to stop. Everyone is counting on us." At Tori's words, Helen's whole face twitched, though what that meant was entirely up to speculation.

There was a brief pause, then Helen found her voice once more. "Everyone is counting on us, which is why we have to stop. Blazing through recklessly could get us hurt, or worse, and if we fail, then what? Ivan has to actually leave the scouts, or drag them along through whatever dangers are still to come. It's late, you're tired, and even using your power to turn sticks into torches, it's getting hard to see. Right now, you're more burden than asset."

The last bit especially stung, since Tori could hardly deny it. She was slowing them down; she was the one Helen had to catch. If they were in a fight, Tori could easily make some careless mistakes in a state like this. Yet every part of her screamed to keep going, keep working, stay ahead of everything.

In the end, Tori decided to split the difference. She needed to rest, but for how long was still open to discussion. A brief respite to recover, and they could get back at it. Nodding in agreement, Tori stepped out of Helen's grip, motioning to an open section of woods not far away. "Want me to build us a fire?"

"We've got nothing to cook and no chill to ward off, but I do love the sound of a nice crackle, so I won't fight you on it. Just sit tight while I grab the kindling."

Moving slowly, eyes watching the ground for further obstacles, Tori wandered over to the minor clearing, which was more a break in the canopy than anything. Once settled, she extinguished what remained of her current torch, a random stick picked up when the last one burned down. Helen had no issues seeing in the dark, her excellent eyes further proving that the glasses were truly cosmetic.

Within a few minutes, Helen had returned, arms filled with various twigs and sticks. Dropping the whole load down in front of Tori, Helen wandered over to a tree and pressed her back against it, finding a semi-lean that in no way appeared comfortable.

One bit of focus, and the fire caught, rippling through the kindling in no time to create a bright, vibrant blaze. It was strangely comforting, even without actual purpose. The monsters wouldn't care, and Helen was right about food and temperature. Still, looking into the flames relaxed Tori, earning a cry of joy from her back as tension slowly faded.

"Resting might not have been the worst idea."

"With age comes wisdom, and that includes the importance of taking breaks."

Tori looked the woman over for the umpteenth time that day, ever since her power had been revealed. "Seeing as you only look a few years older than me, I'm guessing part of that perfect-body package is slower aging?"

"That's definitely one way to look at it," Helen replied. "Without bogging down in details, let's just say I wear my years exceptionally well."

"You and Ivan both. I have to get me some of those anti-aging powers before it's too late. Last thing I need is dementia or arthritis setting in." Tori said it as a joke, yet as the words left her mouth, she wondered... was that on the table? She'd never dug into all the resources the guild offered, focusing on things directly related to her and her goals. Having more time to be young and full of energy sure wouldn't hurt, though.

"They aren't always as great as you might think, but it's case by case." Helen's gaze drifted into the fire, her focus shifting for a brief, unmistakable moment. "Besides, as I see it, you've got quite a useful ability already. Form-phasing, heat control, long-range attacks, flight, and that's just what you've shown so far. If I didn't know better, I might think I was hanging out with a superhero."

The strange notion tickled Tori to imagine, purely for its ridiculousness. "Yeah, that was obviously never on the table for me."

Helen's face grew unexpectedly serious. "With all due respect, that's not true. Anyone can choose to protect the innocent, to fight for those who can't fight for themselves. Not all on the same scale, and not all in the same way, but every sentient creature has the potential to help. To use whatever strengths they have and make the world better."

A strange place for a conversational dig-in, though not entirely shocking. People had strong opinions on capes; often, they'd been saved by one. Even without that personal connection, every person alive had to live with the knowledge that the world only still existed because capes had successfully defended it multiple times. Granted, the threats were usually meta-human or created by said capes, so there was a chicken-and-the-egg question to be asked, but the fact remained that the Earth was still spinning.

"I guess I could have phrased that better. What I meant is that it was never really on the table because I don't have that instinct. If I see things going sideways, my first thought is how to get out safely. After that, I think about how much of the shit I care about can come along, too."

The fire crackled between them. Tori could feel Helen's eyes on her, more focused than ever before. The attention was unexpectedly heavy, and oddly familiar in a way her brain just *refused* to place.

"Is that really how you see yourself, Tori? A selfish coward?"

"I'm a scientist first and foremost. We go by observable data. Historically speaking, that's how I act, so it's the conclusion I draw."

"Sounds to me like you've got a lot of bias in your data collection," Helen countered. "Because my observations have been quite different. I've seen a woman stick by a someone she thought would be nothing more than a burden to drag around. I've watched you show concern for people in danger over yourself, both in theory and in practice. Heck, let's take it from you directly. When I said we should stop a few minutes ago, what did you come back with?"

Tori jumped back in her mind, trying to replay things. "I said there wasn't enough time to stop."

"Close. You said there wasn't time, because everyone is counting on us." This time, there was nothing subtle about the knowing grin on Helen's face. "I've met and known a lot of capes through the years—more than I think you'd believe. 'Everyone is counting on us.' *That* sure sounds like something a superhero would say."

Chapter 83

"Professor Quantum?"

The aide waved, trying to flag him down. Persistent fellow. Most gave up after being ignored the first several times. That meant the matter must be important, at least in the aide's mind. Relenting his constant pace, Professor Quantum turned to the red-faced man waving a document.

"Yes?"

"Sorry to bother you, sir. We've been trying to reach out by phone, but there seems to be an issue." The issue was that Professor Quantum had been ignoring the missives, a fact that both knew and neither would say. "Got a report that came in, flagged high priority. Some kind of orb thing appeared over a Starscout retreat and people are missing. Looks like a Cobblord piece."

At the sound of an older enemy, Professor Quantum allowed his interest to raise its head. He snatched the document from the aide's hand. "Seems as though there's several layers of warped time folded around it, which means breaking through will be quite difficult—as well as unnecessary. We shouldn't get involved."

"Beg pardon?" The aide looked sure that they'd misheard.

Professor Quantum tossed the page back over, paying no attention to if it was caught. "Lodestar has expressed her desire for the Starscouts to be an entity separate from the AHC many times. Since she's so set on that distinction, we wouldn't want to step on toes and go rushing in. I saw that Quorum has already been dispatched, and we all know Lodestar keeps a special eye on that organization. I have no doubt the issue will be handily resolved."

The aide hung in the hallway, staring with mouth agape. To him, it probably seemed as if Professor Quantum were being hard-hearted, but the truth was much simpler. As any enterprise, the Alliance of Heroic Champions had limited resources. There were only so many capes on duty or reachable at any given time, and from that pool, they had to be able to deal with any major threat to the world's safety at often minimal notice.

Considering all that, Professor Quantum could think of few greater wastes of resources than sending reinforcements to Lodestar. Not that the aide had any way of knowing she was there, thanks to that ridiculous secret identity. Truly, the only thing Professor Quantum held in higher esteem than Lodestar's power was Helen's capacity to utterly waste it.

To tell the tale of Fornax was to sing a song of blood. Blood from Ivan, dripping off cuts in his knuckles, running down his chin, pooling in his ears. Blood from the others, felled one at a time by each other's hands. Blood from his captors, taken in their moment of triumph. Blood from their allies, from every member of their cult, every soul connected to the horror of Fornax's creation. So much blood there were days he'd wondered if his eyes had been stained, if he could ever see the world in terms other than flesh to be torn apart.

These creatures had no blood. Ivan drove a fist through the skull-shaped rock of a horned beast the size of a commuter bus, obliterating the head along with the entirety of its body, rocks spraying across the rest of the herd. No blood was a blessing. It made cleanup all the easier. More than that, though, it helped Ivan keep control. The darkness was always there, always pressing to be let out. Whispering that this is who he truly was, where he rightly belonged. Tempting him to go wilder, to enjoy himself. Reminding him of the only thing he'd ever felt made for.

Destruction.

If the trees were painted in viscera, it would have stirred those old memories harder, feeding his worst impulses. This was better, cleaner on multiple levels.

Ivan smashed through the other two giant horned beasts, then shoved past their rubble. He'd been picking off the advance troops as he approached, but staring down the slope he'd reached, Ivan realized that his trek was nearly done. What he was looking at had to be the main force, based on the way the entire forest rippled with their steps. A mishmash of shapes, some animalistic, some humanoid, some truly a design entirely unto themselves. The details didn't matter to Ivan. It was all the same. Rocks to be shattered, enemies to be broken.

This was nothing. Sliding down the dry grass, Ivan leapt into the air, coming down on the back of a horse-sized stone monster covered in spikes. It burst into pieces as his limbs made contact, a wave of power washing out from where Ivan hit the ground, cracking several nearby opponents. Ivan had never cared much for wielding widespread magic, even if his fighting was inherently suited to it. He preferred a one-on-one match, or at least to take down each enemy with his own fists. Tonight wasn't about his preferences, however. It was about keeping that camp protected.

Not even caring what his hand landed upon, Ivan grabbed the nearest stone limb and swung it around, turning the creature into a club he used to bludgeon the first movement that caught his eye. Down here, surrounded by chaos, Ivan's mind couldn't help flashing back to the pit.

Everything was a fight: food, water, a place to sleep. Their captors' favorite method had been to turn everyone loose in the pit, and then allow the winner first choice of their prize while the others were left with scraps. When Ivan showed a bit of talent early on, he inadvertently made himself a target. For years, they would come at him together, making him alone even in a place meant to drive all to isolation.

The limb crumbled in Ivan's tightened grip. He barely even registered the loss, dashing forward, deeper into the thick of combat. He grabbed a pair of gorilla-sized stone monsters by the heads, decapitating both. Multiple opponents meant nothing to him; that was the benefit of surviving all those group attacks. Without meaning to, the others had made him even stronger. By the time the numbers thinned, Ivan had already been winning fights against them collectively. One-on-one... well, there was a reason he was still alive, and they weren't.

Ivan came to a stop, realizing that, without noticing, he'd torn through a bunch of stone spheres held aloft by spider-like limbs. Whatever unexpected function they'd had was lost; their rubble revealed no secrets. Pausing, Ivan forced himself to breathe, mentally getting out of the pit. It was dangerous to lose himself in the past, even for a moment. He couldn't give in, couldn't let that piece of him escape.

Something huge moved in Ivan's periphery. Not quite a stone dinosaur, but the sizes of these things were starting to get ridiculous. It had only been one day, why was the labyrinth pushing so hard on the second wave?

Hesitantly, Ivan felt more power flow into his fists. Releasing condensed waves of pure obliteration magic on every hit would cut down his time, but he loathed using the technique like this. The more destructive Ivan became, the deeper he verged into Fornax's territory. There was a reason that name had stuck, coined as it was for a black hole. In his early days, before he learned better control, Fornax truly was a walking disaster—collateral damage was almost a feature of his abilities. Ivan had already spent a lifetime fighting to win at all costs; paired with the sudden increase in raw strength, he'd barely been able to throw a jab without creating a corpse.

This power was meant to destroy. Always had been, since before it was Ivan's to wield. He'd met its source, overcome that endless appetite to unmake the world with his own will for survival. But putting his burden on a leash didn't change its nature. As Ivan stepped forward, moving toward his giant target, a stone quadruped with long, lashing limbs bounded toward him. A single blow not only shattered his opponent, it sent the shards flying like shrapnel, tearing chunks off the other nearby enemies. Ivan repeated the trick on the next one he could reach, then another, all while moving toward the big beast. It had been a while since he used this technique—a few calibration shots always helped.

The head of this enemy was massive—easily the size of the horned beasts he'd slain not too far back. As for the rest of it, Ivan could see a long stone neck leading to a body he imagined would be covered in thick armor, spines, maybe even some surprise defenses meant to shake off anyone who climbed on board. With his higher vantage point, Ivan opted not to mess with the head. Probably a fake target. The body would be where the real vulnerabilities lay. Cobblord was no rank amateur; he knew how to build a decent monster.

Decent by most people's standards, anyway. To Ivan, these were all the same. The same as those frail cultists whose bones were so easily torn out. The same as so many big-talking opponents who'd raised his hopes only to break after a single blow. The same as the countless challengers who paled in horror upon realizing the fight they'd picked. The same as every piece of fodder these unstoppable fists had effortlessly crushed... until the shining one who was different. Until the punch that was stopped, and everything else that unexpected moment had started.

"Cobblord, I don't know if you can hear me, or if you're monitoring any of this. But just in case, I wanted to pass along a message: you should have let them kill you." Ivan leapt over the head of the monster, toward the main body.

All around it, he could see smaller stone forms, the army circling its strongest asset. How convenient of them all to group together for him.

Landing on its back, Ivan reared back, ready to throw a full-strength punch before thinking better of it. That might crack the entire mechanism of the orb, tripping Cobblord's fiercest defenses, if not a full collapse of their prison. Holding back, Ivan thrust his arm into the nearest patch of stone he saw. The initial hit left a crater, but it was the aftereffect that truly got the show started. Just like the earlier monsters, charged flecks of stone went flying off as shrapnel. Except, thanks to the opponent's greater size, these shards were fist-sized at their smallest, tearing through his massive enemy's inner workings as much as through the peons on the ground.

"Whoever it was, whatever threats they made to get you on board, you should have let them kill you. Because I don't give a shit how much you knew about their plans for this. I'm going to find you. And when I do, I'll show you the folly of your ways. You should have let them kill you, Cobblord. It would have been an easier death than the one I'll bring."

Ivan truly had no idea if Cobblord could watch the happenings of his creations, or if the threat had merely been for his unthinking audience. It was mostly habit, either way. Terrifying an opponent was often an easier way to win than bothering to make a fist. Besides, when it came to both Ivan and Fornax, the words were never really the message.

Explosions of energy tore through the giant monster as Ivan struck again, this time leaving his hand wedged inside. Rocks burst forth, shooting into the nearby hordes and blowing them into rubble. As he stood there atop his giant prey, watching the sea of enemies fall against his power, Ivan tried very, very hard to remember that this was purely a defensive necessity. Otherwise, an especially mad part of him would take too much joy in the spectacle.

Destruction spread like a spiderweb as Ivan rained down more blows, triggering blast after blast. A maelstrom of violence, a parade of obliteration. Like the black hole his other name was stolen from, Ivan wiped out his enemies, the forest, and everything in the surrounding areas. There was no distinction between them; they were all simply objects to be broken.

He wouldn't let one of these things slip past, couldn't risk the life of single scout. Ivan would never be like Lodestar—his powers didn't function the same way. If he had to fight with others around, it put them in danger. Acting before the threat arrived, preemptive annihilation, that was the only real tactic that worked for him. Ivan would be just as meticulous, thorough, and patient as he was at the office. One by one, until the last movement halted, he would crush this army.

So much of his life was about hiding who he was and what he could really do. For tonight, a brief and beautiful moment, Ivan felt united. His better self was determined to protect those kids, whereas his darker impulses were gleeful at the chance to rampage. Everything in him agreed that the only course of action was to wipe these bastards out.

Raising a fist overhead, Ivan felt a mad grin try to wiggle its way onto his face, an impulse he immediately squashed down. This was not Fornax running wild: this was Ivan Gerhardt sending a very clear, explosive message about what happened to anyone who threatened his family.

He hoped Cobblord *was* watching somewhere. Ivan wanted him afraid, wanted him cowering. The reputation of Fornax was one of the few things that kept his family safe. A little wanton decimation here and there was a nice way to remind people why they should be so afraid. Of course, in all likelihood, Cobblord probably wasn't watching. There was so much to keep track of, even if he had surveillance. That was fine, too, though.

When it was all over, Ivan would be sure to hunt him down and explain the error of his ways in person. For as long as Cobblord could endure.

Chapter 84

In spite of her steadily weakening state—a quite natural reaction to extended effort with no nourishment or water—Tori insisted they press on, taking rest only when she had to in the form of a few catnaps, grabbed under the starlight and Helen's watchful eye. At least Tori was accustomed to keeping late hours; it meant they didn't have to worry about drowsiness becoming a factor just yet.

Helen was taking no chances, though. Raising a child through toddlerhood had taught her the power of persistent gab, especially letting loose questions and refusing to be ignored. She wasn't quite as bad as Penelope in her prime, but Helen could force a conversation to stay afloat when needed, especially if it meant keeping someone mentally active. Having Tori out this far into the labyrinth was dangerous enough. If she started making poor judgment calls, it could lead to injury or worse. That wasn't going to happen. Helen would make sure it didn't. This was simply the easiest method of doing so, for the time being.

"—and then he lets his friend go, watching him paddle off into the fifty-year storm, knowing he probably won't come back. Throws his badge into the waves as he fades from sight. Seriously, you have to look this one up when we get out of here. True classic. It got me into surfing for a solid five-year stint."

"I'll add it to the list," Tori replied, tone and words both a bit stiff. Helen had been going hard on Multerion movies for the last hour, veering between ones Tori knew about and far more varied fare. While the topic had started out promising, based on that reaction, it was probably time to switch things up. The chatter wasn't as effective unless it flowed in both directions.

Well… if she wanted to make sure Tori's brain was active and aware, there was a topic she could skirt around that was sure to raise the woman's hackles. It felt a tad like cheating, using her Lodestar knowledge as Helen, but with careful wording, she saw a way forward.

"Let me know how you like it. I've nagged my coworkers enough that I doubt they'll ever give it a real shot. Oh, hey, speaking of coworkers, did you happen to know a man named Donald Moss? The superhero called Cyber Geek?" Conversational subtlety was not a skill Helen particularly cared about utilizing, unless it was absolutely necessary. Sometimes boldness was more effective, anyway.

Like a jolt, Tori's entire body straightened. She really needed to work on that. Had Helen not already known the full story, it would have been a deeply suspicious reaction. Slowly, Tori turned, a forced calm on her face that probably would have been more convincing if she'd had a touch more energy to spare toward acting. "What brought that to mind?"

"Coworkers, sort of," Helen explained. "I know Ivan used to manage him, prior to the career change, so I thought you two might have been acquainted. Had to ask—I mean, how many people know an actual superhero?"

"At this point, I know too many." Tori seemed surprised by her own slip of the tongue, hastily recovering as best she could. "After my kidnapping, I got a protective detail put around me, met a few of the capes doing the work. But yeah, I know Donald, too. He was a friend before his change, and we tried to keep that alive afterward."

"Tried?" That was news to Helen, and Cyber Geek wasn't the stoic sort. If a friendship had broken, he'd likely have worn some visible reaction around the base.

Shoving her way through a dense patch of undergrowth, Tori spared a few moments to form a rough shrug. "Not like we had a big cursing fight and vowed to stop being buds… lately I've been realizing more and more that our lives are heading in different directions. Cyber Geek is going to be a big name one day, and I'll still cheer for him from the sidelines. Just not sure how much longer our worlds will overlap."

To Helen, the hardest feat in the universe was to see someone hurting, be able to help, and simply not. Fornax's life was built upon blood, but Lodestar's foundation was one of loss. Too many times, she'd been unable to help. Too many failures, funerals, tears, and screams. It was what made her the Lodestar she was, and even without her powers in play, that instinct didn't fade. She knew what Tori was saying, *really* saying. A villain and a superhero couldn't be friends. It was a ludicrous notion—to someone in Tori's position.

"If you'll forgive an intrusion from someone who doesn't know you all that well yet, don't be so quick to give up. Life takes strange turns for everyone, sometimes doubling back in directions you'd never imagine. Whether you have overlap or not is a passing occurrence. A good friend, one you trust, who trusts you, and who you want in your life? That's not something to throw away lightly. Even if the circumstances around you change, so long as you value one another, it is possible for a bond to endure."

"Okay, seriously, how old *are* you?" Tori suddenly demanded. "That sounded like someone with a lot more experience than your face shows, even considering the slow aging."

"Old enough to spot a change of topic when I see one." Helen ducked under a branch, not actually bothered by the question. Tori was more engaged than she'd been during the movie talk, which meant she was also more alert. That was the victory Helen had been after in the first place. "Sorry, I don't think I'm especially vain, but I'm still not giving out my age. A gal's allowed a few secrets."

Together, the pair broke through a tree line, only to spot a slight downward slope leading to more forest. There was a path they were following, choppy and thin as it could be at times. Where it was leading, and what would be waiting for them along the way, were mysteries yet to be discovered.

As artificial dawn rose overhead, light returned, making navigation easier, if not faster. Were Ivan running through this place, he'd have blown past them. Then again, he'd also have been forced to leave the kids. Slow, steady, and safe won the day for Helen over brash and reckless. She'd had too many chances to learn better.

"It's not like I want to kick friends out of my life. I've never... I haven't had the chance for many, the way my life has broken. Losing one, even by my own hand, sucks. But it's probably best, in the long run."

Safer, was what Tori really meant. Safer for Hephaestus, less chances to expose a secret. Safer for Cyber Geek, should her secret ever come out and their friendship turn into an anchor around his heels. Safer for Donald and Tori, because the stronger a friendship grew, the more it hurt when the long-buried truths finally came out.

Helen didn't just know this story, she was *exhausted* of it.

"Who you love, trust, and let into your life is ultimately something only you can decide. *But* if you reject anyone who might cause things to get complicated or gums up whatever future roadmap you had in mind, it's going to be a very lonely life to live. That's a steep slope, deciding things are broken before they even have a chance to be tested."

"It's better to leave yourself vulnerable?" Tori was starting to get worked up, which was good for her energy levels, though not so great for keeping her focused. "You might have meta-human aging, but you've got no idea the kind of shit I've seen. I spent years hunkered in holes and hiding in shadows. I've seen plenty of what happens to those so free with their trust. Usually, it ends with them bleeding and screaming, if they're lucky enough to still be alive."

Helen's heart broke as she looked at the fury and pain in Tori's eyes. Though the young villain could have no way of knowing it, Helen had indeed witnessed those sights. When she was new, not yet fully using her abilities, it had been more frequent, but even now, there were times she was too late. Lodestar, for all her power, was still a single person. Even at her fastest, she couldn't be everywhere. She couldn't stop every crime, save every innocent—no matter how much the failures weighed upon her.

"Being vulnerable isn't easy," Helen agreed. "It's why choosing who you trust is such a vital part of the process. But no matter how careful you are, mistakes will happen. Hurts, slights, maybe even betrayals. Nobody's perfect, as a person or a friend. Knowing when to forgive, and how, is a vital part of making those relationships work. Because people can surprise you in good ways, too. You never really know what someone is capable of, who they are, all the way through. People can amaze and astound when given the chance."

"I'm sure that's good advice in a general sense, but this is more complicated than hearing Ivan bust a tune. For my situation, this is what's best for all involved. I think it's the way it has to be."

Through no fault of Tori's, those final words made Helen's jaw clench. She'd heard that phrase many a time in the early days, before she got comfortable in her role as a leader. "I don't believe anything has to be a certain way. This is our world, built by the hands and desires of those who came before us. Now, it's our turn. Whatever you see out there that you don't like: change it. Who creates society if not the people in it? Who shapes this world if not its residents? This is your life, Tori. Your slice of existence. Who do you think has more control over it than you?"

"It's not like I—" Tori was cut off by the long stone spike that shot up from the ground, narrowly missing her left foot. It rose ten feet into the air before stopping completely, reorienting, and slicing down toward Tori yet again. She dodged easily. With so much time to prepare, it was an easy move to make. The stone carved through the dirt, vanishing into the ground. Where it had burrowed, only a small mound remained.

Together, the pair looked ahead at the long stretch of grass and the countless small dirt mounds they were only now paying attention to. If each one represented a similar trap, they might be able to walk through without stepping directly on one. However, Helen hadn't noticed a mound when Tori triggered the first. It was possible those merely represented entry points. The stone spikes were obviously able to navigate this place's underground.

Meaning that any step could trigger an attack.

Eyeing the tree branches, Helen flexed her fingers. It had been a while since she needed to go hopping around. She'd never even heard the term parkour back when Helen was leaping building gaps and free-climbing old brick exteriors. Luckily, being Lodestar meant never getting rusty. With a running start, Helen hopped up, kicking off the nearest trunk, grabbing onto a thick branch before pulling to a squat. She could already see her next two jumps. After that, things would have to get more fluid and improvisational.

"Tori, you okay to fly?"

"Little worn out, but I can manage." As proof, Tori was already halfway into fire form, having read the situation for herself. Helen couldn't help noticing that the change was taking longer this time. Exhaustion was on Tori's heels. Sooner or later, it would catch her.

But not yet. Tori's hands formed fists before vanishing into pure flames, her whole body blazing as she lifted into the sky, careful to go high enough to avoid the treetops. Slow and steady was the way to go. They'd get through this one hurdle at a time.

Unfortunately, just as Helen watched Tori crest over the trees, the blast came. It was pure wind, from the looks of things. That was a new attack, which meant they were probably near the site of the next trial. It had been waiting in the air, so this whole area was meant to be a trap, no matter the route they picked. Given how Ivan favored his leaping techniques, preparing for aerial entry was smart, but it also meant the force was strong enough to theoretically knock an airborne Fornax off-balance. Since Tori's mass was lightened for flight, and she hadn't been prepared to counterblast, the attack shot her forward, well past their current section of forest and toward unknown threats.

Plans of slow and safe movement fell away as Helen accepted what she'd just seen. While she knew Tori to be capable, the younger woman was also running on fumes in a trap made with Fornax in mind. Whatever plans this place had for her were about to be dashed, however. Even if Ivan hadn't asked Helen to watch over her, this wouldn't stand. Tori wasn't here as Hephaestus. She'd come as a normal civilian helping to plan a weekend. Even if that hadn't been enough, she was part of Helen's cluster, and Lodestar's organization.

An innocent civilian was in peril, and Helen was close enough to see it. There was only one way that scenario could end. This was how *she* chose to shape the world—into a place where every cry for help carried with it the genuine hope and knowledge that somewhere out there, at least one person cared. For now, she ran, dropping off her perch and dodging the spikes as they leapt from ground. Hopefully, Helen could make it in time.

But if she couldn't, then Lodestar would.

Chapter 85

It was some kind of vortex, near as Tori could figure. More than just wind, there were small objects being tossed about with her—small bladed ones, from the looks she could snag. Against a normal flying or jumping opponent caught in the wind, these would be a flurry of wounds slicing into one's skin, a constant, unstoppable assault from all angles. Pitted against an intangible target, they were a minor distraction to steal her attention and complicate the process of descent.

The blast had shot her across the forest, above some massive stone circle that seemed to be generating the wind and the blades. That didn't particularly explain how it was shooting wind toward itself. Her hunch was hidden remote stations that were used to create the effect—but being bounced around the sky made it tough to discern precise locations. She had to get low, there was no other choice, but she couldn't manage a clean shot out of the vortex. As carefully as possible, Tori began to solidify parts of herself in bursts, temporarily increasing her weight. The wind could blow all it wanted, gravity always pulled in one direction.

Unfortunately, turning solid even in pieces left her vulnerable. A rogue blade caught her on a solidified shin, while another tore a piece from her shoulder. Nevertheless, Tori was making progress, slowly falling out of the wind's grasp toward the waiting ground below. As she fell, she took a better look at the surroundings.

The forest ended a short way back, leaving only plains of fake grass leading up to the stone circle. Now that she was closer, Tori could see that it was actually several rings laid together, like someone had chopped a section out of a ridiculously oversized rock-redwood. The wind and blades seemed to be drifting up from the cracks between sections—hopefully, this whole thing was just one giant wind generator. Except this place was made with Fornax in mind, and while he did have the ability to fight and travel through the air, this sort of trap would be little more than an annoyance. Then again, wasn't that the point of this entire labyrinth? Even the voice they'd heard hadn't expected it to actually stop him—the whole thing was about sending a message.

Suddenly, the world turned more peaceful as Tori fell out of the wind's grasp. She was below the swirling mass of air, only a few feet from the ground, and the moment was almost serene. Had she been better rested and fed, Tori's sharp mind might have realized how precious such a place was and paused there momentarily before risking any additional movement. Sadly, the toll of her efforts was making itself known, and Tori dropped heavily to the ground, shifting back to human form as she took a dearly needed rest.

No sooner had her feet touched the ground than the noise started, of course. The grinding of stone was like a loud buzzer blaring at the sound of her mistake. In the air, she'd been caught up by happenstance. Landing had obviously tripped some sort of sensor, and having mass when she came down probably didn't help. Part of Tori was glad that Helen had been left further back, even as she wished there was someone else around the help. Limited as that powerset was in terms of scale, Helen had proven adept with it. Still, this would be easier without having to worry about a semi-normal person to keep track of.

That was Tori's thought until she saw the first huge stone leg rise from a rising section of the outermost ring. Ten feet long, with a square, unbalanced body following, along with four more multi-jointed legs. Worse, there wasn't a scrap of greenery she could see on it, meaning that there would be little to burn. *Way* worse were the dozen other legs she saw exiting from around the ring. The last test had been designed to pit Fornax against one massive opponent. This time, it seemed one had to survive being overrun by what would be small fries to someone on his scale. With her suit, Tori felt she could have made a serious go of surviving this. Given her current condition, even escape would take some lucky breaks.

Rustling from behind her had Tori whipping around, fireballs already formed in her hand; however, there was no stealth force approaching from the rear. Instead, she found the dashing form of Helen, who'd sprinted out from the tree line and was racing over. Tori's heart fell to her stomach. This was too dangerous for the kind-hearted cluster leader. Even if Ivan hadn't screamed his request across the sky, she liked Helen. Tori didn't want to see her hurt, or worse, which was looking increasingly likely as more and more crawling cubes came up out of the ground. And that was only the first ring—there were still eight more to go.

"What are you doing?" Tori demanded as soon as Helen made it into earshot range. "Get the fuck out of here! Can you not see those things pouring out?"

The words appeared to catch Helen momentarily off guard, after which she reacted quite oddly. A warm smile was not what one expected in this kind of situation. "Tori, are you trying to put yourself between me and the danger?"

"I'm trying to do what Ivan asked and keep you safe," Tori snapped, eyes darting over to the advancing stone troops. "Go around this area. I'll handle it, but I need time. While I deal with these punks, you sneak ahead and try to find whatever mechanism will end all this. I might not even have to scrap all of them."

It was bullshit, pure and simple. These things would overrun Tori in no time, and with the skies turned chaotic, she couldn't snipe from the air, whatever good that would have done. At best, her fire form would protect her from their attacks, and she could keep them distracted enough for Helen to get away. The woman was shockingly capable. Maybe she actually would activate the exit before Tori's stamina ran out. It was the best chance for everyone, including Ivan and Beth. Tori would figure out a way to survive somehow—it's what she did. That's what she told herself, anyway.

"You want to go charging into an army you've got no way to damage, just because of what Ivan said?" Helen was somehow unaffected by the advancing forces, the entirety of her focus still on Tori.

"Look, lady, this really isn't the time for a deep-dive into my shit. It's been a long, hard, dangerous life. Ivan is the first person in a very long while to genuinely give a fuck about me. He's helped me in ways I don't know how to repay. I'm not letting his friend die while I've still got fight left in these bones." Summoning flames in each hand, Tori turned back to the cubes, drawing steadily closer. Not long left until they'd arrive. "So get out of here and let me get to work." It was an excellent performance, marred only by a minor wobble in her voice at the very end. Given what she was staring down, Tori felt it forgivable that a sliver of fear had made itself known.

"Tori... I'm sorry." Helen stepped to her side, entirely ignoring the directive to run. Something had changed, though. The light joy was gone. In its place was not terror at the nearing onslaught, but rather remorse. "I was selfish. It's been a long time since I could talk with someone like this, a person who knows our world but not my place in it. I never meant for you to feel this kind of fear."

Based on the speed of the advancing cubes on legs, they had less than a minute left, and that was being generous. As if that weren't enough, there were more legs rising from the second stone ring, these even larger than the first design. "Helen, I don't know what the hell you're talking about, but if you've got a plan, now would be a great time to let me in on it."

"Same plan as always, I suppose. Save the day." Facing away from Tori, Helen carefully took off her glasses, folding the legs over one another. A ripple ran across her whole body, like an illusion shifting, except the changes Tori could see were minor, some slight shifts in weight and hair, with perhaps a small alteration in height. Still looking away, Helen continued to speak. "Time for *your* Starscout trivia challenge, Tori. Where does Lodestar's name come from?"

The whole moment was deeply surreal, to the point where Tori was starting to wonder if she'd succumbed to fatigue and passed out without noticing. Dream or reality, her best bet was to play along. Perhaps it would do something about that damned mental itch Helen provoked, the one that was only growing stronger by the second.

"Corvix had just defeated Professor Quantum on national television. A bunch of other capes tried to swarm him, and he started cutting a swath like they were regular humans. Then, in a flash, she was there, putting herself in the path of his blows. He hit her with everything he had and couldn't make so much as a dent. Before she dropped him in a single punch, and Quorum delivered the surprise finish, he asked her how she could be so strong, and Lodestar responded: 'The darker the night, the brighter the stars.'"

"That's the one." Helen looked back, and Tori suddenly realized the shift was more dramatic than she'd noted from the back—it seemed as if several years had dropped away. "Do me a favor, hold these." She extended the glasses, wiggling them slightly, until Tori took them in her grasp. "I'll let you in on two secrets, Tori. The first is that I kind of hated that saying for a long time. It was told to me a lot during a particularly dark time, and didn't quite deliver the hope it was meant to. All of which is to say that the line wasn't planned. It's just what popped out in the moment."

"In the moment?" Tori could almost see the line connecting these obvious, blazing dots, yet her brain refused to connect them, even when it felt like it was *right there*.

"That would be the other secret." Helen began to step forward, changing before Tori's eyes. "I hope you'll forgive minor theatrics. It's not often I get to do these reveals." Light poured out from Helen: blazing, brilliant, and instantly familiar. As her hair and eyes changed hue, Tori was truly struck by how little else shifted. Without the costume, the resemblance was even more uncanny. It was a strange combination of being thunderstruck with shock and also overwhelmed by a feeling she could only describe as "of course." It was like her brain breathed a sigh of relief at finally being able to see what, in hindsight, seemed crazy obvious from the start, followed shortly by the near mind-breaking implication of what this all meant.

Tori had just spent the better part of the day palling around with the strongest superhero on the fucking planet, and that was barely the tip of the iceberg. Thinking about the way Helen and Ivan were around each other, as compared to their other identities, indicated that their story went way deeper than she'd been led to believe. Her brain buzzed with fear about what secrets she might have accidentally let slip, but none could find solid purchase. Part of that was due to overall exhaustion, though it also helped to have far more immediate concerns to focus on. The first wave of cube enemies was drawing close.

Too bad for them, it wasn't Helen and Tori who were waiting to meet them. Instead, the first stone leg came down next to Lodestar, who remained unmoved as it settled down hard into the dirt. She stared the thing up and down, noting the others close on its heels.

"On the off chance there's any sentience in there, now would be the time to give up. All evidence points to you being automated, so if there's more, I'd really like to know before this gets rough."

In response, the cube whipped one of its legs around, slamming it down onto Lodestar's head. At the same time, several panels on its smooth surface opened up, various devices sliding out. What they were or did would remain unknown, however, as Lodestar returned the blow with one of her own. A single punch obliterated her opponent, sending chunks of it screaming into the air, up and through even the vortex of wind.

"Cobblord should be glad I'm the one here, instead of Fornax," Lodestar noted. "He'd be insulted at the idea that these things are a challenge."

"You're not?" Tori asked, really unsure of where the hell else to go with conversation at this point.

"I'm a superhero, which means a whole lot more responsibility in the way I use my abilities." With a motion of her hand, Lodestar formed and flung a ball of energy that detonated on impact, utterly decimating the nearest six cubes that were advancing from Tori's direction. "For me, this is a chance to let loose with no fear about anyone getting hurt. No civilians nearby to protect, no need to worry about injuring my opponent. All I have to do is fight, and I tend to fare pretty darn well on that front."

Truly, that might have been the greatest understatement Tori had ever heard. There wasn't time to comment on it, as Lodestar was already moving forward, heading for the ring where multi-segmented stone lizard-like creatures were rising up. "Stay there and rest. I won't let anything get close. After all, my dear friend Ivan asked me to keep you safe."

Watching Lodestar race off toward the waves of enemies rising off the ground, turning into a shining missile of destruction, Tori finally hit her limit. She half-collapsed to the ground, letting her body rest as her mind went wild, reconciling this new information with everything she already knew. It was a noble effort, but one that quickly gave way to enjoying the spectacle of Lodestar annihilating the stone army.

Sometimes, it was nice to just sit back and watch the destruction unfold.

Chapter 86

It was early for visitors, which narrowed down the number of people potentially knocking on their door. Beverly was the only one up, with Tori at her scout thing and Chloe sleeping in. Everyone in her family tended to be early risers—whether it was genetic or ingrained barely mattered anymore. Whatever the cause, she beat the dawn on many a morning. Today's sunrise had come and gone, at least, so odds were this wasn't some bold robber about to make a hell of a bad choice.

Peering through the peephole—one could never be too careful—she was surprised to see Austin standing in the hallway. Given the early hour and his predilection for manners, she'd assumed if any of the New Science Sentries were going to pull such a move, it would be Ike. She opened the door quickly; Austin wouldn't be here if he didn't have good reason. Only after it was fully ajar did it occur to Beverly that perhaps she *was* the reason. If he'd learned Bahamut's true identity, this could be the start of a very uncomfortable conversation.

Thankfully, Austin seemed his normal self, which was to say that he grew flustered at the appearance of Beverly. It was almost cute, how helpless he was at hiding even his most basic of feelings. At first, she'd taken the whole thing for an act, that he was putting on the "aw shucks" vibe to better sell his cape-image, especially considering whose name he was borrowing. Still, for all her hatred toward Professor Quantum, Beverly refused to be the same kind of bastard he was. She denied herself the easy out of judging someone for the circumstance of their birth rather than the quality of their character, and over time had realized that whatever else Austin had going on, he wasn't putting on an act. Unfortunately, that left her with the obvious dilemma of his not-so-subtle crush. She'd thought getting to know one another would move him past it, or at least lower the awkwardness, but so far, he was proving oddly static in that regard.

After a few moments, Austin had regained his composure, or as much as he ever managed when talking directly to Beverly. "Good morning. Sorry for the early hour. I wasn't sure if calling or gently knocking would wake fewer people."

"A text would also have been fine." Her annoyance was fading to curiosity as Beverly studied Austin further. Shifting body language, eyes darting up and down the hall, there was definitely something off. He had a nervous energy different from the usual infatuation.

"Wish I could, but this was a little too important," Austin replied. "Please let Tori know her security is going to be reduced tonight. I just got a message. There's a big meeting at the AHC. Not sure what's going down, but they're calling in almost everyone. It won't just be us who are gone. There probably won't even be capes nearby if something happens. This is all private, of course. We're not advertising a few hours of weakened forces. Still, I didn't feel right leaving Tori unguarded without her knowing."

Two extremely different parts of Beverly lit up simultaneously. On one side, she was consumed by duty, flooded with worry of what might happen to her friend. However, there was more to Beverly than there had once been. Deep within her, the Bahamut piece of her mind couldn't help whispering that this was also opportunity. If she knew of a time when the capes would be compromised, it meant more dangerous guild jobs could be undertaken. Were Tori there at her side, the Bahamut voice might have been stronger, but concern for her friend ultimately triumphed over her budding villainy.

"Appreciate the heads up. I'll let her know as soon as she gets back from her Starscout thing."

"Any word on how that's going?" Austin was still checking the hallway. Whatever this meeting was about, it clearly had his nerves agitated.

"Didn't expect any. Cell reception outside of civilization isn't exactly renowned for reliability," Beverly explained. "Besides, I can wait until tonight to hear about the fun pinecones they spotted. Only so much interesting stuff can happen on a camping trip."

It was no surprise that Lodestar made short work of her opponents. That was, to Tori's estimation, the *only* part of this hour that wasn't some form of mind-liquefying shock. Helen was Lodestar. Helen, Ivan's good friend. Ivan, who was really Fornax, which Helen *definitely* knew. That whole concept was weird enough; when she factored in the times they seemed to be almost flirting... it was a lot.

Before she'd even realized it, the battle was done. Lodestar annihilated one final stone contraption—twenty feet tall with components of all the other types that had come from the rings—by dropping down from above and shattering it to rubble, before flying swiftly back toward Tori. Fast as she'd been, Lodestar never dipped into super-speed, even now avoiding tripping any of the labyrinth's safeguards.

Floating down to the grass, the glow didn't fade like Tori had expected. Lodestar wasn't hiding anymore. She was unashamedly herself. "From experience, I'm guessing that revelation knocked you somewhat sideways. Would you like to ask questions, or should I start by running down the greatest hits?"

While Tori certainly had questions to pose, she knew better than to pass up freely volunteered information. Asking on her own, she might inadvertently skip something vital. "How about you go first while I compose myself?"

"You mean think of follow-ups," Lodestar pointed out. "Told you, not my first time doing this. I don't mind, there's just no need to bother pretending."

To that, Tori merely nodded. She wasn't sure she trusted her own tongue at this particular moment.

Lodestar sat down, albeit in a peculiar way. She lifted each leg into the air, assuming a cross-legged position, before floating her whole body toward the ground. "The big one to get out of the way is no, you're not stupid, crazy, or wildly imperceptive. Now that you know the secret, it probably seems obvious in hindsight. I've never been great at hiding my identity. I try, but tend to slip up on details. To put it simply: you couldn't see the truth because I hadn't revealed it to you yet."

Now that she'd settled, Lodestar reclined, laying her back against empty air like she was resting in a lounger. "Took a long time to figure that out, but time has proved it true. Something about my power protects my secret. With a few very powerful exceptions, it's impossible to put the pieces together unless I do it for you. Brains refuse to form the connection. Even if someone had been watching us remotely just now, it wouldn't work. They have to be physically present when I knowingly reveal myself, hence why I avoid public transformations. And before you waste a question, no, I don't have any idea how that works. Some of my abilities are harder to understand than others, and I'm still not sure I've found them all."

To Lodestar's credit, her selection of what to address first had been a fine one. Knowing the reason why her brain had been so ceaselessly bothered by Helen put a great deal of things into perspective, and also freed Tori from questioning her own deductive skills. "What's the next big question you normally knock out?"

"Actually, that one we kind of covered," Lodestar said. "The next question is usually if I'm the real Lodestar, the original, and if so, how do I look so young, but you already know that part. All that stuff I told you about my body was true, by the way. I just didn't mention what else I could do."

Behind them, shattered stone minions crumpled further, chunks of rock falling to join their brethren sprayed across the battlefield. An entire army, reduced to garbage in mere minutes. Lodestar paid it no mind, gently tapping the underside of her chin. "After that, things tend to splinter off. Different people have different concerns and reactions. Although, in these sorts of situations, they will eventually get around to asking one more identical question: why me? Why were they chosen to carry this secret?"

"You can skip that. I know a circumstantial emergency when I see one."

"Is that what you think? Tori, I had the entire run over here to change if I wanted to. Even after arriving, I could have slipped behind a tree, or waited until your back was turned. I made a choice to tell you, the same way I have with everyone I choose to share this secret with."

She wasn't entirely sure how to respond to that. Dealing with someone who wielded honesty and forthrightness so expertly compromised many of her usual social tactics. There was nothing to pry at, no secrets or shadows to take conversational refuge in. With few other options, she decided the time for being passive had drawn to a close. If Lodestar was offering answers, then Tori would take them.

"Okay, I'll bite. Why tell me?"

"Because you were afraid, even though I knew you had no reason to be. Because I'm a good judge of character, and have had plenty of time to get to know yours. Because Ivan trusts you, and that puts you in very exclusive company. There aren't many of us." Lodestar paused, visibly taking her time to think. "And because I wanted to. I like you, and I don't enjoy hiding things from people I like. I wouldn't recommend sharing it around, though."

"Obviously. No one will even believe me if you're not the one to show them, right?"

Lodestar seemed momentarily taken aback, though she recovered quickly.

"Well, yes, that too. But mostly because of Ivan. Even despite of my power's protections, he can be a bit overly concerned. There was a near miss some years back—story for another day—however, when the dust settled, he made it a point to crush anyone trying to uncover Lodestar's identity."

The story brought Tori up short, reminding her of the most insane aspect to all of this. Somehow, she had a feeling this particular tidbit wouldn't be covered going through Lodestar's frequently asked questions. "Yeah, on that subject, about Ivan. I mean... what the *fuck*?"

"Can you be a little more specific?"

"I honestly feel like 'what the fuck' summed things up pretty well." Tori took only a moment to consider her phrasing; at this point, interest and curiosity were fast pushing diplomacy to the side. "You're Lodestar. He is... was Fornax. The respect, I get. You were the biggest dogs on the block for a long time, the only ones who could really fight one another. But this is... it's not just some person you used to trade blows with. You two are friends. There's history and banter—hell, he even sang to your kid."

A new thought entered Tori's head, and as it did, her eyes felt like they might break their very sockets with the speed in which they expanded. "Wait a minute... your kid..."

"Let me go ahead and pause this train before it leaves the station. Ivan and I have never even come close to... you know... and therefore certainly couldn't have offspring. Her father died before she was born, and if it's okay, I'd like to leave it there. That's more of a Helen question, and not an easy subject."

It was odd, seeing sadness on the face of Lodestar, even for only a moment. "Sorry, didn't mean to step on old wounds. Just seemed to make the most sense when I put it all together. The idea of Lodestar letting Fornax babysit is still a bit wonky."

"As it should be," Lodestar said. "Because that would never happen. Helen leaning on Ivan, however, happens probably more frequently than it should. In the sense of over-imposing, I mean." Her gaze turned softer, perhaps nearly embarrassed. "As for your 'what the eff' question, I guess I would describe things with Ivan as breaking a candy bar in half to pretend it has fewer calories. Perhaps not always the healthiest choice, though it does make life sweeter. I don't have a lot of constants in this world. Ivan is a rare exception, though sometimes I worry I overburden him too much when things get choppy."

Tori couldn't argue much there. Ivan was nothing if not steady and reliable. Pseudonym and Fornax might be different stories, but the middle manager named Ivan Gerhardt was solid and sturdy enough to build bridges off of. "Why does he do all this..." Tori realized she knew the answer, even as she was forming the question. "Because he feels like he owes you."

Another short flash of surprise from Lodestar, though this was less marked than before. "That's a quick mind you've got there. Ivan credits me with his freedom more than he should, and given what's associated with that freedom, he values it beyond measure. But it would be disingenuous to say that's the root of it all. Truth be told, we even got along well in his Fornax days, when circumstance allowed for civil conversation."

"What possible circumstances could allow for that?" Tori demanded.

"The first time was when we were chosen to represent Earth in a galactic tournament to stop it from being attacked." Given the blasé response, Lodestar had definitely seen some form of this question coming.

Tori folded her arms. "You're fucking with me."

"What a thing to say. Lodestar doesn't really lie, and she certainly doesn't curse. Ask Ivan about it sometime. The whole thing ended up being an evil scheme we had to deal with, but there was a solid bit where Lodestar and Fornax were on the same team." Rising from the grass, which she'd never really even touched, Lodestar stretched out her legs. "That said, since it seems like we've moved past the mental-panic phase of the reveal, how about we fly and talk? Since we didn't get another monologue here and I found another gem when smashing the final boss, it seems this place has given up most of the clues it's going to. Let's wrap this up and get everyone home safely."

Lodestar extended her hand, which Tori grasped. It was unnerving, the ease with which Lodestar lifted Tori up from the dirt. It was as if she had no more substance than a politician's morals; with a single motion, this slender woman could crush Tori to goop. Instead, Lodestar used that strength to pull her close and cradle her gently, taking care to ensure she would be safe as they rose higher into the air. Tori could see more of the fake world stretching out below them, and just before the wind began to howl in her ears, she made out a few half-whispered words from Lodestar.

"Much as I'm a proponent of walking softly, I think the time has come for the big stick."

Chapter 87

With dawn had come the inevitable truth that they were out of food. The last of the scrounged-up rations were doled out among the kids, water making the rounds as well. To their credit, the scouts were holding together well, but hunger was already beginning to put some on edge. Given that they were children who'd been spirited away and were slowly being starved, the fact that they'd stayed this composed was outright miraculous. Ivan couldn't expect it to hold forever.

The lie about being inside a boundary would only work until desperation defeated sense. Pressed into a survival corner, thoughts of monsters would fly out the window, a potential quick death not so bad compared to a slow, certain one. They'd go hunting for food and water, even though neither were here.

It was hard, sitting around, doing nothing, knowing the other two were out there fighting to free them. His hands ached to be fists, furious and powerful. The sidelines were never his place in battle. He belonged in the thick of things, the center of chaos and often, the cause.

Breaking off from the group she'd been talking with, Beth wandered over toward the log where Ivan was resting. Watching her approach, he realized something that should have been obvious.

That brutal position in the middle of a fray was Fornax's place. Ivan didn't belong on a battlefield. Ivan had no place slaying monsters. Given the choice in that moment, he knew he wouldn't have traded places with Helen or Tori without dire cause. Because this was where he *should* be: watching over his daughter, along with the other charges. Were he out there, his mind and heart would be here, constantly distracted by fear for her safety. Better to be focused on the task at hand than let himself be split.

"Some of the kids are starting to get really scared." She sat down next to him, keeping her voice to polite, if not covert, levels. "I keep telling them we'll be saved, but between the noises and the darkness, last night was hard. Being hungry isn't helping. I hope they'll be okay until it's over."

Even in a situation like this one, Beth was more concerned for everyone else. Ivan patted her head, wondering for the umpteenth time how he and Janet had managed to produce these wonderful children. "I suppose that means you're not scared at all."

"A little," Beth admitted. "But that seems selfish. I've got my power and my dad here. Nobody else has either. If I can't be brave, it'll only make the others more scared."

The hug was unexpected, as the best ones often are. Beth's tiny arms encircled his ribs, clutching him tightly, expressing all the fear she was hiding from the others in one single, powerful embrace. "And I know we'll be okay. Even if Lodestar doesn't find a way to save us, my daddy always comes through."

Sitting on that log, Ivan hugged his daughter back, thankful that no one who actually knew him was around to see the swirl of emotions storm across his face. One way or another, they were getting out of this trap. Helen would find a way eventually, but if time ran short, then Ivan would think of something. Destruction was his talent, his burden, his medium. There had to be something he could break to get them out.

Until then, he comforted his daughter, and reminded himself that he wasn't sitting on his ass doing nothing. Ivan was waiting for the inevitable. Lodestar would defeat this place, just like she'd defeated every meta Ivan had ever seen take a swing. It's what she did, and frustrating as that was when set against her, the notion offered a great deal of comfort as one under her care.

It was only a matter of waiting until this labyrinth broke open and Fornax was set free to hunt down the perpetrators. For now, he simply threw all of himself into being Ivan. Each version had a time and a place. Fornax's would come—probably much too soon for the perpetrators. Ivan only hoped he'd have enough self-control to take his time. They'd made his daughter afraid. That earned them the slowest death he could provide.

Something was wrong.

Lozora hung near the edge of the campgrounds, away from the prying eyes of police and capes, just near enough to keep an eye on the floating orb suspended above the track. The sun had fallen and returned, yet still no one had come out. By the estimations they'd been working from, the trap was expected to hold a fully motivated Fornax for only a few hours, ideally. Finding out exactly how long it would take was the whole point of the test; however, this was well outside the bounds of expectation.

With his kid at risk, Fornax would have had to move at top speeds, even if he trusted his apprentice to watch over her. The whole thing should have been done before midnight on the first day, based on what they'd been able to find on Fornax's estimated speed. A few hours here or there was variance, but they were coming up on a full day since the trap had sprung. If Fornax had left the kids alone for that long, odds were at least a few had already been lost, possibly the apprentice, too. What really sent shivers down the cartilage system that functioned as Lozora's spine was the possibility that his daughter was among that kill count.

Crossing Fornax had been a calculated risk, one Lozora didn't take lightly. It was why she'd been careful not to be seen or implicated in any way, and had advocated for a plan that put the kid in as minimal danger as possible. Because the underworld still whispered about the remains of those who crossed Fornax; even now, the Order of the Final Dawn's massacre was told like a bogeyman's tale. Though it wasn't known what they'd done to cross Fornax, he had wiped them from the face of the Earth: every last member, killed and butchered past even the most potent forms of meta-restoration.

Lozora was growing torn with every hour that ticked by. The more she lingered, the greater her chances of discovery, linking her to this crime. But if she fled before seeing the experiment's conclusion, her employer would be aggressively displeased. Despite his attitude already wearing thin on her nerves, Lozora had put in too much to walk away from the endeavor now. Besides, she wanted to see how one of the old legends worked—the ones who never bent a knee to those damned capes.

In the end, it was a matter of weighing risks. While Fornax might be coming out furious, so long as Lozora remained unseen, he'd never know she had a hand in it. Whereas her employer was expecting results and a report, which made him the more pressing danger. Still, it was hard not to wonder just what the hell was going on inside that orb.

"Subtle, it isn't." The massive crater in the ground looked like a sunken amphitheater, with four grooves chopping it into equal quarters. All of it was made of stone, with visible sections that would probably flip over, revealing the inevitable minions within. It was smaller than the series of rings, which Tori found curious until she remembered how weak those had been compared to the first challenge. So far, the labyrinth had tested its prisoners against a single potent threat and many smaller ones. Logically, the next step would be multiple strong enemies.

"If I didn't know better, I'd think it was a trap within a trap. Ivan steps in, puts the gems on those raised chunks in the center, the whole thing locks down after he's worn out from the earlier fights." Lodestar hovered in the air, Tori still clutched carefully, surveying the land—though for what, Tori could only guess. They hadn't seen much in the flight over. All roads seemed to lead here; one more sign that they were on the right trail.

"I guess he would have been taking this faster, with no rests in between," Tori agreed.

Slowly, they began to lower, still a ways off from the giant stone pit. "That wouldn't matter, not against enemies like this. Even if the challenge were great enough that it did briefly work, all it would do is make him mad. No prison can withstand him for long."

"Except Rookstone, obviously." Tori waited, expecting to hear quick confirmation. Instead, she got a very precisely phrased statement.

"In a sense, yes. Ivan never escaped from Rookstone."

With the ground rushing up, it would have been easy to miss the careful parsing of words, but Tori was feeling reenergized and alert after the shocking revelation, along with some time to rest. "That's not the same thing as him being unable to, is it?"

There was scarcely even a jostle as Lodestar landed, lowering Tori onto her own two feet. "No, it's not. I hope you'll understand why we don't broadcast that, though. If people knew there was a meta that jail couldn't technically hold, they'd push for more permanent solutions to be used, and trying that with Fornax, among others, would largely end in bloodshed."

"Trust me, I want the public getting execution-happy with villains even less than you do. Does make me wonder: if Rookstone didn't keep Ivan held, then why did he stay? Fornax broke into and out of government installations before."

"The answer is simple, and exceedingly complicated, depending on how deep one digs. You'll have to do with the succinct version, since we're in a hurry: Ivan stayed because I beat him. Defeated him, I should say. We threw down for real. I proved to be better, and that was my prize. Even as Fornax, he always had his pride. That was why he agreed to the terms, and honored them upon losing. Pride was the only cage I ever found that worked on Fornax, and not even that weakness exists anymore."

"You think Ivan doesn't have pride?" Had those words come from anyone else, Tori might have flushed with anger, but Lodestar knew her teacher better than Tori could even begin to guess. There had to be some meaning to her words outside the obvious read of it as an insult.

"Heavens no, I'm not blind," she corrected. "The *weakness* of it no longer exists. Ivan will cast his pride, his dignity, even his life aside without a second thought when the need is real. If he were suddenly thrown back into Rookstone under similar circumstances, it would only last until the first time Rick or Beth needed help. Pride like that means nothing compared to guarding the ones we love."

Lodestar reached out, taking Tori's hands carefully, giving them a squeeze. "I know, at the outset, this world can be confusing. The labels and legends all seem like they mean so much, the distinctions between cape and villain appear as chasms between us. But here's the truth as I've best discovered: when things get serious, you'll know who your friends are."

"Ah, so we're circling back to Cyber Geek and the New Science Sentries." Tori didn't pull her hands away just yet, even if she was slightly tempted.

"We're circling back to the young woman who told me she didn't think she could keep being friends with people because of circumstance. If that's your choice, then so be it. I just want to make sure you know the decision you're making. The longer you live like this, the less the labels matter. You realize that jerks will chase the glory of being a superhero and good people can end up on the path of villainy. At the end of the day, you'll know who your friends are, because when things inevitably get bad, they'll be the ones you want to protect. The people who, when you see them in danger, a deep, primal part of you simply says ***No***. The world can't have them, can't *take* them. Not while you're there to intervene. You can choose to ignore it, if you like, but you'll never be free of wondering what might have been, had you been a little more honest with yourself and fought when the chance was present."

She released her gentle grip on Tori's hands, looking away quickly, albeit not quite quick enough. "Those the words of experience?" Tori asked.

"Too much experience, honestly. There are days I see why most Lodestars don't last as long as I have." Quickly changing the subject, Lodestar turned back toward the stone circle, gaze turning determined. "So what do you say we put a wrap on this thing? It's either the last trial, or meant to look like it, which means there will probably be some sort of surprise trick. Any thoughts?"

"It's made with Fornax in mind, so my main guess would be violent as hell."

Lodestar licked her finger, shot up into the air a few feet, then dropped back down. "No artificial wind this time. You feeling up to being my eyes in the sky?"

"Hell yes. Here I was thinking I'd have to sit on the sidelines." There was a part of Tori that wondered how essential she could truly be, given who she'd be watching over, but she swiftly dispelled that doubt. This was, after all, a matter of not just getting things done, but getting them done quickly. If her efforts saved even a few minutes for Lodestar, it meant they'd be getting the kids out of danger that much faster.

That was, obviously, the reason Tori was excited as she shifted to fire form and took to the air. As a proper villain, it certainly wouldn't have been anything as silly as the chance to fight alongside a living legend. Well... perhaps Ivan might get some insight into her actual motivations, once the dust had settled.

If anyone could understand, she had a pretty good hunch it would be him.

Chapter 88

Overhead, the scene looked the same as it had floating with Lodestar, only a bit less stable. Tori's tactic of flight didn't allow for the same precision when hovering—not that it mattered much, as she was currently flying rings around the area as Lodestar made her approach toward the pit. The legendary superhero was taking the ground route this time, just like Ivan probably would have. No shifts as Lodestar approached, even when she drew within touching distance of the caveless stalagmite in the stone crater's center.

Pausing to give Tori a brief look, Lodestar placed both gems into grooves on the ground's upward protrusion, each clicking instantly into place.

For as well as she was rolling with the shock, Tori still hadn't fully adjusted to the Helen-Lodestar connection. Even as Tori watched her step into the pit, it was hard to fathom that this was really the same person. The woman who'd hit the dance floor like a tornado of elbows, coordinated constant craft projects, and spent half the night talking about old movies was the most powerful superhero known to Earth. All that saved her from wasting time denying the obvious was knowing that Fornax turned out to be a dependable middle manager, a devoted dad, and a surprisingly skilled cook. Tori was in deep enough now to know that the mask and who was under it didn't always match up, though this *still* felt like a bit much.

Her interest in speculation fell away as movement came from the stone surface. Shifting rocks fired out of the ground, encircling Lodestar, then briefly blocking her from view as they locked together. In the center of each quadrant, a tower appeared, stretching roughly ten feet into the air. One by one, as they completed, small metal objects appeared from hidden compartments in the very top. The whole process took less than ten seconds, and when it was done, Tori was shocked to hear the mysterious voice echo up from below.

"Well done, Fornax. I'm sure you've had a great deal of fun smashing through what must seem like rudimentary obstacles. To escape, however, I'm afraid you'll need something not normally associated with your skill set: delicacy. Around you, I'm sure you've noticed the four pillars that have risen. Atop each is a small puzzle, a minor mental challenge at best, yet you'll need every bit of focus to see the task through. You see, if any of those pillars are destroyed, the labyrinth will self-destruct. Such an explosion wouldn't be enough to kill you, obviously. Anyone else trapped inside likely won't be so lucky."

As the voice was talking, Tori realized the stones on the ground hadn't stopped moving. They were still shifting, and from within the dark spaces, she saw flashes of movement. She started to call out a warning, but unfortunately, her words were drowned out by the loud voice resuming.

"You also won't be the only one in there. We've got plenty more minions for you to play with—though, if you're too occupied, they'll happily attack the towers instead." The first of the new enemies emerged, and for a moment, Tori almost mistook it for a living being; the lizard-like body paired with stretches of moss along the joints created a believable image, at least until it opened its mouth, revealing rows of sharp, gray stone fangs.

"To ensure you continue working with the expediency we've come to expect, let's properly motivate you not to dilly-dally. I think one minute per tower is fair. In fact, we'll round up to an even five."

The center of the pit at last opened up, revealing a modestly sized hourglass. No sooner had it touched the artificial sunlight than the sands began to fall. "Five minutes until everything is annihilated, unless a tower is destroyed or forbidden power used, in which case, it happens immediately. Let us see how the great legend fares with a task beyond pure destruction."

By the time Tori looked back from the hourglass, there was already a spray of stone appendages next to Lodestar, where the first rock-lizard had popped up. More were crawling out across the pit, spacing themselves in what sure seemed to be purposeful inconvenience. Had Ivan been alone, the task would have been trying for him. Kill enough to get breathing room, work on a puzzle, rinse, repeat. Without being called, Tori was already dropping back down. Strong as Lodestar was, she was still a single cape, and with super-speed off the table, they had to pick where best to use her.

"You go low. I'll go high!" Tori all but fell onto the first tower, halting her descent with a powerful blast at the very end. She dared not shift more than her hands to flesh—every pound added increased the work needed to stay airborne, not to mention presented a target for any ambitious enemies. Behind her were the sounds of sneakers skidding, the shatter of rock, but her eyes stayed focused on the puzzle at hand.

It wasn't an especially complex task. With only her first few glances, Tori could see the solution. The test was one of precision more than mental acuity: everything had to be lined up near-perfect to untwist the central cylinder. First try, no luck. Second try, another failure. A spray of shards clipped through the flames of her back, and Tori worked to put the rest of the world out of her mind. This wasn't taking on a meta out of her league or demanding a power she lacked; Tori could do this. It was a test of her ability to concentrate, to think under pressure. That task was within her reach. Failing because she lacked power was one thing. Failing because she couldn't do the damn job—now that was another matter entirely. She mentally pulled back, letting herself take a fresh run at the attempt, just like she had a snagged pole during tent setup.

On her third try, the cylinder twisted, and as it did, the entire puzzle began to dissolve. They didn't get much more "done" than that, so Tori tore back into the air, eyes already hunting for the next tower. Looking around, she was dumbstruck by the number of broken bodies surrounding her position. Evidently, the goons came out in mass when a puzzle was being solved. What would Ivan have done, if he'd really been here all alone? Yank up the whole floor and kill the whole army at once? The notion seemed ludicrous, yet also worryingly plausible.

Hovering near the second tower, Tori noticed that the next puzzle was different from the first. Not unexpected, though part of her had hoped they'd all be the same, since the real test was in the execution. No such luck, so she began to twist the various symbols on the cube, deciphering the pattern as she went. Again, the solution was relatively easy to see, harder to reach. Every movement created countermovements that had to be accounted for. This one, she actually had an easier time with than the first; after all the half-rigged inventions she'd had to keep functioning, working with the overall project vision in mind and thinking several steps ahead were skills she'd polished to a shine.

Flashes of light in her periphery meant that Lodestar was busting out blasts of energy. Tori wrapped up the second puzzle just in time to see flecks of debris hit the ground where presumably a squadron of enemies had stood previously. This time, there were also still a few rock-lizards prowling around, though none near her tower. Lodestar wouldn't have any reason to be slowing down, so the rate they were appearing had to be increasing. Without using her super-speed, there was a limit to how quickly she'd be able to fell them. No wonder she'd switched over to wider-reaching attacks.

As Tori zipped over to the next tower, her vision wandered across the hourglass, which was shedding sand at a worrying rate. Had it really been nearly half the time already, or was it picking up as she cleared each challenge? She had a feeling the voice would pull that stuff, but Helen had been adamant about Cobblord's standards as a creator. Hopefully, accurate timers were part of that.

This time, she found herself staring at a spiked ball where each spike could be twisted anywhere between 180 – 360 degrees. After turning the first few, she was able to pick up on the different sounds each made upon hitting its latches. From there, it was a simple matter of finding the universal noise and dialing all of the spikes to it. Simple, but tedious, and with lots of room for reckless error. In a way, she had to hand it to the designer; given the time and distractions, Ivan really would have had trouble with this, even as detail-oriented as he was. Then again, if he failed, the creator would have a vengeful Fornax with a daughter to avenge, so maybe this wasn't such a great plan after all.

That assumed the threat was genuine, and since they clearly couldn't risk dismissing such a possibility, she had to proceed as though it wasn't a bluff. Whether it truly was or not, she hoped to never find out, dropping the third puzzle as soon as it began to dissolve. Firing away, she scanned the battlefield as she crossed to her final destination.

Save only for the patches where more minions were emerging, Tori could no longer see the ground. It was completely covered by the broken bodies of those that had come before. Like someone had driven a semi through a hall of statues, untold rock limbs lay shattered in piles, surrounding a Lodestar who continued to glow, untouched and unmarred by the relentless assault. Sadly, the hourglass wasn't so unaffected. Her time was definitely running short.

Coming down hard, Tori accidently put a flaming leg into the tower, causing a dark stain along the stone. She pulled back quickly, all attention on the final puzzle: a series of thin rings, brittle enough they'd easily snap, interwoven with strategic gaps in each one. Lining them up required getting the angles precise, and then carefully controlling the force used to pull them apart. There was nothing that said breaking it was against the rules, but given the circumstances, some limitations could be inferred. For as quickly as Tori found the solution, she also realized there was an issue. Hovering roughly had been fine for the first three; however, this task demanded a perfectly steady hand. She couldn't do it while bobbing in the air.

"Going full human. Please keep those things at bay." It was scary, shifting back fully to her human self, grabbing onto one of the many decorative spires along the tower's top, putting her safety entirely in the hands of a cape. Although, if she was trusting herself to any superhero, it would have been hard to pick a better candidate.

Wrapping her legs around the tower's center for stability, Tori didn't bother looking over to the hourglass. At this point, she had the time she had; knowing wouldn't change anything. Working as fast as she dared, one by one Tori pulled the rings apart. A rock whizzed by near her head as she separated the next-to-last pieces, strings of curses filling her mind, then dying on the tongue. Even moving her jaw was unnecessary, and right now, stability mattered more than anything else.

The final two rings had the thinnest of openings, because of course this shit couldn't be easy. Tori shut out the sounds of battle, the protests of pain from her already worn legs, the absolute insanity of her situation overall. She did what she'd always been able to do: close off the world, narrow it to the project before her. Everything else was ancillary. All that mattered was what existed in her hands. With more dexterity than she'd have believed her fingers capable of, the final rings pulled softly apart, neither breaking from the force.

Seconds later, they began to dissolve, though this time, the puzzle wasn't alone. The tower was doing the same thing, as were the bodies Lodestar had beaten. And the active minions, now that Tori was looking around, along with the stone pit and the ground surrounding them. The whole landscape was rippling, like it had been painted on a waterbed that had just been jumped upon.

Before she could shift back, Tori found herself suddenly weightless as Lodestar flew them both up into the air. "Pretty sure it will float us back down, but better safe than sorry. If we start descending normally, I'll let you enjoy the ride."

"What if we all come out of here dropping?"

"Then Lodestar will miraculously swoop in to catch everyone. No more labyrinth rules means I don't have to hold back anymore, and I'm pretty quick when I need to be. Don't worry, I'll set you down as well. There's no need to show anyone your powers unless you choose to."

The words were comforting, despite watching the ground crack and shake below them. Relief was flooding Tori's system; this ordeal truly did seem to be over. Unfortunately, Tori wasn't so short-sighted that she couldn't see there was more on the horizon. Being let in on Lodestar's secret wasn't a minor thing, no matter how the cape herself had tried to downplay it. There was also the fact that the weekend's events constituted a direct, knowing attack on guild leadership. People were going to pay for this, and to her surprise, Tori realized she wanted to be in the thick of it.

That was as far as her thought process went before the world around them suddenly sucked briefly inward, and then exploded.

Chapter 89

One moment, they were gathered in the forest, and then suddenly the ground was shaking. There was barely any time to react before the whole world they were standing on shattered, sending them all flying into what seemed like the sky. The false veneer quickly gave way, opening up to reveal the genuine outdoors. Loud booms were echoing across the campgrounds as the walls of condensed space collapsed, sending out minor shockwaves.

Mercifully, the same effect that had been used during their capture was still functioning, floating them down slowly. Ivan scanned for Beth and found her nearby, holding the hands of several other campers. He readied himself to teleport if gravity suddenly kicked into gear before noticing a familiar light streaking through the sky.

"Oh my god, it's her."

"Look! It's Lodestar!"

"Lodestar saved us!"

The kids were yelling now, moving toward cheering, and it wasn't as if they were wrong. Whether as herself or as Helen, Lodestar had indeed saved the day. Ivan had a great deal of questions for her on how, but resolved himself to waiting. Up here, he could already see the small crowd watching their descent. Her first job would be to update the AHC—official information channels took priority over secret friendships, especially considering she wouldn't want Ivan to get ahead of her on this one. Both had reason to want the perpetrators, but each would have very different plans for what to do with them.

Catching Beth's attention, Ivan gestured to the streaking light, to which he received a few quickly mouthed words: "You were right."

Ivan tried his very best to etch that memory into his brain. If Rick's teen years were any indication, he wouldn't be hearing those words again anytime soon.

As the ground drew nearer, Ivan assessed the crowd, searching for the other missing Starscout personnel. It wasn't hard, as Tori turned out to be less than thirty feet away as they were landing. There was no way she'd been that close when the orb split; although, in all that streaking about, no one would have noticed if Lodestar moved one body to a different position in the sky.

While Lodestar continued to circle the kids as they descended, ensuring that each one landed safely, Tori darted over, grabbing Ivan.

"Glad to see you're okay," he greeted her. "Everything go smoothly?"

"Oh boy, just so much to unpack and tell you about. But first things first, there's some stuff you need to know about what just happened."

With a quick glance, Ivan confirmed there was no one directly near them; however, in the chaos, that could change at any moment. "Perhaps this could wait until we have a more private location?"

"Ivan... you were the target. The old you. Whoever did this knows who you really are, and they also know about Beth."

A different Ivan, one not somewhat tired from a day-long ordeal, not facing down the very apprentice he'd worked so hard to educate on the importance of control, would have potentially ruined an entire swatch of forest with the surge of violent power that rose up inside him. But this was an Ivan who knew the value of control, and of pointing one's vengeance in the proper direction. None of these people deserved to bear his wrath. That would be reserved for the ones who'd incurred it. He could scarcely wait.

"Tell me what I need to know."

By early Sunday evening, the news was pouring from all major outlets: someone had attempted to attack a Starscout event. It had, of course, ended in failure. Details on how they'd been saved were light, but with Lodestar herself appearing on the scene right as the orb shattered and gently dropped its prisoners back to the ground, some assumptions were obvious. Images of slightly dirty children flickered across multiple screens, along with the stern face of Lodestar.

"While we don't have any perpetrators in custody yet, let me assure you, this is a crime the Alliance of Heroic Champions, and I, personally, take quite seriously." Those damned eyes looked right down the camera, like she could see the man going by Wendel Worthington watching in his lair. "I would advise the perpetrators to turn themselves in. Barring that, my recommendation would be to enjoy what freedom you have left. Very soon, you'll be in court—"

He muted the audio feed; threats held no interest for him. His only concern had been the results of the experiment, and whether or not Lozora had been apprehended. Evidently not. If they had a lead to parade in front of the camera, the AHC absolutely would. That was one silver lining; he didn't need to replace his pawn so close to the real game. Unfortunately, the experiment itself had been a massive failure. With Lodestar in the mix, there was no telling if Ivan had even finished the labyrinth himself, or what his speed would be.

Resting on his desk sat a large hunk of rare metal similar in hue to the orb Lozora had been given, yet not quite the same. This was to be material for Cobblord's second draft, a refined version. They could still make it—catching another kid to put in there as the limiter wouldn't be too hard. Hell, it probably didn't even have to be Ivan's own child. The so-called legend had never possessed the ruthlessness to ascend beyond his limitations. But without knowing for certain if it could hold Fornax long enough, the whole effort was useless.

In his youth, this man would have pressed on with the compromised effort. He would have looked at the resources spent, the time and money used to procure these items, and decided it would be folly not to use them. Life and experience had taught him much, including the concept of a sunk-cost fallacy. What mattered wasn't the work put in, but the results obtained. Fornax had to be occupied; otherwise, the whole plan could come apart.

Working the shadows, scheming in secret, it all only held together for so long. Too many villains tried to make this phase last forever rather than accepting what it was: a chance to prepare. Sooner or later, the truth always spilled out, and once it did, there would be a reckoning. Using this time to get ready, to smooth out the path toward his objectives as much as possible, meant that when things did change, he'd still have the upper hand.

If the labyrinth couldn't be counted on, then his best bet was to roll Fornax into the same distraction planned for the AHC. It would shift the timetables, perhaps significantly, but so long as he was efficient, the rest of the plan was still viable. He only needed enough time to do the job and slip away. The real challenge would be forcing himself not to savor the act he'd spent so much work laying a foundation for. Although, this was more about the message than the killing itself, an inherited grudge the owner had no idea had been hung over their head.

Lifting a phone, those thin fingers stalked along the buttons, the anti-tracking equipment wired in making the process slightly cumbersome. It was time to make sure the Guild of Villainous Reformation knew exactly what it was they'd no doubt been tracking for some time now, along with what was hidden from their sensors. Once the guild knew what was coming, they'd have to take steps to interfere, most likely leading with the tip of their spear: Fornax.

After all, this was their world, too. It wasn't as if they could afford to shrug off an impending invasion.

Beth was asleep before she even made it to her room, nodding off on the couch while Ivan brought Janet up to speed. Rick and Juan were out fetching dinner when they arrived, offering Beth a quiet place to rest—probably not a coincidence. Given the look on his ex-wife's face, Ivan imagined this wasn't a conversation she wanted lots of people to be around for. He'd expected to have to wait until Beth wore down; however, a weekend of stress and poor sleep made itself known the instant she felt at home, sending her soaring into slumber.

Nearby, in the kitchen, Janet kept her voice low and controlled, a well-honed skill from their married days, when these discussions were far more frequent. "What the *hell* happened out there?"

"It's like the news says. Someone tossed a maze, and it snagged all of us. I made sure the kids were safe, while the others worked to get us out."

"Uh huh. 'Someone' threw a maze. Weird, how they'd use a device worth millions to the right buyer on a Starscout cluster, run by a middle manager and a whatever-she-pretends-to-be. Just admit it, they were picking a fight with her, and our daughter got caught in the middle, like I always warned you she would." Janet glanced into the living room, making sure the kid in question was still resting. "Well this is the last straw. Tomorrow, we are going to explain to Beth—"

"It was me," Ivan interrupted. He didn't want to agitate her by being rude, but Janet could also be hard to derail once she had momentum going. Better to get the truth out while it was still capable of being considered. "We don't know much yet, but I was able to exchange a few words with Tori after the release. Enough to be aware that *I* was the target, and Beth being in there wasn't a coincidence."

Her head of steam died slowly as Ivan's words sank in. What took its place was far worse, in Ivan's esteem. Janet was past angry, the heat of rage giving way to the pure, unrelenting cold of true fury. When she spoke again, it was with the sort of unnerving calm that had always intrigued Ivan. The facet was, in honesty, part of what had formed their initial attraction.

"You promised me this wouldn't happen. You looked me in the eyes, and you told me they'd stay away. That your identity was secret enough, and even the few who did find out would keep clear. Because no one would *dare* mess with Fornax, or the ones he loves."

The words were all but a slap, and Ivan glanced over himself to be sure that Beth was still conked out. Using that name in her home was not something Janet did lightly.

"Don't think for a moment that I wanted—"

"Our baby just got dragged into an orb in the goddamn sky, I don't give a *fuck* what you want." It was Janet's turn to interrupt, and she hissed the words —likely the only way she could resist from screaming them. "You know I want? I want to spend tonight with my husband and kids, having a nice dinner, not calling a child psychologist who specializes in meta-related trauma. I want to not see that suspicious glint in Rick's eyes every time he looks at either of us these days. I want to stop lying awake every single night wondering when it will all come crashing down, when your secret gets out and their lives become insane—assuming they're lucky enough to make it through. I want our children to be safe, Ivan."

She finally paused, taking a moment to compose herself. Only once Ivan was sure she'd said her piece did he speak once more. "As do I. More than anything in the world. There is nothing I won't do to protect those two."

"Except, apparently, your current plan isn't working. This is the second time in a calendar year our kids have been targeted because of you." Janet was looking more centered now, the initial shock of the revelation giving way to her relentless thought. She seemed to take him in as he stood there, looking over every detail of the aggressively mundane appearance. Her tone softened considerably. "Ivan, no one, not even *her*, knows better than I do how hard you worked to leave Fornax behind when Rick arrived. Whatever issues we might have, you have always been an amazing father to those kids, and I am wowed by the transformation you made. But maybe... maybe right now, they don't need their father as much as they need the demon he used to be."

The words came out heavy, as such a sentiment should be. She never looked away, however. Janet knew what she was saying, asking, in a way that very few could. "People aren't afraid the way they once were. Achievements have turned into history, stories into myths. You did such a good job living in the shadows that Fornax's legend faded."

"Your solution is that I take revenge for this incident, I assume?" Ivan wasn't entirely sure how he felt about the idea she was floating; instead, he focused on making it through the conversation. It had been a very long weekend. He dearly needed some time to decompress.

"Revenge? The kind where your people show up and the perpetrators are never heard from again? No, Ivan. This demands more than death from the shadows. This needs to be a spectacle." Ivan felt a slight chill at Janet's steady, unwavering gaze. "Crack their bones, sear their skin, drop their severed heads onto the tables of their closest allies. *Break* these pieces of shit, the way only the great destroyer can, and make sure the world sees. Show them what happens to anyone who goes against Fornax."

Between the two of them, Ivan was undeniably the greater danger. Even without his meta-human abilities, he had a lifetime of combat training and the willingness to do harm in ways most people could never obtain. However, that didn't mean Janet was some shrinking violet, content to live in willful ignorance. Protecting her children always came first. She knew full well what she was asking, and there wasn't so much as a flicker of doubt.

"If I do something like that, the AHC is going to turn the heat way up. There might be unexpected consequences."

"Glad you mentioned them, actually," Janet replied. "Reminds me—pass a message along to *her*: I want to have a word."

That was a bad idea. A terrible idea, for an abundance of reasons, none of which Ivan could find a tactful way to bring up. Ultimately, he decided to stall for time until he could think of something. "I'll let her know, but she's often busy. Might be a while before she responds."

"Tell her to use that damn super-speed. The way she should have inside that stupid maze, so a bunch of kids wouldn't have spent a weekend being kidnapped."

Though Ivan had gotten a rough outline of the labyrinth's setup and limitations during his brief talk with Tori, he declined to bring any of it up. For the moment, Janet was angry and scared; the facts weren't going to matter. Ivan understood that all too well, because he was feeling exactly the same thing. The fact that Beth had been included on purpose terrified him down to his very core. Life was so fleeting, so easily snatched away, and he couldn't bear the thought of anything happening to either of his kids.

Which was why the anger inside was taking significant effort to hold back. Janet was freer with her emotions, because she could afford to be. Harsh words weren't the same as what slipped loose when Ivan's control wavered. Worse, part of him was already wondering if Janet was right. Was his best move to dole out this punishment publicly? The Apollo fight was a slipup; he hadn't willingly acted as Fornax in years. Perhaps that was part of the reason these new threats felt so emboldened.

Janet had raised some valid points, yet Ivan still remained hesitant. Not because he didn't relish the idea of setting a violent, bloody example of what happened to those who crossed his family—in fact, it was an image he was actively working to keep out of his head. Being Fornax again would be easy, which was why Ivan still felt the need to resist.

Once Fornax was intentionally let out, there might be no putting him back.

Chapter 90

Tori was surprised to see an empty street corner as the car dropped her off. She'd been expecting some of the New Science Sentries to be there, so over-concerned that they insisted on walking her the few feet from sidewalk to front door. Hauling herself out of the car, she looked her brick domicile up and down, appreciating the familiarity. It had taken a while, but arriving here was starting to feel like coming home. Especially knowing that she had friends up there waiting for her.

It was probably a good thing none of the capes were around. Tori still wasn't sure how she felt about learning Lodestar's secret, or the implications it had regarding Ivan, and some time to think through that would be nice. Besides, she needed to reconsider her stance on fraternizing with capes as a whole. The friendships that had seemed so impossible on Friday weren't nearly as remarkable by comparison now, which made them feel far more manageable.

Stepping into the foyer, Tori caught movement from the mail alcove. It wasn't especially subtle, as the figure moved toward her as soon as she appeared. For an instant, her heart leapt at the sight of those kaleidoscope eyes, but the same bit could only be genuinely scary so many times. "Nexus, you are one creepy bastard, you know that?"

"If only," he replied, sounding oddly... wistful? "How was your weekend?"

"What, weren't you posted up on a tree somewhere, watching the whole thing?"

Nexus shook his head hard, causing his long trench coat to shake slightly, sending off small plumes of red dirt. "Others to watch, and Lodestar fights are boring unless they're big. Like... well, odds are you'll see soon enough."

"Great, I'll set my DVR. Anything else, or is this just your creepy hangout for the night?" She should be more scared—Tori knew that rationally. Mad as he seemed, Nexus had endured the full efforts of the guild and the AHC to stamp him out. He was capable of wide-scale destruction like she could only imagine, based on the few displays he'd given.

"One thing, if you're interested." Nexus was smiling in a way that only the truly gleeful and insane could manage: with absolute abandon. "A junction is looming, a point where things tend to go in one of two directions. In one version, several fascinating stories are cut short. In another, they persist, providing more entertainment. The difference in the two is often you."

The unnerving thing about Nexus was that he was mad, not crazy. There *was* logic in those shattered eyes, a process of thought and reason that guided his actions. After a few meetings, she'd gotten enough clues to realize that, at least for now, he was largely acting as a voyeur. Their world was amusing to him, so he watched it for entertainment. Tracking that, when he said stories were cut short... he was probably talking about the people living those tales.

"Who gets hurt?"

"Can't say. Not always the same, you know. But they won't be strangers to you, that much is certain."

It was never that easy. Just enough information to make you do what they wanted: that was how manipulators loved to work. She was very tempted to flip him the bird and walk away, except that afterward, every time she looked at Beverly or Chloe, Tori would wonder if something bad was coming for them, and whether she could have stopped it.

"You can't tell me who is involved, or what will happen, I'm guessing. But somehow, I affect the outcome?"

"A superhero defends what is just; a villain defends what is theirs. Remember who you truly are, and the rest shall flow as it does. I have my preferences, but the show marches on regardless." He twirled once, his massive coat flaring out behind. "Do try to keep it amusing."

Without warning, he was simply gone. Never with flash or spectacle, Nexus moved through space with the same level of grandiose display as when Tori took a step forward. It was mundane to him, as was likely all of this. Who knew how much those fractured eyes had witnessed, and over a span of how long? Yet something impending was fascinating enough to warrant a special trip to Tori. These did happen—she'd been warned as much since he crashed a guild meeting.

Tori's plans for an evening of rest suddenly evaporated as she found a fresh wind. Dinner with her friends, certainly, but after that, it was down to the lab. The Hephaestus suit needed repairing, and she no longer felt safe with it compromised. Something told her she was going to be wearing it again sooner than later.

Curiously, Tori realized this notion had put a thin smile on the edges of her lips. Perhaps Nexus wasn't the only one capable of acclimating to the insanity of this lifestyle.

"Any idea what this is about?" Donald followed Ren through the crowd, his friend's bulk helping clear a path through the array of costumed forms. He couldn't recall ever seeing so many of the AHC's capes in one place. Usually, they were separated by schedules and distance; with a whole world to keep running and only so many capes to lean on, they weren't exactly all walking the same patrol beat. Most of the others seemed excited, though a few appeared nervous.

"I got the same text as you. Major meeting—everyone not on active assignments who can get here needs to report." Ren halted his forward march, having reached the end of space in the crowd. Moving more would demand shoving bodies aside; hardly a polite option, especially around coworkers. This room was enormous, as was the screen dominating an entire wall. Still, even with all the space, they were getting packed in. The AHC had evidently grown since the room was last needed for this purpose.

Scanning the room, Donald noted Irene and Lucy coming in from their individual training sessions. Both were still clad in sweats rather than costumes, Lucy waving as soon as they made eye contact. The two began wading through the sea of bodies, though how long it would take to reach their position was anyone's guess.

Turning his attention toward the front, where the screen was located, he picked out the familiar hue of the New Science Sentries' costumes, all four of them in prime positions. They must have either gotten here in advance or used Presto's teleportation trickery—probably the former. Austin didn't seem the sort to let his people cut ahead. There were other familiar outfits near the front, as well: Dapper Doll, the Ineffable, Glass Cannon, and the unfortunately named Mister Fister, a brawling cape who must be working very hard to ignore the innuendo of his moniker.

At the next figure, Donald almost let out a yelp of shock. Sure enough, that was Lady Shade standing there. She'd been missing since the rebellion. He'd assumed she was booted along with the other traitors. Maybe telling the truth at the end had bought her some leniency? That was more comforting than his other hunch: that they were up against something so dangerous, it demanded all hands on deck. Even the untrusted ones.

Suddenly, the lights flickered, blinking three times. Instantly, the crowd grew silent as every eye turned toward the giant screen. After the third bout of darkness, the lights remained off. What illuminated the room now was a bright, blank screen. Seconds later, Professor Quantum stepped onto the stage, followed by Quorum. Lodestar arrived a few steps behind, her tardiness probably the result of still having to deal with the fallout from the Starscout attack. Donald had sent Tori a text—the most he could do with this meeting filling up his evening. Besides, knowing her, she probably wanted to be alone and relax. Tori would reach out when she was ready; he just hoped his schedule would open up when the moment came.

"Superheroes of the Alliance of Heroic Champions," Professor Quantum began, "today I stand before you with grave news. The purpose for which this organization was founded, to defend the world against threats great and small, shall be put to its fullest test once again. While much of what I'm about to say will eventually leak to the public, it is vital this remain confidential for as long as possible. Failure to control information could lead to mass panic and civilian casualties."

The light, interested vibe of the room shifted quickly. Professor Quantum was never what one would call carefree, but the gravity of these words was undeniable. He was serious, as was their situation. "We have been tracking a migration of ships moving on a course for Earth. These are not Grzzniltan, though we suspect they had some hand in this. Based on information provided by our extraterrestrial sources, we believe these to be the Wrexwren, a species specialized in conquering and combat. Considering their attempt at a stealthy approach and the number of ships present, this is almost certainly an invading force."

Someone in the room obviously had the ability to steal the bottom out from people's stomachs: that was the only explanation Donald could think of for why his gut suddenly dropped to the heels of his shoes. An invasion? An actual attempt to take over their planet? That was crazy. It had been forever since the last time anyone tried that, and the AHC had sent them packing.

Which was exactly what Professor Quantum wanted to have happen again, from the sound of things.

"Before anyone gets too nervous, we do have a plan that we hope will keep things contained," Lodestar announced. "The Wrexwren, like many warring cultures, pride themselves on their strength. Historically, they'll allow a planet's champion to battle their own to earn its salvation. We plan to invoke that, hopefully keeping the fighting entirely contained off-planet."

"However, there is no guarantee this particular force will honor that tradition, or do so fairly," Professor Quantum said, retaking control of his stage. "We must be prepared for the absolute worst we can imagine. Someone is coming to take this planet. From us, from you, from everyone you love. Many things are different across the stars, but conquest is constant. If we aren't prepared, it will be brutal and bloody before you've even got your masks on."

To Donald's surprise, Lodestar actually nodded in agreement this time. "Hope for the best, brace for the worst. There's no such thing as being too prepared. For our newer members, keep in mind that we won't intentionally put you against something you can't handle, but an invasion is a hectic time. We know little about the Wrexwren, their motives, or their potential allies. Trust your instincts. If something feels way out of your league, your first priority is communicating that back to base, not engagement. Information is going to be the name of the game."

"Perhaps we should start at the beginning: expected arrival date." Quorum had to be wearing a mic; there was no way that soft tone traveled so well on projection alone.

His words recentered Lodestar and Professor Quantum, perhaps one of the most essential tasks in all of the AHC. Professor Quantum nodded, then made a motion. The screen behind him suddenly went black, or that was how it initially appeared. After a moment for his eyes to adjust, Donald realized he was looking at an image of stars. A flicker as the image changed, and now he could make out a small patch of Saturn's rings in the photo. Something else, too. A large ship that blended well with the blackness of space, unnatural in design. Too many angles and loops, it had design functions he couldn't even begin to guess at, for a biology he knew nothing about.

The third slide pulled a gasp from Donald, along with several others nearby. Now, they could see more ships, dozens in this one frame alone, with untold more outside the shot. Hearing the word "invasion" was one thing; seeing it stretched out through the vast void of space was an entirely different matter.

"Based on their speed, it is our estimation that the forces will arrive in less than a week's time. While we will of course monitor in case of acceleration, current predications have them entering within range of Earth on Saturday. I hope you all can appreciate the implications." Whether it was needed or not, Professor Quantum opted to go ahead and state the obvious, ensuring that everyone fully grasped the stakes of their situation.

"It means that if we do nothing, this will be humanity's last week in control of its own planet."

All the data was backing it up, ridiculous as the tip had been.

Wade was never one to turn down a solution, so long as he understood all the implications of using it. A random call to a guild-monitored line, leaving explicit information about the invading forces, was all but the literal definition of "suspicious." The thing was, that didn't make the tip incorrect.

People often thought of misinformation as untruths, and while there was certainly a fair bit of that in the mix, there was also more to it than that. On occasion, the right tactic involved giving out real information, but controlling *who* got it, and when. Move the pieces into position, predict their movements, and plot how to use them to the scheme's advantage.

Based on the message he'd gotten, the Wrexwren weren't coming to Earth with no idea of what they were stepping into. They knew the humans had intel, and were planning to challenge them to a duel. They also knew the Earth had an undefeated defender, and they were still coming, which meant they had to think they possessed an effective counter. That part, Wade had been the most curious about, and as test after test returned the predicted results, it seemed he finally had an answer.

"The universe is a scary place, if things like that are just out there wandering around." He looked over the digital image, constructed out of places the transmission vanished, like throwing paint around a hole to get a shape of the void. Without the message's precise frequency to scan, it might have taken him weeks more to manage even this much. Seeing the picture on-screen, Wade felt a rare sense of foreboding.

This was no half-assed effort. Whoever was pulling the strings had accounted for nearly everything, even managing to stymie the guild's power here and there. As much as Wade wanted to wait out the AHC, force them to return on bended knee, begging for even the slightest bit of aid, survival took precedence over grudges. The Wrexwren were coming hard, and so far seemed to be better prepared and informed than the humans they were up against.

The guild would need to be ready to do more than just scavenge and strike. Should the world truly be in peril, it wasn't just the champions with a stake in its defending. His people would be ready, too, prepared to send a message to every alien, cape, and civilian that saw their handiwork.

Even monsters had the right to protect their home.

Chapter 91

The flash in the sky was all she needed. Juan was asleep on the couch with Beth, and Rick had already locked himself in his room for the evening. Still, Janet paused by the door to scoop up the kitchen trash—less an excuse, more being productive with her time. Stepping out into the night, she shivered slightly. Fall was setting in more firmly; the night winds carried a crisp chill. Part of her wondered if she should have grabbed a jacket, though that might have looked odd to simply take out the trash.

Walking around to the side of her house, Janet popped open the large trash can and tossed her bag inside. Out of the corner of her eye, she caught movement coming from the driveway, a figure stepping into the floodlight's range, lighting up a whole section of yard. She'd have been so easy to overlook, had Janet not known the truth.

Adjusting her glasses slightly, the woman waited until the light flickered off, plunging them into darkness once more.

"I heard you wanted to talk."

"Talk?" Janet shoved the trash down harder, resisting the urge to punch and potentially break the bag. With her luck, she'd hit a wine bottle and fracture a knuckle—one more reminder of how human she was. "No, what I want is to be standing over the twisted remains of the people who did this, or living in a world where it never happened in the first place. What I'll settle for is getting some goddamn answers. You were in there the entire time: how *dare* you sit on your hands for a full day and make those children suffer."

Helen didn't rise to the anger. She simply nodded. "I know this is hard to believe, but being careful and going slow was my way of keeping them safe. The labyrinth had failsafes in case certain abilities were used, ones designed to target the kids. Until I knew what they were, I couldn't take the risk of accidentally causing the whole thing to explode."

"How convenient, that it just so happened so that one of the few times Lodestar can't use her speed is one where you're sealed inside a getaway with..." Janet forced herself to take a breath. Going off topic wouldn't help any of this. "Fine. I can accept that in your situation, with Ivan protecting the kids, caution would be the smarter move. My real question is what you intend to do about this moving forward."

"That's a perfectly fair concern," Helen replied. "To answer your question, I've only just started the ball rolling, so there aren't many details yet, but I'm putting together a new division of the Starscouts. Security-based, to ensure that nothing like that happens at one of our events ever again, or barring that, we have people to respond if it does."

Slamming the large trash can lid down, Janet wrinkled her nose at the last whiff of stink. "What a surprise, you went running to your followers. And now that the AHC has its hooks in, it's only a matter of time before they turn it into a recruiting pool."

"Happy to disappoint. This new division still isn't AHC-related." Helen was unfailingly calm, even cheery, despite the implied accusation Janet had just thrown. "Since the Starscouts are an organization open to humans and metas, we have quite a few of the latter who have graduated. I've been reaching out to old members, asking about their time and availability. There's lots of interest so far, but it's much too early to have many specifics in place. Just know that I take what happened this weekend seriously."

Janet wasn't sure why she'd expected anything different. Of course Helen already had a plan and an answer ready to go; not to mention found a way to get the personnel she needed without tapping the AHC. Given the role Helen filled in protecting the world, her efficiency and preparedness were technically positive traits, even if Janet did find them annoying.

"A good start for the Starscouts, but what about my kids?" Janet stepped away from the trash, onto the driveway, inadvertently setting off the floodlight once more. "I know who the target was, and why they chose that event to attack. There's no secret magic protecting their father's identity from getting out, or them from the fallout. If it's already started leaking, then this was only the start of what's to come. Tell me you have a plan to keep them safe."

For a moment, Helen started forward, arms extending like she was reaching out to comfort Janet. That motion lasted for only a brief instant before she halted, just as the floodlight died once more. "I'm sorry, Janet. I know what you want to hear. You want to know your child will be safe, protected, and watched over no matter what. You want to be able to keep the worst of the world away, to drive it off, spare them so many horrible truths. That's why I'm sorry, because I can't give you that. Not even I can be everywhere at once."

Before Janet could begin her tirade, from which there would have been little reprieve, Helen continued, hurrying slightly. "What I *can* do is start by enrolling them in various AHC monitoring services, if you're comfortable with that. We'd set them up with some light surveillance and trackers, along with emergency response beacons they could push to alert us they are in imminent danger. Obviously, these would all be located here; your ex-husband's property is his own business."

"That's it? Your idea is to bug them?"

"I said it was the start," Helen corrected. "I'm happy to work with you to come up with more solutions."

To her credit, she did still have a polite smile fixed in place, but Janet doubted just how "happy" she'd really be if that offer was accepted. Not that it mattered. Hearing her proposal had only set Janet's determination all the more. "Pass."

"On which part?"

"All of it." Janet mimed forming the air into a ball, then tossed it over her shoulder into the closed trash can. "You think I'm giving the AHC even one door into their lives? It's just a matter of time until some cape with an old grudge or burning ambition decides to see how a legend's offspring hold up. Or hell, one might pull an Apollo and outright use them for hostages. My kids *will* have protection, but not from you."

Realization hit instantly. Young as she might look, Helen was concealing a wealth of experience. "As much as I get it—and I do—you understand what you'll be choosing, right? Ivan is not the norm in that organization. He's the leash they're all kept on. I understand the mistrust in the AHC, truly, and if you'd prefer, I can pick the capes assigned to them personally."

"Do... do you honestly think I'd trust *you*?" Janet was sincerely a bit shocked. She and Helen were on far from friendly, or even cordial, terms.

At long last, the veneer slipped, and Helen's forehead pinched in frustration, causing her to run a thumb along the wrinkles that Janet knew would never set. "Outside of your—let me remind you—unfounded suspicions, yes, I would really like to think that if nothing else, you'd believe me when I say I'm trying to protect innocent children. I've got the track record to prove it."

Forcing herself to stay in control, Janet took a few moments to breathe. She couldn't afford to get overly heated. Much as she loathed it, there might very well come a day when Lodestar was the only cape in her kids' corners. Janet knew she should play with at least a minimal amount of diplomacy until then.

"All right, perhaps that was a bit far. I'm standing by my decision, however. No AHC involvement. Maybe the guild won't be as polished or as practiced in their protections, but they'll know the stakes. They'll understand just *who* they're failing if anything happens to their charges. Besides, sooner or later, those two are going to learn the truth. Better they make some inroads with their eventual allies."

Surprisingly, Helen gave another nod rather than keep debating. "Very well, then. It's not the choice I'd have made, but you're their mom. I won't try to tell you what's best for your family. All I can say is that if you ever do decide that we might be able to help, the door will be open so long as I'm there to hold it."

The sentiment was a nice one, and probably the best place to end the conversation. Janet hadn't gotten as much reassurance as she might have liked, but after a point, they would just be empty words. There was, however, one detail of the discussion that she refused to let lie. "I appreciate that, and I appreciate the help you've shown them so far. That said, let's be clear: my suspicions were *not* unfounded."

A loud, weary groan of a sigh escaped from Helen's lungs. "I am several decades too old to stand in a driveway and fight about a boy. I'm sorry you think something went on between us, even though it didn't. No secret affair, no tawdry messages. Ivan and I barely even talked when you two were married. He'd never have done that, and neither would I."

"I know." Janet was surprised to hear the words come from her own mouth. She'd realized all of that long ago, though giving the sentiment words was another step entirely. "I know Ivan would never cheat, because I understand why he was here in the first place. It wasn't an affair I suspected. It was the truth."

"Janet, it's been a long weekend, and I've still got a lot more work before the night is over. Can you maybe skip over being cryptic and just tell me what it is you think happened so I can set the record straight?"

"If that's what you want," Janet agreed. "I 'think' my ex-husband married me because I'd given birth to his son, which is admittedly the same reason I married him. He was a good husband—surprising, given his past—but Ivan is adept at throwing himself fully into things. So he became Ivan the father, Ivan the civilian, Ivan the manager. We had another child, built a life together, and over time, I thought we'd fallen in love. Then that day at the beach came. Horrific as it was, the image I can never seem to forget is what came after, when Lodestar arrived."

There was genuine confusion on Helen's face now, an expression Janet might have relished in other circumstances. As it was, her focus remained on getting to say her piece. "I know how Ivan looks at someone he loves. There's a vulnerability that exists only in those instants. I caught it when he looked at our kids, or as a faraway glint on the rare occasions he'd open up about those he lost in the past. For a long time, I thought he just had a different look for me—one of affection and care, yet still not quite the same. And I was okay with that. You don't wed someone with his baggage without expecting a few oddities. Until that day. Until you landed, racing over to comfort the man who'd just slaughtered an army. Until I saw the way he looked at you."

"I cannot emphasize enough, nothing was going—"

"Do you think that makes it *better* for me?" Janet barely resisted the urge to yell, her hands forming into balls. "I get it. You did nothing wrong, as always. You were perfect, and moral, and continued to live at a standard no one else can touch, and I'm just the horrid monster of an ex who *dared* to want more than a hollow marriage. But he loved you. Loves you still. Don't look me in the eye and pretend you don't realize that."

Some distance off, the sounds of a car's brakes filled the silence of the night air. "Yes, Janet. I know how Ivan feels about me. That's *why* we barely talked when you were together. Both of us understood the danger and avoided it. Because whatever passing affections he might have in my direction, this family is the most important thing in the world to him, as it should be. And I promise you, Ivan never strayed, never even looked off the path. This emotion that you're angry about, I understand, but I'm not sure what more either of us could have done."

"While we're several years and a new, happy marriage past that point, some more honesty might have been helpful. I don't think Ivan is ever going to work past what he feels for you. However, if he'd been open about it, we could have at least tried." A brisk wind caught Janet, causing another shiver. Helen remained unbothered, of course. She lived in the same world as Ivan, filled with beings of incomprehensible power, a realm that mortals could only catch glimpses of.

"On that front, I truly don't know what to say. Getting Ivan to open up is beyond even the greatest of capes. Only he decides when to be vulnerable." Helen took a slight step back, turning on the floodlight once more. Head lifted, she was scanning the skies, preparing to leave.

Tempting as it was to let her go, Janet did have one last bit of curiosity to scratch, especially since answers were flowing. "You know, in all this time, I've only ever gotten to witness Ivan's side of things. That intentional avoiding of each other, was that purely for his sake?"

"Have a good night, Janet. I'll catch you around."

A few hops back out into the darkness, then suddenly, there was a flash of light and an empty driveway.

Janet headed back into the house; question more thoroughly answered than Helen might have intended. Nothing quite said inadvertent guilt like hightailing it out of a conversation at top speed.

Chapter 92

Halfway through her Monday morning wake-up routine, Tori paused to wonder if she even actually had to go in to the office. So far, they'd generally given her a few days off after each life-shaking traumatic event, but a corporation's goodwill could only stretch so far. Then again, she did know the boss, and the guy who owned the whole damn shebang, so perhaps she was receiving more generous time to recover than most. Toothbrush still hanging from her mouth, Tori popped open her phone, a text from Ivan already waiting.

"No office today, but there's still work to do. Meet me outside your building at our usual start time."

Interesting. Tori tossed the phone down and slowly resumed her brushing. No telling for sure what today's activities would entail, though she could make a few general guesses on the subject matter. After a night of sleep and a few thousand actual calories, she was feeling far less wiped, but the new secret she'd uncovered still lay heavy on her mind. Tori was extremely thankful Helen had explained that it was impossible for her to slip up; at least she didn't have to worry about some wrong word or turn of phrase giving away what she knew.

A few solid raps on her door were all the warning she got before Beverly shoved it open. "Hey, you almost ready in here? Chloe got up early to cook you a 'welcome home' breakfast, and I am not facing that alone."

"That was sure... kind of her." Tori had never quite gotten her flames hot enough to manage turning something solid into total ash, which would have made disposal of the goods far easier. Perhaps an invention to consider, once her suit was fully repaired.

"At least you can stall until it's time for your office job," Beverly said, marking one of the few times she'd expressed jealousy for Tori's corporate-cog status. "Speaking of, since my more distracting roommate was gone all weekend, I made a lot of headway on our project. Couldn't sleep after you got home and hit the lab, so I stayed up and got pretty close to being done. By tonight, I should have my part ready for the prototype."

"So soon?" Tori would have expected turnaround like that from herself, which was to say a person with a poor work-life balance and tendency to hurl herself into projects. Beverly was far more reasonable in her passions. Even if she was incredibly skilled, she still must have put in a lot of time to already be near finished.

Beverly affected her best haughty expression, one that actually sat quite well on her finely sculpted face. "You're not the only one capable of knuckling down when the occasion demands." Her face softened, a sliver of weariness cracking through. "Plus, there's been all the stuff with my family reaching out—having something to work on made for a great distraction. After this, I might build us a new dining room table."

"Don't go overcommitting too fast. If the prototype goes well, we're definitely going to need more." Tori stepped into her bathroom, partially to do one last appearance check, and also to buy more time until she had to head into the kitchen. The woman staring back at Tori was one she'd never have imagined possible. Brown suit, long skirt, hair back, stud earrings, and sensible shoes. She was so... boring, and Tori felt a strange swell of pride in her heart at that notion. This was a woman who lived a normal life, worked a boring job, and had the dullest of secrets. Building this image had taken time and effort, not to mention quite a bit of guidance from Ivan.

If everything went well, Tori wouldn't be able to keep playing this angle for much longer. She wouldn't be revealing any heavy truths to the world, but the new role required different features to succeed. That was getting ahead of herself, though. They still had to finish the prototype, impress Wade, and start the ball rolling on production. Nevertheless, Tori took her time examining that reflection, more than just to delay eating Chloe's food.

At the rate her life had been changing, by this time next year, she might have three heads and a tail. Best to appreciate the moment while she was still in it. If Tori had taken no other lesson in her life, she knew that nothing—no time, no phase, no joy—lasted forever. Sooner or later, everything came to end.

Without warning, Chloe's raised voice rang out from the kitchen. "Hey you two, does anyone have an allergy to pimento cheese? I found a waffle recipe online that suggested using it in the batter and thought that sounded fun."

Tori stepped out of her bathroom, locking terrified eyes with Beverly, who reflected her expression nearly as well as the actual mirror had. Hiding was no longer viable; they had to get proactive.

Wordlessly, Tori put up her fist, and Beverly did the same. They each shook the closed hand three times, then reformed it into the finger-symbol of paper, scissors, or rock. Tori won the first match with a last-second scissors, but Beverly took the second thanks to a well-timed rock. The final bout was neck-and-neck, yet Tori's own rock ultimately claimed victory.

"You know what? I think I *am* allergic to that," Beverly called, pausing only to shoot Tori a dirty look. Tori accepted the gaze, along her prize of not having to remember a new fake allergy.

Such were the spoils of victory.

"Excuse me, sir, can I help you?"

Ivan looked up from his phone to see the two figures he'd already clocked approaching standing nearby. The blond was big—not just raw muscle, either. He moved like someone who actually used his body rather than only building it. Next to him was a shorter fellow with brown hair and a lean frame. Given what he knew about Tori's living situation, Ivan had a hunch on who these might be. Still, muscles did not a meta make. It was possible they were normal ruffians planning a robbery. Although, early in the morning, with their arms full of groceries, would certainly be a departure from the mugging norms.

"Appreciate it, but I'm just waiting for someone." Instantly, both men's faces tightened. They were either on guard patrol or were up to shady activities of their own. Clearly, this wasn't a good answer. Deciding to part with slightly more information, Ivan added, "My niece lives here."

The shorter one—Tachyonic, if Ivan was getting this right—stepped forward. "Sorry to say this, but we've had a few incidents surrounding some residents as of late. Perhaps there's somewhere more comfortable you can wait."

"My answer is a polite, firm no." Ivan looked back down at his phone, effectively dismissing them both. "I'm standing on a public sidewalk, not inside the building where you may or may not reside. Since I don't see any badges on display, this doesn't seem to be a discussion of loitering coming from an officer of the law. Unless you two are both secretly superheroes, we're all civilians, and I've got no reason to move."

It was a tad mean, coming so close to calling them out, but they needed to learn to split their identities better. These sorts of discussions had to happen when they were in costume. Without that authority, they just seemed like interlopers bothering strangers, at best.

To their credit, both were flustered, but neither one lost themselves entirely. Instead, the one who had to be Agent Quantum gave a knowing grin, then walked over to the building's brick exterior and placed his back against it. "He's right. We've got no authority to make this gentleman move. But we do have just as much right to stand out here as him, making use of the public sidewalk."

Smarter than the physique indicated, not that Ivan was too surprised. Professor Quantum's attachment to his legacy was legendary among capes and villains alike; the man protected his brand better than an entire PR firm could manage. For him to pass on the mantle, even if only part of his name, was a tremendous vote of confidence in the one who'd be carrying it. Agent Quantum wouldn't have the title if he were merely some hulking bruiser. To earn that, there was no telling what sorts of tests he'd had to endure, let alone pass. Ivan had a hunch that once this kid started showing what he could really do, they'd be in for quite the show. Possibly even a real challenge.

Tachyonic moved slowly—a detail that very nearly caused Ivan to chuckle—stepping over to his friend's side, his eyes never leaving Ivan. He paid them no mind, putting the final touches on his email before hitting send. With that, his schedule had been effectively cleared for the week. Waking up to find he'd been temporarily reassigned, by the head office no doubt, to a special research project had been momentarily confusing, until he noticed the message from Wade. It was vague, as all monitorable guild correspondence tended to be, but the gist came through. Something was up, and while he'd get the details later that day, all indications seemed that it was serious. Wade didn't go around butting into Ivan's schedule willy-nilly; he knew that sort of invasion was only acceptable under extremely necessary conditions.

With work done, Ivan glanced down, noting that the shopping bags were largely filled with various coffees and caffeinated beverages, along with a few sandwich-shaped bundles letting out wisps of steam. Whether it was boredom or simply his office small talk kicking into gear, Ivan found the words leaving his mouth before he'd thought to give them leave.

"Late night?"

That earned a scowl from Tachyonic, yet Agent Quantum nodded without hesitation. "Never a dull moment in Ridge City."

Ivan made a noise in his throat that *could* have been agreement, or simple acknowledgment that the words had been properly heard. It was one of his favorite tools for weathering office meetings, allowing him to handle most questions tossed in his direction without getting bogged down in needless details.

"What about you, mister? Out burning the midnight oil?"

"No, I had a very long, trying weekend. A night of heavy sleep was well-earned." Ivan felt that was true, even though he hadn't gotten one; instead, he'd wasted most of the night digging for any leads on their mystery trapper, only to come up empty. Whoever had thrown that orb was hiding themselves well. Same for Cobblord—no luck, not that Ivan really expected to succeed. He'd never had much talent for locating people. Ivan's skills kicked in once he had a target.

"Sorry to hear that. Hopefully the week ahead will treat you better." Agent Quantum's face twitched, only for a moment, yet in it, Ivan saw his realization. This would not be a normal week—based on Wade's estimates, at least. Seemed like the capes might have finally started letting their people know what was coming.

Ivan gave a shallow nod. "It will certainly be an interesting one."

The slam of a nearby door lifted all their eyes to the same location, which was how they all ended up staring at Tori as she strolled into the afternoon light. He could hear the capes tensing, practically feel it at this proximity. If they thought he was here to do harm, then she would be the chief target for such aggressions. They were waiting to see if he would make a move.

Neither, however, was fully braced for Tori.

"Ivan? What the hell? I thought you meant we'd meet at the office."

"We're heading somewhere else, so this was faster. Special company research project. We've been moved over to it all week."

"As long as it's not more quarterly reviews, I can manage." Seeming to notice the capes for the first time, Tori's eyebrows scrunched together. "Kyle, Austin, why are you guys standing on the sidewalk?"

The flabbergasted look on both Austin and Kyle's faces was such a spectacle, Ivan wished he had a way to snap covert photos. Their gaze went from him to Tori, then back again, as they began to process the implied connection.

"Wait, is this guy your uncle?" Kyle asked, putting a fine point on the issue.

"There's some cousins and marriages in the equation, but yeah, he's pretty much been Uncle Ivan since we met." The proud gleam in Tori's eye made it impossible to miss how well she'd threaded the needle of truth with her carefully chosen words.

After a few more head-turns—too many; he was giving into his speed—Kyle fully faced Ivan. "Sorry for bothering you. We had to be sure you weren't a danger."

With great effort, Tori almost managed to change the harsh bark of laughter that tore from her into a coughing fit, albeit not very convincingly. "You guys were sweating my uncle? What did you think Ivan was going to do, build an organizational spreadsheet of doom?"

Not a bad recovery, at least. Better they think the joke was how comically non-dangerous he was than sniff out anything near the truth.

Austin took a more diplomatic approach, offering Ivan a hand to shake. "I apologize for the inconvenience, if we caused any."

"Not for the act itself?" Ivan accepted the hand, even as he posed the question.

"No, sir. One of our residents has been targeted or endangered multiple times in short succession. I'm glad you were telling the truth; however, you easily might not have been. I'm not sorry for trying to protect this place or the people in it, and I won't do you the disservice of lying about it."

It didn't happen often. In fact, Ivan would say for a long time that it had happened never. On rare occasions, however, he'd get a feeling. Part hunch, part experience, potentially part cosmic connection to the greater forces of the universe. Gripping Austin's hand, looking into the young man's clear eyes, Ivan could sense the barest bit of that old feeling rising from within. A sensation like he was touching his opposite, coupled with recognition of the spirit brimming out from those eyes.

This kid was dangerous. Not in the ways so many of the others feared—raw strength that could be turned against them in force. No, what he had was more insidious, and ineffable. It radiated off of him, that genuine, earnest attitude that made people want to trust. Want to believe. A cape who could lift a mountain was an easy force to predict and contain; one who could inspire others to heroism had a far further reaching impact.

The world before and after Lodestar's arrival was proof enough of that.

Thankfully, Austin was young, and Ivan felt himself questioning the assessment almost as soon as the handshake ended. He had potential, the raw makings were there, but there was still a lot of growing to do before Agent Quantum became a major threat. Ivan would have to keep an eye on him, though. Today's rookies were tomorrow's veterans; the guild would be ready for conflict long before Agent Quantum was.

"I suppose there are worse neighbors than ones who keep an eye on suspicious characters," Ivan conceded.

"Tori's not just our neighbor, she's our friend," Austin corrected. "We'll do our best not to let anything happen to her."

It was a very nice sentiment, largely undercut by their inability to stop any of the attacks she'd suffered so far, not that Ivan could really blame them for those. Someone had been outmaneuvering both the guild and the AHC—expecting four rookies to outperform that went past ridiculous into outright silliness.

Tori made her way over, giving quick high-fives and farewells to Austin and Kyle, then followed Ivan as he led her to the car. Behind them, the heroic duo scooped up their groceries, finally heading indoors after their unexpected delay. Once Tori and Ivan were in the car, they remained silent, waiting until the capes were inside and fully out of view.

"What's up? Is this another day off thanks to the weekend's craziness? 'Cause if so, I think I'd like to head to my lab."

"Not this time. Something is happening, big enough that there's no communications about it going out. We need to head to the guild and see what's going on," Ivan explained.

"Damn, now you've got me all curious." Tori buckled her safety belt and adjusted the car's air vent, lowering the output by half. "Also, I could have used a guild car. I know the weekend was nuts, but you didn't have to drive all the way out here."

Putting the vehicle in gear, Ivan pointed it toward the highway and steeled his courage. There was still a chance to back out, knowledge which forced his tongue to move, lest fear leave it locked in silence. "I picked you up because I thought you might have questions about... well, I'll let you tell me. Given who one of those topics might be about, we can't have the talk on guild property, and not many civilian locations are secure enough to discuss something so sensitive."

Tightening his wheel-grip slightly, Ivan set his will and finished the statement. "This drive is in case you wanted to ask me about Lodestar."

Chapter 93

It was so shocking, Ren had to blink and rub his eyes, despite their above-human vision. Sure enough, this was neither a hallucination nor imagined, which meant the next most likely explanations were a meta with body-possession, copying, or illusion-based abilities. Long shots, sure, but the other choice was to believe what he was seeing.

Donald Moss had beaten him to the gym.

Given the looks of things, not by a tremendous amount; the freckled, pale face of his friend was red, but not yet slick with sweat as he pushed on the weight machine working his chest. For a moment, Ren lingered at the edge of the room, still barely filled on a Monday morning, searching his mind. Had Donald ever even come here on his own before, let alone been first? Not that Ren could recall; it certainly would have stuck out in his memory.

Walking with more grace and precision than he could have dreamed of after his initial shift, Ren approached from the side, waiting until Donald let the bars fall slack and leaned against the seat, panting from effort. How hard had he been going already?

"Vanity, or ambition?"

"Huh?" Donald's face roughly matched the words: bleary-eyed from the combination of a late night and an early morning, along with the surprise arrival of his friend. Ren hadn't slept great either, not after what they'd learned, but he'd plainly done better between the two of them.

"That's not a maintenance workout, and it's not you going through the motions to appease me. This is the first time I've seen you in here with actual drive. Usually, that means someone either decided to sculpt their body, aka vanity, or they found a goal to work for, which I simplified to ambition."

A moment passed before Donald managed to sort the words and put together a proper response. "Fear, I guess." He tried to shove the machine's bars forward, struggling in vain; he'd gone too hard already, and now the current weight was beyond him. "Or maybe frustration? Every time I feel like we're making headway in this job, something reminds me how weak I am. Not being able to help Tori, not being able to stop Hephaestus, and then last night's announcement... there's an invasion coming. People are going to be looking to me to do something about it, trusting me to keep them safe. This isn't busting muggers or doing patrols, Ren. This is war from the stars, and I'm a guy who turns video game items temporarily real. I couldn't sleep, and doing nothing was worse, so I came here."

Sometimes, there were perks to an empty gym, such as unexpected honesty. Given how Donald had opened up, Ren could offer nothing less than his own truth. "I get it. It's really terrifying, when you realize we're part of the line that has to hold. I'm not sure it scares me in the same way, but I do get the drive that kicks in when you feel yourself up against a wall and want to be better."

"Maybe once I get half as strong as you, the fear will ease up a bit," Donald joked.

"You think I'm not as afraid because I'm tougher?" Ren looked around, taking note of the few other bodies present and their current distance. He was pretty sure none of them had meta-hearing, but sometimes, it had to be risked. "Donald, I'm less scared because this job... this is *all* I have. My life, my dreams, even my body got taken away when that meta-storm struck. One day, you might take those talents and do something else, find another way to help, move on to a new phase of life. This, right here, is the best it gets for something like me: still able to help, to make a difference, to matter. There's no leaving that behind. I'll be in this work until the day I fail. It's easier not to be afraid when I already know this job will kill me. It's just a question of how much good I can do before it does."

Donald reached out and grabbed the machine's bars once more, though rather than trying to push, he used his already weary arms to pull himself up, out of the seat. Fully standing, he turned to face his friend in the eye. "Dude, that is *messed* up."

"Pardon?" Ren's inhuman face twisted around, making his version of surprise.

"This is all you have? All you're good for? To *hell* with that. What we do here matters a lot, but you're not some battery to be used up and cast aside for it. I am sorry, man. I didn't realize how hard things still were for you. Been too caught up in my own dumb shit to notice. But the AHC can't be your whole life, and I'm going to help you be okay with that, whatever route it takes. We can even start hunting for a way to reverse the changes. Just because the AHC lacks one doesn't make it impossible."

A night of sleepless anxiety, unknown time sweating at the gym, and Donald's mental state hadn't improved one bit. Less than a minute of having a friend's problem to focus on, and suddenly he was newly alert and engaged. It was strange. Cyber Geek clearly felt unsure in a position of leadership, likely because he didn't have the same talent for combat that some on the team did. Yet in terms of valuing his people, listening to them and considering how they felt, Donald was head and shoulders above countless coaches Ren had suffered through. The guy was like a brace on the other side of a wall: easy to miss, but the support made everything he touched sturdier.

"Thanks. Maybe I need to hear that sometimes. That said, we should table that idea until after the attempted invasion. This seems like a good week to stay focused on the job."

While Donald's face didn't look thrilled, he nodded all the same. "Can't argue well against that. Guess it's time to climb back into this contraption."

Ren snagged his arm, hooking a clawed thumb over to the free weight. "Forget it. Now that you've got a spotter, we're doing the bench. If you're really here to work, I'll show you how to safely get stronger."

With an exaggerated bow, Donald moved from the machine. "Part of me already knows I'll regret this, but lead the way."

"For the most past, I think I've got the basics figured out. She's the Starscout contact you kept mentioning, so after that night with Haywood, you went to see Helen, who pitched leading the cluster as penance. Ostensibly, Lodestar is also there because putting Fornax in charge of impressionable youths would rub people who don't know you the wrong way. The rest sort of falls into place from there, but one thing I haven't figured out yet is why I'm in this, too."

Ivan had remained silent as Tori considered the opportunity and put together a response, only speaking once the pause in Tori's words stretched long enough to be sure it implied a question. "That was Helen's idea. She knew you were at Haywood's office somehow—the AHC has their tricks, as well—and wanted you to get the same lesson: actions have consequences."

Had Ivan dropped that bomb before the first Starscout meeting, Tori might have had a hard time wrapping her head around that as motivation. Even now, her first instinct was to assume it was a trick, part of a larger plan to learn more about her abilities and whether or not she was a threat. But after the weekend she'd spent at Helen's side, Tori understood. Lodestar wanted her to see that there were consequences because she was still hoping to turn Tori away from the path she was on. That thought raised a sudden memory, which created quite the new question.

"Did you know she pitched the idea of me switching over to the capes?"

"Not specifically, but I'm also unsurprised, if that's what you're wondering. Teams change. While usually more tend to flow in our direction than the other, there is precedence. We'd have a few securities put in place, some mental blocks to keep you from accidentally letting anything slip; otherwise, it's a fairly simple process for where you are. Someone like Johnny or Pod Person might have more trouble, but you're only just starting out. Not even an official criminal record yet."

Considering that, Tori could see how it would be viable, yet for all the work joining the guild had taken, could leaving really be that easy? "Guess I'm just surprised you don't put up more of a fight."

Staring in the rearview for several moments, Ivan suddenly changed lanes, then returned to normal speed. "Given your passion for technology, I'm sure you've heard of Tyranny, the inventor who rules over her own country of Indroga."

"Sure. Possibly the greatest meta mind out there, only no one can be sure because Indroga has a massively strict immigration and visitation policy, so we've never gotten a good look at her full potential. She doesn't even allow capes to set foot on Indroga soil."

"Almost," Ivan corrected. "She has one exception: only Lodestar is allowed on Indroga. I had occasion to ask her why that was, once. Her answer is very fitting for this current, and quite a few subsequent, questions. Best as I recall, she said, 'A ruler must have absolute power over their domain. All that occurs within it occurs with their permission. I cannot stop Lodestar from coming, nor do I think any bureaucracy would halt her if she knew there were people in need. Therefore, since she may arrive regardless, and I am Indroga's ruler, she *must* be arriving with my permission.'"

Not a hard story to see the parallels in, especially given her question. When one was facing an overwhelming force, it was often a matter of choosing battles. Yes, the guild could dig in and be shitty if one of their own opted to start doing good, but what would that gain them? Ire from the capes, and a member ripe for turning to treachery. And since it wouldn't look very good to have the AHC dictating terms, deciding it was a mutual policy allowed the guild to save internal face.

"At some point, I definitely want to circle back and hear more about you actually talking to Tyranny."

"I'll save you the time: she was cordial enough, but our conversation centered largely on dealing with capes, many of whom aren't even around anymore. She and Wade had a far more productive discussion that day, if you can ever get him to part with specifics." Another change of lanes, this time paired with acceleration.

Weird driving and inventor tangents aside, Tori tried to focus in on anything she wondered specifically regarding Helen's secret. Other conversations could continue; this one had a shelf-life. Since Ivan had been so forthcoming, and Tori wasn't one to beat around a bush, she decided to just go all in on the obvious.

"Do you love Lodestar?"

"Whether they know it or not, everyone loves Lodestar, in the same way every blade of grass loves the sun. She has single-handedly saved the entire world several times, including all life on it. It's coded into all nature to seek and love the things that keep you alive."

"I've never seen a blade of grass and the sun spend ten minutes making flirty small talk over a bin full of paper mâché," Tori countered. "You're going to tell me there's nothing there?"

"Not nothing, no." Ivan was checking his mirrors more frequently, and Tori was starting to do the same. Something was off, even if he didn't want to address it openly. "Respect, friendship, even trust. There's a tremendous amount of history between Helen and me. Some things are bound to be built atop such a rich foundation."

It was a nice spiel, the kind that almost made one overlook the fact that Ivan had never actually come out and denied Tori's accusation. She decided to let it go for now. The point wasn't to make Ivan sweat with a discussion about feelings, it was to answer her questions and get a clear head.

"She already knew who I was, so I guess nothing has changed in that department. You two have your own thing. Pretty sure I don't want to dig much deeper into that can of worms. I guess my main question left would be... is she for real? The concern, the caring, the way she sees things: I have a hard time believing it's not at least partially an act, but I never saw anything other than sincerity from her. Now that I know her power conceals her identity, I wanted to know if there was a chance that was fake, too."

"Hmm." Ivan's hands drummed the wheel, stopping only once to suddenly jerk the car around a slowed van in front of them rather than reduce speed. "Technically, it is possible that this is one more aspect of the abilities, though it's highly unlikely. I believe I've mentioned that Lodestars are consistent across all the universes we've scanned, and part of it is that they're always trying to do good. Not always Helen's exact brand, that shifts with who holds the power, but they are, at minimum, attempting to work on the side of right. For them all to be fake, the power would have to have no failings in any world we've checked, and then you'd have to ask yourself why? What's the point of pretending to be good if you spend your life saving the world anyway, and at that point, is it even still pretending?"

"I get it, I get it. Morality is hard to gauge in any real sense, but so far as we know, her actions consistently match her attitude." Tori rubbed her left temple, aware the day would end in a headache, yet fighting it off for as long as she could. "Guess this is why we stick to smashing skulls instead of saving worlds."

The exit came fast, but Ivan was ready, jerking the car off the highway, on track to the country club they'd be teleporting out of. "Actually, I did save a world once. Sort of. Not this one… got summoned by mistake, but the experience was more fulfilling than one might expect."

"Wait, what? Forget Lodestar—the hell happened there?"

"Story for another time, I'm afraid. We're being followed, and I wasn't able to shake them."

For an instant, Tori's skin went cold. More attacks, more chaos, more madness, and she'd barely had time to even partially recover from the last. Then, slowly, warmth returned as she remembered that this was no scouting trip stocked with innocent children. To her knowledge, there was only one other meta who could be a real threat to the villain seated next to her, and Lodestar wouldn't need a crappy sedan to follow them in. This was a pothole in their road, not a gaping chasm to leap.

"Should we floor it?"

"Scraping them from our heels was ideal, but the time for that has passed." Ivan's face darkened, and Tori quickly remembered that he'd also had a very shitty weekend, and that currently, they had no clue which of them was the target being tailed.

"Running is for prey. Our kind lay ambushes."

Chapter 94

Their tantrum reached a fever pitch as the camera equipment was torn open, electronic guts dropped roughly onto the gravel. On the television screen, Tori watched as the country club security roughly grabbed one of the photographers that had been on their tail as he lunged for the camera, slamming him to the ground and beginning to administer zip ties.

"This is really legal?" It wasn't that she didn't enjoy watching a pair of parasites being pulled from their car and having their belongings carelessly searched, but it did seem the sort of thing that might come with consequences.

"They drove past multiple signs informing them they were entering private property, with no trespassing permitted and all vehicles subject to search. Given that they were tailing you, a person who has endured multiple attacks in a very short time, it's natural we assume them to be criminals as well and thoroughly check their belongings for hidden weapons or explosives. Resisting the process can only lead to them being detained until the police can arrive to scoop up this refuse." Ivan managed a straightforward tone, despite the not-so-subtle smirk inching along his face.

"I'm just sorry you're still having to deal with this. I'd hoped the fervor would fade quickly. Seems they're either doggedly determined or news you were at the Starscout incident has started to leak." Though they'd done their best to hide the names of those involved, when the bulk of the witnesses were young children, some were going to make slips when asked the right question.

The second paparazzi attempted to make a run, bolting to where one of the guards was yanking out what looked to be an extremely expensive video camera. He grabbed for the equipment, managing to actually pull it away, thanks to the element of surprise. It fared far worse seconds later, as it went flying from his arms, shattering while its owner fell to the ground shuddering, body filled with electrical current. Only once the guard he'd robbed stopped holding down the trigger on his tazer did the twitching at last relent.

"Believe it or not, this kind of works for me. I've got some big plans coming up, and still being part of the public consciousness is in my favor for them. Speaking of, I need to talk with Wade soon. Think he'll be around base today?" With the show winding down, Tori turned from the monitors to the rest of the security room.

It wasn't the actual security wing of this building, rather the mundane one that had existed in its original incarnation. Closed-camera TVs lining the walls, stacks of electronics poorly organized and maintained, even a guard with drooping eyes leaning back in his chair, keeping a sleepy watch on everything happening. Seeing as this employee, like the vast majority of others, was secretly robotic, how open his eyes were didn't actually impact his capacity to do the job. It was simply a small touch of detail. That level of care into every project was part of why Tori admired Doctor Mechaniacal's skills in the first place.

"Wade will definitely be here, though you might have trouble catching him free." Ivan glanced down at his watch, noting that they'd spent a tad longer than they should have enjoying the show. "I've got a meeting with him and the other councilors momentarily, after which, I'll bring you up to speed. While I'm there, I'll see about your meeting… just don't expect anything today."

"Perfect for me. Only looking to get something on the books again. I'm not quite ready either." Tori's mind jumped back to her prototype, now nearly complete. Much as she wanted her suit repaired, she'd also have to make time to properly polish that up. One generally didn't get multiple pitches to multi-billion-dollar corporations, not even with secret villain connections.

Together, they walked through the resort, into the secured teleportation chamber, and crossed untold miles in a single flash. Once at the guild, Tori opted to go grab a breakfast she wouldn't have to pretend to eat while covertly tossing out the window, while Ivan headed up to his meeting—past the residences, the utility rooms, the lounges, all the way to the new Councilors' Chambers.

He was, in a rare anomaly, the last to arrive. Morgana looked tanner since they'd last seen one another—evidently, she was spending a lot of time at the new guild with its ample sunshine. Gork and Xelas were seated next to one another, the latter swiping a hand through the air as she browsed unseen screens. Arcanicus was holding what Ivan deemed to easily be the largest mug of coffee he'd ever seen, his bleary eyes betraying why. Stasis was clad in a surfing outfit, her post-meeting plans very apparent, whereas Wade himself looked as if he was going into the Indigo Technologies offices, clad in tan slacks and a crisp shirt.

It was rare to see Wade like that while in these halls. Knowing him, it meant he'd gotten some new piece of information in his civilian outfit and had been too excited to even consider changing, or probably showering. Although it was a habit that could make Wade hard to room with, it also meant he was good at finding answers, devoting himself entirely to whatever question was currently occupying his brain.

The outfit was one tip-off, the look in his eyes another. It wasn't often that Ivan saw that expression, but when he did, it meant things were about to get extremely complicated, and equally as dangerous.

"Good, we can finally start," Wade said. "Ivan, please shut the door. There's a lot we need to talk about."

Zerle Salvrin's subganwum sacks swelled with pleasure as the orb filled his screen. Blue and green, quite picturesque—if one went in for that sort of thing. He held no particular passion for the aesthetics. What tickled his yerkle were the readings they'd taken from that captured Grzzniltan ship. One of his clawed fingers ran along a panel of dark metal, turning the screen from a picture to a display of that lovely, lucrative data.

Oceans of water, huge tracts of land, an ore-rich core, and billions of lesser lifeforms to serve or feed upon as their talents dictated. A civilization nearing the verge of galactic travel, ripe for the plucking. The Grzzniltans were turned away by a few mere guardians, cowards that they were. Earth would not be so fortunate when it faced the Wrexwren fleet moving toward them.

Two of Zerle Salvrin's eyes kept watch on the communications channel, always waiting for a fresh transmission. Their mysterious Earth informant wasn't the most constant information source, yet what they'd provided thus far had proved valuable. Without the initial broadcast, Zerle Salvrin might never have sent a crew to intercept that Grzzniltan vessel in the first place, leaving this gorgeous celestial pulvin completely unflugged. It was also thanks to their informant that the Wrexwren knew Earth had a special defense, a seemingly unbeatable force.

Changing the screen once more, Zerle Salvrin checked the dispersal of plasma his ships were carefully leaking. One couldn't tame, control, or even direct creatures like that which was following in their wake. All they knew was hunger: perfect machines of function, to Zerle Salvrin's reasoning. The only way to use one was to lead it to the planned destination and turn it into someone else's problem. Whatever supposedly unstoppable defenses the planet had, this would neutralize them nicely.

In a way, Zerle Salvrin was glad this planet had some capacity to put up a fight. His crew had faced far too little adversity in recent conquests, enemies falling like the shards of eslewight that rained down on the Wrexwren's desolate homeworld. Lack of challenge would make them soft. He hoped the Earth would manage to put up enough resistance to demand some effort, though in truth, he expected little. A planet so coddled and cared for would cause most of its inhabitants to lose their edge. Once their champions were broken, the world was essentially done.

Not long to wait, now. They were on course to reach Earth at the appointed moment. They could have arrived weeks early, but the messages were quite specific about the timing, claiming that there was preparation to do. Zerle Salvrin didn't entirely trust this source; however, he also didn't want to alert it to that fact by ignoring the agreed upon plans. They would play along while the source proved to be useful. Once that function lessened, circumstances could be reevaluated. After all, it wasn't as if Zerle Salvrin had told their contact the actual number of Wrexwren ships in the approaching fleet.

By the time Earth realized it was in danger, the conquest would already be done.

In his life, Ivan had seen a great many things. He'd gone briefly to the stars, wandered other worlds, and walked many realms hidden within their own plane. Yet even with his wealth of experience, the sight on-screen caused his heart to hammer. This wasn't just big, wasn't just bad; it was raw, absolute destruction.

Ivan could recognize his metaphorical kin when he saw them. An invasion was one thing—it had certain goals and plans, most of which centered on keeping the planet intact overall as it was being overtaken. This was different. These aliens weren't planning to leave more than a used-up husk behind. They didn't care about losing resources in the name of efficiency. The Wrexwren weren't coming to take over Earth, they wanted to strip it down to the studs.

"Given the new situation, it's safe to say the AHC are not prepared for what they'll actually be facing." Wade was still somehow calm, despite the rundown he'd just delivered on the threats currently en route to Earth. "Most of our people are already planning to be on the ground in the event Wrexwren troops start landing—nothing changes much on that front. The bigger question is what we do about this new intel. While I recognize that we and the AHC are not on our best terms, protecting the planet we live on generally supersedes such momentary grudges."

"You want to tip them off?" Morgana proposed.

"Fuck that. After what Apollo pulled? It'd be good for the AHC to get publicly pantsed again." Xelas, despite her harsh words, didn't sound particularly passionate in her pettiness. "I'm on board with helping keep Earth safe, but we're not their spies or messengers. Let's not start acting like it."

Wade changed the screen, revealing a series of images showing various terrains with specific sections marked. "I'm with Xelas on that front. If they want our help, then they'll at least have to acknowledge it happened. Currently, we have several space-capable weapons locked on the approaching fleet. Attacking preemptively is still an option—break their formation and make them panic. But it risks them turning tail, only to come back better prepared, and again, the AHC can spin things as they see fit. Alternatively, we could sit on our weapons until the ships arrive, then add our firepower to the fray. We won't have the advantage of surprise, however, so active defenses will cut down on how well the attacks work."

It was forming, no matter how Ivan wished it wouldn't: the path to victory, the way ahead, that determination to come out on top that had helped him survive his eighteen straight years of hell. There was a plan coming together, spurred on in no small part by Janet's words still ringing through his mind. "The surprise is obviously for Lodestar. They're hoping to take away Earth's superhero before any sort of duel could officially start. Professor Quantum would never put himself in a position that vulnerable, so he won't step up. Quorum might, but he's also the weakest of the three in combat. They'll either send in someone tough enough to buy time, or give up on the duel entirely, focusing on the armies themselves."

"Tracks with their historical tactics." Gork nodded her large gray head solemnly as she agreed. Her people lived far, far below the planet's surface, meaning that this invasion wouldn't impact them for quite some time. But in a planetary-wide looting, sooner or later, every stone got turned over.

"Seems Ivan and I had a similar train of thought," Wade added. Another slide clicked over, this one showing tech-specs that went sailing right over Ivan's head, but that garnered a whistle from Xelas. "I've reached out to every extraterrestrial contact we have and begun work on a welcome gift for our visitors. Assuming it's completed in time, I would still need proximity to use it. If we were to send our own envoy, along with a champion, it would be a perfect distraction while I put our new tool to work."

Loud slurping from Arcanicus and his oversized mug momentarily broke the tension. He glared right back at several of the looks he received. "What? Does anyone actually think I'm the one getting tapped for this? It's obviously a task for Xelas or Gork—possibly Morgana, if these things have blood."

"I'd prefer to have Xelas with me—should cut down on how long we need." Wade pointedly didn't look at Ivan as he continued. "Whoever we take should be able to withstand some damage. We don't have a firm idea of how strong the Wrexwren are, but it's safe to assume we'll get one of their best, considering the stakes."

When Ivan stood, the room went silent. Now Wade *was* looking in his direction, old friends staring at one another, trying to figure out what the other was thinking. "There's only one choice. We need someone who can endure, can hurt, can survive against nearly any odds. Remember, technically, we're still betting the planet on this fight. Makes sense to try and win."

"Are you sure about this?" Wade asked. "Working as Pseudonym in the shadows is one thing—everyone in the world will be watching when the invasion comes. The AHC will absolutely have some sort of video gear with them; they'd never let PR like this pass undocumented. Depending on what happens and how much is caught, this is a fight where the identity could be easily compromised."

"Then it's a good thing I wasn't proposing Pseudonym take them on." Ivan shut his eyes, not trusting them to remain human in that moment. What Janet had said was true. People weren't scared of him anymore, not of some dusty old monster from the past. They were getting bold enough to come for him, and his children. White-hot rage spiked in Ivan, and he didn't cool it down so much as set it to the side. Fury had ample uses in the right moments, and it seemed he'd be getting such a chance very soon. Because if the world thought they didn't need to be afraid, then he'd just have to remind them why that terror had existed in the first place.

"If they decide to try to step around Lodestar, then the bastards can face Fornax instead."

Chapter 95

Tori found the guild in a lively state upon her arrival. Since the move, she'd been seeing her fellow villains sporadically; it wasn't quite the default clubhouse the old location had been. Yet today, as she helped herself to a breakfast burrito, it was impossible not to notice all the faces, both new and familiar, dotting the halls. Heading to grab some coffee, she found herself in line behind a pair she knew quite well.

"France? You really want to wait in France? Just because they always go for the Eiffel Tower at some point in the movies doesn't mean the real ones bother with landmarks." Johnny Three Dicks rapped a knuckle against Thuggernaut's sizable shoulder, the closest Johnny could get to reaching his head. "You want the biggest population centers you can find. Absolutely going to be a target, and if you don't find any cool alien stuff, there's always looting the normal stores in the chaos."

"You use whatever tactics suit your needs best," Thuggernaut replied. "I've been wanting to visit a good open-air market for weeks. This is a chance to go early and knock out two errands in one trip."

Johnny grumbled, but Tori would bet that when the dust settled, they'd both end up in France. For as much as Johnny talked, he was smart enough to stay near his much larger, more intimidating friend.

Since she saw an opening in the conversation, Tori coughed loudly before asking, "Did someone say aliens? Are the Grzzniltans coming back?"

Thuggernaut and Johnny both turned, expressions softening when they recognized who was speaking. Johnny's sour mood quickly shifted into a mischievous grin. "Well, well, if it isn't Pseudonym's old apprentice. Decided to take a break from being the damsel du jour?"

"I really fucking hope so." Tori's response came out a bit more honest than she intended, so she hurried onward. "Next thing I invent might be a giant firebomb I keep with me at all times. Be a fun surprise for the dumbfucks that try to grab me next." Actually, that wasn't a half-bad idea—she made a mental note to see how viable it was. "Anyway, what was that about aliens?"

While Johnny feigned a confused look, Thuggernaut merely nodded. "Given the potential danger of the outing, only the more experienced members were initially brought up to speed, but I expect that to change soon. The guild has been tracking several alien ships heading toward Earth. We suspect there's an invasion afoot."

The shock on Tori's face was both evident, and completely ignored by Johnny as he took the chance to reinvigorate their prior debate. "That's right, a whole swarm of new marks bringing their favorite goodies for us to snatch. Which is why we should go bigger. No telling how long before they wise up and flee. Have to grab as much as we can while it's here."

"Hang on... are you guys kidding?" Much as Tori wanted to hope for that outcome, both seemed serious, or as serious as a man named Johnny Three Dicks could manage.

"Not in the slightest." Finally, Johnny seemed to register the uncertain fear in Tori's face, his own smile growing wider in response. "Oh my, are you worried? How fun! It's been so long, I've kind of forgotten how that feels. Pulse racing? Starting to get the sweats?"

"Enough." Thuggernaut's voice was calm, but brooked no objections as he silenced his friend. "Sorry. Sometimes, after you've been in this world for so long, you forget what it's like to be new. Johnny is right in one regard, though, you really don't need to worry. Ever since we first learned aliens existed, both the AHC and the guild have prepared for these possibilities. It's not even Earth's first attempted takeover."

He was right. Tori had read up on the prior attempts for herself here and there. Forcibly, she took control of the terror that had reared its head, shoving it aside until she could think more clearly. Her view had been that of a civilian, if not an outright human, fearful of this newly discovered threat. She'd reacted like prey rather than recognizing what else the aliens represented: opportunity. As a predator, what she could see was something slithering in, unprepared for the native beasts already lying in wait.

"Is there a betting pool for how long before they go screaming off into the night?" Tori asked.

"Oooh, look at our optimist here." Johnny stepped forward, the coffee machine finally opening up as he jammed his mug underneath. "The Wrexwren making a successful escape is currently one of the long shot bets, so if you'd like to toss some money on it, I can give you decent odds."

Tempting, though it was always better to have things spelled out to the letter with Johnny. "What defines a successful escape?"

"Retreat with greater than fifty percent of the original forces." Thuggernaut didn't even have to mentally dig around—he had that tidbit ready to go, a subtle tip-off that perhaps Johnny had been trying to coax others toward this wager, as well. "In this case, we'll be counting whatever they land with."

"There's also decent money to be made in the twenty-five to fifty percent range," Johnny added. He moved over to the sugar station, grabbing a handful of various artificial sweetener packets seemingly at random. "Once you get lower than that, we leave the long shot area, and you'll see a steep drop in payout."

While Thuggernaut took his turn at the coffee machine, Tori flipped the situation around in her head. At the end of the day, it was a question of who she thought was stronger: the Earth and its metas, or this extraterrestrial force coming toward them. It was always possible they were outgunned, but if that truly were the case, if these things could overtake people like Lodestar and Fornax, then there was no fight to be had. Earth would be wiped out, likely in a day, and no amount of Tori's fretting would change that. Power at those levels was beyond her ability to deal with, currently.

"Any advice for someone who's apparently about to go through her first invasion?" It seemed prudent to get some guidance from those who'd been there before, and her selection in that range was deeply limited.

Surprisingly, Johnny's expression shifted, turning almost serious. "Be on your guard, and with people you trust. Us being collectively stronger doesn't mean each of us can defeat each of them. Use every advantage, and take nothing for granted. Don't ruin the fun by making us have a funeral after."

His gravity was jarring, enough to remind Tori that these stakes were still life and death. Having powers and the guild didn't change that; they just gave her a better chance to survive. "I'll talk to Glyph, Pest Control, and Bahamut. Guessing they'll be in the same boat, and we can watch out for one another."

"A fine idea," Johnny agreed, instantly softening back to his usual countenance. "The next step would be to determine where you want to wait out the invasion. Somewhere cool and hip—say, the middle of downtown New York—or out in a big, open area with a giant metal art display."

"Your lack of appreciation for art doesn't remove its inherent value." Thuggernaut and Johnny were back in their fight, absentmindedly wandering away from the machine as Tori filled her mug.

As if her week hadn't already been slammed enough, now she had a potential alien invasion to worry about. Part of her wondered why Ivan hadn't told her yet, before realizing that she'd probably stumbled on the very reason they were here today. At least if Wade didn't have time to meet, she would definitely know not to take it personally.

Even for a genius like Doctor Mechaniacal, countering an invasion was one hell of a side project.

Ridge City Grinders was *slammed.* Chloe had no idea if it was the new Electric Conga Cappuccino they were shilling that month or just an especially caffeine-demanding Monday, but her morning had rapidly turned into a blur of grinding, pouring, and handling customers. Most were coping all right with the excessive line, others less so.

"Still waiting on that large latte." The watch he was tapping against the counter cost easily more than any car Chloe had owned, and he definitely knew its value. From suit to shoes, the whole outfit was meant to convey wealth and authority, personality traits that had evidently drifted into his capacity for polite waiting, as well.

Glorious as it would have been to work some small errors into the order, that would only delay things further; he was absolutely the type to kick up a fuss. Putting the final touches on the foam, Chloe set the drink down directly in front of him, motioning to the accessories as she did. "Thank you for your patience, sir. Sugar is on the table, as are lids and straws."

"Lids," he scoffed, grabbing the drink roughly. "I'm not a child or an imbecile. I think I can handle—"

It was truly perfect. Mid-sentence, the cup seemed to suddenly slip in his hand, tipping over toward him. All down the silk shirt and tailored suit the near-boiling coffee ran, drawing screams of both pain and horror from him as he suddenly leapt back. The coffee cup, now all but empty, clattered to the ground in front of him, one final nail in the coffin of his humiliation.

Despite knowing better, Chloe couldn't resist. "There are also napkins, in case you have a spill."

The laughter was quick and contagious, rippling outward like a mocking stone dropped in a lake. There was barely enough time to see the rage and shame in his eyes before he bolted from the shop.

"That guy is definitely going to beat an intern before lunch is over."

That voice was familiar, though unexpected here. Chloe glanced up and realized that Ike and Ellie were in line, the former still chuckling to himself.

"He seems like at least the type to call a manager. If he complains, let us know. We can attest that you were nothing but professional," Ellie added.

"Thanks, but there's cameras all over since the Ridge City Riots. I'm sure we've got footage that shows him spilling on himself." Even as the words left Chloe's mouth, she found herself doubting them. The way he'd lost control of his cup was very strange, almost like someone had moved it while in his grip, causing the container to go tumbling over. "That is what they'll see, right?"

Ike met her gaze without hesitation, offering little more than a shrug. "Sure what it looked like to me. Certainly what the dude deserved, right?"

At his side, Ellie leaned slightly over Ike, turning suspicious. "I suppose, in that case, we could call it karma. Karma that in no way should be emboldened by this and start doing it frequently."

"I doubt it will be an issue. Seems to only happen when people are dicks to someone I like."

"You don't like anyone," Ellie pointed out.

"I like Chloe. She shoots straight and doesn't take bullshit. More people had that attitude, I might not be such a misanthrope." Ike punctuated the statement with a wink, a gesture that Chloe might have found less endearing several minutes prior.

"Says a man who refuses to just admit what he really feels," Chloe replied.

That earned an actual laugh from Ike, along with a snap of the fingers. "See what I mean? Even after that, she refuses to let me skate. Great stuff."

"Sorry about... all of this." Ellie looked back to the sizable line still stretching out behind them, and the other baristas working hard to clear it. "We should probably order and get out of your hair."

"Hope you've still got some warm fuzzies in our direction, because this order is massive." To his credit, Ike wasn't overselling the list he pulled from his pocket; it filled up the front and back of a large sheet of paper.

Looking it over, Chloe noted that since the drinks were built over function rather than form, she could make the bulk of it in batches. There were a *lot* of high-potency drinks on the list, though, stuff generally only ordered by the true addicts, like Tori.

“I can put this together, just going to take a minute. You must be bracing for one hell of an all-nighter.”

There was unquestionably a look exchanged between Ellie and Ike, one that Chloe pointedly chose not to follow up on. Whatever secrets they had were probably AHC-related, and Chloe was more than happy being on the outside of that loop. The more she saw of both sides of the cape-villain coin, the more joy she found in her normal life and job. Ultimately, it was Ellie who spoke, likely not trusting Ike to avoid dropping some manner of hint.

“It’s safe to say that a lot of people won’t be getting much sleep this week.”

By the time Ivan found her, Tori had finished breakfast, done quite a bit of chatting with other guild members, and generally gotten a good grasp of what was heading their direction. An invasion was coming, enough that the guild was expecting troops to land and planning to lie in wait for them. Nobody seemed especially scared about Earth actually losing, which aligned well with Tori’s own deductions. Either their champions could handle it, or the planet would be crushed. At those higher tiers of power, there was no middle ground.

“Done?” Ivan asked. He didn’t sit at the small table where she was clacking away on a tablet, an indication that this would be a walk-and-talk conversation.

“Depends. Do you mean with eating, or with finding out about the invasion you didn’t bother bringing me in on?”

“Both, but mostly the latter. I assumed this would be faster than me explaining, and then you digging around behind my back anyway.” Evidently, Ivan took her response to be confirmation, as his brisk pace resumed.

Tori briefly scrambled, throwing the tablet under her arm as she hopped off the stool and gave chase, catching up to him shortly. “You still could have gotten me up to speed before now. Seems like the whole guild except me had the heads up.”

“All newer members of the guild were left out of that loop. None of you have faced a substantial enough threat to have an accurate combat rating, and we don’t have time to get you trained up before this invasion arrives.” Ivan’s words hesitated, even as his feet continued without pause. “Perhaps some part of me also imagined that keeping you in the dark would hold you apart from the danger such an invasion represents.”

"Gave up on that idea?" Tori found the notion hard to imagine. Ivan sure didn't seem like he'd gotten *less* protective after the weekend's incident.

"In a way. I've realized that my power alone is not enough to protect the people I care for. Had help not been with us for the Starscout incident, the outcome could have been very different. You, alone, might have been killed by those traps and challenges, or we may have lost some of the children in our care. All of which represents a failing on my part."

They came to a stop in front of an elevator. Ivan led her inside. Once there, he tapped a sequence into the buttons, sending the mechanism diagonally, rather than up and down. "I haven't been nurturing your talents the way a mentor should. I taught you the code and survival first, and that was right, but since then, I was content to let you slowly find your own path. My hope was that you would reject this life, find a way back to normalcy. This weekend showed me the folly of that mindset. Unless you are powerful enough to survive our world, you'll never have a chance to leave it behind."

"Hang on, there. I don't necessarily want to go whole hog into the guild," Tori protested. "I like finding my own path. It's the happiest I've been in a long time."

"A journey you are welcome to continue. My concern is not the search for what to do with your life, but rather making sure you live long enough to complete it." The elevator came to a stop, and Ivan punched in another set of numbers. This time, rather than moving, the doors opened to reveal a new room.

Tori's breath caught in her throat at the sight of it. Gleaming metal, flashing screens, a wall stuffed with one strangely shaped tool after another. Tentatively, she stepped out, surveying her surroundings. "Ivan, this is a lab. Not a basement lair, not a retrofitted garage, a *laboratory*." Her voice was caught somewhere between confusion and longing, not daring to approach even the edges of hope.

"Correction: it is *your* laboratory, rented for the next month, though the coming week is the most vital part of that. I expect to see Hephaestus's armor back in working condition at least a day before the first wave of invasion is predicted to arrive."

Given the equipment present, that would be a relatively simple task. So much of the tedium from her work could be automated or simplified with all of this at her fingertips. There might even be time for an upgrade or two, though she was hesitant to put in something untested before a potential fight. Still, the situation nagged at Tori; she didn't trust when anything came too easily.

"Not that I don't appreciate you getting me some nice digs, but mind if I ask why? Do you really expect me to get in danger during the invasion?"

"I do not," Ivan told her. "Nor did I expect you to be taken from the street, or my daughter to end up stuck in a labyrinth. The time for being taken by surprise is at an end. From now on, we are the ones who deliver the shock. Next time something happens, we'll be prepared. You'll have your suit, and I'll be ready to do what's necessary."

Tori could still remember how it felt being in there, watching Lodestar work, realizing how outclassed she was. If she'd had her suit, things would have been different. Tori would have had more options, could have contributed to the fight and gotten them home faster. Much scarier, however, was wondering how it would have gone if Helen hadn't been around. Tori didn't want to need the capes. She had to be capable of handling this insane life on her own. Although, a little help at the start was something she could make peace with.

"Got it. Work starts as soon as I haul over my gear. After the month, do I need to make arrangements with Doctor Mechaniacal to keep paying?"

Ivan merely shrugged. "You'll have to ask him. He seemed to think you might wish for different facilities after that, depending on how your enterprise goes. Your meeting with Wade is set for Wednesday afternoon, by the way."

That tracked. If they were starting something new together, then she might want a more public facility. A concern for later down the line; right now, Tori was staring down a pair of very imposing deadlines. She had a few days to get the prototype finished, and a couple more after that to ensure her meta-suit was in tip-top running condition.

With a gleeful crack of her knuckles, Tori set off to explore her new lab. It was time to get to work.

Chapter 96

He could still hear panting from that inhuman mouth, no matter how hard he ran. It was supposed to be a simple stickup—that couple had the look of a pair with more money than caution. But no sooner had the knife come into view than the creature dropped down from above. Had it been hiding on the rooftops, waiting for a juicy victim? There was no telling. New meta-animals popped up same as humans, each with their own powers and dangers.

All he'd known was that, when it roared, his legs moved. Bolting him from the scene so fast he'd dropped his weapon, racing with all he had, and making what felt like zero progress. Every turn, every street, it was on him. He dared not slow down enough to turn and look, but there were times he could swear there was hot breath splashing across the back of his neck. There was no thought, only running.

Until he hit the wall. In his defense, it was an unexpected obstacle, as this alley was supposed to open up into a wide street. Instead, a frozen blockade smashed against his body, sending him sprawling. There were walls of the same material on either side; only the way he'd come was still open. Spinning around, the would-be mugger prepared to keep running, just to be reminded of why he was fleeing in the first place.

Standing there, backlit by the streetlights, he could finally get a good view of his pursuer. Thick muscles, scales, even a tail: this was no single meta-animal, more like what a mad scientist would create with only a zoo for parts.

That didn't make it any less terrifying as it stepped forward, low rumbling growl rising from deep within.

"I give up! I surrender! Somebody—capes, cops, help! He's going to eat me!"

A slight wince in the approaching monster, before that growl turned into a rough, annoyed voice. "You're in luck, buddy. I'm a superhero with the AHC, so you know what that means."

A big, broad smile revealed a mouth stuffed full of fangs, each somehow larger and sharper than the one before. "It means they only let me eat the ones who don't play nice."

As Medley wrapped up their latest catch with help from Cold Shoulder, Cyber Geek and Hat Trick were seated on a bench, scrolling their AHC-issued phones, checking for any assignment updates. Direct communication was useful in battle, but for assignment coordination, it was hard to beat the convenience of screens and GPS.

"Sounds good. Yeah, we'll be back at the incident point. Meet us when extraction has this one removed." Cyber Geek finished his remote chat with Cold Shoulder, who was keeping an eye on things as Medley's backup. Splitting the team was essential when it came to drawing out these sorts of criminals—few things were lured without bait—but he still disliked how it left them vulnerable. Not even Medley was allowed to run off on his own. Muggers could just as easily have meta abilities, too.

"What's the plan now?" Hat Trick asked. She was, for the most part, unrecognizable as her superhero self, clad in a bright dress too summery for the cooling weather, along with a large designer coat. Hidden within its depths were her hat, wand, and a few other trinkets in case things took a turn for the dire, but on the outside, she looked to be nothing more than a normal woman on a nighttime stroll.

In a rare display of fashion, Cyber Geek matched her well, clad in slacks and a button-down more reminiscent of his cubicle days than his current position. He'd been dressed in a few high-end accessories as well, or at least excellent reproductions, since the AHC didn't seem especially concerned about loaning them out. Together, the duo were playing the part of a couple lost in their affection for one another, blind enough to the world that they'd wandered into a place where dangerous people liked to hunt.

"Probably time to pack in for this operation. Getting so late we won't be believable soon. Besides, I've seen you hurting in those heels, and I'm ready to get in my real uniform, too."

"For the record, it's not the heels," Hat Trick said. "I can walk in heels when I have to, even if they aren't my favorite. It's these designer ones. I don't think they were built for women with all their toes, or even a centimeter of extra ankle."

She leaned against Cyber Geek's shoulder as her hands worked to loosen the tight shoe-straps visibly digging into her flesh. When one latch finally gave, the whole thing seemed to pop, falling away in a series of snaps and straps he could never have hoped to reconstruct.

"Ohhhhh, there it is. That's the good stuff. Don't suppose you've got any shoe-based items I could use?"

"Wish my power worked that way." It would have been incredible, to outfit his team with an endless array of weapons and armor from across the world of gaming. Unfortunately, the items were only real for him. Losing contact with an item was no issue, yet when he tried to give one away, it quickly dissolved back into numbers and sparks. That was something they'd learned in the earliest of experiments, and while it was fun to dream of his power evolving that way over time, so far, there were no indications his ability had any potential to grow in that direction.

Shifting position, yet somehow still with her shoulder against him, Hat Trick released the second shoe with far less effort, scooping it up into her lap before digging around in her pocket. From the coat's depths, she produced her wand, a single black rod with crisp white tips on either end: a magician's wand, to go with the kit she'd purchased that had imbued her abilities. It was strange to imagine gaining powers that way, especially given that Cyber Geek had been nearly deep-fried when obtaining his. The sources of meta-abilities were nearly as varied as the powers themselves—one more reason to always be prepared for the unexpected.

"Not to worry. I've been working on something. Zesto-Chango-Outfit-Rearrangeo!" Hat Trick waved the wand as she spoke, ending with a flourish that tapped the tip of it against her left shoe's heel. A burst of smoke exploded from the footwear, causing both undercover capes to cough and wave their hands.

Once the cloud cleared, Cyber Geek spotted a new pair of shoes waiting where the heels had been. Black, shiny, and made for the stage, Hat Trick had managed to change her designer footwear into the standard shoe of a tuxedo-clad magician.

"Drat. Been working on getting them cuter, but everything comes out like

I'm about to step on a stage." Hooking one of the shoes, Hat Trick slipped it easily onto her foot. "They do fit perfectly, though, and are surprisingly comfortable. I'd make you some, if they didn't all come out in my size."

"That's still amazing." Cyber Geek shook his head, part of him wanting to look around for where the original shoes had been hidden. Magic was fascinating. It played by its own rules even among the metas who wielded it. Evidently, that also made it harder to control than some other abilities, though Hat Trick had been making incredible strides. "I remember when you first started and didn't even use the wand."

"Well, I wouldn't rely on it in a life-or-death situation, but it has proven to be a handy little tool," Hat Trick admitted.

Watching her put on the second shiny shoe, a new thought occurred to Cyber Geek. "Wait, don't you have to turn those back in? I signed out all of my fancy clothes and was warned to bring them back."

"I'm sure Faldica will be mad at me, but maybe if the AHC would start keeping a wider array of sizes on hand for this, I wouldn't have to transform them midway through the night."

Cyber Geek wasn't entirely sure what an appropriate reaction to that would be. While it was true that Hat Trick didn't necessarily have the same frame many female superheroes aspired to, she never seemed bothered by the difference. Since the complaint didn't seem to be coming from a place of insecurity, rather one of annoyance, she probably wasn't looking for reassurance about her appearance, even if he had trusted himself to express such a sentiment without bumbling things into awkwardness, which he did not.

"I'll see what I can file about equipment issues. Having the right gear for us to do the job is part of the AHC's responsibility. If they can make outfits and tech for all the different types of metas we work with, it's not unreasonable to expect them to have shoes that fit."

Hat Trick flushed slightly, easy to spot on the pale skin between her freckles. "You don't have to kick up a fuss on my account."

"Someone on my team isn't getting what they need to do their job safely. If that's not worth kicking up a fuss over, what is?"

Her smile was swift and sudden, shining under the streetlight without warning, so earnest that Cyber Geek found himself looking away after only a few moments. "I suppose I can't argue with our leader on that front. Maybe wait until next week, though. Given what's coming, I think the AHC has bigger issues to focus on at the moment."

It was a thought he'd been trying, and failing, to avoid since the announcement. Only a few days left, and the world would potentially be at war with outside invaders. They knew the fight was coming and were prepared, yet still Cyber Geek's guts twisted when he dwelled on the nearing conflict. With people like Lodestar and Professor Quantum on their side, he had a feeling the Earth would come out victorious overall. But wars didn't just impact the people at the top of the spectrum. There were billions of innocent people who could be swept up in the battle just as easily.

In essence, Cyber Geek wasn't afraid of losing, so much as he was afraid of how much would be lost. That was why his downtime had been largely spent training with Medley. The big capes would take care of the major threats, but it would be on them to keep things safe on the streets. He wanted to be ready this time, or at least as ready as he could be.

"You make a fair point. We can take care of the complaint next week. Until then, we'll stick to costumed patrols."

"Uh huh. Just don't go getting any ideas about signing us up for one tomorrow. Some of us need that occasional bit of downtime." Hat Trick paused, looking around the empty night. "Speaking of, do you have any plans for your day off? I know Wednesdays aren't exactly hopping, but it feels like we should all make good use of it. You know... just in case."

Just in case they lost. Just in case the aliens were stronger than expected. It was a lot scarier, being on this side of the curtain, realizing how many threats he'd been able to live ignorant of by being a civilian. For all the stress it caused, Cyber Geek was pretty sure he preferred it this way. The Ridge City Riots had come out of nowhere, taking him entirely by surprise. A little warning wasn't so bad, in comparison. Especially if it gave him the chance to tackle things he'd been putting off.

"Another excellent point," Cyber Geek agreed. He was scanning the area, so he missed Hat Trick's face lighting up, along with the slight opening of her mouth, as if to speak, before his own response continued. "In fact, there's an appointment for coffee I'm well overdue for. Seems like a good reason to finally make that happen."

He turned back to find Hat Trick wearing a soft grin, with the barest hint of lip caught by one of her upper teeth. "Sounds like a nice idea. I think I'll make the trip to see some family during the day, probably spend that night hanging with the team."

"I bet they'll be overjoyed to—" Cyber Geek trailed off as his phone began to flash, signaling a new alert. "Crap, looks like we've got some sort of meta-bear sighted, and it's near... okay, that has to be a joke."

Checking her own phone, Hat Trick barely suppressed a giggle. "Nope,

I'm seeing the same report. Ten feet tall, looks like a bear that's been rolled in spines, and currently attacking a production center for the BingleBuzzle Honey Corporation out in Brigsby, Utah. Be honest, if we get there, what do you think the odds are it will be wearing a bright red shirt?"

"The real question is if it will *only* be wearing the red shirt," Cyber Geek added. "This one will make Medley happy, if nothing else. He's been complaining that he never gets a real workout in the field lately."

"You think a mere ten feet of bear can challenge our boy?"

"No idea, but I'm willing to sit on the sidelines and cheer as we find out." Cyber Geek tapped the alert on his phone, instantly connecting his earpiece with the appropriate AHC communications facilitator. "Confirming, this is Cyber Geek. We're already in Utah on patrols and can take the bear, just need rapid transport for my team."

Heavy footsteps from nearby signaled to both of them that they weren't alone any longer. Thanks to Medley's sizable shadow, the mystery of who was nearing was quickly solved, as he and Cold Shoulder soon stepped into easy view. "Tell me we've got something interesting this time. I'm tired of slow-chasing these robbers into the iceboxes."

"It does get tedious," Cold Shoulder agreed.

"How about a giant meta-bear attacking a honey factory—that grab you as tedious?" Hat Trick countered.

"Grabs me as you having a laugh." After a moment of looking at Hat Trick's expression, Cold Shoulder lifted an eyebrow. "You're serious?"

"The report is serious. We'll see for ourselves soon enough if the situation is." Cyber Geek had barely finished the words when there was a flash of light nearby.

Standing silently was a man clad in a simple, white cotton outfit. Catching a ride with an AHC asset was rarely the same experience twice—they had too many movement-metas aiding a huge staff in itself, so the odds of getting the same transportations frequently were slim. Upon arrival, this fellow motioned to the area around him, wordlessly indicating that proximity was required.

They headed toward him, Cyber Geek angling himself to arrive next to Medley. "How you holding up? Need a rest or anything?"

"After that chase? I don't even consider myself warmed up, let alone gassed." Medley's claws flexed as he spoke, and his tail gave itself a good long stretch before settling back into position.

"Looks like someone is excited for a good brawl."

"Are you kidding? A fight that might be an actual challenge, and not against another human or sentient creature I've got to hold back against? I'm not just excited, I can *bear*-ly contain myself."

There was just enough time for Cyber Geek to give his friend a dirty look before the light flashed once more, leaving nothing more than an empty street and a single silver buckle that had broken off a designer shoe.

Chapter 97

"I don't give a shit what Gram-Gram says, you need to trust me." Beverly had spent a great deal of effort post-confluence gaining control of her new transforming powers. That was why she was able to still be in human form, not even dragon enough to accidentally shatter the phone in her hand, as the argument dragged on.

"Cancel the damn trip. This isn't the weekend for apple-picking. Be near the house, and have weapons at the ready." She paused, listening to the same reply she'd been getting for nearly an hour. "Because you'll be glad you did! Goddamn it, Ambrose, just keep the fucking family home this weekend. Please."

A crisp knock on the front door pulled Beverly from her pacing, giving her a welcome exit to this frustrating exchange. "I've got someone at the door. We can talk later, but I expect you to get the ball rolling on this. I'm not playing around."

With that, she ended the call, walking over to open the door and reveal Kyle, along with Ellie. Both looked weary, though knowing what was secretly on the horizon for their weekend, Beverly hardly found that surprising. The AHC was likely running itself ragged in preparation for the looming threat.

Since she was supposed to know none of that, having only been brought into the loop by Tori on Monday, Beverly stuck with a simple, noncommittal greeting. "Hey you two, what's shaking?"

"We were hoping to speak with Tori, if she's around," Ellie opened.

"There's some... scheduling issues with this coming weekend. Might be hard to properly guard her, so we wanted to, if she was okay with it, maybe get a little heads up on where she was planning to be."

Given that they'd be handling an invasion, it was actually nice to see that the AHC still took the time to properly cover the people they were actively guarding. There was no chance in hell Tori would go for it, but whatever tactics she used to keep this team at arm's length were hers alone to figure out.

"You'd have to ask Tori herself on that one, and she's not currently around." Beverly checked the clock on the wall, realizing she'd gotten so lost in arguing that she hadn't even noticed the hour change. "It's Wednesday, so she's got a meeting, and I think she mentioned something about grabbing coffee after. That means she'll either be back here or pestering Chloe at Ridge City Grinders. If that doesn't pan out, you could always just use the phone."

Kyle shook his head. "This seems more like a face-to-face conversation. Tori hasn't exactly been shy about liking her privacy, and I don't want to seem like we're prying. We've still got some of the week left, but if I'm near the coffee place, I'll pop in."

He started to turn away, but Ellie remained, staring at Beverly closely. "Actually... you don't have any big plans this weekend, right?"

The conflict was obvious, looking at it, knowing all that Beverly did. Ellie wanted to warn her friend about the upcoming invasion, to make sure Beverly was safe. Except word wasn't supposed to leak out—the AHC would absolutely want to control that narrative, even if only to minimize panic. So now, Ellie was suddenly stuck, the desire to protect weighed against her trust in the AHC that silence was right for now. Perhaps another villain would have taken some pleasure in seeing a cape discomforted, even momentarily, but Beverly felt the pain far too keenly. In a way, it was exactly what she'd just been dealing with regarding her own family.

"Who, me? I have a glorious weekend planned out. Lying around, streaming movies, catching up on work, ordering far too decadent of food—really just two days of indulgence. Sort of a mini-vacation to recharge the batteries. I'll be shocked if I leave this apartment, though you're welcome to come join if work is slow. Kyle, that extends to you too, and the other boys, but I warn you now that I will not tolerate any insubordination on film selection. The rom-coms are happening."

Relief flooded Ellie's face—they *really* had to get better about hiding stuff—as she nodded enthusiastically. "That sounds amazing. I may just take you up on that after... after my work is done." It was a near miss, but Ellie recovered in time, albeit not quite quickly enough to save Kyle from wearing a very nervous expression.

He managed to give a polite wave as they departed. "Have a good day. And please let Tori know we stopped by, in case we don't spot her at the coffee shop."

"Take your time heading over," Beverly advised. "She's probably still got a fair bit of meeting left to go."

Wade examined the item from all angles, running his fingers along the seams, getting close to the pattern, even sniffing one particular section of faux-leather. This went on for ten full minutes as Tori sat, patiently waiting. Having a master of the craft evaluate her work would have been worth it alone, but this was the chance for so much more. If they'd done well enough, this could be the start of something brand new, a place outside of villainy where she could succeed.

"Okay, walk me through it." That was all the guidance Wade gave as he set the prototype back down on the table.

Rising from her chair, Tori approached and scooped up the device, hanging it carefully from her arm. Nearby was a small area with several cardboard dummies. Each had been made up with a classic ruffian face, drawn scruff and painted-on scars unique enough to make Tori wonder if she'd found Wade's secret hobby. Their purpose for today was to serve as stand-ins for real crooks, though Tori wouldn't necessarily have objected to warm bodies for such a test. There was time enough for that after more R&D, she supposed.

"As you can see, from the exterior, this appears to be nothing more than a tasteful purse, and does indeed function as one. For the majority of its owner's life, it could do that job without ever being anything more. But let's say one night I can't catch a car and wind up walking through a particularly dangerous area. Suddenly, I am accosted on all sides by would-be thieves. What's a damsel to do?"

Tori strode over to the cardboard cutouts, mentally replacing them with her actual kidnappers. This device wasn't just marketing bullshit. It mattered to her. Feeling helpless, trapped, unable to fight back—Tori wanted to kick those fears in the fucking teeth. Not just for her, either. For anyone who picked up one of these purses. As an inventor, this was her pride and passion, a chance to actually *do* something the world couldn't ignore. So it had to work, and not just against cardboard. Tori had to feel safe even when mentally facing down a crew of kidnapping metas, because that might very well be what one of these devices went up against.

"The answer is simple. You run your finger along the silver section woven into the handle. There's a specific path to make sure it isn't triggered by accident, but if you're trying, it's easy to do. After that..." Rather than explain, Tori simply activated the trigger. A small piece on the purse's front parted, revealing a spray nozzle that doused the cutouts in green mist. The cardboard was, unsurprisingly, not affected by the spray; however, Wade picked up his phone and began to peruse some sort of display.

"Fascinating. This liquid is unstable, but the effects are quite potent. How many shots per cartridge?"

Waiting until the nozzle was fully spent and the front section had resealed, Tori moved the purse back to her side, tapping the base. "Three per purse, to start. Beverly is working on moving toward a more modular design, something where we could swap out the exteriors and cartridges easily. If it works, you can technically just sell the one purse, and then have separate skins to change out, like phone cases."

They waited a bit longer, until Wade's phone chirped a loud beep at him. "It seems the effects of the spray have now ended. Are there any secondary effects or other features you wish to show?"

Up until that moment, Tori had been feeling pretty good about their work; however, she'd also been hoping for a tad more enthusiasm. Trying to stay optimistic, she shook her head. "That's the basics for now. It's easier to build from here after getting your input than to press forward and have to go back for redesigns."

"A wise choice, as there is still much work to be done," Wade agreed. Not the most encouraging, but if they were continuing work, then it meant the project would still be alive. "Tori, what you have created is quite useful, will certainly have a market, and would never reach shelves in its current incarnation. The design itself is quite nice. What it fails to account for is the potential ramifications."

Wade motioned to the purse, still hanging from Tori's arm. "That weapon is capable of temporarily neutralizing metas with actual power, which makes it useful and dangerous. No sooner would it hit store shelves than we'd see them wielded for robberies, slowing or weakening capes, and all manner of general disarray."

"So... it's a no?"

"Certainly not. There's profit to be made here," Wade corrected. "This, Tori, is where your business education begins. You already know how to build powerful weapons and tools. What you haven't yet experienced is bringing a new product to market without tipping the scales of power or stepping on the wrong toes. This is what you came to me for."

He extended a hand, reaching for the purse. "May I?"

Tori handed it over, watching as Wade's pale hands turned the prototype around several more times. "If I were the creator of such a tool, my first step would be identifying what pieces of the technology were unique, as those are the ones to protect more stringently. Here, everything you've used is fairly straightforward, with the exception of that liquid. Therefore, our main concern is keeping it proprietary, stopping these delivery mechanisms from being used illegally, and ensuring that the cartridges can't be utilized by another device."

"The cartridges are already built to be tamperproof. I'm sure together, we can get them secure. I really don't think anyone can synthesize this liquid; it's spliced-together insanity, and does not play well with other chemicals or equipment. They'd melt a lab and give their eyes a chemical burn before making much progress."

"You'll forgive me if I take a few attempts myself, just to be sure." Wade shifted the weaponized accessory in his hand, moving so that the handle was visible. "For limiting how the purses are used, I recommend adding a fingerprint authentication feature that is set up upon purchase. It will create a record of which purse belongs to which person, so identifying the ones wielded illegally will be a snap for law enforcement, and ensures a stolen purse can't be used. Maybe toss in a GPS as well, along with a beacon that notifies local emergency services that help is needed whenever a spray is activated. We'll also need some wireless charging capabilities to power the new additions. Now you've got a self-defense device that is a pain in the ass to use illegally, but offers even more features to the people who are actually in trouble."

"Sounds expensive," Tori noted.

"It will be, but mass production, along with a few tricks I've picked up, should help reduce costs. Besides, you designed an item often classified as a luxury. With stylish enough designs and the features we're adding, the price tag will justify itself."

He wasn't necessarily wrong, but it still nagged at Tori's conscience. "Let's keep at least a few of the models priced as low as they can go. This isn't about only protecting rich people. No offense."

To her surprise, Tori found Wade was no longer examining the purse, and had instead pointed that scrutinizing stare in her direction. "The desire to create change, to invent something which leaves a lasting mark upon the world… there is nothing wrong with that ambition. In fact, I daresay it's the part of you I find most interesting. But ambition alone does not build an empire. You'll have to make hard choices, and look to the bottom line more than you'll want to. This concession is a small one, and I can easily make it. Understand that in the future, such may well not be the case."

"Got it. If I want my stuff to be universally available, I have to build with that in mind."

"Along with hoping the projects don't change form in development, but that's more of a long-term concern." Gently, Wade handed the purse back over to Tori. "For today, I think it's safe to say we're on an excellent track. If you'd be open to it, I can take a crack at adding the additional features, since I've got more experience building computer components for mass production. However, if you'd prefer to do it all by hand, I understand, and we can schedule another progress meeting down the line."

It was no accident that he'd given the purse back before asking; they both knew Tori's general capacity for trust, especially where her work was concerned. Taking it and adding the suggestions would be doable, but slower than anything Wade could manage, especially with her suit repairs still ongoing. Beyond that, for this partnership to work, at a certain point, Tori would have to let it out of her hands. Since she wasn't planning to make each of these things personally, loosening her grip was simply unavoidable. Better for Wade to show his true colors now, early on, if there was going to be a betrayal. Tori couldn't control that part, though. All she could do was present him with an opportunity.

"I say give it a shot." Tori dropped the purse back on the table, where it had started. "I'll obviously want to look things over, but you can get us a build closer to the mass-market version anyway, so it makes more sense to start from there."

"Your trust is noted, and appreciated," Wade informed her. "I should be able to have something ready by next week. It would be sooner, if not for the upcoming hecticness."

That was certainly one way to categorize a planned alien invasion. Tori might have to steal that the next time she was alluding to an upcoming villain event—at the rate things had been going, the damn things were sure frequent enough.

"Until then, I suggest you focus on personal preparations, especially where self-defense is involved."

"You don't have to tell me twice," Tori concurred. "After one stop at Ridge City Grinders, I'm heading back to the base to keep working."

She pointedly didn't mention why she was stopping for coffee, not that anyone she knew in the guild would require such an explanation. For Tori, it was a perfectly natural detour—would have been stranger if she skipped her favorite java spot. It was much easier to let that assumption slide than to explain she was grabbing a drink with her friend who was also one of the AHC's rising stars. It wasn't a secret, per se, just something she chose not to talk about.

After what she'd learned about Ivan and Helen, Tori was starting to suspect there were a great many things so hidden by the guild members. It was only fair she rack up a few of her own.

Chapter 98

"Mommy? Are you okay?"

With a start, Helen jerked upward, feigning wakefulness as best she could. The effort was severely compromised by the document stuck to her face, pasted there by ill-timed slumbering drool during the unexpected nap. Thankful there were no photographers around to capture this candid moment, Helen yanked the page off, setting it back onto her kitchen table with the others, right where it had been before the boredom and sleepiness overtook her.

"Mommy is doing fine, just taking a short rest when she can. How about you? How's packing coming along?"

Penelope's eyes turned downward, a sure sign that no productive report was impending. "I packed three shirts, twelve socks, and my comfy snow pants."

Sighing, Helen reached down and scooped up her daughter. At six, she was no longer the tiny bundle that could easily fit in a single grip, yet there was no twinge from her back or cry from her arms as she lifted the small human with a squeal of delight. For all that her power had taken through the years, there were other gifts it left behind. Never truly losing the ability to sweep up those she loved in her grasp was one that Helen treasured.

"I know you don't want to go with Miss Theresa this weekend, but she's going to take you somewhere secure. An emergency bunker, with lots of supplies, where you'll be safe no matter what happens."

The small head dug into her collarbone, pressing hard. "But you won't be there."

"No, honey. Mommy can't be down there. Mommy has to do her part to keep everyone safe." She kissed the top of Penelope's head, all too aware that there was no happy end to the conversation in sight. Her daughter was afraid. She knew something bad was coming. For all that Helen wanted to be there with her, telling her that it would be okay, she had to be Lodestar, ensuring that such an outcome was actually possible.

"Can Uncle Ivan come?"

Ridiculous as the notion of Ivan Gerhardt walking into an AHC-owned bunker was, for a moment, Helen found the image deeply comforting. Truth be told, if there had to be one person that wasn't Lodestar watching over Penelope, Ivan would be at the top of the list. Hopefully, he'd be spending the invasion protecting Rick and Beth. This problem was squarely within the AHC's jurisdiction, so she didn't expect much guild activity. Or rather, she hoped there wouldn't be much—because if the guild had a chance to play, it meant that things would have gotten very messy indeed.

"No, honey, Uncle Ivan has another safe place to be. But there will be other kids to play with, new people to meet, and the whole thing shouldn't take more than a day or two. Can you be my brave girl for that long?"

Uncertain squirming made for a potent tell, yet Penelope still screwed her face up into a curiously familiar expression. "I can do it. You go save the world."

In her decades as a superhero, even before fully coming into her powers, there were only a handful of blows that hit as hard as that look. Helen knew that expression, because she'd seen it on her own face so many times throughout the years. It was the face of someone hiding their own pain to put on a brave front for the sake of those watching. Thanks to her job, Helen had worn that mask untold times, but she'd never hated it so fundamentally until she saw her daughter do the same.

"How about I help you pack? We'll pick out some fun outfits you can show everyone, and think of lots of games for you to play with the other kids." It wouldn't make up for being gone when her daughter was scared, but it was something. Helen would deal with the paperwork later; super-speed made for sloppier work, however she didn't especially care. With only a few days left until the world was at risk, Helen was going to spend the time she had where it mattered most.

That was one lesson life refused to stop teaching her.

Almost time.

The man pressed his thin fingers together, hoping the latest round of coverage could contain his excitement until the moment was at hand. The materials for coating himself enough to maintain an appearance of humanity weren't exactly easy to come by, even if he did make the vast majority of them himself. There were still components to consider, some getting rarer by the year. Over time, he'd attempted to adjust the formula, substituting in newer materials for those falling out of availability. Each such experiment ended in disaster. Were he capable of death, several would have likely ended him entirely.

"We just... wait?" Lozora hung in the corner of the room, an attack dog no longer sure of her usefulness. She was wise to be uncertain; her presence was tolerable only so long as it served a purpose. Fortune remained on her side for the moment, as there were still tasks for which she was suitable.

"We are not waiting. We are preparing for the perfect moment to strike," he clarified. "Once the attack begins, some of the assets I've reached out to under my cover identity will move into position, drawing our targets to the appropriate location. Our aim is set, the hammer cocked. It is merely a matter of letting everything properly align to take it all in a single shot."

Her next words were mumbled, perhaps not truly meant for him to hear. "Seems like there are easier ways to kill some capes."

"Countless simpler methods," he agreed instantly. "Yet this is not a job built toward efficiency. It is about the spectacle, the show, and the aftermath of what remains. If simply 'killing capes' were all I had in mind, this would have been finished on the first day. I seek something far more delicious, and difficult."

His thin hands stretched out before him, the pale skin clinging to the finger bones like cheap shrink-wrap. "What I want is to take decades of pain, a lifetime of suffering, an endless torment with no escape, and gift even a small portion of it to someone else. Killing the capes will be the finale, a grand flourish to drive things home. All the hell I put them through before that is the purpose. I want them to know, even briefly, the cost of their power. Only when they understand the truth will death be allowed."

Lozora said nothing to that. She'd been especially quiet since the Starscout incident. She didn't matter, anyway. Her role could be easily filled by multiple lesser minions at this point. The plan was what counted. He'd worked so hard to move everything into position, just to create a perfect opening.

With only a few days left until the fun started, he could scarcely contain himself, as the slow leak of dark smoke rising from his left pinky attested. There was probably enough material left to last for another coating before the invasion, but after that, he'd be running low.

Then again, after the invasion, he might enjoy a little time living in his own visage. After so long spent unseen and unknown, it was well past time he showed the capes what they were really up against.

It took Tori a moment to spot Donald amidst the bustle of Ridge City Grinders. Only the good fortune of Chloe being on shift made things easier, as her roommate gave a pointed nod to a table in the corner, where some douchebag was wearing a hat and sunglasses indoors. On her second look, Tori realized the douchebag in question *was* Donald, which was all the prompting she needed to kick off the conversation.

"You going to a brightly lit baseball game in the next ten minutes, or just auditioning for 'World's Most Obvious Narc'?" Tori smiled down at him, softening the blow slightly.

"Oh, hey!" Donald leapt up, stowing his phone at the apparent realization of her arrival. Working with the AHC was already a busy gig; she had to imagine. With what the weekend was bringing, that was even more the case. It made the fact that he'd coordinated with her schedule for coffee catch-up session to happen all the more impressive, and worrying.

Tori still wasn't sure where she'd landed on the idea of capes and villains being friends. Helen and Ivan were proof that it could work, yet she was smart enough not to base too much of her life around Lodestar and Fornax. Those two tended to be exceptions a lot of the time; it was best to not take them as the standard. Nevertheless, they proved it was possible, for those who put in the work.

As their hug broke apart, she caught the sheepish look on Donald's face. "I... um... I've had to start keeping a lower profile in public lately. Cyber Geek is getting more popular."

"Isn't that a good thing?" She clapped him on the back once, though he didn't seem especially enthusiastic.

"It's not a bad one, but it takes some getting used to. For today, I wanted to be incognito."

"Then I'm glad I caught you before any browser windows were open. Hang on, let me go grab a drink." As Tori turned, she found herself looking at the approaching form of Chloe, who set a large cup on the table in front of her.

She only paused long enough to add a napkin to the top of the cup. "I made you the afternoon usual, plus a little extra. Tell me how the meeting went later tonight." Then Chloe was gone, back into the fray of cranky caffeine consumers.

With no more need for detours, Tori took her seat, sipping the coffee, unsurprised to find it scorching hot. Chloe had probably made the thing, and then tossed it in an oven to stay warm—not like she had to worry about burning Tori's tongue.

"Big day with the Vendallia higher-ups?"

It took Tori a moment to figure out what he meant. She was currently so mentally checked out of her day job that the words almost seemed nonsensical. After a stuttering start, her brain finally kicked into gear, putting together his meaning. Luckily, large sips of coffee were excellent for hiding mental recalibration.

"In a way, sort of, though only in the most technical sense." Tori hesitated. This wasn't a development she was ready to share with the world yet, not even amongst friends. "I'm working on something new, but I don't really want to talk about it until I see if it's going somewhere."

"I've seen the quality of work you can do at a job you tolerate. If it's something you actually care about, I'm sure you'll knock it out of the park." Donald was squirming now, and Tori realized his own drink, an iced coffee turned light from all the added cream, had barely been drunk a quarter of the way, despite his head start. He was... nervous.

Instantly, the scene changed for Tori. Every single body in the building was a potential cape in disguise. Did Chloe know? No, she'd have found to way to slip in some sort of message, or used one of her idioms to escape. What was the plan? Ambush her while the suit wasn't around, subdue her if she was lucky, then drag her to court for... for what, exactly?

Forcing a few deep breaths down under the guise of a *very* long swig, Tori took control of herself. Awareness and fear were useful tools; giving over to full-blown paranoia was another matter entirely. Nerves didn't mean Donald was about to turn on her. He had plenty going on this week to be worried about. And even if she was busted, the only crime Hephaestus was wanted for was a connection to a museum heist, something that the guild lawyers could hopefully handle. More than anything, though, if the AHC wanted to haul her in, Lodestar could have done it whenever she chose.

"Here's hoping you're right." Tori gave a mock toast, which Donald mirrored, albeit on a delay. "Anyway, what wins me time with one of Ridge City's rising capes? Don't get me wrong, it's nice to catch up, but you seemed pretty set on making something happen this week when we were texting."

Of course, Tori knew the reason: Donald was facing down an invasion and was afraid. He was doing what people facing real battle often saw as the best use of their time: spending it with friends and family. Even if she had to feign ignorance, Tori was touched as she realized how important that made their friendship to him—a kind feeling that was followed swiftly by remembering how easily she'd thought him willing to betray her moments ago.

"There's... I've got a mission coming up," Donald said, quite nearly slipping up right out of the gate. "You probably don't need to worry or anything. No one expects me to be in particular danger."

"But life doesn't come with guarantees, especially for capes." That was a truth Tori had understood long before guilds and abilities. She was a smart cookie. Life only had to savagely rip away everyone she loved *once* for the message to sink in.

He nodded, though he didn't seem much more at ease, despite her jumping them to the punch. "That's definitely a big part of it. I've started to really understand how powerful some metas out there are, and how wildly out of my depth I could be with even just one wrong move. I don't want to make the mistake of assuming things will go well, and then end up being wrong."

Softly, Tori reached over and patted him on the forearm. "Dude, you're *allowed* to be scared. These powers aren't a change you asked for. They just happened. The fact that you chose to do something constructive with them at all is amazing. Most people would have kept it to themselves or used it for personal gain. Expecting yourself to take on criminals and monsters without ever being afraid, well, that's just dumb."

"It isn't that kind of fear. I mean, yes, I might get hurt, but that's true any time I go out on patrol. I've had to make peace with that for a while now. My bigger concern is leaving things unsaid."

Without warning, Donald's free hand came down lightly on top of the one Tori had been using to pat his forearm. He looked at her, eyes not quite fully shielded by the reflective glasses, thanks to the angle of the lighting. That was why she could see bits of the terror, and sincerity, in his gaze. Too late, those clues finally gave her an inkling of what this meeting was really about.

"Tori, I asked you here because the truth is... I have feelings for you."

Chapter 99

The first five passes came up empty. Luckily, no one appeared to notice the streak that blasted by Ridge City Grinders multiple times. On try number six, Kyle arrived outside the window just in time to see Tori laying her hand on Donald's arm. His pulse spiked, in a way that had nothing to do with the speeds he was operating at. Unlike many of his peers, Kyle was somewhat in touch with his own feelings, meaning he understood quite well what was happening.

At some point, he'd become taken with Tori. It wasn't all that shocking—his past romantic affections had often landed on headstrong women with forceful personalities. Mix in that she was one of the few people outside of the island who'd treated them all like their positions didn't matter, making her the only outsider he'd ever been able to open up to, and it was practically inevitable.

Recognizing that those feelings existed wasn't the same as giving into them, however. They were in Ridge City to continue a legacy, while building something new of their own. One day, maybe, he could free up enough of himself to put into a relationship, but for now, Kyle knew he would always pick the job and team first, which wasn't fair to any prospective partner. Especially one who clearly had other prospects. So while he did feel his pulse rise, it wasn't accompanied by any sort of impulse to dash over and interrupt.

While a piece of Kyle *was* tempted to slip inside and listen in, he'd already made enough mistakes where Tori was concerned, and for this one, he wouldn't even have the power of self-delusion. Catching a moment in happenstance was one thing; if she caught him purposefully snooping, there rightfully might be no forgiveness.

With one last look through the window, Kyle disappeared in a sudden blur.

Finding the right response was no easy feat. For a dangerous heartbeat, she almost tried to laugh it off, but the look on Donald's face was much too vulnerable. Her next impulse, a new standard in terrible, was to blurt out that she was really Hephaestus. Both were resisted as Tori opted—rather than blow up the conversation and attached friendship— to try to muddle her way through. Not being sure about her future friendship with Donald didn't mean she wanted to hurt him, regardless of how things went.

"Look... I'm about to say something, and it's going to sound like a line, so you have to hear me all the way out, okay?"

"Of course," Donald replied.

Tori took a sip of her coffee to steel her nerves. "You're a great guy, but—"

The groan that slipped out of Donald was plainly unintentional, as his eyes went wide in embarrassed surprise moments later. "Sorry, sorry, just wasn't expecting an *actual* verbatim dumping line."

"Warned you." Tori tossed a small smile on, lightening the mood as much as she dared, given the subject matter. "And like I was saying, you *are* a great guy. The issue is me. I'm... there are a lot of parts of my life that you don't know about. Really, truly messed-up parts."

"I get that things were rough for a long time. Losing your parents, the addiction—I can't imagine what you went through. That said, none of it would change who you are today."

"You're wrong. It's done nothing *but* shape who I am today." Tori felt the rage in her gut rising without provocation, just because she'd dared look into her own history. It was always there, in the spot where happy memories of her family and childhood were supposed to live. The endless blaze of fury over a life stolen from her, not even by something as ineffable as fate, but by simple greed and apathy. One more broken piece in the pile that was Tori Rivas.

"I have a lot of trust issues. I mean, a shitload. Right now, the only way I can seem to make genuine friends is to share some sort of near-traumatic battle with them, which isn't really a healthy or sustainable tactic. As for romantic relationships, they aren't even on my radar. I don't know what sort of emotional bandwidth you need to open up like that, but I don't have it. Not now. Maybe not ever."

It was Donald's turn to use his beverage as a way to buy time, an extra-long slurp punctuating the pause after Tori's words. At last, he lowered it, reply finally formed. "That might be the first time someone has used 'it's not you, it's me' and been entirely sincere."

"Molds were made to be broken."

His gaze softened, despite the bad news. "Clearly." After a moment, he composed himself, looking a tad bashful at the earnest admiration. "If that's how you really feel, then I can respect it. While it's not the answer I wanted, I didn't honestly expect you to feel the same way. I'm sure I've got a type out there, it's just very specific." Donald leaned back slightly, eyes moving toward the shop at large, as if scanning for an exit from this now embarrassing situation.

To no one's shock more than her own, Tori's hand shot out, grabbing him by the wrist. "Hey. Stop. I meant what I said. You *are* a solid guy, Donald. Kind, honest, and loyal to a fault. Even brave, nowadays. You're a damn cape, for god's sake. There is no shortage of women out there who would love to be on Cyber Geek's arm. Just because I'm not one of them doesn't mean I'll let you shit-talk my friend."

"It wasn't much of a shit-talking," Donald protested.

"Sentiment more than words; I can still read between the lines. The point is, you *are* my friend." Tori realized the words were true only as they were tumbling unbidden from her mouth. "Assuming you're okay with that, after my answer."

The response wasn't instantaneous. As Tori pulled her hand back, Donald appeared to give the matter a few seconds of serious thought before finally nodding his head. "I'd love to still be friends. But, fair warning, I also don't think I can turn off my feelings just like that. I won't bring it up again and will try my best not to let anything show; it just might take time. I don't want you to think I'm hanging around in the wings, using our friendship as a way to wait and see if you change your mind."

"If I'd had a few more friends like you throughout my life, I might not be such a fucked-up mess." Tori relaxed a little, now that the conversation was on a more predictable track. "It's okay for you to feel however you want, so long as you respect my own thoughts on the subject."

Despite the positive swing, Donald's face creased, the first time in the whole talk he'd looked genuinely bothered. "Good. Then as your friend, I don't like when you do that."

"Do what?"

"Do what? The exact thing you just got on me about: shit-talking my friend. You're not a 'fucked-up mess,' Tori. You're holding down a job, a social life, an apartment of your own. I know people who haven't been through a tenth of what you have, and they still can't get it together enough to do their own laundry. Give yourself an ounce of credit from time to time."

Her impulse was to deny and defer, pretend all of that was mere happenstance. And to an extent, it was, in the sense that only chance had gotten her on the guild's radar, leading to her apprenticeship with Ivan. Yet that was merely the opportunity; everything from there on had been done by Tori's own hand. She'd endured the guild's trials, she'd survived the Ridge City Riots, she'd built the identity of Hephaestus. Maybe he was right. Perhaps she was a little too hard on herself.

"Well then, how about we both promise to be better about going easy on ourselves, and hold one another accountable to it?" Tori lifted her coffee once more, noting that Donald did the same without even looking. "To friends?"

His reply was as instant as it was earnest. "I'll always drink to that."

"And what makes this place so safe, exactly?" Janet was rubbing the spot above her nose between her eyes, giving Ivan deep flashbacks to the later years of their marriage. That gesture had been in frequent use as the arguments grew more constant. He briefly wondered if she used it around anyone else—it would seem not, if today was any indication. Juan was at work and the kids were in school; this was a meeting solely for those in the know about the greater events of their world. Specifically, the weekend's coming danger.

"Guild owned, heavily reinforced, and with an emergency escape option in the event things go catastrophically wrong." It was all the more galling that they had to hash this out when he *knew* she was going to go along with it in the end. The other options were to take their chances out in the open, or turn to the AHC for help. Intelligence and pride cut off both those paths for Janet.

"Yes, but what good will that do if Earth loses?" Janet persisted. "Death by starvation as we remained trapped in your hidey hole isn't much better than getting wiped out in the initial shot."

It was hard to argue that she wasn't presenting a relevant concern, albeit one Ivan had trouble imagining. Thankfully, the possibility was one he'd also taken into account. "If Earth's defenses fall, then you'll use the escape option.

We have a versal-displacement engine to punch a hole between this part of the multiverse and somewhere safe."

Janet's concern was momentarily tempered by her curiosity—the same trait that had gotten them mixed up together in the first place. "I thought it was near impossible to break through the multiverse barriers anymore."

"Then you also know Wade considers the words 'near impossible' to be the start of a challenge," Ivan explained. "It takes a tremendous amount of power, and the portals only last for a short while, so it's still a huge ordeal. But the technology functions well enough that we built an emergency escape system and established an outpost where we can flee to."

He didn't add that this system wasn't designed with aliens in mind. For all they knew, the Wrexwren were just as far ahead on that front as humanity. No, this safety mechanism was built with a single force in consideration. For all the power Lodestar had, she was completely unable to leave her native universe. All the nooks, subspaces, dimensions, and planes of their own world were fair game, but no Lodestar they'd heard of had ever been able to step beyond the initial universe they inhabited. Which made fleeing to another part of the multiverse the only true way to slip from that powerful, glowing grasp.

"Meaning if things go badly, our best option is to leave the entire world behind?" The words could have sounded patronizing or sarcastic; instead, there was a cold calculation to them. She grasped the stakes at play, and that failure from Earth's defenders meant the entire world they knew could come tumbling down. Janet wanted to be sure she understood the consequences to every action as she made them. It was an attitude Ivan had worked hard to learn from during their time together.

"Yes. If I fall, it means these creatures are incredibly dangerous, and the world is in for a harsh battle. Should Lodestar fall... just get out. If they hold power greater than hers, this planet cannot stand against it."

Janet rolled her eyes with outstanding form; however, not even she bothered to argue on this point. "I do feel better knowing there's a contingency, although it would have been nice to look over the other world's facilities in advance. Our best option is not to need it, to stay put in our own universe. Tell me you're going to win this, Ivan."

"My part is relatively simple. The harder tasks fall upon Wade, Xelas, and Lodestar."

"That's not what I said." Janet rose from her kitchen table, striding over to the corner of the room and plucking up a set of framed photos. She walked back, thumb resting on the image in the rightmost corner. "Do you remember that day?"

He took the photos from her hands. Janet appeared to be standing on a dusty road, in front of a natural rock formation, posing with the infant version of Rick. All of that was true and accurate; what was unseen, just outside of frame, were the front gates of Rookstone, where Ivan had been imprisoned at the time. The picture was from the day he'd first met his son, taken less than an hour prior to the event.

"I could never forget." He remembered every piece of it. The uncertainty in Janet's eyes, the sharp sting of the cleaning spray lingering in the prison air, the tiny fingers that grabbed at his hands before balling up into a fist, clenching on the orange fabric of Ivan's uniform until Rick was taken away. Even then, the small hand hung on, tugging the collar in a way that had never truly gone from Ivan's mind.

"Do you remember what you told me before I left?"

"I won't let anything happen to him."

The sharp "tsk" hissed out of Janet's closed teeth instantly. "Those weren't your words."

Ivan's eyes traveled from the starting photo to the rest of the frame. He was missing in most of these, but there was no shortage of pictures documenting his children's lives. Babies, to toddlers, now one nearing her teens and the other verging toward adulthood.

"I will kill every meta, every monster, every world, if it means keeping our child, our children, safe. No price is too high, no blood is too sacred. I *will* protect them."

"That's what I wanted to hear." Janet gently plucked the photograph from his hands, looking up at him with a small touch of her former admiration. "Now, you're ready to fight."

Chapter 100

Contact came on Friday. Specifically, Friday morning, just between when Professor Quantum wrapped his current project of upgrading his flight belt and when he returned to the lab with an ultra-energy bar. He'd already half unwrapped the glowing treat when he stepped into his facilities to find every piece of communications equipment lighting up. Those tricky little invaders were trying to send it worldwide, stirring up panic among the masses before they'd even set a single ship in Earth's space.

Such a mass broadcast was impossible without tripping the AHC's blocking equipment, and while there were, admittedly, a few other metas capable of bypassing the media defense, the days of screens suddenly filling with criminals were largely long-past. There were obvious exceptions, like that traitor Apollo teaching Balaam the ways around it for their little rebellion, but those were insider tricks. An alien force wouldn't have knowledge of such tactics, so for the moment, this message was only for the AHC, and anyone else who'd rigged up a functioning interstellar communications array.

Looking over the content of the message as his automated translator was spitting it out, there was nothing surprising thus far. This was a twenty-four hour notice: the battle would begin in a day's time. Earth was allowed to send up a champion if they so chose, losing would forfeit their planet to be plundered—all the standard bits they were already expecting. The only real unknown to be revealed was the timetable. A single day, enough to technically give the planet a chance to ready their defenses, yet still with most of the benefits of a surprise attack.

There was sharp crack and a minor flash of light as Professor Quantum took a large bite from his bar, the crumbs dissolving as soon as they hit the ground. Now that they knew the invasion was planning to move soon—within a day, if they were telling the truth—it was time to bring the public in on what was happening. In the old days, they'd have just let the sky fill up with aliens and tell people to have faith. Now, everyone expected these sorts of things to be added right to their calendar. Lodestar coddled this world too much. Professor Quantum was of the mindset that tribulation built character. Not a fight worth having on this front, though, especially not when the issue would have the public on her side.

Instead, he activated the preprogrammed sequence, sending out the recorded video across the world, the computer redubbing over their voices in various languages to ensure it was understood by all who saw. While he might not have loved the necessity of communication, Professor Quantum would never permit his work to fall below acceptable quality.

On his screen, and across millions stretching out through every corner of the globe, a new image suddenly appeared. On it was himself, Quorum, and at the front, speaking, was Lodestar. Time to bring the world up to speed on what the weekend held in store.

Across the world, people drew near to their screens and speakers, all too aware of what an announcement like this foretold. Families huddled closer, souls were searched, and each person faced the momentary possibility that everything they'd ever known or loved could be destroyed in a single day's time. Then, for the most part, they continued on with their respective days. An invasion on the horizon was all well and good, but it didn't change the work ahead of them, and once the AHC kicked the attackers back to the far reaches of space, things would be back to normal by Monday.

Some took the news more seriously than others. In one particularly well-armed Ridge City household, for example, the entire family was engaged in cleaning and checking their entire stock of weapons. Ambrose watched the screen as he reassembled a rifle, not needing his eyes for a task so well burned into his muscles. Beverly had called it, and days before the AHC. Something big was coming all right, and she'd wanted to make sure her family was ready for it. Part of him wondered if he should be probing deeper into *how* exactly she'd had access to that sort of information, but they were already in the process of getting reestablished after the transformation incident. Better to let her reveal the truth in time. For now, he had plenty to keep busy with.

Beth and Rick saw the announcement on their phones, inside a car already headed out of town. Beth was mostly interested and excited, while Rick couldn't help thinking about this trip they'd mysteriously decided to take beforehand. It all tied back to his dad's secret somehow, though for the moment, he was content to let that sleeping dog lie. Learning just a taste of the truth had terrified him to the core of his soul. Right now, he was happy to have Ivan just be his dad. Yet even as he held that thought, Rick's eyes wandered out the window to the blue sky overhead. When the dust settled, did he really expect a man who'd killed—or rather, *slaughtered* an entire army, to just sit back and watch?

Sitting at his stool, surrounded by terrified locals, Grantham watched the old tube set flickering as it blasted out the message in a language he'd only picked up the basics of. He'd been around long enough to get the essentials: there was a fight coming, and the AHC was trying to keep it off-world. Keeping his beer soundly on the table, Grantham flexed his left hand into a fist. Veins bulged an icy blue hue, a shade that spread across the arm, swelling it with muscle at even the merest thought of combat. Smiling, he used his right hand to take a sip of beer, not even caring that it had dropped by several degrees. He wasn't ready to take on the AHC yet, but Jokull might have fun tearing through some easier targets.

Chloe watched the announcement along with everyone else at Ridge City Grinders. It was strange, seeing this message while practically sitting in the AHC's shadow. People were obviously scared, yet not sure how afraid they should really be. Daunting as the concept was, it was hardly the first time Earth had been attacked at large, and so far, the capes had succeeded in repelling back every major threat. Then again, they only had to lose once for the planet to be wiped out, a fact that everyone was trying hard not to think about. Her customers absorbed the message like a small blow, then each began the process of walking it off. The rest of the world would deal in its own way; this was just part of what it took to build a life in Ridge City.

Sitting atop the Statue of Lizardy, which rested directly across from the Statue of Liberty, Captain Bullshit's hand stayed, despite being moments away from summoning the sarsaparilla storm clouds. The clunky old mobile television was easily four times bigger than a modern phone, and with far worse picture, but it still held a signal well enough to get the message. While he was disappointed to scrap the performance, such a display was no longer needed today. The world had already been reminded to expect the unexpected; to strike again at their cocoons of repetition would be mental assault, rather than the art of cerebral elevation. This could wait for another day, when the masses' minds were properly aligned for radical shocks.

On an island nation off the coast of Australia's Shattered Shores, the message was blazing on a huge screen, higher in definition than most people even realized was possible. The figure seated upon a mechanical throne took in every detail, face inscrutable through her meta-suit's seamless helmet. It flowed into the rest of the armor, which coated every inch of the wearer's body. Her fingers tapped heavily against the armrest, calculating the odds of AHC failure. Chances were strong they would repel the threat, though whether or not they would succeed without the Earth taking damage was more in question. Whatever the outcome, Tyranny was confident in her nation's defenses. Her land would either endure, or tear off the enemy's flesh on their way out. Leaning over, she whispered to a figure at her side, the only person in the chamber with her. Confident or not, there were preparations to be made.

Nexus had no grand view to watch from for this part. He was only around happenstantially, in case this was one of the versions where Captain Bullshit went ahead with the storm. Standing on the street, he could see the image playing on several screens in various stores and windows, none of which he paid attention to. The message wasn't inherently fascinating, especially after hearing countless prior versions of it. What came next, now *that* he would have several good seats for. This was little more than the curtain call. With no sarsaparilla storm on the horizon, Nexus soon vanished, popping out of the world like he'd been digitally removed. Only for a bit, though.

Come tomorrow, this would be an event he dared not miss.

Tori and Ivan didn't see the announcement. They weren't intentionally avoiding it; however, there were no television screens in the testing chamber, and neither had elected to bring a phone along with them for this.

Zipping through the air, Tori adjusted her flight path, nimbly getting around one of the cardboard protrusions popping down from the ceiling. As she did, a fresh target popped into view, earning a short blast from the gauntlet on her left arm.

In all but title and a few small suit pieces, she was once more Hephaestus—or at least, she would be once this test was complete. It wasn't really for Ivan; he'd simply wanted to see where she was at. The real assessor was Tori herself, keenly observing every detail of her suit's performance post-repair. So far, it was holding up splendidly, the few limitations she hit being ones of design and fatigue. No amount of repairing would change the fact that she'd put the armor through more than its initial materials were meant to endure. Between learning in the field and access to superior components, Tori was slowly coming around to the fact that soon, she'd need to build an entirely new meta-suit. Projects like this were never done. Each design reached the full extent of its potential, and from that knowledge, a next step forward could be taken.

Reorienting with a quick spin, Tori fired at two more targets with the left gauntlet. Her right was cycling into its large beam weapon. For all the work she'd done on efficiency, there was still a sizable charging time before her big shots could be used. Not ideal in the field, so she needed to make a habit of keeping one blast ready to go whenever possible. The rapid turns earned her groans from the suit's dark metal. Between fighting with metas and the strain of flying at high speeds, she was going to have to go far more durable for the next incarnation, assuming she could find something both strong and light enough—there was no way she was parting with flight.

Settling into a rough hover, Tori scanned around, isolating two more targets as they flopped out into view. A pair of shots, and both were smoldering pieces of cardboard seconds later. Carefully, keeping a close eye on her stabilizers, Tori brought her suit back down to the ground, coming to a halt roughly ten feet from Ivan. She disengaged the helmet's latches, popping it off as her body reformed to flesh and bone. "Now that's a way to start a morning! What did you think?"

"Very impressive." Ivan didn't actually *sound* terribly impressed, though Tori knew that if she was waiting for that to happen, her next invention had better be the world's comfiest chair. "Your mobility is constantly increasing as you improve the flight systems, and the gravitational distorters have even made you light on your feet. Aim seems accurate, force is adequate, though I notice you didn't test the major weapons."

Even without her helmet showing the indicator, Tori could tell her gauntlet was still charged; there was a crackling, static-like energy running along the length of her arm. Crap, that meant she needed to reinforce the shielding before there was a major rupture. That issue would have shown in the charging, though, so it was probably still safe-ish to use. "Wasn't quite sure what these walls were rated for. Figured Wade had enough on his plate without me cutting a hole in the base."

"A bit overconfident, though you do make a good point." Ivan took several steps back, then raised his hands out in front, like he was pushing an invisible wall. "Whenever you're ready."

"For mime-work? Hate to be the bearer of bad news, but you're going to be holding that position for a hell of a long time."

Ivan sighed with the exhausted resolve that only a parent raising a teen was capable of. "For the fully charged beam. We're testing all of your suit. That certainly includes your ace in the hole. The walls' durability can be called into question. Mine is a known quantity, especially when braced. So, as I said, whenever you're ready."

There was no reason why Tori's arm hesitated before shifting into position. Ivan was, so far as she knew, borderline indestructible. Her absolute best efforts might be able to put a scratch or a burn on him, but causing actual damage was currently a pipe dream. All the same, it was momentarily difficult to point her greatest weapon at the man who'd fast become one of the few positive constants in her life, even knowing how silly her fear was.

In that moment, just before she fired, Tori finally understood how Ivan could feel protective over Lodestar, despite how fantastically nonsensical and pointless it was. Whatever the rational brain might know, it didn't quiet the fearful voice that lived much deeper down, the whispering tone terrified to lose someone its owner cared about.

The beam of energy scorched the air, blazing through the short distance between them in a flash. That was the furthest it went, however. Ivan's hands, still stretched before him, didn't just stop the beam, they contained it. It was like he'd hefted some invisible shield, which wasn't the worst way to describe magical wards, soaking up all the power she'd sent hurtling in his direction.

Finally, when the beam cut out, Ivan waited a few seconds, then lowered his arms. His hands were rubbed against one another, then shaken out, like they'd been slept on and had to be roused from numbness. "I could feel that."

"What does that mean?" Her gauntlet was smoking—she definitely needed to tweak the shielding before the invasion kicked off. Still, Tori felt the first whispers of pride rising in her chest, wondering if she'd managed something especially impressive.

"Many things. That you've increased the power from the last time I took one of these shots by quite a bit. That you'll be capable of damaging all but the most durable of metas." A hand landed on the armor of her shoulder, patting her twice. "And it certainly means that, should you choose to enter the fray tomorrow, I won't have to worry about Hephaestus making it through safely. That villain will have more than enough power to survive."

Good as the praise made Tori feel, she wasn't quite sure that survival would be her only goal once the invasion started. The majority of her life had been focused on having no attachments, caring for nothing, so that she couldn't be hurt by losing it again. For better or worse, the last year had chipped away at that tactic, one friendship at a time. Helen was right. She could keep pretending to not give a shit, but that wouldn't actually lessen the pain she'd feel to have someone taken away. If she wanted to protect the people she cared for, it was time to have a hard, honest reflection about who those folks really were.

Once she knew, Hephaestus could decide in the moment how to react to whatever the invaders threw at them. Tori might not have much insight into their game plan, but she had a pretty good idea of her own: defend what was hers, and show any dumb sonsabitches who tested Hephaestus why it was *never* a good idea to try to steal from a villain.

Chapter 101

"Those of you assembled before me, your primary task in the coming event is to maintain peace and stability among Earth's citizens. When something like this occurs, there will always be those who assume the Alliance of Heroic Champions is too busy to deal with lower-tier crimes. On top of that, some people may give in to genuine panic, taking actions that endanger themselves and those around them. You are going to be out there, en masse, making sure there's help for anyone who needs it."

Lodestar floated before the massive assembly, more capes than Cyber Geek had even realized were working at their level. Then again, with the rotating shifts and ways they were spread out, there were plenty of other members he passed like a ship in the night. Plus, the AHC was always adding new members, albeit not in the same flood that had been around when Donald first joined. To his left was Medley, on his right were Hat Trick and Cold Shoulder. They'd arrived that evening as a unit, ready to receive orders for the coming madness.

"In the event that our visitors decide to take the fight to Earth, your focus should be on guiding and protecting civilians. We have more experienced superheroes standing by to deal with an actual invasion force—that's not where you'll do the most good. Those of you who've gone through evaluation and done well may be tasked with slightly more difficult jobs as needs demand; however, it is highly unlikely we will ask you to get into the fray."

Her form rotated through the air, working to make eye contact, however fleeting, with each person in the crowd. Neither Professor Quantum nor Quorum were present, not that Cyber Geek had expected them to be around. Given what the planet was facing, it already felt like a waste to have Lodestar here breaking things down. But then, the real trouble was still a sunrise away.

"Should they invade, for most of you, this will be your first experience in anything similar to true war. In the heat of combat, pitted against an enemy with ruthless intentions, you may be forced to make difficult ethical decisions. I can't tell you how much force is the right amount, or if the final line has to be crossed. The circumstances you'll be facing will have to inform that decision. Just remember that there are no undoes in this world. A life that's taken can never be reclaimed."

It was a notion that had been sitting heavy in Cyber Geek's gut ever since he learned about the planet's current threat. He'd had no issue blasting through a monster that Nexus conjured from another world, but since then, he'd been largely dealing with humans who required a far more gentle touch. Killing an alien was a notion that left him feeling uncomfortable, yet was still something he could imagine. Were it a human, Cyber Geek was fairly sure he wouldn't be able to go through with it. He really hoped he wouldn't have to find out if it was in him to kill a sentient being.

"We're going to be working in rotations, since the chaos this causes will reach well outside the timetable we were given. First teams go out tonight, then back before dawn for some rest and recovery while the secondary teams work. It'll go like that until we're in the clear. I can't promise we won't hit an all-hands-on-deck situation at some point, so make sure to use your downtime well. There might only be so much of it."

"First teams! Find a coordinator and get your starting position assignments. Second teams, hit the beds. You're up in just a few hours." This announcement came from one of the many people wearing polos bearing the AHC logo. Support staff were essential to keeping this place running, especially since so many other capes lacked Cyber Geek's experience with office drudgery, along with his honed planning skills.

The crowd broke into movement instantly; they'd all had enough training to understand that speed was a factor in dangerous situations. By the time he looked back up to the ceiling, Lodestar was gone, zipped off to another of what had to be countless pre-invasion tasks. The polo-wearing staff were moving fast, too, dispatching teams and individuals to patrol areas with blazing efficiency. When his team's turn came, there wasn't even a chance to speak.

"Ah, Cyber Geek's quartet—just one moment, please." The bespectacled man was slender and meek in a way that reminded Cyber Geek of himself less than a year prior. "Looks like you're on the home team. You'll be running patrols in Ridge City. No teleport needed. We'll route you as the night goes on. For starting off, let's have you begin near Ridge City Savings and Loan, swing wide around the Alfred Settler Memorial Plaza, then head up to Denny's Diamond Depot on fourth. By then, you'll have new directions waiting."

With their orders received, the team headed toward the main exit, a different direction than the vast majority of their peers, who were all being relocated to various locations. To his surprise, Cyber Geek noticed another group of four heading in the same direction. Waving, he caught the attention of Agent Quantum, who was walking with his own team. The big man returned the gesture, though there was still a bit too much crowd between them for anything verbal.

"At least we've got some heavy hitters hanging around," Medley noted. It was, by Cyber Geek's estimation, the first real compliment he'd ever paid the New Science Sentries.

"Let's just hope we don't need them," Hat Trick added.

"Because the threats are so weak, or we're so strong?" Cold Shoulder held up a bicep, perhaps intentionally showing off the results of her own training. Medley and Cyber Geek weren't the only ones hitting the gym lately.

"Ideally, because no one is in danger at all. I guess I'd settle for them being weak, though, since that would be easier for the average person to deal with." It was more or less the answer he'd expected from Hat Trick, though that didn't make her point any less salient.

It wasn't so long ago he'd been one of the normal humans, and he could still remember how terrifying it was in moments like these, when forces so far beyond anything he could fathom were gathered to determine his—along with the rest of the world's—fate. Hat Trick was spot on: the best outcome was one where nobody was in danger. Barring that, the next best thing was to make sure that if someone *was* in trouble, then there would be a superhero nearby to save the day.

"Everyone, grab a snack or some caffeine if you need it. We've got a lot of work to do."

"Mobile, or fortified?" It was a strange question for Beverly to ask at a kitchen table next to bowls of Chloe's half-burned spaghetti, even with the few empty beers scattered around. Lying in front of Beverly was a rough sketch of the neighborhood, with their building at the center. Based on the assessment they'd done over dinner, it was clear that holding this place during an invasion would be tricky. Like most apartment buildings, it wasn't designed to resist real assault, only to keep unwanted trespassers out.

"With my hop-skip-and-jump phrase, we could change entire countries as needed. Even if the aliens come, there's no way they can be everywhere," Chloe pointed out. "Still a lot of planet to cover."

Curious as she was about alien tech, Tori had been through one too many close calls lately to find any appeal in flying around, trying to hunt down invaders. Truth be told, in other circumstances she'd likely have holed up in the guild and let the whole ordeal pass, except they couldn't very well bring Chloe along. She and Beverly had made sure to keep their friend off of both guild and AHC radar, since Chloe wanted to keep her normal life, extremely potent ability and all.

Considering the nature of the threat, mobile was absolutely the safer move. They could pop into some towns in the middle of a flyover state, the sort of place low on any invasion's target list. Even if they picked wrong, Chloe could give them another shot within seconds. Mobile made them both efficient and safe.

And yet, Tori still felt a hitch in her stomach at the idea of fleeing. Ivan's house had felt like her first home in a long while, and it had been destroyed—technically by her—during the last of these major catastrophes. This apartment, for all its faults, was *hers*. She'd chosen it with her friends, declared it to be her home, and even found herself missing it when she was away. Nexus had said it himself: a villain defends what was theirs. What was the point of having power if she was going to let some interstellar assholes push her around and wreck her home?

"I can't speak for you two, but I don't like the idea of running off and leaving this place for scavengers or aliens. If we try to stay here, we don't lose our teleportation option. I propose we start by hunkering down, and then, if it becomes clear there's no holding the line here, we bail out."

"Running's never really been my style, either," Beverly agreed. Both eyes turned to Chloe, who was the heavier voice to weigh in on this discussion. She had no meta-suit, nor dragon-shifting. Her ability was strong, but strange, and certainly not the kind that could be counted on to keep her safe.

Scooping up two of the spaghetti bowls, Chloe brought them into the kitchen and dropped them on the counter, before returning, albeit not empty-handed. She'd grabbed the pink and black umbrella that always managed to somehow be in the same room or area as Chloe, despite none of them ever seeing it move, or even disappear. Sitting back down, she laid the umbrella down on the table.

"Last time I got involved in meta-human stuff, I accidentally exploded the top half of someone and ended up haunted by their indestructible umbrella. I definitely don't want to do any fighting again, especially with outcomes like that, but I do have a little protection. I'll stay with you two until it's time to leave, and then we get clear. Fair?"

"Can't reasonably ask for more than that," Beverly agreed. "I think it's a good plan. While we're bracing for a fight, our exit strategy is impeccable. At the worst, we can strike hard, and then retreat."

"Which brings us to our next question. We've got a single night to work with: what sort of defenses can we get in place before then?" Tori paused, looking over the rough diagram once more. "Ideally ones that don't kill our neighbors or tip off the capes that there's some sort of diabolical genius sharing the building with them."

That earned her a raised eyebrow from Beverly. "Isn't it a bit egotistical to call yourself a diabolical genius?"

"Humility is a virtue, so that shit is for the capes."

"Touché." A flash of thought darted through Beverly's eyes. "Speaking of, should we expect any interference from them? Given that the New Science Sentries are on protective detail around you, they might be sticking close during an invasion."

Crap. In all the madness of approaching aliens, Tori had forgotten their duty to her. Then again, if aliens ended up attacking the world, there was little chance the New Science Sentries wouldn't get called to pitch in. No way they'd let a team like that ride the pine guarding one woman and her apartment. It was a thought that felt true, yet didn't quite reassure her fully.

"Nothing to be done. We have no idea where the AHC will put them, or even if aliens will show up at all, let alone come here specifically. But I think a good rule should be that we stay civilian until the first contact is reported, just in case they check in. An invasion would mean shit hitting the fan, so they'll have way more on their plate to deal with than me."

"There's always—" Chloe was cut off by a burst of sudden, fast knocking on the door, like someone was trying to pound out a rhythm.

Tori rose, putting the pieces together in short order. That sound was really just someone knocking normally, only sped up significantly. Unless the legendary Ricky Rocket had suddenly run back *into* reality, she had a pretty good hunch who this would be.

Sure enough, the door opened to reveal Tachyonic, looking almost jittery with the way he was fidgeting. Someone must have their speed cranked up substantially. The energy didn't extend merely to his body, even Tachyonic's voice came out at an accelerated pace.

"Hey Tori sorry to bother you in a bit of a hurry we're technically on patrol but I zipped over to let you know the AHC has us patrolling the city so please keep your head down and stay safe since we won't be next door plus I also snagged an emergency response clicker in case anything happens just hold the button down for five seconds and we'll get an alert okay gotta get back on patrol bye."

The words were a flurry, ending in a burst of wind as Tachyonic dashed back out to wherever it was he was actually supposed to be. Resting in Tori's hand was a small electronic button, like a stylized garage door opener: silver and with a large AHC logo emblazoned across the top. For a moment, she felt dirty, holding a thing like that, but the notion was quickly followed by intrigue. This was something that tapped into the AHC's communications network. If Professor Quantum had designed it, there would no doubt be safeguards on top of safeguards, but logically, he couldn't make every single piece of tech the AHC used. Some had to be crafted by other, lesser minds that weren't so skilled at protecting their creations.

Shutting the door, Tori turned back to her friends, who were watching with curious expressions. "Good news: I don't think we'll have to worry about any capes. Now, if we can just convince the aliens to stay away, we might finally manage to have ourselves a goddamn peaceful weekend."

Her friends laughed, and Tori chuckled as well, though there wasn't really much mirth in her at the moment. Tomorrow brought an element of unpredictable chaos, and there was no guarantee that when the dust settled, things wouldn't have changed. As someone who finally liked where her life was at, the idea scared Tori, the same fear that had helped act as a drive during her suit repairs.

When Tori felt afraid, her instinct was not to curl up and hide. Whatever was out there and coming to fuck with her, or the few people she cared about, would find a mad-eyed woman willing to fight tooth and nail to protect what was hers. Well, she'd certainly be willing to break *somebody's* teeth and nails, at any rate.

Whatever the Wrexwren were planning, Tori sure hoped they knew the fight they were in for. Otherwise, the savagery they were facing almost wouldn't feel fair.

Chapter 102

When the Wrexwren ships first entered Earth's space, it was a very different event than the Grzzniltan visitation. Since the last extra-worldly visitors hadn't been bringing a fleet, there had been substantially less concern. This time, it seemed all but a given that there was a fight looming, and the citizens of Earth had endured too many such frays to be caught unaware. Families sheltered in place where possible, or banded together in large community centers. Weapons were passed out, and those with meta-human abilities were assigned roles best fitting to their talents. The world at large prepared to weather a storm from the far reaches of outer space.

Quorum and Professor Quantum were in the same room as Lodestar, where they'd been waiting and talking for the past hour, until this moment arrived. Another message lit up the equipment, a new transmission from the Wrexwren. On the large screen, dozens of imposing ships filled the sky: strange and alien, yet with the familiar hallmarks of machines made for war. Weapons, shielding, maneuverability—the exact shape might change, but the generalities remained the same. In the center was a larger vessel, almost like four balls of metal yarn: one at the center and three linked with tubing that seemed much too thin to exist outside the weightlessness of space.

"Signal source confirms, that's our mothership." Professor Quantum ran a finger along the readout, checking carefully. "Whatever big object they're dragging, it's still managing to stay hidden from our censors. We can at least tell it is significantly behind them, though."

"Which may or may not matter, depending what it is and how fast it can move," Quorum added. "All we can safely presume is that it will not be something that turns the tide in our favor."

"Doesn't really change anything, does it? I go handle the fight, you two take care of anything they try to pull while I'm gone. Any surprises, we roll with." Lodestar couldn't help staring at that void in their readings, even as she dismissed it. All of this felt too well-organized. For off-world invaders, everything seemed to be running smoothly. They had a plan, and while she didn't know it yet, Lodestar also wasn't convinced that things would go as easily as they hoped. Although, that could have easily just been the inner voice of experience.

Standing nearby, Professor Quantum finished reading over the communication. "Seems they're ready to host guests. We've got thirty minutes to present a champion and claim the right to duel; otherwise, the invasion begins."

"You're getting ever faster at translations," Quorum complimented.

"Yes, but also, they sent it in multiple Earth languages." Professor Quantum seemed unbothered by the news—they'd already suspected the Wrexwren to have advanced information. This merely confirmed it.

"Half an hour isn't a lot of time." It wasn't a concern, but Lodestar wanted to make sure she understood as much as possible. Once these things got going, there usually wasn't a chance for reflection.

Professor Quantum tilted his head in agreement. "My best guess would be it's a remnant of their culture too sacred to disregard, while also deeply inconvenient to the act of world-conquering, so they honor it in a cursory fashion. Whatever the case, no one sets a time limit that short and plans a grace period."

No point in wasting her window, then. Lodestar did one last equipment test, checking her communicator, Professor Quantum's newest galactic translator, the long-range scanning goggles, and other tidbits that helped make her job easier. Everything came back singing, as she'd expected. Professor Quantum had a lot of traits that caused friction between the two of them; his dedication to the work was never among them.

"This is Lodestar. Preparing to initiate contact."

"Lodestar, we're reading you loud and clear. Good luck, and godspeed."

The voice on the other end represented one of the countless support staff who would be monitoring her feed, along with that of all the other active superheroes, as they tried to keep this situation contained. With a clock ticking down and all her prep work out of the way, there was only one thing left to do.

Lodestar leapt into the air, defying gravity like she took pleasure in it, which was accurate. In the ceiling, she slipped through one of the hatches designed for expressly this purpose. When the world *needed* Lodestar, it was often time sensitive, so after the tenth roof she'd burst through, the new design rule was to leave her some escape options.

Once clear of the AHC's base, she rose up, higher into the sky. Ridge City spread out below, a beautiful tapestry of roads, homes, businesses, communities—a society of people going about their lives. As she rose, Lodestar could pick out familiar landmarks: her own home, currently empty as Penelope waited elsewhere, watching the television to see her mommy fly. Without meaning to, her eyes swept further out, to the under-construction lot that was Ivan's house. More locales filled her vision: Penelope's favorite yogurt shop, Mr. Bando's karaoke bar, and a small patch of seemingly inconsequential street not far from downtown where a significant punch was once thrown.

Rising higher, more of the world came into view. Human eyes could never have taken it all in, but Lodestar was decades past being human. She could see most of her home nation, from the quiet hamlet of Canple, where her first life had started and ended, to the bustling metropolis of Faucet Hills, where she learned to be a cape. So many places, where she'd fought so many dangers. Higher and higher, until she was past the atmosphere, out into the true vacuum of space.

She loved this spot. In the early Lodestar days, before she learned to completely control her abilities, it was her quiet place. Up here, with the right angle, it was like she could literally hold the entire world in her palm. It would be so much easier to protect that way. Sometimes, she liked to imagine a version where things were that simple. Today wasn't about peace, however. Someone had gone and parked a fleet of warships much too close to her relaxing place for Lodestar's tastes.

Time to give them a proper Earth greeting.

Just as she turned, Lodestar caught a flash from below—that would have to be trusted to the other superheroes. She had a deadline to beat. Flying over to the mothership, Lodestar scanned for anything that seemed like it might be a docking port. While she could survive the crushing void of space without issue, not every species fared so well, and ripping a hole in their ship was a bit extreme before the fight had officially started.

Near what she thought of as the top of the pseudo-yarn ball, Lodestar spotted what appeared to be a large opening with some sort of energy barrier in front. Trusting that to be for keeping space out rather than ships or visitors, she set course and soared through, causing a commotion of surprised noises from the various Wrexwren gathered in what looked like their version of a hangar.

It was her first time seeing a Wrexwren, and they were certainly a sight to behold. Much like their ship, there was no real front or back: four huge arms, four squat legs, a thick torso, and heads without any visible features, all completely covered in what appeared to some sort of natural armor. It was sort of akin to stone, except far shinier. They began to speak to each other hurriedly, platelets in the armor of their face opening and closing quickly to create shrill tones that her translator picked up perfectly. They were surprised, but not flabbergasted.

"Somebody called for a champion from Earth. I'm here to take up the fight."

More tones, though with less panicked energy. After a few moments, a new Wrexwren stepped out from an archway. This one was larger than the others, his armor a dark hue with spiked sections poking out. Perhaps it had to do with their roles in the society, or maybe genetics was as fickle a mistress on other worlds as it was on Earth.

"You are the Lodestar." The voice didn't come out of the face, which made the same tones as the others. It had a small blue device ringed around its neck, and that was where the words originated from.

"Guess my reputation precedes me," she replied. "May I ask your name?"

This time, there was a delay between the whistles and the translator, as if it were processing. "My true name is unpronounceable in your tongue. The closest translation would be Salvrin, and I am the Zerle of this vessel."

"Got it. Nice to meet you, Salvrin."

Two of the arms sort of... shimmied, in a way Lodestar had no idea how to interpret. "A name is a thing given to all. I hold no pride in it. Zerle is a title of great honor. I will not be addressed without it."

"My apologies, Zerle Salvrin. Your culture is a new one to me. I meant no offense." Evidently, shaking arms indicated annoyance; that was probably a good note to file away. For now, she had to play nice. No matter how obvious their intentions were, she wouldn't give them an excuse to start anything.

"Of little matter. You will follow. Time runs short." Zerle Salvrin motioned for Lodestar to come with him, moving with surprising grace for those stubby legs. She also noted that his fingers had claws, a distinction from the other Wrexwren visible; one more feature to mark him as dangerous.

Walking through the ship was bizarre, even by Lodestar's extraterrestrial-vehicle standards. Riddled with loops and repeated sections, it was akin to a maze of mirrors, only without actually needing any mirrors to function. When Zerle Salvrin finally came to a halt, however, it was not in some reinforced room, as Lodestar was expecting. Instead, they appeared to be at a communications station, based on the number of screens and flickering holograms.

At her arrival, nearly every other Wrexwren filed out, until it was only her, Zerle Salvrin, and a few other Wrexwren that also had spikes on their armor. His clawed hands began to tap at the screen.

"Before you formally accept this challenge, you should know that leaving once it begins is akin to a forfeit. Should you flee, for any reason, the victory goes to the Wrexwren."

Without warning, the other Wrexwren let out a high-pitched tone. There was no translation in her ear for that one, which meant it was probably just the sound of them cheering.

Something was off, that was obvious by now. The hidden package they were towing, the specific condition, all of it was part of a plan. Unfortunately, she didn't see any way around it. Her only option was to be strong and fast enough to neutralize their scheming.

Zerle Salvrin kept right on clicking as he talked, laying out the question like a hunter setting down steel jaws. "Knowing that, do you, Lodestar, accept the role as Earth's defender?"

"Objection!" This was not a Wrexwren voice, or Lodestar's, but it was one she knew quite well. Half-surprised, and then surprised at the fact that she *was* surprised, Lodestar turned to see the unmistakable form of Doctor Mechaniacal in full meta-suit strolling up casually, with Xelas on his heels. Thinking back to that flash from below, she realized they must have been flying a ship that launched only a few minutes behind her. "That message you sent out made the invitation to any of Earth's citizens. Who says Lodestar gets to take the job just because she was here first? It's our home, too, you know. We do have a stake in this."

Several of the other Wrexwren moved position slightly, the most active one suddenly finding a seared patch of flesh roasting on his arm. Across the communications station, Xelas wiggled a still glowing finger. "Ah-ah-ah. We came here nice and chummy, playing by your rules. I'd be very certain of myself before deciding you want to play by ours."

Zerle Salvrin held up one of his four fists, and the other Wrexwren relaxed. "Very well. Do you wish to challenge her for the right? If it is not settled by the time limit, then Earth will have no defender."

"Me?" Doctor Mechaniacal put a hand on his metal chest, causing a clang.

"Oh no. I'm not much of a fighter, especially not compared to these two. But I like a *good* fight, you see. One with real stakes and effort. Having you spring this on Lodestar and send her flying off would have killed all the fun." With one motion, Doctor Mechaniacal hit a button on his suit. A holographic image suddenly bloomed from a light in his hand.

The creature was massive and hideous, like a giant mouth hooked to a long body with various limbs stretching out, none quite like the others. "No idea what this thing is called, but I've been able to figure out quite a bit of other information. It appears to survive on plasma, and based on the energy readings of what they've been using to lure it along, my guess is it's the sort one finds in stars. Seems to eat every signal and light we shine on it—that's why it stayed hidden, like a living black hole."

Doctor Mechaniacal's words felt like tumblers clicking into place. A threat she couldn't ignore, even with the stakes established, one so powerful that Lodestar was the only person who might be able to stop it. But bringing in something to eat their sun? That was beyond invasion. They were willing to leave this world as nothing more than a cold husk.

"Is it who I think?" Lodestar didn't look at Doctor Mechaniacal. Her eyes were still on the monster, one that was flying not nearly far enough behind this very ship, heading toward the Earth's sun.

"Indeed, and he will be along shortly. We had him make sure the hangar was closed to any other potential interruptions."

"You have ruined our surprise, but it matters not," Zerle Salvrin declared. "Earth's hero must still choose. Defend your world from us, or from the Scralthor. Time runs short."

It was hopeless. She knew that already. The die was cast, and there would be no going back, but she still had to try. Lodestar saved people. It was who she was. "Listen to me, Zerle Salvrin. Whatever you think you're doing, you're wrong. I know how this sounds, and it must seem like prey in a trap begging for its life. But you are the one with the jaws closing in. While there's still time, send that creature away. Sit down and talk with us as visitors, not invaders. Please, you have no idea what you're getting your people into."

This time, the pitches oscillated, high and low, long and short. Without fully understanding how she knew, Lodestar was certain she was hearing the Wrexwren version of laughter. "Pathetic. We'd been warned to no end of how dangerous Earth's great champion is, yet she merely begs."

Being a superhero was as much about accepting limits as challenging them. Lodestar couldn't be everywhere, couldn't do everything. Sometimes, she had to make the hard choices, and this was no exception. Shaking her head, she turned from Zerle Salvrin. "Remember, this was the path you wanted."

The footsteps came from the same hall as Doctor Mechaniacal and Xelas had. This entity had no desire to sneak, however. He came strolling in, knocking a few globs of green-blue blood from his hands. It had been a long time since Lodestar saw the full outfit—as much as one could call it that. There had never been much of a formal costume: dark clothes, sometimes a leather jacket tossed on, an ensemble built for function over fashion. There was no need to glitz up the outfit when the mask already stood out so well. Blood red—because in the beginning, it had been actual blood; even his disguise referenced the sort of mess his fights had left behind. The eyes were still normal, but she'd seen the trick enough to know that they could change at a moment's notice.

Her breath caught in her throat. When Lodestar asked if it was who she expected, she'd meant Pseudonym. This was so, so much worse. What happened with Apollo was one thing, losing control in a fit of rage over his children.

If Ivan had donned that mask in advance, it was a declaration of intent.

Walking past, too aware of the clocks on them both, Lodestar whispered as lightly as she dared. "If there's any mercy to be shown, try to find it."

"They had their chance for mercy. Now, they get me."

Roughly the answer she'd expected. Which meant her only option was to go deal with the Scralthor fast enough to still make a difference here. Not an easy task by any means, but being the strongest superhero meant Lodestar got the hardest jobs. As she flew away, back through the ship and out of the now wrecked hangar, Lodestar wasn't quite quick enough to miss Doctor Mechaniacal's words.

"My dear extraterrestrials, and the countless millions watching this stream at home, allow me to present Earth's defender for this duel: Fornax."

Chapter 103

"There's something up." Beverly couldn't say exactly why the sensation was there. It was no singular element, no suspicious figure walking past the same alley three times, nor covert whispers being traded by unsavory characters. She couldn't put her finger on it, but it felt like there was too much foot traffic around them, given what was happening. And she was pretty sure *some* of the faces had repeated. Then, there were the oddities, like a man in a full suit trying to hide what looked like neck tattoos, and the businesswoman whose dress showed the telltale outline of a knife. Part of her brain whispered for her to ignore the hunch, but her family had long ago taught her that intuition was often your gut being smarter than your head. Always worth at least a listen.

"You think?" Tori said, eyes wide as she sat next to Chloe on the couch. "Not only is Doctor Mechaniacal streaming a live feed of their assault on the Wrexwren, motherfucking Fornax just walked on-screen. What the living shit are they up to?"

Beverly kept her eyes on the street, watching the way the people flowed. Less than half an hour prior, a new link had appeared all over the internet, popping up on major sites as well as social media. The stream kicked on with a spaceship like four tied-together balls showing up on screen, and from there, the viewership had only begun to soar. Enough that it was strange so many people apparently had business around their building when there was a live invasion-attempt to watch.

"Show of force. When the AHC came for us, we lost some cred. Being hauled out into the street like that, losing our anonymity—it made us seem weak. I'd guess that's why the rules are getting pushed more. The Council wants to turn that trend around." Beverly craned her head, still focused on the street as she spoke.

"Got it." A dark joy spread across Tori's face. "We're going to remind them that the secrecy and systems were never the reason they should be afraid of us. Can't imagine a better messenger for that job."

There was a loud crunching sound as Chloe helped herself to a handful of popcorn. "At this point, anyone fighting for the same planet where I live is good with me. Go Team Earth!"

No question about it: Beverly was seeing more groups massed up as they walked by. Whatever was going on, it was escalating. Technically, there were several other buildings, other apartments, that this trouble could be addressed toward. If only that damned intuition would let her believe it.

"Tori, I know what we said about waiting until the aliens moved, but you might want to at least get in costume, if not your full suit."

To her credit, Tori's response held no hesitation. "On it. What's up?" She was already moving toward her room, where both outfits were waiting.

Beverly moved the curtains slightly aside, noting the way a select few of the walking masses reacted. Some of them had noticed, which meant they were watching her right back. "Not sure yet, just looks like trouble."

"Here I thought we rookies were going to miss out on all the fun." Tori slammed the door behind her, hurrying to change.

Lozora was learning it was hard to control a collection of individuals; they were far less cohesive than an actual group. Unfortunately, when one was hiring freelance violence, package deals were harder to come by. That was why her employer had procured a great deal of individual talent—more than really felt necessary to scare a few metas. Most of them were competent, mercifully, even if it had required hours of dressing to make them passable for normal civilians.

It was important to get the timing right. They had to strike during the initial wave, when chaos would be the highest. Even their long-laid preparations—the blocking technology in place, the teams ready to cause distractions elsewhere—would only work during the right window of opportunity. Move too soon, and too many capes could be brought in for assistance. They needed to wait until resources were at their limit before the trap would be ready. All of the work that had been done—drawing in the aliens, testing the equipment, even tipping off the guild to move Fornax off of Earth—everything was in service to this singular goal. Lozora didn't care about the outcome in a personal sense. This was her employer's grudge entirely; her motivation was largely monetary.

Although, it would be a lie to say she was in it for the cash alone. After seeing what her fellow villains had begun, their sad little clubhouse with its long list of rules, the idea of setting a counter-example appealed to her greatly. This was a chance to remind the world what true villains looked like.

Killing several capes would be the perfect way to drive such a message home.

More high-pitched notes, laughter, coming from the Wrexwren. Zerle Salvrin made one motion, and the noise came to an instant halt. He was a commander in total control of his ship; there was no question about that.

"This is your choice? Be certain. Once he dies, your only hope is lost. Pick someone strong, and do not mistake the crew you have encountered as a sample of what you are to face." Zerle Salvrin drew himself up to full height, which was quite impressive, and stretched those spiked limbs out. "I have endured many battles, forged my strength in the deadly terrains of untold planets. You do not fathom the danger I represent."

Another round of laughter—only this time, it wasn't the Wrexwren. Xelas, showing the reason Doctor Mechaniacal had likely brought her along, was leaning on a wall, letting out peals of howling laughter. "Oh my god, you have to stop. I'm going to pee, and I don't even do that."

Doctor Mechaniacal kept to the more professional approach. Reading a species without faces wasn't easy, but the way some arms crossed and bodies shifted, they didn't seem to be fans of mockery when it was turned around. "Our selection is adequately strong."

"Very well then, we formally accept your challenge." Zerle Salvrin tapped one button on a nearby console, and suddenly, the ship rumbled slightly. "Should you defeat me, the invasion will be halted."

A long pause filled the silence of the ship, until Doctor Mechaniacal finally piped up. "Are you waiting for us to cry out in surprise? Something like, 'Oh no, they're going to attack until you win, splitting your focus during the bout,' or other tripe? Happy to disappoint, but we counted on that from the start. Before Lodestar stopped us, humanity had a real passion for making war. The ships are impressive and the discipline is respected, but you're nowhere near humans when it comes to the mindset of combat."

That earned some low pitches from the assembled Wrexwren, but Zerle Salvrin sounded unmoved. "All you have shown me so far is your talent for empty boasting. Come, Fornax. Let us see what the defender of Earth is capable of delivering. Your attendants may wait here, out of the way."

"One moment." Doctor Mechaniacal reached into a suit compartment and produced three small orbs. Each one glowed and quickly flitted out of his hand, hovering in the air, taking up a gentle orbit around Fornax. "I presume there are no objections to broadcasting the bout? Since you expect to win, it will be an excellent way to break the spirits of those watching below."

"Or be a source of inspiration if I fall. A transparent effort, but I will win, so it matters not."

It was a very good thing no one could see Wade's actual smile. It would have given away the game right then and there. "Your grace is greatly appreciated."

That earned him a short, shrill tone with no translation, probably akin to a grunt. Zerle Salvrin left the room with Fornax in tow, walking him along a stretch of various paths and routes, all of which were recorded and mapped by Doctor Mechaniacal as the cameras followed. It required fiddling with lots of settings and unseen screens, so to an outsider, he might have appeared to be pawing at empty air. Even if it left him looking silly at times, Doctor Mechaniacal still preferred this to display screens others could see, largely for situations precisely like this one.

While Fornax was being led away, he made a few motions not related to any camera work. No, these had more to do with the ship's systems as a whole, and the remote access module Xelas had planted on their way in. It had taken a lot of work and every ounce of extraterrestrial tech information they could get a hold of, but as the connection established, Doctor Mechaniacal felt a deep satisfaction ripple through his bones. There was truly nothing like the feel of a plan coming together.

Access was only the first step, however. There was still quite a bit of work to do before the real scheme could kick in. Until then, Fornax, and Earth as a whole, were just going to have to endure.

Against the dark backdrop of space, it was easy to spot the hundreds of smaller ships alighting out of the fleet, their first wave of attack heading for the surface. Lodestar wanted to turn back, to knock them all from the sky before they could ever touch down, but she had *much* bigger concerns. The Scralthor, as Zerle Salvrin had called it, still looked mostly like a dark patch of space to Lodestar, but with every passing moment, she was catching more and more details.

Huge was an understatement. This thing could have easily tossed a comet without thinking twice. Its motions were like living ink on a map of the stars —it was more emptiness than being. Leading it by some distance, she spotted a pair of Wrexwren ships, spitting out small sprays of what appeared to be glowing liquid. Bait, meant to lure it closer to its targets. This close, there couldn't be much more guidance needed. Not for a creature that had evolved to eat stars. Most predators had means of finding their prey.

In earlier days, Lodestar would have been awash in self-doubt, wondering if she had the necessary power to defeat this threat. Having enough strength was no longer a fear she held, but wielding that power appropriately was another matter. For all she knew, this was a sentient, thinking creature that had merely been led to destruction by the Wrexwren. Just because something looked scary didn't make it evil. Using the kind of power it would take to stop the Scralthor came with risks; she'd much rather convince it to change course.

Should that fail, then force would be resorted to—hopefully just enough to scare it away before she had to get serious. So many steps to get through, and all while the Earth was fighting off an invasion. At least they weren't unprepared for it. If the Wrexwren thought her planet had put all of its eggs into the dueling basket, they were in for a sun-eating-sized shock of their own.

Across the world, skies burned with the glow of alien ships breaking through the atmosphere. For some, they came out of clouds, ruining a blue-sky day. Others saw their strange curves descending under moonlight. Citizens of all walks of life, in nearly every country, felt the tight clamp of fear bind their chests as the invaders landed around the globe. That terror drove some inward, deeper into their safehouses and bunkers to ride out the storm. For a different sort, rage was hot on fear's tracks, a fury borne from the fact that some interloping bastards would come try take this planet.

Wrexwren ships began to touch down; the first reports were already hitting the internet. The crews emerged clad in a foam-like exterior that was evidently their spacesuit, swinging strangely shaped objects that soon proved to be dangerous weapons. For a terrible moment, it felt like a true invasion, as though the aliens might get a foothold it would be impossible to drive them out of.

Lozora cared for none of that. Her orders were simple on this front. Now that the Wrexwren were beginning to move, the AHC was reacting. The digital feed scanner showed her capes suddenly popping up in all corners of the Earth. The Wrexwren invasion had officially, finally, kicked off. With their giant smokescreen in place, it was time to get to work on their actual objective.

"Listen up, everyone. I want to be crystal clear on this: the goal is to make them afraid. Corpses do not help us. Unconscious bodies, do not help us. Mutilated leftovers... well, that one is probably circumstantial, but we are not going to risk it." Lozora looked at her crew, the hodgepodge of miscreants her employer had managed to recruit. She'd have liked some heavy hitters, even one other Rookstone escapee, more for their experience than power. Half of this lot looked like they'd start slicing and never look back once they had a target.

"To put as fine a point on this as I can, anyone who breaks that rule can expect to have a long session with me, and Mr. Worthington, when this is over."

Even the hardest of faces blanched at that. There was an aura to the man, a coldness that went deeper than any she'd seen before. It wasn't that he was strong—that was common enough in the meta-human world. It was that he had an unmistakable mix of ruthlessness and competence. Encountering someone who claimed they would do anything to see their goals met wasn't a total rarity, but meeting someone who actually seemed capable of following through on such schemes was another matter. Her employer was such a man, and she was quite curious to see how one of his plans looked when it came to fruition.

After months of work and laying low, she was starting to feel like a proper criminal again. An excellent sign, since the day was only just getting started. Lozora gave one last look at the building, then back to her stitched-together crew.

"Remember: above all, we want them scared. Afraid for their very lives. So terrified, in fact, that they're even willing to call the capes for help." Once the real targets showed up, that was when things would get interesting.

With a nod, Lozora dismissed her crew, and they moved toward the building as one. No more need for skulking about, hiding, or subtlety. At long last, it was time for a fight.

Chapter 104

"They're coming." This time, it was Tori who gave the report, though only barely. Between the full mask and costume, along with nearly every piece of her meta-suit, she was as close to being Hephaestus as possible without fully making the switch. Sitting at her side rested her helmet, waiting for the moment when it was donned.

On her laptop, she could see the crowd moving through the remote camera feeds they'd set up. With limited time to work in, most of their preparations had been focused on expanding their information-gathering capabilities. A few traps were waiting as well, but they'd all been built with the intention of halting robbers, or perhaps a few rogue aliens. As things stood, they were facing dozens of enemies, and with their civilian disguises falling away, it looked like at least some had experience with violence.

"Best guess on what they want?" Beverly had also changed, her usual flair for fashion replaced by the thick armor that would shift with Bahamut's various dragon forms.

"This feels like the kind of force you'd see for guild business, except I can't think of anyone we've pissed off enough to warrant the effort." Tori paused, thinking things over. "Well, no one still around, or who has these kinds of resources."

Clad in combat boots, thick pants, a flak jacket that Beverly had produced without explanation, and of course, holding her pink and black umbrella, Chloe was pacing around in the back, thinking hard. Her face was mostly covered by a wool balaclava, with a set of Tori's telescope-goggles added to obscure her eyes, yet one could still make out the worried lines of her forehead if they searched carefully. "Maybe they're friends of that gang who kidnapped you and got slaughtered?"

"Publicly, that was on Nexus. Privately, on the guild. Either way, I'd be a weird retribution target. Not impossible, though." Something snagged in Tori's brain, a memory from that dark time when she'd been taken against her will. "But that gang never wanted me in the first place. I was just bait, put in a trap to lure the New Science Sentries out, because they thought Tachyonic and I were an item."

"Which many people online still do," Beverly pointed out.

Finally, they'd hit an angle that had even the smallest bit of legs. Tori watched as strangers moved toward the building steadily, methodically, ensuring every exit was covered. The crowd didn't even care how visible they now were. Definitely not the actions of people who were walking in expecting a fight. If she was right, that definitely meant they were here for Tori, not Hephaestus. What they would find, now that was a matter still to be decided.

Tapping carefully at a key with her gauntlet-covered hand, Tori cycled through the camera angles once more, getting a full sweep of the area. "Whether or not this is about the New Science Sentries, I don't think they know who they're coming for. Maybe they want to make enough commotion that Agent Quantum and the others show up; maybe they're here to kill the whole building. The question is, what are we going to do? If there's running to be done, this is our prime chance. They can show up to find an empty apartment."

There was a look on Beverly's face that Tori was starting to learn. It happened when they hit a point where her life and her nature were forced to be at odds with one another. The truth of the matter was, Beverly didn't have the right disposition for villainy. She was too nice, too responsible—only her absolute hatred of the AHC had kept her from viewing the other side as an option. As a result, Beverly was caught in a difficult situation: trying to live as a villain while still being true to the decent person she was.

"We aren't the only ones who live here." It was Chloe who put voice to the issue, briefly changing Beverly's expression to one of relief. "What if they find us gone and burn the whole place down, or we're not even the targets?"

"Besides, you really want those pieces of shit touching all your stuff?" Beverly added.

The smart move, the survivor's move, was to leave now. Use Chloe's power, get out of Ridge City, spend the invasion holed up in some backwater bar, watching it all play out on television. The villain's move, on the other hand, would be to obliterate her would-be attackers, sending a message to all who tried next. Prey, or predator. Tori had fought like hell to claim the title of villain. It was time to start defining what that truly meant for her.

"We're going to use Chloe's power," she announced. The faces of both her colleagues were momentarily disappointed, though the expression changed as soon as she wrapped one armored hand around her helmet. "We're just going to use it a little differently than originally planned."

As the Wrexwren landed, out came the orders: different parts of the city, suddenly flaring up with various issues. The more experienced superheroes were sent to handle the actual landing sites, while Cyber Geek and his team ran to clear rubble from the road. A nearby building had been clipped by a landing ship, causing a massive obstruction in the roadway.

Medley and Cold Shoulder teamed up to haul the debris, the latter in her giant ice-armor to make lifting easier. Hat Trick was directing traffic around them, and as for Cyber Geek himself, he was making use of Autom's Eye from the latest *Sneak Soldiers Semi-Solid* game. In a franchise built around stealthing into various places and bases, there was no shortage of useful goodies to play around with, and this one was a real doozy, capable of floating through the air, scanning within set parameters, even feeding the images back into his eyeball display. Thanks to Autom's Eye, he was able to note that there were no Wrexwren approaching their position, though the humans nearby were getting antsy.

"Cyber Geek, what's your status?" The voice came over his communicator, one of the support staff that was too numerous to learn purely by voice.

"Cleanup is nearly complete, at least for the big chunks. Team is ready for our next assignment."

"We've got reports of an unusually large crowd massing up in a residential block to your east. Could be people collectively banding together in case they're attacked, but the old lady who called it in sounded spooked. Better make sure we don't have early rioters striking in the chaos. Sending location."

On his camera feed, Cyber Geek saw a Wrexwren wander into frame, directly to their northwest. His whole body went cold, the understanding that the battle was near landing on him in a way that seemed perhaps too familiar, given how long he'd been at this. It was a small mercy that the Wrexwren arriving were nowhere as intimidating as Zerle Salvrin, the leader whose face and name were all over the internet thanks to that livestream. Why in the hell the villains were up there, let alone squaring off with the Wrexwren, he hadn't the faintest idea. There was no time to sit and watch the unfoldings, so all of his intel was coming from what could be gleaned from short snippets of information.

Quick as the threat had arrived, it vanished, punched out of frame by someone wearing a brilliant emerald cape. With a small breath of relief, Cyber Geek activated the team channel on his communicator. "Be aware, there's some extra threats to the north. Exilor has got it handled from what I can see, but still, stay careful. There could be more around. Our orders are to head east —we've got a crowd that apparently needs controlling. We're not sure if they've just scared or up to no good, so diplomacy first until we know for sure. There's plenty of people afraid right now, the last thing we need is a misunderstanding."

Medley dropped a sizable hunk of bricks onto the sidewalk, out of the roadway, before spinning a few times to get his bearings. "You said east of where we are now?"

"Yeah, why?"

The buzz on Cyber Geek's phone proved to answer the question at the same time as Medley did, even though his teammate couldn't see the mini-map that had just appeared, showing their next destination.

"I'm pretty sure that's where we went to your friend's pool party."

Whether it was his animal abilities or merely a good sense of direction, Medley was spot on. While the map only gave a general zone based on the report received, it couldn't be a coincidence that Tori's building was smack dab in the middle of the estimated area.

"Everyone, move out. We've got civilians in potential danger." Despite keeping his words calm and professional, it took everything Cyber Geek had not to put on his jetpack at that very moment. Getting there ahead of his team would only make things harder, however, and rationally, he knew that. Nevertheless, after failing to be there for Tori twice already, Cyber Geek refused to go for three.

This time, he was going to save his friend.

"Get me every space-faring meta we have up there, knock those ships down before they ever break the atmosphere. Defense team, why are our beam-cannons missing so many of these vessels? How is our ground response going?"

From the sea of nameless workers, a voice rose up. "We're working on counters for some of shielding and blocking tech they've employed, sir, but it's… well, it's like they know exactly what to defend against."

Professor Quantum stood in the center of the chaos, watching every monitor, hearing every tidbit screamed or spoken his way, constantly calculating. In terms of raw power, he was now on the higher side of the scale, although he'd started much closer to Agent Quantum before decades of self-betterment. Even after all of that, his physical capabilities could never hold a candle to the talents of his mind. The world was filled with metas of all shapes and manners, but only he, only Professor Quantum, had gotten there on his own. He'd broken the world, yes, and by doing so introduced the meta-elements and shifted physics that made such impossibilities real, but he'd had to do it before those things existed. His power had come through old-fashioned hard work and genius, traits that were only amplified after the change.

Today, he was acting as the nerve-center of the response, issuing orders and tactics, conducting the entire fray like a lab-coat wearing maestro. Out there, he was one more set of highly capable fists. In here, he was an electric charge to the system, speeding everything up and handling issues as they arose. No one had objected to him taking on the role; in fact, most were delighted by it. Even Lodestar agreed it was the right call, and they were so often at philosophical odds that alone counted as a small miracle.

Yet it was not entirely for the greater good of the AHC that Professor Quantum had taken his place in the communications hub on this occasion. Somewhere, in the deepest recesses of his brain, a small voice whispered that he should see as much as he could. This tiny, oft-ignored voice represented what remained of Professor Quantum's self-doubt—a voice that whispered there was *one* enemy out there who could have been at work behind the scenes. Thought to be dead, but then, wouldn't be the first time, would it? With his massive intellect absorbing every detail from the multitude of informational streams, this ensured that if any clues did pop up, Professor Quantum would be the one to catch them first.

How he would deal with such an issue if it arose remained to be seen. There would be situational details to consider, but Professor Quantum would want to have a hand in the response regardless. If that annoying little voice did prove to be right, it only be proper that he deal with it.

This was no mere common criminal capitalizing on an opportunity. This was a chance to deal with an old friend.

For good.

At long last.

It was hard to tell if he was being led purposefully on a long route, or the winding nature of the ship simply made it seem that way. Around Ivan the orbs swirled, sending video of him and Zerle Salvrin, still leading the way, back home to Earth. The broadcast idea had been a hard sell, but Wade won out in the end. As he pointed out, the purpose of this was visibility, reminding everyone why the guild was nothing to trifle with. If they allowed the AHC to control the narrative, then any achievements the guild earned would either be minimized, ignored, or outright robbed of their due credit, depending on what suited the organization best. This way, there was no chance for them to spin. It gave the guild control of their own message, but also demanded Ivan rise to the challenge of live theatre. Fornax's performance would be key to making this worth the effort.

Zerle Salvrin made no attempts at chitchat or conversation. If Ivan was reading his general energy right, the Wrexwren leader seemed more put out than anything. Likely, he'd expected to join the invasion fun once Lodestar was off handling the giant space-monster. One of great many disappointments Ivan planned to deliver before the day was over.

At last, they reached a pair of large doors covered in various markings. Zerle Salvrin tapped a clawed finger on the entrance, producing an unexpectedly harmonious *ping*. "Perzolic ore. Very rare. Source unknown, chunks have been found spread across the galaxy. Once forged, indestructible. Every master-warship must include such a chamber. The only way to have a proper battle while traveling."

The message was clear: no need to hold back. This cell could handle whatever they dished out—in theory, anyway. Zerle Salvrin stepped back as the doors parted and revealed an entire room made of the same gleaming metal. Given the rarity Salvrin described, Ivan could only speculate how many worlds worth of conquering this represented. Maybe there were a few shards of Perzolic ore buried on his planet as well, scraps the Wrexwren were eager to get their claws on.

He stepped inside, followed by Zerle Salvrin. Once they were through, the doors shut loudly and melodically in one sweeping clang. Scanning around,

Ivan noted that there were no screens or windows—hardly surprising given the room's purpose, but inconvenient for the plan he had in mind.

"Perhaps you technologically sophisticated pillagers have some sort of way to watch the outside world. Lodestar versus a monster that eats suns, I *have* to see that one play out." The grin he gave was not for Zerle Salvrin; very little of any of this was. All of the pageantry was for the masses watching at home, ones who'd know quite well about Fornax's history battling Lodestar.

"You wish to see your champion devoured before being broken yourself. What a strange challenger they have sent me this time."

On the ceiling above them, an image suddenly snapped into focus. Darkness, the void of space stretching on endlessly… until the flash of light. Lodestar, blazing through the sky, on a crash course with an alien creature of untold size and power. Didn't even seem fair, really.

"Do you have more requests, or are you prepared to begin?" Zerle Salvrin did little to hide his lack of patience, so perhaps the walk to get here really was just that long after all.

"I was prepared upon arrival, there—"

The movement was instantaneous, so much faster than the unwieldy size betrayed. Zerle Salvrin struck as soon as Ivan confirmed he was ready, mix of limbs twisting into a strange pretzel of crooks and angles. There was only a second to realize that this must be a kind of Wrexwren martial art before the first blow caught Ivan in the face, blasting him across the room where he banged off the far wall, leaving not so much as a scratch in the surface. He did note that the ringing sounds were far less enjoyable when conjuring them with one's own skull.

"Pathetic." Zerle Salvrin was standing a bit back, still twisted up, waiting to see what his opponent would do. After all that boasting, Ivan was really hoping for a paper tiger; unfortunately, Zerle Salvrin lived up to his own hype. That punch had packed a *wallop*.

Rising to his feet, Ivan brushed off his shirt and ran a hand along Fornax's mask, as if checking the placement—not that it had any potential to move with all the latches and charms keeping it in place. "Not bad, for a sucker punch. You might make this fun yet."

Again, no hesitation as Zerle Salvrin charged, although he did let out one quick response before unleashing a flurry of blows. "Pity, I do not hold the same expectations for you."

Chapter 105

For a bunch of randoms, Lozora's motley collection of crooks was sticking to the plan surprisingly well. They'd all remembered their approaches and areas to guard, ensuring there was no chance of escape. After that, it was a matter of turning up the pressure until the women caved and called for help.

"Boss, we got an issue. The team that was supposed to be ahead of us isn't here." The communicators, like all the tech these minions were using, were hand-made by her employer. A little shoddy on appearance, yet they carried a clear signal from within the building to Lozora's position down the street, where she was keeping watch.

The message came from one of the front-teams, second only to the actual first wave. "Are there any clues?"

"We thought we heard a scream and something heavy falling, but that's it. No signs of a struggle. They're just gone."

Teleportation? Or perhaps just a hidden pit or latch that covered up the captured contents. Either way, what the hell? Who had put traps inside an apartment building? After a moment's consideration, Lozora reasoned that there must have been defensive measures put in when the New Science Sentries took up residency.

"Careful, the AHC might have added a few tricks around there. Can't be too dangerous, though, not in a public residence. Watch where you're going, and I'm sure you'll be fine."

"Sure" was something of an overstatement, and for a moment, Lozora felt the uncomfortable sensation of guilt slither through her. It wasn't based on morality in particular—these assets were expendable, that was the reason they were here, and she didn't tend to hold mammalian life in high regard to start. Yet she did dislike finding herself doing to others what she herself especially loathed. Keeping a team in the dark made her feel a bit too much like her employer. The man barely gave her any information to go off of, keeping nearly all the tidbits that might make her job that much easier to himself. At least they knew who the bait was versus the real target... probably.

This time, she caught part of a boom on her communicator, in the split second before it cut out. After waiting a few moments, she tapped the broadcaster to send out a wide message. "Everyone, be advised: it seems there are some traps in place. Two of our advance teams are down already."

She imagined that riled them slightly. Most had been equipped with some level of offensive equipment, although those were for when the capes arrived, making these lower-powered goons feel like real threats for a change. Only now they would start realizing that a shiny new toy wasn't enough to change the odds entirely, not in a world like theirs. There might be threats they never even saw coming, to say nothing of having time to pull a trigger.

Because of her vantage point away from the building, only Lozora saw the approach. A figure in black metal descended from the sky, coming down with unexpected grace on the sidewalk outside. For a moment, she dared hope the job might be done, only to quickly realize this wasn't the cape they were fishing for. Didn't look like any cape she knew, in fact. She might have seen a suit like that one in the Ridge City Riots footage, but who could keep track of every metal-based costume?

Regardless, this wasn't their target: only an interloper and potential cause of trouble. Luckily, that was why the pawns had been equipped. This should be a threat they could handle, with the aid of technology.

"Perimeter Team Two, there's a meta-suit that just landed near your exit. Send a few with firepower to deal with it."

Almost instantly, they came from the nearest doorway's shadows. Three of her people, all packing some manner of ranged weapon. The one at the vanguard had a red serpent tattooed along the length of his body, poking out of the neck and ending on his skull. She'd seem him bring that tattoo to life when another member of the crew spoke with disrespect; it manifested as nine feet long and incredibly venomous. And that was nothing compared to what the mini-molecule detonator he was aiming would do to all but the hardiest of flesh. Behind him were a pair of tough metas with fun guns of their own. She practically felt bad for the poor idiot who'd chosen the wrong landing point.

Running up on their quarry, they didn't bother with such pleasantries as a warning. Red Snake raised his gun, getting a line on the target, ready to shoot. Lozora was so focused on watching her people, she didn't catch the source of the beam. All she saw was the flash of light as a searing energy burst forth, sweeping along to make sure it hit all three of the approaching forms. In seconds, it was over, and what remained of Lozora's attackers was writhing on the ground.

No warning. Not even a word said. They saw a weapon aimed and responded with zero hesitation, employing what was inarguably *far* too much force. That was definitely not a cape—even the worst of them couldn't get away with that kind of response. Yet the power of the weaponry employed spoke to a professional, someone a cut above from the general rabble of ne'er-do-wells.

The only minor mercy was that, by luck or intent, the beam had been fired at a low angle, targeting the bottom halves of the would-be attackers and ensuring only some melted street in collateral damage. Lozora also noticed a lack of blood, and quickly realized that the wounds were cauterized as they formed. The end result was that all three were technically alive, for the moment, though none were as whole as they'd been moments prior.

"What the living fu—" Lozora didn't hear the rest of the message. It was cut off, though she was fairly certain her excellent ears detected something like a roar coming from within the building. More than just one, they were coming in succession. Screams, as well.

After a moment, she got a more coherent message. "Boss, something is in here! It's green, and huge, and it's breaking people in half. We can't even get a clean shot."

"Then take a dirty one," Lozora snapped. Months of work, planning, scheming, and all of it was getting immediately fucked up by some unknowns crashing the party. She didn't really care about success or failure on a personal level, but her employer would be sure to blame her for any issues, and this project represented too much work to miss out on her payday.

Like most of the crew, this member proved to be more adept than expected at following orders. Less than five seconds later, part of the building's third floor exterior wall exploded outward, sending brick and debris spraying into the empty street. The newly formed window showed Lozora a peek at what was going on, and it was not a pleasant sight. What few of her people she could even still see were either leaning on a wall or one another, clearly nursing injuries. One of them lifted a staff overhead, preparing an attack, only to go sailing back from an unseen blow. The strike carried him off his feet, and would have slammed him into a wall, if only the wall was still there.

Instead, he went sailing out the new third-story expedient exit, crashing with a wet thud on the sidewalk below. Lozora was fairly certain he'd been an extra tough meta, so there was a chance he might walk it off. The same couldn't be said for what remained of the advance teams, who'd been cut through at a rapid rate.

While Lozora was distracted, the black meta-suit had advanced, making it all the way to the front entrance. She didn't see the charge, but evidently, one of her people tried to hold the perimeter. The suit threw a punch, grabbed an arm and twisted its hips, hurling the adversary into plain view as they were tossed over the suit's shoulder, into the street. Blood ran down the goon's mouth, indicating where that first punch had landed. Walking back over, the suit leaned down, and then stomped on both of the man's elbows. Between the impact and the audible *crunch*, it was clear he wouldn't be getting back into the fray.

Much as she respected the efficient brutality, they were clipping through her pawns at a rapid rate, and the real party hadn't even kicked off yet. She was going to have to slow this down, which meant getting her own hands dirty. It would make things tougher later on, but this had to last until the cavalry was called for.

"Hephaestus!" The voice rang out from the sky, the descending form of Cyber Geek soaring into view, jet plumes firing off a pack strapped to his back. He bore down on the suit almost like he planned to crash, before pulling up short just in time, coming to a sharp halt. "What have you done?"

"Self-defense." Hephaestus, the suit's evident name, tilted their helmet down to the man still writhing in pain. "Maybe slightly aggressive self-defense."

"You call this slightly?" He motioned to the downed man, even as more were appearing from within the building, taking note of the injured among their peers.

"Look buddy, if someone points a gun at me, I'm not taking the gun. I'm taking the whole fucking arm."

Nearly on cue, one of the rabble from the building raised an impact isolater, firing at where Hephaestus and Cyber Geek were standing. The explosion of force sent Cyber Geek flying backward, causing a flicker of blue light where he landed, while Hephaestus was merely knocked back a few paces, the differences in their mass causing variant reactions.

Two more goons had their weapons at the ready, and Lozora felt a sense of relief as things got back on track. The giant wall of ice that suddenly formed, blocking line of sight between her crew and their targets, stole the relief away just as quickly. Multicolored scarves shot out from a nearby alley, ensnaring and plucking the weapons from the attackers' hands. A hulking beast of a creature ran over, scooping Cyber Geek up and putting him back on his feet.

"What's going on?" Now that she could see him better, Lozora recognized Medley, along with Hat Trick and Cold Shoulder. They'd managed to summon a team of capes, as intended, just not the right ones.

"No idea. Some kind of attack, and it doesn't seem like aliens," Cyber Geek relayed.

Scanning the field, Medley caught sight of Hephaestus and let out a growl, stepping forward before Cyber Geek's hand snagged his furry shoulder. "Hang on. He's not with them. They shot at both of us."

"Of course I'm not with them. These bastards came at me. I'm just showing them the folly of their ways." Without warning, Hephaestus fired another beam, this one directly into the ice wall. It exploded the entire structure, turning the shards of frozen water into shrapnel flying directly at the formerly gun-toting trio. This time, there was quite a lot of blood, as jagged hunks of ice didn't seal their wounds the way an energy beam did.

"Stop that!" Cyber Geek yelled, growing visibly distressed. "You're going to kill someone."

"Do you think those guns fired beams of candy canes and rainbows? Wake up, dipshit. Those people were aiming for our heads. They are not here to play the game of capes and villains. They came with a purpose and will happily leave you cold on the street if you get in their way."

So, this suit was a man named Hephaestus, and he was observant, as well as able to comprehend the true stakes on the table. A complication, no doubt about that, yet in the end, things had still worked out well enough. The targeted woman calling for help would have been ideal, as it was the least complicated version of the plan. However, there was no reason it couldn't be multiple factors that drew the New Science Sentries over: fellow capes asking for backup would be an excellent motivator.

Double-checking her laptop feed, Lozora confirmed that the AHC's resources were largely deployed. The goal was to limit how many options could even come to help; otherwise, they might end up with more unwanted additions. Based on what their systems were able to gather, the capes appeared to be stretched damn thin. For every three Wrexwren landing sites, there would be only one unit to respond. The aliens could certainly take direction well—they were overwhelming the exceptional skills of any individual cape purely by being too numerous to be effectively dealt with.

With so much to handle, the only teams likely to respond would be other capes stationed in Ridge City. Between the location and the team needing assistance, she couldn't see any possible way to stack the deck harder for getting the New Science Sentries. Since there were no more variables to tweak, that meant it was time to advance.

"Secondary team, now."

Had they possessed a capable teleporter, her first choice would have been to drop the additional troops in suddenly, with no warning. Since that was not a skill her employer possessed, however, they'd gone with another, more classic method. All around the street, car doors began to open and bodies poured out. Using the same cloaking tech they'd tested with the kidnappers, every vehicle had been fitted to hide any life signs from even the most potent of scans. In a night of pre-invasion revelry around town, it had been a simple matter to have them parked and waiting.

Just like that, the capes and Hephaestus found themselves surrounded on all sides. These were more formidable opponents, the ones considered to be not quite so easily replaced, and as such, her employer had gifted them with higher-valued equipment. If these annoyances thought all the fights would be so easy as the first wave, they would be in for quite the surprise.

"Come on, already," she muttered, idly checking the streets and sky for movement. The sooner they arrived, the sooner the real work could start. One way or another, they were going to pull the New Science Sentries here.

It was just a matter of finding the screams that would bring them running.

Chapter 106

Ducking beneath the cracked remains of a lamppost, Jean huddled in the shadows, hoping that the unnatural forms wandering nearby wouldn't notice. They'd already landed their ship in the middle of his block, opening fire on the nearby citizens with their strange, sizzling weapons. Jean was trying to slip out. He was the only one of his family here; he just *had* to move to the big city for University. Already, his mind was on the village kilometers away, hoping it was as peaceful and idyllic as his heavily panicked memory was recalling. He had to get there, had to make it away from the landing site. The Wrexwren couldn't be everywhere. It was just a matter of staying unseen.

The pair nearby were pawing at the front of a jewelry store window that had been smashed open in the chaos. One with armor in a light green hue plucked a sapphire earring from the display. It made high-pitched whistles to its magenta counterpart, who echoed similar sounds right back. Green took the gem in its eight-digited hand, then slammed the butt of its weapon down onto it, causing a spark. Lifting its arm high, Green dropped the chunks of sapphire down into its face, all the various holes opening wide to accept the offering.

Silence, then loud, sharp whistles as the green Wrexwren shook its head violently, clearly unhappy with the choice of snack. While they were distracted, Jean started to creep back, slowly and steadily shifting his feet one after another. Not too fast, focus on being silent. Every step had to be sure... which made the sudden arrival of the curb behind him so unfortunate.

Although he momentarily lost his footing, Jean managed to avoid taking a tumble. He didn't even whirl his arms or nearly keel over. What he did, however, was produce a loud yelp in the brief instant where he felt the ground slip out from under him. The moment his foot was stable, he looked back at the Wrexwren, whose heads were suddenly stiff and alert.

All efforts at planning flew away in an instant. Jean simply turned and ran for everything he was worth. Stubby legs slamming onto cobblestones marked the pace of his pursuers, and it was horrifyingly swift. They were catching up already as he took the first corner, using his knowledge of the area to aim for narrow, twisting alleys. If he could lose them on the angles and find a nook to hide inside, he might see that farm again one day after all.

Part of him wanted to look upward, to search the skies, wondering where the hell all the capes were at. What was the point of the AHC having a branch here if Sir Vitesse couldn't even marshal the superheroes into helping out? Jean already knew the answer, though. They were out there dealing with the hundreds of other ships that had come crashing to Earth. He'd just been unlucky enough to be one of the people left on their own.

Ducking along a narrow stone wall, Jean hunkered down, listening to the sounds of heavy steps now no longer dashing. Had he managed to lose them?

That delusion lasted only until the first nearby wall exploded in a shower of mortar and rubble. Ten feet over, and Jean would have been caught in the detonation. Through the gap, he could just make out the form of the Wrexwren. Magenta had a weapon still pointed at the wall, whereas Green was selecting a target. A sharp whistle and shifting head confirmed that the window had worked both ways; they'd seen Jean at the same time he spotted them. Not that it would have mattered, since they were obviously happy to destroy the whole neighborhood for the fun of running down their quarry.

Nowhere else to run, and little hope of superheroes happening by to offer salvation. This was it, then. To his surprise, Jean felt calmer than he would have expected; once the future became certain, fear was something of a useless concept. He started to lift his arms into fists, thin as they were, before thinking better of it. From the rubble, Jean lifted a hefty chunk of stone. It felt almost fitting, to fight with a rock, humanity's very first evolutionary tool pitted against these better-equipped sci-fi conquerors.

Magenta raised its weapon once more, making sure Jean knew he would have limited time to use that rock. Then, without any warning, the Wrexwren was gone. In its place was an exploded pile of viscera and organs, none of which appeared even vaguely human. Green was still there, swiveling its head around quickly. It very nearly got a guard up in time before the hulking man stepped out of the alley's shadows. The Wrexwren struggled as those meaty hands broke apart its attempts to block, this giant man gripping the whistling head like he was palming a basketball. A grunt of effort slipped out as he turned the arm—and the Wrexwren's head—steadily counter-clockwise. Several crunches and pops made it seem as if the job was done, but when he yanked at the end and took the head off entirely, there could be no doubt that the fight was definitely won.

"Anything fun?" The voice didn't come from the giant. It was further up the alley, and had spoken in English. Jean knew quite a bit from his studies, so he listened closely, unsure of whether this was truly better than what he'd been facing or not. Mindless murdering monsters were horrifying in their own right, but there were some truly scary humans out there, as well.

"More exploders, from the looks of things." The huge man hunkered down and lifted up the light green Wrexwren remains, gently plucking the weapon hanging from its claws.

"I'm not mad at that. These are pretty fun. Can definitely find some buyers once the dust has settled. I do hope we find something a little more special, though. One of these has to be their version of a higher rank with fancier gear." The second speaker having now stepped fully into view, Jean realized he was human—in appearance, if nothing else. Slim, cheerful, clad in a pinstripe suit, a Wrexwren weapon slung over his shoulder. That explained what happened to Magenta, at any rate.

The larger man let out a low harrumph. "I still wish they hadn't destroyed the outdoor market on entry. Such a waste."

"Tell you what, after we fence all this tech, let's pick up a case of truffles and snails or whatever," his friend replied.

Moving as slowly as he could manage, Jean backed away, toward a gap in the debris where he could squeeze past. Tempting as it was to run to these two for help, capes didn't rip the heads off opponents' bodies and then loot the corpses. Whoever this duo was, they represented a different meta-human element, one that Jean had no desire to learn more about.

Just as he was about to slip through the break, Jean looked up to see that the small man was standing over the puddle that had once been a magenta Wrexwren, watching him move. For a second, they held eye contact before Jean bolted, scurrying through a break in the debris and sprinting the moment he was on the other side.

It wouldn't be until several hundred meters later that he would finally slow down, and only then realize that perhaps the run might have been easier if he hadn't held on to the huge rock.

Seeing the crowd rise from the cars, Hephaestus dearly wished they hadn't left Chloe, who was going by Cliché in her makeshift costume, up on the roof. The plan made sense, in theory. Since the people attacking thought their targets were trapped in the apartment, all attention was focused on keeping them inside. By repositioning themselves to the rear and staying hidden in the halls, they were able to strike from the angles no one was expecting. Unfortunately, as the second wave reminded her, they weren't the only ones allowed to get clever. She did have to wonder, who the hell was committing this much force to what sure felt like fishing for small fries?

Weapons were being pulled, and she could see several metas drawing on their abilities, including one who appeared to be absolutely sizzling with energy. Before the battle could start in earnest, Hephaestus fired off a quick shot, right into the glowing one's torso. Anyone showing off that much would be more trouble than it was worth.

While certainly not planned, the shot did turn out to be helpful. All that crackling energy exploded out from the now dead meta, striking at the others nearby and causing momentary confusion. It was an unexpected window of opportunity; the question was what Hephaestus should do with it. If she zipped up to the roof and grabbed Cliché, they could pick through the interior stragglers, scoop up Bahamut, and get clear. Of course, that would mean leaving their home, along with Cyber Geek and his team, totally undefended.

Running was always an option—she wasn't ready to give up on fighting just yet, especially not when things were getting interesting. They did need to regroup, however.

Racing over, Hephaestus clapped Cyber Geek on the arm.

"Come on. We have to go inside. We'll be overwhelmed out here."

"What?" Cyber Geek had produced a large shield in a shower of sparks and numbers. He was trying to get between the crooks and the others before they recovered. "Why would you help us, and why would I trust you?"

"How about because neither of us has ever tried to kill the other, which I can't say about any of those assholes." Hephaestus cocked a thumb at the already recovering crowd, driving home the point. "Do you really want one more enemy in this situation when you could have an ally?"

Shots came from the goons—some bullets, some blasts of strange color, all crashing into the surroundings with various destructive effects. Cyber Geek took one right on the shield, drawing a loud beep and sparks, even as the protection held together. "I suppose that old 'enemy of my enemy' bit doesn't endure for no reason. Fine, we'll go inside with you, but if you try anything—"

"You'll scold me and call the coppers?" Hephaestus interrupted. "Save the empty threats for someone who doesn't know how capes work. Now, let's get in the damn building already."

Together, the five avoided most of the shots as they scrambled for the entrance. Too many of the shots, in fact—only Medley took a few bullets, and those didn't even break his scales. Hephaestus had a hunch they were shooting to wound, at most. If they were still holding back even after she'd wantonly been breaking their troops, then they didn't have whatever it was they wanted yet. More and more, the evidence was pointing toward this being about someone else, and it was hard to imagine who it could be other than the New Science Sentries.

Huddling in the mail room, Hephaestus clicked off her helmet's outward speaker and activated its communicator. The device was connected to a similar model expertly woven into Bahamut's mask. Since Cliché wasn't a guild villain, however, she had no such equipment on hand. They'd had to improvise a little to keep her in the loop.

"Bahamut, what's your situation? We've got reinforcements surrounding the building, and these look more competent than the last wave. Cliché, everything okay up there?" With the helmet speaker disabled, Hephaestus was effectively able to have a private conversation, despite all the capes in proximity.

"I'm okay, but there's a lot of people around us." Patching a toy walkie-talkie into their communication system hadn't been easy, but it was also a trick Tori had lots of experience with. When it came to listening in undetected, there were few things as convenient to crack as a radio signal. Guild lines were too encoded for a direct tap, but patching a signal through her helmet and relaying it to Bahamut made the whole system more or less function, at least well enough for what they needed in the moment.

After a few seconds, the deep hush of Bahamut's voice joined in. "Pretty sure I've cleaned out most of the first wave, but there's bound to be a few stragglers holed up. Have to be careful moving around inside from here on. Where do you want to regroup?"

That was an excellent question. Their own place was out, for obvious reasons. Roof would provide easy exits in a pinch, but also opened them up to fire from a distance. Given that Cliché could get them out easily enough, there was no reason to risk that yet. Ducking into a random apartment would be the easiest move, except she didn't know which ones would be occupied, and adding civilians to the mix was only going to make things messier. They needed somewhere safe, ideally secure, and not currently occupied.

Instantly, Hephaestus knew where they were heading. "Group up at the New Science Sentries' apartment. If anywhere in here has extra protections, that'll be the place, and most importantly we know it's not currently in use. Bahamut, open the door and rough up the scene so it looks like an empty place you stumbled upon mid-battle. Can't risk letting on that we know who actually lives there. Cliché, if you want to keep an eye on things up top, it's fine, but get out of there if there's even a whiff of danger."

"So far, no one seems to have noticed me," Cliché replied. "I don't mind keeping guard. It's better than watching that video stream."

"Why, what's going on with the video?" Had Ivan already lost control and gone on a rampage? That would be a surprise, but if he was wearing that mask again, then there was no telling what was on the table. Hephaestus was prepared for anything.

"It's Fornax. He's... he's losing. And it looks like it's starting to hurt."

Halted dead in her tracks by the cold chill of shock, Hephaestus realized she wasn't as "prepared for anything" as she'd thought.

Chapter 107

Zerle Salvrin delivered a blow to Ivan's stomach, slipping through his guard with those twisting movements and hurling him back against the far wall. Most metals would have dented, or at least shown a scratch after so much damage, yet their chamber remained intact no matter how many times Ivan was roughly slammed into the material.

Thus far in the fight, Ivan had learned quite a bit about Zerle Salvrin's combat abilities. The alien had prodigious strength, exceptional reflexes, an outstanding capacity to read an opponent, and one could only presume durability on par with the rest of his abilities. The reason Ivan had to make guesses on the hardiness of his opponent was that he'd yet to land a substantial blow.

Punch after punch, he would try to dodge, block, or otherwise counter, only to be slammed from some unexpected angle, clobbered across the room until he scrambled up and the whole dance began once more. There were times Zerle Salvrin could have pushed the attack but chose not to. Perhaps he was being cautious, making sure that Ivan didn't have some hidden tricks up his sleeve. Or, as one who'd clearly reached a level of strength which surpassed that of his peers, maybe Zerle Salvrin was merely savoring the chance to let loose against a sturdy opponent. It was a sentiment Ivan understood perfectly.

"What a disappointment." Zerle Salvrin's words were still coming out translated—whether for Ivan or the audience watching at home was anyone's guess. "The rumors of Earth's strength had me intrigued. There are whispers about this section of the galaxy, tales of exploratory forces that vanished entirely. Yet when we arrive, what do we find? An overconfident champion and a pitiful substitute."

The laugh that rose from his throat was not Ivan's. It was too expressive, too mad, and much too joyous. A small drop of blood slipped from the corner of his mouth, one of the small wounds this battle had already imparted. Ivan caught it with his tongue, running the red along the stretch of his teeth. It was a very familiar flavor, one that called up parts of him he'd spent decades trying to bury. He held it back, not denying what welled up within, merely halting it for the moment. This wasn't yet the time.

"You laugh?" Zerle Salvrin was confused, though it was unclear if he was wondering why Ivan was laughing, or if he was checking to see that that's what the sound was.

"I do. I laugh at you, Zerle Salvrin. I laugh at your idiocy, your ignorance, and your pride. I laugh because you still have no idea where this is going. And I laugh at your pitiful idea of strength. You cannot fathom the power we've all been struggling against, nor how we've grown as a result."

No more talking: the banter earned Ivan a fresh round of punches, this time catching him directly in the ear. He spun across the room, slapping the wall once more and sliding down. Lying there, he took a brief moment to catch his breath, eyes scanning the ceiling screen to check on Lodestar's progress. She was getting close, tearing through space at speeds no rocket could hope to match. Still going to be a while, knowing her. Even against something like that, Lodestar would try to talk. To reason. To find a way forward that didn't require violence. It was a habit that was easy to dismiss or mock, and there had been no shortage of capes or villains who'd done both through the years.

But silly an idea as it seemed, Ivan could never say that it was pointless. Because every now and then, she was right. There was a solution other than punching, a compromise to find where everyone could be satisfied. A spark of goodness in a criminal the world was willing to write off. She had her way, and Ivan could endure until the time was right.

For the show they had planned, they required a perfectly set stage. Until then, Ivan would have to deal with the beating and wait for his cue.

The alert in Tachyonic's ear came just as he finished yanking the weapons from a pair of Wrexwren clutches. Powerful as their tech was, once it was stripped away, they were only marginally stronger than regular humans, which was nowhere near powerful enough to hang with the New Science Sentries.

Agent Quantum brought down the first Wrexwren with a pair of punches, while the other tried to flee. A searing beam of energy caused the alien to skid to a halt, moments before Agent Quantum appeared overhead, dropping heavily down and subduing his second target.

Presto popped into view nearby; now that the threats were handled, he didn't have to manipulate from behind the scenes. "Okay, I tried again and felt like I was going to burst a blood vessel. These things are either way denser than they look or have some natural resistance to teleportation. I'd wipe myself out just shifting one, forget about popping them around."

Half-ignoring Presto, Tachyonic listened carefully to the message relay. It wasn't an official dispatch, technically speaking. But he'd put in a request to be notified if there was significant activity in a certain area of Ridge City. Based on the timestamp at the end, sending it over hadn't been high priority.

"Sentries, it sounds like something might be going down back at our off-site base. There was a report of a large crowd gathering, and a team was sent out to check on it. Nothing reported back yet."

"Which could mean they're busy dealing with the threat," Plasmodia suggested.

"Or that they were wiped out in an instant," Presto countered.

Agent Quantum looked over his team, first at the pair debating, then at Tachyonic himself. His gaze lingered there, briefly, before giving his oldest friend a knowing nod. "Regardless, we have a responsibility in that building, civilians we gave our word to protect. Our track record on that front has been frankly terrible. Seems like we've finally got a chance to do this right, so let's make sure we use it well."

"I'll scout. You relay our position shift and catch up." Tachyonic was gone so fast he imagined himself getting ahead of his own words, though that was impossible at his system's current settings. Nevertheless, he blasted through the increasingly familiar streets of Ridge City, along the nearly vacant highway, past the buildings of people hunkered down, until he neared the downtown section stuffed with residences, including one old apartment building that now hosted a giant hole in the third floor.

Skidding to a halt, Tachyonic resisted the urge to go in swinging, especially once he caught sight of the crowd that awaited. Dozens of people, none of whom looked friendly, wielding the same cobbled-together tech they'd been picking off the street for weeks. Except, this was no selection of minor wares; every person out there was geared up with at least one device. Some had multiple. That was without counting the ones showing clear meta-powers, like the woman hovering, or the guy talking to four frogs the size of hubcaps.

"Team, we've got more than just a group out here. Looks like someone assembled and outfitted a small army—none of them alien, at least visually." Tachyonic's speedy brain zipped through the possibilities. This organized and malicious group made it seem like something that villain's guild would be a good fit for, except he didn't recognize any of the milling faces. Based on the Ridge City Riots footage, most of the guild members had existing famous careers or were fairly distinctive, none of which applied to this rabble. It could be a meta-gang out to grab territory in the chaos, but this was a strange place to try to claim, especially considering the AHC headquarters wasn't too far off. It didn't track. There was nothing about this place valuable enough to warrant such force, which meant it was more likely about one of the building's tenants.

The most probable explanation was that they were here for the New Science Sentries. If their identities had leaked and someone figured out their address, that might explain the attack force. Only... much as Tachyonic hated to admit it, they hadn't really done anything to warrant this yet. Since arriving, the vast bulk of their time had been spent dealing with low-tier muggers and goons, not the kind of people who could access armies for vengeance. There was also the chance the crowd was here for Tori, if they were connected to the other gang and had decided to hold her responsible for the slaughter, since Nexus was well out of reach.

Over the communicators, he heard an unexpected, familiar voice pipe up. "Tachyonic, did you come into range?"

AHC communicators functioned on multiple levels, and while dedicated channels to the home base and one's team were always useful, there was also value in a simple proximity system, making sure they knew when they had allies in the area.

"Cyber Geek, is that you? What's your location?"

"Currently inside, hunkered down and figuring out what to do next. They've been like this for the last few minutes, penning us in but not advancing."

Tachyonic peeked around a corner, able to carefully scan the surroundings in a fraction of the time most would need. "It's weird. They're all staying ready to react, but there's no movement toward the front. Any idea who these jerks are? My best guesses were a gang out for revenge or part of that villain guild."

"The first is possible. The second one is probably out, though," Cyber Geek replied.

"What makes you so sure?"

"Because we've got two of that guild's members here with us, and they're both pissed about the situation."

That lined up with what little they knew about the guild—one feature of which *was* that very lack of information. If the guild did deal with internal issues, they certainly weren't public about it; this was exactly the kind of situation that drew AHC's attention. The fact that Cyber Geek was stuck with a pair of villains didn't sit well with Tachyonic, however. It was possible they were there as moles, or even the ones who'd put all of this together in the first place. He'd have liked to simply trust Cyber Geek's judgment, but with civilians in the building too, it was best to avoid chances as much as possible.

"Which two members do you have, exactly? Knowing what they can do gives us more options. I can do some quick research while the others are on their way."

"I don't imagine that will be necessary. Your team is already familiar with the skills of Hephaestus and Bahamut."

Of course—of fucking course—it would be them. Taking a moment to steady himself, Tachyonic reasoned that there were two versions of this scenario: either the villains were truly with them, or part of the attack. While the latter would be highly problematic, the flipside was that he knew those two were capable: smart, tough, and motivated to survive. If the pair really were with them for this fight, it added more to their desperately mismatched team sizes. Ten versus a small army wasn't a lot better than eight, but it *was* an improvement.

"Any sign of our mutual friends?"

"There's some sort of blockade between us and their room, with a few people already skewered on it. We assumed you'd put some defenses in. I've texted her a few times since we arrived. Seems like she and the others are sheltering in place. I warned her to keep everyone indoors and away from the windows until we give the all-clear."

A text wasn't as good as eyes-on, but in the current situation, it still took a huge burden from Tachyonic's mind. His charge was out of harm's way, which meant they'd be able to take a more offensive approach to handling the issue. Once his team arrived, they could figure out a plan of attack. Because, with so many civilians in the area, evacuation was out. Even if they could get to just Tori and her friends, there were too many others to reach. Protecting this area meant driving out the threat, and based on how armed they were, he had a hunch this crowd wouldn't respond to politely spoken requests.

"Good thinking, Cyber Geek. Let's keep them out of this as much as possible. Now, we've got about five minutes before the rest of my team will be able to catch up. That's how long we have to come up with what to do next."

It was strange, watching what looked like a parade-viewing crowd gather up on the streets below, all with their attention on her building. Cliché peered carefully over the sides of the roof in short stints, making sure not to draw their attention. Her umbrella was clutched carefully in her left hand, ready to defend if the moment demanded. The right hand, she'd left unencumbered, which was why the sudden appearance of a revolver in her fingers was such a surprise.

Spinning around, she trained the weapon on her target, only for the barrel to start immediately shaking. What the hell good was a gun supposed to do against him?

The kaleidoscope eyes of Nexus stared back at her as he cocked his head in an almost curious manner. After a moment, he snapped his fingers.

"Forewarned is forearmed. When a potential threat approached, you got a weapon. Very clever, haven't seen one of you use that in ages." He paid her and the weapon no mind, waltzing to the rooftop's edge, peering over with none of the same caution Cliché had been employing. "Shoot if you like, but I'm not here for you. You're almost never worth it."

The whiplash of going from shocked to terrified, relieved to slightly offended, had Cliché's head swimming. Lowering her gun, she dropped it to the rooftop, where it soon vanished. The umbrella, conversely, she gripped tightly, ready to swing at a moment's notice. It would likely fare as well as the gun, but it at least had a chance of working.

"What do you mean, I'm not worth it?"

He waved a hand in her general direction, eyes still on the crowd below. "What's the point in a power you go out of your way not to master? Where's the thrill in seeing someone give half their effort? Entertaining as you could potentially be, I've seen that possibility squandered untold times, because you fear what you might become."

Stepping slightly forward, Cliché tried to angle herself so she could keep a lookout over the roof's edge, too; if she wasn't keeping watch, there was no point to even staying up here. "Let me guess, this is where you tell me all my fears are ridiculous and ungrounded?"

"Certainly not. You are perceptive, with yourself, as well as others, and the potential you see is far from imagined. There are worlds where you embrace your power, plumb its fullest depths, and truly master the gifts you have been given. In some of those iterations you even manage to retain what you think of as your current sense of self. But the best of the lot, the ones I consider personal favorites, are exactly what you fear: beings cut off from the laws of reality, unbound by the same limits as the rest of the world. Sometimes, Cliché, you become an even greater monster than you can imagine, and she is *glorious*. You may be of little interest, but Edict is always worth watching."

Chapter 108

At long last, she was near enough to see, and Lodestar's stomach twisted at what awaited her. Up close—or at least as close as she could get without losing sight of the massive creature—the Scralthor was a mind-twisting array of features. The dark exterior captured and reflected the void of space, masking it near perfectly, even from the AHC's advanced instruments. Long limbs, like a mix of a spider's leg, an octopus tentacle, and a sucker mouth, stretched off the vast main body. No eyes that she could see, though it did have various plates with a slightly different reflective sheen.

The most distinguishing, disgusting feature was easily its true mouth, not the sucker-like endings on its limbs. It was easy to miss on the approach, a void within a void, the place where the Scralthor stopped reflecting space and instead embodied it. Cavernous, surrounded by endless rows of grasping teeth, seemingly with no end, that was the maw Lodestar would expect from a creature that lived by surviving off of suns. Hanging there, staring at what was closer to a celestial body than a creature in terms of mass, Lodestar was momentarily struck by the sheer impossibility of her task.

It was ludicrous—to even compare their differences as an ant versus a human drastically undersold the gap in scale. Ant versus blue whale wouldn't have even properly captured it. This was no person, or meta, or even something as grand as a natural disaster. She was gazing upon a fundamental force of the galaxy, something powerful and ancient, well beyond the constraints of what a single planet could contain.

Cupping her hands to her mouth, Lodestar let out a loud yell. She was perfectly aware that sound didn't travel through the vacuum of space under normal circumstances, but this was one more area where the limits of reality had become iffy after Professor Quantum's famous experiment. Besides, the idea of standing in this creature's path was absolute lunacy to begin with. Attempting to start a conversation wasn't really all that much more ridiculous, comparatively.

"Hey there!" Decades of this, and she never felt like she'd gotten the hang of starting the awkward pre-fight discussions. It was hard to find a cordial greeting for a being one was likely about to exchange blows with, yet she still persisted, because sometimes, those greetings were enough to keep the punches from being needed. "I don't suppose you're a talker?"

No reaction, which was more or less what Lodestar had expected. Even the ones who did eventually listen needed their attention grabbed first, and there was really only one universal method to that end. Keeping the power low, just enough to be felt, Lodestar fired off three shots at one of the limbs, which was wiggling through the sky in a very gut-churning fashion. Her shots hit their mark, but produced no reaction that she could see. Even the limb itself was unmarked. The blasts may as well have been more awkward small talk.

About what she'd anticipated; anything that was eating suns wouldn't be that vulnerable to simple energy blasts. Part of her hoped that would have been enough to garner a kernel of attention, though, and in a way, she was right. Red beams caught her directly in the torso while her attention remained on the Scralthor, pushing her back a full inch in surprise. Glancing up, she noticed the Wrexwren ships that had been leading the cosmic monstrosity were now pointing in her direction, one charging to follow the first's shot.

Moving faster than either ship could dream of tracking, she raced right past, twisting around behind the pair and letting off a shot of her own from each hand. Unlike the Scralthor, these alien crafts were not made of some nigh indestructible natural armor, a truth that was proven nicely as Lodestar sliced up their engines, leaving them both adrift until the main forces could send someone to scoop them up.

That done, she turned back to the Scralthor, which was quite easy to do, because this close, it occupied more of the space around her than less. "Just you and me now, big guy. Please give me some kind of sign that there's sentience in there." Her right hand was already formed into a fist, too aware of the inevitable outcome she was staring down. Still, she *had* to try. With power like hers, it was so easy to turn force into the default solution. Only by attempting to make peace could she truly be free to fight, certain that there was no other way available in the moment.

No response as the creature continued to swim through nothingness, path unchanged even as its guides fell by the wayside. So be it, then. Time to see how the Scralthor held up against direct strikes.

Of all the suit capabilities Hephaestus hadn't expected to need today, texting was proving to be the underdog MVP. Responding to Cyber Geek's—and soon Tachyonic's—rapid requests for assurance that she was okay was all that kept them from charging down the hall to confirm Tori's safety in person, which was a very good thing for Hephaestus and Bahamut. She added a line about spotty service to both of them, hoping that would buy some breathing room if they tried to chat mid-fight. Covertly responding inside her suit wouldn't be quite so easy while also battling for survival.

"At least we're in an older building, from when they made them to last rather than break safely." Cold Shoulder was running her hands along the exposed brick wall, getting as close as she dared to the window and scoping out a view. She nearly knocked over one of several empty ice cream containers poking out of a trash can, a caloric giveaway that someone with super-speed lived here. "Want me to ice-wall over that and limit our exposure?"

"Not yet. If anyone spots it from outside, we've basically given away our position, and right now, we need the advantage of surprise." Cyber Geek was cycling back and forth, coordinating with Tachyonic as they waited for the rest of the New Science Sentries to arrive. He'd ended up in something of a pacing circle around Austin's go-to chair, like he was trying to conjure help here faster with a slapdash summoning circle.

It was more or less the outcome they'd specifically been trying to avoid—this outdoor assemblage of assholes had managed to bait the real targets nearly into the open. Once the New Science Sentries were known to be on the scene, Hephaestus had a hunch that the rules of the game were going to change. Everything so far had been about drawing them in. Once it was time to spring the trap, there was no more need for niceties.

As Hephaestus saw it, every plan they formed would come from one of three foundations: send away the New Science Sentries and let the siege continue, use them as mobile bait to draw away the attackers, or let them join the fight. The second option was easily her favorite, and the one she knew would be all but impossible to talk anyone into. Even if they trusted her while under this helmet, there was no way the New Science Sentries would run off and leave another team of capes surrounded by criminals, in a room with a pair of villains, along with the civilians they were supposed to be protecting. Maybe, if they knew the whole situation, it would be viable, but this was one cost of living a double life: she couldn't tell people everything she knew, even when it would be extremely helpful information for them to have.

Finishing a sweep of the perimeter, Bahamut circled back around, sidling up next to Hephaestus under a giant light-up beer display that they both instinctively knew was Ike's. Medley had been watching them both without pause, barely even blinking, and they had no lack of understanding as to why: he expected them to turn traitor at any moment. In truth, Hephaestus couldn't even say it was a farfetched concept. Her goal was to get everyone she liked through this day alive; whether or not they were fond of the meta-suit-wearing villain in the end wasn't a central part of that equation. It did mean they had to choose every word carefully, though, since these were going to be very public conversations.

"How's the fight going?" Bahamut asked.

The short answer was "bad." A small section of the helmet's inner screen was showing a muted version of the fight stream, and when Hephaestus could bring herself to look, what she saw was her mentor getting smacked around, thrown into walls, even dripping blood. Part of her kept insisting that this had to be a trick, part of some grand villain scheme, but the bright streaks of red made that idea harder to cling to. The mere fact that the Wrexwren leader could even make Fornax bleed spoke to the power in those alien blows.

"The same," Hephaestus replied finally. "I'm sure he's got a plan."

That garnered a snort from Medley. "If that's the real Fornax, then I doubt it. His whole deal was being a walking disaster. He isn't one to plan, and sure not the sort to get his ass kicked by a lone alien. That's either a fake, or he's gone soft."

"You have—and I cannot stress this enough—absolutely no *fucking* idea what you're talking about." She was coming back at him too hard, could even feel herself doing it, yet the rage couldn't be stopped. It wasn't even anger, really, just fear. The oldest fear she had, the one she thought would never apply to someone like Ivan: she was afraid to lose a person she cared about, and the semi-parental shape of their relationship only made the ache hit all the deeper. "That's the real Fornax, and he's going to win. It's what he does. There's only one exception to that rule, and it sure as shit isn't that Wrexwren bastard."

"I'm sure he'll be fine." Hat Trick wandered over, laying a careful hand on Hephaestus's arm. The rest kept their distance from Hephaestus and Bahamut, but she seemed entirely unconcerned by their villain status. "Lodestar wouldn't have left it in his hands otherwise."

Still positioned semi-near the window, Cold Shoulder shook her head. "Didn't seem like she had much of a choice in the matter."

"When you're as powerful as they are, you always have choices," Bahamut said. "For right now, let's trust that the ones more experienced than us are making smart calls, even if we can't grasp their significance yet. Our bigger concern is the mini-army outside. With Agent Quantum, myself, and Medley on the scene, we have a good amount of heavy hitters, plus Cold Shoulder if she makes that big ice body. Plasmodia and Hephaestus can snipe for us, putting Presto, Tachyonic, and Hat Trick in flex positions. Cyber Geek, given your array of tools, I'd assume you can fill any of those roles as needed, so let's decide where we're weakest and shore things up."

Nearby, Cyber Geek blinked in visible surprise. "That's surprisingly close to what Tachyonic and I have come up with."

"I know." Bahamut tapped the side of her head, where ears would be. She seemed to realize the absence at the same time as everyone else. "Er, you get what I mean. Good hearing, even for hushed phone conversations, and it's not a hard composition to sort out."

"The bigger question is what do we do with those teams?" Medley interjected. "How do we drive off this mob while not plunging everyone on this block into a meta-brawl?"

That was an exceptional point, but thankfully, one Hephaestus already saw the fix for. "While we don't know for sure what or who they want, it's clearly all focused on this building. If the New Science Sentries join us, it ensures that the focus stays trained here. At that point, it becomes a game of funneling them where we can and picking through. Snipers on the roofline to keep them from swarming, heavies in the halls to block their progress, and so on."

"Too risky," Cyber Geek replied. "Holing up while under fire is one thing, but we can't bring a brawl inside knowing there are also civilians sheltering here, too."

Between seeing her mentor getting beaten and feeling trapped in her own home, Hephaestus was not in a patient enough mood to deal with moral objections. This was a survival situation. "Then you get out there and scare them off, superhero. You go show us whatever power you have that's going to send them screaming into the night. Because as far as I can tell, they're here to do some damage, and aren't inclined to leave. This fight is happening, Cyber Geek. The question is if it's on our terms, or theirs."

"That said, we do have another asset in the building, unofficially. A friend who is pitching in, and could theoretically guide the survivors somewhere safe," Bahamut offered. "I believe a lot of the underground parking spots here are concrete-enclosed cubes, the perfect spot for hiding out from a riotous mob."

Cyber Geek and his team looked at one another, the unspoken question so obvious they may as well have just used words. Trusting the villains was one thing; trusting the villains to handle evacuation, and with an asset they'd never even met—that was asking a lot. Especially considering that the capes believed they had friends hiding out in another room, as well.

"When the Ridge City Riots happened, we ended up having to work with a different pair of villains, Glyph and Pest Control," Medley stated. "I didn't like it at the time. Still don't fully, to be frank, but I can't say they didn't hold up their end of the bargain. If you can be like them, then we can walk away from all of this on the same terms. But if you betray us—"

"You'll carry a grudge that will shine through all eternity and will harass us at every turn until one or both parties are dead. Yeah, man, I'm in a guild of villains. How do you *think* the people I'm around respond to being betrayed? Our friend will get people somewhere safe; they've got ways of moving around and staying unseen. Will that put you at ease enough to accept the inevitable?"

Surprisingly, Cyber Geek nodded to the affirmative. "According to Tachyonic, the rest of the New Science Sentries just arrived, and the outer crowd is getting restless, starting to look at nearby buildings. We have to get their attention and keep it. Everyone ready?"

He looked around, first to his team, then to the pair of villains sharing the room with them. No one objected. They understood where this was heading and were ready to stop cowering.

"Let's go over starting positions, then get into them as fast as we can. The New Science Sentries are going to arrive with a splash. While we wait, let's put that free-roaming asset of yours to work. There's an apartment near here you'll need to start with."

"Should be no problem," Hephaestus confirmed. She said a silent prayer of thanks to Bahamut, who'd just made their lives much, much easier. Not only would “moving” Tori out of supposed proximity lower her chances of being caught, it came with a perfect excuse to let the texting drop. Once her other identity was expected to be surrounded by concrete, even the best phone would have trouble keeping a signal. This was a chance to put Tori out of the way and let Hephaestus have full rein.

She only hoped their efforts fared better than Fornax’s had so far.

Chapter 109

The sound of Wrexwren mirth was grating on Doctor Mechaniacal's nerves, aided in no small part by watching his oldest friend get beat to hell. The experience couldn't be pleasant for anyone who cared about Ivan, yet Doctor Mechaniacal felt it all the more keenly, because it was *his* fault. While the plan had placed huge burdens on others, like Ivan, it was Doctor Mechaniacal and Xelas who were handling the most important piece. Without them, this invasion would simply end, and that would be that. The prime opportunity they'd been handed would slip away, and in a few months, they'd be dancing the same jig with a new set of challengers.

That was why he made no objection or sounds of his own as the Wrexwren let out their whistling titters at Fornax's beating. There was better use for such mental energy. Because while it appeared that he and Xelas were standing there like good little escorts, watching what looked to be an inevitable defeat, in truth, they were both hard at work. Getting access to the systems had only been the first step. From there, it was a matter of finding what they needed, running digital tests until they found the right settings, and then making sure the implementation was flawless. Given that they were working with alien technology, it was an insane idea, even for meta-genius intellect like his own.

Now, two meta-genius intellects, with years of experience and trust deepening their connection, working in perfect tandem—*that* was another story. For as rambunctious as she could be, Xelas also possessed one of the most sophisticated digital minds in existence, thanks largely to years of self-directed upgrades and improvements. With her considerable processing power added in, the task went from "utterly impossible" to just "mostly impossible," and those were odds Doctor Mechaniacal felt quite at home with. Especially considering the progress they were making.

A little bit more. Ivan just had to hang in there for a touch longer, and things would change. He hoped the rest of the guild was out there working hard in this window, because once their plan sprang, the Wrexwren would start behaving very differently. Better to grab all they could before the aliens realized the situation they were really in. At least he didn't have to worry about most of them getting caught up in the streaming show; they knew Fornax well enough not to expect he'd really go down like this. But based on the numbers ticking by on his helmet screen, quite a few people were tuning in.

That was just as expected, and planned. Seeing Fornax lose would certainly be curious and novel enough to draw more viewers, expanding the size of their audience. They needed to set the stage well and get as many live eyes as possible on the broadcast—the AHC would definitely attempt to purge this footage once the day was done.

And really, given how horrific it would be, Doctor Mechaniacal wasn't even sure he blamed them.

The small town of Kerber was nestled perfectly between two highways, so as to be convenient for neither. Once it had held a key farm road running through it, but when the new interstate came, the travel business in the town dried up. It managed to hang on thanks to stubborn citizens and enough agriculture to get by, but it would never be a major metropolis. They had no Alliance of Heroic Champions outpost, no superheroes nearby, not even a meta-human among the population. Their law enforcement consisted of a small Sheriff's outpost, most of which was already burning.

With no real defenses, the town of Kerber had been completely unprepared when a Wrexwren ship crashed into Old Man Gaffleston's cornfield. Four had emerged, wielding unnatural weapons and whistling in those horrific high-pitched tones. They swept like fire, destroying all they came across as the citizens fled, most holing up in the church near the edge of town.

One member of the city did not go to the church, however. Mrs. Croskey cursed her age as the uphill walk sapped her legs' strength. She pushed herself onward, ignoring the sounds of buildings collapsing and the Wrexwren whistles, even as it seemed like they were getting closer. Roots tore at her feet, nearly tripping her twice as she pressed farther into the small grove. The third time, she fully tilted over, catching herself on a nearby tree trunk, scraping her hand badly in the process.

The pain didn't matter, nor did the ache in her lungs. She had to keep going. This was the town's only hope. None of the others knew such a chance existed; they believed their only meta-residents in history had left, never to return. Only Mrs. Croskey had gotten the visit years later, along with the gift. She'd buried it away, thinking such things best left forgotten. It was an act she regretted all the more with every step.

At last, Mrs. Croskey arrived. Her thin, wrinkled hands plunged into the dirt beneath the gnarled old tree, winding into a small gap of two intertwined roots. The Wrexwren noises were drawing near. If they found her, then they found her. What mattered was the task at hand. Arms already shaking from the overall effort, Mrs. Croskey kept digging, kept hoping, until she felt the cold metal of the box she was searching for.

With the last of her strength, she yanked it out, turning the combination tumblers to their proper position, all while hearing the aliens approach. It took more struggling than she wanted, but finally, the box opened, revealing a small silver device with a single button. On it was a stylized droplet of blood, which was soon covered by the smear of the genuine article Mrs. Croskey's scraped hand left as she smashed the button down, drawing a brief light under the symbol.

It was done. She collapsed back against a nearby tree, panting so heavily it felt like she might never catch her breath. That was possible. Her body had given too much in the run; perhaps the cost would overwhelm her. It was far from ideal, yet also a chance Mrs. Croskey knew she'd been taking. Her only wish was that she knew everyone would be safe. Devices and promises were one thing, but could she really expect that after so long—

"I'm going to need some field healing. No, a civilian. That's fine. I'll go out of pocket. This one is under my protection."

It was impossible. She'd hit the button less than a minute ago—surely this was a delusion. Yet it seemed quite real as the shadow leaned over, then crouched to look Mrs. Croskey right in the eye. In the years since she'd last seen that gaze, much had changed, but not the determination looking back at her.

"How did you get here... so fast?" The pause for breath mid-question only drove home how depleted Mrs. Croskey was.

"I've got friends who are handy at transportation, and I promised that if you needed me, I'd be here."

"The town... needs you."

That earned Mrs. Croskey a frown, along with a resigned sigh. "Fine. But keep my name out of it, if you can. I don't want them thinking it's some bit of hometown pride. Personally, they could raze this place and I wouldn't bat an eye." She leaned in, lightly kissing the older woman on the forehead. "Except I know how much it would hurt you."

She stood back to her full height, then lifted a finger. From the wound on Mrs. Croskey's hand came a small tendril of blood, which wound its way around Morgana Le Faye's finger, before shaping itself into a dagger. The Blood Witch of the villains' guild clutched her weapon tightly, then turned back to the forest.

"Now then, let's deal with the dead pieces of shit who dared to wound my favorite teacher."

Agent Quantum looked up at the roof again and frowned. "You sure you can get an angle on that? Seems like the closest point we can see would have you both dropping a good distance to the ground below, not to mention drawing attention."

"Have a little faith. This is my one trick, and I'm pretty damn good at it," Presto replied. "I'll squeak us over the edge of the roof so we don't have far to go. There's no way around the visibility part, though. If I can see it, then I can teleport there, but I do *have* to see it. Which means when we pop out, we'll be in plain view before the fall starts."

"Which is exactly why, when they do that, you and I are charging in the front door." Tachyonic was fiddling with his bracer, getting the output settings just right. Once this battle started, there wouldn't be many chances for casual recalibration, so it was important he start off properly. "I'll run defense, you go right for the entrance. Once we're in, the roof team starts laying down cover, breaking up the crowds that charge after us. Plasmodia, you still okay getting teamed with a villain?"

She hesitated for only a small moment before giving a blonde-hair-bouncing nod. "Not ideal, but what about this is? So long as he keeps shooting at the people attacking, we'll be good. If he tries anything, I'll pop that can open and see how tough our villain is then."

The four superheroes exchanged glances once more, before looking out to the small army blocking them from their goal. It was not the first time they'd faced such a situation, if one counted training. Professor Quantum had been relentless in preparing them for what he considered to be the most vital part of superhero work: efficiently neutralizing threats. After weeks in the real world, they'd begun to understand all the gaps such training had left in their knowledge, gaps that had caused the sorts of mistakes that had put them on the wrong foot with this town. But for all their failings, the New Science Sentries still knew how to fight. Today, it looked as though they might finally have a chance to work in their element.

Slowly, one by one, the eyes all turned to Agent Quantum, their unquestioned leader. Not because he was the most dangerous, which went to Plasmodia, or the fastest, obviously Tachyonic, or even the most perceptive, a title all would begrudgingly give to Presto. Not even because he was the one chosen by Professor Quantum to head the team.

Agent Quantum was their leader because, above all else, he had their trust. They believed in him, in the way he saw the world, in the team he wanted to lead. He might not always lead them to safety—that was the price of being a superhero—but each knew he would give every drop of blood in his veins to bring them back alive, and the feeling was reciprocated.

"The time is here. New Science Sentries: attack."

In terms of rallying cries, there was room for improvement, but the results could hardly be questioned. Agent Quantum and Tachyonic burst from their hiding place, loudly drawing attention in a way no real attackers would. The plan worked flawlessly, as suddenly, dozens of heads swiveled in their direction. Worse, they didn't just turn, the faces reacted. Lit up, in fact, at the sight of what should have been a sign that the party was over. Instead, they all looked like someone was rolling in with a truck of fresh food and drink, a few actually rubbing their palms together like greedy cartoon characters.

Nearby, Agent Quantum caught sight of several raising their unusual weapons—these resembled junkyard scraps welded into roughly gun-like shapes, similar to what they'd seen on the streets lately. None of them got raised higher than mid-waist before the blur zipping through the crowd struck. Sometimes it knocked the guns away; others received swift kicks to the back of their knees to send them sprawling; and a few just got flat-out coldcocked into unconsciousness. Agent Quantum had no idea how Tachyonic was picking which target to give which strategy; perhaps he was trying all three on each person and seeing what worked. It had to be taxing. Even with his speed, there were so many opponents to keep track of.

Agent Quantum made the job as easy on his teammate as he could, weaving wide to avoid fights and focus on speed. Some confrontations were unavoidable, however, as a one-eyed man with horns along his skull tried to halt Agent Quantum's charge. Tough as he looked, a single blow to the ribs was enough to send him hurling back, and Agent Quantum realized he'd forgotten to factor his current momentum into the punch. It was stronger than needed, but had the side effect of scaring a few nearby threats, so Agent Quantum seized the opportunity and bolted ahead.

He glanced up to the roofline just in time to catch Plasmodia's legs going over the side, out of view. That meant the sniper team was now in position, and no one appeared to be reacting to the roof, so hopefully, they'd slipped by unseen. With the distraction done, his only task remaining was to make it through the front door.

Pumping his legs, Agent Quantum didn't bother hitting the next person who jumped in his way, mostly because he'd plowed over them before there was even a chance to react. Something stung his back, fluorescent yellow strings that seemed to sear wherever they touched extending from a nearby crook's arm. It was tempting to deal with, but the lone glance back showed Agent Quantum how many of the momentarily stunned enemies were recovering both their wits and their weapons, all with their attention on him.

With the top speed he could muster, Agent Quantum barreled ahead, lowering his shoulder and knocking aside a few hefty gentlemen that tried to block him with mere mass. The effect was similar to a bowling ball cleaving through pins, sending them scattering and opening up a clear path inside. Agent Quantum took it, continuing to bolt forward until he turned a corner and nearly collided with a scaly green wall.

Except, it wasn't actually a wall. It was Bahamut, the dragon who'd managed to fight him to a stalemate only a few weeks earlier. Normally, Agent Quantum wouldn't have been so happy to see someone so dangerous, but if they were going to team with villains, better they at least pull their own weight.

"Agent Quantum," the dragon greeted. "You should follow me. There's quite a few people on your heels, and this isn't the place to deal with them."

Lozora didn't especially care about how they'd done it. All that mattered was that the New Science Sentries had gotten inside. Really, she'd done everything but leave a neon sign and a key in the lock, but they'd managed it eventually. With them in position, the preamble could finally come to an end. It was time to get down to business.

On her phone, she sent a single message: "The piñata is stuffed." With that, her employer was officially notified. Nearby, blocking devices keyed to specific signals engaged, triggered by her message. In other parts of the city, different teams were turned loose, creating a buffer of crime in case any passing patrol might head their way. The capes wouldn't be able to call for any more backup. From this point on, they were stuck with what they had until the man who'd put it all together arrived. She still wasn't sure how he would make the approach—perhaps by air, or maybe burrowing up from under the street. It wouldn't really even shock her if he simply walked out of a coffee shop and strolled up to the front door. The man loved to keep secrets, even from those in his employ, and that included his own entry methods. It didn't especially matter; Lozora had kept her end of the bargain and brought the target into the trap. If her employer failed from this point on, there was no one to blame but himself.

Nevertheless, she still rose and prepared to take a more active role if needed. Whether the blame would be deserved or not, she'd dealt with enough despots to know they rarely saw fault within themselves. Making sure this stayed on the rails was how she ensured there were no snafus in her payday.

Besides, after working so hard to put this piece on the board, there was no way Lozora was going to miss the actual game.

Chapter 110

It was kind of like watching the inception of a parade. As Agent Quantum ran, the rest of the crowd came alive, realizing something of note was happening. If there'd been any doubt in Hephaestus's mind who they were here for, it vanished at the obvious reactions from the hodgepodge army. This was their target all right, and they pursued him with the gusto one would expect after so much milling around. Together, they surged forward on his heels, slowed by their own numbers but giving chase nonetheless, forming a river of bodies in Agent Quantum's wake.

The gauntlets were primed and ready, and from the glow rippling off Plasmodia, she was in a similar state. Cyber Geek sat posted up on the actual edge of the roof, hidden by a cloak he'd pulled out as he kept an eye on the goings on through the scope on his huge *Blaster Brahs* gun. Only Presto didn't look ready to fire, since he had an entirely different job to do.

"Once Agent Quantum and Tachyonic are clear, aim for the middle of the crowd. Let's break them up and limit how many get inside." Cyber Geek gave the orders, since obviously the villains weren't being trusted to *that* extent, though Hephaestus had no objection to the situation. Between the two of them, Cyber Geek had logged far more hours in actual combat with just this last year, to say nothing of Donald's love for games that required tactics and strategy. And it meant she was free to break off if need be without leaving them in the lurch. "Remember, stunning shots only."

That last bit was obviously directed at Hephaestus, who rolled her eyes even though no one else could see through the helmet. "I bet that's what all their weapons are set at, too."

"Doesn't matter," Cyber Geek rebutted. "We aren't them. We're superheroes. No more bloodshed than is absolutely necessary."

There was the end of their discussion, as Agent Quantum finally made it through the front door, a blur on his heels less than a second later. No one needed the cue—they'd all just gotten it—and almost in unison, the shots burst forth.

Hephaestus's gauntlet beams didn't really have a "stun" setting, so instead, she fired a few feet in front of the crowd, creating visible damage in the concrete and pulling most of them up short. Some kept right on going, only to be smacked aside by bright bolts blasting out of Plasmodia's hands. Based on how hard they were being sent flying from those shots, Hephaestus had a hunch they were only just barely on the non-lethal side, perhaps the weakest Plasmodia could manage.

For the bulk of the group that stopped at the sight of Hephaestus's beams, Cyber Geek had something special. He fired directly into the center of them, releasing an explosion of crackling blue light that sent nearly every crook hit down to the ground, twitching. They couldn't have asked for a better opening shot, which was a good thing, because with eyes twisting upward, their advantage of surprise was officially spent.

No more freebies. Now, they were getting fired back on. Chunks of brick exploded into the air as they all ducked down, save for the lone member who hadn't fired a single shot yet. Smacking his hands on his costume's pants, Presto tilted his head up to the sky. "Looks like that's my cue."

He vanished, reappearing some distance off, much higher up. That position lasted only a moment before he was gone again. Hephaestus carefully approached the roof's edge as the shots tapered off, poking her helmet up while making sure to stay in flame form inside, just to be safe. What greeted her was a scene of masterful chaos.

Presto was there, popping around, moving the crooks along with him. Whenever he saw one taking aim to shoot, they'd suddenly find themselves reoriented, firing into a fellow criminal. Not only were they taking one another out, but the ersatz betrayals were causing fights among their ranks. He darted around like that for nearly a full minute before vanishing, only to reappear overhead, then pop directly to their sides once more.

"That should give you all a little breathing room. We can do this trick maybe twice more before they wise up and really focus fire on the roof. Also, heads up to the indoor team, I saw a few slipping in the front during the confusion." While he kept the panting out of his voice, Presto's chest was rising and falling quickly—using so much power had left him winded.

"Good. It means we're doing our job right," Plasmodia said. "Break them up into manageable chunks for the rest to handle."

Hephaestus tilted a head to the well-manicured hands that were rippling with energy. "I think you could break them into literal chunks. Those sure seem easier to handle."

"I told you, we're not doing that," Cyber Geek snapped.

"You say that now, while things are going well. What if the tide starts to turn? What are you willing to do when your team's lives are at risk?"

She'd expected another canned reply, but that was her own failing. This was not just a generic cape, no matter how often he could fall into the habits of one. Donald Moss was a man who loved superheroes, yes, but who also thought deeply about the things he did. "I know that sometimes, there is no getting around a lethal shot in this job. I had to kill an interdimensional monster on my first time out, but that same situation could have easily happened with a meta-human. Even Lodestar has had to throw that final punch a few times. Whether or not it's in me to kill another person, I don't think I'll know until the moment comes, but I refuse to take that step a single moment before it becomes absolutely necessary."

"Agent Quantum would make the same call." It was perhaps the first time Hephaestus had noticed Plasmodia really look at Cyber Geek since arriving on the roof.

Even Presto seemed a tad impressed, if one paid more attention to his tone than his words. "Yeesh, now we've got another of them to compensate for."

There was clearly no winning this battle, so Hephaestus opted to let it go, though she couldn't resist one final bit of parting wisdom. "I admire your resolution and dedication to your ideals. Just remember, there's a cost to taking the high road."

Cyber Geek's eyebrows pinched as he pointedly looked up and down the armored suit. "As opposed to your way?"

"Oh no, my road has its own costs, too. I imagine they all do." Hephaestus returned to the roofline, gauntlets charged to fire once more. "But I live my life prepared to pay them. Be sure you're ready to do the same."

This was, in Medley's estimation, total bullshit. Being behind Agent Quantum's combat skills had been one thing. He was the inheritor of a legacy team, and had clearly been provided with ample training as part of that. The fact that Medley could fight on nearly the same level was almost a point of pride, even if Agent Quantum was clearly ahead. But now, before his eyes, Medley was realizing that he wasn't the second strongest member of this motley combat team: he was third.

As it turned out, Bahamut was quite a great deal more adept at brawling than Hephaestus. While the former used his suit's bulk and weapons to make up for gaps in skill, Bahamut had no such failings to cover. Despite the size, he was quick and sure, cracking the man emitting smoke from his ears hard in the ribs, sending him tumbling to the ground. A huge fellow with some kind of cobbled-together electro-axe swung for Bahamut's flank while he should have been distracted, except the green dragon ducked under the blow, striking back with a kick to the knees that earned a horrific yowl from the axe-wielder as he crumpled to the ground.

It was to Medley's disadvantage that he was on the side of the capes in this contest. Unlike Bahamut, he and Agent Quantum were putting their targets down with as little damage as they could manage, while the dragon seemed to be paying a passing effort at most to not being lethal. Near Agent Quantum, a goon produced dripping purple blades from his arms, angling them directly for the cape. He never even came close, as Bahamut grabbed him from behind, spun the man's arms, and sank both blades into the limbs of two other crooks, both of whom dropped to the ground immediately.

"Oh, that stuff is dangerous," Bahamut noted. He twisted the arms inward, the captive struggling vainly against the dragon's superior might, until the blades were plunged into the wielder's own legs. While it did appear to hurt, he didn't have the same reaction as the first pair.

"Stupid fucking lizard, of course I'm immune to my own poison."

"Guess that does make sense." The *crack* turned Medley's stomach, even before he looked to confirm. Sure enough, Bahamut had snapped poison-blade's arms at the elbow; both were hanging limply at his sides. "Looks like you're not immune to broken bones, though. Or concussions."

That was the only warning before Bahamut's fist smashed into his face, sending the broken man flying back into a wall, where he wouldn't be able to sneak up on them with those potent blades. Agent Quantum looked aghast, but in the midst of a fray, he didn't exactly have the spare time to object.

As for Medley, he deflected a pair of bone-daggers hurled by one of his nearest opponents, then noticed they were still airborne, floating around to his rear. Somebody was pairing with a telekinetic; a smart combination, but less useful once noticed. Medley dropped to a crouch, his body's natural pouncing position, then leapt, jumping over the bone thrower to an inconspicuous invader who'd been hanging to the sides. A surprised face, one swift punch, and just like that, the daggers clattered down once more. The physical threats were straightforward to deal with; they had to handle anyone who could throw curves as soon as possible.

So far, things had been going well. In fact, they'd gone so well that Medley didn't trust it. In the months since he'd been changed and joined the Alliance of Heroic Champions, there had been a great many lessons to learn; one of the earliest was that battles never went to plan. Out in the field, things were chaotic, messy, unpredictable. Plans were meant to be shapes of things, general guides to trust and use as a compass. Details always shifted on the fly. Yet somehow, while totally surrounded and trapped, it was all working flawlessly. The outer team was slowing the slew of entrants enough to where just three of their fighters could handle it, and apparently, none of the crooks considered the idea of taking another route inside.

No, something was definitely off. The only way things went this well if it was a piece of *both* parties' plans. Except, Medley couldn't see what gain there was to this setup. How did letting them whittle away at the troops help whoever had put this all together? Were the bodies booby-trapped, or rigged to suddenly regain consciousness and heal? They smelled normal enough, so far as he could tell, but with metas, there was never truly a way to be sure.

Unfortunately, Medley's only current available tactic was the "wait and see" move. Once he knew what the point of all this was, he could start working more directly against whoever was pulling the strings. Until then, he had to play the game long enough to reach the end, which meant keeping up with Agent Quantum and Bahamut as they took down new threats.

Tachyonic appeared in the room, zipping in from another hallway. "You've got a team on the way. I took out two of them, but three more are still coming. A new group just entered—I'll lead them around a bit until you're clear." As quickly as he'd arrived, the speedster was gone, back to running in-building interference.

That, like everything else, was working well. Medley had a hunch that things would continue to keep going their way, until the trend very abruptly stopped. Sooner or later, the synchronized plans would diverge, and these criminals' real goal would come into focus. When that moment arrived was when the deadliest part of the fight began.

The Wrexwren ship was flying over a long stretch of ocean, searching for a viable landing target, when a message hit their comms system. It was from another Wrexwren vessel, reporting that they'd discovered an excellent find not far away. Little defense, ample resources, even natural features that would make a sustained occupation more viable; they were calling for reinforcements to help raid and hold their discovery. Redirecting course, the pilot angled for the other ship's beacon, homing in and locking the location.

In a matter of minutes, they'd shot across the sky, arriving at what appeared to be a huge chunk of land surrounded by ocean—an island, as the humans called them. This island had a great many human-built structures, the most striking of which was a massive castle that gleamed wherever light struck, metal coating most, if not all, of its surface. The Wrexwren pilot looked to the rest of his crew; this was certainly not what the transmission had promised. Something was amiss, and with no backup anywhere nearby, the prudent call was to evacuate.

As he tried to steer them away from the island, however, it became clear that the ship was no longer in control of its own movements. Below, they could see energy lashes dig into the sides of their vessel, pulling it roughly down from the sky, onto a metal pad waiting below. They prepared themselves for combat, readying weapons to make a final stand and show these humans the might of the Wrexwren fighting spirit.

Sadly, such a fight was never to occur. When the ship got with fifteen feet of the circle below, a pulse shot up, delivering a tremendous dose of electrical current to everything inside it. Some of the Wrexwren initially survived, but they had no time to recover before the ship was pulled all the way down and the roof roughly opened. Mechanical limbs reached in, yanking out the pilot's crew as he struggled vainly to reach for them, arms barely even capable of a twitch.

"Looks like we've got one that can still move. Put him in the observation tank. The rest are dead or dying—get them directly to our dissection room. Our leader wants these as fresh as possible."

Above the Wrexwren, a human face appeared, looking at him with none of the typical sentiment they'd been told to expect from this species. The human examined him once, then moved its skull in a side-to-side motion. "Really, if you're falling for tricks this simple, someone really must have fed you a lot of misinformation about Earth. Did they paint us a simple rubes in the backwater of the galaxy, huddling together out of fear of the unknown? Our planet is much like this place, the island built by Tyranny. Lovely to gaze at, yet so much more deadly than appearances would ever let on."

The human made a noise, a light series of expulsions from its mouth—perhaps this was their version of laughter. “I’m sure that sounds ridiculous to a mighty invader like yourself, but in time, I think you’ll understand. You see, the ones currently being dragged away were fortunate. For them, this nightmare is already done. Fate was not nearly so kind to you.” He leaned back, motioning to someone unseen. “All right, get him moving. We need to reset the trap for the next batch.”

Metal reached into the cab, tearing the Wrexwren pilot out of his seat, dragging him into the damp Earth air as his screeching whistles echoed through the night.

Chapter 111

Where in the hell was he? All this work, weeks of scheming, planning, luring in an entire alien invasion to serve as a distraction, and now, when the goal was at hand, her employer was late? That didn't track. No way would he miss this. Catching the New Science Sentries had been all he focused on, the lone goal driving every action. Something was up, and Lozora didn't like it, especially when she'd yet to be paid.

Finishing her coffee, she dropped a few bills on the table and rose, striding out to the street all other civilians were steering clear of. Shots rained down from the apartment building's rooftop, receiving return fire that tore at the brick exterior of the building. Real guns would have little to no impact, which was why her crew was outfitted with more effective options. Given enough time, they could clear out the whole wall running along the roofline. Hence why the capes shooting back were being certain not to give the gang that kind of opportunity.

Lozora moved easily through the road, steering clear of the brawl like any normal person would. She slipped up a few streets, circling around and coming at the building from the other side. A few others could be spotted using the same tactic, though for the most part, everyone was sticking at the front. Well, they hadn't been hired for their on-the-job thinking skills. Mostly, they were just intended to be fodder, though for what purpose still remained a mystery to her. Unlike the others, she went unnoticed until reaching the building itself. Using her strength, it was a small matter to scurry up the exterior to a second-story window, then smash her way inside.

She'd chosen a dark apartment, and it appeared to be currently unoccupied, which was perfect. Lozora wasn't necessarily going to join the battle—that wasn't what she'd been contracted for—but she had no intention of letting her employer get everything he wanted and then skip out on the bill. For as little as she knew about his plans as a whole, one way or another, it would end with the New Science Sentries. So long as she stayed near them, her employer would turn up.

Until then, it was a matter of laying low. When he inevitably arrived, there was truly no telling what might happen, save only that the New Science Sentries were unlikely to survive it.

Finally.

Doctor Mechaniacal reran the simulation again and again, testing external variables for differing results, yet none of it seemed to matter. So long as the meltdown process was started properly, minor details like position and active velocity had no impact whatsoever. They'd found their move, but there were still a few more details to handle. It wouldn't do to give away the turn too early.

The first preparation step was to take control of the ship's communications. Blocking the signals from Earth had been a minor chore to set up before they left; this was quite a bit more comprehensive. From the Wrexwren version of cameras currently trained on Lodestar, to the actual signals being relayed between ships, Doctor Mechaniacal took control of every last scrap. As of this moment, the Wrexwren on the main vessel would see and hear only what he permitted.

With that done, he scanned the general chatter as Xelas dummied up a few programs to simulate the same amount of mid-battle noise. It wouldn't fool anyone truly perceptive, and even the slower ones would catch on eventually, but it wasn't as if this charade needed to stand the test of time. It didn't particularly matter if they saw through it, really; the damage would be done, except this would give Fornax a more powerful tool to use when the time was right.

Control established, preparations in place, and the right sequence discovered. There was no need for he or Xelas to move their physical heads, not when they were already working together so closely in digital space. They did pause for a moment to confer, making completely sure that both were ready to proceed. Once they made the call, there was no turning back on multiple fronts.

Together, unseen by any of the Wrexwren who were still laughing as they watched Zerle Salvrin smack around Fornax, Doctor Mechaniacal and Xelas activated their creation.

It was, at its heart, only a signal. A signal carrying specific programming, one designed to bypass the Wrexwren security completely and cause a series of sequential activations within the engines. Just a signal, yet with it, the Wrexwren invasion functionally came to an end, even if it would take the aliens some time to fully understand the loss they'd incurred. Most would die with no idea of what had even happened—a small blessing that proved Doctor Mechaniacal wasn't entirely heartless.

Since there was no more need to play nice, he and Xelas both raised their weapons, unnoticed by the Wrexwren who'd written them both off entirely. A few bright flashes and some whistle-screams, then they were alone, that annoying rabble of laughter muted at long last. It felt good, but not nearly so fine as the sensation of broadcasting a message to his friend's ears, letting him know the first part of the fight was over. No more sandbagging.

"Fornax, this is Doctor Mechaniacal. Injury has been accomplished. You are free to proceed with adding Insult."

Despite the distance, she saw them go. Lodestar was burning bright with power, operating at what most of the world thought to be her maximum. They were close on that front, as this was what she considered to be her terrestrial maximum—things got dangerous if she swung much more power than this around while planet-side. But the truth was, so far as she knew, a Lodestar had no true limit. There was always more power to be drawn. The only question was how much of the person would remain afterward.

Using her power was like stealing some primal force of the universe to make herself bigger, in a metaphysical sense rather than a literal one. The more she drew, the greater her capabilities, but the less of *her* there was in comparison. As the power flowed in, it became harder and harder to stay Helen. That was how Lodestars changed, based on the multiverse research they'd managed. One drew in more than they could find their way back from.

There was a time even brushing against her current level might have caused some concern, but that was very long ago indeed. She was, to her knowledge, one of the longer-lived incarnations of Lodestar, and had a very strong hunch as to why. Most Lodestars were cut off, their tremendous power and responsibility making it near impossible for them to feel truly connected with anyone else. Who could possibly relate to that kind of burden? But she was different. Friends, family, the simple thought of her daughter, all of it bonded her to that world, to the life she lived outside this costume.

She was Helen, who served as the Lodestar, while knowing *exactly* who she was. And right at that moment, she was furious. With Ivan and the guild, for what they'd just done. With the Wrexwren, for putting them in that position to begin with. With herself, more than anything. Maybe there was a way it didn't have to be like this. A world where, if she'd been stronger, faster, or smarter, there would be less bloodshed. It was a very familiar anger, one that had burned in her since the first day she woke with these powers, and *without* her parents or brother.

Earth-maximum was clearly not going to cut it. Still, she had to press on incrementally. Trying to kill this creature outright because of her own fury would make her just as bad as the guild. But those increments were about to start increasing sharply, by necessity if not intent.

Truth be told, when she started using this kind of power, not even Lodestar could completely control it. For the Scralthor's sake, she really hoped it was smart enough to run while it still had a chance.

Doctor Mechaniacal's voice in his ear was both welcome and terrifying. Welcome, because even Ivan was starting to get weary of taking blow after blow constantly. Terrifying, because compared to what came next, that was the equivalent of sitting on a park bench on a sunny afternoon. He was going to have to do something genuinely horrifying, and there was simply no way around it.

With so many meta-humans and people watching at home, no subterfuge would go undiscovered, no trickery could slip the collective consciousness. The plan called for Fornax, which was why he'd donned the mask and name once more. Except, the reputation wasn't enough. For this to work, for the message to get through, he couldn't be Ivan playing pretend. Everything had to be real, so there were no loose threads to unravel.

Pretending wasn't enough. Today, he had to *be* Fornax once more. And that was what made Ivan so scared, as the darkness filled his eyes and runes appeared in their place: how incredibly easy it was for that first mad giggle to come bounding past his lips, like it had been waiting just below the surface for a chance to rise.

It was a strange time to laugh, given that he was currently leaning against the wall, having been sent there by Zerle Salvrin's mighty fists. The Wrexwren was struck by the sound, turning its head in some manner—though without eyes, it was hard to view any section as the "front" with certainty.

"Zerle Salvrin, I came here expecting to be disappointed, but you... you *are* worthy." Fornax rose, not bothered by the blood dripping from parts of his face. That was what the mask was for, and anyway, it wasn't as if he hadn't fought through far worse pain than this.

"I need be worthy to kill one so pitiful as you?" He seemed insulted by the idea, charging right up with a fresh attack. Only, this one didn't land like all the others. Despite the twisting madness of his movement, Zerle Salvrin found one arm caught by Fornax, while the red-masked man dodged the other strikes. There was a brief moment as they looked upon one another, before Fornax's fist sent Zerle Salvrin flying back to the other side of the chamber.

"You are worthy of being broken." Fornax was smiling now, genuine glee as he took in the rasped, unsteady nature of the Wrexwren's whistles. He might have hit whatever their version of lungs was. "Only the strong can truly be destroyed, you see. The weak have too much bend. They lack suitable pride to be humbled, confidence to shatter. Even the things they love, they understand might be stolen away by fate or another. Not like the strong, who believe we can push against the very will of the universe when what's ours is threatened."

Zerle Salvrin didn't simply lie on the ground and suffer abuse. He was up in short order, but approached with far greater caution this time. The movements were closer to his initial attacks, before he'd felt certain in his victory: guarded, probing, a much more defensive tactic now that he knew his opponent was capable of hitting back. Fornax allowed three blows to land on various points of his body, and in return, he slammed a fist into the same spot he'd hit the first time, sending Zerle Salvrin flying again with a fresh round of rasping.

"You think you can kill me that easily?" Zerle Salvrin was already rising again. It looked as if he could take as hard as he gave—no wonder this being had attained such a high position among his species.

"Kill you? My good Zerle, you truly have zero grasp on what is happening. If someone wanted you killed, there is no shortage of options available to us. We could have obliterated you from the ground weeks ago. You are not so fortunate as to get an executioner. I am Fornax, and my one true gift is destruction. Death is easy. Instead, I am going to break every piece of who you are. Then, if you ask very nicely, I may just grant you an ending."

The whistle had a very snarl-like quality as it rang out, which matched the aggressive posture Zerle Salvrin was adopting, visibly prepared for another bout. "Empty threats. Even if you are stronger than I, my people have well prepared me for torture. I've endured it on missions more than once. There is no breaking of Zerle Salvrin."

Fornax's smile grew substantially wider. "Excellent. That's right, tell me how pointless it is. Tell me how you will absolutely, unquestionably triumph. Show me your strength, Zerle Salvrin. Show my world your power, so that your shattering will be all the greater."

This time, Fornax didn't counter the attacks. He merely dodged them, stepping nimbly out of the way so the myriad of Wrexwren limbs struck only air. "But you know, I really can't stand fighting in all this silence. Down on Earth, things are messy and chaotic. By now, we'd have people screaming and yelling, possibly even a few interlopers to deal with. Doctor Mechaniacal, would you be so kind as to give us a soundtrack?"

This time, the voice didn't reply over the communicator. Doctor Mechaniacal's reply echoed through the entire chamber, broadcast along whatever system was still showing Lodestar squaring off with the Scralthor overhead. "My pleasure, Fornax. In fact, I have just the thing."

The closest sound Fornax could compare to what came next was a truckload of whistles crashing in a hurricane, which then blew through each one. A cacophony of crunching, crashing, shrill noises, most of which were all nonsense. Only a few soundbites were clear enough for his translator to make them out.

"They're everywhere. We can't get out!"

"—large teeth and glowing red eyes, killed—"

"—entire crew eviscerated—"

"—a trap!"

"Seems like this was planned—"

"Zerle, this is a world woven of death."

That last one was rather poetic, assuming it was the Wrexwren's actual words and not the translator's approximation. Zerle Salvrin, however, was not reacting nearly so well to these new sounds. Given that he understood all of them, it was probably quite the bloody accounting of how their invasion was going so far. Selectively blocking the signals had been vital, both to keep the Wrexwren cocky and to ensure Zerle Salvrin was properly caught off guard.

Now, he was learning the truth of how his people were faring, or at least, the relative few that might still be alive.

"If you want to break someone at their core, you must first understand what makes up their foundation. From where do they draw their strength. As you informed Lodestar, you are a Zerle, an earned rank, no doubt connected to your position on this ship. I do wonder, how many are required under your command to be a Zerle? Is there a specific number needed? How about you count the ones we hear actually die, and you tell me when I need to start addressing you by another title."

This noise was nearly a train whistle, a furious burst from Zerle Salvrin which served as the only warning before he sprang, a wild mass of limbs moving faster than any blow thrown before. As planned, he was now fighting for real. No more putting on a show or taking his time; Zerle Salvrin was swinging for the kill. That too was an important part of the process: he had to bring his very best to the fight.

Because that would make Fornax crushing him all the more painful.

Chapter 112

Between the trickle of goons making it through only to be smacked down, the shots on the roof doing some damage on their own, and the few smart enough to leave after they noticed that dozens had gone into the building without anyone reemerging, they were making a surprisingly good pace through the siege's attackers. A worryingly good pace, if Tachyonic was being honest. For as relatively new to the field as he was, it wasn't as if Vomisa were without any dangers of its own. Tachyonic had been in enough tight spots to trust his instincts, all of which were screaming that something was off. Whoever had thrown this together put in a lot of effort. There was virtually no chance it would be settled so easily.

That's why Tachyonic was doing a thorough sweep while he had the opportunity, making sure that none of the crooks were secretly planting explosives or setting up meta-tech devices while everyone else was distracted. Thus far, he'd come up entirely empty. The only things he was passing as he ran were the toppled bodies of criminals that had already been taken out. They were scattered through the halls, most in various states of unconsciousness, with a few showing more substantial injuries—largely the ones who'd been unlucky enough to fight Bahamut.

He paused near an electrical panel that was slightly askew, stepping over three knocked-out minions to get at it. Maybe they'd been doing something when they were interrupted, and the others hadn't noticed? Yanking open the door, he scanned over the interior, finding nothing amiss. While he wouldn't have been capable of puzzling out the workings of some complex device, he trusted himself to at least tell if the wires had been yanked out and messed with.

Unfortunately, all that focus on the panel took away from other potential threats, though it wasn't as if he'd have paid much attention to a defeated foe in the first place. That's what made it such a perfect hiding space.

The pain was instant, swift, and terrifying: a burning spike driven directly through his left ankle, forcing Tachyonic to lean against the wall as his leg suddenly refused to bear weight. Spinning around, he saw one of the bodies calmly rising to its feet. It appeared to be a largely unremarkable man—plain clothes and simple looks, not even any meta-tech on hand. On the subject on hands, Tachyonic noticed that this fellow did have one very distinguishing feature: his left hand was gaunt, almost skeletal, with dark wisps of smoke rising off it. The smoke was quite similar to a small tendril drifting out of Tachyonic's new ankle-hole, making the puzzle of what had happened a simple solve.

Struggling, Tachyonic tried to move, hopping slightly away. To his shock, the man made no immediate lunge, but rather followed slowly, as if he had no reason in the world to hurry. Did he not realize that with enough time, Tachyonic could call for backup?

No. He wanted the call for backup to go out. Suddenly, it all made much more sense. Whoever this was had been lying in wait, next to a trap that would draw in any superhero doing a perimeter sweep. He'd hobbled their fastest member in a single blow—that was not a coincidence. Having the power to do such a thing meant nothing if one couldn't create opportunity. This was someone with a plan, and there was little hope that playing into it worked out well for the New Science Sentries.

The trouble was, if he radioed and warned everyone, there was a strong possibility they might come anyway. Were he to know a friend was in danger, Agent Quantum wouldn't turn back, and the others would be hot on his heels. Their best shot was if Tachyonic could escape and warn them in person. It might still come down to a fight; the goal was just not to have it on this mystery attacker's terms.

Running on an ankle with a hole in the middle would be painful as hell, but the real problem was how much it would slow him down. Still, he'd be limping at super-speeds, so hopefully that beat out the ambusher's running pace. Tilting forward, Tachyonic took off, bolting himself forward. Except something was wrong, more than just his foot. His speed was diluted, weakened, even with the bracer confirming that he was indeed getting a constant setlium output.

He'd barely gotten ten steps down the hall when a strong hand fell upon his shoulder, jerking him back effortlessly. Tachyonic flew into drywall as he was tossed, leaving a sizable dent and receiving a good rattle to the skull. By the time he looked up, the attacker was standing above him once more, staring down with a smile that didn't fit the skin of his face.

"One of life's cruel humors; I am the opposing element to your power source. That potent setlium crackling in your cells is suddenly not working so well now that my energy is in the mix, corrupting the bonds that fuel your abilities. The good news is that the effects will fade, eventually. Assuming you survive."

It was not his smoking left hand, but his still human-looking right that reached forward. Although Tachyonic tried to struggle from the ground, it was useless. This man wasn't just strong in the sense of Agent Quantum: he was on a whole other level, closer to Professor Quantum. Nothing Tachyonic did, from pulling at his arms to a full-force punch in the face, made any impact. The superhero might as well have been a stiff breeze. The attacks were short-lived, as he soon found his head pressed against the wall as the stranger waved a device next to his ear. When his attacker spoke again, Tachyonic realized with horror that he didn't just hear it nearby, it was coming through the communicators, as well.

"Good morning, New Science Sentries. I'm pleased at how well you've done with the warm-up exercises, but the time has come to take things to the next level. We now know you to be capable of the basics for superhero work. Let us next test your bravery. I have taken Tachyonic, and he won't be escaping without help. Playing with him will likely keep me occupied for some while, long enough that the rest of you might get away. Time for your first choice, New Science Sentries. Come save your friend, or live to fight another day. You have five minutes to find us. After that, I'll put a new hole in him for every minute the entire team isn't present. Oh, and as you can tell, I'm tapped into your lines. If anyone decides to try to reach the AHC, I'll leave Tachyonic's body in the lobby. His head... now that you'll have to search for."

Fighting through the pain, Tachyonic stared into those cold, distant eyes. "Why are you doing this? We don't know you. There's no grudge here."

"Poor little pawn. He's so cruel as to send you out into the world with no idea what you'll truly be facing, yet somehow, I'm the monster?" While the words might have crafted a veneer of sympathy, there was no touch of humanity in those words. "Take heart, because this isn't really about you. It never could have been—not if you'd spent decades building to the New Science Sentries' legacy. He would have never let it be that way. You were always destined to die a footnote, just one more person for Professor Quantum to step over in his quest for greatness."

It might not be the nicest sentiment, but at least it made sense. The New Science Sentries hadn't gotten into nearly enough trouble to have grudges like this held against them. The Science Sentries in their original incarnation, especially with Professor Quantum in the lead, would be a very different story. And as someone who'd grown up around Professor Quantum, Tachyonic had no trouble believing someone could hate the man that much. In other circumstances, it might even have been a point of bonding.

"Look, I'm sorry if Professor Quantum screwed you over in some way. That's just who he is. You're one of countless. But it has nothing to do with us."

"So very wrong, on multiple levels," the attacker countered. "You became part of it when he gave you that name, when he decided to add to his legacy using you four as tools. You are connected to his accomplishments—which is to say, his ego—and nothing hurts him more than being attacked there. Besides which, I am not 'one of countless' as you implied. I am, without question, the first one destroyed by Professor Quantum's ambition."

"What makes you so sure of that?" Tachyonic spat, half hoping to keep him distracted, half trying to keep his mind off the pain in his ankle.

There was a placidness to the man as he spread his arms, one hand normal, the other letting off plumes of dark smoke. "Because on the day he betrayed me, his name was still Vernon."

Sunshine covered the green landscape, where verdant trees and lush grass grew in every direction. As the Wrexwren moved, it noted the structure up ahead: simple, yet large and well-maintained. This was a lived-in area, which made it more dangerous. The rest of the team would be circling, ensuring they took the occupants by surprise.

In front of the structure, many tiny humans were running about, wasting their already short lives on frivolity. Such energy would be better used in industries across the galaxy, once the Wrexwren understood how much labor a human body could endure at various levels of growth. There would be trial and error, but there was no shortage of subjects to learn from.

Stepping out of the woods, the Wrexwren leader began to raise his weapon, only to have his view cut off. The rest of his team was around him—only, chunks of their bodies had been torn out. Worse, there were more appearing: the Stropolof warriors they'd mowed through, the devoted innocents who'd been wiped out by his fire on Tregle-9. More and more, the past appeared, all of it looking right at him, deadly hatred in their eyes.

Together, the mass of unseen horrors descended upon the Wrexwren leader, viciously tearing him apart as they had the rest of his crew. None of the playing children witnessed any of this, however. They were busy making a fort with their current caretaker, a grown man with dirty-blond hair. He alone looked to the dying Wrexwren, no pity whatsoever present on that serene face. For a moment, in the pain of death, the alien believed he saw something else, like a pair of metal wings extending behind the peaceful man.

Kristoph handed out fresh crayons to a child drawing the landscape, not a single Wrexwren or ship to be seen in the artwork. Taking a role of protection had made the most sense for him on this chaotic day. While the Wrexwren invasion would no doubt have casualties among every age group, there was little purpose to hunting them down.

The guild was already making sure that when the day was done, the Wrexwren would thoroughly answer for their crimes.

"Holy shit." Presto stopped cold, and Plasmodia looked as though she might be ill. The smaller cape's face was hidden by his mask, yet the anger made it into his words without any obstruction whatsoever. "Oh, this guy is so dead."

"He could be bluffing." Plasmodia's rebuttal was weak—she didn't believe it. This was a moment's respite in brief denial.

"Not on our communication channel, he isn't." Presto started for the roofline, only to be snared by Cyber Geek.

Hephaestus, for her part, was mostly trying to keep the blasts raining down, though the available targets were getting thin. After a prolonged period of firing and letting them past in batches, most were either inside, injured, or had decided this was not worth the effort and bailed. "Anyone want to loop me in on what's going on? Temporary allies and all?"

She was unprepared for the furious dervish who suddenly appeared next to her, Presto grabbing her helmet and trying to force it into his eye-line. "You! If you had anything to do with—"

Hephaestus jerked her helmet forward. She nearly smashed Presto in the nose until he leapt away at the last moment, though she did succeed in her attempt at breaking his grip. "I have about had it with the goddamn threats. In case you didn't notice, I am not a fucking cape, and I do *not* have to be here putting up with your shit. Flying out has been an option from the start. Now, will you cut the posturing and tell me if there's anything new I need to know about?"

"Someone captured Tachyonic and sent a message over the nearby AHC communicators." The response came not from Presto, who was still fuming, but rather from Cyber Geek. "They're going to torture him until the New Science Sentries come help. And apparently kill him if we attempt to call in any backup."

Suddenly, Presto's rage made a great deal more sense. What she comprehended less, however, was the unforeseen surge of anger that suddenly tore up from Tori's gut. There was a time when she wouldn't have understood what it meant, but Lodestar's words still hung heavy on her mind. She could put up all the walls, pretend that there weren't bonds, and go through her entire life acting as if she had no human connections. Lying to herself was the only area where it was doomed to fail. Because deep down, she knew when she felt that instinctive reaction, that every part of her was saying *No.* Tachyonic... Kyle... was intrusive, often said the wrong thing, and had generally made her life more complicated since he'd arrived in it.

But he was her friend. She could accept that now, while there was still time to act, or later, when nothing she did would matter.

Just like that, the world made sense again. It didn't matter if he was a cape, or a villain, a meta-human, an alien, a god, or a demon. She wanted him around, alive, and that made him *hers*, in a sense. If there was one thing that defined Tori Rivas, one truth carved into her soul as she endured the beeping hell of watching her parents slowly fade away, it was this:

No one stole from her. No one took what was hers, be it items, ideas, or people she cared for. Whoever this person was, they had made a huge mistake. It wasn't merely the capes they'd pissed off with that move, they'd caught the attention of a dangerous villain, as well.

"Then why the hell are you all still standing here? Shouldn't we be sweeping for him?"

The three capes looked at her, visible worry in their eyes. Hephaestus been an ally so far, but also an adversary in the past. With the stakes suddenly dire, their tenuous trust was stretched thin, torn between the need for more bodies in the fight versus pairing with people they actually trusted.

"I feel like one of you is about to threaten me yet again, which is not only unneeded, at this point, it's actively rude. You don't like me, fine. Don't trust me, that's fair too. But you're all smart enough to understand that I'm a guild member, meaning that there are rules I play by. Torturing and killing capes is not a part of that. Whoever this person is, they're disrespecting my organization, as well. Now, that's not the same as 'kidnapped friend' for motivation, sure, but it's more than enough reason to plant my beam in the base of their skull."

"Let Hephaestus come. What matters most is getting Tachyonic back. Anything else, we can deal with after." Presto headed toward the rooftop doorway, his only way into the building since they lacked a clear line of sight. "But we stay together as we move. Anyone capable of taking down Tachyonic is not to be underestimated."

The mere fact that Presto, of all people, was being so serious drove the gravity of the situation home. Hephaestus followed the capes from the roof, leaving the few straggling goons waiting for shots that would never come. They had a new threat to deal with, and this one was not nearly so easily countered.

Chapter 113

"The new guy is kind of intense." Pest Control directed his swarm of meta-hornets into the Wrexwren cockpit, drawing more whistle-screams from within. Whatever physical characteristics the aliens had, immunity to insects that had been mutated by a chemical spill was not among them. Since adding these specimens to his arsenal, the villain's deadliness had gone up considerably, though this was his first chance to really cut loose with them.

Nearby, Glyph snapped in triumph as a different Wrexwren soldier stepped into one of the hidden magical runes placed along the ground. Without warning, he turned on his comrade, firing onto the other Wrexwren who'd trusted their leader with their lives, killing several before they managed to shoot back and bring it all to an end. "Yeah, he's really racking up the bodies."

From the trees, the humanoid form dropped, sinking claws into a Wrexwren's neck before savagely digging further, sending sprays of alien liquid all along the lush grass. He leapt off the still-standing corpse, laying his fangs into another Wrexwren while pointing its own weapon toward more invaders. As pain took over, the alien tensed, sending errant shots sizzling through the air.

"Emory hasn't had much chance to test himself in the field yet—he's got to rebuild his sense of power and self, especially after the training he went through." Arcanicus reinforced the magical shield around them, a form of power which the Wrexwren were showing no capacity for whatsoever. If they hadn't even been prepared for mystical forces, they were woefully unready to try to take on Earth.

"We all had training," Pest Control pointed out.

"You had a group experience. Emory has been entirely in the hands of his mentor to mold." Arcanicus had to look momentarily away as their newest guild apprentice ripped the scaly exterior from a Wrexwren's body, drawing horrific noises in the process. He usually didn't mind watching over the newer members—they weren't ambitious or competent enough to cause much trouble yet—but this bout was making him wish he'd prepared a stomach-soothing potion.

Glyph appeared to have a similar reaction, shaking his head at the carnage on display. "Who exactly was his mentor, anyway? A walking flesh-blender?"

"Close guess, actually. He learned from Xelas." Arcanicus wasn't sure how he felt about the immediate understanding that settled into both rookies' faces at that revelation. He was of the opinion that perhaps the guild didn't need to be bone-chillingly scary to function effectively, but that put him in the minority of their leadership. The guild's current plan was built out of reestablishing precisely that horrific reputation, so Xelas and her methods were clearly a good fit for the organization.

As a spray of alien viscera landed on his shoes, Arcanicus muttered darkly under his breath. Carnage was one thing; they needed to teach him how to aim the consequences better. If the guild was going to be home to the world's greatest horrors, then Arcanicus could ensure they were well-trained unnatural disasters, if nothing else.

Moving the apartment building's residents around was surprisingly easy. One of the benefits to living in Ridge City: everyone was accustomed to meta-fights and evacuations. With minimal prompting, they were willing to accept the aid of a woman in what could be generously described as a makeshift costume. By opting to be "**Better lucky than good**," Cliché managed to avoid almost every threat as they walked down into the garage, depositing her neighbors into their respective concrete cubes or whatever ones were unoccupied. On the few occasions where someone did spot them, her umbrella easily deflected any ranged attacks they sent, and soon, the attackers had one of the capes to worry about.

She tried hard to put Nexus and his cryptic warning out of her mind as she worked. There had been no sign of him since leaving the roof, but that offered little comfort when it came to a man who could appear from nowhere. Scary as Nexus was, he didn't appear to be taking an active role today, which made him more annoyance than threat. When everyone else was coming to kill, creepy predictions didn't carry quite the same oomph.

The scream caught her off guard. Having already checked all of the rooms down this hall, Cliché was heading back toward the roof to report a successful evacuation. It didn't sound like a mid-fight scream, especially considering she'd glimpsed Bahamut and Agent Quantum a floor above minutes prior. Maybe she'd missed someone, and they'd gotten caught? Except, something about that voice was almost... familiar. Umbrella at the ready, Cliché crept forward, taking each step with care until she came around a corner and nearly gasped in shock.

Tachyonic was down. Not just down, trying to crawl on his back, eyes tilted upward at the twisted face of the man staring down at him. Smoke drifted from the man's left arm, dark and gaunt all the way to the elbow. By the way Tachyonic was dragging his leg, this didn't seem like any sort of ploy; he'd been seriously injured. For someone with his skillset, Tachyonic was functionally out of the fight, a huge blow to the New Science Sentries' collective strength.

"It's such a pretty narrative. One man's genius breaks the very foundations of reality, ushering in a new age of limitless potential. The laws of physics and the universe are altered, allowing what was once impossible to become commonplace. Except it all ignores the simple truth that some things are *supposed* to be impossible. What was unleashed has far more capacity to corrupt, destroy, and ruin rather than elevate. How many monsters have risen out of our world, chasing or fueled by the power he unleashed?"

"So you're the good one? Going to tell me how, somehow, all of this is because *you* were really in the right? Look, you'll never have to sell me on Professor Quantum being a callous, cold, calculating asshole. But he still turns his power toward the greater good, so why don't you spare me the moralizing. I know who the superhero is between the two of you."

The man advanced, stomping down a foot next to Tachyonic's shin that shattered the wood beneath. Oh crap; he was strong on top of whatever was going on with his hand. Cliché leaned slightly forward, shifting her footing in case she needed to help. Thus far, the umbrella had been able to take everything thrown at it. Hopefully, this was not the day she discovered its limits.

"You're so young, barely more than a child. It's no wonder you still believe in such ridiculous concepts. There are no heroes in this world, super or otherwise. Only powerful people playing games to amuse themselves, the mundane serving as little more than pieces and prizes. The entire premise is a fabrication, a trick that lets them rule while upholding the illusion of service. The only difference between your people and the guild is that yours were more effective in seizing power."

Cliché said a small prayer of thanks in her heart to whoever the god of monologuing was, for they'd been blessed with a talker. That was time not spent maiming or killing; Tachyonic just needed to play into the rant and keep him going until help could arrive. Help other than her—someone with real power to swing around.

"I might be young, but you are categorically *wrong*." Tachyonic somehow managed to find a defiant expression, despite his prone, vulnerable position. "Are a lot of capes like that? Hell yes. Most of us are in this career for the wrong reasons, from pure ambition to having no normal job options. But there are some who live up to the word superhero, whose hearts are in exactly the right place, who take up this fight because they can't imagine standing by when they have the power to help. I know it with absolute certainty; it has been my privilege to work under just such a person."

A sharp hiss and crackle drew Cliché's attention to the looming man's left arm, which was sending up even more smoke. Strangely, the skin along his arm turned crisp, then flaked away, unlike any transformation she'd seen before. It was more like he was burning off an outer shell of flesh.

Leaning down, his right hand flew out, snaring Tachyonic by the skull, holding his head locked in place. "Do you still think he's going to save you? That there's any hope you will all make it out of this?"

"The entire point of being a superhero is giving people hope even in the most dire of lost situations," Tachyonic replied. "Maybe he won't make it in time to save me, but he's absolutely going to stop you."

They stayed like that for a long moment, until the grip on Tachyonic's skull was suddenly released. "Very brave, little pawn. Trying to goad me into killing you in the hopes of taking away my hostage. Your friends still would have died, but I will admit, it might have been harder to draw them all in. Now, I shall teach you the cost of bravery. Everything below your right knee seems an adequate price."

He lifted his smoking left arm, and Cliché realized her bystander time was officially over. Either she let this happen or stood up: both options represented a choice. Praying dearly that the mask and goggle combo adequately hid her face, Cliché dove out from her hiding spot, racing forward with umbrella at the ready.

Whether it was uncertainty as to who she was or merely confusion at the motley ensemble running in his direction, the man actually did pause to see what the hell was happening. It was enough of a gap for Cliché to leap between him and Tachyonic, popping her umbrella out to full extension, barely fitting inside the narrow confines of the hallway.

"Get out of here! He's too strong." Tachyonic tried to send her away; however, the effort was significantly compromised by his inability to stand or walk.

"I think that's in our favor. The worse I am in comparison, the luckier I should be." Cliché wasn't entirely sure if that was how her current saying actually worked, but it felt like it *could* be true as an interpretation. If the power really was shaped by her perceptions of it, then that was how she chose for the phrase to interact with the world.

Then again, if she was wrong, it probably wouldn't take too long to figure out.

The man examined Cliché once with detached interest before coldly remarking, "You are not a New Science Sentry. There is no purpose in killing you slowly." His left hand slashed down, intercepted by the umbrella as the bone-like digits raked off what should have been nothing more than dark fabric. Mercifully, the makeshift shield held, though the reaction that came next was completely unexpected.

"*What*?!?" The man bellowed, his voice ringing off the walls around them, all composure suddenly gone. He struck again, that smoking hand scratching at the handheld barrier between them, only to slide harmlessly off. "This can't be. No mere object can withstand my corrosion. Even the skin I wear is temporary. You... *dare* to challenge me?"

The next blow that came was not a scratch; instead, it was like a sledgehammer. Having raised up his arms, the man struck with tremendous force, driving Cliché and her legs deep into the wooden floor. Snapping sounds were her only warning before suddenly, there was no ground beneath her feet. The stomp he'd delivered earlier had substantially weakened the structure; this second blow was more than the old building could bear.

Through the air she and Tachyonic tumbled, down onto the unexpectedly soft landing pile of blankets and pillows. They'd ended up in a bedroom a floor below, the lush mattress easily breaking both of their falls. Up above, she could still see the man, staring down through the hole he'd just accidentally made, twisted in rage and glaring down at both of them. Well, she was certainly on his radar now.

"The hell just happened?" Tachyonic fought his way out from under a pile of pillows, rising back to a seated position just before they heard the gentle *thud* of another body hitting the ground, their attacker landing only feet away.

"You managed to buy yourself another few minutes." Everything from his left shoulder down was smoking now, as were small sections of his face where the peeling process had begun. "That's all your vain struggling managed to accomplish."

This time, there was nothing gentle about the noise that rang out from the floor upon landing. Given the new form's size and muscles, it was no surprise the wood struggled to uphold what crashed down heavily upon it, and if rage had any mass, then Agent Quantum would have caused the floorboards to buckle right then and there.

"They also made enough noise to be easily found." Agent Quantum looked across the room to Tachyonic's injured form. The anger hardened as his gaze turned to the smoking-armed attacker. Cliché had never seen an expression like that on his face, in or out of costume. It was, curiously, the first time she'd even noticed any resemblance at all between Agent and Professor Quantum.

Despite the evident fury, he still didn't come out of the gate swinging. "You get one chance: surrender, and come in quietly. Don't try to fight me right now. I'm not at all confident I can hold back."

"He's our weakness!" Tachyonic hurriedly yelled from the bed. "Don't let him touch you—it messes with our abilities. Just get the others clear. He won't stop until he has us all."

"Well, yes and no," the man corrected, his calm voice and face once more fixed in place. Whatever dark impulses Cliché had stirred up, Agent Quantum was clearly of higher priority. "The weakness part is true, and I fully intend to do some killing, but only you are truly essential, Agent Quantum. Only you carry *his* blood."

Up above, Cliché could make out the forms of Medley and Bahamut. They must have heard the noise, as well. Perhaps they were waiting for the right moment to strike, which she hoped would arrive soon. Tempting as it was to teleport out, she wasn't going anywhere until at least her roommates were present. Besides, at least here, she could influence things slightly. She just hoped it would be for the better.

"That mean you'll let the others go?" Agent Quantum asked.

"Obviously not. My point is just that I don't especially care about them, so it's possible they could escape. Flee and cower—that will shame the Science Sentries brand nearly as well as their deaths. That means the longer you 'distract' me, the better their chances of escape."

Lifting his arms, Agent Quantum took a position that clearly indicated a fight was about to begin. "Seems we both believe ourselves to be the stronger in this fight. How 'bout we skip the bluster and find out who's right?"

"You lack his prudence and intelligence, yet you managed to retain the arrogance. I shall take great pleasure in this."

Agent Quantum charged, and the battle was on.

Chapter 114

The noise was fading, not that it mattered. Zerle Salvrin remained enraged, swinging like he intended to knock Fornax's skull from his shoulders. The cries for help from his people, all beyond his reach, had done their job and rattled his certainty. Had Ivan been the one running this show, he would have ended things soon after. To his thinking, it was enough. Sadly, for Zerle Salvrin, this was a Fornax mission, and he was only just beginning to have fun. Besides, this show wasn't really for Zerle Salvrin, and Fornax couldn't start the conclusion until the star performance had occurred.

A dull ringing echoed through the room as Zerle Salvrin's fists collided with the wall, failing yet again to land a blow on Fornax. The Wrexwren anatomy and martial art was certainly unique, involving tactics that had demanded time to fully grasp, but Fornax had been born in battle. His entire life until the change was nothing but fighting: constantly, endlessly, without even the hope of it ceasing. Adapting to new forms of attack was one of the reasons Ivan had been the lone survivor, and some habits were far too ingrained to be weathered away by a few mere years of peace.

"While my world chips away at your title, I can move on to breaking the next of your foundations: that strength in which you place so much value. Tell me, Zerle Salvrin, were you the strongest of your people?""

Zerle Salvrin was in no mood for chitchat. He kept pressing the attack, limbs swirling in all manner of directions, like an inescapable cloud. Fornax struck directly through the attempt, knocking two arms aside as he sent the

Wrexwren hurtling back hard into the wall. "I asked you a question. Don't get boring on me, or I'll have to find other ways to entertain myself."

Whether it was the actual threat, or just the desire for a few seconds of rest, Zerle Salvrin eventually replied as he slowly pulled himself back to standing. "I am among the elite, yet there are greater threats still among my people. Do not think this will save your planet. Even if our forces are driven back, the Wrexwren will never stop."

"Oh?" Fornax didn't sound as if he was afraid of the prospect. In fact, he was bordering on excitement. "How I wish you were right about that. What I wouldn't give for an endless stream of your people coming to Earth, providing me with new fun. Because I am *not* the strongest of my people."

He pointed overhead, to where the screen showed Lodestar glowing brighter than before, still attempting to fight back the cosmic horror on a crash course for the Earth's sun. "Our planet is like a pressure cooker, and that is the lid. We host a constant building of power and force that should spill forth into the greater universe, except for the insurmountable barrier that holds us all back. It spurs us on to greater heights, building more pressure as we try and fail to overtake her. As iron sharpens iron, meta sharpens meta, all so we can break our blades on that incomprehensible wall named Lodestar."

"You believe weakness is a thing to boast of?" Zerle Salvrin came in for another round, but this time, Fornax didn't wait for the attack. He dashed forward, hitting his opponent in the torso yet again. He didn't permit the alien to fly back, however. Instead, he took hold of one of the four arms, pulling it taut until it nearly separated from the body.

"I don't think you get the point. My species hasn't been dominating the galaxy for untold years, attacking less-advanced cultures and calling that superiority strength. We are a combative, violent race that struggles endlessly to be mightier. In just fighting with each other and trying to reach that impossible standard set by our champion, we have already grown well past the point where the Wrexwren could ever have been a real threat."

Kicks came from the multiple legs, but Fornax didn't bother trying to dodge. He let the blows rain down, wards blocking most of the damage, yet not all. It was a gamble, allowing some injury now in the hopes it would strip away Zerle Salvrin's will to fight. After telling him he was weak, refusing to show any reaction to the alien's blows only drove the point further home.

"If we are no threat, then why did your greatest defender come to meet us?" Zerle Salvrin demanded. It might have been a real question, or a ploy to take whatever the Wrexwren version of a breather was. Either way, that was a good enough opening to Fornax.

"She is the world's true superhero, and will defend it from any threat, big or small. It's why the people of that planet can live such peaceful lives despite the chaos and madness of their reality: deep down, they all know that they have Lodestar's protection. Which is the same reason why I'm up here today. Because you... *don't*."

The sound was wetter than he'd expected, given all the rough armor on the exterior, but it turned out the Wrexwren had a goopier inside than anticipated, at least around their limbs. Whatever noises Zerle Salvrin was making, there was no direct translation available, and perhaps that was a small mercy.

Not letting go of his prize, Fornax slapped Zerle Salvrin across the head with the newly detached arm, still flinging green goop all over the place. "*You* don't have her protection, mighty Zerle. Since you came declaring war, none of your people do. What you considered an invasion, we think of as a pleasant diversion. You've given the Earth's metas some new amusement, toys we can break to our heart's content without fear of the blinding light interrupting the fun."

Throwing his head back, Fornax let out a good old-fashioned villainous cackle. It came naturally, as did every part of this. That was the problem, being Fornax was *too* easy. There was no helping it for now, though. Making this work meant selling the part, so he allowed the dark impulses to wash over him. "You thought she was protecting us from the greater galaxy, didn't you? Never once did it occur to you that perhaps Earth is home to innumerable monsters that would chew through what the rest of the cosmos considers to be threats. She's not protecting *us* from the greater universe. She's protecting the rest of you from things like *me*. That cute little ploy with your giant monster, what you likely thought to be a stroke of genius, was really just you sending away the only being who could have saved your people from this outcome."

Another smack with the arm, more to horrify than to hurt. The job wasn't yet done, and wouldn't be until Lodestar completed her task. Fornax could break many things—he truly was an artist of the medium—but destroying hope was another matter. For that, he needed the power of a Lodestar. Until then, Fornax would simply have to amuse himself further.

"You lie... this is a trick..." Zerle Salvrin didn't have quite the same confidence he had earlier in the fight—even his anger was being drowned out by uncertainty. They'd have to rekindle that flame soon, though not quite yet. Fornax preferred to hit him with the heaviest blows in rapid succession.

"Lying is for people too weak to own their truths. I am Fornax, one of the planet's strongest combatants, renowned killer, and infamous villain. No tricks, no deceit. I'm just better. The only reason you aren't dead yet is that I haven't finished destroying you. Well, that..."

The blow was sudden and savage, a direct kick to the Wrexwren's leg that completely shattered the lower half of the limb. Zerle Salvrin went sprawling, down to three functional appendages on both the upper and lower halves of his body. More harsh whistle-screams rang out as Fornax walked around him slowly, savoring each screech.

"That," Fornax continued, "and I like the funny noises you make. Let's see just how entertaining a Zerle can really be."

"This might be getting a little violent." Juan reached for the remote, intending to click away from the stream on the television. The hideout Ivan had sent Janet and the others to resembled a simple hotel on the fringes of a farming museum—not that there were any tours going on, given the day's events. Everyone was huddled inside, though no Wrexwren ships had been seen anywhere near their vicinity. Or if they were, the security forces were handling it.

Janet's hand moved before she'd thought it all through, snatching the remote away first. "You're right. This is probably a bit much for Beth. Why don't you two go to the lobby and get us some lunch?" She couldn't turn away. Part of this was on her—she'd told Ivan the world needed to fear Fornax again. If anyone owed him a duty as witness, it was Janet. Besides, for all that had passed between them, some shard of her would always love Ivan, even if it was only the pieces of him she saw reflected in their children. He was fighting for the fate of the world and his family—at the very least, she could watch him do it.

"What about me?" Rick asked.

A month ago, it would have been such a simple question. Make him leave, keep him in the dark, as far from the truth as humanly possible. Now, he'd begun to unravel the shawl draped over their past. Sooner or later, there was a very real chance Rick was going to discover who his father was. He was going to hear horrible things about the man he called "Dad"—and worse, most of them would be true. Today would do little to alter that perception; watching Fornax torture a living creature, invader or not, would leave a sour taste in many people's mouths. Then again, there would also only be so many times he might get to see his father helping to save the world, and whether people liked the methods or not, Fornax was pitching in. Based on the horrific stream of cries from the Wrexwren in that broadcast, it seemed as if the entire guild was.

"It's up to you," Janet decided and declared in the same breath. "Violent as it is, I can't say this isn't a historic moment for our planet. There is some value in watching it unfold." Rick's journey of discovery had thus far been largely self-directed, so Janet decided to let that trend continue.

"I'll stay and watch. Finding out Fornax was alive was crazy enough. I never thought I'd get to see him cutting loose. Where the hell has he been all these years?" The flicker was brief, dispelled instantly by a brain not willing to contemplate such truths, yet Janet saw it all the same. A moment of concern, terror, on Rick's face as he'd briefly entertained what no doubt seemed like a ridiculous possibility. Pity for him; the longer he mulled it over, the less implausible it would sound.

As Juan and Beth headed out, Janet changed her position. Moving from the chair, she sat down on one of the bed's edges, next to Rick. If asked, she'd have said it was to get a better view—except Rick didn't ask. Probably because he'd reached that conclusion already, or the fight on-screen was simply too engrossing.

Or, deep down, Rick knew why she'd moved into easy hugging range and didn't yet want to face it. Janet, for her part, said nothing more. She didn't trust herself not to give everything away, even with how close Rick was to the truth. All she could do was be there for her son no matter if he chose discovery or ignorance, and try to mend what remained if his entire world fell down around him.

Lozora slipped along, moving toward the sound of the fracas. Her employer should be where the action was by this point. The few advances she'd gotten were fine, but the bulk of her pay still hung in the balance, so he'd better have managed to make it on time. At least she didn't have to worry about him losing upon arrival. There were capes who could potentially deal with him as a threat—temporarily, if nothing else—but they were all handling the much larger issue of an alien invasion. It was the most ludicrous, over-the-top distraction she'd ever even heard of, and it had been a large chunk of what convinced her to take the job. Anyone with that kind of ambition would be fun to watch whether they succeeded or flamed out spectacularly.

Her slender limbs made little sound as she crept, peering around a corner to spot Medley and some humanoid-dragon meta both looking through a hole in the floor. Dollars to cents, that would be where she found her target. How to approach was more complicated. Medley was no pushover, and the dragon certainly possessed the build of a bruiser. As a physical-based meta herself, two-on-one would put her at a disadvantage, even if they were individually weaker than she. Part of surviving meant avoiding needless risks, so Lozora eased back out of their sight.

The retreat lasted until she felt cold metal press into her back, and saw flashing lights in the corner of her eye.

"Tell us who the fuck you are right now, or I remodel your torso with an outside view. Whatever is left, Plasmodia can dice into pieces."

"Hephaestus, that isn't how superheroes work." Cyber Geek stepped into view, some device that looked like a lantern with earmuffs fading back to sparks. That explained how they'd snuck up on her, though it didn't really help the current predicament.

"Someone just captured a New Science Sentry and threatened to cut off his head. You'd better harden up fast, Cyber Geek. These people are not playing around." The voice from behind, Hephaestus, was spot on, not that Lozora could tell any of them that.

Raising her hands slowly, Lozora made her posture as nonthreatening as possible. "I'm sorry! I'm sorry. I didn't mean to trespass, but there were aliens and a bunch of people with weird weapons, so I was trying to find somewhere to hide. Please, I can leave. I don't want any trouble."

"Horseshit. You, a clear meta-human, broke into a building surrounded by a violent battle in an attempt to escape danger? Tell me neither of you capes are buying this."

Plasmodia stepped forward, the sharp light emitting from her hand forcing Lozora to blink and look away. "Honestly, no. I don't believe it either." The light suddenly dimmed, and Plasmodia shifted her hand away. "But being a superhero isn't just about protecting honest people. She doesn't have a weapon and didn't try to attack either of our allies. At worst, I think we have a robber with bad taste. At best, a civilian with terrible luck."

"Either way, you're staying with us," Cyber Geek declared. "It's too dangerous to let you wander off if you really are a civilian, and too risky for us if you're not. Stay close, out of the fight, and when this is all over we'll see you to safety."

Almost incapable of believing her luck, Lozora waited for the coldness on her back to move. It finally did, though not before the helmet came within touching distance, brushing against the side of her head. "Give me a reason. I dare you."

The voice didn't try to whisper, which made the need for proximity curious, but when the threat was delivered, Lozora found herself not being poked by the weapon, which she considered excellent progress. Not only did it sound like she'd found her employer, Lozora had also procured a front-row seat. If things went south, she might even be willing to jump in and help the plans stay running smoothly.

For an additional fee, of course.

Chapter 115

Agent Quantum's swing went wide, sailing over the strange man's head as he easily side-stepped the attempted blow. Crawling, Tachyonic tried to make it to the edge of the bed, unsure of what he'd even do once he was off it, but certain that he had to try *something*. He'd already known their enemy was powerful. Now, they were learning things was even worse: this bizarre man also had training.

Thus far, he hadn't even delivered a single blow to Agent Quantum. There had been no need, when he could dodge every attack. It wasn't that he was just fast, however. For all the capabilities taken from Tachyonic by being hobbled, he could still perceive things at near super-speed. Watching the fight in slow motion, it was easier to notice the small details, like how this man wasn't actually quicker than Agent Quantum. He started reacting to the attack before it actually arrived, which could mean prophetic abilities, making them all the more screwed. Except sometimes, he had to tweak his dodges on the fly, meaning he didn't know exactly what was coming, only the general shape. Strangely, the attacks that came closest were when Agent Quantum got sloppy and broke his form.

Taking it all in and processing through a sped-up brain, Tachyonic quickly reached the most viable explanation he could find. "Agent Quantum! This guy knows our playbook. That's how he's reading your moves."

"*Your* playbook?" A hideous glare twisted around to Tachyonic, hatred flowing like the smoke drifting from cracks in his face. "These tactics are no more yours than the team name or costumes. I have fought the real Science Sentries, tracked their every development through the decades. If the true creators of your techniques were unable to defeat me with them, the sickly imitations will fare no better."

The speech bought Agent Quantum a few moments to breathe, which he wisely utilized. Sounds came from overhead, and Tachyonic caught blurs of movement from Bahamut and Medley, along with what appeared to be more goons. Right, there were still a few stragglers around. Those two were probably holding the perimeter. He looked away just as a flash tugged at the corner of his eyes, but the smoking-armed man was much too dangerous to leave unwatched.

When Agent Quantum came again, he was moving differently. Not nearly as smooth or polished, he'd broken out of his usual form and was shifting more to a brawling style. Unrefined, true, but also less predictable. The first punch still missed, but the second managed to land. A solid uppercut that caught their enemy on the chin, resulting in a *snap* that brought warmth to Tachyonic's heart... until he saw Agent Quantum grip his own fist in pain.

Before Agent Quantum could retreat, his opponent's right hand snapped out, grabbing him by the shoulder and squeezing so hard it drove the big cape to his knees. "I'm afraid hitting me is only the first hurdle. You'd also have to be strong enough to inflict damage. Seems we've reached your limits already. How disappointing, and after your dear friend gave such an impassioned speech about how you'd stop me for certain."

Agent Quantum tried to struggle, but it was no use. He was simply far weaker than his enemy. This was the difference in strength that existed in the meta-world.

Tachyonic pulled toward the end of the bed where that umbrella woman was huddled up, her odd yet effective shield fully extended, just in case. Nearly to the edge, Tachyonic had to jerk his head back as a fully masked face appeared in front of him.

Hunkering low, his small stature at last a boon, Presto put a finger to where his lips would be, pointing up through the hole as he slipped an arm around both of them. Tachyonic began to object, until Presto quickly whispered, "We have to get you both out so there's room to fight. Why do you think the other heavies are waiting?"

Knowing it was the right tactic, Tachyonic bit his tongue. They weren't running. They were getting out of the way… no matter how much it felt like abandoning a friend.

"Look, Agent Quantum. Your friends are so quick to leave you, perhaps there's more in common with you and the original than I suspected."

It was a good thing Presto looked up out of the hole and teleported at that moment, as Tachyonic might have tried to claw his way over. They popped out barely past the perimeter of the hole; at the angles Presto was working with, this was the best line-of-sight he could manage. All three collapsed in a heap, but Tachyonic was on his back, scoping things out before the others.

Throughout the hall there were a few newly downed crooks, as well as the entirety of their AHC forces, minus Agent Quantum below. Medley was already halfway through the hole, Bahamut right behind. Flanking either side of the floor's entrance were Hephaestus and Plasmodia, both with arms up and energy at the ready. Further down one hallway, Tachyonic spotted Cold Shoulder forming an ice wall, cutting off potential avenues of attack, just like she'd done when they were controlling the flow of crooks getting in. Above him, Hat Trick and Cyber Geek were both looking down, the former wearing her concern plain on every part of her face not covered by a mask.

"Can you do anything?" She wasn't talking to him, instead to Cyber Geek, who was making motions in the air like there was something only he could see.

"Got an idea, just haven't had much chance to test it." Cyber Geek produced a sci-fi-looking implement in a shower of blue sparks and numbers. "No outright healing items I've tried have worked on anyone because they were consumables, but status effects are another matter, like with my freeze ray. This is the Rally Rod from *Galactic Conquest 9*, an item that temporarily numbs pain and boosts the energy of every troop you use it on. It won't fully heal you, but it might get you back in the fight for a little while."

"Do it." Tachyonic had to force himself to slow down enough to make the words comprehensible to these two.

A flicker of hesitation from Cyber Geek. "Thing is, I haven't tried it yet, and in-game, it's not described a pleasant experience—"

"My best friend is down there getting stomped because *I* got my stupid ass captured. Use the goddamn staff, *now*!" Medley and Bahamut were already through, yet Tachyonic knew it wouldn't be enough. That guy was just too strong. Even getting momentarily healed, he had no idea what difference his speed could even make in the fight.

None of which mattered. There was no way in hell he was letting Austin face a match like that without his backup. He held on to that thought as Cyber Geek's staff made contact and the incredible waves of pain began to flow from his ankle. It was all that kept him from passing out immediately.

Medley was only a few steps in front of Bahamut, yet he sprang with such ferocity upon landing that he reached the target substantially ahead of her. The strange man was unbothered by their appearance—given the wide smile on his smoking face, he might have even been happy to see them. Medley's first round of blows were taken without flinching, before his opponent delivered a single backhand that sent the sizable cape sailing into, and through, one of the apartment walls. He crashed in the kitchen, creating a cacophony of pots and pans.

Slowing her own charge, Bahamut reconsidered the plan. That kind of strength was no joke, especially considering Medley's general heft. Between that trick and the fact that their target was still holding Agent Quantum prone, it was evident they'd yet to push this stranger anywhere close to his limits. That didn't mean all was lost; they did have a rudimentary plan in place, but brute force wouldn't be enough.

"The guild's new dragon is here, too, I see. You may want to scamper home, little lizard. I'm no more afraid of your organization than I am of theirs. Riding the reputations of your betters will do you no good in the real world."

It was an obvious attempt to get under her skin, but it presumed she'd put far more sense of self into her villainy and strength than Beverly had even approached. That those were the targets he went for first was informative, however. People often attacked what they considered to be their own weak spots on others, because that was what they thought of as being most vulnerable.

"You've got some nerve to talk about riding reputations. How many pawns did you need just to make it this far and get Agent Quantum in your clutches? All that effort to take on what you call a sickly imitation of the real team. Guess that makes *you* an imitation of the original Science Sentries' actual villains. No wonder you had to settle for going after the kiddie version when you couldn't cut it against the real deal."

Facially, there was little change. Dermatologically, it was a terrifying show as the skin along his neck and face rapidly eroded, revealing gaunt, dark features. The more of him that was exposed, the surer Bahamut became that there was nothing other than bones waiting to greet them. It made the smile even more horrifying as a corner of the mouth fell away completely.

To her surprise, his next move was not to bolt over to her. Instead, he released Agent Quantum, who darted away and back to his feet in seconds. "How silly of me. I was caught up in the action, eyes on my prize, and nearly forgot to relish the experience. In front of a guild representative, no less. You're quite right. This demands far more cruelty and torment. I shall play with you all for a bit longer, with one caveat. Agent Quantum, if you run, I'm going to kill everyone here, then start lopping off the heads of civilians, one per hour, until we finish this."

Whoever this guy was, nothing gave the impression he was bluffing. Bahamut's eyes flickered to Agent Quantum, noting the way his arm wasn't hanging quite right. The grip on his shoulder had left damage, and that wasn't even with the smoking arm. A single blow from this guy could take them out of the fight, or cave their very skulls in, depending on how much he put into it. They were outside their league right now, and all of them could feel it. But life wasn't merely an equation with numbers plugged in. There was strategy and tactics to consider. Plus, they had the advantage of greater forces, and that opened up more options than working alone.

Rustling from the other room was all the warning they got before Medley came bursting out of the kitchen rubble, bounding on all fours as he came at the enemy. Bahamut charged, too, ready this time to make it a multi-pronged assault. Since she and Medley had no experience working together or fighting alongside one another, they'd elected for a simple division of combat labor.

As Medley went low, aiming for the legs, Bahamut went high, sending precise blows toward the torso. There was an uncomfortable crumpling as Medley hit the legs, his body collapsing in on itself from the resistance. Still, with claws dug in for grip, he managed to force the back of their enemy's knee slightly forward, shifting his center of balance. Seeing the opening, Bahamut let loose a real punch, not holding back one bit. If she blasted the walls with his brains, then that was a good turn so far as she was concerned. Not one worth worrying about, however, as the strike sent pain tearing through her arm. It was like she'd hit a steel beam, except she suspected that would have hurt less.

For as strong as he was, the enemy did still use two legs to stand on. That meant shifting his balance in one direction while pushing hard in another was enough to leave him unsteady. On their own, that probably would have been the limit of their offensive, but there was still one more ally to account for. Agent Quantum came barreling in, showing no fear despite his recent failings, following up Bahamut's blow with one of his own.

The trio of attacks was enough to do what on their own none could have managed: they knocked the stranger onto his back. Unfortunately, the plan had to adapt. Originally, this was when they would have helped Agent Quantum escape, getting everyone out and to safety. After that ultimatum, she had a hunch he wouldn't go that easily. There was one idea from the old plan that could be repurposed, however: the way they'd planned to hold this guy off if he tried to follow.

Reaching down, Bahamut grabbed the man by his ankles, planning to easily chunk him through the air. Instead, she felt as if she were lifting a boulder. He was dense in a way that wasn't quite weight, yet still made him hard to move. Putting everything she could manage into it, Bahamut used her whole body to force the throw, weakly slamming him into the wall at the far end of the room.

Upon landing, he rose to his feet, brushing some of the dust from what remained of his shirt. The left section had largely burned away, revealing that the smoking bits of flesh were now well past the left shoulder and into the torso. "If you're about done, I think I've given you ample chance for your turn at offense."

"That's wasn't my offense," Bahamut corrected. "That was just optimal repositioning."

He had almost enough time to realize the throw had placed him almost directly under the hole in the ceiling. Had he made it in time, that revelation might not have mattered much, given that the toughest fighters from every team were already down with him. But he didn't share in Bahamut's knowledge, namely that they had a pair of long-range damage dealers who were positioned right overhead, ready to fire if their opponent had tried to pursue.

She didn't even have to call out the order. Both of the women watching had pieced it together; they'd heard the same threat to Agent Quantum as Bahamut. From above, multiple streams of concentrated energy rained down. Hephaestus's beams were familiar by this point, and also visibly outclassed by the ridiculous torrent of energy flowing from Plasmodia. Clearly, she didn't appreciate her team leader being threatened.

The combined assault was too much for Bahamut to look at; the guy's body was essentially glowing. At last, the lights faded, and Bahamut was able to blink her way back to vision. In a way, she wished she hadn't, because the first thing she saw was that their opponent was still standing. Only, he didn't look much like the one they'd started the battle with.

Almost all the skin was gone, save for a few patches here and there, one hanging on just above his right eye, if it could be called that. An inky, dark orb easily mistaken for a void filled the socket, resting in a face with no nose, ears, or other decoration. Only a dark sinew ran between the black limbs, not like any form of muscle Bahamut had encountered before. Smoke rose from his entire body now, and she noticed the ground where he stood was warping and cracking.

There was no more smile—Bahamut realized there had never been one to start. Only a skull's haunting, unmoving grin with a thin veneer of false flesh stretched atop. She really hoped the craftier members of their groups had something in mind. Her well of ideas ran dry just as he took a step forward.

"As I was saying, I think you've had a fair shot at offense, and should now realize just how impossible the fight is. However, I'm not done playing yet, so let's make this a bit more fun. Something classic seems in order. Should you manage to guess my name, I'll grant your wish and let everyone go. Even Agent Quantum."

The words might have been heartening, if not for the malicious glee absolutely dripping from each word. No one was even surprised when he continued. "Just be warned, I take a toll of flesh for every attempt. Try as many times as you like, for as long as you can bear it."

Chapter 116

Nothing. Not a scratch, not a dent, not a crack. Even Ivan had shown a small mark on his hand, and that was from a much earlier model of this blaster. Granted, he wasn't exactly in full combat mode at the time, but this guy hadn't employed any tricks that Hephaestus could discern either. It sure seemed like he'd just taken the entire blast of energy, near point-blank, without flinching. Given the intensity in her attack and the shock on her face, Hephaestus had a hunch Plasmodia was experiencing similar feelings.

Noises came from down the hall, where Cyber Geek and Cold Shoulder were taking care of another batch of straggling enemies. Hat Trick and Presto were still nearby; their powers tended to be more situational, so they'd been stuck guarding the unexpected trespasser. While it was impossible to read Presto's face through the mask, Hat Trick's expression made it clear she felt as flummoxed as they did. Not far away, Cliché was on her phone, scrolling like the wind, though what she was looking at, Hephaestus had no clue. By virtue of distraction, Cliché was one of two who missed the terrifying display of durability. The other was Tachyonic, who was slowly coming around, but was still visibly out of it from Cyber Geek's staff.

"We didn't even annoy him. He's ignoring us." Plasmodia looked down at her hands, still glowing with what should be deadly power.

It was an experience Hephaestus had known was coming, yet the arrival was no more pleasant to endure: she was against someone above her abilities. Dealing with people like Ivan and the council, it was impossible to delude herself into believing her current meta-suit and some fire powers would be enough to overcome every challenge. Some metas existed on an entirely different scale than she did, for now. The man below was obviously one such example.

As panic swept through the others, she forced herself to stay calm. Terrifying as the moment was, all was not yet lost. Because the truth was, her original gift wasn't beam-shooting gauntlets, or a homemade combat suit, or fire powers, or even meta-genius. From the very beginning, her one true talent was the capacity to look at a situation and keep thinking until she found a way through: intelligence born of willfully stubborn determination. This smoking bone-man had bested the suit. That wasn't the same as beating her.

What did she have to work with? One cape with the powers of a stage magician, one with line-of-sight teleportation, a living plasma battery, topped off by commanders of ice and video games, respectively. She also had Cliché, who might be handy if they could hit upon the right saying. For most of those present, Hephaestus knew too little about their abilities and training to make proper use of them, but as she looked from her own hands to Plasmodia, an idea took shape. The same idea, in a way, only reformed and hopefully improved.

Below them, Bahamut tried to knock the legs out from under the enemy with a sweep, only to have her own leg kicked back so hard there was no question the bone would be fractured. Fast as she healed in that form, it would still hurt like hell. And that was nothing compared to what might happen if this guy really let loose. He was toying with them, openly so, and once the fun dried up, what came next wouldn't be pretty. Agent Quantum and Medley ran in to help, but Hephaestus already knew how it would end. They were fighting a losing battle, unless she could change the equation.

"Anyone have guesses on the name?" Hat Trick asked. "I don't think he'd really let us go, but it might give them some space, or create an opportunity."

"No, which is troubling." Presto sounded unlike himself. This might have been the first time Hephaestus heard him take a fight seriously. "I've studied the Science Sentries more than anyone but the most devoted superhero expert, and this guy is ringing zero bells. Even though he acts like he's been around forever."

While this wasn't the time to say it, Hephaestus was having similar thoughts. Someone with this much power should have left an impression throughout history; the fact that he was such an unknown meant that either he'd been working in secret all this time, or another power had wiped out any traces of him. Neither boded well for what they were facing.

"Doesn't matter. When we guess it, he'll just find another excuse. Nobody having this much fun is just going to let the game end, especially after a plan this complicated to get here. If we want this asshole gone, the only way is to drive him out." Hephaestus pointed to Plasmodia, who was slowly coming back to herself. "I need your help."

"For what? Soldering? I just hit him with the strongest blast I've got. I could go bigger, but if that intensity didn't work, then... there's nothing I can do." Plasmodia was also hitting the wall of her own limitations, and wasn't nearly as prepared for it as Hephaestus had been.

Ordinarily, she'd have let the cape get over it in her own time, except Hephaestus needed Plasmodia if her idea had even a chance of working. "Why? Because your power doesn't work? You fucking capes. It's always about the abilities. Who gives a shit if he's got us beat on that angle? We've got limbs, lungs, and most of all, brains. He's stronger than us, fine. Let's make ourselves stronger than him. Meta or not, we're all humans at our base level, and there is nothing more human than using tools and wit to overcome a challenge outside our own abilities."

She noticed Presto start to do a mock-clap, then halt himself. Perhaps because he agreed with the sentiment or just appreciated the impact it was having. Plasmodia no longer looked so unsure; instead, her face was creasing in anger. It might have been more ideal if that rage was pointed down into the hole, but Hephaestus would take the progress she could get.

"How the hell are we supposed to do that? I watched your attack do just as much nothing as mine, so it's not like you've got an ace up your sleeve."

"Funny you should mention sleeves." Hoping this wouldn't be a time when she looked back with deep regret, Hephaestus released the interlocking systems on her left gauntlet, reaching over to pull it free from the suit with her right. The removal of a suit piece revealed her hand and forearm, covered entirely by the costume she'd donned before her suit. Staying concealed was still ideal, as it would keep anyone from realizing Hephaestus was a woman, which made keeping her identity secret so much easier.

Lifting up the device, Hephaestus nodded to it. "If I work fast, I can retool my own blaster. Get rid of everything except for the amplification systems, put all of it into making the strongest shot possible. The more powerful a beam we start with, the greater the final output."

"Who knows if that will even work? Or how long it will take?" Plasmodia couldn't keep her eyes out of the hole, where they could see Agent Quantum take a particularly bad blow that sent him spinning. "If I went down there now, I couldn't do anything, could I? I'd just be another target."

"Let him take a crack at it," Presto said. "Not like he's trying to mess with any of our gear, and as you said, at this point, what do we risk? Even reaching out to try to teleport that guy felt like lifting a mountain. I'd probably explode my heart getting him across the street. It's all I can do to minimize damage."

Paying closer attention, Hephaestus realized that Presto was indeed doing more than throwing cursory looks at the trespasser in their care. When one of the downstairs combatants got knocked toward anything too dangerous or sharp, he would shift them over slightly, conserving energy while keeping the wounds they took as limited as he could.

"Anything." This voice didn't come from any that had been speaking. It belonged to Tachyonic, who had finally managed to bring himself back to consciousness. "Try anything. Doesn't have to be a good plan. Doesn't have to be a smart one. If it might work, that's enough." Sweating from the effort of sudden injury and temporary recovery, Tachyonic struggled to his feet, using the wall to lean on and discovering his ankle would tolerate the weight of a leg once more, albeit barely.

"I am not letting that bastard win. We save our friends, which means stopping this threat. Find a way, if you can. It's the most any of us can do." With barely a glance down to aim for the bed, Tachyonic leapt through the hole in the ground, reentering the fray as soon as he was able. There were bursts of speed as he scrambled off the bed, but he was definitely not back to full strength.

Shuffling through her sleeves and vest, Hat Trick sorted an array of magical items, plainly searching for anything that might be of aid. Her hands fell upon the wand, terror flickering in her gaze. "I've never used actual attack magic before. It would be a risk, but he might be vulnerable."

"Knowing the way your new tricks tend to go before you master them, that might not be the best use of us," Presto suggested. "I know how you're feeling. Getting stuck on the sidelines is the worst. Welcome to being a support member: you have to watch the people you care about take the risks you aren't able to."

Those words, more than anything else, seemed to convince Plasmodia as she listened to them talk. "Hell with it. Sure, let's try your plan. If it fails, we're in exactly the same situation as right now. Just hurry. I think our enemy is getting bored."

"I'll work fast, but it's still going to take a minute." More than a minute, really. While she'd loaded up the suit with tools for repair and modifications in the field, these were still less ideal conditions than a lab. Add in that she'd essentially be working one-handed, with her other in the gauntlet, and things would be even slower. That was what she expected, anyway.

The second set of hands were familiar, largely because Tori recognized the high-end leather gloves around them. After all, she'd been there when Beverly loaned Chloe the accessories to complete her ensemble. Cliché was smiling nervously at Hephaestus, phone finally put away. "Don't worry. I think I found a way to help." Looking down again, she blinked, then pulled off the device hiding her eyes, setting them to the side. "Probably easier without the ultra-telescope goggles, though."

"Much as I appreciate the sentiment, this is specialized equipment that demands expertise-level knowledge and skill to work with." It was as close as she could get in a public setting to calling out Cliché's total lack of understanding when it came to meta-suits.

Lowering her voice, Cliché leaned in, speaking directly to Hephaestus. "Look, my friends are down there, giving everything they can to keep us safe. It's time for me to stop being so afraid of my power and see if it can do something of value, like helping stop that jerk. From behind the scenes, though, ideally."

"Lovely as the sentiment is, that doesn't change the fact that you have no idea how to work on this equipment." Hephaestus was half-scared, half-curious on where this was leading. Knowing the ability Cliché possessed, it could truly be anything.

"Not at the moment, sure, but you're forgetting one important fact: **Anything you can do, I can do better**."

It was the first time Hephaestus had seen an immediate physical shift accompany Cliché's empowered words—even the aesthetic change had been slightly delayed. This time, it was a bizarre experience as Hephaestus watched a familiar pair of eyes suddenly look back at her from Chloe's sockets. She knew them in an instant, and had there not been a helmet between them, the same eyes would have been staring right back at Chloe. They were, after all, the eyes of Tori Rivas.

For a moment, the stolen irises stared back, until they began to dissolve like shimmering flames, drawing into Cliché's pupil, revealing her own eyes once more. Suddenly, she grabbed the sides of her head, wincing in visible pain as her whole body began to shake.

"Gaaaah, okay, okay, I think I'm—crrraaaaap." She swayed, and for a moment, Hephaestus feared her friend would collapse entirely. "Hang on. Little longer. I think... nearly there." At last, her eyes opened, tears streaming down her face. "Wow. That was like an ice-cream headache multiplied by a root canal. So *much* getting crammed in at once. I think this one might be tougher depending on how much power I'm copying." Shaking off the last of her brain pain, Cliché's gaze fell upon the removed gauntlet. "Oh, hey, looks like you misaligned one of the connectors. That's going to make this feel sluggish when you need full dexterity."

It took a tremendous amount of self-control not to bristle at that, remembering that her saying had purposefully called out being better than the subject from whom the talents were taken. Part of her wondered how that would have worked if she'd targeted the smoking bone-man instead. Given the painful reaction for just Hephaestus, it was probably best she hadn't tested the power on someone that powerful. Even if it worked, publicly using such an ability would mean Cliché would definitely no longer be under anyone's radar—not if she had a power that allowed her to suddenly jump entire leagues in terms of danger.

"Glad to know, but let's focus on getting this thing capable of handling Plasmodia's output. Efficiency is more of a refining concern than an immediate worry."

From below, there tore a scream. This wasn't like the muffled thuds of bodies and blows being thrown. Someone had just been hurt, and based on the voice, that person was Agent Quantum. Presto, Hat Trick, and even their pseudo-prisoner were all staring with rapt attention through the hole. Plasmodia, however, was striding over to join them.

"What happened?" Cliché asked.

"He forced them to make a guess, and it went poorly." Plasmodia sat down, crossing her legs like she was settling in for a session of yoga. "You two keep working. I'm going to work on building up my energy. If we're betting it all on one shot, then I'm going to put every last bit of intensity I have into the attack." The crackling glow of power radiated up from her hands, stretching across her entire body inch by inch.

The message was clear: if they wanted to save everyone, time was running out. Once the smoking stranger was no longer amused by playing with his toys, he'd begin breaking them. On a small, muted video still playing in a corner of her helmet screen, Fornax was giving a live demonstration of exactly what happened when a real monster grew bored. Unless they wanted one of their own to end up like Zerle Salvrin, they had to change the situation.

Activating the soldering torch in the finger of her right gauntlet, Hephaestus cracked into her creation and got to work.

Chapter 117

The scream had belonged to Agent Quantum. As he went in next to Medley, the two of them attempting to knock their enemy off-balance, the opponent suddenly shifted in ferocity. One hand shot out, slamming into Medley's torso and sending him through a wall, shattering a bathtub. Agent Quantum wasn't so lucky as he found his own blow caught, the arm being squeezed so hard it drove him to his knees in moments.

"That's enough pondering. Time for you to make a guess. Any takers, or should I move right on to the penalty for failure?" As their opponent raised his smoking, gaunt hand, no one knew exactly what the punishment would be, but they could all make educated guesses that it would hurt.

Agent Quantum twisted his head, meeting what technically qualified as the man's eyes. "How about Mr. Bones?" Although the name was patently ridiculous, Agent Quantum had heard stranger. Besides, he didn't expect to be right. If the name were really guessable, the offer never would have been put forth.

"Thematic, yet incorrect." The man's eyes darted over to where Bahamut was slowly shaking off the last round of attacks, and to the shifting debris of a bathroom covering Medley. "Now we move on to the fun part of the game. Tell me, Agent Quantum, who shall be punished for this failure? It can be you, another cape, or even one of these villains you've formed a shaky alliance with."

"Your problem is with me. Leave them out of it."

Not quite a laugh, not quite a cackle, the hideous amusement that brimmed from that lipless mouth was almost as terrifying as the threats. "Exactly the answer I would expect from a superhero of your caliber. But the first one is easy. Let's see how noble you remain after understanding what you're in for."

His movement was sudden, smoking right hand extended so the bony fingertips were pointed forward, then thrust into the meat of Agent Quantum's left shoulder. The scream was immediate, like it had been pushed out by force of the blow. It wasn't merely pain, though; everyone in the room had taken enough injuries to understand what that looked like. Agent Quantum was leaned over, barely hanging on as his whole body twitched and seized. Finally, the man yanked his hand free, leaving Agent Quantum collapsed on the ground. He didn't stay there long, stirring soon, but the point was made.

"As your friend warned you, I am your weakness. That doesn't just mean my ability lessens yours, ironically enough, but also that it hurts tremendously in the process. Now then, once you're able to speak, let's hear your next guess. I hope it's better—"

The speech trailed off as the form of Tachyonic suddenly dove through the hole in the ceiling, landing roughly on the bed then scrambling off of it. Standing at a visible lean, there was no pretending he was able to fight at full strength, but he *was* standing. Given the state of his leg minutes before, that in itself was impressive enough.

"Perfect. It's so much more enjoyable when someone personally invested has to watch. A coworker and a temporary ally aren't the same as being taken apart in front of someone who believes in you." The man's eyes lingered on Agent Quantum, despite him making no forward movements. Now that the game was in full swing, he was enjoying himself far too much to rush it. The Wrexwren weren't even dealt with yet, and once they were, the chaos would last for hours. Plenty of time to savor his triumph.

At last, Bahamut was back up, visibly groggy yet upright nonetheless. From the bathroom, Medley's tail broke through, sweeping off shards of porcelain as he rose. Agent Quantum had made it to a turned-over chair and was using that to haul himself up. Just like when Tachyonic has been stabbed by those digits, Agent Quantum was visibly weakened, more than what just pain could manage.

Wobbling forward, not fully trusting his own leg yet, Tachyonic held up his hands and made a "come get some" motion. "Hey asshole, how about Round Two? Only this time, no sucker punch."

"Do you know why it is prudent to take out the team's speeder first? It isn't because they're dangerous—few ever manage to do significant damage against real threats. Your kind are simply annoying, dashing about in the middle of a fight. And *you* especially have a talent for failure. Being my hostage was perhaps the closest you've come to doing something right."

The man turned away, facing Agent Quantum once more. "You are beneath me, Tachyonic, as are the rest of this silly ensemble. But you aren't even entertaining enough to break. Stay patient. You'll die when I get around to it."

The wet *smack* was not the blow the smoking man, or anyone else, was expecting. Tachyonic became a momentary blur as he ran to the kitchen's garbage can, yanked out a semi-full bag, and slapped it over his opponent's head. No one was entirely sure what the owner of this kitchen had made the night prior, only that it was very sauce-heavy. Unidentifiable green and red liquids dripped down the lengths of the near-skeleton, whose smoke suddenly increased in amount and darkness.

"You dare—"

"You're goddamn right I dare!" Tachyonic was right there, in his face, so aggressive it seemed to knock their opponent momentarily off-balance. "Where do you get off, strutting around like the big shit in town? Do you know why your little game works? Because none of us know who the fuck you are! All these big claims about fighting the original Science Sentries—except we've gone through all of their old cases and fights as part of our training. If you really were around, then you left so little impression it didn't even warrant mentioning."

In a flash of movement, Tachyonic dashed back several feet, wincing at the end as his leg nearly gave out. Ignoring the pain, he repeated his previous hand-motion, once more inviting their opponent to trade blows. "You're a nobody. Nothing but forgotten trash. You don't *deserve* to face Agent Quantum yet. Team leaders are reserved for actual threats, the kinds with real reputations, not sad fantasies they've concocted."

In terms of subtlety, there was a lot of room for improvement. Tachyonic might as well have been waving a red flag and wearing a matador's outfit. That was the upside to blunt attacks, though: they didn't have to be refined to be effective.

Plumes of dark smoke rose from the man, searing off all the garbage on his person into a sizzling residue that clung to the floor where it landed. He stared at Tachyonic, all others momentarily forgotten.

"Such a dear, devoted friend you are, taking my wrath all for yourself. Very well, Tachyonic, I'll grant your wish. My statement holds true: you aren't worth the entertainment. Yet I think it will be rather enjoyable to watch Agent Quantum's face as I tear his most devoted supporter limb from limb."

In spite of being less an arm and down a leg, Zerle Salvrin refused to buckle. His assaults continued, their techniques changing on the fly. The Zerle even scored a few hits with unexpected movements, making use of the now missing appendage's space. Fornax let him come, parrying here, knocking back there, but otherwise keeping him at bay and suffering. There was a next step to this process; however, it couldn't be initiated by Fornax. Moving forward had to begin with Lodestar or Zerle Salvrin himself.

As it turned out, the latter arrived first. After taking a rough punch to where his hips would be on a human, the Wrexwren leader did not immediately attempt to spring back up. Instead, he sat, leaning his head and back against the cool metal of the chamber's walls.

"My pride as a fighter can deny it no longer. You are indeed stronger than I, Fornax." Zerle Salvrin made a motion with his hand, though what it was or what it meant, Fornax could only speculate. Perhaps a gesture of respect?

"Is this your way of calling it quits? I must say, I didn't see that coming from you." He paused, rune-filled eyes sweeping across the alien enemy. "Still don't, actually."

"Nor should you. I will never admit defeat, nor permit you to take victory." Zerle Salvrin made the noise Fornax felt reasonably sure was laughter, albeit low and subdued. "My people saw the command given. As we speak, they are already training their weapons on this ship. We will be annihilated together, along with the entirety of the crew, but you will not triumph today." Having taken a breather, the Wrexwren got up, keeping weight off his broken leg. "I hope now you understand the Wrexwren people's commitment to victory. Not even our own leaders are of greater importance."

The whistle was sharp and high, nearly a Wrexwren voice, except it came from Fornax's puckered lips. "Hell of a move. Rather die than lose. Believe it or not, I get that. Even respect it, in the right circumstances. Of course, I could always kill you before the attack hits."

"Which is why I took my time explaining. It's already too late. The blast will arrive at any moment." Zerle Salvrin raised his remaining arms, determined to hold out until mutual destruction took them both.

Fornax made no move to follow up on his threat, turning his attention to the floating cameras instead.

"Well then, it seems our only recourse is to patiently wait for the end to come. In these, my final moments of life, I would like to leave all of you viewers with a simple bit of advice: never start a war with the most dangerous species in the galaxy."

With that, Fornax turned, facing Zerle Salvrin as they waited for the ship to explode. After ten seconds, Zerle Salvrin began to get worried. After a full minute, true terror set in. Finally, he broke, the question bursting forth as he watched the absolute lack of concern remain in Fornax's grin. "What have you done?"

"Me? I've been in here with you, having a grand old time. But I'm not the only villain out there with stress to relieve. In fact, while we were playing around, my old friend Doctor Mechaniacal was working on his own project. Doc, you want to take it away?"

From all around them, broadcast over the Wrexwren's own communications system, the answer came. "Gladly. After some basic analysis, I discovered quite a number of weaknesses in the design and programming used in your ships. Redundancy is all well and good; however, the trouble with using identical components over and over is that they all have the same vulnerabilities. For example, did you know it was possible to create an overload sequence in the engines, leading to catastrophic detonation? Ten seconds, and any Wrexwren ship is nothing more than debris in the void."

"An entire ship... you wouldn't. There is no honor in such a tactic."

Fornax laughed at that, loud and cruel. "You don't get to say shit about honor. Tricking Earth's champion, launching the invasion before our duel, even trying to cheat at the last minute when losing became inevitable. You have held to whatever code the Wrexwren have in only the most technical sense. I will say this much, though: you're right. We *wouldn't* do that."

The smile widened as new images flashed into existence all around; Doctor Mechaniacal was really getting the hang of the Wrexwren systems. The entire invasion fleet still in space, from the largest warship to the tiniest landing vessel, were being detonated before Zerle Salvrin's eyes, the scenes played over and over on a constant, repeating loop.

"We wouldn't, because we already did." Fornax spread his arms, gesturing to the cornucopia of destruction surrounding them. "What sort of creature would do a thing like that? Kill an entire army when peace is still on the table? What sort of species would even conceive of such a notion, wiping out their enemy without prudence or partiality? It's the same one that fell upon your people the moment they landed. A species born in war and conflict, with millennia to hone both their skill and the darkest parts of their souls. You would shrivel in disgust to know what we have done to each other, for crimes no greater than a hue of skin or a place of birth. What did you think would be waiting for monstrous invaders such as yourselves?"

He faced the floating cameras once more, and for the first time, Zerle Salvrin began to understand that this wasn't really about him at all. Whoever was on the other side of those orbs, that was the target Fornax was trying to reach. Ordinarily, he'd have considered that useful information for controlling the tide of the fight. As it was, Zerle Salvrin was momentarily lost in the horror of seeing his entire force purged so completely. Much as he wanted to think it all a trick, the fact that they were still here meant the other ships had failed to fire. Zerle Salvrin's life was proof of his people's death.

"My advice earlier was genuine," Fornax continued, speaking directly into the cameras. "It is indeed prudent not to start a war with the galaxy's most dangerous species. Only, the Wrexwren are not the holders of that title. They are a simple, brute force: effective at their own tasks, yet inherently limited by their own rules. No, the true danger would be creatures capable of planning, deception, and untold death, all without a moment's pause. An imagination that can conceive of terrible ideas, the sort no decent species would ever consider, let alone put into use. Beings who can justify any atrocity, so long as they come out on top."

Pointing back over his shoulder, Fornax drew attention to the array of exploding images all around him and Zerle Salvrin. "Meet humanity: the most twisted, murderous, foul species in the entire cosmos. We are the ones you should have avoided conflict with. Now, you get to be a warning for the rest of the galaxy, a tale to tell over whatever the alien versions of campfires are. The once mighty Wrexwren, destroyed by one simple, poor decision: they decided to fuck with Earth."

Finally managing to gather some of his thoughts, Zerle Salvrin glared back defiantly. "Do not think one kolitre is the entirety of the Wrexwren force. There will be more to follow, to avenge our failing."

"My dear Zerle, don't be so impatient. We'll get to that, when the time is right. A being like you, possessing such willpower and strength, must be broken properly." Fornax started forward, a fresh look of excitement in his rune-filled eyes. "Have no fear, you are in the hands of a professional. I will make sure to see the job done *right*."

Chapter 118

This world was a hellscape. Humans were not the docile, simple creatures that had been painted for the Wrexwren forces. They fought like prexles, a notoriously ferocious pest on the Wrexwren home world, famous for its willingness to lash out when dying rather than flee. Prexles would prefer to wound their enemy in death than to survive, and somehow, it felt like humanity had stolen that philosophy from across the stars.

Even the ones that lacked abilities were armed, opening fire on the trio of Wrexwren as they ran through the streets, fleeing their pursuers. The ship was lost, blown up minutes after landing. The team's only hope was to find somewhere to hunker down and call for rescue. Not that they felt great about the odds, given how many similar cries for help were pinging their own systems. With every passing step, the effort of running became more and more futile.

Just when a few of the Wrexwren were pondering the prexle route themselves, something strange happened. The team was advancing on a dilapidated old building with dozens of vehicles in front of it, and as they drew closer, their pursuers started to fall away. Together, the aliens ran faster, and saw the trend continued. No explanation to be had; perhaps this ground was somehow cursed or sacred to the native species. After a day full of the worst sorts of surprises, none of the three was willing to argue with a turn of good fortune. Together, they raced up to the front and burst through the door.

For a moment, the first Wrexwren thought it was some sort of human design choice. Red splashes all over the floors and walls, bits and chunks spread around to create a messy ambience. It was a forgivable initial mistake; they were hardly familiar with much human anatomy. Upon spotting an arm, however, the Wrexwren reassessed the situation, along with estimating roughly how many humans would be required to create this much debris.

"What happened?" The whisper came from one of the others, communicated in the softest of their whistles as possible.

"Somebody didn't live up to the hype." This response came from deeper in the building, and while they had translation software equipped, it was unneeded. Whoever the mysterious being was, they'd replied in the native Wrexwren tongue. Footsteps rang out from further in the building, unseen in the thin strips of light streaming through from outer streetlamps. Darkness was in swing on this section of the planet, though all of the aliens suddenly wished they had a bit of sunshine on their side.

Raising their weapons, too aware that this might be a chance where they only got a single shot, the Wrexwren at the front called out. "Who goes there?"

"This was a meta-mercenary base. True war might be banned, but countries still have conflict, and this team was often hired to fill a given side's ranks. They were quite renowned, especially their leader: a man wielding a magical sword, said to be one of the most skilled fighters on the planet."

From the shadows an object came, tossed much too short to come within striking distance of the team, yet they all tensed just the same. It landed with a clatter—or rather, they landed. It turned out to be two objects which had once been whole. A golden sword, sparks of fading power crackling along the edges, sliced cleanly in two.

"I waited so patiently for a chance to strike in secret, a time when the blame could be put elsewhere, like an invading force. Such pains making sure not to lose Captain Bullshit's veil, only for this absolute disappointment to be my reward. Not a good day. Not a good day at all."

A spray of sparks came from the darkness, metal being run along concrete. For the first time, the aliens saw who they'd been speaking with. He appeared human, save for the twisted expression on his face. Mundane clothes, no visible armor, equipped with a single weapon: another sword, this one with a slight curve to the blade. The Wrexwren weren't especially familiar with the names of Earth's out-of-date weaponry, but there was enough context to expect it would be dangerous.

"I know you won't be any better. I do. But after waiting this long for such a worthless taste, I can't be satisfied with just this." The sparks ended, and suddenly, the man was in front of the first Wrexwren. His blade moved a single time, and the would-be invader felt his upper body sliding, leaving the lower portion behind. There was just enough mental function to hear his next words in the alien's final moments.

"After so long trapped in its sheath, my sword *thirsts*."

Grantham was mildly surprised by the small army waiting outside the bar. They were not made of Wrexwren—in fact, everyone present was either human or meta. Sipping his beer, he bristled at the chill hitting his lips. Damnit, he'd held the glass for too long.

"Diego, what's the deal with the battalion?"

His bartender, a svelte man with dangerous tattoos running up and down both arms, jumped slightly at being directly addressed. Thus far, he'd been one of the only people Grantham had bothered to learn the name of and occasionally talk to, largely because Diego also spoke English. Neither Diego nor the others were sure if that made him safer, or more in peril. All they knew for certain was that this was not a child to cross.

"They are from a neighboring compound and seek to lay claim on our holdings, attacking during the confusion. Word has probably spread about the prior owners being slaughtered."

"Yet nobody thinks to wonder if the thing that did the slaughtering is still around." Spinning on his stool, for a brief moment, it was possible to forget the absolute power this kid had used to rule them with since arriving; he looked like any other normal child. The effect ended as soon as he stopped, and Diego could see the icy-blue shining in his eyes. "What the hell—I could use a workout, and I doubt this will count as making a scene."

As his feet touched the ground, his skin changed, turning the blue of one lost and frozen in the deepest tundra. Muscle bulged in his limbs as his height shot up, reaching and passing that of an adult's stature in no time. A bushy beard of frost sprouted on his no longer childish face. He was out of the bar before fully transforming, largely because the door couldn't accommodate his modified bulk.

From outside, the deeper, older voice thundered. "Look at this pathetic lot! Such a pitiful offering. Your bodies will serve as warning to those who come next. Only the strong can face Jokull!"

Groggily, the lone surviving Wrexwren struggled back to consciousness. He'd been with a team of four. One had been killed on landing, forcing them to flee. The forest had seemed like a good place for cover, until they reached a patch where the ground gave way. Between the fall and the blunted stone triangles at the bottom, the others died on impact. Only a bit of fortune had influenced the survivor's fall, shattering a pair of legs and one arm rather than his head. It was a curious choice for a trap—sharp objects at the bottom would have a much higher lethal success rate.

Overhead, something new came into view. It appeared to be one of Earth's native species, called a bear, except the alien felt almost positive bears didn't have horns, or opposable thumbs on a huge, hairy hand. Most of the creature was off in some way, yet it moved with certainty as it grabbed the living Wrexwren and began to drag the captive along.

For a while, the ground was dirt, then slowly stones started showing up. Tighter and tighter they grew, until it was as if they were on some stone-cobbled path. Strange as that was, it had nothing on the door they reached: huge, dense, and a striking shade of white that stood out amidst the darkness of the subterranean lair. The bear-like creature knocked once, and instantly, the door gave way.

Inside was a room lit by electric lanterns. White shelves lined the walls, decorated with various knickknacks and pops of color. Chairs in the same white hue were lined up next to a matching table, not far from an actual bed. To the sides of the room, tunnels were visible, some smaller than what a human could fit through, others too large even for bear-sized creatures. Seated on a pillow in the center, preparing herself a cup of liquid from some sort of white cup-and-jug set, was what appeared to be a human woman.

She wore a lavender dress, barely fitting over her visibly emaciated frame. Frail, thin, he could see her bones moving through the skin as she reached for her cup and took a tentative sip, letting out a sharp squeak.

"It's hot," she said by way of explanation, the Wrexwren's translator conveying the general meeting. "I suppose we should start with an apology. I'm afraid you're going to find me a terrible host today."

Bad as this was, perhaps all hadn't yet been lost. If she was the meta controlling this beast, then killing her could set it free. That would put him alone with a wild animal, but that was still a better fight than having it puppeteered by someone with intelligence.

"I wish I could offer you some wonderful options to replace what you've broken. Unfortunately, laying low means I haven't been able to collect any human or meta parts. All my lovies have come from the nearby forest."

At her words, new sounds came from within the tunnels. Few approached the flickering light of the electric lanterns; however, there were enough misshapen shadows to know that none of these creatures were currently in the same configuration as they'd been born.

"Even that might not be so bad, except Sissy doesn't like to help me build anymore. I can't do nearly as clean of work without her. Modern medicine helps bridge the gap, but her ability made things so much more stable. And *far* less messy."

Deciding that this was his only shot, the Wrexwren slammed his remaining three arms into the ground, shooting up and kicking off with his pair of working legs. The effort was successful, in that he managed to get clear of the bear-monster's reach. That was the end of the positive outcome, and the Wrexwren's advancement, however.

From the table and each chair came a spear, molding from their very material, firing out and piercing directly into the Wrexwren's flesh. Four lances where the dining area had been, skewering him in place, lifting up slightly so he was unable to even use the ground for traction.

"While I did say I was going to be a terrible host, I can't believe I forget to introduce myself. My friends call me Cathy, but I guess you'd probably be more interested in my professional title. Before I got locked away and had my old lovies taken, people used to call me the Bone Mage."

The shadows were slinking out from the tunnel, a menagerie of warped creations, each spliced together in a hideous hodgepodge. From her pillow, Cathy rose as well, stepping lightly over to take a closer look at her newly captured specimen. When she reached out, the Wrexwren tried to jerk its head back. That earned him a gentle smile, as well as a hand delicately running along his torso.

"There's no need to fear. I'm going to take good care of you, or as much of you as I can. Alien physiology is tricky. Luckily, I've got the rest of your friends to experiment on first. Don't worry. I'll get all the mistakes out before it's your turn. We'll make you stronger than you ever were before. Relax, be at peace, and look forward to what the future holds."

That gentle smile sharpened, and her wide eyes shined down like mad moons, like they couldn't wait to unveil the horrors lying in store. "I just *know* you're going to enjoy being one of my lovies."

Clad in a scat-brown suit and bowler hat, no one would mistake this man as an icon of fashion… not that the gentleman clad in such an ensemble gave even the smallest of notions to the opinions of the masses on any topic, including clothes. Compliance with the herd was a practice for the weak. Those with power lived in whatever way suited them best. This was simply one more way he marked himself as above them. Although, not quite so far above them as the woman currently on screen.

Unlike the rest of the world, he had no interest in watching Fornax piss about—the man had been insufferable enough when they shared a prison together. Trying to view Lodestar with magic was a fool's errand, so they'd simply found the Wrexwren broadcast and tuned in to that with the help of a peon. Other metas often looked down on those with powers focused more toward utility than combat, while those of wisdom knew it was always handy to keep such talents around.

"Worried she might not win?" This man wore simple garments with a high collar—almost a priest's outfit, yet not quite.

"For a meta who uses the name 'Faithful,' you certainly express a great deal of doubt." In truth, he knew why Faithful wore such a moniker, and the history that made it such a hideous joke. One did not align with Faithful unless there was good reason, and it was *never* wise to fully trust him. Yet Faithful's power was so great, sometimes the risk was worth it to gain access to his abilities.

With a completely sincere expression, Faithful lowered his head in apology. "Consider me chastised. Against such a tremendous threat, I thought perhaps even the Lodestar might have some trouble."

"*A* Lodestar, certainly, but not *that* Lodestar. She's already ascended to greater heights than this. If she were dispatched by such a base, rudimentary threat, she wouldn't be the prize worth pursuing."

The bowler hat tipped back, revealing a face worn by the years, unlike Faithful, who remained young and spry no matter how much time piled up on top of him. "My mistake the first time was moving too fast. This is no ordinary cape to bring low; it was folly to think of her that way. One does not snare an apex predator the same way they catch meager prey. This will be a long hunt. Keep that in mind if you get any urges to make a spectacle and lose yourself Captain Bullshit's veil."

"My urges are entirely in check, until they aren't," Faithful replied, as if that settled the matter. "I'm more curious on how, precisely, you expect to snare her. Not even my ability was able to overcome that cape, and I was among the most offensively powerful in Rookstone."

The bowler hat dipped down as its owner nodded in agreement. “The trouble was that you came at her head-on, as did I, as did almost everyone else. We all forgot a truth as simple as a nursery lullaby.” He hummed a few bars to himself, watching as Lodestar grew brighter, hitting her opponent over and over to no effect.

“If you seek to catch a star, first you have to make it fall.”

Chapter 119

This enemy should be beyond her. Lodestar understood that, as another attempt to even dissuade it from the current course failed to draw so much as a reaction. It existed on a scale beyond what humans were designed to fathom, let alone challenge. To stand against the Scralthor was like seeking to halt a sun's meltdown mid-nova. These were not forces they were meant to have control over. And yet, for better or worse, she was permitted to break that limit. Human-shaped wasn't the same as human.

For even another Lodestar, this creature likely represented a final task. Tapping that deeply into the power would be enough to wipe out any trace of the person wielding it, all but guaranteeing that someone else would be burdened with the mantle. Under normal circumstances, this would be her last bout: going out in a final blaze of glory to keep her planet safe.

Except that Helen had a secret that not even most of the other capes knew. Over a decade before, she'd floated in the depths of space, squaring off against another seemingly unbeatable opponent: Orion. With his speed, power, and semi-intangible nature, even her abilities hadn't been enough to fully stop the former scientist bent on destroying the world. At least, not at first. Not until the fight neared its climax, and she finally understood her place in the cosmos.

Not until she broke the rules.

"You're just hungry." She said it to no one but the vast monster. Even the Wrexwren ships that had been leading the Scralthor were gone now, blown up with all the others—no doubt the guild was somehow responsible. "This isn't your fault, and I get that. Someone is using you. This was never a fight you wanted any part of. As much as I can, I'll try to hold back. With what I'm about to do, there are no promises."

She blasted off, soaring into space, tightening her focus as she moved. It was easier to access while active, gave her somewhere to channel the excess energy as it was building. Distance traveled didn't matter. By the time she was ready, it would largely be a question of how fast she chose to move. Still, she had to be focused. This was only her second occasion going past the current limit.

Last time, there had only been the absolute injustice of the situation to focus on, and her own unwillingness to bend to it. That was the night she learned that roles were just words, and that even a Lodestar could be greedy. Today was different. She could already feel that as the heightened levels of power flowed into her, trying to drown out the woman at their center.

Between the daughter, friends, and history on that planet, there was no chance she was letting the Scralthor plunge it into darkness. Scorching through the void, Lodestar wasn't just glowing anymore. She'd begun to shine.

Cyber Geek and Cold Shoulder arrived back at the hole just in time to catch the end of their mystery attacker's threat toward Tachyonic. He wasn't making empty overtures, either—those bony hands came grabbing for Tachyonic immediately. Luckily, he was still mobile enough to dodge, albeit poorly. He wasn't as sluggish, though whether that was from the staff or the fact that the power-weakening attack had begun to fade was up in the air.

"What's going on?" Cyber Geek asked as Tachyonic scrambled away from the claw-like hands.

"Mystery asshole says he's going to kill everyone unless we guess his name, then probably kill everyone anyway." Hephaestus didn't look up from the glove she and Cliché were hunched over, the pair working in near perfect tandem. "Unless you have something more powerful than me and Plasmodia blasting at once, save the ammo. Delay and holding tactics would be greatly appreciated."

To their surprise, it was Cold Shoulder who perked up. "Looks like that's me." She started for the hole, but Presto suddenly appeared in front of her.

"Shoot from up here. He's strong enough that he can kill any of us with one hit. Ice-armor isn't likely to change that, and I don't think he's going to react well if you actually do hinder him."

Cold Shoulder hesitated, until Plasmodia jumped in, still seated and building her charge. "Presto doesn't joke around when we're losing, and he's actually got a good head on his shoulders. That guy is toying with them. Let's not give him any more targets, especially less durable ones."

That evidently convinced her, as she perched at the edge and watched the battle unfold, swirls of frost dancing in her hands as she waited for the opportunity to strike. Plasmodia and Presto were by her side, neither of them paying proper attention to the green trespasser in their care, who was mostly poking her head over to watch the same show play out.

Meanwhile, Cyber Geek was hung up on the rest of the conundrum, trying to guess the attacker's name. There were so many games where avatar names popped up automatically, and he knew that some interface components came over when he used head-covering items from specific games. Unfortunately, so far, none had name-revealing properties; otherwise, he'd have known who was really under Hephaestus's mask. This was where he needed more item variety, the kinds of situations where his power could truly excel, if only he knew the right option to use.

"Do we have any clues on mystery man?" Cyber Geek wasn't expecting much, but knowing he was too weak to fight directly and apparently not powerful enough to fire an effective shot, this was all he could think of to do.

"Well, he looks like that, so there's a starting point," Presto noted. "Says he fought the original Science Sentries, seems to really hate Professor Quantum, basically untouchable in terms of strength, and his power directly weakens those with abilities derived from setlium exposure. That's all we know."

Plasmodia's head popped up as something occurred to her. "And it's ironic that he has that effect on setlium—at least to him. I'm ninety percent sure he said that."

Tachyonic's voice came over the communicators, a sharp reminder they were still broadcasting locally, words spit fast between pants for air. "He also claimed to know Professor Quantum before the change. Said he was the first destroyed by the professor's ambition."

Who could have lived that long and still remained unknown? For that matter, why would it be anything other than pure convenience to have an ability that neutralized not only one of the most legendary capes in existence, but also hindered everyone sharing the same source of powers? A sudden notion scratched at Cyber Geek's mind, intuition cobbling together the pieces he was too frantic to see. There was one thread of an idea firm enough to pull on, so that's what he did, yanking out his AHC phone and opening up a quick tab for research. It certainly didn't feel heroic, skimming the internet as his friends were fighting for their lives, but Cyber Geek was fast learning not to give a shit about what did and didn't feel like cape-work.

If it had even a chance of keeping someone alive, then it was time well spent. Besides, this didn't have the feeling of a wild goose chase. Cyber Geek was on to something. The question was if he'd figure it out in time to matter.

The dodges were working, at a cost. Between the injured ankle and the residual effects of being weakened, it was taking everything Tachyonic had to avoid the clawed blows. From behind, Medley ran up on their attacker, throwing the entirety of his bulk into one of the bony man's joints. It was truly the only technique he'd managed with any effectiveness, knocking his opponent briefly off-balance before a smoking leg kicked Medley across the room and into a wall.

If not for incredible endurance and rapid healing, Medley and Bahamut would both be out of the fight already, likely in shape similar to Agent Quantum. Tachyonic felt pangs of guilt as he backpedaled, equally aware of what these distractions were costing them, and how badly they were needed. Without those two drawing occasional focus so he could rest, the dance would already be over.

Sadly, there weren't many steps left to it either way. Tachyonic zipped around, grabbing a meat tenderizer from the kitchen. He tried to break it over the man's skull, hoping to annoy more than hurt at this point, keeping focus away from Agent Quantum. As he made the approach, Tachyonic's ankle hit a poor position and suddenly buckled. Not enough to send him sprawling, though that was largely because of the strong, gaunt, smoking hands that grabbed onto Tachyonic before he could land.

"At last, my little fly, you've wandered too close. Let's see what we can do about pulling off those wings."

"Rob Bob." The name was nonsense to Tachyonic, as well as everyone else in the room based on their expressions, yet Agent Quantum didn't pause before throwing out another. "Todd Williams. William Todds. Jack Crack. Is that enough guesses for a penalty yet?"

Injured or not, Agent Quantum was on his feet, dragging himself to a standing position thanks to the wall. "That's the game, right? Guess and take the penalties. Well I just earned myself four, and they're all coming to me. Unless you'd rather play with Tachyonic than finish trying to break me."

For a face lacking flesh, the stranger did an excellent job of showing his momentary indecision. "You are already beaten."

"If this was about crushing me, you could have done that on a street corner in the middle of the night. Whatever you're after, I don't think it's just proving you can take us in a fight, and I'm positive it has nothing to do with my friend. You want to hurt Professor Quantum, right? I'm the one walking around wearing part of his name and using some of his DNA. I'm the one you want to hurt."

Medley and Bahamut, both slowly having shaken off their last blows, were nearby, watching the act play out silently, unwilling to move and risk tipping whatever gambit was in play. If either was surprised by the revelation of Agent Quantum's origins, they had more important matters at the forefront of their minds.

"Yes, you are," the man agreed. "But unlike Professor Quantum, it seems you truly care for your team. And there are many ways to hurt someone."

"Maybe so, but you challenged me to take the pain until I caved and gave it to someone else. Maim Tachyonic, and it's the same as admitting you couldn't defeat me. Not the way you wanted to."

For a delicate moment, no one moved, all of them too aware that this man could squash Tachyonic's head in a single motion if he so chose. Finally, the dark skull turned back to its captive. "I suppose it would be disappointing, to come all this way and not see you ultimately turn on those who trust you. Though I've had enough of this pest flitting around."

The sharp tips of his left hand broke the skin on Tachyonic's arm, and he stabbed his right fingers into the thigh on the cape's non-injured leg—a short combo that drew a brief yelp of pain before Tachyonic collapsed. Between the new injuries and the power-weakening effects, he'd done his last running of the battle. Their enemy stepped over Tachyonic's writhing form, shifting toward Agent Quantum.

"Now then, about those penalties."

Before the man was fully turned, Medley sprang, launching at their enemy's head. Between the fur, bulk, and general confusion, he was able to hang on long enough to hammer home a few blows before getting roughly hurled through a wooden beam. Loud creaks came from overhead, as Medley dimly realized how many of the support structures on this floor had been already taken out.

Futile as the attack seemed, it gave Bahamut enough time to run in and drag Tachyonic away. She even managed to return as Medley was getting thrown, grabbing a chunk of broken granite from what had once been a kitchen counter and smashing it against the bone man's back. He spun around, surprisingly quick when he wanted to be, and snared one of her arms. That was all it took, so great was the strength difference between them. For the first time since she'd been transformed into a dragon against her will, Bahamut was truly feeling the limits of her power, and it was not an experience she had any interest in repeating.

Dragging her along, the man looked back to Agent Quantum. "What about this one? Are you also willing to suffer in place of a villain? Who knows the number of innocents these claws and teeth have drawn blood from, how many injustices they've perpetrated. You're a superhero; surely it serves the greater good for me to hobble criminals and leave you at full strength."

"There's nothing good about passing my problems on to someone else, greater or otherwise. Maybe he deserves what you'd give, but if I bought into that philosophy, I'd never have become a superhero in the first place. We're not here to punish. We're here to protect. Now, are you done wasting time with these distractions? I'm half-recovered from that last attack; you'd better get moving if you want to stand a chance."

A plainly empty bluff, yet Bahamut was still released from the iron grip, all interest from her captor instantly lost. "You put on a better show than he did, I'll give you that. Which will make it all the more enjoyable as I rip that façade of nobility away and show them all who you truly are."

In an unexpected bound, the man crossed the gap between him and Agent Quantum, easily snaring the weakened cape by the back of his neck and holding him roughly in place. "Which brings us to your punishments. Can't take your tongue yet—I'll need to hear you talk so you can cave—and most of the senses will be vital in watching your own body torn apart. A limb might be a good start, though I do worry you may bleed out too soon."

The sharp fingers traced along Agent Quantum's face, leaving a red abrasion wherever they ran, until stopping on the bridge of his nose. "Then again, I suppose you could still see your team butchered with only one eye. The real question is, which one to take? I have just the solution, one that Professor Quantum would find great appreciation in." His finger began to tap under each eye in succession as he spoke. "Eenie... meenie... miney..."

"Alfred!"

What should have been a random name being shouted in desperation instead had a very curious effect. Their attacker halted, finger still halfway between eyes for the next tap, all attention shifting to the hole above, where Cyber Geek's head was poking through.

"That's who you are. Alfred Settler, the member of Professor Quantum's team supposedly killed in the experiment that created meta-humans. You're the man setlium was named after."

Chapter 120

Laughter. That was the bone man—or rather, Alfred's—response. Tittering chuckles that oozed from his mouth as he looked from Agent Quantum, still held tightly in his grip, to the virtually unknown cape that had awkwardly blundered into such a revelation. Unfortunately, this was not the kind of mirth that signaled a positive shift in mood. If anything, he appeared even more dangerous.

"Alfred Settler is supposed to be dead," Agent Quantum said from his prone position, searching his captor's fleshless face as though there were clues to be found. "When Professor Quantum's experiment changed the world, most of the team with him became the first meta-humans. Alfred was killed, and Professor Quantum named what he saw as his greatest discovery in honor of their fallen team member."

"Yes, that *is* the story." Without warning, Alfred hurled Agent Quantum through yet another chunk of wall, drawing groans from bits of ceiling overhead. While the cape struggled to his feet, blood dripped from fresh wounds; in his weakened state, even the lesser attacks were causing damage. "Because the truth casts such a hideous light on the great, beloved Professor Quantum. I wasn't just some assistant caught in the blast. Nearly half the work on that experiment was *mine*! *I* was the one who saw the greater potential, who warned your supposed hero that there were dangers he wasn't considering. *I* was the lone voice of caution who stood against the experiment, and *this* is how fate repaid me."

He gestured to himself, to the smoking skeleton with the barest bits of muscle tissue keeping it held together. "I'm sure they thought me dead. My body had become corrosive to everything, in varying degrees, and looked like this. By the time I woke up, I was entombed in a metal box and buried under literal tons of rock, the same way we treated nuclear materials at the time. But that's the upside to being corrosion incarnate: nothing can hold you forever."

Having a receptive audience, Alfred had fallen into one of the oldest villain habits in the book: monologuing. No one dared to interrupt. This was a chance for them to catch their breath and think a few steps ahead. Had Alfred gone through guild training, he'd have been warned on the dangers of such an indulgence, especially when the fight was not yet won.

Lifting a thin hand, he pointed directly to Agent Quantum. "Yet what should await me when I emerged? A world enamored with the same selfish, irresponsible, arrogant bastard who made me this way!" The wood under his feet turned dark and cracked at the sudden flash of anger, forcing Alfred to move closer to Agent Quantum. "Whereas I am nothing more than a footnote. Even my name he warped and corrupted to serve his own goals. What a great man, to honor the colleague he killed and erased from history by naming something I never wanted to exist after me. Of course, by the time I reemerged and the humor in that became evident, it was too late for a renaming."

Another step closer, causing everyone watching to tense up. The truth was, if he made a run for Agent Quantum, they couldn't stop him. Slow him down, maybe, but there were no delusions left to dispel; everyone present knew he'd simply been taking his time and having fun. Unless they came up with something soon, the moment he got serious, they would have to face the hard choice: flee, or die fighting.

"We were across from each other, in almost exact opposite points of the room. I wonder sometimes if that's why it worked out this way. Perhaps we inadvertently freed the entire spectrum of meta-elements in that one moment and have slowly been discovering what was in Pandora's Box. He got setlium, whereas I got the opposite. This horrible, eroding energy that kills everything except the man who would welcome it. The exact opposite of what infuses your cells with their ability. I call it: vernium. What do you think?"

Agent Quantum went momentarily stiff, drawing another round of terrible chuckles from Alfred. "That was just in case any of you thought I was spinning a yarn. I am glad to be able to tell you all this, before your end. It's been so long since I shared that story, and I think it will add to the experience of watching your friends die. If nothing else, you'll understand why I'm going to leave them as nothing more than skeletons. A message to the man I'm playing with."

"You think he'll see this as a game?" Medley demanded. It might have been telling that the one who doubted such a sentiment was a cape who'd never worked with Professor Quantum before.

"The game is what he and I have been playing for decades. This is only a single move—though an excellent one, if I do say so myself." To their surprise, Alfred started walking again, but not toward Agent Quantum. He was heading away from everyone, toward one of the holes into the hallway punched by flinging bodies. "As for games, I suppose there is a prize that is owed. Cyber Geek, you and your team are permitted to escape, assuming you are able. Because now that my secret is out, I find it's nearly time to draw things to a close."

He didn't step through the hole, as a few might have been expecting or hoping he would. Rather, he grabbed a support beam on either side, two of the few in the area left standing, holding up everything currently over their head, including the rest of the capes and villains. "Everyone in the pool. It's time to sink or swim."

A pulse of dark energy washed over the beams—the first time they'd seen him intentionally use the corrosive power. In less than a second, the thick wooden supports were nothing more than black ash. Overhead, a loud *snap* could be heard, followed by a series of groans and crackling, before a huge chunk of the ceiling—and everyone who'd been sitting on it—came crashing down.

Bloopston was pinned down. Separated from Big Swing by the sudden Wrexwren ship that had slammed down to Earth, weakened by having to run through a burning hallway, and now with four aliens drawing close to his position. The call for help had gone out minutes prior, but hope was restrained. There was so much going on right now, and a limited amount of backup to spread around.

Just as the first Wrexwren rounded the corner, face aimed right at Bloopston, something fell from the top of the building, landing directly in front of the creature. On first glance, it appeared to be a normal person. No costume, no mask, nothing to mark this man as exceptional, not until he threw a single glance backward, permitting Bloopston to get a look at his face.

No wonder there wasn't a costume: Quorum didn't wear one. His identity, much as one could call it that, was on public display. Despite the tense situation, he still sounded calm, as another Wrexwren joined the first, sounds of the other two drawing near.

"I know you have translators. This is your only chance. Surrender now, and we can attempt to protect you. The invasion has failed, your people are beaten, but as individuals there might be a path of peace for you moving forward."

In response, the first Wrexwren took a swing at Quorum, who deftly leaned out of the way before returning a blow to a spot on the left side of its chest. As the alien choked, two more hits came, striking a specific point in the torso, and one just above where two of the legs joined. Three quick strikes, and his opponent was lying on the ground, making a sound Bloopston felt reasonably sure was gasping.

Seeing its ally injured, the second alien began to raise a weapon. The attempt was leagues too slow, as Quorum had the speed and perception of over a thousand people piled into the single space his body occupied. Twisting the weapon out of the Wrexwren's claws, Quorum used it as a blunt instrument, delivering one sharp blow to the head and sending his opponent down in a heap.

"Go." Quorum had turned to Bloopston, still unfazed. "Along that alley, turn left by the fountain, keeping heading north until you see the other AHC members. We're consolidating our forces to root out the nearby remaining invaders. I'll be there shortly."

He was gone, around the corner, off to meet more Wrexwren head-on before they arrived. Bloopston, still shaken, did as he'd been instructed, forcing his webbed feet to move along the paved stone streets. As much as Lodestar and Professor Quantum tended to be the larger profiles at the AHC, this particular cape felt a great deal of gratitude to the less-assuming member of the Champions' Congress, who was out here getting his hands dirty. Granted, Lodestar's fight was obviously essential as well, but Professor Quantum could have made a real difference out in the field. Who knew how many capes wouldn't be coming home tonight because their calls for backup had gone unanswered?

If the big capes were busy, then that just meant the rest of them had to pick up the slack. Bloopston poured more effort into his legs, eager to find the others. Assuming they had some healing power on hand, he could recover and get back out into the field. Being trapped and helpless, only to have salvation arrive unexpectedly, was an excellent reminder of what it meant to be a superhero.

Time to pay it back. There were others out there who needed help, and next time, Bloopston would be the one running in to save the day.

Hovering in the air, Cliché held in one arm, the in-progress gauntlet in the other, Hephaestus couldn't believe there was a time she hadn't considered flight an essential suit function. She blasted back, toward a hopefully stable section of the remaining floor, and set both down. "You okay?"

"Not especially. That guy sounds serious about killing us all, and I'm not sure this is going to work," Cliché admitted. "Oh, you meant physically. Little bruised on the ribs from your grip, but doing much better than I would be if I'd taken the tumble." Tenderly poking herself in the side, Cliché appeared momentarily confused. "Actually, wait—maybe not a full bruise?"

"If you copied my powers along with my brains, then your body is tougher than normal right now, and will heal quickly. Really wish we had more time to play with the fire-based stuff, but eyes on the prize. As of now, I think this bad boy is our last shot."

Reaching over, Cliché put a hand on the cold metal of Hephaestus's shoulder. "What if it fails?"

It was something she'd been trying not to think about. Calling the guild was out, since most of them were dealing with the invaders, just like the major capes, so they couldn't count on backup. If this didn't work, she was officially out of ideas. Sure, with enough time and tech, there might be a solution; however, with what they had on hand, it simply might be impossible to beat the enemy who'd clawed his way out of the past. Should that be the case, it was important to remember that they weren't the capes here.

"Teleport out as many of them as will go. Bahamut and I should be able to escape on our own. I don't think Alfred really gives a damn either way, since we aren't with the AHC. Regardless, the guy lacks wings. Take anyone who's willing to teleport somewhere far—another country if you can manage it. Aim for big cities. The kinds of places where capes will have to be present, dealing with invaders. Then get away from the superheroes fast, because we don't want any part of this grudge spilling onto us."

The sudden groan of floorboards had both of them expecting another collapse, until they glanced behind and saw the familiar pattern of kaleidoscope eyes peering past them, into the rubble below, where bodies were already beginning to stir.

"Not a good time for cryptic bullshit, Nexus," Hephaestus spat, focus swiftly returning to the gauntlet-in-progress.

"Then I am pleased to say that I have none to offer. This is merely the point where things grow most interesting, so I've come to see your version."

"Still a little cryptic," Cliché pointed out, though her tone was gentler than Hephaestus's. "I'm surprised you're here, though. With Lodestar fighting a big monster and Fornax dueling an alien champion, aren't there more interesting things to watch?"

Nexus gave a small nod, never looking away from the shifting debris where Medley's tail had just emerged. "Both are worthy of witnessing, which is why I am doing just that. There are a great many tales being told in this chaotic backdrop, and I am carefully observing all of the most entertaining ones."

Very nearly, Cliché almost asked how—except she sensed that that would start a journey down a rabbit hole they very much did not have time for. Instead, she helped Hephaestus with the gauntlet, rewiring at incredible speed, despite her previous lack of familiarity with the task. This was quite a potent saying to keep on hand, assuming the next attempt didn't split her head open like she felt the last one still might.

A voice rang out from below, filled with confidence, perhaps even a dash of joy. Unfortunately, that voice belonged to Alfred, and only made their situation worse. "Lozora, is that you? Here I assumed you'd have scampered off into a hole once the work began. Turns out, you managed to sneak in. A dedicated helper to the end."

Hephaestus knew that voice. It was one she'd clung closely to, making sure not to forget a single syllable, and as she listened to Alfred speak, his tone finally landed in her memories. It hadn't sounded quite the same through the magical fire and distortion of the room, but there was no mistaking that air of shitty smugness. This was the voice they'd heard in the labyrinth, meaning that she'd finally found the one responsible for attacking the Starscouts.

That might be useful in the long term for getting him on Lodestar's radar, but in the moment, it meant their "trespasser" was exactly what Hephaestus had feared: an enemy in disguise. In fact, her skin's inhuman hue triggered another bit of memory from the flaming pit's speech—this Lozora woman was likely the "green little helper" he'd mentioned. Worse, based on everything she'd managed so far, Lozora might also be competent, as well. They were already on the ropes; one more enemy who knew what they were doing could very well put the nail in this coffin.

"So considerate of you. Saves me the trouble of hunting you down later."

After Alfred's words came a sharp screech, and Hephaestus felt a tad less worried. This was why villains used the guild, for protections against exactly this type of betrayal.

It wouldn't take him long to finish with his former ally—or anyone else, for that matter. Hephaestus scanned the gauntlet again, searching for any potential way to increase the output. There was no chance the weapon would survive; they'd get a single shot out of this, at most. It had to be cranked to the absolute maximum.

Because if this didn't work, the only choice they had left was to run, and Hephaestus knew deep down that not all of them would get away. Alfred's bony hands wouldn't let them escape.

Chapter 121

From the wounded body of Zerle Salvrin came a series of higher-toned whistles, what Fornax had begun to suspect indicated the presence of mirth. Moments later, the translator kicked in as words sprang forth. “Behold, your mighty champion. She has realized the fight is hopeless, and is fleeing for her life.”

The mistake was understandable. Zerle Salvrin had no context for what he was seeing, no history to pull from. To Fornax, this sight also represented the nearing of the end, though not in the same way his opponent anticipated.

As he was looking up at the ceiling’s screen, Zerle Salvrin launched an attempted surprise attack. To his credit, several blows managed to land before Fornax hit back, once, stunning the Wrexwren momentarily.

By the time Zerle Salvrin recovered, he was being held, head pointed upward, directly facing the screen.

“Fun as playing with you is, this is the sort of thing one rarely gets to witness,” Fornax said. “It’s about time you understood just what your species is truly up against.”

Together, they stood, watching the light burn brighter as it rose through the sky, waiting to see what came next.

The rubble should have been nothing, not to him. From the early days, he'd been strong. Before he learned, trained, grew, and evolved into the man who could lead the New Science Sentries, he'd been born strong. Pressing his hands against the floor, the weight bore down on top of him, trying to hold him back. Out there, he could discern muffled voices, followed by a scream. It could be one of his team, or the other superheroes, even one of the villains giving aid. There was no way to tell through all the debris blocking his ears.

A small voice inside whispered that perhaps it was better this way. Covered as he was, the situation was actually a momentary respite from the beating he'd been taking. The voice lit something in his belly, a self-directed fury at even being capable of such a notion. Pushing harder, arms straining, he forced his muscles to work, despite being weakened by Alfred's energy. Staying put, laying low, none of those were acceptable options for a superhero.

His head swam from the effort, threatening to pass out entirely, and he refused it. Through the blurry vision and near unconsciousness, he could still see the faces of his team... his friends. Ike, so jaded and broken when he'd first arrived, now fighting to protect others. Ellie, starting so nervous and quiet, they initially thought she had stealth powers; it had taken years for her shell to crack and the powerful superhero to emerge. Kyle, who'd been with him from the very beginning, a pair of kids shooting for the impossible goal of carrying on a legacy.

Just when it felt like his arms would fail, one last face swam into view, followed by her gentle voice. "I don't like the idea of you following his footsteps, especially knowing how dangerous it can be. That said, I trust you, and I know this is where your heart is set. So just promise me one thing. Don't be like him, a figurehead playing a role. Be true to who you really are: my superhero."

Something in his back tore, a pain that barely registered amidst the accumulation of wounds piled atop him, as Agent Quantum managed to shove aside a massive hunk of unseen material pinning him. He burst forward, getting most of his torso out into the open air. What greeted him was an array of groans and slow movement as a few of the others pulled themselves free. It seemed Agent Quantum had been under one of the densest sections, though there were some still hidden beneath the debris.

Nearby, Alfred was holding some tall woman with skin the color of an old lime underneath. Her face was twisted in pain—no surprise given the way one of her legs was dangling, refusing to bear any weight. Neither paid the newly emerged cape much attention; they were busy dealing with one another.

"You traitorous shit. Why?"

"Same old Lozora, needing explanations instead of just accepting the commands. Because you annoyed me, I wanted to kill you, and now that the job is done, there's no reason not to. As a bonus, it saves me some pest nipping at my heels, demanding payment that was never going to come."

As they were fighting, a sudden creak next to Agent Quantum tipped him off to Presto's arrival before the other man spoke—though not by much. "Things are looking rough. We've got one real card left to maybe play. After that, our only option is to hope we can escape."

Spinning around, he noticed Presto was lightly coated by dust, having taken at least part of the tumble with everyone else. There was also a curious set of goggles wrapped around his left wrist, much too cobbled-together for the New Science Sentries aesthetic. "You heard him—if we run, he'll kill random civilians until I show up."

"I'm not so sure about that. Look at when he took his shot: mid-invasion, when all the bigger capes are busy. I don't think he can afford to draw that much attention to himself. Because next time we show up, it'll be with the full Champions' Congress at our backs. That's the whole point of being in an alliance."

It was a good point; with backup, this fight could go very differently. And in truth, Agent Quantum didn't really expect Alfred to manage a nonstop murder rampage if they got out. But people *would* die for it, he had no doubt there. This was an enemy who delighted in hurting them. He'd never miss such an opportunity to twist the knife.

"Thank you, Presto. I know what you're trying to do, and I appreciate it. Get everyone else out safely. That's an order." Turning from his ally, Agent Quantum shoved his legs through the rubble, yanking himself fully free as he faced their attacker once more. "Hey, Alfred! I thought we were mid-game. Get bored of me already?"

At the sound of Agent Quantum's voice, Alfred hurled Lozora over his shoulder without the slightest care; she hit a wall and slid softly down. "*Never*, my boy. I will never tire of tormenting anyone who wears even a piece of that name."

Moving with intent, Agent Quantum stepped away from the site of the collapse. The others were managing, but they needed time. If he could keep Alfred's interest, it would give them a chance to recover, and hopefully escape. "It doesn't have to be like this. What happened to you is clearly a tragedy, but the AHC has resources. They might be able to find a cure."

"A cure? A *cure*?" Another section of floor darkened moments before

Alfred shot forward, backhanding Agent Quantum so hard the cape stumbled back several feet. "What possible need do I have for a cure? Shall I go return to my family, all of whom are long dead? Perhaps I can visit the graves of my friends, marvel at the results of my stolen legacy, or mourn for what might have been. A cure—what a childish notion. The only things in this world that are still mine are this power, and that mid-city patch of ugly concrete they slapped my name upon."

"This is better?" Agent Quantum wiped the blood from his mouth, or as much as would come away, as he struggled to regain his balance. "Hurting people you don't even know, hoping the pain carries over to Professor Quantum. Which is *pointless*. Whatever you do to me, we both know he won't really care."

For a very strange moment, something passed between them. On as many aspects as these men were polar opposites, there was a shared understanding common to both. They knew the man behind the legend, understood what it was to live in the shadow of the great Professor Quantum. In their own way, both had been scarred by the experience—only one of them wore that pain on the outside.

"I do know." There was almost a tenderness to Alfred's tone, which did not match the punch he delivered to Agent Quantum's ribs, shattering several. "But having his precious legacy ripped violently apart so soon after their debut will hurt the Science Sentries' reputation. Let the years pile on as they may: pride has always been Professor Quantum's one true weakness, the place where he can suffer."

Morose though the moment was, Agent Quantum's heart suddenly fluttered as he caught sight of a dark armor floating down from the ceiling. Alfred glanced back once, allowing Agent Quantum a chance to strike, which he didn't take. Knowing the effect such a blow would have, it wasn't worth the injury to his hands. Right now, he needed to stay whole for as long as possible—taking the beating was the only way he could hold Alfred's interest.

"Oh, are the others planning something? How cute. Perhaps you're buying them enough time to attempt an escape, now that you've all finally grasped how hopeless things will be? Guess that means you'll have to keep me busy, then." Another punch, this time to the left shoulder, breaking it and sending Agent Quantum reeling.

Even through the pain, however, he kept watching the others. Hephaestus had brought down some woman with a ski-mask and an umbrella just after Alfred turned away, and together, they were rooting through the rubble, searching for someone. Agent Quantum tried to raise both fists, but the shattered shoulder refused to work properly, so he settled for getting the right hand up.

"That's right, I will. Keep it coming. Almost got your timing down."

A bony palm to the sternum cracked it on impact, as well as sending Agent Quantum stumbling back. He was saved from the floor only by virtue of crashing into some of the few remaining kitchen cabinets. Breath was suddenly tight in his lungs—the air had been knocked out of him, adding rasping to injury.

Behind Alfred, light burst forth from the debris. They'd uncovered Plasmodia, who was seated like she'd been meditating, energy crackling along her entire body. Agent Quantum wasn't even sure she'd realized the floor collapsed. Plasmodia was building a charge, focused enough to manage through the chaos. Hephaestus and the strange woman hurriedly grabbed her attention.

"Bastard though he is, at least Professor Quantum is capable of adapting to a challenge. Look at you, the situation so clearly hopeless, yet you persist on playing hero. Do you really intend to take this all the way to the end?"

"Absolutely." Sweat and blood were dripping into Agent Quantum's right eye; he must have cut his head on impact. It didn't even matter. Seeing the punches coming wasn't helpful in this fight. Half-vision was plenty. "I know what happens when you start choosing yourself over everyone else. I've seen what lies at the end of that road. If my choices are to be a real superhero for this one moment or spend decades as a fraud... well, I think I've already made my decision on that front clear."

Ignoring the pain screaming across his body, Agent Quantum lifted his working arm into a fist once more. The others were to his right, in the blurred-out section of his vision, so he had no clue where they were in whatever scheme they had planned. All he could do was keep standing, and have faith in his team.

Alfred, on the other hand, was in clear view as he lifted a hand, fingers fully extended. That was the form he used for stabbing blows, and gauging by the angle, Agent Quantum had a gut feeling he'd be feeling this one in the gut. "Such a noble sentiment, yet in the end, what did all your suffering accomplish?"

"Well, he bought us enough time to beat you, so that's something." Hephaestus's voice rang loudly through the room, clearly meant to be heard. At the sound, Alfred twisted back toward it, and Agent Quantum was able to adjust his gaze. Now he could make out Hephaestus and the woman wearing the ski-mask, both directly behind Plasmodia, who'd donned one of

Hephaestus's metal gloves. Both she and the device were glowing like a sword pulled from the hearth, his fellow New Science Sentry staring pure death at their attacker.

Interestingly, it was the ski-mask stranger that seemed to rile Alfred the most, pointing directly at her. "You! The gall to be in my presence again, and with that vile item in hand no less." To Agent Quantum's shock, Alfred began to stalk across the room, interest momentarily shifted.

While this did move him closer to the others, it also put distance between him and Agent Quantum, meaning Plasmodia had an easier shot. From the whine of the metal glove, it sounded as if she'd hit the same conclusion.

"Really? More of this pointless pageantry. Very well. These are your final moments. Waste them as you see fit." Alfred kept right on walking, and given how unassailable he'd been through the whole fight, it was hard to blame him. Odds were, this would be just like all the other attacks: entirely pointless.

Hephaestus grabbed Cliché as the threat drew near, no longer shouting, the voice still easily carried through the small space. "Weapon is out of our hands now. Can you think of anything to give it some extra juice?"

There was something familiar about the twinkle of her eyes as the ski-mask woman stared down the approaching skeleton, but Agent Quantum was in no headspace to place it, even with the aid of her voice.

"In times like these, only one pops to mind, and I can't think of anything more fitting. **The darker the night, the brighter the stars**." No sooner had the words left her mouth than the woman tipped over as she passed completely out, saved from hitting the ground only by Hephaestus's quick reaction time.

Amidst the madness, Plasmodia paid neither of them any mind. Every ounce of her focus was on the still-advancing form of Alfred. She was letting him draw close, making sure there was no chance the shot could miss, even if it meant she'd be in danger afterward.

"On behalf of the New Science Sentries, the original Science Sentries, the Alliance of Heroic Champions, and everyone else you've hurt with your horrible scheme, consider this a message from the bottom of our hearts: Fuck you back to the grave."

Plasmodia fired, and the entire world exploded in light.

Chapter 122

It had never been like this before. Not anything close. Usually, Chloe felt the power shift around a touch with each new saying, like a mild change in the breeze. Even the ones that impacted her physically, she registered differently than the power itself. This was no breeze, however. It was a tornado, yanking her out of metaphorical Kansas and whipping Chloe through what felt like a dozen different spaces all packed into one.

When she finally stopped, there were no sights to behold. Everything was sensation; she was well past the boundaries of the physical world. There was a shape to this place, a form, even shifting as it was. Mentally groping around, Chloe felt a small divot, a break in what should be. At her touch, words drifted into mind—her own words, in fact, spoken to Hephaestus back in that hallway, when they needed to work on the gauntlet.

This was a mark left from using her power. Wherever she was, it was connected to that ability. As she pondered what it could mean, Chloe also realized something else: the break was shrinking. Self-repairing, soon it would be no more than a memory. Continuing on, Chloe tried to get her bearings, to create a sense of this place. There was no time here, making it impossible to say how long she wandered. She only knew that something was leading her forward. It was a peaceful, nearly serene trip... until she reached the edge.

No mere divot this time. Instead, she was at the lip of a crater. Standing there, she could feel her own power flowing into the fracture of reality, reinforcing something much larger and bigger than she was capable of generating on her own. Slowly, Chloe put the puzzle of her situation together. Before, she'd been the one creating the breaks, her own pockets of the world where things functioned differently. This time, she'd stumbled onto someone else's efforts, and that made for a very different experience.

Today was turning out to be quite the learning opportunity. Not only had she discovered a new use for her abilities, Chloe also learned she wasn't the only one out there who could create these sorts of effects. Except, whoever had made this one was worlds stronger than her—though, with Nexus's warning fresh on her mind, it was hard not to wonder if that gap could be closed. Especially considering the other truth she was realizing.

Based on how much was flowing from her into the crater, Chloe had a *lot* more power than she'd been using, far more than had been leaking out of her last effort. She could feel the connection, and had an intuition that it could be severed when she desired, but Chloe made no attempts to halt the power. Might as well see how much she really had to throw around.

Besides, if this was working as she imagined, then there was no phrase to use where her efforts would bear better fruit. She wouldn't change the tide of the invasion—that had already been sewn up—but there were still untold smaller fights going on across the planet, countless forces facing dangerous odds, seemingly unbeatable forces. This crater was already a thumb on the cosmic scale. Chloe was just turning that thumb into something a little heftier.

Now it was just a matter of seeing how heavy she could go.

Two-on-one were bad odds, even without an injured leg, something that Dapper Doll tried not to dwell on as she leapt to the side, narrowly avoiding fire from their blasters. She had the advantage in physical power, but the ranged weapons kept forcing her back, scoring minor damage from shrapnel when she wasn't quick enough. With buildings to her rear, however, room to maneuver was running out.

There was one shot she could think of: do the unexpected, sprint *toward* them and try to dodge the incoming fire. Absolute lunacy, there was no way she had the dexterity or reflexes to pull off something like that. And yet, in that moment, something in her stirred. A newfound... confidence wasn't the right word. Certainty. This was the only path forward. She simply had to find a way to make it work.

Hearing the footsteps draw near, Dapper Doll sprang, her feet unexpectedly swift. Whether it was terror or adrenaline, she was faster than she'd ever been before, clocking the movements of her opponents as they aimed their weapons. At the last second, she dropped into a slide, narrowly avoiding the pair of shots that went clear overhead. That got her within swinging distance of the first Wrexwren, just the proximity she was aiming for. A pair of punches sent it reeling; funny, the last one she fought had been a bit tougher, but an upper hand was an upper hand.

One kick to the head put it down to the ground hard, revealing that the other Wrexwren had been drawing a bead on Dapper Doll. That should have been it, end of the line, a shot point-blank into her torso. Except that her instincts had a mind of their own. Rather than duck down like she had before, Dapper Doll used her enhanced strength to push off the ground, leaping into a standing somersault. The Wrexwren shot had been angled low, expecting her to dodge downward, which meant it missed her entirely.

Her move, on the other hand, landed Dapper Doll only steps from the enemy, steps she took quickly, sending the alien down with a few well-placed blows. Scanning the area for more threats, she saw nothing. "Everyone, come on out. Let's keep moving to the evacuation point."

Out of nooks and crannies all along the street, civilians appeared, the ones she'd been leading to safety when the pair attacked.

Now that the fight was done, her hands were starting to tingle, the post-battle drain setting in. Moments later came the pain in her leg, the injury exacerbated by all the acrobatics. Dapper Doll was glad for it, though, because moments prior, she hadn't been expecting to make it through the night. It seemed someone out there was keeping watch over the capes today.

Lodestar was nearing the edge of safe terrain, the limits of what she could wield without substantial risk. With power like this, it was very possible to lose herself, even rooted as she was. Feeling the flood of new energy wash over her, filling her relatively miniscule form with the fundamental forces of the universe, she mentally turned away from the Scralthor and all the fighting.

To hold on in moments like this, the key lay in remembering who Helen truly was. The first faces pained her heart: Mom, Dad, and David. Why did her mind always go to that night, that hill, where they were waiting for her with the telescope? Next came a vision of Mackenzie, trying to hide her tear-stained eyes as Helen awoke in the hospital.

Lodestar began to fly once more, no longer away from the Scralthor, now on a direct course. Helen's mind flashed ahead, to Faucet Hills on that fateful day she'd been forced to accept and wield the same power that had killed her family. Because the other option had been to standby helpless as Corvix butchered her friends. That was the moment she swore to never be helpless again.

Her shine, already blazing so brightly, only intensified as the memories flew by. After Corvix came Quorum, the loss and gain he simultaneously represented. Faces flitted by faster, friends and people she'd saved, anchors that helped her stay grounded as the world grew enamored with Lodestar. Battles, challenges, enemies, adversaries, one after another they fell, until Fornax.

Ivan's face swam before her, coated in a red mask, staring in absolute shock that his blow hadn't sent her spinning back through the air. In fairness, her face had also been a mask of confusion; it had been so long since anyone threw a punch she really *felt*. From there, it was a chaotic swirl of Fornax and Ivan, sometimes an enemy, sometimes an ally, yet somehow almost always a friend.

New pain filled her as she remembered the way he'd stared up during their final bout, eyes filled with the apology he didn't know how to voice, fully aware of how much it wounded her to bring their dance to an end. To leave her alone on the top of the mountain once more. It was short-lived, soon replaced by the image of Ivan hanging in the void of space, wielding more power then she'd even known he possessed, holding Orion locked in position. The moment he'd helped her see who it truly was that set their roles in this life. For a fleeting moment, she could hear his voice, reaching through the chasms of time.

Even the Lodestar is allowed to be greedy.

Things grew brighter from there, as did the soaring Lodestar, now on a crash course with the Scralthor and only picking up more speed. At last, she'd reached the foundation of her world, the cornerstone that would not give: images of Penelope's newly born, scrunched-up, crying face filled Helen's mind. Fast on its heels were countless memories of holding, teaching, playing, dancing, all with the daughter that was never supposed to be.

The same daughter who was probably watching right now, along with the rest of the world, worrying about what would happen if Lodestar failed. She was counting on the world's greatest hero, yes, but also on her mother. Without a sun, their world would wither and die, and at the even idea of Penelope suffering, Lodestar drowned all the forces of the universe vying to overwhelm her. This thing, this being—whatever it was—would not yield until it was fed, or beaten.

That fear in Penelope's heart wasn't hers alone. It stretched across the entire planet, *her* planet. It had lingered over all of them for long enough. Lodestar locked her fist in position as she increased her speed, charging toward the otherworldly abomination.

Seemed she needed to remind everyone, cape or villain, alien or human, cosmic beast or god or anybody else that wanted to step up, just *who* this planet was protected by.

Across the world, countless small fights suddenly turned, the forces seeking to protect gaining ground on those who were after conquest. It wasn't always enough to shift the tides, but for a great many, that extra bit of speed or oomph in a punch was enough to snatch victory.

In the room with Chloe's unconscious body, a much more direct contest was occurring. Plasmodia's beam wasn't simply hitting Alfred with no effect, like last time. No, this was leagues more powerful, physically driving the near skeleton back, forcing him to raise his hands in defense. A scent of burning bone drifted up from the air, and something gave way, flying off from Alfred. Whatever snapped, he'd had enough, diving out of the shot, which instantly carved through the back wall, opening them up to a view of the outdoors. Plasmodia angled the beam upward as it died out, making sure not to hit anyone below.

The gauntlet fell off her arm in pieces, the entire contraption burned away from the beam's intensity. That had been everything they had, and then some, but it wasn't enough. Alfred was still there, rising slowly to his feet. No one moved, because what move was there left to make? That was their final gambit, and it failed.

"You..." He wasn't beaten, but he also wasn't the same, twisting toward Plasmodia like a serpent rearing to bite. "This cannot be. I have stood against the Science Sentries countless times, wiped out capes and villains alike, even survived an encounter with Fornax. After all of that, I *refuse* to believe the first true injury dealt to me came from one of Quantum's whelps."

As he spoke, the keen-eyed in the room realized something had changed. On his left hand, the ring finger was now missing. Plasmodia's beam hadn't been enough to kill him outright, but she had managed to cause a wound. To his ego more than his body, unfortunately. There was no revelry or humor as he began to stalk directly toward her, hands already extended.

"There's only one solution. I'll just have to kill you all and rewrite history.

Starting with the one who caused this unacceptable embarrassment." Suddenly, he wasn't walking anymore, but rather bolting forward on a direct course with Plasmodia.

It was too fast for almost anyone to act. Even if he'd been at full strength, Agent Quantum couldn't have caught up in time. Most of the team was still crawling their way out of the debris, and while Hephaestus was at Plasmodia's side, what kind of aid could be offered? Those bony hands would likely tear through metal just as easily as everything else. There wasn't even room to dodge as Alfred barreled down on her. Plasmodia merely faced the threat head-on, watching as his arm reared back and struck.

Before it could hit, the arm was slowed by a sudden new obstacle in its way. Presto stood there, strange goggles over his eyes and blood dripping from his stomach where the arm went cleanly through, Alfred's hand poking out the other side. Shocked, the room was silent, meaning they heard the slight sizzle as Presto leaned forward, grabbing on to Alfred's forearm, his own flesh burning on contact.

"There's a funny thing about having a power that can kill you if pushed too hard: that issue only matters when there's not something you'd die to protect. For as much of a limit as it's been, the upswing is I've got one hell of a single-use trick, and you're along for the ride, asshole." Presto sucked in a deep breath, then jerked his head upward, staring past Alfred, into and past the sky, the stolen goggles peering at the dark depths of space.

"One last time, for the people in the cheap seats... ***Big Finish***!"

This was unlike any other time Presto teleported. Normally, he simply vanished, and that was that. On this occasion, be it due to effort, mass being pulled, or overall effect, there was a snap of a moment where the spaces connected. Cold burst forth as air flowed in, a fraction of a nano-second enough to feel the wave of emptiness ripple out from their destination.

The silence that followed felt false. It couldn't be over, not just like that. But it was.

Plasmodia's hand was reaching out, grasping at the point where her teammate had been moments prior. "Presto... why...?"

"Not to be indelicate, but the why is pretty obvious. He knew what we all knew: there was no winning this fight." Hephaestus looked at the still-smoldering hole in the building. While her current system couldn't see much, the goggles he'd grabbed were capable of far more impressive views, daylight be damned. If Presto had really used enough power to die, then there was no telling how far into the cosmos Alfred had been flung. What was more impressive was that he'd had the presence of mind to grab and test new equipment, then formulate a last-ditch plan, all in the midst of Alfred's chaos. He'd had a brain with lots of potential, all of which was now lost.

"No." The voice was near a whimper, and it didn't come from Plasmodia. Agent Quantum was leaned against a set of wrecked cabinets, tears running down his face as he pressed his working arm's fist to his forehead. "Damn it, Ike. Damn it." He swallowed, trying to find some level of composure. "I'm sorry. I should have been better. I should have found a way."

Emotional a scene as it was, Hephaestus's perspective afforded her a good view of the sky, which had suddenly grown *much* brighter. Weirdly, the sun appeared to have shifted position as well, moving at an alarming rate. Except, when Hephaestus checked again—nope, the sun was still in its expected position. Too preoccupied to noticed how Fornax was holding his captive on the livestream, she turned to the others. "Not to undercut the moment, but should we be worried about that?"

Following her pointing finger, Plasmodia looked up as well, damp eyes going suddenly wide in shock. "Oh my god. It's just like the Day of Two Stars."

That name was familiar, something Tori had uncovered in her initial research of Fornax; after all, it was all but impossible to learn about her mentor without also reading the history on his greatest rival. As she recalled, the Day of Two Stars was what some people called the fight with Orion, alleging that Lodestar had blazed so bright, the planet's two light sources became indistinguishable.

Seeing it for herself, Hephaestus could certainly understand how the nickname had formed. There was something horrifying and humbling to see so much power being wielded that it was literally visible from space. Yet even that paled in comparison to what came seconds later.

With most of the Earth still watching, the sky suddenly shattered.

Chapter 123

The term "Scralthor" was a Wrexwren word without direct translation. To the creature itself, such a combination of noises would have had no meaning. The sharp shrills of smaller beings weren't even loud enough to be an annoyance. Merely background, like the songs of the stars and the hideous buzz lurking within black holes. It had no concern or thought for them as it swam, gobbling up small morsels on its way to a larger meal. Flashes of light and minor impacts had caught what passed for its eye, but they were no more than minor meteor strikes, impossible to break through its tremendous hide.

As it swam, however, the creature noticed a new sound. Rich, deep, melodic, and loud. Increasing in volume, at that. Shifting its attention, the creature could not believe what its senses were saying. Since being spawned in the flickers of a dying nebula, the being had swum and devoured, devoured and swum. Others of its kind were challengers, an occasional threat, but space was large enough for all to swim.

This was not a challenger. This was not of its kind, nor was it fully of the tiny ones. The song thundered all around, inescapable and undeniable. Power, a power that was far older than the creature or any of its kin, rippling forth like the fabric of the universe could scarcely contain it. While the creature had been alive for time untold, it was still growing, still learning.

In that moment, seeing a force so much greater than itself, the creature had just enough time to experience genuine terror. Seconds later, a blow that seemed to fracture reality itself rang out, the shred of light stretching through the darkness of space. It made no sense, that a being so small could wield such power, but the pain radiating forth would tolerate no second-guesses.

For the first time in its existence, the endlessly devouring creature born from the void of space was being genuinely challenged.

"That's..."

The first translated whistle reached Fornax's ears moments after Lodestar's initial blow. Before their eyes, a tremendous burst of energy tore forth from the point of impact, like a crack made of light splintering across the windshield of the universe. That was merely the spectacle, however. What was visible when the light cleared was the real show.

"That's..."

Against all known reason and sense, the Scralthor had been sent reeling back, blasted away from its shining snack by one true blow from Lodestar. It opened its mouth, letting out some unseen howl lost in the distance of the void. The creature turned to face this blazing threat, taking it seriously at last, far too late. Another blow sent it hurtling further away, Lodestar proving she had plenty more punches to throw, if needed.

"That's..."

In truth, Fornax didn't even need the translator for these words. He'd heard them spoken over and over again through the decades. Sometimes, the language changed, or the voice, or even the form of speech, yet the feeling was always the same. It was the sound of understanding setting in, the audible crunch as delusions of grandeur were smashed apart. Scheming scientists, aspiring gods, invading monsters, horrific villains: they all sounded alike when the reality of what they were facing finally landed.

"That's impossible!" Finally, Zerle Salvrin got the words out, joining a rich Earth tradition he had no idea he was even part of. The words Fornax had been waiting for, the signal that his work could at last draw to a conclusion.

"Yes, it is, not that she gives a damn. This is what it means to stand against the Lodestar," Ivan explained. "That is the lid on the pressure cooker of our planet, the limit we cannot rise above, the force that rises to meet *every* challenge. Barrage of giant robots, summoned army of demoids, or even asteroid-sized monsters from space. It doesn't matter. It *never* matters. All hope of victory has been stolen. No amount of training, or planning, or effort will ever be enough, regardless of how hard any of us try. Do you understand now, Zerle Salvrin, why the day was lost before it began? Even if there are any Wrexwren left out there, they'll never be a threat to Earth. Getting past her only means dealing with all the hungry beasts of the planet that eagerly await fresh targets."

Fornax couldn't destroy hope, but Lodestar did it by her nature. While inspiring those she protected was all well and good, being on the other end of that equation wasn't nearly so nice. It forced one into the simple realization that some walls could never be climbed, certain challenges left forever unmet. Watching her beat a natural force of the cosmos away like nothing more than a shoplifter's hand reaching for a candy bar, Fornax himself felt the same wave of despair as Zerle Salvrin and anyone else who dreamed of being the strongest. Once they knew how high that bar really was, the impossibility of the task became unshakable.

"There *will* be more Wrexwren." Zerle Salvrin was whistling sharply now, trying to twist his head away from the screen; however, Fornax kept it held firmly in place. "They will find a way to deal with your planet's defender, and you will suffer for this day."

Taking a moment to be sure there were no sudden surprises in store with the Lodestar fight, Fornax moved slowly around, putting his head in Zerle Salvrin's line of sight. By no coincidence, this also gave the floating cameras a good view of both Fornax and Zerle Salvrin's faces as they looked into one another.

"In truth, they wouldn't," Fornax corrected. "Whatever tricks they'd have brought would be irrelevant. Trust me, if anyone, on this subject: Lodestar rises to the challenge. Not that it matters, anyway. Because no more Wrexwren are coming, Zerle Salvrin. You see, we didn't tell you everything about that destructive wave from earlier, did we, Doc?"

The voice came immediately, finally tipping off some of the viewers at home to just how planned all of this had been. Fornax was never in danger; they were toying with the alien who'd challenged Earth, drawing the fight out to make him suffer.

"As a matter of fact, there was one tidbit we omitted. What we used wasn't merely some sort of short-range attack; it was coded into a signal. And my, you Wrexwren have just as robust an interstellar communications array on your warships as I was hoping for. Capable of reaching across innumerable light years in a matter of moments. I've been watching their systems detonate one after another, never even aware they were under attack. I'll scroll some of their identification codes on the screen, just in case you need proof."

Twisting against Fornax's grip, Zerle Salvrin tried to look away, not that there were any good alternatives to the horror in his gaze. Above, he saw

Lodestar smacking down what was meant to be his ace in the hole, now with alien symbols flashing on the side of the image, the names of more downed ships across the stars. Next to him was the twisted joy in Fornax's face, eager to dole out more suffering. Even looking to nothing held no escape, as his mind filled with images of all his kin dying in space without warning.

"You would not do such a thing. To destroy our ships, murdering untold soldiers far from conflict… that is beyond the scope of war."

"Beyond the scope of *your* war, maybe. Humans are a truly unforgivable species. Then again, you came here to invade, to wipe us out. Did you expect to have fewer stakes in the fight? Think we'd be content with merely driving you off? Ridiculous dreams. Ours is not such a benevolent way of thinking. Our kind would sooner rip the moon in half than let a chance for vengeance go unfulfilled. Come for this planet, and know you do so with the life of everyone you care for riding along. Consider the preemptive genocide of the Wrexwren army our version of a warning shot to the galaxy at large."

Finally, Fornax shifted his gaze away from Zerle Salvrin, turning to the cameras. "Because this isn't only being broadcast to the citizens of Earth. Doctor Mechaniacal is using your ship to send this video out to every receiving system out there. A galactic hello, from the hellpit of Earth, in case any other eager aliens have thoughts about sending more invaders." His eyes shifted back, down to the rattled form of Zerle Salvrin. "We'll get to them. First, I believe you and I have some unfinished business."

The truth was settling in. Their previous demonstration proved that not only could they remotely blow up ships, but they absolutely had zero compunctions in doing so. Zerle Salvrin raised an arm, half-forming a claw to strike with, only for the appendage to drop heavily. Nearly there. Just a bit more to finish out the job.

"Zerle Salvrin, I present you with a rare opportunity. Based on the state of your ships and the conditions waiting for your invaders, even the few who survive our signal won't be able to withstand the wrath of all those other planets you attacked. There is a real chance you may end up being the last of the Wrexwren army. Yet all hope is not lost. Doctor Mechaniacal can still halt the signal before every ship is reached. I'm willing to offer a way out, and make no mistake, this is your only chance to save countless Wrexwren soldiers. Let us see if you are a leader who can also be humbled. Accept that your people are helpless, that you live or die only by our pleasure, that your strength is nothing. I will permit you to beg for your life."

Releasing the grip on Zerle Salvrin's head, Fornax slowly took a few steps back, visibly unworried about potential attacks. First, he'd broken Zerle

Salvrin's faith in his physical strength, showing that Fornax was unquestionably the more powerful of the two. Then, he'd broken Zerle Salvrin's sense of strength in numbers, decimating the forces that had earned him his title. Next, Lodestar destroyed any hope he had that the Wrexwren people would ever be able to overcome this obstacle, making sure he would die for nothing, not even a potential new invasion target. Now, they'd come to the hardest part for beings like Zerle Salvrin, the reason Fornax had needed to knock away every other support before arriving to this point: it was time to break his pride.

A being like Zerle Salvrin would never beg for himself. That was a truth Fornax understood to his bones. Yet the experience of Ivan also gave insight, because even the staunchest of warriors had something they would beg to save—he knew that firsthand. Being the final survivor of the invasion would be a heavy enough burden to carry; to be the last warrior of his species was a concept beyond horrific. A battle that couldn't be won by strength, the only chance for victory was in weakness, contrary to what seemed to be every facet of the Wrexwren culture.

Unable to read the emotions on what passed for Zerle Salvrin's face, Fornax nevertheless watched the storm of them flow. Eventually, the Wrexwren leaned forward, using one hand to extend his head slightly, while dropping the three working legs into all right angles, creating a sort of suspended crouch. Not quite a bow by human standards, yet clearly meant to convey vulnerability in the same way. Head angled toward the floor, Zerle Salvrin's whistles echoed around the room before being translated.

"I ask... on behalf of the Wrexwren species... for time to discuss terms of surrender."

"Terms? What terms do you think there will be? Which pieces of you we dissect versus which ones we try eating? Terms are for people with leverage, Zerle Salvrin. You don't have that." Fornax paused, waiting a moment for reply before deciding the wound needed a dash more salt. "Want to know what's really funny? There was *never* a point where you had a chance. The only reason you're here is that someone on my planet wanted to occupy the AHC, so they sent bait to lure you down. And my people decided to make better use of you. Do you understand what I'm saying, Zerle Salvrin? You didn't even warrant a warning shot. Instead, you *are* the warning we're giving to rest of the universe. All you've been from the start are pawns in an Earth scheme. Countless Wrexwren slaughtered, for nothing more than a game."

There was a moment where Zerle Salvrin appeared to be on the edge of taking a swing, only to feel the confidence that would back such a play suddenly absent. Every other avenue of hope had been cut off by Fornax. There was no fighting a way out of this, no rescue was coming, and even if he escaped, where would Zerle Salvrin flee to? A cosmos full of formerly conquered planets would have quite a few entities looking for payback against the last known Wrexwren soldier. The only hope of living long enough to preserve his people's legacy was in front of him—that was the conclusion there was no skirting around.

"Mighty Fornax, great warrior of Earth. I humbly beg of you, please spare me. Let me live on in my shame, a worthless coward weakling. We greatly erred in challenging this world. Your power was more than even the Wrexwren could handle. Please, let my cowering life serve as testament to the collective strength of Earth."

It had taken some time, yet Fornax delivered as promised. The leader of the invading alien forces, hunkered over, pleading for his life, with most of Earth and unknown viewers across the galaxy tuned in for the show. Beating Zerle Salvrin would have been simple and proved just as little. Breaking him completely was far more terrifying, all the more so to any who'd faced the Wrexwren and their seemingly endless pride.

"That was excellent," Fornax said, peering down at his former opponent. "You held nothing back. I couldn't ask for a more earnest, sincere pleading. Well done, Zerle Salvrin." The words were slightly softer, encouraging the alien to look up, providing a momentary view of Fornax's boot lifted high overhead. "But my answer is no."

One stomp, a spray of liquid, and Zerle Salvrin was nothing more than a headless torso flopping about on the ground. Soon even those movements slowed.

Fornax, however, was only getting started, gaze darting between the body and the cameras.

"No, because the Wrexwren were garbage, nothing but a species of brutish fodder. You died the way you were always meant to: cut down effortlessly by those with real power. Yet in your death, and the death of your entire species' armed forces, you will serve one actual function: our warning message to the rest of the universe. Because if those of you out there watching haven't realized it yet, Earth is not a place for amateurs. To even face us, you have to get past Lodestar, and the lesser capes at her aid. So if you'd like to test your mettle, feel free to come take a swing."

Fornax lifted Zerle Salvrin's body from the floor, hurling it against the wall, where it collided with a damp thud, largely splattering across the gleaming metal. "But unless you're already the strongest being in your corner of the galaxy, don't bother. We don't want your refuse. We want your conquerors, your kings, your gods and demons. Prey worthy of sinking our fangs into, something that can offer up a proper challenge."

Grabbing the middle camera, Fornax pulled it in close, making sure his rune-covered eyes filled up the entirety of the shot. "Earth is riddled with monsters, and we are all so very... *hungry*."

Rick was shaking. Not violently, not even noticeably, if one wasn't paying close attention. His mother's arms slipped over his shoulders, and even as the logical part of his brain insisted that she was part of this too, it was drowned out by how much of him needed that hug.

How had he not seen... because why would he? How would he? In what world could his dad, Ivan Gerhardt, the plain, dull, middle manager be... no, even the thought was too much. But those words floated back up: "rip the moon in half." Who talked like that? Ivan did, when he was being serious. Such a stupid turn of phrase, yet it had been like a pin pricking the side of a balloon, and now, there was no way to put back all the realizations that were escaping.

Twisting, he meant to speak to his mother, only to recoil in horror at the expression on her face. Was that pride? Admiration? It absolutely was not the appropriate reaction to a man saying he'd wiped out part of a species and then brutally murdering a beaten foe.

"Why?" That was surprising—he'd thought the question of how would win out, but much of Rick's brain was working on autopilot at the moment. "Why is he doing this?"

"On the immediate level, to help keep the world safe," Janet replied. Not one sliver of hesitation to her voice. She'd been ready and waiting. "In a longer term sense, to help keep us safe."

Now, Rick did throw off her arm, physically scooching over on the sheet. "How does that have anything to do with us?"

Never had Rick seen an expression like what darted over his mother's face. Dark, harsh, determined and set, he wondered how many times she'd had to wear that, given who she'd evidently married. "It has everything to do with us. Your father just walked onto a stage in front of the universe and sent two very clear messages. The first is not to challenge Earth idly, which should give any other potential invaders a long pause before they pester us. The second message is what happens specifically to anyone who crosses Fornax. After seeing what he just did to someone he had no grudge against, would you ever want to incur that man's true wrath?"

There wasn't an easy answer for that. Rick had a hunch it would be a long while before he found any easy answers at all, in fact. Laying his face in his hands, Rick closed his eyes, trying to clear his mind so he could think.

Instead, all that waited for him in the darkness were those horrible eyes with the glowing red runes. Only now, he couldn't stop seeing them embedded on his father's face.

Chapter 124

The sudden cold of metal shocked Lozora nearly as much as the force being exerted. Someone was yanking on her shoulder, trying to pull her up to a standing position, despite her weakened leg. She turned to find Hephaestus staring down, gauntleted hand on her, while the free digits motioned back to where everyone else was either stricken with grief or slowly emerging from the pile of collapsed debris.

"We should be gone."

Given the state of the superheroes, Lozora could see the wisdom there. Logic said she'd just been double-crossed by the same person who'd attacked them, putting everyone on the same side. But they'd just watched a friend die to save them all. Logic wasn't necessarily the current captain of decision-making. With emotions running this high, the last thing they needed was an outlet.

Much as she detested the help, there was no way she could escape with her leg's current condition. Doing her best not to appear annoyed by the gracious assistance, she allowed herself to be hauled up onto Hephaestus's shoulder and steadily walked out into the hallway. No one seemed to notice or follow. They were all lost in the moment, looking up to the sky, though whether it was searching for their lost ally or admiring Lodestar's handiwork was anyone's guess. Only the dragon appeared unconcerned, gently lifting up the ski-mask woman, who was still sleeping soundly.

Together, Lozora and Hephaestus trudged down the hall, weaving their way through the groaning, injured bodies of her former crew. The capes weren't going to come down easy on this group, not with one of their own now dead. All the better to get clear before they started arriving. Nevertheless, she didn't trust such a kind gesture, even as she needed it.

"I'm surprised you didn't want to stay with your friends back there," Lozora noted. "One of them seemed to have gotten knocked out."

"Which is why Bahamut's job is to take her somewhere to get help," Hephaestus explained. "Sorry to disappoint, but you weren't the first item on my checklist when the dust settled. You're not even the first thing I picked up. Still, with the capes always having each other's backs, we villains have to look out for one another occasionally, too. Otherwise, those saps will always have the upper hand."

Though "enemy of my enemy" wasn't the most original reason to lend aid, it was one Lozora could wrap her head around. Desperation formed strange alliances; she'd seen that borne out a great many times through her unnatural life. Besides, it wasn't as if she had some item or information worth stealing. With her employer disposed of, Lozora would have to start all over again. Perhaps this next time, she'd take a few solo jobs to build up some funds, then form her own crew.

"The way you say villain, I take it to mean you're part of the club." This meta-suited fellow was clearly not Fornax—aside from him being broadcast on television for everyone to see, he would never hide in a fake identity when a real fight presented itself. Plus, Fornax shouldn't even know she'd had a hand in trapping him and his daughter. Nevertheless, it didn't hurt to sniff around, just in case.

"Only in the most technical sense. I made it through initiation, haven't really done much since then. Getting access to backup is great, though. Makes this life not so scary, having people to turn to, especially considering how capable some of them are."

There was no arguing that point. Even Alfred—such a strange name to put to the man she'd known all these weeks—had acknowledged the strength of the guild. That was why he'd taken pains to keep them busy. Finding herself suddenly helpless and in need of aid, Lozora was less dismissive of the notion than normal. "You may be right. Perhaps it's time I gave consideration to the benefits of working together." Turning down a new hallway, they were nearly to the stairs, which Lozora's leg was already groaning about.

"You should know up front, getting in isn't without risk. Some of the tests can kill you, and even with the help of a mentor, there's no promising you'll make it through."

Lozora bit back a scoff only by necessity; she couldn't risk offending the person hauling her around. "I've been on the scene longer than this admittedly embarrassing situation might indicate. Normally, I'm quite a force to be reckoned with. The man was simply... anomalous." Some metas were just too strong. The world didn't play fair, not every fight *was* winnable. Learning that early on was one of the keys to surviving in their world.

Round a new bend, only to find a pile of moaning bodies and huge, torn-out chunks of wall blocking the path. "Crap, looks like Medley or Bahamut got rowdy over here. We'll have to circle around." Together, they continued back down the last hall, passing the turn-off to the blockade. There was another set of stairs at the far end of the building, made for fire emergencies. Not as spacious, but it would work, or failing that, a window could allow them to fly out.

Lozora was so lost in thoughts of escape, she didn't quite notice the way Hephaestus adjusted his grip on her, the same way he'd had to several times already. That this movement also shifted the position of his gauntlet ever so slightly was a detail that would have grabbed her attention on a day with less occupying her mind.

At last, they neared the edge of the hallway, one that would give them access to the outside. Lozora felt so thrilled, her leg even seemed to stop hurting for a moment. "Seems as if we're fr—"

The sound of blasting energy and sizzling flesh interrupted Lozora, followed swiftly by horrific pain rising out of what used to be the middle of her torso. She collapsed, already dying, yet kept conscious by her own damned durability, which even now struggled to save what was plainly lost.

"Like I mentioned, the guild sometimes gives mentors to new members. Some are better than others, and at first, I thought mine was a terrible fit. Still might be, on a technical level. But Fornax has been the only person consistently in my corner since a very long time ago, and we do share at least one core philosophy." Hephaestus paused, looking right into the dying eyes of Lozora.

"Actions have consequences. You fucked with my mentor, which was bad, but understandable. Then you brought his kid into it. So you don't get to die in a grand battle or display. You don't deserve to face a living legend and fall by his hand. Your ending is here, led to a hallway far enough away that the capes wouldn't have arrived in time, even if they had heard the shot. Die alone, helpless, knowing you'll be forgotten, and understand that this is still getting off easy."

Hephaestus couldn't fathom what Ivan would have done in her place.

Something more creative, and certainly more painful, but she was working with what she had. An energy beam at point-blank range left minimal room for delicacy. Didn't hurt to be safe, so Hephaestus headed back to a section where bodies were piled up. From one, she rooted around and produced a gleaming object, its sharpness flashing in the flickering hallway lights.

Who brought a machete to a meta-fight in the first place? Well, it wasn't like she had room to complain. This would make hauling out her second prize of the day much easier. Moving swiftly, Hephaestus hurried back to the corpse, already aware of the wicked work that awaited her.

The stream cut out just before Ivan turned away from the camera, forcibly reasserting control. That had been a dangerous dance. More than once, his darker impulses threatened to overwhelm the proceedings, but the staged nature of the pageantry helped Ivan keep his head straight. Having a pseudo-script kept his mind on the next task, prevented it from reveling in the pain of the moment.

Across the chamber, the giant doors parted to reveal Doctor Mechaniacal and Xelas, both of whom were splattered in some of the Wrexwrens' internal workings, though neither looked nearly as much of a fright as Ivan.

"How are we doing?" Ivan asked.

"Based on reports from the ground, the initial invasion waves broke against our shores as expected. Most have already been killed or captured. How well they're being treated depends on who snatched them up. There are a few still trying to go down in a blaze of glory, but mostly the AHC is now dealing with humans who sought to take advantage of the confusion."

Stepping in, Xelas added, "Plus, we blew up every ship in our solar system not originating from Earth, so there are no reinforcements to send."

"Which just leaves..." Ivan trailed off, looking up to the screen overhead. The Scralthor was retreating; there was no other possible interpretation of the situation. This massive beast was sent fleeing by the burning light coursing through the stars. In a very odd way, Ivan felt kinship with the creature. He knew that feeling, that fear, it was experiencing far too well. "Seems Lodestar has the Scralthor handled."

"Which means she'll soon turn her attention to Earth, and us, so we should be gone before then," Doctor Mechaniacal suggested. "Anyone need to use the restroom before we get in the ship? Mostly looking at you, Fornax, as you're the only flesh-and-blood body up here."

It took some doing for Ivan to tear his eyes away from the screen. Seeing her like this stirred up a lot of memories, not that this was the appropriate time for any of them. Ivan yanked his gaze away, looking to his allies. "I'll hold it somehow. It's not like we've got a long trip."

Together, the three of them hurried through the vessel, occasionally passing scenes of grim carnage telling the story of what happened to the ship's remaining crew. Evidently, he hadn't been the only one cutting loose up here. Ivan couldn't even imagine what sort of havoc the guild as a whole had wreaked upon their targets.

No sooner was Doctor Mechaniacal's ship safely out of range than the final Wrexwren vessel detonated, blast briefly lighting the sky before it became nothing more than a mass of floating wreckage. Some would make it to Earth, but the AHC had systems in place to break up any chunks that were too large, so they'd burn up one way or another. That would be the final reminder of the Wrexwren invasion: a bastion of debris that occasionally lit the sky when a piece tumbled into the atmosphere.

It was, to Ivan's thinking, exactly the sort of memorial he wanted. A clear warning to any extraterrestrials who came calling of what they could expect from starting trouble with the planet called Earth.

Chloe's eyes snapped open without warning, followed by her drawing a large gasp of air, despite the fact that she'd been breathing steadily the entire time. It was like she'd burst forth from a deep pool, blinking at the sudden onslaught of light and sound.

In seconds, Beverly was there, holding her friend steady by the shoulders in case of vomit.

It took a few seconds for Chloe to come all the way back, to leave that unreal place fully behind. She wasn't sure she succeeded, in truth. Something felt different from before, like she was more connected to whatever systems her power influenced. She worked hard to put that out of her mind for the moment, along with deeper concerns of what she'd seen. Chloe was neither cape nor villain, and had no serious desire to be either—at least, for the moment. Digging into the sorts of questions her vision raised would invariably drag her deeper into that world, so she simply chose to ignore it. Sometimes, the classic tactics were still the best.

Able to pay some attention to her surroundings, Chloe realized they weren't at the apartment, or a hospital. For a fleeting moment, she was seized with terror that Beverly, unaware of what else to do, had brought her to the guild. That notion was quickly dispelled. She didn't imagine the guild guest quarters to have a huge antique sewing machine, or pictures of family that bore a striking resemblance to Beverly.

"What happened? Where are we?"

"My guess on what happened is you used too much power in a short span of time. I don't think we've ever heavily cycled your sayings like that before —might be a toll, though you'd know better than me on that front." Beverly paused, looking around her surroundings as if seeing them for the first time. "As to where... I wasn't sure what to do with you. Everything seemed stable, but you wouldn't wake up. I figured step one was to get you somewhere safe, a place I could trust, then find someone to help once they wrapped up dealing with the invasion."

Loud noises came from some ways outside the door, a commotion of bustling and voices all yelling over one another, until a quiet one silenced them all. Beverly, looking more sheepish than Chloe had ever seen her, seemed to take that as a cue to press on. "I brought you to my family's house. A few of them have field medic training, in case you took a turn for the worse, and there are enough munitions to drive back an actual force of aliens, let alone the scraps wandering the streets."

Chloe was still moving sluggishly, like her energy couldn't catch momentum. Realizing where some of that juice might be flowing, she hurriedly switched her active saying. "**A penny saved is a penny earned**." The change wasn't instantaneous, but there *was* a change. Instead of her power flowing out of her like a sinking rowboat, it felt more akin to a giant jug, one where the overflow began to accumulate. While she wasn't suddenly bursting with gusto, the dull ache in her head did quickly vanish.

"Where are the others? Did everyone make it out okay?"

The pain that flickered across Beverly's face gave away the ending of her tale before the first word was spoken. "We won, in a way. But there was a price."

Before the conversation could spiral into the true depths of despair, noise rose from outside once more, this time closer to the door. Beverly looked from her patient to the room's entrance, visibly doing speedy mental math on how this would play out. "It wasn't Tori. I'll explain the rest later. For now, it looks like it's time to meet the family."

Perhaps on cue, the door burst open and nearly a dozen people poured through, all eager to meet Beverly's newest friend, and perhaps discuss why their kin had arrived in the shape of a flying dragon.

Chapter 125

Upon return to the guild, Ivan was both surprised and grateful to hear that Tori was waiting for him in his office. Pausing only long enough to call Janet, checking in to be sure his kids were safe, Ivan hurried to the designated meeting space, one he rarely had use for in these facilities. It wasn't as if Pseudonym welcomed many callers, or made efforts to. He truly hoped that wouldn't change now that Fornax had made a special appearance, but life had taught him the world was rarely so kind.

The first thing he noticed after walking through the door was the state of her armor: banged up, missing a gauntlet, and with more than a few pieces torn out, exposing bits of wiring. The second thing he noticed, which *should* have been the first, was the burlap sack oozing a green puddle on the corner of his desk.

"What... who is that?" Ivan had seen enough decapitated heads to know what they looked like when stuffed into a bag. Why one was on his desk was a genuine mystery, on the other hand. Tori had been expected to lay low during the invasion. If things turned messy, that would be understandable, but it didn't account for why she would bring a severed head to him like this.

"It's a thank-you present," Tori explained. "For everything you've done. For being around even after the mentorship ended and you didn't have to. For teaching me how to be a villain."

After a day like this one, Ivan had more or less run out of tolerance for things like cryptic hints. He opened the bag himself, stunned in confusion by the unexpected bolt of familiarity. "Lozora?" Ivan's head shot up, looking Tori over in a brand new light. "How... Tori, did you kill her?"

"I had some help. Her employer pulled the oh-so-shocking double-cross and left her injured. I took advantage of her weakness and confusion, then blasted a hole through her middle. The head was easier to transport. Plus, it just felt right, considering the context."

The context? Tori had no idea about the context this implied. Lozora was not some no-name minion. She'd been around for decades, and that was before being hurled into Rookstone. His former apprentice had just taken out an actual player in their game, the sort of move others would take note of, to say nothing of the allies who might come looking for payback.

"I see. Mind if I ask how, exactly, this is a present for me?" Troublesome as it all was, Tori was nothing if not rational. With everything she did, there was a reason. What remained to be seen was if it was a good one, or not.

Any traces of a smirk fell from Tori's face as she looked back to the bag. "Her employer was the mystery man who set up that whole Starscout-labyrinth situation, and that green bitch was the trigger-woman. She's the one who put Beth in danger."

Whatever trains of thought Ivan had been engineering were instantly knocked off-track by that revelation. It changed a great many things about the circumstances, including how much fallout he would allow to get near Tori. Killing wantonly wasn't something he'd wanted to encourage, but paying back what was owed? That was a different matter entirely. "Tell me everything."

Which was exactly what Tori did, laying out the labyrinth voice's cryptic hints, the visit from Nexus, the attack on her apartment, and the revelation regarding Alfred Settler, a tidbit which actually managed to draw surprise from Ivan when it was reached. She wrapped things up by explaining how the fight ended, quickly detailing her moment of thievery followed by tricking Lozora, then escaping. The only bits she may have skimmed over were those involving Chloe's power, where possible.

"Damn." As she spoke, Ivan had pulled some plastic wrap from in his desk, coating the head-bag and putting triple layers on his desk to prevent more general ooze drippage. "Some capes dying today was inevitable, but I'd have preferred all of the blame to be on the wiped-out aliens. At least this guy wasn't one of ours. If anything, we can cite our members who offered critical help in dealing with him."

"Did you know about him? Alfred Settler?"

Ivan finished cleaning the head juice and wiped off his fingers, exuding a moment of magic to burn his hands clean—not that the rest of him wasn't still coated in Zerle Salvrin's internal workings. From within his desk, he produced a bottle of fine liquor, one he reserved for special occasions. "I knew about Alfred Settler in the same way as everyone else: a piece of history that died in our new world's creation. The meta you're describing rings a bell. We crossed paths here and there—I once had to belt him to send a message, but I punched a lot of people in my heyday. He wasn't part of the Order of the Final Dawn, though, meaning I never had any reason to care beyond that."

"So you wouldn't know... or maybe, could make a guess..."

"I have no idea if he's alive or not," Ivan intervened, saving her from finding a way to ask the question without sounding afraid. Of course she was afraid. Tori was too smart to experience something like that and not better understand her place in the world. She was stronger than humans, yes, but in the world of metas, Hephaestus was still barely starting out. Understanding the difference between what power lay at the summit and how much she could muster would make anyone afraid. "Were I to guess, I'd say yes. Doesn't seem like the type to need air or food, and given the durability you've described, space alone may not finish the job. That said, while he might still be alive, Alfred has effectively been taken out."

From another drawer, Ivan produced a pair of glasses, setting them both down in succession. Tori watched the act, waiting until he was about to pour before speaking. "Just a sip for me. I've got more work after this."

With a nod, he poured her enough for one toast—all they would need. As he moved on to his own glass, which got substantially more, Tori continued, "How do you figure he's gone, if he might not be dead?"

"Between our respective run-ins and the general rumors I've heard of such a figure, he has no movement-based powers to speak of. No flight, no teleportation, nothing that would permit him to navigate the far reaches of space. If he is alive, he's stuck out there, waiting to be found. The only ones capable of such a feat are ourselves, and the Alliance of Heroic Champions. If they find him, he gets Lodestar. If we find him, he's going to wish the AHC had. Either way, won't be much of an issue."

There was an implied "for now" that neither chose to comment on. In a world like theirs, when reality was such a fickle enforcer, nothing could ever really be taken for granted—not until they were dead, like Lozora. That was the price of living in a world of miracles.

Shifting forward, Ivan set the less-filled glass in front of Tori, then lifted his own. "I didn't know Presto, either as a cape or a person. In truth, he likely would have been an enemy in almost every circumstance imaginable. Yet today, his bravery and determination helped keep my former apprentice... my friend, safe. To Presto, one who deserved to chase the title of superhero."

"To Ike." Tori whispered the words, more to herself than to Ivan, before gulping down the single mouthful of liquor. It was excellent, yet horrible, for reasons that had nothing to do with flavor. "Okay, and with you brought up to speed, it's time for both of us to go clean off. I need to meet with Doctor Mechaniacal in a few. This is the perfect chance to kick off our new project, and we're not going to miss it. After that, don't expect to see me around outside the lab for a bit."

"Got new plans in mind?"

There was real danger in Tori's smile, a look Ivan knew all too well. When faced with a power that much greater than themselves, most people's reactions fell into one of three camps. The vast majority were scarred by it, forever made afraid by the knowledge that there were some limits they simply couldn't overcome. Some took that pain and grew, however, resolving to be as strong as they could, to minimize how many times that gap would appear. Then there was the third group, the ones who saw how high the mountain stretched and were filled with one all-consuming notion: if they can be that strong, then so can I.

"Lots," Tori confirmed. "It's time for a updated model—past time, really. Especially now that I've got a lead on a new material. One that can stand up to the leagues I want to play in. A long road ahead on that front, though, so I'm jumping in as soon as possible. Not going to have as much free time pretty soon."

Ivan watched as she set the glass back down, keeping it a healthy distance from the head-bag. "Care to elaborate?"

"Nah, it'll be more fun to let you see with everyone else. Time for a shower, anyway." Tori slowly pulled herself from the chair, suit not moving with the usual grace in its current condition.

"Before you go..." Ivan wasn't quite sure how to phrase this. It had the potential to be taken wrong, but he and Tori generally understood one another fairly well. Sometimes, it was best to just plug ahead. "Tori, are you *sure* you want Hephaestus to be the one who killed Lozora? She is not unknown, nor without friends. I won't deny you the glory you've earned, but there is much less baggage if Fornax did the deed. Otherwise, you should expect eventual consequences."

"When the guild reopened, you asked me what kind of villain I want to be." Tori's eyes darted from the bag to her right hand, still clad in the killer gauntlet. "That head is my answer. I want to be the kind of villain people fear, because they should. The person no one dares to fuck with, knowing what awaits them. The world needs bogeymen, things to rightly fear. I want everyone to understand what happens to those who cross Hephaestus, or her guild."

It was a path Ivan knew all too well, one he'd just recommitted himself to on intergalactic television; he had no room to cast judgment, no matter how much he wished she'd found a safer road to travel. But Tori Rivas didn't want normality or safety, and only she could live the life that was best for her. Even if it meant one that might end up significantly shorter.

"Then we tell the truth. Hephaestus killed Lozora. Make sure that new suit is a good one, Tori. You *will* have enemies coming to test it."

The first coherent thought Donald had was when the cocoa burned his tongue. That sharp jolt of pain finally yanked him from his reverie—a mix of injury, exhaustion, and emotional fatigue. By the time all of the other superheroes climbed free, the fight was over. Presto was gone, and the rest of the New Science Sentries were near inconsolable. Since then, Cyber Geek had been running on what felt like autopilot, forcibly putting one foot in front of the other.

Backup arrived eventually—they'd caused too much destruction to not get noticed—and from there, they'd all largely been swept into more experienced hands. He'd gotten some texts from Tori that they were evacuated, but safe, which left him with nothing to do except dwell on the fight they'd just had. On how, once again, he'd been ultimately useless when the threat turned severe.

The gruff voice in his ear might have caused him to leap right up, if the cocoa hadn't already brought him partially out of the fugue. "It wasn't your fault." Ren's rough hand fell on his back a moment later.

"How did you know?" Donald didn't even glance up from his Styrofoam cup. He couldn't stand the same zoned-out stares on the faces of the other capes in this area: a place for those who'd seen too much this night to decompress.

"Because Ren feels the same way, just like the rest of us." Lucy plopped down to his right, still clad in her costume, save only for the mask. "We're all aspiring superheroes. We all take too much responsibility when things go wrong. He's right, too. In this case, there was no victory to be had. Presto... he saved us."

Tears welled up in Donald's eyes. He'd barely even known Ike, but this was the first time he would be burying a fellow superhero. That fact alone was scary enough to draw the waterworks. "There might have been ways to escape."

"There weren't." Irene took the final spot near him, sitting closer than she normally preferred. "Not without risking innocent lives. Presto saw the chance to make a difference. He had the ability to matter, the opportunity to act, and the willpower to see it through. That's what it takes to be a superhero, if only for a moment. He made the hard call to keep us alive."

In a way, that was true, but largely by coincidence. The real people he'd been protecting were the New Science Sentries, none of whom were currently in the same room. Probably off for a debrief—the same treatment his team would be in for once they'd had a chance to recover. With the chaos of the day, everything had to be tackled in waves. The ones who needed more time were shuffled around to the end of the queue.

Last time he'd been in a real pinch, he'd made it through thanks to the power of his team. Today, it was thanks to another superhero, one who wouldn't be around to pitch in next time. Donald was tired of being saved, frustrated to feel like he was making progress only to hit one wall after another. Yet painful as it was, his other choice was to accept that weakness, to simply say that this was the league where he could play and leave it at that. Be left behind by the friends who were taking time to make sure he was all right, even after living through the same hell themselves.

He had to get stronger; only now, Donald was starting to understand that this wasn't some temporary condition. For as long as he lived in this world, he'd forever be climbing, striving, reaching just a bit higher, all in the hopes that the next time they hit a major threat, he'd be the one making a difference, not another person getting saved.

Presto had perished protecting them all. Next time, Cyber Geek wanted to make sure no one had to die. Not if he could become strong enough.

Epilogue

"I'd like to thank you all for being here today."

That opening was the only traditional thing about the morning's event, the strangest funeral Tori had ever attended, though she'd really only been to a few. None of those had been in bars, however, let alone ones rented out for private mourning. The others had also had dead bodies present; in the case of her parents, barely recognizable ones, but bodies all the same. While this was not a traditional funeral, it did feel fitting. Presto hadn't really been a traditional cape.

"I put a lot of thought into what I could say about Ike Pemberton, whether I should lay more emphasis on the man or the mask to eulogize him properly. In the end, I realized that to honor my friend, there was only one clear choice: I have to emphasize the truth. Because almost above all else, Ike hated bullshit."

Austin's line drew a small chuckle from the audience, meager as it was. Aside from her, Beverly, and Chloe, all seated at one small table, the crowd largely consisted of the remaining New Science Sentries, Cyber Geek's team, and a few strangers Tori didn't recognize, along with one she very much did. As a newer cape, Presto had gotten little time to make an impression. The world would mourn their hero through the AHC's public memorial and upcoming ceremony for all those lost in the invasion. Today was for those who knew the man beneath the moniker.

"That trait could make him abrasive, hard to work with, and even harder to befriend. It also kept him honest, upfront, and one of the few voices I could always trust to tell me when I was making a mistake. Ike valued truth over sentiment, and would hate nothing more than being held up as a saint just because he passed. Ike was our dear friend, and also an asshole much of the time."

A loud sniff from Ellie in the front, though she was holding up better than Kyle, who was already crying openly. Some folks cracked smiles at the sudden swearing, but there were no titters this time. The moment no longer felt right for such mirth.

"I'm not going to stand here and tell you that Ike had the natural disposition of a superhero, that he was always fated to fight for the side of good. None of that. Yet even though he didn't especially like them, he still used his power to help people. In the end, Ike passed us all up, going out in the most heroic way I could imagine, saving the rest of his team."

Chancing a glance over her shoulder, Tori noted that the woman standing at the edge of the room wasn't crying. The look on her face was more severe, almost guilty looking. There was no logical reason for the woman to wear such an expression, but Tori understood why it was there. This sort of failing probably always felt personal to her.

Standing at the bar, which they were treating as a makeshift podium, Austin lifted his glass, and the others followed suit. Tori wondered what the capes would say if they were to learn that the world's most feared villain had lifted his glass to Presto in the same manner. Sadly, posing such a query would essentially be opening a case of worm-filled-cans, so some things had to remain a mystery.

"To Ike, a reminder that the seeds of true heroism can spring from any one of us, when defending what we love. I'm sorry you had to save us, and I promise we're not going to waste the second chance you provided."

An echo of "To Ike" rumbled through the bar as everyone tipped back a glass, toasting to the cape missing from the room. Since the invasion, apparently the AHC had begun scanning space, searching for Alfred or Presto's remains. No luck so far, which was about as expected, given how much area they had to scour. It meant there was no corpse to lay to rest, however. Instead, they were gathered around one of Presto's spare costumes, laid out artfully inside a glass case.

With Austin's speech done, some of the crowd headed over to the bar for refills, while others trekked to the bathroom with relief in mind. As for Tori, she decided it was time for light mingling, making her way around to the back of the room where the lone figure had been watching from the shadows. Her target made no effort to escape, even as Tori drew close enough to speak softly.

"I didn't think Ike warranted a personal appearance from Lodestar at his funeral."

"He most certainly did. Unfortunately, when she shows up, the focus shifts from where it's meant to be, so I'm here instead," Helen replied. She wasn't in a disguise, necessarily, though her outfit was more stuffy and professional than Tori would have expected, creating a different vibe altogether. Tori wondered if she'd have recognized Helen were she not in the know about her secret, and just how potent that identity cloaking of hers really was.

"Do you always go to cape funerals?"

"Not always. Job often gets in the way. All the ones I can though, yes. It's the least I owe them."

Did she really feel guilty over not being there for Ike? The woman had been battling a space monster intent on eating their sun, a fight that only she could have won, protecting the entire planet as a whole. Maybe that was what it cost to be so powerful; when you could do anything, it meant what you chose to save was all the more important.

"How have you been?" Helen broke Tori out of her reverie with a slight turn and a friendly smile. "With Starscout meetings temporarily suspended, we haven't gotten to catch up in a couple of weeks. I was glad to see you made it through alive. Especially knowing what a good helper you can be to your friends."

Her eyes darted pointedly to the rest of the room, making it clear she knew what Hephaestus had done but had no intent of airing that secret out here. It was bizarre, realizing Lodestar was keeping tabs on her. That was likely unavoidable, one of the encumbrances of being Fornax's apprentice.

Thinking of Ivan made Tori uncomfortable. She had no idea how Lodestar reacted to the guild's move against the Wrexwren. News outlets had called it horrific, unconscionable, an extreme overreaction. Tori, on the other hand, had gotten to see the results. It wasn't as if the world had suddenly become a clean and sparkling utopia—there were still a great deal of criminals out there, all at varying degrees of morality. However, after Fornax's appearance, the guild was suddenly deluged by debts being repaid and oaths of loyalty being reaffirmed. Most of the rule-skirting had thinned out quickly, helped along by the guild's new commitment to enforcing their edicts. They would never be powerful enough to influence every action of every criminal, but they were once again a threat to be considered. Worse than before, in many ways. Under the old system, they'd been a rumor; now, they were fact.

"I've been okay. Mostly busy with work. In fact, I've got a big event later today. Thankfully, they didn't set this at the same time."

"Glad to hear it," Helen replied. She rummaged around in her pocket, producing a small white card. "In all our time together, I don't think I ever gave you my number. Shoot me a call if you need anything, Tori. Even just perspective or guidance."

Despite an initial wave of hesitation, Tori accepted the card. Odd as it might be, having direct access to Lodestar was not something she was dumb enough to pass up. There might well come a day when that phone call saved her life, or the lives of her friends. "Holding out hope I'll switch over?"

"Let's just say that I think anyone willing to put their lives on the line in a fight that isn't even theirs has superhero potential. You can call about other issues, too." She checked her watch, then noted that the official part of the funeral seemed to have wrapped up with the speech. "As for me, time to get back to it."

Tori was mostly braced for the hug farewell—she'd gotten accustomed to Helen enough after their few weeks together—though it was still bizarre knowing who had their arms around her. After pocketing the card, she turned to find Kyle walking over, a pair of beers in hand.

"Do I see Tori making new friends of her own free will?" He handed over the spare drink as he arrived, which Tori accepted. In truth, it was hard staying sober at this event, not only because of the palpable sadness in the air. The timing couldn't have been worse. After working so hard to get things ready so fast, their big premiere *had* to come on the day of Ike's farewell.

"More like making small talk." Tori instantly realized she should have come up with a better lie—by this point, Kyle knew she hated that sort of chitchat—but the words were already out, so she took a long drink to cover them. "How are you holding up?"

At her question, he paused to wipe his shining cheeks. The tears had halted, but their effects remained. "Good as can be expected. The AHC was able to mend my injuries, so at least I'm not out a job, too, but losing Ike was a bigger blow than any of us were prepared for. Doesn't help that Professor Quantum already wants to start interviewing replacements."

That did seem soon, after little more than a week and change. Then again, how long was a superhero team expected to operate a member down? Getting a replacement might be safer, not that Tori was quite socially inept enough to voice such a notion.

"I'm not sure if I ever said this or not, but I wanted to come over and apologize," Kyle continued, halting only for a healthy sip of his own drink.

"Our team was the reason you all got put in danger. They were using you to draw us out." A dark laugh slipped past his lips. "It seems like every other time we talk, it's me apologizing for putting you in danger."

"Yeah, seems about right," Tori agreed. "Maybe you should stop."

The words hit like she'd kneed him in the groin, so Tori hurried to elaborate. "Stop apologizing. You fucked up once and got me exposed, there's no sugarcoating that, but it was only once. Everything the world does following that isn't on your shoulders."

"Be that as it may, we're not going to let it happen again. When the apartment building is repaired, we won't be there. Another team can take over protective detail, one with less baggage of their own, inherited or otherwise."

Had this news come on any other day, there was a good chance Tori would have leapt upon it. A chance to be free of the New Science Sentries, with no suspicion on her in the process? But today wasn't that day. Not with what they'd lost, and with the twist of the knife she knew was still coming. She couldn't steal this, too.

"Look, the water takes forever to get warm, our front door lock sticks, and people keep pissing in the alley out back, but it's not that bad of a place to live. No need to go running back to your fancy superhero lair just like that."

"Tori, I meant—"

"I got what you meant. You want to move to keep me safe. Well, guess what: I'm *not* safe. Because the world isn't safe. Shit happens, human or meta, and we all do our best to muddle through. You want to leave, by all means go ahead, just don't do it for me. Live where you want to live, how you want to live."

This time, the drink nearly drained half of Kyle's glass. "Maybe it's just because of where we are, but that almost sounds like something Ike would say."

"He was a smart guy, when he wanted to be." Tori checked her own watch, realizing that time was nearly up. Crap. She'd wanted to talk to Donald, too, give him a proper warning. "Listen, I have a meeting to get to. Sorry to duck out early."

"No, we understand. The perils of holding it on a weekday. Just when we could get the time; things have been crazy since the invasion." Between rebuilding, missing persons, and general chaotic fallout, Tori could imagine how thin the capes were spread at this point. The world was steadily coming back together, though. That was the silver lining of surviving multiple worldwide catastrophes: humanity was getting adept at bouncing back.

Tempting as it was to bolt on that, Tori had to say something; otherwise, it would go over even worse. "Before I head out, I wanted to let you know... look, Kyle, I think of you guys as friends. Ellie, Austin, Donald, Kyle—those people. Not the masks you wear. Keep that division in mind, and please believe me when I say none of it is personal."

"What does that mean?" Kyle said, noting the way she was already edging toward the door.

"You'll see. And this time, for what it's worth, I'm the one who's sorry."

Sitting outside the house, Rick thought the day was too nice. This wasn't how the world was supposed to feel after horrific revelations. It was expected to be gloomy, drab, morose, tainted by the new perspective he'd obtained. Instead, there was sunshine and mild winds, a perfect final day before fall's true onslaught. The world didn't care that everything had changed for him. It just went right on turning how it pleased.

A slam of a car door jolted him into the moment, one brief warning sign before Beth came scampering up the drive, clad in a hat with a stuffed shark on it. Not far behind was Ivan, Rick's father and a homicidal villain who'd tortured a sentient being on live television, only to eventually crush his head. If only those were separate entities, instead of being crammed all into one body.

"We missed you at the aquarium today. They had some new exhibits, one last big event before school restarts."

Ivan sat down next to him on the bench, one Janet had picked up years ago and restored to sit outside her home. Or had it been stolen from a dead superhero's lair? Rick really had no idea how much of what he thought to be true actually was, save for some points he'd have much rather lacked clarity on.

"I wasn't feeling up to it."

"That's what your mother said." Ivan sat there, listening closely as Beth dashed through the house, on a direct track for the bathroom after getting a whale-sized soda. He waited until he was sure she'd left earshot. "You figured it out."

"Is it that obvious?" Rick wasn't sure what words were coming out of his mouth next, nor why he'd waited out here in the first place. Things had spun so far out of control, he barely understood his own thoughts at this point, let alone actions.

Slowly, Ivan nodded. "Frankly, yes, but I knew it was just a matter of time. You've got too much of your mother's wiles to not put the pieces together eventually. There is more to the story than you know, than my old reputation would let on. Though it doesn't change what I did, nor excuse it. I am a man who has lived a strange, terrible, occasionally wonderful existence, and I own every choice within that life. Including last week's display."

"Dis*play*?" The word got choked halfway through, like even his own throat couldn't believe that that's what Ivan was calling it. "I watched my dad beat someone to the brink of death, make them get down and beg to live, then kill them anyway. I don't... what the hell am I supposed to *do* with that? With who you really are?"

"Make peace with it, or reject me from your life entirely. Those are my guesses for how this eventually goes," Ivan replied. Still calm and steady, same as he'd always been. Except now, Rick knew how deep those still waters ran, and what sorts of terrors were waiting down below.

Could he do that? Kick his dad entirely out of his life? It was entirely viable, given his age and his mother's awareness of the situation; Rick just wasn't sure he had it in him. Because on top of the images of Fornax wreaking havoc, he couldn't stop seeing flashes of Ivan, of his dad. Nights spent on homework, working as a chaperone on school trips, offering support and guidance wherever possible. Rick's father was a rock in his life, something he'd always counted on, and the idea of losing it scared him nearly as much as knowing about Fornax. "Would you be okay with that, if I did reject you?"

"Okay with it?" The calm demeanor cracked, and for a flash, Rick could see just how deeply hurt the idea of that left Ivan. "It would break my heart losing even a piece of you. To be cast out entirely would leave a wound no meta-human or monster could ever dream of matching. No, I would never be okay with it, but I *would* respect your choice. I grew up being forced at every turn, chained to my destiny. Your life is yours, and if I'm no longer welcome in it, then it's on me to deal with that fact. I did my best as a father, but sometimes, the past refused to stay buried."

"You're the one who dug it up. Who went on TV, who wore that mask... Fornax was gone. Supposedly dead long enough that he was more legend than history. You brought him back, Dad."

Sounds from inside betrayed that Beth was done, and Ivan didn't want to be lingering on this conversation if she popped back out for a second goodbye hug. Best to be heading out, anyway; his day wasn't finished yet. "Yes, I did. A choice I made; one I don't regret. Because even if you never understand why, Ivan had just as much reason to be in that fight as Fornax. They were coming for our planet, threatening *my* children."

Another break in the calm; however, this wasn't a flash of pain. Instead, Rick saw his father's determination laid bare, and even a glimpse of that was staggering. Staggering, and ferocious. There was no limit in that gaze, only absolute will. Whatever was demanded of him to keep them safe, Ivan would rise to the occasion, even if he had to stand on Fornax's shoulders to do it.

"Oh yeah, that's what I feel right now. Overwhelmingly safe."

Ivan rose to his feet, departure imminent. "When you look at the stars, are you afraid of what might be out there? Given that a previously unknown sentient race tried to invade us barely more than a week ago, it would make perfect sense."

To that, Rick said nothing. He realized the answer in his heart, as did Ivan, but speaking it was a step further. Instead, he managed to shake his head, just barely.

"No. Because you know the monsters that any aspiring invaders will have to get through first. And now, so does the rest of the galaxy. It will break me to lose you from my life, Rick, but understand that no matter how things go between us, I will never stop keeping you safe, protecting you, and loving you. None of the powers, title, accomplishments—nothing in that world matters more to me than you and Beth."

"Then *why* did you choose to resurrect Fornax?" Rick demanded.

"He was necessary, and though it would make my life somewhat easier, I truly hope you never have to understand why." Ivan started to go in for a hug out of habit, then halted when he caught Rick's stiffened posture. "If you ever have questions, want to know more, or want to just talk, I'll answer them honestly. No more secrets worth hiding, not after that one. Until then, I'll give you space to think."

Ivan didn't look back as he walked to his car. It was a silly point of pride, but he loathed to let anyone see him cry.

"Are you sure? The results keep ending up the same." Beverly stared at her friend, concern evident on her face.

She and Chloe were alone in their apartment, despite the building still undergoing repairs. A huge tarp still clung to the side of the brick complex, even as people came and went through the front door. It was incredible, the speed with which their home was being rebuilt. Only two nights in a hotel were needed, then they'd been able to move back in to their miraculously untouched apartment. Several areas were closed off, and obviously, the owner of the room where the New Science Sentries had fought Alfred Settler was going to take a lot longer for repairs, but other than the steadily shrinking hole in the building's side, Beverly was amazed at the rate of their home's recovery. Amazed to the point of suspicion, in fact. Since Thuggernaut assured her that the guild wasn't gassing things along, her current guess was that the AHC was speeding the process through for the sake of the New Science Sentries.

"Only from your side," Chloe replied. "I can feel myself making progress. Not as much as I might like, but every time we do it, I hold out a little longer."

"And that's worth the migraines?" The skepticism on Beverly's face made it clear how she felt, especially as the one who had to carry Chloe's unconscious body every time. "You really want access to dragon forms that badly?"

Looking away, Chloe chewed her lower lip for a few seconds, mulling over the question. "It isn't about your powers, specifically; they just happened to be the right setup I needed. Something out of reach, but not by an impossible amount. What I'm really trying to figure out is if I'm capable of growth. Can I get better, my power stronger, or is this what I'm working with for the rest of my life?"

"Be certain that's a rabbit hole you want to go down. The stronger you get, the harder it is to stay on the sidelines," Beverly cautioned.

This time, Chloe didn't need consideration time for her response. Instead, she lifted the pink and black umbrella resting at her side. "I accidentally killed someone in my first real fight, when I got this souvenir. Then, it managed to block an attack from the otherwise unstoppable bone-guy, pissing him off in my direction. Whether I like it or not, sometimes this is a dangerous world, and I'm not going to ignore my power when it could help save my life or that of someone I care about. Still no desire to do that professionally, I'm just tired of feeling helpless on the sidelines. If I'm going to use this power, then I have to be able to control it, maybe one day even understand how it works. All which is to say... yes, I think figuring out growth potential is worth the migraines, even if it does cause me more trouble down the line."

Worried as Beverly was, she couldn't find much fault in Chloe's logic. With everything that had happened, it was no wonder she didn't want to feel helpless, to her power or the strength of others. Besides, the truth of the matter was that this was now the second time having Chloe around might well have saved her life, the first being that same fight where Chloe had distracted the umbrella's original owner. Without her helping Tori on the gauntlet, drawing

Alfred's fury to Plasmodia and causing Presto to make the ultimate sacrifice, Beverly genuinely wasn't sure if any of them would still be alive.

More than that, though, she realized Chloe's sentiment echoed her own. Fighting Alfred had been a stark reminder of how far behind the meta-curve all of them were in the grand scheme of things. Beverly herself had begun experimenting again, attempting to draw out new dragon forms without luck. Knowing her own frustration, she didn't have it in her to refuse someone else the chance to make progress.

At last, Beverly relented. "Fine, but only just the once. Last time we went for two, your nose started bleeding." She walked over, sitting down on the couch next to Chloe, who was already propped up carefully with her back braced on cushions.

Taking deep breaths, Chloe centered herself and looked Beverly in the eye. "**Anything you can... do...**" Her eyes were attempting to take on the sharp green of a dragon's iris, warping and flexing, shifting in place, yet unable to stabilize. "**I... can—**" Chloe's shifting eyes snapped shut as she collapsed backwards into the cushions, passed out on the spot.

It was the result Beverly had been expecting, the same one they'd gotten every time Chloe tried this since the day of the invasion. A phrase that let her copy someone's capabilities—not just their power, but something like Tori's talent for mechanics—was incredibly powerful, and Beverley had been as eager as her friend to see someone else take on a dragon form. Unfortunately, it appeared there were some limits in place as to how much Chloe could handle. Someone who could do a single phase-shift was evidently not as draining as turning into a multi-formed magical shifter. Or perhaps it was something to do with their power sources. As Tori had put it, "With only two points of data to consider, any conclusion we draw is basically a glorified guess."

But the activity hadn't been entirely a waste. As Chloe's training partner for this exercise, Beverly had kept careful track of just how far into that saying she could get before losing consciousness. Although Beverly hadn't been sure at first, today was the first time she found real certainty in her observations. Chloe had been squeaking ahead a syllable at a time, and today, she got out a full word further than she had on their first try.

It might take a tremendous amount of time and effort, but she had a hunch that Chloe was indeed capable of growing stronger. Beverly wasn't sure if she was more curious or terrified to see what that power could do when fully realized, but she was damn glad it was in the hands of a friend rather than those of an enemy. Fists and fangs, even strength like Alfred's, she could wrap her head around. The power to do near anything, assuming one could find the right words—that was *truly* terrifying.

Ivan and Tori were together backstage, waiting for the call. There was no technical reason for him to be present. The project was publicly between Wade and Tori, secretly between Doctor Mechaniacal and Hephaestus—neither situation called for Ivan's talents. No, there was no need for him to be here, but after everything they'd gone through, Tori and Ivan no longer felt much requirement to justify their presence around one another. He was her teacher, her friend, and in some ways would always be her mentor. Given how long Tori had been entirely on her own, it was nice to feel like she finally had someone to lean on.

"Nervous?" He knew it was a silly question, one asked purely for the sake of talking. Tori's pacing through the room made her emotional state plenty clear without any words needing to be spoken.

"Terrified," she admitted. "The hell was I thinking? I can't go on camera. On live TV, at that. I come off as surly with just normal socializing—add in nerves and I'll probably call the host a pig-fucker or something."

With minor effort, Ivan smothered a chuckle before it could reach his lips. "Give yourself a little credit. You're not the same thief with an attitude problem Wade put in front of me. Over the months, you've grown exceptionally well into your civilian identity, even getting along with our most mundane of coworkers. Besides, the hard part was shot last week, and editing can make anyone charming. All you have to do is go out there with Wade and do the introduction. After that, everyone's focus will be on the screens."

"Uh huh. See, I know that rationally, but the twisting nerves in my stomach just refuse to listen to reason." Tori glared down at her own stomach, as if angry at her body for not being more stalwart. "Let's talk about something else. Any news on Presto or Alfred?"

Solemnly, Ivan shook his head. Considering that the cape's death had saved two of the guild's own members, it was deemed appropriate to use some resources to search for Presto's remains, as well as the potentially still-living Alfred Settler. Ivan was a man who believed in repaying debts, both the positive and the negative. He owed both of those men proper burials, though one might take more work to prepare for the grave.

"Figured that was a long shot. How about Lodestar? Have you heard anything?"

"Still haven't been able to get in touch. She's been busy helping put the world back in order. I imagine whatever fate she has planned for me, or should I say, Fornax, she'll get to it when time permits." Ivan resisted touching his phone, checking for a text or phone call that he knew wouldn't be there. Thus far, he'd only gotten one communication from Helen, a single text reading "We'll talk later" and nothing more.

Tori's pacing slowed momentarily. "Fornax's fate? The hell are you talking about? You fought back an alien invasion, put yourself at risk to keep the entire world safe, and covered the AHC's ass in the process. Hell, you even praised their leader for the world to see. What are they going to charge you with, defending the Earth?"

"In the eyes of the law, I've done no wrong," Ivan agreed. "But Lodestar is not the law. Her power is far beyond such human concepts and limitations. I think now, at last, you all better understand that."

The flash of terror in Tori's eyes told him she was remembering the same sight that the rest of the world had seen play out on video screens billions of times since the invasion. Although no one knew where the recording had come from, thanks to Wade's technological adeptness, a mysteriously high-res video of Lodestar's triumph over the space monster began circulating before the invasion day was even finished. Ivan had spent too long being the only one who truly understood just how strong Lodestar was; it was nice to have company in that existential dread.

"Yeah, that was... well, impossible seemed to capture it best." Tori hesitated, her curiosity and fear battling with one another over the prospect of more information. In the end, as it always did, her curiosity took the upper hand. "Can she really do anything?"

"Not anything," Ivan corrected quickly. "There are a few limits we've learned through the years. She's bad with intangible enemies, can't travel through the multiverse, and at the end of the day, she's still only one person, with all the limitations that implies. However, if she truly believes in what she's doing, that she's in a fight that must be won, then she *will* triumph. That's why I live in fear of the day Helen no longer wears that title."

Her pacing had come to a total stop as Tori grew more invested in the conversation, her focus helping to settle her nerves quite a bit in the process. "About that. I get that you like Helen, and so do I, but you've said the power passes on. We'd still have a Lodestar, right?"

"Yes, we would, and they would be a force of good—the power always seeks a suitable host. That said, what is and isn't 'good' has many subjective pieces. We've scanned the multiverse time after time for various reasons, and while every person who carries that power is on the side of the capes, they don't always share Helen's sense of empathy and compassion. To put it bluntly… now that you understand just how powerful Lodestar really is, that *none* of us could stand against her, how many people do you know that you would trust with that strength? With that level of unchecked, absolute power keeping watch on the world? Because for me, the answer is exactly one."

Tori's anxious energy dissipated as she sat heavily on the couch across from Ivan, a thousand-yard stare settling down in her eyes. "Now that, I get. A more authoritarian Lodestar could reshape our whole world in a matter of years, especially with the AHC at their disposal."

"Precisely. Add in that Helen is an actual friend, and you can see my concern, admittedly misplaced as it is. Even among the Lodestars of the other worlds, Helen is exceptional." Ivan should know. He'd been there when she bucked the system and broke the rules—except, that wasn't really how it worked for Lodestar. She didn't break the rules. Even when she thought she did, it was far scarier than that. Lodestar *changed* the rules, sometimes without even realizing she'd done it.

Tori leaned forward in her seat, pushing the couch cushion to a precarious edge. "Why is that?" Most in the guild would have let the cryptic statement hang, but Tori's love of learning easily outpaced any sense of respect for unspoken secrets. Luckily, she was clued in enough that he could give her part of the answer.

"A few factors, but the most important of which is her bonds to other people. This is, admittedly, some speculation, but I believe Lodestars are designed to slowly lose their connections to the world they protect. As time goes on, the job wears them down, the burden of that power becomes too heavy to bear. Being the absolute strongest is a lonely proposition, especially when the whole world counts on you. Slowly, they lose the fire to fight, and the next time they're pushed, the power moves on, finding a fresh host filled with the desire to make a difference. Even Helen had some rough patches along the way, but she managed to stay connected to friends, enemies, and some who fall in the middle. She's held her sense of self for an already impressive amount of time, which let her grow into the power more than most. But all of that was just the warm-up, because *very* few Lodestars have children. She didn't even think it was possible for decades."

"With Penelope in the mix, there's no way Helen will run out of will to fight," Tori realized. Unfortunately, she also had the mind of a villain, as well as someone who'd recently seen the depths some criminals would stoop to.

"That also makes the kid a vulnerability, though. If anything happened to Penelope, would Helen be able to hold on?"

There wasn't an easy answer for that, so Ivan didn't try to give one. "I've no idea, and have worked very hard over the last few years to not find out. That is not a version of Helen, or Lodestar, I ever want to see."

Leaning back into her couch, Tori let out a long breath. "Well, that's sure not going to keep me up at night or anything. Thanks for the eventual existential crisis, Ivan."

"You could always look on the bright side," he suggested.

"Which is?" Tori's words were barely out before the knock at the door brought her jerking back to the reality of the situation, just in time to see the wily smirk on Ivan's face.

"I took your mind off the stage fright, didn't I?"

The gun clattered onto the concrete, knocked away by a barely seen blur as it whipped by, seconds before a powerful blow knocked the crew's muscle two feet off the ground before landing, visibly dazed. With their muscle pushed back, the others were exposed. They turned toward the street, hoping to find some passersby that might serve as makeshift human shields. None were within reach, and as the blur did a sweep around the perimeter of the bank, they realized that was no coincidence. The New Science Sentries hadn't just been drawing fire. Tachyonic was clearing civilians every time they were distracted.

Agent Quantum walked up to their stunned brick of meta-muscle and executed a simple trip, sending him to the ground without inflicting any more damage than necessary. Half the crew tried to make a break for it, only to have the ground in front of them sear and bubble as burning hot beams of focused energy tore forth from Plasmodia. There was no getting away that easily, not unless they were willing to take their chances on her aim, which didn't really have to be *that* good to hit under these conditions.

The blur stopped next to Agent Quantum, marking the first time in the fight Tachyonic had slowed down enough to be seen. "Area is clear. No civilians left to be in danger."

"Good job. That means we can wrap things up." Agent Quantum looked over the crew, many of whom were still reared up and spoiling for a fight, not content to be taken out so easily by some rookie team with a spotty record. Eyes flicked to Plasmodia, guarding the rear, and Tachyonic, always at his side. The missing presence pained him. No taunting voice or vanishing form. Perhaps that was why the words found their way to his tongue and felt strangely right perched there. Agent Quantum wasn't especially prone to improvisation, but he knew when to listen to his heart.

"New Science Sentries..." Despite the ache in his soul, Agent Quantum's mouth still twisted into a smile as the words broke free, a moment he liked to think Ike would have appreciated. "Time for the Big Finish."

"Isn't that Tori?"

Lucy's voice startled Donald. The team had been largely silent for the last hour, seated in the general AHC facilities, mentally recovering from Presto's funeral. The New Science Sentries were already back on patrol—everyone handled grief in their own way, and it seemed that team was the type to work through it. As for Donald's group, they had no pressing business, and after a morning of heavy workouts all around, had simply fallen into a state of rest, save for Ren, who was doing pushups in the corner next to Irene reading her book.

Only Lucy had been paying much attention to the communal television, set to a local news station in case of emergency information being broadcast. Donald had appeared to be napping, though he was in fact cycling through his lists of items and games, trying to find something that might have helped in the battle with Alfred Settler. It had become his new hobby, or a reincarnation of his previous one. Before the powers and items, Donald was just a guy who loved gaming, and one component of that was loss. Failure was part of games; it was why they had multi-life mechanics. But he'd yet to find any item trustworthy enough to bet a self-resurrection on, which meant he had to make sure to learn his lessons well when he was lucky enough to survive. He'd keep digging until he found a viable strategy. Even if Settler was gone, there were other dangerous threats out there—no reason a sound tactic couldn't be used elsewhere.

Pausing the programs with an opening of his eyes, Donald realized that Lucy was right, that was indeed Tori on the screen. The subtitles were a few seconds behind, so he missed the initial context. It seemed like she was being interviewed in a nice place, lots of natural light and gleaming fixtures. When the camera cut away, it was to a genial face framed by a fading hairline of copper. Donald nearly fell back in his chair. What in the hell was Tori doing on the news with famous billionaire Wade Wyatt?

Hopping up from his seat, he darted over to the side table near Irene, where the remote was sitting, quickly turning up the volume. His movement also got Irene and Ren's attention, both of them taking note of a familiar face on the screen. Finally, Donald found the sound button and clicked it.

"—which is what inspired me to reach out through the corporate chain and speak to Mr. Wyatt," Tori finished. She was clearly nervous, though not rattled, voice surprisingly calm and steady despite her body's occasional fidget.

The screen cut back to the reporter, a generic, handsome face Donald couldn't have picked out of a news anchor lineup. "Is it standard policy for the company's owner to hear out such requests from employees?"

Another cut, this time to Wade Wyatt, who was in no way showing the slightest bit of unease. He looked as if he'd been born on camera, a genial grin fixed in place and a sparkle of brilliance shining from his eyes. "As a matter of fact, Indigo Technologies and all subsidiaries have many programs for advancement that self-starters like Tori have used to get attention on their excellent ideas, though her case was indeed special. Learning what one of our employees went through, I reached out to see if there was anything she needed that we could provide. And lo and behold, what does she say? Not a request for more time off, or even a joke about hazard pay. No, Tori Rivas took that opportunity and told me she didn't want this to happen again. More than that, she had ideas for how to make a difference, if I was willing to listen."

Tori looked almost sheepish as the camera returned to her for a few seconds, circling around to Wade Wyatt once more soon after. "I think we've teased this out enough, don't you? Let's let Tori tell us, in her own words, about the new product line from Indigo Technologies."

"The hell is all this?" Irene had closed her book, getting up from the chair just as the interview cut out, switching over to prerecorded footage.

"Genuinely no idea," Donald replied. The screen was currently showing footage of Tori's kidnapping, the event that had catapulted her right into the public's eye after Tachyonic gave her the initial bout of exposure. Watching the attack on his friend hurt, filling Donald with a desire to show those jerks what-for, if any of them were still alive.

The clip didn't show it all, just the highlights, as Tori's voice began to play. "My name is Tori Rivas, and if you know me, it's as the woman who recently got snatched off the streets of Ridge City— despite me having training." The clip showed Tori's attacks to the kidnappers' joints, brutal and accurate as she made them work for their prize. "Despite the crowds nearby." A new angle, flashing on the multitude of bystanders who'd stood idly by as the fight took place, some even having produced their phones. "Despite all of this happening in the Alliance of Heroic Champions' same neighborhood." Now the shot was of a sweeping view of the city, giving context for the few blocks that separated Tori's point of abduction from the home base of what was supposed to be the greatest superhero organization in the world.

Tori was on-screen again, but not in cobbled-together found-footage, nor as the stiff woman giving a live interview. This was still prerecorded, and apparently, with enough time and takes, she could manage to smother her discomfort. She looked right down the barrel of the camera, expression bordering on severe. "We live in a dangerous world. A world where the balance of power swings wildly from person to person, and often, there's no telling who, or what, you're up against until it's too late. While we appreciate the help of superheroes and their organizations, there's no denying the fact that they can't save everyone. In light of the recent invasion, that has become all the more clear."

"What is she talking about?" Ren was no longer working out, a true testament to how attention-grabbing Tori's interview was. "We fought the Wrexwren back on the first wave."

"We won," Lucy agreed, a touch of melancholy in her tone. "Just not for free. Innocents still died, people lost their loved ones. The big victory doesn't always seem so worth it when you're the one who has to pay the price."

Much as Donald felt like he should ask more about that, Tori was speaking again, and this wasn't a situation where he wanted to miss the details.

She was standing now, walking forward down a white hallway. "What you might not know about me is that I'm more than the internet's favorite damsel of the moment. I'm also an inventor, a problem solver. So, after experiencing that terror for myself, I decided that next time would be different. And thanks to the generous support of Indigo Technologies, we've been able to make that ambition into a reality."

A podium appeared in frame as she kept walking, holding what appeared to be a handbag and collection of accessories. Tori scooped up the bag, showing it off to the camera. Under her breath, Donald heard Lucy whisper "So cute!", probably without realizing she'd spoken aloud.

"This was our starting point, the product launching this week, from which we've already grown. A seemingly simple purse capable of releasing a toxin that will render all but the most powerful of metas incapable of action while you make your escape. It's also compliant with all federal regulations for self-defense weaponry, and specifically engineered to keep it from being used by even the most fashionable of criminals."

Her hand wandered now, tapping on a few of the featured accessories. “A small preview of some upcoming options we think you’ll find especially useful: video-recording earrings with remote cloud storage for evidence, lipstick that can create incredibly painful dermal abrasions, watches with sonic charge capabilities—an entire arsenal hidden in plain sight. If you’re like me, if you feel the same fear of this world’s dangers, then you don’t just want a weapon. You want an armada, an ambush waiting in your hand for the next time someone decides you look like an easy target.”

Gesturing to the display, Tori graced the camera with her first real smile of the whole spectacle. “With great pleasure, I’m honored to announce Indigo Technologies’ newest line: the Rivas Personal Defense System. Because it’s about time we were allowed to save ourselves.”

Ivan hadn’t been sure what to expect from the knock at his door. Most people who knew this address would also be the type to reach out before heading over. Of course, the surprise made more sense when Ivan saw who was standing on the other side. After over a full week of radio silence, some conversations needed to be done in person.

“Helen,” he greeted, looking around his townhome’s entrance courtyard to see if there were any other people to overhear. “Would you like to come in?”

“Sorry, can’t stay for long.” She rummaged around in her purse, producing a small stack of pages and handing them over. “Just came to give you these. Congratulations, Ivan, your sentence as a Starscout leader has officially come to an end. When the cluster reopens, they’ll have new, permanent staff for the kids. I already vetted everyone myself. There won’t be a repeat of the Haywood incident.”

Moving without thinking, Ivan accepted the papers, unfolding them to reveal exactly what had been described—an official notice from the Starscouts thanking him for his time and explaining the leadership handoff process. “Thank you. Stability will be good for Beth, especially after all the excitement.”

“Of course. Any child welcome *means* any child welcome, and so long as that organization uses my likeness, they’re going to uphold that tenet.” Helen looked him over, not quite able to hide the awkwardness that now lay between them.

Tempting as it was to let her walk away while the mood was still polite, Ivan couldn’t permit the moment to pass. He had no idea when the next chance might arrive. "About the other stuff..." he began, before Helen put a single hand on his chest.

"Ivan, I have always known who you are, and what you're capable of. Do you really think you need to explain this to me, of all people? That I don't already know it was for your kids, yes, but also about maintaining order the only way you knew how. I think, deep down, maybe even a little bit of you thought it was for me, saving me the trouble of working toward peace with invaders that had no taste for it. I understand your reasoning. I just... can't accept it."

"The world is safe," Ivan pointed out.

"At what cost?" Helen looked up, and he realized that her eyes were watering. "Even beyond the loss of life you caused, did you ever think that maybe there were things beyond this planet worth knowing about? Technologies, medicines, new ways of living we could benefit from, all of which are likely lost to us now, because you just painted Earth as a backwater hellpit that no sensible species would come within a hundred lightyears of."

He nodded, already aware of the effect such a message would have. "A necessary risk to ensure our planet is left undisturbed."

The hand against his sternum turned into a finger, poking him roughly. "Because *you* decided it should be that way. *You* made that choice for all of humanity, for untold generations to come. That wasn't your right to decide."

"Forgive me if I have trouble taking that critique from *you*."

The tears were fading fast now as anger began to outpace sadness on Helen's emotional spectrum. "Do you think I sought those choices out? That I ever wanted to make them? I am tormented daily by the fears that I made the wrong decisions along the way and set something in motion to doom us all. But at least I was trying to think of everyone when I made them. All you were thinking about was yourself, about the kind of world you wanted. Congratulations, Ivan. You got your way."

Her rage petered out toward the end. Fury was never Helen's strong suit, unless she was truly motivated, and on those occasions, even Ivan ran for cover. Part of him wanted to reach out to her, yet once again that day, Ivan felt the distance separating them keenly.

"Helen, I did what I thought was necessary to keep the world safe. I'm sorry if you don't agree with my methods, but the low body counts alone speak to how efficient it was."

"I know you did, Ivan. Like I said up front, I've always known who you are," Helen said, a distinct tinge of sadness unmistakable in her voice. "It had just been so long, I guess I let myself pretend otherwise." The sigh from Helen was long, as her hand finally moved away from his chest. "Even if you break a chocolate bar in half, it still has the same calories."

A fear unlike any Ivan had experienced in battle gripped his heart. "What does that mean?"

"It means that you and I are a pair of unlikely friends. Best friends, sometimes, when things aren't so complicated. After everything we've gone through with and for one another, I don't see that changing quite so easily. But you also reminded me why that's the most we can ever be, no matter how nice these last few weeks have been."

She didn't need to explain herself any more than that; not to him. He too had been enjoying their temporary partnership, a facsimile of domestic life that perhaps other versions of them could have enjoyed. Unfortunately, no matter how Ivan and Helen felt, Lodestar couldn't take up with Fornax. Even their friendship pressed at the edges of acceptable morality. Lodestar was the golden standard the world looked to—a scandal like that could undo literal decades of positive work for the world.

Moving carefully, watching for any sign of resistance, ready to halt, Ivan reached out and lifted Helen's chin, their eyes meeting in the lonely courtyard. "I understand."

"I *know* you do. That's part of why it hurts." She put her hand over his, gripping it tightly. "Another world, another life, huh?" Wielding inner strength that had nothing to do with Lodestar, Helen pushed Ivan's hand back to his chest, patting it once. It wasn't the first time either had spoken those words to one another, though the occasions never seemed to get any easier.

"Who knows what could have been," Ivan said, finishing out the phrase. "I'll give you some space for a while."

Helen nodded, despite the pained look on her face. "Penelope has a dance recital next month she'd hate for Uncle Ivan to miss. Let's see how we're feeling then." For a moment, she looked over her shoulder to turn before pausing. "Goodbye, for now."

"See you in a few weeks." Ivan had wanted to say goodbye, as well; however, his tongue betrayed him, refusing to form the words. Not to her. For Helen, this was the most he could manage.

Ivan stood in his doorway, watching her leave, waiting until the courtyard gate clanged closed, and for five minutes afterward before finally closing the door and heading inside.

Sparks flitted from the shattered television, remote still embedded in the glass near dead center. Professor Quantum paid them no mind. He'd get around to fixing or replacing it when the need arose. For now, the art-piece on the nature of rage soothed him every time he looked at it. How dare that ungrateful little whelp use her position to slander their reputation in an attempt to build her own. Was it not enough that the AHC had given her and that guild adequate room to commit their atrocities thanks to "respecting the law?" Had they not dispatched Lodestar to her aid, in spite of knowing there were resources already willing to save her? This was her repayment? A line of products built on the assumption that the superheroes would fail?

His office door opened without warning, which meant there was one of two people who should be walking in. Only fellow members of the Champions' Congress were permitted such free entrance, and moments later, he was relieved to see Quorum appear. The last thing he needed right now was one of Lodestar's tiring speeches.

"Afternoon," Quorum greeted. "Stopping by to let you know we moved the call with the Defense Department to five—only time we could get everyone you wanted on at once."

"I am up to date with all emails and changes to the schedule." Professor Quantum tapped his device—calling it a phone would be a genuine injustice to the amount of technology bundled inside. "I'm also too busy to bother with politeness. What do you need that had to be said in person?"

The brusqueness didn't bother Quorum—who knew if anything did, really. He was truly impossible to get a handle on, the amalgamation of over a thousand unique voices and perspectives creating something wholly unique, and unnatural. "Very well. I came to tell you not to make any moves against the woman."

While Professor Quantum briefly entertained the notion of playing dumb, there was little purpose. Quorum might not be a meta-genius; however, he had excellent observation and deductive skills, not that the embedded remote left much need for speculation.

"I could hardly help it if someone anonymously tipped off a few reporters about the new Indigo Technologies spokeswoman living a secret, villainous life. It's not as if her identity is protected by the Orion Protocols the way that beast's is."

"Which would accomplish nothing, at this point," Quorum explained, having already seen the situation from that and untold more angles. "Tori has no warrants for her arrest; she is at most wanted in connection to a minor museum robbery that insurance has already paid for. If you expose her now, she can pivot, using the chance to come out into the open about just *how* advanced her creations can be. Building a suit for self-protection already fits into the narrative she's spinning, and currently, you'd have little support internally for trying to move against her. Hephaestus was on-site helping the New Science Sentries in their battle. None of them will care more about one potential heist than that."

It was frustrating, being told that what should be such a simple fix would only end in error, but one ignored Quorum's insight at their own peril. "I suppose you'll advocate we take the high road and only strike through proper channels."

"There would be no point in speaking such words to you," Quorum replied, not incorrectly. "What I am advising is patience. Let her continue working in the shadows, sowing the seeds of her own destruction. There are no warrants for Hephaestus, currently. In time, thinking she's slipped our notice, chances are strong she'll take larger risks. Once there is a crime Hephaestus has committed, one significant enough to weaken the public's approval and her own support within the AHC, then drawing a link between the villain and Tori could produce the results you're after. Move too soon, lose the chance before it's ripe. Not to mention, we don't need the guild angry right now."

Professor Quantum had been looking over the same reports, and the data was almost undeniable. Between the guild's threat, Lodestar's showy battle, and the AHC's exceptional response to the alien invasion, crime was trending down once more. Even the misconduct still being committed was generally more low-key—the New Science Sentries had run down the first bank robbers of the week earlier that day. Peace was good. It kept the AHC looking effective and made the public more docile, easier to manage. The current situation was tenuous; tipping the guild to retribution could indeed cause more harm than momentary vengeance would be worth.

"Very well. I'll wait for a better opportunity to strike with her identity. Until then, I'll have to busy myself by checking each and every one of her devices for the slightest violation of federal defense statutes. Perhaps we can get them all recalled." Hitting his keyboard without delay, Professor Quantum pulled up Indigo Technologies' website, now with Tori's face and new product line splashed across the front page. A few clicks, and suddenly, a distinct frown settled on the usually distinguished face.

"Something wrong?" Quorum asked.

While still professional, it was impossible to miss the terse annoyance sliding through Professor Quantum's voice. "It seems the launch announcement struck a chord. There's already a two week backorder."

The guild was bustling. Tori had no sooner walked up from the teleportation chamber than she nearly collided with Gork, who pivoted her tremendous mass with delicate grace, stepping to Tori's side at the last moment.

"Whoops, sorry," Tori quickly sputtered.

"Happens to everyone." Gork readjusted her position, revealing Stasis and Arachno Bro, who'd both been blocked by her substantial size.

Pointing up to the ceiling, Stasis gestured. "We need to get one of those office bubble-mirror thingies installed there, make it easier to see who is coming from every angle. Also, going to need a high-five from Hephaestus over here. Caught your commercial this afternoon and *loved* it. 'Save ourselves,' that's going to piss the capes right off."

Tori accommodated the high-five, hitting one with Arachno Bro as well when he lifted one of his several arms, the others largely encumbered with a large metal case. It was somewhat off-putting, hearing her villain name bandied about like that, but then, she did generally use the official nomenclature for everyone aside from Ivan or the other rookies. It was part of guild protocol, though not the code specifically, which made enforcement far more voluntary among the ranks.

"Thanks. I tried to walk the line and not seem like I was coming after them. Figured that would bring down more heat than we wanted." To say nothing of how it would impact the friends she had in that organization, hearing her speak those words. In the end, Tori had found her peace with the marketing strategy in the simple facts of the matter: everything she'd said was true. The AHC *had* failed to save her, because they *couldn't* be everywhere at once. Beyond that, Tori sincerely did believe her inventions could help others from ending up in the same situation. If the capes had a real problem with the fact that they weren't able to protect everyone, then maybe they should take it as a sign to step up their game.

Gork gave her a slow, unmissable nod. "Doc wouldn't let you cross any lines. With apologies, we have a facility appointment to keep."

"That's right!" Stasis slapped the metal box in Arachno Bro's arms, causing an unexpectedly harmonic note to ring out. "We hired the Bytes to play around with some of the Wrexwren tech so handily left on their corpses —need a place with special shielding to test this out."

"Gonna be loud," Arachno Bro added, adjusting his many-armed grip to ensure the device was perfectly snug. He was putting in enough effort to make Tori wonder what would happen if it was dropped, and how close she should really be standing.

With a wave, Tori opted to take the graceful exit they'd presented. "Have fun! I'm off to go do some tinkering myself."

The trio headed out, barely missing getting run into by Pod Person and Killcitate as they emerged from the teleportation chamber, proving that Stasis was indeed right about the need for a bubble-mirror. Tori went another way, winding her way along the exterior path even though there were more direct routes inside.

It was startling to realize how much the island had changed just since its unveiling. New buildings were added to the town, a fresh green bubbling pit of unknown goop had appeared to the north, and it appeared that some sort of trees with faces were beginning to dot the nearest shoreline. The rest of the guild had been busy with their own activities and projects, most of which were likely even more bizarre than her own. Perhaps it was time to start spending more time around her fellow villains. The bonds formed here wouldn't necessarily be any less complicated, but at least they'd be on the same side. Unless another insurrection formed, anyway.

Rounding a corner, Tori caught sight of Lance and Warren, or maybe Pest Control and Glyph. She needed to start thinking of them in their villainous roles with or without the costumes, but it wasn't as if the other guild members weren't familiar with one another. Maybe she'd just ask if they cared; sometimes, there were upsides to a reputation for bluntness.

The duo were part of a quartet hauling a giant red cube lashed onto a hefty cart, with one person manning each corner, shoving it along. Both offered a sweaty wave, forgoing verbal greetings due to their gulping breaths. Tori walked a bit further and found herself looking at an identical cube, only this one was being pushed by a single meaty hand belonging to Thuggernaut.

"Looky here, we got ourselves a celebrity." Johnny Three Dicks poked his head around the side, making no pretense that he'd been in any way helping with the task. "What's the going rate on one of those handbags paired with your signature?"

"I'm going to shoot straight with you, Johnny: you don't have the shoulders to pull off that model."

He clutched his chest, reeling back as if struck. "I like the attack, but you'll have to pick a target other than these perfect shoulders if you want to land a blow. Besides, the design is a bit too splashy for me. I like clean lines. I was going to sell the thing online—you do know there's already a backorder, right?"

"What Johnny means is congratulations on your new endeavor. It sounds like it's already been very successful," Thuggernaut stepped in to add.

The eye roll of Johnny Three Dicks was so perfect, it very well might have qualified as a superpower in itself. "Spoilsport. Anyway, nice to see you, but we've got to get these... materials to... a place or something will... are meltsplosions officially a thing? Can't remember how the voting went."

"We're on a schedule. Good to see you, Tori, and congratulations from me, as well." Thuggernaut resumed pushing the block, which had darkened slightly in hue, unless Tori was mistaken. She gave them a wide berth to head past her.

Watching the odd pair wander down the slope, Tori momentarily marveled at how normal the whole exchange had felt. Less than a year with these maniacs, and she was already getting accustomed to the madness. Craving it, at times, especially when normal life was fraught with more complex problems. Dealing with a meta-suit that wasn't strong enough: simple. Start upgrading one piece at a time until one reached the desire level. It was people who made things complicated.

On her phone, an unanswered text from Donald lingered. A simple, short message: "Saw the commercial, congratulations on starting your new business. Let me know if you want to go celebrate." She'd implied the entire enterprise he was devoting his life to wasn't adequately doing its job, and he'd responded with an olive branch. That was the trouble with capes—they took the higher path, which made her feel all the more shitty about the slight. Were they just going to ignore it? Because her gut said the rest of Cyber Geek's team might have different words the next time they all hung out. She didn't know what to say back, which was why the message lingered, every passing minute potentially making the reply all the more awkward.

Suddenly looking around, Tori realized she'd taken a wrong turn. Instead of her initial destination, she'd veered off toward the council offices, where one might find Pseudonym when he was around. Of course, Ivan didn't have an express reason to be here, so he wouldn't be. Tori spun around, absolutely secure in that knowledge right up until she nearly collided with Ivan's elbow.

He didn't dodge, merely vanished and reappeared in a different point. Sometimes, she forgot he could do short-range teleports at will—one more talent piled atop so many others. If she wanted to climb into that league, the world where people like Alfred Settler couldn't make her feel powerless, then there was very long trek ahead, and today was only one step of countless.

"Didn't expect to see you here," Ivan greeted, stealing her own line quite effectively. "Don't you want to go out and celebrate the new endeavor? I imagined Beverly would have put together an enjoyable outing for you all."

"Fancy dinner and unfancy drinks at some swanky place uptown." Tori was already annoyed by the dress code, but it wasn't as if she hadn't gotten accustomed to office attire at Vendallia; she could certainly muddle through for a high-end meal. "It's on Indigo's dime, at least. Now that I'm a public figure, Wade wants me seen around town more, flaunting the merchandise."

"Making yourself a target for anyone who wants to give them a test," Ivan pointed out.

The idea had occurred to Tori, and she responded with a mild shrug. "I was a target before, I'm still a target now. The difference is, if the AHC lets me get attacked, they give me a chance to show off while also proving that they can't always be there. The smart money is I'm going to be very protected by the superheroes until they figure out a countermove."

"Which means it will be dangerous to act as Hephaestus." Lifting his hands, Ivan gestured around them to the villainous volcano lair in which they stood. "Part of why I thought you might take a little time to lay low. There are a lot more eyes on Tori Rivas than there once were."

"But only a fraction of the ones on people like Wade Wyatt," she countered. "You are sort of half-right. I'm planning to lay low on the villain stuff for a while. The suit is due for an overhaul. Between everything I've learned and the new resources I've got access to, it no longer represents my best efforts. Doing a new build right takes time, so Hephaestus can take a breather while Tori gets her empire running."

Ivan let out a half-sigh, half-chuckle as he shook his head. "It's my own fault for expecting anything less. I'll let you get to it then."

He started to step past her, but Tori shifted her weight to block him. Despite the fact that he'd moments ago proven that she was no obstacle, Ivan still allowed her to halt his progress. "Hang on there, bucko, what are you doing here? There's no council meeting I'm aware of, not with Gork and Stasis on some weird weapons test, and no pressing emergencies to handle. That tends to be all that draws you to this place."

It was bizarre, seeing Ivan look uncertain, like watching a mountain crack a joke. He shifted back slightly, scratching under his chin. "In truth... I was a bit bored. The kids are with their mom, no Starscouts work to do, and even the office is still closed until next week." Although Ivan didn't mention the other friend he might have wanted to spend time with, Tori already knew things were tense with Helen; no need to rub salt in the wound. "I thought perhaps there might be tasks to do around here, get ahead of things for a change."

Whether or not it was wise for Ivan to spend more time here, Tori couldn't be sure. He clearly needed to keep himself busy, and being around friends was a good move in rough times, but this place had a way of drawing people deeper in. Ivan himself had been the one to warn her about that. Still, if anyone could handle the balance, it was likely to be one of the guild's own founders. There were surely better places to direct her concern.

"You know I'm not going to be coming into the office anymore, right?" Tori had already been transferred off Vendallia's payroll—though since it was an Indigo Technologies subsidy, she was technically getting heavily promoted rather than changing companies.

Ivan nodded. As her manager and former mentor, Wade had probably looped Ivan in before even she got the final confirmations. "I may never find a more competent, or surly, assistant."

"Oh, you absolutely will not," Tori agreed. "My point was that I'm glad you'll be around here, since I won't see you as much in the outside world. Probably still going to need a lot of advice, now that I'm a small-time celebrity on top of being one of the world's most promising new supervillains."

The lifted eyebrow of skepticism was much more akin to the Ivan expression Tori was used to, and she even took some comfort in the mild incredulity of his tone. "Decided on that title for yourself?"

"I stood against one of Professor Quantum's old nemeses and killed a crook with a much grander reputation than my own. If any of the other newbies can top that, they're welcome to claim the title for themselves."

"They can't." Ivan's words were praise, yet the ones that followed were tinged with warning. "For now."

"Like I said, I'm already in the process of making sure I don't fall behind the pack." Tori checked her watch, realizing that all these delays had put her behind schedule, and she did *not* want to make Beverly late. Her roommate could be a tad tyrannical about staying on time—at least when it was something Beverly wanted to do. "On that note, better hustle. Let's do a dinner around here next week, though. I heard Scrap-Rabble opened a spot on the island with food like no one has ever tasted before."

A momentary look of mock-fear washed over Ivan's face. "Knowing Scrap-Rabble, that could encompass a great many options indeed." The pseudo-terror was fast replaced by a genuine smile. "I'll look forward to it."

They broke apart on that note, Tori wasting no more time on winding paths. All that slowed her pace was a short text reply to Donald reading: "Love to. I'll call you tomorrow and we can talk schedule." No sense in having a mentor if she wasn't going to learn from him, and Ivan was a prime example on the importance of balance. Maybe staying friends with someone on the other side would prove to be impossible long-term; however, she still wanted to try. Aside from everything she'd gone through with some of the capes, having bonds outside the guild would keep her from slipping in too deep as well—something important to keep in mind while laying low.

That done, she made as direct a line as possible to her guild laboratory, now hers long-term thanks to the deal with Wade. He'd comped her a year for free, after which, they'd revisit the issue and see if the space still suited her needs. By the time she needed to pay actual rental rates, money from the venture would be rolling in, though most of it was already earmarked for meta-suit development.

Finally making her way inside, Tori went straight to the reason she'd popped in for a visit: her new material was ready. She powered up the huge machine carefully, checking to see that everything had executed as programmed before opening the release chamber. Considering the unknown substance she'd been working with, there was a chance her creation could be toxic, if not outright destructive.

Resting atop a large podium ten feet away, suspended in a miniature gravitational field, was the bony finger of Alfred Settler. Even disconnected from the main body, it was corrosive—the damn thing had eaten through nearly all of her suit's hidden compartments by the time she got it back to the apartment lab, and rigging up transport to the guild had taken half a day. From there had come the material scans, trying to figure out precisely what this nigh-indestructible substance was made from, and how much could be replicated.

Several of the elements the scanner found were totally foreign, unlike anything Tori had ever seen. Others were rarer, certain trace meta-minerals like erlestrite and cadinphode that were formed by exposing more common materials to meta-elements, such as setlium. Or vernium, apparently, since Alfred's own internal energy must have formed them in his body. Those would be integrated in later versions, when Tori had the cash to spare.

Right now, she'd found a hopefully stable build at around a seventy percent structural match. Replacing the missing elements had been the hardest part; up until today, every attempt had resulted in a pile of sludge, at best. Getting an alert that one of the sequences had produced something viable was all it took to send her rushing back to the guild.

Hitting the final buttons, a section of the large machine spun away from the wall, revealing a tightly sealed chamber. After a few seconds and some loud clangs, the door began to release its locks before slowly swinging open. Tori waited as the soft hiss of smoke cleared, showing her a rectangular hunk of metal. All readings indicated it was non-corrosive, but she still tapped it gently with a pinky finger, waiting for any telltale burn or tingle. Nothing: only cold metal, though Tori wondered if it shouldn't be a tad colder. Trusting her instruments, she lifted the material up, bringing it out into the bright lights of the laboratory.

"Guess it's a good thing my suit was already black." She'd anticipated as much, given the coloration of the source material, but this was a step further than expected. More than dark, it absorbed a higher amount of light than anything she'd seen short of specialized cloaking fabrics. Handy for working at night, she supposed.

Setting the material against a far wall, Tori headed over to a table, where the remains of her meta-suit were splayed out. A few bits would be salvaged for version number two; however, most of it was going to need to be rebuilt from the ground up. She was planning to do cosmetic repairs on this one, even if it was getting retired, then see about procuring a glass case for display. Just because it was time to move on didn't mean she wasn't proud of where she'd started.

From the table, Tori plucked her still-functioning gauntlet, the only piece of the suit to already receive full repairs. As the strongest weapon she had, it was also the best option for testing her new metal. Alfred had taken this kind of shot without missing a step, and soon, she'd be able to do the same. Because that was the danger in fighting a thief and letting them live. A good one never walked away entirely empty-handed.

Tapping the side of her laptop to wake it up, Tori clicked on the recording program and activated various scanners. The silver lining to a week of failed attempts, she'd had plenty of time to prep for once something stable came along. "Hephaestus Version Two, Settler Metal Test Number One." Flexing the gauntlet, she fueled it with power, flames cascading off her hidden hand and into the system. Without the helmet on, there was no indicator signal—she'd just used the weapons enough to learn the timing. Bit by bit, the energy level climbed as Tori got herself into position, drawing a direct line on the square of metal waiting across the room. By the time she was ready, so was the gauntlet, and she saw no reason to keep Beverly waiting with needless delays.

"Let's see just how tough I'm going to be."

With EMTs keeping the driver calm and his car set safely back on the ground, Lodestar was preparing to leave. There wasn't any crime to record, just a tired driver on a mountain road who'd tried too sharp of a turn. Lucky for him, Lodestar was flying the skies.

She'd been doing that quite a few times over the past week—whenever a certain young woman named Penelope was otherwise occupied, in fact. It was getting excessive, and she knew it, but for the moment, it was nice to have control over some part of her life. As Lodestar, she could always make a difference, always be of use, always know the right path forward. It was the human side where things got muddled. Yet that same uncertainty and confusion were what made it essential. Humans weren't sure of every move they made—losing that would mean losing a piece of what kept her... Helen.

A step down a path she was determined to avoid for as long as absolutely possible.

Before she could take to the skies, a figure appeared next to her. If the sudden emergence from nowhere and the dirty overcoat hadn't tipped her off, the kaleidoscope eyes would have. Nexus was a thorn that couldn't be plucked, not permanently. Beating him didn't matter. He always came back, the same as before. Lodestar decided to open politely tonight. She didn't want there to be any more conflict than necessary, especially given the scales of destruction Nexus could operate on.

"Out for an evening stroll?"

"Countless," he agreed. "Though only the one with you. This you, anyway. Others who wear the name, or the power, there are scant few worth watching. This world is special, however."

"I'm already aware that we have multiple Singulars, just like I know that I'm not one of them. What else can I help you with?"

He stalked around the grass at the road's side, looking with eyes that saw far more than even his most cryptic ramblings went on. It would be easy to dismiss Nexus, as many had early on, except that he constantly knew more than anyone should. Not always accurate information, but often enough that he couldn't be fully ignored, no matter how much smarter a tactic that might be. "You can heed my warning: you need to be more careful. I have seen what happens when a Lodestar dies, and do not wish for a world as interesting as this one to share the same fate."

Something in her, a piece of human fear long left dormant, stirred slightly. "Lodestars don't die. You can get rid of the person, not the power. Basically every villain I went against with any multiverse access hunted for weaknesses, and the results always came back the same."

"Ah, yes, no worlds where a Lodestar has fallen. But that doesn't mean such worlds didn't exist. I saw it happen, in a place many degrees separated from your universe, yet you wouldn't find entirely unfamiliar. Another world with multiple Singulars, such a pleasure to watch unfold. When they decided to use their abilities in tandem, I expected the same result as you, but to my surprise, they succeeded at the seemingly impossible task. Combining talents found solely in their world, the trio managed to slay their version of Lodestar. It was such a battle, the very planet shook by the end. I was enraptured at the pageantry. Then, it ended."

"That's it? In a different corner of the multiverse, somebody allegedly killed a Lodestar, and you were so concerned that it seemed prudent to give me a warning?" Was he playing at something? Madness didn't mean Nexus couldn't be cunning. Perhaps this was part of a larger plan.

Something like a sad cackle split from Nexus's lips as he stared at her with those shattered eyes. "There are plenty like you to watch, same story of self-denial and sadness echoed over and over. But this world has Singulars which make it fascinating, because their presence renders everything harder to predict, yet also means you might be killable here. That is why I came to give my warning. I do not want to see this world share the same fate."

Thinking back on Nexus's exact words, Lodestar caught a turn of phrase she'd initially missed, and suddenly, she felt as nauseated as if she'd been using super-speed for too long. "Nexus, when you say *it* ended, you do mean the fight, don't you?"

Reaching into the roadside grass, Nexus tore up a handful, then blew it into the wind, each piece drifting over the mountain's edge. "Gone, in a matter of moments. One light after another simply faded away, an entire universe collapsed into nothingness. Some of me barely made out it; some didn't at all. I felt it to the end, the crushing obliteration. That power you wield may well be each universe's greatest defense, but in balance, it also represents a critical weakness. No one can find a universe where Lodestar has died, because to kill a Lodestar is to end that universe. They do not leave remains, only emptiness."

It was an absolutely lunatic statement—except deep down, part of Helen always knew there *had* to be a cost. That was the way things worked, or had worked, for a long time. Just the act of wielding the power had taken nearly everything from her, time and time again. That its existence represented a danger as well as a defense... it tracked with her understanding. However, that didn't mean she was going to take Nexus at face value.

"I suppose it would be pointless to ask you for proof."

"Very much so. I have none to offer, save only for the truth in my words." He lumbered toward her, half lunge, half fall, stopping a few feet short. "Take care, Lodestar, and if I arrive to give you caution, then heed it. This world is too entertaining. I'm not yet ready for the curtain to fall."

Then he was gone, as instantly as he'd arrived.

Lifting off, Lodestar flew up into the night sky, trying not to dwell too hard on his ramblings. Even if the story was true, the world he'd cited had needed multiple Singulars to accomplish the task, and by definition, none of them would be present here. Nevertheless, she already knew this was a lead that had to be chased down, as discreetly as possible. If her death would put the entire universe in danger, then that was something she'd quite like to know.

Floating up higher, she looked down upon the planet below. So messy, chaotic, flawed, and human, Helen loved this world so very much. Even now, people were making mistakes, getting into danger, looking to the heavens in the hopes of some sudden miracle to save the day. And she, of all people, was lucky enough to be able to give that help, to offer that second chance when it was needed most. Despite all it had taken from her, Lodestar enjoyed this view and everything that came with it. Even the burdens of the role were familiar weights at this point.

Shooting down from the sky, her eyes scanned about, searching for those in peril. Theoretical deaths could wait for another day. Right now, she had an entire world to keep safe. In a burst of light, Lodestar shot down into the city, flying toward a cry for help that was about to be answered in spectacular fashion.

End of Villains' Code: Book #2

About the Author

Drew Hayes is an author from Texas who has now found time and gumption to publish a few books. He graduated from Texas Tech with a B.A. in English, because evidently he's not familiar with what the term "employable" means. Drew has been called one of the most profound, prolific, and talented authors of his generation, but a table full of drunks will say almost anything when offered a round of free shots. Drew feels kind of like a D-bag writing about himself in the third person like this. He does appreciate that you're still reading, though.

Drew would like to sit down and have a beer with you. Or a cocktail. He's not here to judge your preferences. Drew is terrible at being serious, and has no real idea what a snippet biography is meant to convey anyway. Drew thinks you are awesome just the way you are. That part, he meant. You can reach Drew with questions or movie offers at NovelistDrew@gmail.com Drew is off to go high-five random people, because who doesn't love a good high-five? No one, that's who.

Read or purchase more of his work at his site: DrewHayesNovels.com

www.ingramcontent.com/pod-product-compliance
Lightning Source LLC
Chambersburg PA
CBHW020720310726
48979CB00004B/999

* 9 7 8 1 9 5 4 4 5 3 0 0 5 *